To Sleep,
Perchance to Dream . . .
NIGHTMARE

To Sleep, Perchance to Dream . . . NIGHTMARE

THIRTY TERRIFYING TALES

Edited by
Stefan R. Dziemianowicz,
Robert Weinberg
& Martin H. Greenberg

BARNES & NOBLE BOOKS
NEW YORK

This edition published by Barnes & Noble, Inc.,
by arrangement with Martin H. Greenberg.

1993 Barnes & Noble Books

Book design by Charles Ziga, Ziga Design

ISBN 1-56619-926-3

Printed and bound in the United States of America

M 9 8 7 6 5 4 3 2 1

Acknowledgments

Grateful acknowledgment is made to the following for permission to reprint their copyright materials: "Three Lines of Old French" by A. Merritt. Copyright 1919, renewed 1947 by Popular Publications Inc.; reprinted on behalf of the Merritt Estate by permission of Agent Forrest J Ackerman, 2495 Glendower Ave., Hollywood, CA 90027-1110. "Beyond the Door" by J. Paul Suter. Copyright 1923 by Rural Publications. Reprinted by permission of Weird Tales, Ltd. "The Shadows" by Henry S. Whitehead. Copyright 1927 by the Popular Fiction Publishing Co. Reprinted by permission of the agents for the author's Estate, the Scott Meredith Literary Agency, Inc., 845 Third Ave., New York, NY 10022. "The Black Stone" by Robert E. Howard. Copyright 1931 by the Popular Fiction Publishing Company for WEIRD TALES, November 1931. Copyright renewed © 1959. Reprinted by permission of Glenn Lord, agent for the heirs of Robert E. Howard. "Ubbo-Sathla" by Clark Ashton Smith. Copyright 1933 by the Popular Fiction Publishing Co. Reprinted by permission of the agents for the author's Estate, the Scott Meredith Literary Agency, Inc., 845 Third Ave., New York, NY 10022. "The Watcher in the Green Room" by Hugh B. Cave. Copyright 1933 by the Popular Fiction Publishing Co. for WEIRD TALES, September 1933. Reprinted by permission of the author. "The Lady in Gray" by Donald Wandrei. Copyright 1933 by the Popular Fiction Publishing Co. Reprinted by permission of Lindquist & Vennum Attorneys At Law. "Scarlet Dream" by C. L. Moore. Copyright 1934, renewed © 1962 by C. L. Moore, © 1990 by Thomas Reggie. Reprinted by permission of Don Congdon Associates, Inc. "The Dreams in the Witch House" by H. P. Lovecraft. Copyright 1933 by the Popular Fiction Publishing Co. Reprinted by permission of the agents for the author's Estate, the Scott Meredith Literary Agency, Inc., 845 Third Ave., New York, NY 10022. "The Isle of the Sleeper" by Edmond Hamilton. Copyright 1938 by the Popular Fiction Publishing Co. Reprinted by permission of The Spectrum Literary Agency. "Prescience" by Nelson S. Bond. Copyright 1941 by Street & Smith Publications, Inc., renewed © 1969; by arrangement with the author's agent, Forrest J Ackerman, 2495 Glendower Ave., Hollywood, CA 90027-1110. "The Dreams of Albert Moreland" by Fritz Leiber. Copyright 1948, renewed © 1976 by Fritz Leiber. Reprinted by permission of Richard Curtis Associates, Inc. "The Unspeakable Betrothal" by Robert Bloch. Copyright 1949, renewed © 1977 by Robert Bloch. Reprinted by permission of the Scott Meredith Literary Agency, Inc., 845 Third Ave., New York, NY 10022. "Lover When You're Near Me" by Richard Matheson. Copyright 1952, renewed © 1980 by

Richard Matheson. Reprinted by permission of Don Congdon Associates, Inc. "Perchance to Dream" by Charles Beaumont. Copyright © 1958, renewed © 1986 by Christopher Beaumont. Reprinted by permission of Don Congdon Associates, Inc. "The River of Night's Dreaming" by Karl Edward Wagner. Copyright © 1981 by Stuart David Schiff for WHISPERS III. Reprinted by permission of the author. "The Depths" by Ramsey Campbell. Copyright © 1982 by Ramsey Campbell. From DARK COMPANIONS. Reprinted by permission of the author. "Dream of a Mannikin" by Thomas Ligotti. Copyright © 1983 by Thomas Ligotti. Reprinted by permission of Robinson Publishers, London. "Never Visit Venice" by Robert Aickman. Copyright © 1968. Reprinted by permission of the Pimlico Agency, Inc. "The Dream of the Wolf" by Scott Bradfield. Copyright © 1984 by Scott Bradfield. Reprinted by permission of Curtis Brown, Ltd. "The Last and Dreadful Hour" by Charles L. Grant. Copyright © 1986 by Charles L. Grant. Reprinted by permission of the author. "Dream Baby" by Bruce McAllister. Copyright © 1987 by Bruce McAllister. Reprinted by permission of the Scott Meredith Literary Agency, Inc., 845 Third Ave., New York, NY 10022. "The Heart's Desire" by Chet Williamson. Copyright © 1990 by Chet Williamson. Reprinted by permission of the Scott Meredith Literary Agency, Inc., 845 Third Ave., New York, NY 10022. "In the Flesh" by Clive Barker. Copyright © 1985 by Clive Barker. From BOOKS OF BLOOD. Reprinted by permission of Little, Brown & Co. (U.K.), Ltd.

CONTENTS

INTRODUCTION

To Sleep, Perchance to Dream . . . Nightmare is the first collection of its kind to mine the rich vein of horror and fantasy literature concerned with nightmares. Spanning a century and a half, these thirty tales provide an overview of the various bad dreams the genre has dreamt up over the years, and the uses to which horror writers have put them.

Readers tend to think of horror fiction in terms of the most familiar monsters—the vampire, ghost, werewolf, mummy, and the zombie. There is, however, at least one horror motif that predates all of these imaginary creatures and rivals them in popularity: the nightmare.

Although as prevalent in horror fiction as any supernatural monster, the nightmare is generally overlooked because it is a *natural* phenomenon used in a great many non-horror stories. Yet one couldn't ask for a more perfect manifestation of the weird and uncanny. Like more tangible horrors, it strikes in the dark when victims are at their most vulnerable. But it is more difficult to defend oneself against this product of the unconscious mind than something made of flesh and blood, and no one, no matter how innocent or evil, is immune. More important, perhaps, this byproduct of sleep and dark fancy perfectly represents the willing suspension of disbelief that supernatural fiction demands of the reader. As Thomas Ligotti has written, "Once you're trapped in a nightmare—I mean a really good nightmare—nobody has to ask you to suspend disbelief in the horror that is about to overwhelm you."

The earliest story here, "The Drunkard's Dream" (1838), is one of a handful of tales related by Irish fantasist Joseph Sheridan Le Fanu as an account of the experiences of Reverend Francis Purcell of Drumcoolagh. A master of ambiguity, Le Fanu shows the nightmare to have been tailor-made for a century that preferred its horrors subtle, by leaving to the reader the correct interpretation of the story's climax. Is Pat Connell's vision a "mere chimaera of a sleeping fancy" turned into self-fulfilling prophecy through liberal quantities of alcohol and religious superstition; or are the circumstances surrounding it too coincidental for it to be understood as anything less than a premonition of divine judgment?

Not all Victorian writers were as intent as Le Fanu on questioning the validity of the nightmare, but most followed his lead by focusing on the disturbing relationship between dreams and waking life. For example, there is no question in Wilkie Collins' "The Dream Woman" (1859) that Isaac Scatchard has experienced a bad dream, but these very literal events are dismissed as the harmless figment of a fanciful mind. Only when the details gradually begin to insinuate themselves into his daily life is the dream revealed to be a symbol of the ineluctability of his personal fate. In contrast, Bram Stoker encodes Jacob Settle's nightmare in "A Dream of Red Hands" (1914) with imagery that can be deciphered only in terms of the guilty secret he has harbored all his life. The story's ironic ending reveals the dream as little more than an instrument of moral rectification.

By the end of the nineteenth century, the nightmare was a stock theme in horror fiction, serving most prominently as either a portent of impending doom or a window upon the guilty conscience. But American writers Ambrose Bierce and Robert W. Chambers recognized a hitherto unexplored potential of the nightmare when they tried to replicate its logical illogic in their narratives. Bierce's profoundly disquieting "The Death of Halpin Frayser" (1893) can be read as a tale of dreams come true, but it is more remarkable for the use of dream imagery redolent with taboo sexuality that blurs the boundary between conscious experience and subconscious desire. A similar interweaving of dream and life is seen in Chambers' "The Yellow Sign", (written in tribute to Bierce) (1895) in which the artist's discussion of his aesthetics and bohemian lifestyle approximates the disoriented rhythms of the nightmare that eventually overwhelms his waking life.

Still another way writers expanded the possibilities of the nightmare tale was to combine dreams with other genre motifs and to synthesize a final horror that would total more than the sum of its parts. An example is E. F. Benson's "The Room in the Tower," which begins as a conventional nightmare story, becomes increasingly more ominous as the nightmare overlaps with the narrator's daytime life, and then unexpectedly shifts its locus of horror to a surprise for which the repeating nightmare turns out to have been just a stage setting.

Benson's experiment anticipates the sort of imaginative exploration of the nightmare that the authors of pulp fiction stories were to indulge in. The main source of popular fiction in America between 1920 and 1950, the pulps published hundreds of thousands of stories by almost as many authors in every genre imaginable. Originality was one means by which authors could guarantee their survival in such a competitive market, and the nightmare story proved a popular attraction for some of the most inventive fantasy and horror writers of the period.

Although largely forgotten today, A. Merritt was a highly respected fantasist who made his mark with the "lost world" fantasy, a story type in which human beings find themselves transported to a forgotten realm where magic and exotic adventure are the order of the day. The seeds of this fantasy subgenre can be seen in his early tale "Three Lines of Old French" (1919), which transmutes the trance of a shell-shocked soldier into a dream experience where his dream of the afterlife is more reassuring than the nightmare that reality has become. Fifteen years later, C. L. Moore followed up on this same idea of dream-as-alternate-reality in "Scarlet Dream," an adventure in her saga of intergalactic gunslinger Northwest Smith. Elaborating an idea first tackled by Edgar Rice Burroughs in his tales of John Carter of Mars, Moore uses the dream as a vehicle for extraterrestrial travel, and portrays the fabulous imagery and preposterous logic of the dream setting as landmarks of an alien environment.

A popular type of dream story in the pulps employed the psychic residues left by earlier events and their influence on the unprotected subconscious. In J. Paul Suter's "Beyond the Door" (1924) and Henry S. Whitehead's "The Shadows" (1927), naive characters become unwitting witnesses to past atrocities through nightmares that prey upon their ignorance of local history. In contrast, Hugh Cave's "The Watcher in the Green Room" (1933) depends on the protagonist's complicity in a heinous crime for which he feels no pangs of conscience, in order that his guilt might express itself through oblique but highly disturbing dream fancies. In all of these stories, the nightmare plays the role once reserved for the avenging specter of Gothic horror fiction.

One of the most popular phenomena to emerge from the weird fiction pulps was a series of loosely interconnected tales written by H. P. Lovecraft and his colleagues and referred to today as "the Cthulhu Mythos." The underlying premise of these tales is that the human species lives in blissful ignorance of its insignificant place in the cosmos, a true appreciation of which would result in total insanity. The preferred mode by which luckless characters were made aware of mankind's plight was an encounter with extradimensional monstrosities that mocked all scientific theories of life. Occasionally, though, Lovecraft and his disciples used the crude symbolism of dreams to reveal cosmic truths in mercifully muted forms. So it is that the narrator of Robert E. Howard's "The Black Stone" (1931) lives to tell of what he saw revealed in a pagan ceremony dreamed of on Walpurgisnacht, and the ill-fated protagonist of Clark Ashton Smith's "Ubbo-Sathla" (1933) discovers the true origins of organic life when he becomes trapped in a dream of ancestral regression. Lovecraft's own "The Dreams in the Witch House" (1935) is undoubtedly the most profoundly far-reaching of these stories, with its assertion that human conceptions of dreams and the occult are mere misinterpretations of otherworldly sciences.

Of course, not all nightmare stories published in the pulps fit into such subcategories. Some, such as Donald Wandrei's "The Lady in Gray" (1933), with its narrator who becomes so acclimated to the landscape of his dreams that nightmare and reality become interchangeable forms of perception, rely on the potency of repeated dream imagery to overwhelm the discriminative faculties of both the fictional character and the reader. Others, like Edmond Hamilton's "The Isle of the Sleeper" (1938), play with the sort of paradox that might arise were a dream character to realize that his existence is only a fantastic projection of a dreamer's mind. Still others, like Nelson Bond's "Prescience" (1941) and Robert Bloch's "The Unspeakable Betrothal," written decades after Sigmund Freud's *Interpretation of Dreams*, imply that there are more things in heaven and earth than are dreamt of in psychoanalysis.

In the years immediately following World War II, horror fiction underwent a conceptual shift as writers sought to assimilate new fears that had shaken hitherto secure world views. Nightmare stories followed suit, as can be seen in Fritz Leiber's "The Dreams of Albert Moreland" (1947), where one man's dream of his tireless involvement in a cosmic chess game comes to represent the inexorable cosmic processes that grind human endeavor into meaningless dust. And as many fantasy writers began applying their skills to science fiction (a genre that grew exponentially following the explosion of the atom bomb in 1945), the once wondrous vistas of outer space became tarnished by horror fiction's archetypal fear of the unknown. Thus Richard Matheson in "Lover When You're Near Me" (1952) imagines an interplanetary frontier where the vulnerable human psyche crumbles under the onslaught of a telepathic race that has learned to manipulate dreams. In many ways, this story anticipates the horrors of Bruce McAllister's "Dream Baby" (1987), in which the kinship between telepathy and dreaming creates an exploitable weapon during the Vietnam War.

The overriding concern of horror fiction in the postwar years is the overwhelming sense of doubt that colors every aspect of human life: identity, sexuality, morality, even sanity. In place of the struggle between good and evil or the exploration of man's relationship to the universe which defined so much earlier horror fiction, most contemporary stories substitute anxiety over intimate matters concerning the home, the family, and the neighborhood. Implicit in the nightmares described in this book's last ten stories is how these anxieties grow inevitably into powerful forces of psychological dislocation and alienation.

The entanglement in dreams within dreams that plagues the therapy patient in Charles Beaumont's "Perchance to Dream" (1958) suggests a world in which the worst horrors are the subtly disarming ones revealed on the psychiatrist's couch. Taken one step further by Karl Edward Wagner in "The River of Night's Dreaming" (1981) (a direct homage to Robert W. Chambers' "The Yellow Sign"), the mind deprived of an outlet to express those horrors either loses control over the ability to distinguish between the real and not-real—or worse, discovers that there was no distinction to begin with.

The extremes to which such reasoning can lead are embodied in the paranoid delusions of the writer in Ramsey Campbell's "The Depths" (1982), who becomes convinced that he can prevent his nightmares from becoming reality if only he can transcribe them onto paper, or the solipsistic nightmare of Thomas Ligotti's "Dream of a Mannikin," (1983), in which the narrator cannot be convinced that he is anything more than the idle thought of a dreaming entity that delights in self-torture.

In contrast to the extraordinary experiences of these characters, which give way effortlessly to the surreality of nightmares, the bland existence of characters in other stories finds a perfect analogy in dreams. The repressed protagonist of Robert Aickman's "Never Visit Venice," (1968), and the character frustrated by the mundanity of his life in Scott Bradfield's "Dream of the Wolf," (1988), find their dreams preferable to life as they live it, regardless of the consequences. Yet their fate proves no better than that of Michael Lindstrom in Chet Williamson's "The Heart's Desire," (1990), who finds in a devastating epiphanic moment that some dreams are better left buried beneath life's false veneer of contentment and self-satisfaction. The final word on this paradox of modern life can be found in Charles L. Grant's "The Last and Dreadful Hour," (1986) in which it is discovered that the failure to dream for something better than one's lot, no matter how painful the inability to realize it, can render a person as ephemeral as the substance of dreams themselves.

The culmination of horror fiction's longstanding fascination with nightmares can be found in Clive Barker's "In the Flesh" (1986). Working in a literary tradition where it is commonly assumed that waking life is a state which nightmares perpetually try to invade and overwhelm, Barker intimates instead a realm in which waking life is itself the intrusive dream, and the moral principles of good and evil nothing but fragments of a dream logic lacking any application outside the dream. Barker's reflection on the interplay between dream and reality brings the focus of the nightmare story full circle: from the dreamer's dream, to the dreamer dreamed.

One word of caution: the stories that follow sometimes interpret the term "dream" liberally. But whether they deal with nightmares, daydreams, visions of the hopeful, or fancies of the fevered mind, all are guaranteed to disturb. Although is the nature of dreams that they can never come true, it is the nature of nightmares that they will always *seem* true. Pleasant dreams.

Stefan Dziemianowicz
New York, 1993

The Drunkard's Dream

J. Sheridan Le Fanu

*Being a Fourth Extract from the Legacy
of the Late F. Purcell,*

P. P. of Drumcoolagh

*All this he told with some confusion and
Dismay, the usual consequence of dreams
Of the unpleasant kind, with none at hand
To expound their vain and visionary gleams.
I've known some odd ones which seemed really planned
Prophetically, as that which one deems
'A strange coincidence,' to use a phrase
By which such things are settled now-a-days.*
—Byron

Dreams—What age, or what country of the world has not felt and acknowledged the mystery of their origin and end? I have thought not a little upon the subject, seeing it is one which has been often forced upon my attention, and sometimes strangely enough; and yet I have never arrived at any thing which at all appeared a satisfactory conclusion. It does appear that a mental phenomenon so extraordinary cannot be wholly without its use. We know, indeed, that in the olden times it has been made the organ of communication between the Deity and his creatures; and when, as I have seen, a dream produces upon a mind, to all appearance hopelessly reprobate and depraved, an effect so powerful and so lasting as to break down the inveterate habits, and to reform the life of an abandoned sinner. We see in the result, in the reformation of morals, which appeared incorrigible in the reclamation of a human soul which seemed to be irretrievably lost, something more than could be produced by a mere chimaera of the slumbering fancy, something more than could arise from the capricious images of a terrified imagination; but once prevented, we behold in all these things, in the tremendous and mysterious results, the operation of the hand of God. And while Reason rejects as absurd the superstition which will read a prophecy in every dream, she may, without violence to herself, recognize, even in the wildest and most incongruous of the wanderings of a slumbering intellect, the evidences and the fragments of a language which may be spoken, which *has* been spoken to terrify, to warn, and to command. We have reason to believe too, by the promptness of action, which in the age of the prophets, followed all intimations of this kind, and by the strength of conviction and strange permanence of the effects resulting from certain dreams in latter times, which effects ourselves may have witnessed, that when this medium of communication has been employed by the Deity, the evidences of his presence have been unequivocal. My thoughts were directed to this subject, in a manner to leave a lasting impression upon my mind, by the events which I shall now relate, the statement of which, however extraordinary, is nevertheless *accurately correct.*

About the year 17—having been appointed to the living of C——h, I rented a small house in the town, which bears the same name: one morning, in the month of November, I was awakened before my usual time, by my servant, who bustled into my bed-room for the purpose of announcing a sick call. As the Catholic Church holds her last rites to be totally indispensable to the safety of the departing sinner, no conscientious clergyman can afford a moment's unnecessary delay, and in little more than five minutes I stood ready cloaked and booted for the road in the small front parlour, in which the messenger, who was to act as my guide, awaited my coming. I found a poor little girl crying piteously near the door, and after some slight difficulty I ascertained that her father was either dead, or just dying.

"And what may be your father's name, my poor child?" said I. She held down her head, as if ashamed. I repeated the question, and the wretched little creature burst into floods of tears, still more bitter than she had shed before. At length, almost provoked by conduct which appeared to me so unreasonable, I began to lose patience, spite of the pity which I could not help feeling towards her, and I said rather harshly, "If you will not tell me the name of the person to whom you would lead me, your silence can arise from no good motive, and I might be justified in refusing to go with you at all."

"Oh! don't say that, don't say that," cried she. "Oh! sir, it was that I was afeard of when I would not tell you—I was afeard when you heard his name you would not come with me; but it is no use hidin' it now—it's Pat Connell, the carpenter, your honour."

She looked in my face with the most earnest anxiety, as if her very existence depended upon what she should read there; but I relieved her at once. The name, indeed, was most unpleasantly familiar to me; but, however fruitless my visits and advice might have been at another time, the present was too fearful an occasion to suffer my doubts of their utility as my reluctance to reattempting what appeared a hopeless task to weigh even against the lightest chance, that a consciousness of his imminent danger might produce in him a more docile and tractable disposition. Accordingly I told the child to lead the way, and followed her in silence. She hurried rapidly through the long narrow street which forms the great thoroughfare of the town. The darkness of the hour, rendered still deeper by the close approach of the old fashioned houses, which lowered in tall obscurity on either side of the way; the damp dreary chill which renders the advance of morning peculiarly cheerless, combined with the object of my walk, to visit the death-bed of a presumptuous sinner, to endeavour, almost against my own conviction, to infuse a hope into the heart of a dying reprobate—a drunkard, but too probably perishing under the consequences of some mad fit of intoxication; all these circumstances united served to enhance the gloom and solemnity of my feelings, as I silently followed my little guide, who with quick steps traversed the uneven pavement of the main street. After a walk of about five minutes she turned off into a narrow lane, of that obscure and comfortless class which are to be found in almost all small old fashioned towns, chill without ventilation, reeking with all manner of offensive effluviae, dingy, smoky, sickly and pent-up buildings, frequently not only in a wretched but in a dangerous condition.

"Your father has changed his abode since I last visited him, and, I am afraid, much for the worse," said I.

"Indeed he has, sir, but we must not complain," replied she; "we have to thank God that we have lodging and food, though it's poor enough, it is, your honour."

Poor child! thought I, how many an older head might learn wisdom from thee—how many a luxurious philosopher, who is skilled to preach but not to suffer, might not thy patient words put to the blush! The manner and language of this child were alike above her years and station; and, indeed, in all cases in which the cares and sorrows of life have anticipated their usual date, and have fallen, as they sometimes do, with melancholy prematurity to the lot of childhood, I have observed the result to have proved uniformly the same. A young mind, to which joy and indulgence have been strangers, and to which suffering and self-denial have been familiarised from the first, acquires a solidity and an elevation which no other discipline could have bestowed, and which, in the present case, communicated a striking but mournful peculiarity to the manners, even to the voice of the child. We paused before a narrow, crazy door, which she opened by means of a latch, and we forthwith began to ascend the steep and broken stairs, which led upwards to the sick man's room. As we mounted flight after flight towards the garret floor, I heard more and more distinctly the hurried talking of many voices. I could also distinguish the low sobbing of a female. On arriving upon the uppermost lobby, these sounds became fully audible.

"This way, your honor," said my little conductress, at the same time pushing open a door of patched and half rotten plank, she admitted me into the squalid chamber of death and misery. But one candle, held in the fingers of a scared and haggard-looking child, was burning in the room, and that so dim that all was twilight or darkness except within its immediate influence. The general obscurity, however, served to throw into prominent and startling relief the death-bed and its occupant. The light was nearly approximated to, and fell with horrible clearness upon, the blue and swollen features of the drunkard. I did not think it possible that a human countenance could look so terrific. The lips were black and drawn apart—the teeth were firmly set—the eyes a little unclosed, and nothing but the whites appearing—every feature was fixed and livid, and the whole face wore a ghastly and rigid expression of despairing terror such as I never saw equalled; his hands were crossed upon his breast, and firmly clenched, while, as if to add to the corpse-like effect of the whole, some white cloths, dipped in water, were wound about the forehead and temples. As soon as I could remove my eyes from this horrible spectacle, I observed my friend Dr. D——, one of the most humane of a humane profession, standing by the bed-side. He had been attempting, but unsuccessfully, to bleed the patient, and had now applied his finger to the pulse.

"Is there any hope?" I inquired in a whisper.

A shake of the head was the reply. There was a pause while he continued to hold the wrist; but he waited in vain for the throb of life, it was not there, and when he let go the hand it fell stiffly back into its former position upon the other.

"The man is dead," said the physician, as he turned from the bed where the terrible figure lay.

Dead! thought I, scarcely venturing to look upon the tremendous and revolting spectacle—dead! without an hour for repentance, even a moment for reflection—dead! without the rites which even the best should have. Is there a hope for him? The glaring eyeball, the grinning mouth, the distorted brow—that unutterable look in which a painter would have sought to embody the fixed despair of the nethermost hell—these were my answer.

The poor wife sat at a little distance, crying as if her heart would break—the younger children clustered round the bed, looking, with wondering curiosity, upon the form of death, never seen before. When the first tumult of uncontrollable sorrow had passed away, availing myself of the solemnity and impressiveness of the scene, I desired the heart-stricken family to accompany me in prayer, and all knelt down, while I solemnly and fervently repeated some of those prayers which appeared most applicable to the occasion. I employed myself thus in a manner which, I trusted, was not unprofitable, at least to the living, for about ten minutes, and having accomplished my task, I was the first to arise. I looked upon the poor, sobbing, helpless creatures who knelt so humbly around me, and my heart bled for them. With a natural transition, I turned my eyes from them to the bed in which the body lay, and, great God! what was the revulsion, the horror which I experienced on seeing the corpse-like, terrific thing seated half upright before me—the white cloths, which had been wound about the head, had now partly slipped from their position, and were hanging in grotesque festoons about the face and shoulders, while the distorted eyes leered from amid them—

A sight to dream of, not to tell.

I stood actually rivetted to the spot. The figure nodded its head and lifted its arm, I thought with a menacing gesture. A thousand confused and horrible thoughts at once rushed upon my mind. I had often read that the body of a presumptuous sinner, who, during life, had been the willing creature of every satanic impulse, after the human tenant had deserted it, had been known to become the horrible sport of demoniac possession. I was roused from the stupefaction of terror in which I stood, by the piercing scream of the mother, who now, for the first time, perceived the change which had taken place. She rushed towards the bed, but, stunned by the shock and overcome by the conflict of violent emotions, before she reached it, she fell prostrate upon the floor. I am perfectly convinced that had I not been startled from the torpidity of horror in which I was bound, by some powerful and arousing stimulant, I should have gazed upon this unearthly apparition until I had fairly lost my senses. As it was, however, the spell was broken, superstition gave way to reason: the man whom all believed to have been actually dead, was living! Dr. D—— was instantly standing by the bedside, and, upon examination, he found that a sudden and copious flow of blood had taken place from the wound which the lancet had left, and this, no doubt, had effected his sudden and almost preternatural restoration to an existence from which all thought he had been for ever removed. The man was still speechless, but he seemed to understand the physician when he forbid his repeating the painful and fruitless attempts which he made to articulate, and he at once resigned himself quietly into his hands.

I left the patient with leeches upon his temples, and bleeding freely—

apparently with little of the drowsiness which accompanies apoplexy; indeed, Dr. D—— told me that he had never before witnessed a seizure which seemed to combine the symptoms of so many kinds, and yet which belonged to none of the recognized classes; it certainly was not apoplexy, catalepsy, nor *delirium tremens,* and yet it seemed, in some degree, to partake of the properties of all—it was strange, but stranger things are coming.

During two or three days Dr. D—— would not allow his patient to converse in a manner which could excite or exhaust him, with any one; he suffered him merely, as briefly as possible, to express his immediate wants, and it was not until the fourth day after my early visit, the particulars of which I have just detailed, that it was thought expedient that I should see him, and then only because it appeared that his extreme importunity and impatience were likely to retard his recovery more than the mere exhaustion attendant upon a short conversation could possibly do; perhaps, too, my friend entertained some hope that if by holy confession his patient's bosom were eased of the perilous stuff, which no doubt, oppressed it, his recovery would be more assured and rapid. It was, then, as I have said, upon the fourth day after my first professional call, that I found myself once more in the dreary chamber of want and sickness. The man was in bed, and appeared low and restless. On my entering the room he raised himself in the bed, and muttered twice or thrice—"Thank God! thank God." I signed to those of his family who stood by, to leave the room, and took a chair beside the bed. So soon as we were alone, he said, rather doggedly—"There's no use now in telling me of the sinfulness of bad ways—I know it all—I know where they lead to—I seen everything about it with my own eyesight, as plain as I see you." He rolled himself in the bed, as if to hide his face in the clothes, and then suddenly raising himself, he exclaimed with startling vehemence— "Look, sir, there is no use in mincing the matter; I'm blasted with the fires of hell; I have been in hell; what do you think of that?—in hell—I'm lost for ever—I have not a chance—I am damned already—damned—damned——." The end of this sentence he actually shouted; his vehemence was perfectly terrific; he threw himself back, and laughed, and sobbed hysterically. I poured some water into a tea-cup, and gave it to him. After he had swallowed it, I told him if he had anything to communicate, to do so as briefly as he could, and in a manner as little agitating to himself as possible; threatening at the same time, though I had no intention of doing so, to leave him at once, in case he again gave way to such passionate excitement. "It's only foolishness," he continued, "for me to try to thank you for coming to such a villain as myself at all; it's no use for me to wish good to you, or to bless you; for such as me has no blessings to give." I told him that I had but done my duty, and urged him to proceed to the matter which weighed upon his mind; he then spoke nearly as follows:—I came in drunk on Friday night last, and got to my bed here, I don't remember how; sometime in the night, it seemed to me, I wakened, and feeling unasy in myself, I got up out of the bed. I wanted the fresh air, but I would not make a noise to open the window, for fear I'd waken the crathurs. It was very dark, and throublesome to find the door; but at last I did get it, and I groped my way out, and went down as asy as I could. I felt quite sober, and I counted the steps one after another, as I was going down, that I might not stumble at the bottom. When I came to the first landing-place, God be about us always! the floor of it sunk under me, and I went down, down, down, till the senses almost left me. I do not know how long I was falling, but it seemed to me a great while. When I came rightly to myself at last, I was sitting at a great table, near the top of it; and I could not see the end of it, if it had any, it was so far off; and there was men beyond reckoning, sitting down, all along by it, at each side, as far as I could see at all. I did not know at first was it in the open air; but there was a close smothering feel in it, that was not natural, and there was a kind of light that my eyesight never saw before, red and unsteady, and I did not see for a long time where it was coming from, until I looked straight up, and then I seen that it came from great balls of blood-coloured fire, that were rolling high over head with a sort of rushing, trembling sound, and I perceived that they shone on the ribs of a great roof of rock that was arched overhead instead of the sky. When I seen this, scarce knowing what I did, I got up, and I said, 'I have no right to be here; I must go,' and the man that was sitting at my left hand, only smiled, and said, 'sit down again, you can *never* leave this place,' and his voice was weaker than any child's voice I ever heerd, and when he was done speaking he smiled again. Then I spoke out very loud and bold, and I said—'in the name of God, let me out of this bad place.' And there was a great man, that I did not see before, sitting at the end of the table that I was near, and he was taller than twelve men, and his face was very proud and terrible to look at, and he stood up and stretched out his hand before him, and when he stood up, all that was there, great and small, bowed down with a sighing sound, and a dread came on my heart, and he looked at me, and I could not speak. I felt I was his own, to do what he liked with, for I knew at once who he was, and he said, 'if you promise to return, you may depart for a season'; and the voice he spoke with was terrible and mournful, and the echoes of it went rolling and swelling down the endless cave, and mixing with the trembling of the fire overhead; so that, when he sate down, there was a sound after him, all through the place like the roaring of a furnace, and I said, with all the strength I had, 'I promise to come back; in God's name let me go,' and with that I lost the sight and the hearing of all that was there, and when my senses came to me again, I was sitting in the bed with the blood all over me, and you and the rest praying around the room." Here he paused and wiped away the chill drops of horror which hung upon his forehead.

I remained silent for some moments. The vision which he had just described struck my imagination not a little, for this was long before Vathek and the "Hall of Iblis" had delighted the world; and the description which he gave had, as I received it, all the attractions of novelty beside the impressiveness which always belongs to the narration of an *eye-witness,* whether in the body or in the spirit, of the scenes which he describes. There was something, too, in the stern horror with which the man related these things, and in the incongruity of his description, with the vulgarly received notions of the great place of punishment, and of its presiding spirit, which struck my mind with awe, almost with fear. At length he said, with an expression of horrible, imploring earnestness, which I shall never forget—"Well, sir, is there any hope; is there any chance at all? or, is my soul pledged and promised away for ever? is it gone out of my power? must I go back to the place?"

In answering him I had no easy task to perform; for however clear might be my internal conviction of the groundlessness of his fears, and however strong my scepticism respecting the reality of what he had described, I nevertheless felt that his impression to the contrary, and his humility and terror resulting from it, might be made available as no mean engines in the work of his conversion from profligacy, and of his restoration to decent habits, and to religious feeling. I therefore told him that he was to regard his dream rather in the light of a warning than in that of a prophecy; that our salvation depended not upon the word or deed of a moment, but upon the habits of a life; that, in fine, if he at once discarded his idle companions and evil habits, and firmly adhered to a sober, industrious, and religious course of life, the powers of darkness might claim his soul in vain, for that there were higher and firmer pledges than human tongue could utter, which promised salvation to him who should repent and lead a new life.

I left him much comforted, and with a promise to return upon the next day. I did so, and found him much more cheerful, and without any remains of the dogged sullenness which I suppose had arisen from his despair. His promises of amendment were given in that tone of deliberate earnestness, which belongs to deep and solemn determination; and it was with no small delight that I observed, after repeated visits, that his good resolutions, so far from failing, did but gather strength by time; and when I saw that man shake off the idle and debauched companions, whose society had for years formed alike his amusement and his ruin, and revive his long discarded habits of industry and sobriety, I said within myself, there is something more in all this than the operation of an idle dream. One day, sometime after his perfect restoration to health, I was surprised on ascending the stairs, for the purpose of visiting this man, to find him busily employed in nailing down some planks upon the landing place, through which, at the commencement of his mysterious vision, it seemed to him that he had sunk. I perceived at once that he was strengthening the floor with a view to securing himself against such a catastrophe, and could scarcely forbear a smile as I bid "God bless his work."

He perceived my thoughts, I suppose, for he immediately said, "I can never pass over that floor without trembling. I'd leave this house if I could, but I can't find another lodging in the town so cheap, and I'll not take a better till I've paid off all my debts, please God; but I could not be asy in my mind till I made it as safe as I could. You'll hardly believe me, your honor, that while I'm working, maybe a mile away, my heart is in a flutter the whole way back, with the bare thoughts of the two little steps I have to walk upon this bit of a floor. So it's no wonder, sir, I'd thry to make it sound and firm with any idle timber I have."

I applauded his resolution to pay off his debts, and the steadiness with which he pursued his plans of conscientious economy, and passed on.

Many months elapsed, and still there appeared no alteration in his resolutions of amendment. He was a good workman, and with his better habits he recovered his former extensive and profitable employment. Every thing seemed to promise comfort and respectability. I have little more to add, and that shall be told quickly. I had one evening met Pat Connell, as he returned from his work, and as usual, after a mutual, and on his side respectful salutation, I spoke a few words of encouragement and approval. I left him industrious, active, healthy—when next I saw him, not three days after, he was a corpse. The circumstances which marked the event of his death were somewhat strange—I might say fearful. The unfortunate man had accidentally met an early friend, just returned, after a long absence, and in a moment of excitement, forgetting everything in the warmth of his joy, he yielded to his urgent invitation to accompany him into a public house, which lay close by the spot where the encounter had taken place. Connell, however, previously to entering the room, had announced his determination to take nothing more than the strictest temperance would warrant. But oh! who can describe the inveterate tenacity with which a drunkard's habits cling to him through life. He may repent—he may reform—he may look with actual abhorrence upon his past profligacy; but amid all this reformation and compunction, who can tell the moment in which the base and ruinous propensity may not recur, triumphing over resolution, remorse, shame, everything, and prostrating its victim once more in all that is destructive and revolting in that fatal vice.

The wretched man left the place in a state of utter intoxication. He was brought home nearly insensible, and placed in his bed, where he lay in the deep calm lethargy of drunkenness. The younger part of the family retired to rest much after their usual hour; but the poor wife remained up sitting by the fire, too much grieved and shocked at the recurrence of what she had so little expected, to settle to rest; fatigue, however, at length overcame her, and she sunk gradually into an uneasy slumber. She could not tell how long she had remained in this state, when she awakened, and immediately on opening her eyes, she perceived by the faint red light of the smouldering turf embers, two persons, one of whom she recognized as her husband noiselessly gliding out of the room.

"Pat, darling, where are you going?" said she. There was no answer—the door closed after them; but in a moment she was startled and terrified by a loud and heavy crash, as if some ponderous body had been hurled down the stair. Much alarmed, she started up, and going to the head of the staircase, she called repeatedly upon her husband, but in vain. She returned to the room, and with the assistance of her daughter, whom I had occasion to mention before, she succeeded in finding and lighting a candle, with which she hurried again to the head of the staircase. At the bottom lay what seemed to be a bundle of clothes, heaped together, motionless, lifeless—it was her husband. In going down the stairs, for what purpose can never now be known, he had fallen helplessly and violently to the bottom, and coming head foremost, the spine at the neck had been dislocated by the shock, and instant death must have ensued. The body lay upon that landing-place to which his dream had referred. It is scarcely worth endeavouring to clear up a single point in a narrative where all is mystery; yet I could not help suspecting that the second figure which had been seen in the room by Connell's wife on the night of his death, might have been no other than his own shadow. I suggested this solution of the difficulty; but she told me that the unknown person had been considerably in advance of the other, and on reaching the door, had turned back as if to communicate something to his companion—it was then a mystery. Was the dream verified?—whither had the disembodied spirit sped?—who can say? We know not. But I left the house of death that day in a state of horror which I could not describe. It seemed to me that I was scarce awake. I heard and saw everything as if under the spell of a nightmare. The coincidence was terrible.

THE DREAM WOMAN

WILKIE COLLINS

ONE

I had not been settled much more than six weeks in my country practice, when I was sent for to a neighbouring town, to consult with the resident medical man there on a case of very dangerous illness.

My horse had come down with me at the end of a long ride the night before, and had hurt himself, luckily, much more than he had hurt his master. Being deprived of the animal's services, I started for my destination by the coach (there were no railways at that time), and I hoped to get back again, towards the afternoon, in the same way.

After the consultation was over, I went to the principal inn of the town to wait for the coach. When it came up it was full inside and out. There was no resource left me but to get home as cheaply as I could by hiring a gig. The price asked for this accommodation struck me as being so extortionate that I determined to look out for an inn of inferior pretensions, and to try if I could not make a better bargain with a less prosperous establishment.

I soon found a likely-looking house, dingy and quiet, with an old-fashioned sign, that had evidently not been repainted for many years past. The landlord, in this case, was not above making a small profit, and as soon as we came to terms he rang the yard-bell to order the gig.

"Has Robert not come back from that errand?" asked the landlord, appealing to the waiter who answered the bell.

"No, sir, he hasn't."

"Well, then, you must wake up Isaac."

"Wake up Isaac!" I repeated; "that sounds rather odd. Do your ostlers go to bed in the daytime?"

"This one does," said the landlord, smiling to himself in rather a strange way.

"And dreams too," added the waiter; "I shan't forget the turn it gave me the first time I heard him."

"Never you mind about that," retorted the proprietor; "you go and rouse Isaac up. The gentleman's waiting for his gig."

The landlord's manner and the waiter's manner expressed a great deal more than they either of them said. I began to suspect that I might be on the trace of something professionally interesting to me as a medical man, and I thought I should like to look at the ostler before the waiter awakened him.

"Stop a minute," I interposed; "I have rather a fancy for seeing this man before you wake him up. I'm a doctor; and if this queer sleeping and dreaming of his comes from anything wrong in his brain, I may be able to tell you what to do with him."

"I rather think you will find his complaint past all doctoring, sir," said the landlord; "but if you would like to see him, you're welcome, I'm sure."

He led the way across a yard and down a passage to the stables, opened one of the doors, and, waiting outside himself, told me to look in.

I found myself in a two-stall stable. In one of the stalls a horse was munching his corn; in the other an old man was lying asleep on the litter.

I stooped and looked at him attentively. It was a withered, woebegone face. The eyebrows were painfully contracted; the mouth was fast set, and drawn down at the corners. The hollow wrinkled cheeks, and the scanty grizzled hair, told their own tale of some past sorrow or suffering. He was drawing his breath convulsively when I first looked at him, and in a moment more he began to talk in his sleep.

"Wake up!" I heard him say, in a quick whisper, through his clenched teeth. "Wake up there! Murder!"

He moved one lean arm slowly till it rested over his throat, shuddered a little, and turned on his straw. Then the arm left his throat, the hand stretched itself out, and clutched at the side towards which he had turned, as if he fancied himself to be grasping at the edge of something. I saw his lips move, and bent lower over him. He was still talking in his sleep.

"Light grey eyes," he murmured, "and a droop in the left eyelid; flaxen hair, with a gold-yellow streak in it—all right, mother—fair white arms, with a down on them—little lady's hand, with a reddish look under the finger-nails. The knife—always the cursed knife—first on one side, then on the other. Aha! you she-devil, where's the knife?"

At the last word his voice rose, and he grew restless on a sudden. I saw him shudder on the straw; his withered face became distorted, and he threw up both his hands with a quick hysterical gasp. They struck against the bottom of the manger under which he lay, and the blow awakened him. I had just time to slip through the door and close it before his eyes were fairly open, and his senses his own again.

"Do you know anything about that man's past life?" I said to the landlord.

"Yes, sir, I know pretty well all about it," was the answer, "and an uncommon queer story it is. Most people don't believe it. It's true, though, for all that. Why, just look at him," continued the landlord, opening the stable door again. "Poor devil! he's so worn out with his restless nights that he's dropped back into his sleep already."

"Don't wake him," I said; "I'm in no hurry for the gig. Wait till the other man comes back from his errand; and, in the meantime, suppose I have some lunch and a bottle of sherry, and suppose you come and help me to get through it?"

The heart of mine host, as I had anticipated, warmed to me over his own wine. He soon became communicative on the subject of the man asleep in the stable, and by little and little I drew the whole story out of him. Extravagant and incredible as the events must appear to everybody, they are related here just as I heard them and just as they happened.

TWO

Some years ago there lived in the suburbs of a large seaport town on the west coast of England a man in humble circumstances, by name Isaac Scatchard. His means of subsistence were derived from any employment that he could get as an ostler, and occasionally, when times went well with him, from temporary engagements in service as stable-helper in private houses. Though a faithful, steady, and honest man, he got on badly in his calling. His ill luck was proverbial among his neighbours. He was always missing good opportunities by no fault of his own, and always living longest in service with amiable people who were not punctual payers of wages. "Unlucky Isaac" was his nickname in his own neighbourhood, and no one could say that he did not richly deserve it.

With far more than one man's fair share of adversity to endure, Isaac had but one consolation to support him, and that was of the dreariest and most negative kind. He had no wife and children to increase his anxieties and add to the bitterness of his various failures in life. It might have been from mere insensibility, or it might have been from generous unwillingness to involve another in his own unlucky destiny; but the fact undoubtedly was, that he had arrived at the middle term of life without marrying, and, what is much more remarkable, without once exposing himself, from eighteen to eight-and-thirty, to the genial imputation of ever having had a sweetheart.

When he was out of service he lived alone with his widowed mother. Mrs.

Scatchard was a woman above the average in her lowly station as to capacity and manners. She had seen better days, as the phrase is, but she never referred to them in the presence of curious visitors; and, though perfectly polite to everyone who approached her, never cultivated any intimacies among her neighbours. She contrived to provide, hardly enough, for her simple wants by doing rough work for the tailors, and always managed to keep a decent home for her son to return to whenever his ill luck drove him out helpless into the world.

One bleak autumn, when Isaac was getting on fast towards forty, and when he was, as usual, out of place through no fault of his own, he set forth from his mother's cottage on a long walk inland to a gentleman's seat where he had heard that a stable-helper was required.

It wanted then but two days of his birthday; and Mrs. Scatchard, with her usual fondness, made him promise, before he started, and he would be back in time to keep that anniversary with her, in as festive a way as their poor means would allow. It was easy for him to comply with this request, even supposing he slept a night each way on the road.

He was to start from home on Monday morning, and, whether he got the new place or not, he was to be back for his birthday dinner on Wednesday at two o'clock.

Arriving at his destination too late on the Monday night to make application for the stable-helper's place, he slept at the village inn, and in good time on the Tuesday morning presented himself at the gentleman's house to fill the vacant situation. Here again his ill luck pursued him as inexorably as ever. The excellent written testimonials to his character which he was able to produce availed him nothing; his long walk had been taken in vain: only the day before the stable-helper's place had been given to another man.

Isaac accepted this new disappointment resignedly and as a matter of course. Naturally slow in capacity, he had the bluntness of sensibility and phlegmatic patience of disposition which frequently distinguish men with sluggishly-working mental powers. He thanked the gentleman's steward with his usual quiet civility for granting him an interview, and took his departure with no appearance of unusual depression in his face or manner.

Before starting on his homeward walk, he made some inquiries at the inn, and ascertained that he might save a few miles on his return by following a new road. Furnished with full instructions, several times repeated, as to the various turnings he was to take, he set forth on his homeward journey, and walked on all day with only one stoppage for bread and cheese. Just as it was getting towards dark, the rain came on and the wind began to rise, and he found himself, to make matters worse, in a part of the country with which he was entirely unacquainted, though he knew himself to be some fifteen miles from home. The first house he found to inquire at was a lonely roadside inn standing on the outskirts of a thick wood. Solitary as the place looked, it was welcome to a lost man who was also hungry, thirsty, footsore, and wet. The landlord was civil and respectable-looking, and the price he asked for a bed was reasonable enough. Isaac therefore decided on stopping comfortably at the inn for that night.

He was constitutionally a temperate man. His supper consisted of two rashers of bacon, a slice of home-made bread, and a pint of ale. He did not go to bed immediately after this moderate meal, but sat up with the landlord, talking about his bad prospects and his long run of ill luck, and diverging from these topics to the subjects of horse-flesh and racing. Nothing was said either by himself, his host, or the few labourers who strayed into the taproom, which could, in the slightest degree, excite the very small and very dull imaginative faculty which Isaac Scatchard possessed.

At a little after eleven the house was closed. Isaac went round with the landlord and held the candle while the doors and lower windows were being secured. He noticed with surprise the strength of the bolts and bars, and iron-sheathed shutters.

"You see, we are rather lonely here," said the landlord. "We never have had any attempts made to break in yet, but it's always as well to be on the safe side. When nobody is sleeping here, I am the only man in the house. My wife and daughter are timid, and the servant-girl takes after her missuses. Another glass of ale before you turn in? No! Well, how such a sober man as you comes to be out of place is more than I can make out, for one. Here's where you're to sleep. You're our only lodger to-night, and I think you'll say my missus has done her best to make you comfortable. You're quite sure you won't have another glass of ale? Very well. Good night."

It was half-past eleven by the clock in the passage as they went upstairs to the bedroom, the window of which looked on to the wood at the back of the house.

Isaac locked the door, set his candle on the chest of drawers, and wearily got ready for bed. The bleak autumn wind was still blowing, and the solemn, monotonous, surging moan of it in the wood was dreary and awful to hear through the night-silence. Isaac felt strangely wakeful. He resolved, as he lay down in bed, to keep the candle alight until he began to grow sleepy, for there was something unendurably depressing in the bare idea of lying awake in the darkness, listening to the dismal, ceaseless moaning of the wind in the wood.

Sleep stole on him before he was aware of it. His eyes closed, and he fell off insensibly to rest without having so much as thought of extinguishing the candle.

The first sensation of which he was conscious after sinking into slumber was a strange shivering that ran through him suddenly from head to foot, and a dreadful sinking pain at the heart, such as he had never felt before. The shivering only disturbed his slumbers; the pain woke him instantly. In one moment he passed from a state of sleep to a state of wakefulness—his eyes wide open—his mental perceptions cleared on a sudden, as if by a miracle.

The candle had burnt down nearly to the last morsel of tallow, but the top of the unsnuffed wick had just fallen off, and the light in the little room was, for the moment, fair and full.

Between the foot of his bed and the closed door there stood a woman with a knife in her hand, looking at him.

He was stricken speechless with terror, but he did not lose the preternatural clearness of his faculties, and he never took his eyes off the woman. She said not a word as they stared each other in the face, but she began to move slowly towards the left-hand side of the bed.

His eyes followed her. She was a fair, fine woman, with yellowish flaxen hair and light grey eyes, with a droop in the left eyelid. He noticed those things and fixed them on his mind before she was round at the side of the bed. Speechless, with no expression in her face, with no noise following her footfall, she came closer and closer—stopped—and slowly raised the knife. He laid his right arm over his throat to save it; but, as he saw the knife coming down, threw his hand across the bed to the right side, and jerked his body over that way just as the knife descended on the mattress within an inch of his shoulder.

His eyes fixed on her arm and hand as she slowly drew her knife out of the bed: a white, well-shaped arm, with a pretty down lying lightly over the fair skin—a delicate lady's hand, with the crowning beauty of a pink flush under and round the finger nails.

She drew the knife out, and passed back again slowly to the foot of the bed; stopped there for a moment looking at him; then came on—still speechless, still with no expression on the blank beautiful face, still with no sound following the stealthy footfalls—came on to the right side of the bed, where he now lay.

As she approached she raised the knife again, and he drew himself away to the left side. She struck, as before, right into the mattress, with a deliberate perpendicularly-downward action of the arm. This time his eyes wandered from her to the knife. It was like the large clasp-knives which he had often seen labouring men use to cut their bread and bacon with. Her delicate little fingers did not conceal more than two thirds of the handle: he noticed that it was made of buck-horn, clean and shining as the blade was, and looking like new.

For the second time she drew the knife out, concealed it in the wide sleeve of her gown, then stopped by the bedside, watching him. For an instant he saw her standing in that position, then the wick of the spent candle fell over into the socket; the flame diminished to a little blue point, and the room grew dark.

A moment, or less, if possible, passed so, and then the wick flamed up, smokingly, for the last time. His eyes were still looking eagerly over the right-hand side of the bed when the final flash of light came, but they discerned nothing. The fair woman with the knife was gone.

The conviction that he was alone again weakened the hold of the terror that had struck him dumb up to this time. The preternatural sharpness which the very intensity of his panic had mysteriously imparted to his faculties left them suddenly. His brain grew confused—his heart beat wildly—his ears opened for the first time since the appearance of the woman to a sense of the woeful ceaseless moaning of the wind among the trees. With the dreadful conviction of the reality of what he had seen still strong within him, he leaped out of bed, and screaming "Murder! Wake up, there! wake up!" dashed headlong through the darkness to the door.

It was fast locked, exactly as he had left it on going to bed.

His cries on starting up had alarmed the house. He heard the terrified, confused exclamations of women; he saw the master of the house approaching along the passage with his burning rush candle in one hand and his gun in the other.

"What is it?" asked the landlord breathlessly.

Isaac could only answer in a whisper. "A woman, with a knife in her hand," he gasped out. "In my room—a fair, yellow-haired woman; she jobbed at me with the knife twice over."

The landlord's pale cheeks grew paler. He looked at Isaac eagerly by the flickering light of his candle, and his face began to get red again; his voice altered, too, as well as his complexion. "She seems to have missed you twice," he said.

"I dodged the knife as it came down," Isaac went on, in the same scared whisper. "It struck the bed each time."

The landlord took his candle into the bedroom immediately. In less than a minute he came out again into the passage in a violent passion.

"The devil fly away with you and your woman with the knife! There isn't a mark in the bedclothes anywhere. What do you mean by coming into a man's place, and frightening his family out of their wits about a dream?"

"I'll leave your house," said Isaac faintly. "Better out on the road, in rain and dark, on my road home, than back again in that room, after what I've seen in it. Lend me a light to get my clothes by, and tell me what I'm to pay."

"Pay!" cried the landlord, leading the way with his light sulkily into the bedroom. "You'll find your score on the slate when you go downstairs. I wouldn't have taken you in for all the money you've got about you if I'd known your dreaming, screeching ways beforehand. Look at the bed. Where's the cut of a knife in it? Look at the window—is the lock bursted? Look at the door (which I heard you fasten yourself)—is it broke in? A murdering woman with a knife in my house! You ought to be ashamed of yourself!"

Isaac answered not a word. He huddled on his clothes, and then they went downstairs together.

"Nigh on twenty minutes past two!" said the landlord, as they passed the clock. "A nice time in the morning to frighten honest people out of their wits!"

Isaac paid his bill, and the landlord let him out at the front door, asking, with a grin of contempt, as he undid the strong fastenings, whether "the murdering woman got in that way."

They parted without a word on either side. The rain had ceased, but the night was dark, and the wind bleaker than ever. Little did the darkness, or the cold, or the uncertainty about the way home matter to Isaac. If he had been turned out into a wilderness in a thunderstorm, it would have been a relief after what he had suffered in the bedroom of the inn.

What was the fair woman with the knife? The creature of a dream, or that other creature from the unknown world called among men by the name of ghost? He could make nothing of the mystery—had made nothing of it, even when it was midday on Wednesday, and when he stood, at last, after many times missing his road, once more on the doorstep of home.

THREE

His mother came out eagerly to receive him. His face told her in a moment that something was wrong.

"I've lost the place; but that's my luck. I dreamed an ill dream last night, mother—or maybe I saw a ghost. Take it either way, it scared me out of my senses, and I'm not my own man again yet."

"Isaac, your face frightens me. Come in to the fire—come in, and tell mother all about it."

He was as anxious to tell as she was to hear; for it had been his hope all the way home, that his mother, with her quicker capacity and superior knowledge, might be able to throw some light on the mystery which he could not clear up for himself. His memory of the dream was still mechanically vivid, though his thoughts were entirely confused by it.

His mother's face grew paler and paler as he went on. She never interrupted him by so much as a single word; but when he had done, she moved her chair close to his, put her arm round his neck, and said to him,

"Isaac, you dreamed your ill dream on this Wednesday morning. What time was it when you saw the fair woman with the knife in her hand?"

Isaac reflected on what the landlord had said when they had passed by the clock on his leaving the inn; allowed as nearly as he could for the time that must have elapsed between the unlocking of his bedroom door and the paying of his bill just before going away, and answered,

"Somewhere about two o'clock in the morning."

His mother suddenly quitted her hold of his neck, and struck her hands together with a gesture of despair.

"This Wednesday is your birthday, Isaac, and two o'clock in the morning was the time when you were born."

Isaac's capacities were not quick enough to catch the infection of his mother's superstitious dread. He was amazed, and a little startled also, when she suddenly rose from her chair, opened her old writing-desk, took pen, ink, and paper and then said to him,

"Your memory is but a poor one, Isaac, and now I'm an old woman, mine's not much better. I want all about this dream of yours to be as well known to both of us, years hence, as it is now. Tell me over again all you told me a minute ago, when you spoke of what the woman with the knife looked like."

Isaac obeyed, and marvelled much as he saw his mother carefully set down on paper the very words that he was saying.

"Light grey eyes," she wrote, as they came to the descriptive part, "with a droop in the left eyelid; flaxen hair, with gold-yellow streak in it; white arms, with a down upon them; little lady's hand, with a reddish look about the finger-nails; clasp-knife with a buck-horn handle, that seemed as good as new." To these particulars Mrs. Scatchard added the year, month, day of the week, and time in the morning when the woman of the dream appeared to her son. She then locked up the paper carefully in her writing-desk.

Neither on that day nor on any day after could her son induce her to return to the matter of the dream. She obstinately kept her thoughts about it to herself, and even refused to refer again to the paper in her writing-desk. Ere long Isaac grew weary of attempting to make her break her resolute silence; and time, which sooner or later wears out all things, gradually wore out the impression produced on him by the dream. He began by thinking of it carelessly, and he ended by not thinking of it at all.

The result was the more easily brought about by the advent of some important changes for the better in his prospects which commenced not long after his terrible night's experience at the inn. He reaped at last the reward of his long and patient suffering under adversity by getting an excellent place, keeping it for seven years, and leaving it, on the death of his master, not only with an excellent character, but also with a comfortable annuity bequeathed to him as a reward for saving his mistress's life in a carriage accident. Thus it happened that Isaac Scatchard returned to his old mother, seven years after the time of the dream at the inn, with an annual sum of money at his disposal sufficient to keep them both in ease and independence for the rest of their lives.

The mother, whose health had been bad of late years, profited so much by the care bestowed on her and by freedom from money anxieties, that when Isaac's birthday came round she was able to sit up comfortably at table and dine with him.

On that day, as the evening drew on, Mrs. Scatchard discovered that a bottle of tonic medicine which she was accustomed to take, and in which she had fancied that a dose or more was still left, happened to be empty. Isaac immediately volunteered to go to the chemist's and get it filled again. It was as rainy and bleak an autumn night as on the memorable past occasion when he lost his way and slept at the road-side inn.

On going into the chemist's shop he was passed hurriedly by a poorly-dressed woman coming out of it. The glimpse he had of her face struck him, and he looked back after her as she descended the doorsteps.

"You're noticing that woman?" said the chemist's apprentice behind the counter. "It's my opinion there's something wrong with her. She's been asking for laudanum to put to a bad tooth. Master's out for half an hour, and I told her I wasn't allowed to sell poison to strangers in his absence. She laughed in a queer way, and said she would come back in half an hour. If she expects master to serve her, I think she'll be disappointed. It's a case of suicide, sir, if ever there was one yet."

These words added immeasurably to the sudden interest in the woman which Isaac had felt at the first sight of her face. After he had got the medicine-bottle filled, he looked about anxiously for her as soon as he was out in the street. She was walking slowly up and down on the opposite side of the road. With his heart, very much to his own surprise, beating fast, Isaac crossed over and spoke to her.

He asked if she was in any distress. She pointed to her torn shawl, her scanty dress, her crushed, dirty bonnet; then moved under a lamp so as to let the light fall on her stern, pale, but still most beautiful face.

"I look like a comfortable, happy woman, don't I?" she said, with a bitter laugh.

She spoke with a purity of intonation which Isaac had never heard before from other than ladies' lips. Her slightest actions seemed to have the easy, negligent grace of a thorough-bred woman. Her skin, for all its poverty-stricken paleness, was as delicate as if her life had been passed in the enjoyment of every social comfort that wealth can purchase. Even her small, finely-shaped hands, gloveless as they were, had not lost their whiteness.

Little by little, in answer to his questions, the sad story of the woman came out. There is no need to relate it here; it is told over and over again in police reports and paragraphs about attempted suicides.

"My name is Rebecca Murdoch," said the woman, as she ended. "I have ninepence left, and I thought of spending it at the chemist's over the way in securing a passage to the other world. Whatever it is, it can't be worse to me than this, so why should I stop here?"

Besides the natural compassion and sadness moved in his heart by what he heard, Isaac felt within him some mysterious influence at work all the time the woman was speaking which utterly confused his ideas and almost deprived him of his powers of speech. All that he could say in answer to her last reckless words was that he would prevent her from attempting her own life, if he followed her about all night to do it. His rough, trembling earnestness seemed to impress her.

"I won't occasion you that trouble," she answered, when he repeated his threat. "You have given me a fancy for living by speaking kindly to me. No need for the mockery of protestations and promises. You may believe me without them. Come to Fuller's Meadow to-morrow at twelve, and you will find me alive, to answer for myself—No!—no money. My ninepence will do to get me as good a night's lodging as I want."

She nodded and left him. He made no attempt to follow—he felt no suspicion that she was deceiving him.

"It's strange, but I can't help believing her," he said to himself, and walked away, bewildered, towards home.

On entering the house, his mind was still so completely absorbed by its new subject of interest that he took no notice of what his mother was doing when he came in with the bottle of medicine. She had opened her old writing-desk in his absence, and was now reading a paper attentively that lay inside it. On every birthday of Isaac's since she had written down the particulars of his dream from his own lips, she had been accustomed to read that same paper, and ponder over it in private.

The next day he went to Fuller's Meadow.

He had done only right in believing her so implicitly. She was there, punctual to a minute, to answer for herself. The last-left faint defences in Isaac's heart against the fascination which a word or look from her began inscrutably to exercise over him sank down and vanished before her for ever on that memorable morning.

When a man previously insensible to the influence of women forms an attachment in middle life, the instances are rare indeed, let the warning circumstances be what they may, in which he is found capable of freeing himself from the tyranny of the new ruling passion. The charm of being spoken to familiarly, fondly, and gratefully by a woman whose language and manners still retained enough of their early refinement to hint at the high social station that she had lost, would have been a dangerous luxury to a man of Isaac's rank at the age of twenty. But it was far more than that—it was certain ruin to him—now that his heart was opening unworthily to a new influence at that middle time of life when strong feelings of all kinds, once implanted, strike root most stubbornly in a man's moral nature. A few more stolen interviews after that first morning in Fuller's Meadow completed his infatuation. In less than a month from the time when he first met her, Isaac Scatchard had consented to give Rebecca Murdoch a new interest in existence, and a chance of recovering the character she had lost by promising to make her his wife.

She had taken possession, not of his passions only, but of his faculties as well. All the mind he had he put into her keeping. She directed him on every point—even instructing him how to break the news of his approaching marriage in the safest manner to his mother.

"If you tell her how you met me and who I am at first," said the cunning woman, "she will move heaven and earth to prevent our marriage. Say I am the sister of one of your fellow-servants—ask her to see me before you go into any more particulars—and leave it to me to do the rest. I mean to make her love me next best to you, Isaac, before she knows anything of who I really am."

The motive of the deceit was sufficient to sanctify it to Isaac. The stratagem proposed relieved him of his one great anxiety, and quieted his uneasy conscience on the subject of his mother. Still, there was something wanting to perfect his happiness, something that he could not realize, something mysteriously untraceable, and yet something that perpetually made itself felt; not when he was absent from Rebecca Murdoch, but, strange to say, when he was actually in her presence! She was kindness itself with him. She never made him feel his inferior capacities and inferior manners. She showed the sweetest anxiety to please him in the smallest trifles; but, in spite of all these attractions, he never could feel quite at his ease with her. At their first meeting, there had mingled with his admiration, when he looked in her face, a faint, involuntary feeling of doubt whether that face was entirely strange to him. No after familiarity had the slightest effect on this inexplicable, wearisome uncertainty.

Concealing the truth as he had been directed, he announced his marriage engagement precipitately and confusedly to his mother on the day when he contracted it. Poor Mrs. Scatchard showed her perfect confidence in her son by flinging her arms round his neck, and giving him joy of having found at last, in the sister of one of his fellow-servants, a woman to comfort and care for him after his mother was gone. She was all eagerness to see the woman of her son's choice, and the next day was fixed for the introduction.

It was a bright sunny morning, and the little cottage parlour was full of light as Mrs. Scatchard, happy and expectant, dressed for the occasion in her Sunday gown, sat waiting for her son and her future daughter-in-law.

Punctual to the appointed time, Isaac hurriedly and nervously led his promised wife into the room. His mother rose to receive her—advanced a few steps, smiling—looked Rebecca full in the eyes, and suddenly stopped. Her face, which had been flushed the moment before, turned white in an instant; her eyes lost their expression of softness and kindness, and assumed a blank look of terror; her outstretched hands fell to her sides, and she staggered back a few steps with a low cry to her son.

"Isaac," she whispered, clutching him fast by the arm when he asked alarmedly if she was taken ill, "Isaac, does that woman's face remind you of nothing?"

Before he could answer—before he could look round to where Rebecca stood, astonished and angered by her reception, at the lower end of the room, his mother pointed impatiently to her writing-desk, and gave him the key.

"Open it," she said, in a quick, breathless whisper.

"What does this mean? Why am I treated as if I had no business here? Does your mother want to insult me?" asked Rebecca angrily.

"Open it, and give me the paper in the left-hand drawer. Quick! quick, for Heaven's sake!" said Mrs. Scatchard, shrinking farther back in terror.

Isaac gave her the paper. She looked it over eagerly for a moment, then followed Rebecca, who was now turning away haughtily to leave the room, and caught her by the shoulder—abruptly raised the long, loose sleeve of her gown, and glanced at her hand and arm. Something like fear began to steal over the angry expression of Rebecca's face as she shook herself free from the old woman's grasp. "Mad!" she said to herself; "and Isaac never told me." With these few words she left the room.

Isaac was hastening after her when his mother turned and stopped his farther progress. It wrung his heart to see the misery and terror in her face as she looked at him.

"Light grey eyes," she said, in low, mournful, awestruck tones, pointing towards the open door; "a droop in the left eyelid; flaxen hair, with a gold-yellow streak in it; white arms, with a down upon them; little lady's hand, with a reddish look under the fingernails—*The Dream-Woman,* Isaac, the Dream-Woman!"

The faint cleaving doubt which he had never been able to shake off in Rebecca Murdoch's presence, was fatally set at rest for ever. He *had* seen her face, then, before—seven years before, on his birthday, in the bedroom of the lonely inn.

"Be warned! oh, my son, be warned! Isaac, Isaac, let her go, and do you stop with me!"

Something darkened the parlour window as those words were said. A sudden chill ran through him, and he glanced sidelong at the shadow. Rebecca Murdoch had come back. She was peering in curiously at them over the low window-blind.

"I have promised to marry, mother," he said, "and marry I must."

The tears came into his eyes as he spoke and dimmed his sight, but he could just discern the fatal face outside moving away again from the window.

His mother's head sank lower.

"Are you faint?" he whispered.

"Broken-hearted, Isaac."

He stooped down and kissed her. The shadow, as he did so, returned to the window, and the fatal face peered in curiously once more.

FOUR

Three weeks after that day Isaac and Rebecca were man and wife. All that was hopelessly dogged and stubborn in the man's moral nature seemed to have closed round his fatal passion, and to have fixed it unassailably in his heart.

After that first interview in the cottage parlour no consideration would induce Mrs. Scatchard to see her son's wife again, or even to talk of her when Isaac tried hard to plead her cause after their marriage.

This course of conduct was not in any degree occasioned by a discovery of the degradation in which Rebecca had lived. There was no question of that between mother and son. There was no question of anything but the fear-fully-exact resemblance between the living, breathing woman, and the spec-tre-woman of Isaac's dream.

Rebecca, on her side, neither felt nor expressed the slightest sorrow at the estrangement between herself and her mother-in-law. Isaac, for the sake of peace, had never contradicted her first idea that age and long illness had affected Mrs. Scatchard's mind. He even allowed his wife to upbraid him for not having confessed this to her at the time of their marriage engagement, rather than risk anything by hinting at the truth. The sacrifice of his integrity before his one all-mastering delusion seemed but a small thing, and cost his conscience but little after the sacrifices he had already made.

The time of waking from this delusion—the cruel and the rueful time— was not far off. After some quiet months of married life, as the summer was ending, and the year was getting on towards the month of his birthday, Isaac found his wife altering towards him. She grew sullen and contemptuous; she formed acquaintances of the most dangerous kind in defiance of his objections, his entreaties, and his commands; and, worst of all, she learned, ere long, after every fresh difference with her husband, to seek the deadly self-oblivion of drink. Little by little, after the first miserable discovery that his wife was keeping company with drunkards, the shocking certainty forced itself on Isaac that she had grown to be a drunkard herself.

He had been in a sadly desponding state for some time before the occurrence of these domestic calamities. His mother's health, as he could but too plainly discern every time he went to see her at the cottage, was failing fast, and he upbraided himself in secret as the cause of the bodily and mental suffering she endured. When to his remorse on his mother's account was added the shame and misery occasioned by the discovery of his wife's degradation, he sank under the double trial—his face began to alter fast, and he looked what he was, a spirit-broken man.

His mother, still struggling bravely against the illness that was hurrying her to the grave, was the first to notice the sad alteration in him, and the first to hear of his last worst trouble with his wife. She could only weep bitterly on the day when he made his humiliating confession, but on the next occasion when he went to see her she had taken a resolution in reference to his domestic afflictions which astonished and even alarmed him. He found her dressed to go out, and on asking the reason received this answer:

"I am not long for this world, Isaac," she said, "and I shall not feel easy on my death-bed unless I have done my best to the last to make my son happy. I mean to put my own fears and my own feelings out of the question, and to go with you to your wife, and try what I can do to reclaim her. Give me your arm, Isaac, and let me do the last thing I can in this world to help my son before it is too late."

He could not disobey her, and they walked together slowly towards his miserable home.

It was only one o'clock in the afternoon when they reached the cottage where he lived. It was their dinner-hour, and Rebecca was in the kitchen. He was thus able to take his mother quietly into the parlour, and then prepare his wife for the interview. She had fortunately drunk but little at that early hour, and she was less sullen and capricious than usual.

He returned to his mother with his mind tolerably at ease. His wife soon followed him into the parlour, and the meeting between her and Mrs. Scatchard passed off better than he had ventured to anticipate, though he observed with secret apprehension that his mother, resolutely as she controlled herself in other respects, could not look his wife in the face when she spoke to her. It was a relief to him, therefore, when Rebecca began to lay the cloth.

She laid the cloth, brought in the bread-tray, and cut a slice from the loaf for her husband, then returned to the kitchen. At that moment, Isaac, still anxiously watching his mother, was startled by seeing the same ghastly change pass over her face which had altered it so awfully on the morning when Rebecca and she first met. Before he could say a word, she whispered, with a look of horror,

"Take me back—home, home again, Isaac. Come with me, and never go back again."

He was afraid to ask for an explanation; he could only sign to her to be silent, and help her quickly to the door. As they passed the bread-tray on the table she stopped and pointed to it. "Did you see what your wife cut your bread with?" she asked, in a low whisper.

"No, mother—I was not noticing—what was it?"

"Look!"

He did look. A new clasp-knife, with a buck-horn handle, lay with the loaf in the bread-tray. He stretched out his hand shudderingly to possess himself of it; but, at the same time, there was a noise in the kitchen, and his mother caught at his arm.

"The knife of the dream! Isaac, I'm faint with fear. Take me away before she comes back."

He was hardly able to support her. The visible, tangible reality of the knife struck him with a panic, and utterly destroyed any faint doubts that he might have entertained up to this time in relation to the mysterious dream-warning of nearly eight years before. By a last desperate effort, he summoned self-possession enough to help his mother out of the house—so quietly that the "Dream-woman" (he thought of her by that name now) did not hear them departing from the kitchen.

"Don't go back, Isaac—don't go back!" implored Mrs. Scatchard, as he turned to go away, after seeing her safely seated again in her own room.

"I must get the knife," he answered, under his breath. His mother tried to stop him again, but he hurried out without another word.

On his return he found that his wife had discovered their secret departure from the house. She had been drinking, and was in a fury of passion. The dinner in the kitchen was flung under the grate; the cloth was off the parlour table. Where was the knife?

Unwisely, he asked for it. She was only too glad of the opportunity of irritating him which the request afforded her. "He wanted the knife, did he? Could he give her a reason why? No! Then he should not have it—not if he went down on his knees to ask for it." Further recriminations elicited the fact that she had bought it a bargain, and that she considered it her own especial property. Isaac saw the uselessness of attempting to get the knife by fair means, and determined to search for it, later in the day, in secret. The search was unsuccessful. Night came on, and he left the house to walk about the streets. He was afraid now to sleep in the same room with her.

Three weeks passed. Still sullenly enraged with him, she would not give up the knife; and still that fear of sleeping in the same room with her possessed him. He walked about at night, or dozed in the parlour, or sat watching by his mother's bedside. Before the expiration of the first week in the new month his mother died. It wanted then but ten days of her son's birthday. She had longed to live till that anniversary. Isaac was present at her death, and her last words in this world were addressed to him:

"Don't go back, my son, don't go back!"

He was obliged to go back, if it were only to watch his wife. Exasperated to the last degree by his distrust of her, she had revengefully sought to add a sting to his grief, during the last days of his mother's illness, by declaring that she would assert her right to attend the funeral. In spite of all that he could do or say, she held with wicked pertinacity to her word, and on the day appointed for the burial forced herself—inflamed and shameless with drink—into her husband's presence, and declared that she would walk in the funeral procession to his mother's grave.

This last worst outrage, accompanied by all that was most insulting in word and look, maddened him for the moment. He struck her.

The instant the blow was dealt he repented it. She crouched down, silent, in a corner of the room, and eyed him steadily; it was a look that cooled his hot blood and made him tremble. But there was no time now to think of a means of making atonement. Nothing remained but to risk the worst till the funeral was over. There was but one way of making sure of her. He locked her into her bedroom.

When he came back some hours after, he found her sitting, very much altered in look and bearing, by the bedside, with a bundle on her lap. She rose, and faced him quietly, and spoke with a strange stillness in her voice, a strange repose in her eyes, a strange composure in her manner.

"No man has ever struck me twice," she said, "and my husband shall have no second opportunity. Set the door open and let me go. From this day forth we see each other no more."

Before he could answer she passed him and left the room. He saw her walk away up the street.

Would she return?

All that night he watched and waited, but no footstep came near the house. The next night, overpowered by fatigue, he lay down in bed in his clothes, with the door locked, the key on the table, and the candle burning. His slumber was not disturbed. The third night, the fourth, the fifth, the sixth passed, and nothing happened. He lay down on the seventh, still in his clothes, still with the door locked, the key on the table, and the candle burning, but easier in his mind.

Easier in his mind, and in perfect health of body when he fell off to sleep. But his rest was disturbed. He woke twice without any sensation of uneasiness. But the third time it was that never-to-be-forgotten shivering of the night at the lonely inn, that dreadful sinking pain at the heart, which once more aroused him in an instant.

His eyes opened towards the left-hand side of the bed, and there stood—

The Dream-Woman again? No! His wife; the living reality, with the dream-spectre's face, in the dream-spectre's attitude; the fair arm up, the knife clasped in the delicate white hand.

He sprang upon her almost at the instant of seeing her, and yet not quickly enough to prevent her from hiding the knife. Without a word from him—without a cry from her—he pinioned her in a chair. With one hand he felt up her sleeve, and there, where the Dream-Woman had hidden the knife, his wife had hidden it—the knife with the buck-horn handle, that looked like new.

In the despair of that fearful moment his brain was steady, his heart was calm. He looked at her fixedly with the knife in his hand, and said these last words:

"You told me we should see each other no more, and you have come back. It is my turn now to go, and to go for ever. I say that we shall see each other no more, and *my* word shall not be broken."

He left her, and set forth into the night. There was a bleak wind abroad, and the smell of recent rain was in the air. The distant church-clocks chimed the quarter as he walked rapidly beyond the last houses in the suburb. He asked the first policeman he met what hour that was of which the quarter past had just struck.

The man referred sleepily to his watch, and answered, "Two o'clock." Two in the morning. What day of the month was this day that had just begun? He reckoned it up from the date of his mother's funeral. The fatal parallel was complete: it was his birthday!

Had he escaped the mortal peril which his dream foretold? or had he only received a second warning?

As that ominous doubt forced itself on his mind, he stopped, reflected, and turned back again towards the city. He was still resolute to hold to his word, and never to let her see him more, but there was a thought now in his mind of having her watched and followed. The knife was in his possession; the world was before him; but a new distrust of her—a vague, unspeakable, superstitious dread had overcome him.

"I must know where she goes, now she thinks I have left her," he said to himself, as he stole back wearily to the precincts of his house.

It was still dark. He had left the candle burning in the bed-chamber; but when he looked up to the window of the room now, there was no light in it. He crept cautiously to the house door. On going away, he remembered to have closed it; on trying it now, he found it open.

He waited outside, never losing sight of the house, till day-light. Then he ventured indoors—listened, and heard nothing—looked into kitchen, scullery, parlour, and found nothing; went up, at last, into the bedroom—it was empty. A picklock lay on the floor, betraying how she had gained entrance in the night, and that was the only trace of her.

Whither had she gone? That no mortal tongue could tell him. The darkness had covered her flight; and when the day broke, no man could say where the light found her.

Before leaving the house and the town for ever, he gave instructions to a friend and neighbour to sell his furniture for anything that it would fetch, and apply the proceeds to employing the police to trace her. The directions were honestly followed and the money was all spent, but the inquiries led to nothing. The picklock on the bedroom floor remained the one last useless trace of the Dream-Woman.

At this point of the narrative the landlord paused, and, turning towards the window of the room in which we were sitting, looked in the direction of the stableyard.

"So far," he said, "I tell you what was told to me. The little that remains to be added lies within my own experience. Between two and three months after the events I have just been relating, Isaac Scatchard came to me, withered and old-looking before his time, just as you saw him to-day. He had his testimonials to character with him, and he asked for employment here. Knowing that my wife and he were distantly related, I gave him a trial in consideration of that relationship, and liked him in spite of his queer habits. He is as sober, honest, and willing a man as there is in England. As for his

restlessness at night, and his sleeping away his leisure time in the day, who can
wonder at it after hearing his story? Besides, he never objects to being roused
up when he's wanted, so there's not much inconvenience to complain of,
after all."

"I suppose he is afraid of a return of that dreadful dream, and of waking
out of it in the dark?" said I.

"No," returned the landlord. "The dream comes back to him so often that
he has got to bear with it by this time resignedly enough. It's his wife keeps
him waking at night, as he has often told me."

"What! Has she never been heard of yet?"

"Never. Isaac himself has the one perpetual thought about her, that she is
alive and looking for him. I believe he wouldn't let himself drop off to sleep
towards two in the morning for a king's ransom. Two in the morning, he
says, is the time she will find him, one of these days. Two in the morning is
the time all the year round when he likes to be most certain that he has got
that clasp-knife safe about him. He does not mind being alone as long as he is
awake, except on the night before his birthday, when he firmly believes
himself to be in peril of his life. The birthday has only come round once since
he has been here, and then he sat up along with the night-porter. "She's
looking for me," is all he says when anybody speaks to him about the one
anxiety of his life; "she's looking for me." He may be right. She *may* be
looking for him. Who can tell?"

"Who can tell?" said I.

A Dream
of Red Hands

Bram Stoker

The first opinion given to me regarding Jacob Settle was a simple descriptive statement, 'He's a down-in-the-mouth chap': but I found that it embodied the thoughts and ideas of all his fellow-workmen. There was in the phrase a certain easy tolerance, an absence of positive feeling of any kind, rather than any complete opinion, which marked pretty accurately the man's place in public esteem. Still, there was some dissimilarity between this and his appearance which unconsciously set me thinking, and by degrees, as I saw more of the place and the workmen, I came to have a special interest in him. He was, I found, for ever doing kindnesses, not involving money expenses beyond his humble means, but in the manifold ways of forethought and forbearance and self-repression which are of the truer charities of life. Women and children trusted him implicitly, though, strangely enough, he rather shunned them, except when anyone was sick, and then he made his appearance to help if he could, timidly and awkwardly. He led a very solitary life, keeping house by himself in a tiny cottage, or rather hut, of one room, far on the edge of the moorland. His existence seemed so sad and solitary that I wished to cheer it up, and for the purpose took the occasion when we had both been sitting up with a child, injured by me through accident, to offer to lend him books. He gladly accepted, and as we parted in the grey of the dawn I felt that something of mutual confidence had been established between us.

The books were always most carefully and punctually returned, and in time Jacob Settle and I became quite friends. Once or twice as I crossed the moorland on Sundays I looked in on him; but on such occasions he was shy and ill at ease so that I felt diffident about calling to see him. He would never under any circumstances come into my own lodgings.

One Sunday afternoon, I was coming back from a long walk beyond the moor, and as I passed Settle's cottage stopped at the door to say 'How do you do?' to him. As the door was shut, I thought that he was out, and merely knocked for form's sake, or through habit, not expecting to get any answer. To my surprise, I heard a feeble voice from within, though what was said I could not hear. I entered at once, and found Jacob lying half-dressed upon his bed. He was as pale as death, and the sweat was simply rolling off his face. His hands were unconsciously gripping the bedclothes as a drowning man holds on to whatever he may grasp. As I came in he half arose, with a wild, hunted look in his eyes, which were wide open and staring, as though something of horror had come before him; but when he recognised me he sank back on the couch with a smothered sob of relief and closed his eyes. I stood by him for a while, quite a minute or two, while he gasped. Then he opened his eyes and looked at me, but with such a despairing, woeful expression that, as I am a living man, I would have rather seen that frozen look of horror. I sat down beside him and asked after his health. For a while he would not answer me except to say that he was not ill; but then, after scrutinising me closely, he half arose on his elbow and said:

'I thank you kindly, sir, but I'm simply telling you the truth. I am not ill, as men call it, though God knows whether there be not worse sicknesses than doctors know of. I'll tell you, as you are so kind, but I trust that you won't even mention such a thing to a living soul, for it might work me more and greater woe. I am suffering from a bad dream.'

'A bad dream!' I said, hoping to cheer him; 'but dreams pass away with the light—even with waking.' There I stopped, for before he spoke I saw the answer in his desolate look round the little place.

'No! no! that's all well for people that live in comfort and with those they love around them. It is a thousand times worse for those who live alone and have to do so. What cheer is there for me, waking here in the silence of the night, with the wide moor around me full of voices and full of faces that make my waking a worse dream than my sleep? Ah, young sir, you have no past that can send its legions to people the darkness and the empty space, and I pray the good God that you may never have!' As he spoke, there was such an almost irresistible gravity of conviction in his manner that I abandoned my remonstrance about his solitary life. I felt that I was in the presence of some secret influence which I could not fathom. To my relief, for I knew not what to say, he went on:

'Two nights past have I dreamed it. It was hard enough the first night, but I came through it. Last night the expectation was in itself almost worse than the dream—until the dream came, and then it swept away every remembrance of lesser pain. I stayed awake till just before the dawn, and then it came again, and ever since I have been in such an agony as I am sure the dying feel, and with it all the dread of tonight.' Before he had got to the end of the sentence my mind was made up, and I felt that I could speak to him more cheerfully. 'Try and get to sleep early tonight—in fact, before the evening has passed away. The sleep will refresh you, and I promise you there will not be any bad dreams after tonight.' He shook his head hopelessly, so I sat a little longer and then left him.

When I got home I made my arrangements for the night, for I had made up my mind to share Jacob Settle's lonely vigil in his cottage on the moor. I judged that if he got to sleep before sunset he would wake well before midnight, and so, just as the bells of the city were striking eleven, I stood opposite his door armed with a bag, in which were my supper, an extra large flask, a couple of candles, and a book. The moonlight was bright, and flooded the whole moor, till it was almost as light as day; but ever and anon black clouds drove across the sky, and made a darkness which by comparison seemed almost tangible. I opened the door softly, and entered without waking Jacob, who lay asleep with his white face upward. He was still, and again bathed in sweat. I tried to imagine what visions were passing before those closed eyes which could bring with them the misery and woe which were stamped on the face, but fancy failed me, and I waited for the awakening. It came suddenly, and in a fashion which touched me to the quick, for the hollow groan that broke from the man's white lips as he half arose and sank back was manifestly the realisation or completion of some train of thought which had gone before.

'If this be dreaming,' said I to myself, 'then it must be based on some very terrible reality. What can have been that unhappy fact that he spoke of?'

While I thus spoke, he realised that I was with him. It struck me as strange that he had no period of that doubt as to whether dream or reality surrounded him which commonly marks an expected environment of waking men. With a positive cry of joy, he seized my hand and held it in his two wet, trembling hands, as a frightened child clings on to someone whom it loves. I tried to soothe him:

'There, there! it is all right. I have come to stay with you to-night, and together we will try to fight this evil dream.' He let go my hand suddenly, and sank back on his bed and covered his eyes with his hands.

'Fight it?—the evil dream! Ah! no, sir, no! No mortal power can fight that dream, for it comes from God—and is burned in here;' and he beat upon his forehead. Then he went on:

'It is the same dream, ever the same, and yet it grows in its power to torture me every time it comes.'

'What is the dream?' I asked, thinking that the speaking of it might give him some relief, but he shrank away from me, and after a long pause said:

'No, I had better not tell it. It may not come again.'

There was manifestly something to conceal from me—something that lay behind the dream, so I answered:

'All right. I hope you have seen the last of it. But if it should come again, you will tell me, will you not? I ask, not out of curiosity, but because I think it may relieve you to speak.' He answered with what I thought was almost an undue amount of solemnity:

'If it comes again, I shall tell you all.'

Then I tried to get his mind away from the subject to more mundane things, so I produced supper, and made him share it with me, including the contents of the flask. After a little he braced up, and when I lit my cigar, having given him another, we smoked a full hour, and talked of many things. Little by little the comfort of his body stole over his mind, and I could see sleep laying her gentle hands on his eyelids. He felt it, too, and told me that now he felt all right, and I might safely leave him; but I told him that, right or wrong, I was going to see in the daylight. So I lit my other candle, and began to read as he fell asleep.

By degrees I got interested in my book, so interested that presently I was startled by its dropping out of my hands. I looked and saw that Jacob was still asleep, and I was rejoiced to see that there was on his face a look of unwonted happiness, while his lips seemed to move with unspoken words. Then I turned to my work again, and again woke, but this time to feel chilled to my very marrow by hearing the voice from the bed beside me:

'Not with those red hands! Never! never!' On looking at him, I found that he was still asleep. He woke, however, in an instant, and did not seem surprised to see me; there was again that strange apathy as to his surroundings. Then I said:

'Settle, tell me your dream. You may speak freely, for I shall hold your confidence sacred. While we both live I shall never mention what you may choose to tell me.'

He replied:

'I said I would; but I had better tell you first what goes before the dream, that you may understand. I was a schoolmaster when I was a very young man; it was only a parish school in a little village in the West Country. No need to mention any names. Better not. I was engaged to be married to a young girl whom I loved and almost reverenced. It was the old story. While we were waiting for the time when we could afford to set up house together, another man came along. He was nearly as young as I was, and handsome, and a gentleman, with all a gentleman's attractive ways for a woman of our class. He would go fishing, and she would meet him while I was at my work in school. I reasoned with her and implored her to give him up. I offered to get married at once and go away and begin the world in a strange country; but she would not listen to anything I could say, and I could see that she was infatuated with him. Then I took it on myself to meet the man and ask him to deal well with the girl, for I thought he might mean honestly by her, so that there might be no talk or chance of talk on the part of others. I went where I should meet him with none by, and we met!' Here Jacob Settle had to pause, for something seemed to rise in his throat, and he almost gasped for breath. Then he went on:

'Sir, as God is above us, there was no selfish thought in my heart that day, I loved my pretty Mabel too well to be content with a part of her love, and I had thought of my own unhappiness too often not to have come to realise that, whatever might come to her, my hope was gone. He was insolent to me —you, sir, who are a gentleman, cannot know, perhaps, how galling can be the insolence of one who is above you in station—but I bore with that. I implored him to deal well with the girl, for what might be only a pastime of an idle hour with him might be the breaking of her heart. For I never had a thought of her truth, or that the worst of harm could come to her—it was only the unhappiness to her heart I feared. But when I asked him when he intended to marry her his laughter galled me so that I lost my temper and told him that I would not stand by and see her life made unhappy. Then he grew angry too, and in his anger said such cruel things of her that then and there I swore he should not live to do her harm. God knows how it came about, for in such moments of passion it is hard to remember the steps from a word to a blow, but I found myself standing over his dead body, with my hands crimson with the blood that welled from his torn throat. We were alone and he was a stranger, with none of his kin to seek for him and murder does not always out —not all at once. His bones may be whitening still, for all I know, in the pool of the river where I left him. No one suspected his absence, or why it was, except my poor Mabel, and she dared not speak. But it was all in vain, for when I came back again after an absence of months—for I could not live in the place—I learned that her shame had come and that she had died in it. Hitherto I had been borne up by the thought that my ill deed had saved her future, but now, when I learned that I had been too late, and that my poor love was smirched with that man's sin, I fled away with the sense of my useless guilt upon me more heavily than I could bear. Ah! sir, you that have not done such a sin don't know what it is to carry it with you. You may think that custom makes it easy to you, but it is not so. It grows and grows with every hour, till it becomes intolerable, and with it growing, too, the feeling that you must for ever stand outside Heaven. You don't know what that means, and I pray God that you never may. Ordinary men, to whom all things are possible, don't often, if ever, think of Heaven. It is a name, and nothing more, and they are content to wait and let things be, but to those who are doomed to be shut out for ever you cannot think what it means, you cannot guess or measure the terrible endless longing to see the gates opened, and to be able to join the white figures within.

'And this brings me to my dream. It seemed that the portal was before me, with great gates of massive steel with bars of the thickness of a mast, rising to the very clouds, and so close that between them was just a glimpse of a crystal grotto, on whose shining walls were figured many white-clad forms with faces radiant with joy. When I stood before the gate my heart and my soul were so full of rapture and longing that I forgot. And there stood at the gate two mighty angels with sweeping wings, and, oh! so stern of countenance. They held each in one hand a flaming sword, and in the other the latchet, which moved to and fro at their lightest touch. Nearer were figures all draped in black, with heads covered so that only the eyes were seen, and they handed to each who came white garments such as the angels wear. A low murmur came that told that all should put on their own robes, and without soil, or the angels would not pass them in, but would smite them down with the flaming swords. I was eager to don my own garment, and hurriedly threw it over me and stepped swiftly to the gate; but it moved not, and the angels, loosing the latchet, pointed to my dress, I looked down, and was aghast, for the whole robe was smeared with blood. My hands were red; they glittered with the blood that dripped from them as on that day by the river bank. And then the angels raised their flaming swords to smite me down, and the horror was complete—I awoke. Again, and again, and again, that awful dream comes to me. I never learn from the experience, I never remember, but at the beginning the hope is ever there to make the end more appalling; and I know that the dream does not come out of the common darkness where the dreams abide, but that it is sent from God as a punishment! Never, never shall I be able to pass the gate, for the soil on the angel garments must ever come from these bloody hands!'

I listened as in a spell as Jacob Settle spoke. There was something so far away in the tone of his voice—something so dreamy and mystic in the eyes that looked as if through me at some spirit beyond—something so lofty in his very diction and in such marked contrast to his workworn clothes and his poor surroundings that I wondered if the whole thing were not a dream.

We were both silent for a long time. I kept looking at the man before me in growing wonderment. Now that his confession had been made, his soul, which had been crushed to the very earth, seemed to leap back again to uprightness with some resilient force. I suppose I ought to have been horrified with his story, but, strange to say, I was not. It certainly is not pleasant to be made the recipient of the confidence of a murderer, but this poor fellow seemed to have had, not only so much provocation, but so much self-denying purpose in his deed of blood that I did not feel called upon to pass judgment upon him. My purpose was to comfort, so I spoke out with what calmness I could, for my heart was beating fast and heavily:

'You need not despair, Jacob Settle. God is very good, and His mercy is great. Live on and work on in the hope that some day you may feel that you have atoned for the past.' Here I paused, for I could see that sleep, natural sleep this time, was creeping upon him. 'Go to sleep,' I said; 'I shall watch with you here, and we shall have no more evil dreams tonight.'

He made an effort to pull himself together, and answered:

'I don't know how to thank you for your goodness to me this night, but I think you had best leave me now. I'll try and sleep this out; I feel a weight off my mind since I have told you all. If there's anything of the man left in me, I must try and fight out life alone.'

'I'll go tonight, as you wish it,' I said; 'but take my advice, and do not live in such a solitary way. Go among men and women; live among them. Share their joys and sorrows, and it will help you to forget. This solitude will make you melancholy mad.'

'I will!' he answered, half unconsciously, for sleep was overmastering him. I turned to go, and he looked after me. When I had touched the latch I dropped it, and, coming back to the bed, held out my hand. He grasped it with both his as he rose to a sitting posture, and I said my good-night, trying to cheer him:

'Heart, man, heart! There is work in the world for you to do, Jacob Settle. You can wear those white robes yet and pass through that gate of steel!'

Then I left him.

A week after I found his cottage deserted, and on asking at the works was told that he had 'gone north', no one exactly knew whither.

Two years afterwards, I was staying for a few days with my friend Dr. Munro in Glasgow. He was a busy man, and could not spare much time for going about with me, so I spent my days in excursions to the Trossachs and Loch Katrine and down the Clyde. On the second last evening of my stay I came back somewhat later than I had arranged, but found that my host was late too. The maid told me that he had been sent for to the hospital—a case of accident at the gas-works, and the dinner was postponed an hour; so telling her I would stroll down to find her master and walk back with him, I went out. At the hospital I found him washing his hands preparatory to starting for home. Casually, I asked him what his case was.

'Oh, the usual thing! A rotten rope and men's lives of no account. Two men were working in a gasometer, when the rope that held their scaffolding broke. It must have occurred just before the dinner hour, for no one noticed their absence till the men had returned. There was about seven feet of water in the gasometer, so they had a hard fight for it, poor fellows. However, one of them was alive, just alive, but we have had a hard job to pull him through. It seems that he owes his life to his mate, for I have never heard of greater heroism. They swam together while their strength lasted, but at the end they were so done up that even the lights above, and the men slung with ropes, coming down to help them, could not keep them up. But one of them stood on the bottom and held up his comrade over his head, and those few breaths made all the difference between life and death. They were a shocking sight when they were taken out, for that water is like a purple dye with the gas and the tar. The man upstairs looked as if he had been washed in blood. Ugh!'

'And the other?'

'Oh, he's worse still. But he must have been a very noble fellow. That struggle under the water must have been fearful; one can see that by the way the blood has been drawn from the extremities. It makes the idea of the *Stigmata* possible to look at him. Resolution like this could, you would think, do anything in the world. Ay! it might almost unbar the gates of Heaven. Look here, old man, it is not a very pleasant sight, especially just before dinner, but you are a writer, and this is an odd case. Here is something you would not like to miss, for in all human probability you will never see anything like it again.' While he was speaking he had brought me into the mortuary of the hospital.

On the bier lay a body covered with a white sheet, which was wrapped close round it.

'Looks like a chrysalis, don't it? I say, Jack, if there be anything in the old myth that a soul is typified by a butterfly, well, then the one that this chrysalis sent forth was a very noble specimen and took all the sunlight on its wings. See here!' He uncovered the face. Horrible, indeed, it looked, as though stained with blood. But I knew him at once, Jacob Settle! My friend pulled the winding sheet further down.

The hands were crossed on the purple breast as they had been reverently placed by some tender-hearted person. As I saw them my heart throbbed with a great exultation, for the memory of his harrowing dream rushed across my mind. There was no stain now on those poor, brave hands, for they were blanched white as snow.

And somehow as I looked I felt that the evil dream was all over. That noble soul had won a way through the gate at last. The white robe had now no stain from the hands that had put it on.

THE DEATH
OF HALPIN FRAYSER

AMBROSE BIERCE

ONE

For by death is wrought greater change than hath been shown. Whereas in general the spirit that removed cometh back upon occasion, and is sometimes seen of those in flesh (appearing in the form of the body it bore) yet it hath happened that the veritable body without the spirit hath walked. And it is attested of those encountering who have lived to speak thereon that a lich so raised up hath no natural affection, nor remembrance thereof, but only hate. Also, it is known that some spirits which in life were benign become by death evil altogether.—*Hali.*

One dark night in midsummer a man waking from a dreamless sleep in a forest lifted his head from the earth, and staring a few moments into the blackness, said: "Catherine Larue." He said nothing more; no reason was known to him why he should have said so much.

The man was Halpin Frayser. He lived in St. Helena, but where he lives now is uncertain, for he is dead. One who practices sleeping in the woods with nothing under him but the dry leaves and the damp earth, and nothing over him but the branches from which the leaves have fallen and the sky from which the earth has fallen, cannot hope for great longevity, and Frayser had already attained the age of thirty-two. There are persons in this world, millions of persons, and far and away the best persons, who regard that as a very advanced age. They are the children. To those who view the voyage of life from the port of departure the bark that has accomplished any considerable distance appears already in close approach to the farther shore. However, it is not certain that Halpin Frayser came to his death by exposure.

He had been all day in the hills west of the Napa Valley, looking for doves and such small game as was in season. Late in the afternoon it had come on to be cloudy, and he had lost his bearings; and although he had only to go always downhill—everywhere the way to safety when one is lost—the absence of trails had so impeded him that he was overtaken by night while still in the forest. Unable in the darkness to penetrate the thickets of manzanita and other undergrowth, utterly bewildered and overcome with fatigue, he had lain down near the root of a large madroño and fallen into a dreamless sleep. It was hours later, in the very middle of the night, that one of God's mysterious messengers, gliding ahead of the incalculable host of his companions sweeping westward with the dawn line, pronounced the awakening word in the ear of the sleeper, who sat upright and spoke, he knew not why, a name, he knew not whose.

Halpin Frayser was not much of a philosopher, nor a scientist. The circumstance that, waking from a deep sleep at night in the midst of a forest, he had spoken aloud a name that he had not in memory and hardly had in mind did not arouse an enlightened curiosity to investigate the phenomenon. He thought it odd, and with a little perfunctory shiver, as if in deference to a seasonal presumption that the night was chill, he lay down again and went to sleep. But his sleep was no longer dreamless.

He thought he was walking along a dusty road that showed white in the gathering darkness of a summer night. Whence and whither it led, and why he traveled it, he did not know, though all seemed simple and natural, as is the way in dreams; for in the Land Beyond the Bed surprises cease from troubling and the judgment is at rest. Soon he came to a parting of the ways; leading from the highway was a road less traveled, having the appearance, indeed, of having been long abandoned, because, he thought, it led to something evil; yet he turned into it without hesitation, impelled by some imperious necessity.

As he pressed forward he became conscious that his way was haunted by invisible existences whom he could not definitely figure to his mind. From among the trees on either side he caught broken and incoherent whispers in a strange tongue which yet he partly understood. They seemed to him fragmentary utterances of a monstrous conspiracy against his body and soul.

It was now long after nightfall, yet the interminable forest through which he journeyed was lit with a wan glimmer having no point of diffusion, for in its mysterious lumination nothing cast a shadow. A shallow pool in the guttered depression of an old wheel rut, as from a recent rain, met his eye with a crimson gleam. He stooped and plunged his hand into it. It stained his fingers; it was blood! Blood, he then observed, was about him everywhere. The weeds growing rankly by the roadside showed it in blots and splashes on their big, broad leaves. Patches of dry dust between the wheelways were pitted and spattered as with a red rain. Defiling the trunks of the trees were broad maculations of crimson, and blood dripped like dew from their foliage.

All this he observed with a terror which seemed not incompatible with the fulfillment of a natural expectation. It seemed to him that it was all in expiation of some crime which, though conscious of his guilt, he could not rightly remember. To the menaces and mysteries of his surroundings the consciousness was an added horror. Vainly he sought by tracing life backward in memory, to reproduce the moment of his sin; scenes and incidents came crowding tumultuously into his mind, one picture effacing another, or commingling with it in confusion and obscurity, but nowhere could he catch a glimpse of what he sought. The failure augmented his terror; he felt as one who has murdered in the dark, not knowing whom nor why. So frightful was the situation—the mysterious light burned with so silent and awful a menace; the noxious plants, the trees that by common consent are invested with a melancholy or baleful character, so openly in his sight conspired against his peace; from overhead and all about came so audible and startling whispers and the sighs of creatures so obviously not of earth—that he could endure it no longer, and with a great effort to break some malign spell that bound his faculties to silence and inaction, he shouted with the full strength of his lungs! His voice broken, it seemed, into an infinite multitude of unfamiliar sounds, went babbling and stammering away into the distant reaches of the forest, died into silence, and all was as before. But he had made a beginning at resistance and was encouraged. He said:

"I will not submit unheard. There may be powers that are not malignant traveling this accursed road. I shall leave them a record and an appeal. I shall relate my wrongs, the persecutions that I endure—I, a helpless mortal, a penitent, an unoffending poet!" Halpin Frayser was a poet only as he was a penitent: in his dream.

Taking from his clothing a small red-leather pocketbook, one-half of which was leaved for memoranda, he discovered that he was without a pencil. He broke a twig from a bush, dipped it into a pool of blood and wrote rapidly. He had hardly touched the paper with the point of his twig when a low, wild peal of laughter broke out at a measureless distance away, and growing ever louder, seemed approaching ever nearer; a soulless, heartless, and unjoyous laugh, like that of the loon, solitary by the lakeside at midnight; a laugh which culminated in an unearthly shout close at hand, then died away by slow gradations, as if the accursed being that uttered it had withdrawn over the verge of the world whence it had come. But the man felt that this was not so—that it was near by and had not moved.

A strange sensation began slowly to take possession of his body and his mind. He could not have said which, if any, of his senses was affected; he felt it rather as a consciousness—a mysterious mental assurance of some overpowering presence—some supernatural malevolence different in kind from the invisible existences that swarmed about him, and superior to them in power. He knew that it had uttered that hideous laugh. And now it seemed to be approaching him; from what direction he did not know—dared not conjecture. All his former fears were forgotten or merged in the gigantic terror that now held him in thrall. Apart from that, he had but one thought: to complete his written appeal to the benign powers who, traversing the haunted wood, might some time rescue him if he should be denied the blessing of annihilation. He wrote with terrible rapidity, the twig in his fingers rilling blood without renewal; but in the middle of a sentence his hands denied their service to his will, his arms fell to his sides, the book to the earth; and powerless to move or cry out, he found himself staring into the sharply drawn face and blank, dead eyes of his own mother, standing white and silent in the garments of the grave!

TWO

In his youth Halpin Frayser had lived with his parents in Nashville, Tennessee. The Fraysers were well-to-do, having a good position in such society as had survived the wreck wrought by civil war. Their children had the social and educational opportunities of their time and place, and had responded to good associations and instruction with agreeable manners and cultivated minds. Halpin being the youngest and not over robust was perhaps a trifle "spoiled." He had the double disadvantage of a mother's assiduity and a father's neglect. Frayser *père* was what no Southern man of means is not—a politician. His country, or rather his section and State, made demands upon his time and attention so exacting that to those of his family he was compelled to turn an ear partly deafened by the thunder of the political captains and the shouting, his own included.

Young Halpin was of a dreamy, indolent and rather romantic turn, somewhat more addicted to literature than law, the profession to which he was bred. Among those of his relations who professed the modern faith of heredity it was well understood that in him the character of the late Myron Bayne, a maternal great-grandfather, had revisited the glimpses of the moon—by which orb Bayne had in his lifetime been sufficiently affected to be a poet of no small Colonial distinction. If not specially observed, it was observable that while a Frayser who was not the proud possessor of a sumptuous copy of the ancestral "poetical works" (printed at the family expense, and long ago withdrawn from an inhospitable market) was a rare Frayser indeed, there was an illogical indisposition to honor the great deceased in the person of his spiritual successor. Halpin was pretty generally deprecated as an intellectual black sheep who was likely at any moment to disgrace the flock by bleating in meter. The Tennessee Fraysers were a practical folk—not practical in the popular sense of devotion to sordid pursuits, but having a robust contempt for any qualities unfitting a man for the wholesome vocation of politics.

In justice to young Halpin it should be said that while in him were pretty faithfully reproduced most of the mental and moral characteristics ascribed by history and family tradition to the famous Colonial bard, his succession to the gift and faculty divine was purely inferential. Not only had he never been known to court the muse, but in truth he could not have written correctly a line of verse to save himself from the Killer of the Wise. Still, there was no knowing when the dormant faculty might wake and smite the lyre.

In the meantime the young man was rather a loose fish, anyhow. Between him and his mother was the most perfect sympathy, for secretly the lady was herself a devout disciple of the late and great Myron Bayne, though with the tact so generally and justly admired in her sex (despite the hardy calumniators who insist that it is essentially the same thing as cunning) she had always taken care to conceal her weakness from all eyes but those of him who shared it. Their common guilt in respect of that was an added tie between them. If in Halpin's youth his mother had "spoiled" him, he had assuredly done his part toward being spoiled. As he grew to such manhood as is attainable by a Southerner who does not care which way elections go the attachment between him and his beautiful mother—whom from early childhood he had called Katy—became yearly stronger and more tender. In these two romantic natures was manifest in a signal way that neglected phenomenon, the dominance of the sexual element in all the relations of life, strengthening, softening, and beautifying even those of consanguinity. The two were nearly inseparable, and by strangers observing their manner were not infrequently mistaken for lovers.

Entering his mother's boudoir one day Halpin Frayser kissed her upon the forehead, toyed for a moment with a lock of her dark hair which had escaped from its confining pins, and said, with an obvious effort at calmness:

"Would you greatly mind, Katy, if I were called away to California for a few weeks?"

It was hardly needful for Katy to answer with her lips a question to which her telltale cheeks had made instant reply. Evidently she would greatly mind; and the tears, too, sprang into her large brown eyes as corroborative testimony.

"Ah, my son," she said, looking up into his face with infinite tenderness, "I should have known that this was coming. Did I not lie awake a half of the night weeping because, during the other half, Grandfather Bayne had come to me in a dream, and standing by his portrait—young, too, and handsome as that—pointed to yours on the same wall? And when I looked it seemed that I could not see the features; you had been painted with a face cloth, such as we put upon the dead. Your father has laughed at me, but you and I, dear, know that such things are not for nothing. And I saw below the edge of the cloth the marks of hands on your throat—forgive me, but we have not been used to keep such things from each other. Perhaps you have another interpretation. Perhaps it does not mean that you will go to California. Or maybe you will take me with you?"

It must be confessed that this ingenious interpretation of the dream in the light of newly discovered evidence did not wholly commend itself to the son's more logical mind; he had, for the moment at least, a conviction that it foreshadowed a more simple and immediate, if less tragic, disaster than a visit to the Pacific Coast. It was Halpin Frayser's impression that he was to be garroted on his native heath.

"Are there not medicinal springs in California?" Mrs. Frayser resumed before he had time to give her the true reading of the dream—"places where one recovers from rheumatism and neuralgia? Look—my fingers feel so stiff; and I am almost sure they have been giving me great pain while I slept."

She held out her hands for his inspection. What diagnosis of her case the young man may have thought it best to conceal with a smile the historian is unable to state, but for himself he feels bound to say that fingers looking less stiff, and showing fewer evidences of even insensible pain, have seldom been submitted for medical inspection by even the fairest patient desiring a pre-scription of unfamiliar scenes.

The outcome of it was that of these two odd persons having equally odd notions of duty, the one went to California, as the interest of his client required, and the other remained at home in compliance with a wish that her husband was scarcely conscious of entertaining.

While in San Francisco Halpin Frayser was walking one dark night along the water front of the city, when, with a suddenness that surprised and disconcerted him, he became a sailor. He was in fact "shanghaied" aboard a gallant, gallant ship, and sailed for a far countree. Nor did his misfortunes end with the voyage; for the ship was cast ashore on an island of the South Pacific, and it was six years afterward when the survivors were taken off by a venture-some trading schooner and brought back to San Francisco.

Though poor in purse, Frayser was no less proud in spirit than he had been in the years that seemed ages and ages ago. He would accept no assistance from strangers, and it was while living with a fellow survivor near the town of St. Helena, awaiting news and remittances from home, that he had gone gunning and dreaming.

THREE

The apparition confronting the dreamer in the haunted wood—the thing so like, yet so unlike his mother—was horrible! It stirred no love nor longing in his heart; it came unattended with pleasant memories of a golden past—inspired no sentiment of any kind; all the finer emotions were swallowed up in fear. He tried to turn and run from before it, but his legs were as lead; he was unable to lift his feet from the ground. His arms hung helpless at his sides; of his eyes only he retained control, and these he dared not remove from the lusterless orbs of the apparition, which he knew was not a soul without a body, but that most dreadful of all existences infesting that haunted wood—a body without a soul! In its blank stare was neither love, nor pity, nor intelligence—nothing to which to address an appeal for mercy. "An appeal will not lie," he thought, with an absurd reversion to professional slang, making the situation more horrible, as the fire of a cigar might light up a tomb.

For a time, which seemed so long that the world grew gray with age and sin, and the haunted forest, having fulfilled its purpose in this monstrous culmination of its terrors, vanished out of his consciousness with all its sights and sounds, the apparition stood within a pace, regarding him with the mindless malevolence of a wild brute; then thrust its hands forward and sprang upon him with appalling ferocity! The act released his physical energies without unfettering his will; his mind was still spellbound, but his powerful body and agile limbs, endowed with a blind, insensate life of their own, resisted stoutly and well. For an instant he seemed to see this unnatural contest between a dead intelligence and a breathing mechanism only as a spectator—such fancies are in dreams; then he regained his identity almost as if by a leap forward into his body, and the straining automaton had a directing will as alert and fierce as that of its hideous antagonist.

But what mortal can cope with a creature of his dream? The imagination creating the enemy is already vanquished; the combat's result is the combat's cause. Despite his struggles—despite his strength and activity, which seemed wasted in a void, he felt the cold fingers close upon his throat. Borne backward to the earth, he saw above him the dead and drawn face within a hand's breadth of his own, and then all was black. A sound as of the beating of distant drums—a murmur of swarming voices, a sharp, far cry signing all to silence, and Halpin Frayser dreamed that he was dead.

FOUR

A warm, clear night had been followed by a morning of drenching fog. At about the middle of the afternoon of the preceding day a little whiff of light vapor—a mere thickening of the atmosphere, the ghost of a cloud—had been observed clinging to the western side of Mount St. Helena, away up along the barren altitudes near the summit. It was so thin, so diaphanous, so like a fancy made visible, that one would have said: "Look quickly! in a moment it will be gone."

In a moment it was visibly larger and denser. While with one edge it clung to the mountain, with the other it reached farther and farther out into the air above the lower slopes. At the same time it extended itself to north and south, joining small patches of mist that appeared to come out of the mountainside on exactly the same level, with an intelligent design to be absorbed. And so it grew and grew until the summit was shut out of view from the valley, and over the valley itself was an ever-extending canopy, opaque and gray. At Calistoga, which lies near the head of the valley and the foot of the mountain, there were a starless night and a sunless morning. The fog, sinking into the valley, had reached southward, swallowing up ranch after ranch, until it had blotted out the town of St. Helena, nine miles away. The dust in the road was laid; trees were adrip with moisture; birds sat silent in their coverts; the morning light was wan and ghastly, with neither color nor fire.

Two men left the town of St. Helena at the first glimmer of dawn, and walked along the road northward up the valley toward Calistoga. They carried guns on their shoulders, yet no one having knowledge of such matters could have mistaken them for hunters of bird or beast. They were a deputy sheriff from Napa and a detective from San Francisco—Holker and Jaralson, respectively. Their business was man-hunting.

"How far is it?" inquired Holker, as they strode along, their feet stirring white the dust beneath the damp surface of the road.

"The White Church? Only a half mile farther," the other answered. "By the way," he added, "it is neither white nor a church; it is an abandoned schoolhouse, gray with age and neglect. Religious services were once held in it—when it was white, and there is a graveyard that would delight a poet. Can you guess why I sent for you, and told you to come heeled?"

"Oh, I never have bothered you about things of that kind. I've always found you communicative when the time came. But if I may hazard a guess, you want me to help you arrest one of the corpses in the graveyard."

"You remember Branscom?" said Jaralson, treating his companion's wit with the inattention that it deserved.

"The chap who cut his wife's throat? I ought; I wasted a week's work on him and had my expenses for my trouble. There is a reward of five hundred dollars, but none of us ever got a sight of him. You don't mean to say—"

"Yes, I do. He has been under the noses of you fellows all the time. He comes by night to the old graveyard at the White Church."

"The devil! That's where they buried his wife."

"Well, you fellows might have had sense enough to suspect that he would return to her grave some time."

"The very last place that anyone would have expected him to return to."

"But you had exhausted all the other places. Learning your failure at them, I 'laid for him' there."

"And you found him?"

"Damn it! he found *me*. The rascal got the drop on me—regularly held me up and made me travel. It's God's mercy that he didn't go through me. Oh, he's a good one, and I fancy the half of that reward is enough for me if you're needy."

Holker laughed good humoredly, and explained that his creditors were never more importunate.

"I wanted merely to show you the ground, and arrange a plan with you," the detective explained. "I thought it as well for us to be heeled, even in daylight."

"The man must be insane," said the deputy sheriff. "The reward is for his capture and conviction. If he's mad he won't be convicted."

Mr. Holker was so profoundly affected by that possible failure of justice that he involuntarily stopped in the middle of the road, then resumed his walk with abated zeal.

"Well, he looks it," assented Jaralson. "I'm bound to admit that a more unshaven, unshorn, unkempt, and uneverything wretch I never saw outside the ancient and honorable order of tramps. But I've gone in for him, and can't make up my mind to let go. There's glory in it for us, anyhow. Not another soul knows that he is this side of the Mountains of the Moon."

"All right," Holker said; "we will go and view the ground," and he added, in the words of a once favorite inscription for tombstones: " 'where you must shortly lie'—I mean, if old Branscom ever gets tired of you and your impertinent intrusion. By the way, I heard the other day that 'Branscom' was not his real name."

"What is?"

"I can't recall it. I had lost all interest in the wretch, and it did not fix itself in my memory—something like Pardee. The woman whose throat he had the bad taste to cut was a widow when he met her. She had come to California to look up some relatives—there are persons who will do that sometimes. But you know all that."

"Naturally."

"But not knowing the right name, by what happy inspiration did you find the right grave? The man who told me what the name was said it had been cut on the headboard."

"I don't know the right grave." Jaralson was apparently a trifle reluctant to admit his ignorance of so important a point of his plan. "I have been watching about the place generally. A part of our work this morning will be to identify that grave. Here is the White Church."

For a long distance the road had been bordered by fields on both sides, but now on the left there was a forest of oaks, madroños, and gigantic spruces whose lower parts only could be seen, dim and ghostly in the fog. The undergrowth was, in places, thick, but nowhere impenetrable. For some moments Holker saw nothing of the building, but as they turned into the woods it revealed itself in faint gray outline through the fog, looking huge and far away. A few steps more, and it was within an arm's length, distinct, dark with moisture, and insignificant in size. It had the usual country-schoolhouse form —belonged to the packing-box order of architecture; had an underpinning of stones, a moss-grown roof, and blank window spaces, whence both glass and sash had long departed. It was ruined, but not a ruin—a typical Californian substitute for what are known to guide-bookers abroad as "monuments of the past." With scarcely a glance at this uninteresting structure Jaralson moved on into the dripping undergrowth beyond.

"I will show you where he held me up," he said. "This is the graveyard."

Here and there among the bushes were small inclosures containing graves, sometimes no more than one. They were recognized as graves by the discolored stones or rotting boards at head and foot, leaning at all angles, some prostrate; by the ruined picket fences surrounding them; or, infrequently, by the mound itself showing its gravel through the fallen leaves. In many instances nothing marked the spot where lay the vestiges of some poor mortal —who, leaving "a large circle of sorrowing friends," had been left by them in turn—except a depression in the earth, more lasting than that in the spirits of the mourners. The paths, if any paths had been, were long obliterated; trees of a considerable size had been permitted to grow up from the graves and thrust aside with root or branch the inclosing fences. Over all was that air of abandonment and decay which seems nowhere so fit and significant as in a village of the forgotten dead.

As the two men, Jaralson leading, pushed their way through the growth of young trees, that enterprising man suddenly stopped and brought up his shotgun to the height of his breast, uttered a low note of warning, and stood motionless, his eyes fixed upon something ahead. As well as he could, obstructed by brush, his companion, though seeing nothing, imitated the posture and so stood, prepared for what might ensue. A moment later Jaralson moved cautiously forward, the other following.

Under the branches of an enormous spruce lay the dead body of a man. Standing silent above it they noted such particulars as first strike the attention —the face, the attitude, the clothing; whatever most promptly and plainly answers the unspoken question of a sympathetic curiosity.

The body lay upon its back, the legs wide apart. One arm was thrust upward, the other outward; but the latter was bent acutely, and the hand was near the throat. Both hands were tightly clenched. The whole attitude was that of desperate but ineffectual resistance to—what?

Near by lay a shotgun and a game bag through the meshes of which was seen the plumage of shot birds. All about were evidences of a furious struggle; small sprouts of poison-oak were bent and denuded of leaf and bark; dead and rotting leaves had been pushed into heaps and ridges on both sides of the legs by the action of other feet than theirs; alongside the hips were unmistakable impressions of human knees.

The nature of the struggle was made clear by a glance at the dead man's throat and face. While breast and hands were white, those were purple— almost black. The shoulders lay upon a low mound, and the head was turned back at an angle otherwise impossible, the expanded eyes staring blankly backward in a direction opposite to that of the feet. From the froth filling the open mouth the tongue protruded, black and swollen. The throat showed horrible contusions; not mere finger-marks, but bruises and lacerations wrought by two strong hands that must have buried themselves in the yielding flesh, maintaining their terrible grasp until long after death. Breast, throat, face, were wet; the clothing was saturated; drops of water, condensed from the fog, studded the hair and mustache.

All this the two men observed without speaking—almost at a glance. Then Holker said:

"Poor devil! he had a rough deal."

Jaralson was making a vigilant circumspection of the forest, his shotgun held in both hands and at full cock, his finger upon the trigger.

"The work of a maniac," he said, without withdrawing his eyes from the inclosing wood. "It was done by Branscom—Pardee."

Something half hidden by the disturbed leaves on the earth caught Holker's attention. It was a red-leather pocketbook. He picked it up and opened it. It contained leaves of white paper for memoranda, and upon the first leaf was the name "Halpin Frayser." Written in red on several succeeding leaves—scrawled as if in haste and barely legible—were the following lines, which Holker read aloud, while his companion continued scanning the

dim gray confines of their narrow world and hearing matter of apprehension
in the drip of water from every burdened branch:

> "Enthralled by some mysterious spell, I stood
> In the lit gloom of an enchanted wood.
>   The cypress there and myrtle twined their boughs,
> Significant, in baleful brotherhood.
>
> "The brooding willow whispered to the yew;
> Beneath, the deadly nightshade and the rue,
>   With immortelles self-woven into strange
> Funereal shapes, and horrid nettles grew.
>
> "No song of bird nor any drone of bees,
> Nor light leaf lifted by the wholesome breeze:
>   The air was stagnant all, and Silence was
> A living thing that breathed among the trees.
>
> "Conspiring spirits whispered in the gloom,
> Half-heard, the stilly secrets of the tomb.
>   With blood the trees were all adrip; the leaves
> Shone in the witch-light with a ruddy bloom.
>
> "I cried aloud!—the spell, unbroken still,
> Rested upon my spirit and my will.
>   Unsouled, unhearted, hopeless and forlorn,
> I strove with monstrous presages of ill!
>
> "At last the viewless—"

Holker ceased reading; there was no more to read. The manuscript broke
off in the middle of a line.

"That sounds like Bayne," said Jaralson, who was something of a scholar in
his way. He had abated his vigilance and stood looking down at the body.

"Who's Bayne?" Holker asked rather incuriously.

"Myron Bayne, a chap who flourished in the early years of the nation—
more than a century ago. Wrote mighty dismal stuff; I have his collected
works. That poem is not among them, but it must have been omitted by
mistake."

"It is cold," said Holker; "let us leave here; we must have up the coroner
from Napa."

Jaralson said nothing, but made a movement in compliance. Passing the end of the slight elevation of earth upon which the dead man's head and shoulders lay, his foot struck some hard substance under the rotting forest leaves, and he took the trouble to kick it into view. It was a fallen headboard, and painted on it were the hardly decipherable words, "Catherine Larue."

"Larue, Larue!" exclaimed Holker, with sudden animation. "Why, that is the real name of Branscom—not Pardee. And—bless my soul! how it all comes to me—the murdered woman's name had been Frayser!"

"There is some rascally mystery here," said Detective Jaralson. "I hate anything of that kind."

There came to them out of the fog—seemingly from a great distance—the sound of a laugh, a low, deliberate, soulless laugh, which had no more of joy than that of a hyena night-prowling in the desert; a laugh that rose by slow gradation, louder and louder, clearer, more distinct and terrible, until it seemed barely outside the narrow circle of their vision; a laugh so unnatural, so unhuman, so devilish, that it filled those hardy man-hunters with a sense of dread unspeakable! They did not move their weapons nor think of them; the menace of that horrible sound was not of the kind to be met with arms. As it had grown out of silence, so now it died away; from a culminating shout which had seemed almost in their ears, it drew itself away into the distance, until its failing notes, joyless and mechanical to the last, sank to silence at a measureless remove.

THE YELLOW SIGN

ROBERT W. CHAMBERS

*LET THE RED DAWN SURMISE
WHAT WE SHALL DO,
WHEN THIS BLUE STARLIGHT DIES
AND ALL IS THROUGH.*

ONE

There are so many things which are impossible to explain! Why should certain chords in music make me think of the brown and golden tints of autumn foliage? Why should the Mass of Sainte Cécile send my thoughts wandering among caverns whose walls blaze with ragged masses of virgin silver? What was it in the roar and turmoil of Broadway at six o'clock that flashed before my eyes the picture of a still Breton forest where sunlight filtered through spring foliage and Silvia bent, half curiously, half tenderly, over a small green lizard, murmuring: "To think that this also is a little ward of God!"?

When I first saw the watchman his back was toward me. I looked at him indifferently until he went into the church. I paid no more attention to him than I had to any other man who lounged through Washington Square that morning, and when I shut my window and turned back into my studio I had forgotten him. Late in the afternoon, the day being warm, I raised the window again and leaned out to get a sniff of air. A man was standing in the courtyard of the church, and I noticed him again with as little interest as I had that morning. I looked across the square to where the fountain was playing and then, with my mind filled with vague impressions of trees, asphalt drives, and the moving groups of nursemaids and holiday-makers, I started to walk back to my easel. As I turned, my listless glance included the man below in the churchyard. His face was toward me now, and with a perfectly involuntary movement I bent to see it. At the same moment he raised his head and looked at me. Instantly I thought of a coffin-worm. Whatever it was about the man that repelled me I did not know, but the impression of a plump white grave-worm was so intense and nauseating that I must have shown it in my expression, for he turned his puffy face away with a movement which made me think of a disturbed grub in a chestnut.

I went back to my easel and motioned the model to resume her pose. After working awhile I was satisfied that I was spoiling what I had done as rapidly as possible, and I took up a palette knife and scraped the color out again. The flesh tones were sallow and unhealthy, and I did not understand how I could have painted such sickly color into a study which before that had glowed with healthy tones.

I looked at Tessie. She had not changed, and the clear flush of health dyed her neck and cheeks as I frowned.

"Is it something I've done?" she said.

"No—I've made a mess of this arm, and for the life of me I can't see how I came to paint such mud as that into the canvas," I replied.

"Don't I pose well?" she insisted.

"Of course, perfectly."

"Then it's not my fault?"

"No. It's my own."

"I'm very sorry," she said.

I told her she could rest while I applied rag and turpentine to the plague spot on my canvas, and she went off to smoke a cigarette and look over the illustrations in the *Courier Français*.

I did not know whether it was something in the turpentine or a defect in the canvas, but the more I scrubbed the more that gangrene seemed to spread. I worked like a beaver to get it out, and yet the disease appeared to creep from limb to limb of the study before me. Alarmed I strove to arrest it, but now the color on the breast changed and the whole figure seemed to absorb the infection as a sponge soaks up water. Vigorously I plied palette knife, turpentine, and scraper, thinking all the time what a séance I should hold with Duval who had sold me the canvas; but soon I noticed that it was not the canvas which was defective nor yet the colors of Edward. "It must be the turpentine," I thought angrily, "or else my eyes have become so blurred and confused by the afternoon light that I can't see straight." I called Tessie, the model. She came and leaned over my chair blowing rings of smoke into the air.

"What *have* you been doing to it?" she exclaimed.

"Nothing," I growled, "it must be this turpentine!"

"What a horrible color it is now," she continued. "Do you think my flesh resembles green cheese?"

"No, I don't," I said angrily, "did you ever know me to paint like that before?"

"No, indeed!"

"Well, then!"

"It must be the turpentine, or something," she admitted.

She slipped on a Japanese robe and walked to the window. I scraped and rubbed until I was tired and finally picked up my brushes and hurled them through the canvas with a forcible expression, the tone alone of which reached Tessie's ears.

Nevertheless she promptly began: "That's it! Swear and act silly and ruin your brushes! You have been three weeks on that study, and now look! What's the good of ripping the canvas? What creatures artists are!"

I felt about as much ashamed as I usually did after such an outbreak, and I turned the ruined canvas to the wall. Tessie helped me clean my brushes, and then danced away to dress. From the screen she regaled me with bits of advice concerning whole or partial loss of temper, until, thinking, perhaps, I had been tormented sufficiently, she came out to implore me to button her waist where she could not reach it on the shoulder.

"Everything went wrong from the time you came back from the window and talked about that horrid-looking man you saw in the churchyard," she announced.

"Yes, he probably bewitched the picture," I said, yawning. I looked at my watch.

"It's after six, I know," said Tessie, adjusting her hat before the mirror.

"Yes," I replied, "I didn't mean to keep you so long." I leaned out of the window but recoiled with disgust, for the young man with the pasty face stood below in the churchyard. Tessie saw my gesture of disapproval and leaned from the window.

"Is that the man you don't like?" she whispered.

I nodded.

"I can't see his face, but he does look fat and soft. Someway or other," she continued, turning to look at me, "he reminds me of a dream,—an awful dream I once had. Or," she mused, looking down at her shapely shoes, "was it a dream after all?"

"How should I know?" I smiled.

Tessie smiled in reply.

"You were in it," she said, "so perhaps you might know something about it."

"Tessie! Tessie!" I protested, "don't you dare flatter by saying that you dream about me!"

"But I did," she insisted; "shall I tell you about it?"

"Go ahead," I replied, lighting a cigarette.

Tessie leaned back on the open window-sill and began very seriously.

"One night last winter I was lying in bed thinking about nothing at all in particular. I had been posing for you and I was tired out, yet it seemed impossible for me to sleep. I heard the bells in the city ring ten, eleven and midnight. I must have fallen asleep about midnight because I don't remember hearing the bells after that. It seemed to me that I had scarcely closed my eyes when I dreamed that something impelled me to go to the window. I rose, and raising the sash leaned out. Twenty-fifth Street was deserted as far as I could see. I began to be afraid; everything outside seemed so—so black and uncomfortable. Then the sound of wheels in the distance came to my ears, and it seemed to me as though that was what I must wait for. Very slowly the wheels approached, and, finally, I could make out a vehicle moving along the street. It came nearer and nearer, and when it passed beneath my window I saw it was a hearse. Then, as I trembled with fear, the driver turned and looked straight at me. When I awoke I was standing by the open window shivering with cold, but the black-plumed hearse and the driver were gone. I dreamed this dream again in March last, and again awoke beside the open window. Last night the dream came again. You remember how it was raining; when I awoke, standing at the open window, my night-dress was soaked."

"But where did I come into the dream?" I asked.

"You—you were in the coffin; but you were not dead."

"In the coffin?"

"Yes."

"How did you know? Could you see me?"

"No; I only knew you were there."

"Had you been eating Welsh rarebits, or lobster salad?" I began laughing, but the girl interrupted me with a frightened cry.

"Hello! What's up?" I said, as she shrank into the embrasure by the window.

"The—the man below in the churchyard;—he drove the hearse."

"Nonsense," I said, but Tessie's eyes were wide with terror. I went to the window and looked out. The man was gone. "Come, Tessie," I urged, "don't be foolish. You have posed too long; you are nervous."

"Do you think I could forget that face?" she murmured. "Three times I saw the hearse pass below my window, and every time the driver turned and looked up at me. Oh, his face was so white and—and soft? It looked dead—it looked as if it had been dead a long time."

I induced the girl to sit down and swallow a glass of Marsala. Then I sat down beside her, and tried to give her some advice.

"Look here, Tessie," I said, "you go to the country for a week or two, and you'll have no more dreams about hearses. You pose all day, and when night comes your nerves are upset. You can't keep this up. Then again, instead of going to bed when your day's work is done, you run off to picnics at Sulzer's Park, or go to the Eldorado or Coney Island, and when you come down here next morning you are fagged out. There was no real hearse. That was a soft-shell crab dream."

She smiled faintly.

"What about the man in the churchyard?"

"Oh, he's only an ordinary unhealthy, everyday creature."

"As true as my name is Tessie Reardon, I swear to you, Mr. Scott, that the face of the man below in the churchyard is the face of the man who drove the hearse!"

"What of it?" I said. "It's an honest trade."

"Then you think I *did* see the hearse?"

"Oh," I said, diplomatically, "if you really did, it might not be unlikely that the man below drove it. There is nothing in that."

Tessie rose, unrolled her scented handkerchief, and taking a bit of gum from a knot in the hem, placed it in her mouth. Then drawing on her gloves she offered me her hand, with a frank, "Good-night, Mr. Scott," and walked out.

TWO

The next morning, Thomas, the bellboy, brought me the *Herald* and a bit of news. The church next door had been sold. I thanked Heaven for it, not that it being a Catholic I had any repugnance for the congregation next door, but because my nerves were shattered by a blatant exhorter, whose every word echoed through the aisle of the church as if it had been my own rooms, and who insisted on his r's with a nasal persistence which revolted my every instinct. Then, too, there was a fiend in human shape, an organist, who reeled off some of the grand old hymns with an interpretation of his own, and I longed for the blood of a creature who could play the doxology with an amendment of minor chords which one hears only in a quartet of very young undergraduates. I believe the minister was a good man, but when he bel-lowed: "And the Lorrrd said unto Moses, the Lorrrd is a man of war; the Lorrrd is his name. My wrath shall wax hot and I will kill you with the sworrrd!" I wondered how many centuries of purgatory it would take to atone for such a sin.

"Who bought the property?" I asked Thomas.

"Nobody that I knows, sir. They do say the gent wot owns this 'ere 'Amilton flats was lookin' at it. 'E might be a bildin' more studios."

I walked to the window. The young man with the unhealthy face stood by the churchyard gate, and at the mere sight of him the same overwhelming repugnance took possession of me.

"By the way, Thomas," I said, "who is that fellow down there?"

Thomas sniffed. "That there worm, sir? 'E's night-watchman of the church, sir. 'E maikes me tired a-sittin' out all night on them steps and lookin' at you insultin' like. I'd a punched 'is 'ed, sir—beg pardon, sir——"

"Go on, Thomas."

"One night a comin' 'ome with 'Arry, the other English boy, I sees 'im a sittin' there on them steps. We 'ad Molly and Jen with us, sir, the two girls on the tray service, an' 'e looks so insultin' at us that I up and sez: 'Wat you looking hat, you fat slug?'—beg pardon, sir, but that's 'ow I sez, sir. Then 'e don't say nothin' and I sez: 'Come out and I'll punch that puddin' 'ed.' Then I hopens the gate an' goes in, but 'e don't say nothin', only looks insultin' like. Then I 'its 'im one, but, ugh! 'is 'ed was that cold and mushy it ud sicken you to touch 'im."

"What did he do then?" I asked, curiously.

"'Im? Nawthin'."

"And you, Thomas?"

The young fellow flushed with embarrassment and smiled uneasily.

"Mr. Scott, sir, I ain't no coward an' I can't make it out at all why I run. I was in the 5th Lawncers, sir, bugler at Tel-el-Kebir, an' was shot by the wells."

"You don't mean to say you ran away?"

"Yes, sir; I run."

"Why?"

"That's just what I want to know, sir. I grabbed Molly an' run, an' the rest was as frightened as I."

"But what were they frightened at?"

Thomas refused to answer for a while, but now my curiosity was aroused about the repulsive young man below and I pressed him. Three years' sojourn in America had not only modified Thomas' cockney dialect but had given him the American's fear of ridicule.

"You won't believe me, Mr. Scott, sir?"

"Yes, I will."

"You will lawf at me, sir?"

"Nonsense!"

He hesitated. "Well, sir, it's Gawd's truth that when I 'it 'im 'e grabbed me wrists, sir, and when I twisted 'is soft, mushy fist one of 'is fingers come off in me 'and."

The utter loathing and horror of Thomas' face must have been reflected in my own for he added:

"It's orful, an' now when I see 'im I just go away. 'E maikes me hill."

When Thomas had gone I went to the window. The man stood beside the churchrailing with both hands on the gate, but I hastily retreated to my easel again, sickened and horrified, for I saw that the middle finger of his right hand was missing.

At nine o'clock Tessie appeared and vanished behind the screen with a merry "good-morning, Mr. Scott." When she had reappeared and taken her pose upon the model-stand I started a new canvas much to her delight. She remained silent as long as I was on the drawing, but as soon as the scrape of the charcoal ceased and I took up my fixative she began to chatter.

"Oh, I had such a lovely time last night. We went to Tony Pastor's."

"Who are 'we'?" I demanded.

"Oh; Maggie, you know, Mr. Whyte's model, and Pinkie McCormick— we call her Pinkie because she's got that beautiful red hair you artists like so much—and Lizzie Burke."

I sent a shower of spray from the fixative over the canvas, and said: "Well, go on."

"We saw Kelly and Baby Barnes the skirt-dancer and—and all the rest. I made a mash."

"Then you have gone back on me, Tessie?"

She laughed and shook her head.

"He's Lizzie Burke's brother, Ed. He's a perfect gen'l'man."

I felt constrained to give her some parental advice concerning mashing, which she took with a bright smile.

"Oh, I can take care of a strange mash," she said, examining her chewing gum, "but Ed is different. Lizzie is my best friend."

Then she related how Ed had come back from the stocking mill in Lowell, Massachusetts, to find her and Lizzie grown up, and what an accomplished young man he was, and how he thought nothing of squandering half a dollar for ice-cream and oysters to celebrate his entry as clerk into the woollen department of Macy's. Before she finished I began to paint, and she resumed the pose, smiling and chattering like a sparrow. By noon I had the study fairly well rubbed in and Tessie came to look at it.

"That's better," she said.

I thought so too, and ate my lunch with a satisfied feeling that all was going well. Tessie spread her lunch on a drawing table opposite me and we drank our claret from the same bottle and lighted our cigarettes from the same match. I was very much attached to Tessie. I had watched her shoot up into a slender but exquisitely formed woman from a frail, awkward child. She had posed for me during the last three years, and among all my models she was my favorite. It would have troubled me very much indeed had she become "tough" or "fly," as the phrase goes, but I never noticed any deterioration of her manner, and felt at heart that she was all right. She and I never discussed morals at all, and I had no intention of doing so, partly because I had none myself, and partly because I knew she would do what she liked in spite of me. Still I did hope she would steer clear of complications, because I wished her well, and then also I had a selfish desire to retain the best model I had. I knew that mashing, as she termed it, had no significance with girls like Tessie, and that such things in America did not resemble in the least the same things in Paris. Yet, having lived with my eyes open, I also knew that somebody would take Tessie away some day, in one manner or another, and though I professed to myself that marriage was nonsense, I sincerely hoped that, in this case, there would be a priest at the end of the vista. I am a Catholic. When I listen to high mass, when I sign myself, I feel that everything, including myself, is more cheerful, and when I confess, it does me good. A man who lives as much alone as I do, must confess to somebody. Then, again, Sylvia was Catholic, and it was reason enough for me. But I was speaking of Tessie, which is very different. Tessie also was Catholic and much more devout than I, so, taking it all in all, I had little fear for my pretty model until she should fall in love. But *then* I knew that fate alone would decide her future for her, and I prayed inwardly that fate would keep her away from men like me and throw into her path nothing but Ed Burkes and Jimmy McCormicks, bless her sweet face!

Tessie sat blowing rings of smoke up to the ceiling and tinkling the ice in her tumbler.

"Do you know that I also had a dream last night?" I observed.

"Not about that man," she laughed.

"Exactly. A dream similar to yours, only much worse."

It was foolish and thoughtless of me to say this, but you know how little tact the average painter has.

"I must have fallen asleep about 10 o'clock," I continued, "and after a while I dreamt that I awoke. So plainly did I hear the midnight bells, the wind in the tree-branches, and the whistle of steamers from the bay, that even now I can scarcely believe I was not awake. I seemed to be lying in a box which had a glass cover. Dimly I saw the street lamps as I passed, for I must tell you, Tessie, the box in which I reclined appeared to lie in a cushioned wagon which jolted me over a stony pavement. After a while I became impatient and tried to move but the box was too narrow. My hands were crossed on my breast so I could not raise them to help myself. I listened and then tried to call. My voice was gone. I could hear the trample of the horses attached to the wagon and even the breathing of the driver. Then another sound broke upon my ears like the raising of a window sash. I managed to turn my head a little, and found I could look, not only through the glass cover of my box, but also through the glass panes in the side of the covered vehicle. I saw houses, empty and silent, with neither light nor life about any of them excepting one. In that house a window was open on the first floor and a figure all in white stood looking down into the street. It was you."

Tessie had turned her face away from me and leaned on the table with her elbow.

"I could see your face," I resumed, "and it seemed to me to be very sorrowful. Then we passed on and turned into a narrow black lane. Presently the horses stopped. I waited and waited, closing my eyes with fear and impatience, but all was silent as the grave. After what seemed to me hours, I began to feel uncomfortable. A sense that somebody was close to me made me unclose my eyes. Then I saw the white face of the hearse-driver looking at me through the coffin-lid———"

A sob from Tessie interrupted me. She was trembling like a leaf. I saw I had made an ass of myself and attempted to repair the damage.

"Why, Tess," I said, "I only told you this to show you what influence your story might have on another person's dreams. You don't suppose I really lay in a coffin, do you? What are you trembling for? Don't you see that your dream and my unreasonable dislike for that inoffensive watchman of the church simply set my brain working as soon as I fell asleep?"

She laid her head between her arms and sobbed as if her heart would break. What a precious triple donkey I had made of myself! But I was about to break my record. I went over and put my arm about her.

"Tessie dear, forgive me," I said; "I had no business to frighten you with such nonsense. You are too sensible a girl, too good a Catholic to believe in dreams."

Her hand tightened on mine and her head fell back upon my shoulder, but she still trembled and I petted her and comforted her.

"Come, Tess, open your eyes and smile."

Her eyes opened with a slow languid movement and met mine, but their expression was so queer that I hastened to reassure her again.

"It's all humbug, Tessie, you surely are not afraid that any harm will come to you because of that."

"No," she said, but her scarlet lips quivered.

"Then what's the matter? Are you afraid?"

"Yes. Not for myself."

"For me, then?" I demanded gayly.

"For you," she murmured in a voice almost inaudible, "I—I care for you."

At first I started to laugh, but when I understood her, a shock passed through me and I sat like one turned to stone. This was the crowning bit of idiocy I had committed. During the moment which elapsed between her reply and my answer I thought of a thousand responses to that innocent confession. I could pass it by with a laugh, I could misunderstand her and reassure her as to my health, I could simply point out that it was impossible she could love me. But my reply was quicker than my thoughts, and I might think and think now when it was too late, for I had kissed her on the mouth.

That evening I took my usual walk in Washington Park, pondering over the occurrences of the day. I was thoroughly committed. There was no back out now, and I stared the future straight in the face. I was not good, not even scrupulous, but I had no idea of deceiving either myself or Tessie. The one passion of my life lay buried in the sunlit forests of Brittany. Was it buried forever? Hope cried "No!" For three years I had been listening to the voice of Hope, and for three years I had waited for a footstep on my threshold. Had Sylvia forgotten? "No!" cried Hope.

I said that I was not good. That is true, but still I was not exactly a comic opera villain. I had led an easy-going reckless life, taking what invited me of pleasure, deploring and sometimes bitterly regretting consequences. In one thing alone, except my painting, was I serious, and that was something which lay hidden if not lost in the Breton forests.

It was too late now for me to regret what had occurred during the day. Whatever it had been, pity, a sudden tenderness for sorrow, or the more brutal instinct of gratified vanity, it was all the same now, and unless I wished to bruise an innocent heart my path lay marked before me. The fire and strength, the depth of passion of a love which I had never even suspected, with all my imagined experience in the world, left me no alternative but to respond or send her away. Whether because I am so cowardly about giving pain to others, or whether it was that I have little of the gloomy Puritan in me, I do not know, but I shrank from disclaiming responsibility for that thoughtless kiss, and in fact had no time to do so before the gates of her heart opened and the flood poured forth. Others who habitually do their duty and find a sullen satisfaction in making themselves and everybody else unhappy, might have withstood it. I did not. I dared not. After the storm had abated I did tell her that she might better have loved Ed Burke and worn a plain gold ring, but she would not hear of it, and I thought perhaps that as long as she had decided to love somebody she could not marry, it had better be me. I, at least, could treat her with an intelligent affection, and whenever she became tired of her infatuation she could go none the worse for it. For I was decided on that point although I knew how hard it would be. I remembered the usual termination of Platonic liaisons and thought how disgusted I had been whenever I heard of one. I knew I was undertaking a great deal for so unscrupulous a man as I was, and I dreaded the future, but never for one moment did I doubt that she was safe with me. Had it been anybody but Tessie I should not have bothered my head about scruples. For it did not occur to me to sacrifice Tessie as I would have sacrificed a woman of the world. I looked the future squarely in the face and saw the several probable endings to the affair. She would either tire of the whole thing, or become so unhappy that I should have either to marry her or go away. If I married her we would be unhappy. I with a wife unsuited to me, and she with a husband unsuitable for any woman. For my past life could scarcely entitle me to marry. If I went away she might either fall ill, recover, and marry some Eddie Burke, or she might recklessly or deliberately go and do something foolish. On the other hand if she tired of me, then her whole life would be before her with beautiful vistas of Eddie Burkes and marriage rings and twins and Harlem flats and Heaven knows what. As I strolled along through the trees by the Washington Arch, I decided that she should find a substantial friend in me anyway and the future could take care of itself. Then I went into the house and put on my evening dress, for the little faintly perfumed note on my dresser said, "Have a cab at the stage door at eleven," and the note was signed "Edith Carmichel, Metropolitan Theatre."

I took supper that night, or rather we took supper, Miss Carmichel and I, at Solari's and the dawn was just beginning to gild the cross on the Memorial Church as I entered Washington Square after leaving Edith at the Brunswick. There was not a soul in the park as I passed among the trees and took the walk which leads from the Garibaldi statue to the Hamilton Apartment House, but as I passed the churchyard I saw a figure sitting on the stone steps. In spite of myself a chill crept over me at the sight of the white puffy face, and I hastened to pass. Then he said something which might have been addressed to me or might merely have been a mutter to himself, but a sudden furious anger flamed up within me that such a creature should address me. For an instant I felt like wheeling about and smashing my stick over his head, but I walked on, and entering the Hamilton went to my apartment. For some time I tossed about the bed trying to get the sound of his voice out of my ears, but could not. It filled my head, that muttering sound, like thick oily smoke from a fat-rendering vat or an odor of noisome decay. And as I lay and tossed about, the voice in my ears seemed more distinct, and I began to understand the words he had muttered. They came to me slowly as if I had forgotten them, and at last I could make some sense out of the sounds. It was this:

"Have you found the Yellow Sign?"

"Have you found the Yellow Sign?"

"Have you found the Yellow Sign?"

I was furious. What did he mean by that? Then with a curse upon him and his I rolled over and went to sleep, but when I awoke later I looked pale and haggard, for I had dreamed the dream of the night before and it troubled me more than I cared to think.

I dressed and went down into my studio. Tessie sat by the window, but as I came in she rose and put both arms around my neck for an innocent kiss. She looked so sweet and dainty that I kissed her again and then sat down before the easel.

"Hello! Where's the study I began yesterday?" I asked.

Tessie looked conscious, but did not answer. I began to hunt among the piles of canvases, saying, "Hurry up, Tess, and get ready; we must take advantage of the morning light."

When at last I gave up the search among the other canvases and turned to look around the room for the missing study I noticed Tessie standing by the screen with her clothes still on.

"What's the matter," I asked, "don't you feel well?"

"Yes."

"Then hurry."

"Do you want me to pose as—as I have always posed?"

Then I understood. Here was a new complication. I had lost, of course, the best nude model I had ever seen. I looked at Tessie. Her face was scarlet. Alas! Alas! We had eaten of the tree of knowledge, and Eden and native innocence were dreams of the past—I mean for her.

I suppose she noticed the disappointment on my face, for she said: "I will pose if you wish. The study is behind the screen here where I put it."

"No," I said, "we will begin something new"; and I went into my wardrobe and picked out a Moorish costume which fairly blazed with tinsel. It was a genuine costume, and Tessie retired to the screen with it enchanted. When she came forth again I was astonished. Her long black hair was bound above her forehead with a circlet of turquoises, and the ends curled about her glittering girdle. Her feet were encased in the embroidered pointed slippers and the skirt of her costume, curiously wrought with arabesques in silver, fell to her ankles. The deep metallic blue vest, embroidered with silver, and the short Mauresque jacket, spangled and sewn with turquoises, became her wonderfully. She came up to me and held up her face smiling. I slipped my hand into my pocket and, drawing out a gold chain with a cross attached, dropped it over her head.

"It's yours, Tessie."

"Mine?" she faltered.

"Yours. Now go and pose." Then with a radiant smile she ran behind the screen and presently re-appeared with a little box on which was written my name.

"I had intended to give it to you when I went home tonight," she said, "but I can't wait now."

I opened the box. On the pink cotton inside lay a clasp of black onyx, on which was inlaid a curious symbol or letter in gold. It was neither Arabic nor Chinese, nor as I found afterwards did it belong to any human script.

"It's all I had to give you for a keepsake," she said, timidly.

I was annoyed, but I told her how much I should prize it, and promised to wear it always. She fastened it on my coat beneath the lapel.

"How foolish, Tess, to go and buy me such a beautiful thing as this," I said.

"I did not buy it," she laughed.

"Where did you get it?"

Then she told me how she had found it one day while coming from the Aquarium in the Battery, how she had advertised it and watched the papers, but at last gave up all hopes of finding the owner.

"That was last winter," she said, "the very day I had the first horrid dream about the hearse."

I remembered my dream of the previous night but said nothing, and presently my charcoal was flying over a new canvas, and Tessie stood motionless on the model stand.

THREE

The day following was a disastrous one for me. While moving a framed canvas from one easel to another my foot slipped on the polished floor and I fell heavily on both wrists. They were so badly sprained that it was useless to attempt to hold a brush, and I was obliged to wander about the studio, glaring at unfinished drawings and sketches until despair seized me and I sat down to smoke and twiddle my thumbs with rage. The rain blew against the windows and rattled on the roof of the church, driving me into a nervous fit with its interminable patter. Tessie sat sewing by the window, and every now and then raised her head and looked at me with such innocent compassion that I began to feel ashamed of my irritation and looked about for something to occupy me. I had read all the papers and all the books in the library, but for the sake of something to do I went to the bookcases and shoved them open with my elbow. I knew every volume by its color and examined them all, passing slowly around the library and whistling to keep up my spirits. I was turning to go into the dining-room when my eye fell upon a book bound in serpent skin, standing in a corner of the top shelf of the last bookcase. I did not remember it and from the floor could not decipher the pale lettering on the back, so I went to the smoking-room and called Tessie. She came in from the studio and climbed up to reach the book.

"What is it?" I asked.

"'The King in Yellow,'"

I was dumbfounded. Who had placed it there? How came it in my rooms? I had long ago decided that I should never open that book, and nothing on earth could have persuaded me to buy it. Fearful lest curiosity might tempt me to open it, I had never even looked at it in book-stores. If I ever had had any curiosity to read it, the awful tragedy of young Castaigne, whom I knew, prevented me from exploring its wicked pages. I had always refused to listen to any description of it, and indeed, nobody ever ventured to discuss the second part aloud, so I had absolutely no knowledge of what those leaves might reveal. I stared at the poisonous mottled binding as I would at a snake.

"Don't touch it, Tessie," I said; "come down."

Of course my admonition was enough to arouse her curiosity, and before I could prevent it she took the book and, laughing, danced off into the studio with it, I called to her but she slipped away with a tormenting smile at my helpless hands, and I followed her with some impatience.

"Tessie!" I cried, entering the library, "listen, I am serious. Put that book away. I do not wish you to open it!" The library was empty. I went into both drawing-rooms, then into the bedrooms, laundry, kitchen and finally returned to the library and began a systematic search. She had hidden herself so well that it was half an hour later when I discovered her crouching white and silent by the latticed window in the store-room above. At the first glance I saw she had been punished for her foolishness. "The King in Yellow" lay at her feet, but the book was open at the second part. I looked at Tessie and saw it was too late. She had opened "The King in Yellow." Then I took her by the hand and led her into the studio. She seemed dazed, and when I told her to lie down on the sofa she obeyed me without a word. After a while she closed her eyes and her breathing became regular and deep, but I could not determine whether or not she slept. For a long while I sat silently beside her, but she neither stirred nor spoke, and at last I rose and entering the unused store-room took the book in my least injured hand. It seemed heavy as lead, but I carried it into the studio again, and sitting down on the rug beside the sofa, opened it and read it through from beginning to end.

When, faint with the excess of my emotions, I dropped the volume and leaned wearily back against the sofa, Tessie opened her eyes and looked at me.

We had been speaking for some time in a dull monotonous strain before I realized that we were discussing "The King in Yellow." Oh the sin of writing such words,—words which are clear as crystal, limpid and musical as bubbling springs, words which sparkle and glow like the poisoned diamonds of the Medicis! Oh the wickedness, the hopeless damnation of a soul who could fascinate and paralyze human creatures with such words,—words understood by the ignorant and wise alike, words which are more precious than jewels, more soothing than music, more awful than death!

We talked on, unmindful of the gathering shadows, and she was begging me to throw away the clasp of black onyx quaintly inlaid with what we now knew to be the Yellow Sign. I never shall know why I refused, though even at this hour, here in my bedroom as I write this confession, I should be glad to know *what* it was that prevented me from tearing the Yellow Sign from my breast and casting it into the fire. I am sure I wished to do so, and yet Tessie pleaded with me in vain. Night fell and the hours dragged on, but still we murmured to each other of the King and the Pallid Mask, and midnight sounded from the misty spires in the fog-wrapped city. We spoke of Hastur and of Cassilda, while outside the fog rolled against the blank window-panes as the cloud waves roll and break on the shores of Hali.

The house was very silent now and not a sound came up from the misty streets. Tessie lay among the cushions, her face a gray blot in the gloom, but her hands were clasped in mine and I knew that she knew and read my thoughts as I read hers, for we had understood the mystery of the Hyades and the Phantom of Truth was laid. Then as we answered each other, swiftly, silently, thought on thought, the shadows stirred in the gloom about us, and far in the distant streets we heard a sound. Nearer and nearer it came, the dull crunching wheels, nearer and yet nearer, and now, outside before the door it ceased, and I dragged myself to the window and saw a black-plumed hearse. The gate below opened and shut, and I crept shaking to my door and bolted it, but I knew no bolts, no locks, could keep that creature out who was coming for the Yellow Sign. And now I heard him moving very softly along the hall. Now he was at the door, and the bolts rotted at his touch. Now he had entered. With eyes starting from my head I peered into the darkness, but when he came into the room I did not see him. It was only when I felt him envelop me in his cold soft grasp that I cried out and struggled with deadly fury, but my hands were useless and he tore the onyx clasp from my coat and struck me full in the face. Then, as I fell, I heard Tessie's soft cry and her spirit fled: and even while falling I longed to follow her, for I knew that the King in Yellow had opened his tattered mantle and there was only God to cry to now.

I could tell more, but I cannot see what help it will be to the world. As for me, I am past human help or hope. As I lie here, writing, careless even whether or not I die before I finish, I can see the doctor gathering up his powders and phials with a vague gesture to the good priest beside me, which I understand.

They will be very curious to know the tragedy—they of the outside world who write books and print millions of newspapers, but I shall write no more, and the father confessor will seal my last words with the seal of sanctity when his holy office is done. They of the outside world may send their creatures into wrecked homes and death-smitten firesides, and their newspapers will batten on blood and tears, but with me their spies must halt before the confessional. They know that Tessie is dead and that I am dying. They know how the people in the house, aroused by an infernal scream, rushed into my room and found one living and two dead, but they do not know what I shall tell them now; they do not know that the doctor said as he pointed to a horrible decomposed heap on the floor—the livid corpse of the watchman from the church: "I have no theory, no explanation. That man must have been dead for months!"

I think I am dying. I wish the priest would——

The Room in the Tower

E. F. Benson

It is probable that everybody who is at all a constant dreamer has had at least one experience of an event or a sequence of circumstances which have come to his mind in sleep being subsequently realized in the material world. But, in my opinion, so far from this being a strange thing, it would be far odder if this fulfilment did not occasionally happen, since our dreams are, as a rule, concerned with people whom we know and places with which we are familiar, such as might very naturally occur in the awake and daylit world. True, these dreams are often broken into by some absurd and fantastic incident, which puts them out of court in regard to their subsequent fulfilment, but on the mere calculation of chances, it does not appear in the least unlikely that a dream imagined by anyone who dreams constantly should occasionally come true. Not long ago, for instance, I experienced such a fulfilment of a dream which seems to me in no way remarkable and to have no kind of psychical significance. The manner of it was as follows.

A certain friend of mine, living abroad, is amiable enough to write to me about once in a fortnight. Thus, when fourteen days or thereabouts have elapsed since I last heard from him, my mind, probably, either consciously or subconsciously, is expectant of a letter from him. One night last week I dreamed that as I was going upstairs to dress for dinner I heard, as I often heard, the sound of the postman's knock on my front door, and diverted my direction downstairs instead. There, among other correspondence, was a letter from him. Thereafter the fantastic entered, for on opening it I found inside the ace of diamonds, and scribbled across it in his well-known hand-writing, 'I am sending you this for safe custody, as you know it is running an unreasonable risk to keep aces in Italy.' The next evening I was just preparing to go upstairs to dress when I heard the postman's knock, and did precisely as

I had done in my dream. There, among other letters, was one from my friend. Only it did not contain the ace of diamonds. Had it done so, I should have attached more weight to the matter, which, as it stands, seems to me a perfectly ordinary coincidence. No doubt I consciously or subconsciously expected a letter from him, and this suggested to me my dream. Similarly, the fact that my friend had not written to me for a fortnight suggested to him that he should do so. But occasionally it is not so easy to find such an explanation, and for the following story I can find no explanation at all. It came out of the dark, and into the dark it has gone again.

All my life I have been a habitual dreamer: the nights are few, that is to say, when I do not find on awaking in the morning that some mental experience has been mine, and sometimes, all night long, apparently, a series of the most dazzling adventures befall me. Almost without exception these adventures are pleasant, though often merely trivial. It is of an exception that I am going to speak.

It was when I was about sixteen that a certain dream first came to me, and this is how it befell. It opened with my being set down at the door of a big red-brick house, where, I understood, I was going to stay. The servant who opened the door told me that tea was going on in the garden, and led me through a low dark-panelled hall, with a large open fireplace, on to a cheerful green lawn set round with flower beds. There were grouped about the tea-table a small party of people, but they were all strangers to me except one, who was a schoolfellow called Jack Stone, clearly the son of the house, and he introduced me to his mother and father and a couple of sisters. I was, I remember, somewhat astonished to find myself here, for the boy in question was scarcely known to me, and I rather disliked what I knew of him: moreover, he had left school nearly a year before. The afternoon was very hot, and an intolerable oppression reigned. On the far side of the lawn ran a red-brick wall, with an iron gate in its centre, outside which stood a walnut tree. We sat in the shadow of the house opposite a row of long windows, inside which I could see a table with cloth laid, glimmering with glass and silver. This garden front of the house was very long, and at one end of it stood a tower of three stories, which looked to me much older than the rest of the building.

Before long, Mrs. Stone, who, like the rest of the party, had sat in absolute silence, said to me, 'Jack will show you your room: I have given you the room in the tower.'

Quite inexplicably my heart sank at her words. I felt as if I had known that I should have the room in the tower, and that it contained something dreadful and significant. Jack instantly got up, and I understood that I had to follow him. In silence we passed through the hall, and mounted a great oak staircase with many corners, and arrived at a small landing with two doors set in it. He pushed one of these open for me to enter, and without coming in himself, closed it behind me. Then I knew that my conjecture had been right: there was something awful in the room, and with the terror of nightmare growing swiftly and enveloping me, I awoke in a spasm of terror.

Now that dream or variations on it occurred to me intermittently for fifteen years. Most often it came in exactly this form, the arrival, the tea laid out on the lawn, the deadly silence succeeded by that one deadly sentence, the mounting with Jack Stone up to the room in the tower where horror dwelt, and it always came to a close in the nightmare of terror at that which was in the room, though I never saw what it was. At other times I experienced variations on this same theme. Occasionally, for instance, we would be sitting at dinner in the dining-room, into the windows of which I had looked on the first night when the dream of this house visited me, but wherever we were, there was the same silence, the same sense of dreadful oppression and foreboding. And the silence I knew would always be broken by Mrs. Stone saying to me, 'Jack will show you your room: I have given you the room in the tower.' Upon which (this was invariable) I had to follow him up the oak staircase with many corners, and enter the place that I dreaded more and more each time that I visited it in sleep. Or, again, I would find myself playing cards still in silence in a drawing-room lit with immense chandeliers, that gave a blinding illumination. What the game was I have no idea; what I remember, with a sense of miserable anticipation, was that soon Mrs. Stone would get up and say to me, 'Jack will show you your room: I have given you the room in the tower.' This drawing-room where we played cards was next to the dining-room, and, as I have said, was always brilliantly illuminated, whereas the rest of the house was full of dusk and shadows. And yet, how often, in spite of those bouquets of lights, have I not pored over the cards that were dealt me, scarcely able for some reason to see them. Their designs, too, were strange: there were no red suits, but all were black, and among them there were certain cards which were black all over: I hated and dreaded those.

As this dream continued to recur, I got to know the greater part of the house. There was a smoking-room beyond the drawing-room, at the end of a passage with a green baize door. It was always very dark there, and as often as I went there I passed somebody whom I could not see in the doorway coming out. Curious developments, too, took place in the characters that peopled the dream as might happen to living persons. Mrs. Stone, for instance, who, when I first saw her, had been black-haired, became grey, and instead of rising briskly, as she had done at first when she said, 'Jack will show you your room: I have given you the room in the tower,' got up very feebly, as if the strength was leaving her limbs. Jack also grew up, and became a rather ill-looking young man, with a brown moustache, while one of the sisters ceased to appear, and I understood she was married.

Then it so happened that I was not visited by this dream for six months or more, and I began to hope, in such inexplicable dread did I hold it, that it had passed away for good. But one night after this interval I again found myself being shown out on to the lawn for tea, and Mrs. Stone was not there, while the others were all dressed in black. At once I guessed the reason, and my heart leaped at the thought that perhaps this time I should not have to sleep in the room in the tower, and though we usually all sat in silence, on this occasion the sense of relief made me talk and laugh as I had never yet done. But even then matters were not altogether comfortable for no one else spoke, but they all looked secretly at each other. And soon the foolish stream of my talk ran dry, and gradually an apprehension worse than anything I had previously known gained on me as the light slowly faded.

Suddenly a voice which I knew well broke the stillness, the voice of Mrs. Stone, saying, 'Jack will show you your room: I have given you the room in the tower.' It seemed to come from near the gate in the red-brick wall that bounded the lawn, and looking up, I saw that the grass outside was sown thick with gravestones. A curious greyish light shone from them, and I could read the lettering on the grave nearest me, and it was, 'In evil memory of Julia Stone.' And as usual Jack got up, and again I followed him through the hall and up the staircase with many corners. On this occasion it was darker than usual, and when I passed into the room in the tower I could only just see the furniture, the position of which was already familiar to me. Also there was a dreadful odour of decay in the room, and I woke screaming.

The dream, with such variations and developments as I have mentioned, went on at intervals for fifteen years. Sometimes I would dream it two or three nights in succession; once, as I have said, there was an intermission of six months, but taking a reasonable average, I should say that I dreamed it quite as often as once in a month. It had, as is plain, something of nightmare about it, since it always ended in the same appalling terror, which so far from getting less, seemed to me to gather fresh fear every time that I experienced it. There was, too, a strange and dreadful consistency about it. The characters in it, as I have mentioned, got regularly older, death and marriage visited this silent family, and I never in the dream, after Mrs. Stone had died, set eyes on her again. But it was always her voice that told me that the room in the tower was prepared for me, and whether we had tea out on the lawn, or the scene was laid in one of the rooms overlooking it, I could always see her gravestone standing just outside the iron gate. It was the same, too, with the married daughter; usually she was not present, but once or twice she returned again, in company with a man, whom I took to be her husband. He, too, like the rest of them, was always silent. But owing to the constant repetition of the dream, I had ceased to attach, in my waking hours, any significance to it. I never met Jack Stone again during all those years, nor did I ever see a house that resembled this dark house of my dream. And then something happened.

I had been in London in this year, up till the end of July, and during the first week in August went down to stay with a friend in a house he had taken for the summer months, in the Ashdown Forest district of Sussex. I left London early, for John Clinton was to meet me at Forest Row Station, and we were going to spend the day golfing, and go to his house in the evening. He had his motor with him, and we set off, about five of the afternoon, after a thoroughly delightful day, for the drive, the distance being some ten miles. As it was still so early we did not have tea at the club house, but waited till we should get home. As we drove, the weather, which up till then had been, though hot, deliciously fresh, seemed to me to alter in quality, and became very stagnant and oppressive, and I felt that indefinable sense of ominous apprehension that I am accustomed to before thunder. John, however, did not share my views, attributing my loss of lightness to the fact that I had lost both my matches. Events proved, however, that I was right, though I do not think that the thunderstorm that broke that night was the sole cause of my depression.

Our way lay through deep high-banked lanes, and before we had gone very far I fell asleep, and was only awakened by the stopping of the motor. And with a sudden thrill, partly of fear but chiefly of curiosity, I found myself standing in the doorway of my house of dream. We went, I half wondering whether or not I was dreaming still, through a low oak-panelled hall, and out on to the lawn, where tea was laid in the shadow of the house. It was set in flower beds, a red-brick wall, with a gate in it, bounded one side, and out beyond that was a space of rough grass with a walnut tree. The façade of the house was very long, and at one end stood a three-storied tower, markedly older than the rest.

Here for the moment all resemblance to the repeated dream ceased. There was no silent and somehow terrible family, but a large assembly of exceedingly cheerful persons all of whom were known to me. And in spite of the horror with which the dream itself had always filled me, I felt nothing of it now that the scene of it was thus reproduced before me. But I felt the intensest curiosity as to what was going to happen.

Tea pursued its cheerful course, and before long Mrs. Clinton got up. And at that moment I think I knew what she was going to say. She spoke to me, and what she said was:

'Jack will show you your room: I have given you the room in the tower.'

At that, for half a second, the horror of the dream took hold of me again.

But it quickly passed, and again I felt nothing more than the most intense curiosity. It was not very long before it was amply satisfied.

John turned to me.

'Right up at the top of the house,' he said, 'but I think you'll be comfortable. We're absolutely full up. Would you like to go and see it now? By Jove, I believe that you are right, and that we are going to have a thunderstorm. How dark it has become.'

I got up and followed him. We passed through the hall, and up the perfectly familiar staircase. Then he opened the door, and I went in. And at that moment sheer unreasoning terror again possessed me. I did not know for certain what I feared: I simply feared. Then like a sudden recollection, when one remembers a name which has long escaped the memory, I knew what I feared. I feared Mrs. Stone, whose grave with the sinister inscription. 'In evil memory', I had so often seen in my dream, just beyond the lawn which lay below my window. And then once more the fear passed so completely that I wondered what there was to fear, and I found myself, sober and quiet and sane, in the room in the tower, the name of which I had so often heard in my dream, and the scene of which was so familiar.

I looked round it with a certain sense of proprietorship, and found that nothing had been changed from the dreaming nights in which I knew it so well. Just to the left of the door was the bed, lengthways along the wall, with the head of it in the angle. In a line with it was the fireplace and a small bookcase; opposite the door the outer wall was pierced by two lattice-paned windows, between which stood the dressing-table, while ranged along the fourth wall was the washing-stand and a big cupboard. My luggage had already been unpacked, for the furniture of dressing and undressing lay orderly on the washstand and toilet-table, while my dinner clothes were spread out on the coverlet of the bed. And then, with a sudden start of unexplained dismay, I saw that there were two rather conspicuous objects which I had not seen before in my dreams: one a life-sized oil-painting of Mrs. Stone, the other a black-and-white sketch of Jack Stone, representing him as he had appeared to me only a week before in the last of the series of these repeated dreams, a rather secret and evil-looking man of about thirty. His picture hung between the windows, looking straight across the room to the other portrait, which hung at the side of the bed. At that I looked next, and as I looked I felt once more the horror of nightmare seize me.

It represented Mrs. Stone as I had seen her last in my dreams: old and withered and white-haired. But in spite of the evident feebleness of body, a dreadful exuberance and vitality shone through the envelope of flesh, an exuberance wholly malign, a vitality that foamed and frothed with unimaginable evil. Evil beamed from the narrow, leering eyes; it laughed in the de-

mon-like mouth. The whole face was instinct with some secret and appalling
mirth; the hands, clasped together on the knee, seemed shaking with suppressed and nameless glee. Then I saw also that it was signed in the left-hand
bottom corner, and wondering who the artist could be, I looked more
closely, and read the inscription, 'Julia Stone by Julia Stone.'

There came a tap at the door, and John Clinton entered.

'Got everything you want?' he asked.

'Rather more than I want,' said I, pointing to the picture.

He laughed.

'Hard-featured old lady,' he said. 'By herself, too, I remember. Anyhow
she can't have flattered herself much.'

'But don't you see?' said I. 'It's scarcely a human face at all. It's the face of
some witch, of some devil.'

He looked at it more closely.

'Yes; it isn't very pleasant,' he said. 'Scarcely a bedside manner, eh? Yes; I
can imagine getting the nightmare if I went to sleep with that close by my
bed. I'll have it taken down if you like.'

'I really wish you would,' I said.

He rang the bell, and with the help of a servant we detached the picture
and carried it out on to the landing, and put it with its face to the wall.

'By Jove, the old lady is a weight,' said John, mopping his forehead. 'I
wonder if she had something on her mind.'

The extraordinary weight of the picture had struck me too. I was about to
reply, when I caught sight of my own hand. There was blood on it, in
considerable quantities, covering the whole palm.

'I've cut myself somehow,' said I.

John gave a little startled exclamation.

'Why, I have too,' he said.

Simultaneously the footman took out his handkerchief and wiped his hand
with it. I saw that there was blood also on his handkerchief.

John and I went back into the tower room and washed the blood off; but
neither on his hand nor on mine was there the slightest trace of a scratch or
cut. It seemed to me that, having ascertained this, we both, by a sort of tacit
consent, did not allude to it again. Something in my case had dimly occurred
to me that I did not wish to think about. It was but a conjecture, but I fancied
that I knew the same thing had occurred to him.

The heat and oppression of the air, for the storm we had expected was still
undischarged, increased very much after dinner, and for some time most of
the party, among whom were John Clinton and myself, sat outside on the
path bounding the lawn, where we had had tea. The night was absolutely
dark, and no twinkle of star or moon ray could penetrate the pall of cloud

that overset the sky. By degrees our assembly thinned, the women went up to
bed, men dispersed to the smoking- or billiard-room, and by eleven o'clock
my host and I were the only two left. All the evening I thought that he had
something on his mind, and as soon as we were alone he spoke.

'The man who helped us with the picture had blood on his hand, too, did
you notice?' he said. 'I asked him just now if he had cut himself, and he said
he supposed he had, but that he could find no mark of it. Now where did
that blood come from?'

By dint of telling myself that I was not going to think about it, I had
succeeded in not doing so, and I did not want, especially just at bedtime, to
be reminded of it.

'I don't know,' said I, 'and I don't really care so long as the picture of Mrs.
Julia Stone is not by my bed.'

He got up.

'But it's odd,' he said. 'Ha! Now you'll see another odd thing.'

A dog of his, an Irish terrier by breed, had come out of the house as we
talked. The door behind us into the hall was open, and a bright oblong of
light shone across the lawn to the iron gate which led on to the rough grass
outside, where the walnut tree stood. I saw that the dog had all his hackles up,
bristling with rage and fright; his lips were curled back from his teeth, as if he
was ready to spring at something, and he was growling to himself. He took
not the slightest notice of his master or me, but stiffly and tensely walked
across the grass to the iron gate. There he stood for a moment, looking
through the bars and still growling. Then of a sudden his courage seemed to
desert him: he gave one long howl, and scuttled back to the house with a
curious crouching sort of movement.

'He does that half-a-dozen times a day,' said John. 'He sees something
which he both hates and fears.'

I walked to the gate and looked over it. Something was moving on the
grass outside, and soon a sound which I could not instantly identify came to
my ears. Then I remembered what it was: it was the purring of a cat. I lit a
match, and saw the purrer, a big blue Persian, walking round and round in a
little circle just outside the gate, stepping high and ecstatically, with tail
carried aloft like a banner. Its eyes were bright and shining, and every now
and then it put its head down and sniffed at the grass.

I laughed.

'The end of that mystery, I am afraid,' I said. Here's a large cat having
Walpurgis night all alone.'

'Yes, that's Darius,' said John. 'He spends half the day and all night there.
But that's not the end of the dog mystery, for Toby and he are the best of

friends, but the beginning of the cat mystery. What's the cat doing there? And why is Darius pleased, while Toby is terror-stricken?'

At that moment I remembered the rather horrible detail of my dreams when I saw through the gate, just where the cat was now, the white tomb-stone with the sinister inscription. But before I could answer the rain began, as suddenly and heavily as if a tap had been turned on, and simultaneously the big cat squeezed through the bars of the gate, and came leaping across the lawn to the house for shelter. Then it sat in the doorway, looking out eagerly into the dark. It spat and struck at John with its paw, as he pushed it in, in order to close the door.

Somehow, with the portrait of Julia Stone in the passage outside, the room in the tower had absolutely no alarm for me, and as I went to bed, feeling very sleepy and heavy, I had nothing more than interest for the curious incident about our bleeding hands, and the conduct of the cat and dog. The last thing I looked at before I put out my light was the square empty space by my bed where the portrait had been. Here the paper was of its original full tint of dark red: over the rest of the walls it had faded. Then I blew out my candle and instantly fell asleep.

My awaking was equally instantaneous, and I sat bolt upright in bed under the impression that some bright light had been flashed in my face, though it was now absolutely pitch dark. I knew exactly where I was, in the room which I had dreaded in dreams, but no horror that I ever felt when asleep approached the fear that now invaded and froze my brain. Immediately after a peal of thunder crackled just above the house, but the probability that it was only a flash of lightning which awoke me gave no reassurance to my galloping heart. Something I knew was in the room with me, and instinctively I put out my right hand, which was nearest the wall, to keep it away. And my hand touched the edge of a picture-frame hanging close to me.

I sprang out of bed, upsetting the small table that stood by it, and I heard my watch, candle and matches clatter on to the floor. But for the moment there was no need of light, for a blinding flash leaped out of the clouds, and showed me that by my bed again hung the picture of Mrs. Stone. And instantly the room went into blackness again. But in that flash I saw another thing also, namely a figure that leaned over the end of my bed, watching me. It was dressed in some close-clinging white garment, spotted and stained with mould, and the face was that of the portrait.

Overhead the thunder cracked and roared, and when it ceased and the deathly stillness succeeded, I heard the rustle of movement coming nearer me, and, more horrible yet, perceived an odour of corruption and decay. And then a hand was laid on the side of my neck, and close beside my ear I heard quick-taken eager breathing. Yet I knew that this thing, though it could be perceived by touch, by smell, by eye and by ear, was still not of this earth, but something that had passed out of the body and had power to make itself manifest. Then a voice, already familiar to me, spoke.

'I knew you would come to the room in the tower,' it said. 'I have been long waiting for you. At last you have come. Tonight I shall feast; before long we will feast together.'

And the quick breathing came closer to me; I could feel it on my neck.

At that the terror, which I think had paralysed me for the moment, gave way to the wild instinct of self-preservation. I hit wildly with both arms, kicking out at the same moment, and heard a little animal-squeak, and something soft dropped with a thud beside me. I took a couple of steps forward, nearly tripping up over whatever it was that lay there, and by the merest good-luck found the handle of the door. In another second I ran out on the landing, and had banged the door behind me. Almost at the same moment I heard a door open somewhere below, and John Clinton, candle in hand, came running upstairs.

'What is it?' he said. 'I sleep just below you, and heard a noise as if—Good heavens, there's blood on your shoulder.'

I stood there, so he told me afterwards, swaying from side to side, white as a sheet, with the mark on my shoulder as if a hand covered with blood had been laid there.

'It's in there,' I said, pointing. 'She, you know. The portrait is in there, too, hanging up on the place we took it from.'

At that he laughed.

'My dear fellow, this is mere nightmare,' he said.

He pushed by me, and opened the door, I standing there simply inert with terror, unable to stop him, unable to move.

'Phew! What an awful smell,' he said.

Then there was silence; he had passed out of my sight behind the open door. Next moment he came out again, as white as myself, and instantly shut it.

'Yes, the portrait's there,' he said, 'and on the floor is a thing—a thing spotted with earth, like what they bury people in. Come away, quick, come away.'

How I got downstairs I hardly know. An awful shuddering and nausea of the spirit rather than of the flesh had seized me, and more than once he had to place my feet upon the steps, while every now and then he cast glances of terror and apprehension up the stairs. But in time we came to his dressing-room on the floor below, and there I told him what I have here described.

*   *   *

The sequel can be made short; indeed, some of my readers have perhaps already guessed what it was, if they remember that inexplicable affair of the churchyard at West Fawley, some eight years ago, where an attempt was made three times to bury the body of a certain woman who had committed suicide. On each occasion the coffin was found in the course of a few days again protruding from the ground. After the third attempt, in order that the thing should not be talked about, the body was buried elsewhere in unconsecrated ground. Where it was buried was just outside the iron gate of the garden belonging to the house where this woman had lived. She had committed suicide in a room at the top of the tower in that house. Her name was Julia Stone.

Subsequently the body was again secretly dug up, and the coffin was found to be full of blood.

Three Lines
of Old French

A. Merritt

But rich as was the war for surgical science," ended Hawtry, "opening up through mutilation and torture unexplored regions which the genius of man was quick to enter, and, entering, found ways to checkmate suffering and death—for always, my friends, the distillate from the blood of sacrifice is progress—great as all this was, the world tragedy has opened up still another region wherein even greater knowledge will be found. It was the clinic unsurpassed for the psychologist even more than for the surgeon."

Latour, the great little French doctor, drew himself out of the depths of the big chair; the light from the fireplace fell ruddily upon his keen face.

"That is true," he said. "Yes, that is true. There in the furnace the mind of man opened like a flower beneath a too glowing sun. Beaten about in that colossal tempest of primitive forces, caught in the chaos of energies both physical and psychical—which, although man himself was its creator, made of their maker a moth in a whirlwind—all those obscure, those mysterious factors of mind which men, for lack of knowledge, have named the soul, were stripped of their inhibitions and given power to appear.

"How could it have been otherwise—when men and women, gripped by one shattering sorrow or joy, will manifest the hidden depths of spirit—how could it have been otherwise in that steadily maintained crescendo of emotion?"

McAndrews spoke. "Just which psychological region do you mean, Hawtry?" he asked.

There were four of us in front of the fireplace of the Science Club—Hawtry, who rules the chair of psychology in one of our greatest colleges, and whose name is an honored one throughout the world; Latour, an immortal of France; McAndrews, the famous American surgeon whose work during the war has written a new page in the shining book of science; and myself. These are not the names of the three, but they are as I have described them; and I am pledged to identify them no further.

"I mean the field of suggestion," replied the psychologist. "The mental reactions which reveal themselves as visions—an accidental formation in the clouds that becomes to the overwrought imaginations of the beholders the so-eagerly-prayed-for hosts of Joan of Arc marching out from heaven; moonlight in the cloud rift that becomes to the besieged a fiery cross held by the hands of archangels; the despair and hope that are transformed into such a legend as the bowmen of Mons, ghostly archers who with their fantom shafts overwhelm the conquering enemy; wisps of cloud over No Man's Land that are translated by the tired eyes of those who peer out into the shape of the Son of Man himself walking sorrowfully among the dead.

"Signs, portents, and miracles; the hosts of premonitions, of apparitions of loved ones—all dwellers in this land of suggestion; all born of the tearing loose of the veils of the subconscious. Here, when even a thousandth part is gathered, will be work for the psychological analyst for twenty years."

"And the boundaries of this region?" asked McAndrews.

"Boundaries?" Hawtry plainly was perplexed.

McAndrews for a moment was silent. Then he drew from his pocket a yellow slip of paper, a cablegram.

"Young Peter Laveller died today," he said, apparently irrelevantly. "Died where he had set forth to pass—in the remnants of the trenches that cut through the ancient domain of the Seigniors of Tocquelain, up near Bethune."

"Died there!" Hawtry's astonishment was profound. "But I read that he had been brought home; that, indeed, he was one of your triumphs, McAndrews!"

"I said that he *went* there to die," repeated the surgeon slowly.

So that explained the curious reticence of the Lavellers as to what had become of their soldier son—a secrecy which had puzzled the press for weeks. For young Peter Lavaller was one of the nation's heroes. The only boy of old Peter Laveller—and neither is that the real name of the family—for like the others, I may not reveal it—he was the heir to the grim old coal king's millions, and the secret, best beloved pulse of his heart.

Early in the war he had enlisted with the French. His father's influence might have abrogated the law of the French Army that every man must start from the bottom up—I do not know—but young Peter would have none of it. Steady of purpose, burning with the white fire of the first Crusaders, he took his place in the ranks.

Clean-cut, blue-eyed, standing six feet in his stocking feet, just twenty-five, a bit of a dreamer, perhaps, he was one to strike the imagination of the poilus, and they loved him. Twice he was wounded in the perilous days, and when America came into the war he was transferred to our expeditionary forces. It was at the siege of Mount Kemmel that he received the wounds that brought him back to his father and sister. McAndrews had accompanied him overseas, I knew, and had patched him together—or so all thought.

What had happened then—and why had Laveller gone back to France, to die, as McAndrews put it?

He thrust the cablegram back into his pocket.

"There is a boundary, John," he said to Hawtry. "Laveller's was a border-land case. I'm going to tell it to you." He hesitated. "I ought not to, maybe; and yet I have an idea that Peter would like it told; after all, he believed himself a discoverer." Again he paused, then definitely made up his mind, and turned to me.

"Merritt, you may make use of this if you think it interesting enough. But if you do so decide, then change the names, and be sure to check description short of any possibility of ready identification. After all, it is what happened that is important—if it is important—and those to whom it happened do not matter."

I promised, and I have observed my pledge. I tell the story as he whom I call McAndrews reconstructed it for us there in the shadowed room, while we sat silent until he had entered . . .

Laveller stood behind the parapet of a first-line trench. It was night—an early April night in northern France—and when that is said, all is said to those who have been there.

Beside him was a trench periscope. His gun lay touching it. The periscope is practically useless at night; so through a slit in the sand-bags he peered out over the three-hundred-foot-wide stretch of No Man's Land.

Opposite him he knew that other eyes lay close to similar slits in the German parapet, watchful as his were for the least movement.

There were grotesque heaps scattered about No Man's Land, and when the starshells burst and flooded it with their glare these heaps seemed to stir, to move—some to raise themselves, some to gesticulate, to protest. And this was very horrible, for those who moved under the lights were the dead—French and English, Prussian and Bavarian—dregs of a score of carryings to the red wine-press of war set up in this sector.

There were two Jocks on the entanglements; killed Scots, one colandered by machine-gun hail just as he was breaking through. The shock of the swift, manifold death had hurled his left arm about the neck of the comrade close beside him; and this man had been stricken within the same second. There they leaned, embracing—and as the star-shells flared and died, flared and died, they seemed to rock, to try to break from the wire, to dash forward, to return.

Laveller was weary, weary beyond all understanding. The sector was a bad one and nervous. For almost seventy-two hours he had been without sleep— for the few minutes now and then of dead stupor broken by constant alarms was worse than sleep.

The shelling had been well-nigh continuous, and the food scarce and perilous to get; three miles back through the fire they had been forced to go for it; no nearer than that could the ration dumps be brought.

And constantly the parapets had to be rebuilt and the wires repaired—and when this was done the shells destroyed again, and once more the dreary routine had to be gone through; for the orders were to hold this sector at all costs.

All that was left of Laveller's consciousness was concentrated in his eyes; only his seeing faculty lived. And sight, obeying the rigid, inexorable will commanding every reserve of vitality to concentrate on the duty at hand, was blind to everything except the strip before it that Laveller must watch until relieved. His body was numb; he could not feel the ground with his feet, and sometimes he seemed to be floating in air like—like the two Scots upon the wire!

Why couldn't they be still? What right had men whose blood had drained away into the black stain beneath them to dance and pirouette to the rhythm of the flared? Damn them—why couldn't a shell drop down and bury them?

There was a château half a mile up there to the right—at least it had been a château. Under it were deep cellars into which one could creep and sleep. He knew that, because ages ago, when first he had come into this part of the line, he had slept a night there.

It would be like reentering paradise to crawl again into those cellars, out of the pitiless rain; sleep once more with a roof over his head.

"I will sleep and sleep and sleep—and sleep and sleep and sleep," he told himself; then stiffened as at the slumber-compelling repetition of the word darkness began to gather before him.

The star-shells flared and died, flared and died; the staccato of a machine gun reached him. He thought that it was his teeth chattering until his groping consciousness made him realize what it really was—some nervous German riddling the interminable movement of the dead.

There was a squidging of feet through the chalky mud. No need to look; they were friends, or they could not have passed the sentries at the angle of the traverse. Nevertheless, involuntarily, his eyes swept toward the sounds, took note of three cloaked figures regarding him.

There were half a dozen of the lights floating overhead now, and by the gleams they cast into the trench he recognized the party.

One of them was that famous surgeon who had come over from the base hospital at Bethune to see made the wounds he healed; the others were his major and his captain—all of them bound for those cellars, no doubt. Well, some had all the luck! Back went his eyes to the slit.

"What's wrong?" It was the voice of his major addressing the visitor.

"What's wrong—what's wrong—what's wrong?" The words repeated themselves swiftly, insistently, within his brain, over and over again, striving to waken it.

Well, what *was* wrong? Nothing was wrong! Wasn't he, Laveller, there and watching? The tormented brain writhed angrily. Nothing was wrong—why didn't they go away and let him watch in peace? He would like it much better.

"Nothing." It was the surgeon—and again the words kept babbling in Laveller's ears, small, whispering, rapidly repeating themselves over and over: "nothing—nothing—nothing—nothing."

But what was this the surgeon was saying? Fragmentarily, only half understood, the phrases registered:

"Perfect case of what I've been telling you. This lad here—utterly worn, weary—all his consciousness centered upon just one thing—watchfulness . . . consciousness worn to finest point . . . behind it all his subconsciousness crowding to escape . . . consciousness will respond to only one stimulus—movement from without . . . but the subconsciousness, so close to the surface, held so lightly in leash . . . what will it do if that little thread is loosed . . . a perfect case."

What were they talking about? Now they were whispering.

"Then, if I have your permission—" It was the surgeon speaking again. Permission for what? Why didn't they go away and not bother him? Wasn't it hard enough just to watch without having to hear? Something passed before his eyes. He looked at it blindly, unrecognizing. His sight must be clouded.

He raised a hand and brushed at his lids. Yes, it must have been his eyes—for it had gone.

A little circle of light glowed against the parapet near his face. It was cast by a small flash. What were they talking about? What were they looking for? A hand appeared in the circle, a hand with long, flexible fingers which held a piece of paper on which there was writing. Did they want him to read, too? Not only watch and hear—but read! He gathered himself together to protest.

Before he could force his stiffened lips to move he felt the upper button of his greatcoat undone, a hand slipped through the opening and thrust something into his tunic pocket just above the heart.

Someone whispered, "Lucie de Tocquelain."

What did it mean? That was not the password.

There was a great singing in his head—as though he were sinking through water. What was that light that dazzled him even through his closed lids? Painfully he opened his eyes.

Laveller looked straight into the disk of a golden sun setting over a row of noble oaks. Blinded, he dropped his gaze. He was standing ankle-deep in soft, green grass, starred with small clumps of blue flowerets. Bees buzzed about in their chalices. Little yellow-winged butterflies hovered over them. A gentle breeze blew, warm and fragrant.

Oddly he felt no sense of strangeness then—this was a normal home world —a world as it ought to be. But he remembered that he had once been in another world, far, far unlike this one; a place of misery and pain, of blood-stained mud and filth, of cold and wet; a world of cruelty, whose nights were tortured hells of glaring lights and fiery, slaying sounds, and tormented men who sought to rest and sleep and found none, and dead who danced. Where was it? Had there ever really been such a world? He was not sleepy now.

He raised his hands and looked at them. They were grimed and cut and stained. He was wearing a greatcoat, wet, mud-bespattered, filthy. High boots were on his legs. Beside one dirt-incrusted foot lay a cluster of the blue flowerets, half crushed. He groaned in pity, and bent, striving to raise the broken blossoms.

"Too many dead now—too many dead," he whispered; then paused. He *had* come from that nightmare world! How else in this happy, clean one could he be so unclean?

Of course he had—but where was it? How had he made his way from it here? Ah, there had been a password—what had it been?

He had it: "Lucie de Tocquelain!"

Laveller cried it aloud, still kneeling.

A soft little hand touched his cheek. A low, sweet-toned voice caressed his ears.

"I am Lucie de Tocquelain," it said. "And the flowers will grow again— yet it is dear of you to sorrow for them."

He sprang to his feet. Beside him stood a girl, a slender maid of eighteen, whose hair was a dusky cloud upon her proud little head and in whose great, brown eyes, resting upon him, tenderness and a half-amused pity dwelt.

Peter stood silent, drinking her in—the low, broad, white forehead; the curved, red lips; the rounded, white shoulders, shining through the silken web of her scarf; the whole lithe, sweet body of her in the clinging, quaintly fashioned gown, with its high, clasping girdle.

She was fair enough; but to Peter's starved eyes she was more than that—she was a spring gushing from the arid desert, the first cool breeze of twilight over a heat-drenched isle, the first glimpse of paradise to a soul risen from the centuries of hell. And under the burning worship of his eyes her own dropped; a faint rose stained the white throat, crept to her dark hair.

"I—I am the Demoiselle de Tocquelain, *messire*," she murmured. "And you—"

"Laveller—Peter Laveller—is my name, *mademoissel*," he stammered. "Pardon my rudeness—but how I came here I know not—nor from whence, save that it was—it was a place unlike this. And you—you are beautiful, *mademoiselle!*"

The clear eyes raised themselves for a moment, a touch of roguishness in their depths, then dropped demurely once more—but the blush deepened.

He watched her, all his awakening heart in his eyes; then perplexity awoke, touched him insistently.

"Will you tell me what place this is, *mademoiselle*," he faltered, "and how I came here, if you—" he stopped. From far, far away, from league upon league of space, a vast weariness was sweeping down upon him. He sensed it coming—closer, closer; it touched him; it lapped about him; he was sinking under it; being lost—falling—falling—

Two soft, warm hands gripped his. His tired head dropped upon them. Through the little palms that clasped so tightly pulsed rest and strength. The weariness gathered itself, began to withdraw slowly, so slowly—and was gone!

In its wake followed an ineffable, an uncontrollable desire to weep—to weep in relief that the weariness had passed, that the devil world whose shadows still lingered in his mind was behind him, and that he was here with this maid. And his tears fell, bathing the little hands.

Did he feel her head bend to his, her lips touch his hair? Peace came to him. He rose shamefacedly.

"I do not know why I wept, *mademoiselle*—", he began; and then saw that her white fingers were clasped now in his blackened ones. He released them in sudden panic.

"I am sorry," he stammered. "I ought not touch you—"

She reached out swiftly, took his hands again in hers, patted them half savagely. Her eyes flashed. "I do not see them as you do, Messire Pierre," she answered. "And if I did, are not their stains to me as the stains from hearts of her brave sons on the gonfalons of France? Think no more of your stains save as decorations, *messire*."

France—France? Why, that was the name of the world he had left behind; the world where men sought vainly for sleep, and the dead danced.

The dead danced—what did that mean?

He turned wistful eyes to her.

And with a little cry of pity she clung to him for a moment.

"You are so tired—and you are so hungry," she mourned. "And think no more, nor try to remember, *messire,* till you have eaten and drunk with us and rested for a space."

They had turned. And now Laveller saw not far away a château. It was pinnacled and stately, serene in its gray and lordly with its spires and slender turrets thrust skyward from its crest like plumes flung high from some proud prince's helm. Hand in hand like children the Demoiselle de Tocquelain and Peter Laveller approached it over the greensward.

"It is my home, *messire,*" the girl said. "And there among the roses my mother awaits us. My father is away, and he will be sorrowful that he met you not, but you shall meet him when you return."

He was to *return,* then? That meant he was not to stay. But where was he to go—from whence was he to return? His mind groped blindly; cleared again. He was walking among roses; there were roses everywhere, great, fragrant, opened blooms of scarlets and of saffrons, of shell pinks and white; clusters and banks of them, climbing up the terraces, masking the base of the château with perfumed tide.

And as he and the maid, still hand in hand, passed between them, they came to a table dressed with snowy napery and pale porcelains beneath a bower.

A woman sat there. She was a little past the prime of life, Peter thought. Her hair, he saw, was powdered white, her cheeks as pink and white as a child's, her eyes the sparkling brown of those of the *demoiselle*—and gracious —gracious, Peter thought, as some *grande dame* of old France.

The *demoiselle* dropped her a low curtesy.

"*Ma mère,*" she said, "I bring you the Sieur Pierre la Valliere, a very brave and gallant gentleman who has come to visit us for a while."

The clear eyes of the older woman scanned him, searched him. Then the stately white head bowed, and over the table a delicate hand was stretched toward him.

It was meant for him to kiss, he knew—but he hesitated awkwardly, miserably, looking at his begrimed own.

"The Sieur Pierre will not see himself as we do," the girl said in half merry reproof; then she laughed, a caressing, golden chiming. "*Ma mère,* shall he see his hands as we do?"

The white-haired woman smiled and nodded, her eyes kindly, and, Laveller noted, with that same pity in them as had been in those of the *demoiselle* when first he had turned and beheld her.

The girl touched Peter's eyes lightly, held his palms up before him—they were white and fine and clean and in some unfamiliar way beautiful!

Again the indefinable gaze stifled him, but his breeding told. He conquered the sense of strangeness, bowed from the hips, took the dainty fingers of the stately lady in his, and raised them to his lips.

She struck a silver bell. Through the roses came two tall men in livery, who took from Laveller his greatcoat. They were followed by four small black boys in gay scarlet slashed with gold. They bore silver platters on which were meat and fine white bread and cakes, fruit, and wine in tall crystal flagons.

And Laveller remembered how hungry he was. But of that feast he remembered little—up to a certain point. He knows that he sat there filled with a happiness and content that surpassed the sum of happiness of all his twenty-five years.

The mother spoke little, but the Demoiselle Lucie and Peter Laveller chattered and laughed like children—when they were not silent and drinking each other in.

And ever in Laveller's heart an adoration for this maid met so perplexingly grew—grew until it seemed that his heart could not hold his joy. Even the maid's eyes as they rested on his were softer, more tender, filled with promise; and the proud face beneath the snowy hair became, as it watched them, the essence of that infinitely gentle sweetness that is the soul of the madonnas.

At last the Demoiselle de Tocquelaine, glancing up and meeting that gaze, blushed, cast down her long lashes, and hung her head; then raised her eyes bravely.

"Are you content, my mother?" she asked gravely.

"My daughter, I am well content," came the smiling answer.

Swiftly followed the incredible, the terrible—in that scene of beauty and peace it was, said Laveller, like the flashing forth of a gorilla's paw upon a virgin's breast, a wail from deepest hell lancing through the song of angels.

At his right, among the roses, a light began to gleam—a fitful, flaring light that glared and died, glared and died. In it were two shapes. One had an arm clasped about the neck of the other; they leaned embracing in the light, and as it waxed and waned they seemed to pirouette, to try to break from it, to dash forward, to return—to dance!

The dead who danced!

A world where men sought rest and sleep, and could find neither, and where even the dead could find no rest, but must dance to the rhythm of the star-shells!

He groaned; sprang to his feet; watched, quivering in every nerve. Girl and woman followed his rigid gaze; turned to him again with tear-filled, pitiful eyes.

"It is nothing!" said the maid. "It is nothing! See there is nothing there!"

Once more she touched his lids; and the light and the swaying forms were gone. But now Laveller knew. Back into his consciousness rushed the full tide of memory—memory of the mud and filth, the stenches, and the fiery, slaying sounds, the cruelty, the misery and the hatreds; memory of torn men and tormented dead; memory of whence he had come, the trenches.

The trenches! He had fallen asleep, and all this was but a dream! He was sleeping at his post, while his comrades were trusting him to watch over them. And those two ghastly shapes among the roses—they were the two Scots on the wires summoning him back to his duty; beckoning, beckoning him to return. He must waken! He must waken!

Desperately he strove to drive himself from his garden of illusion; to force himself back to that devil world which during this hour of enchantment had been to his mind only as a fog bank on a far horizon. And as he struggled, the brown-eyed maid and the snowy-tressed woman watched—with ineffable pity, tears falling.

"The trenches!" gasped Laveller. "O God, wake me up! I must get back! O God, make me wake!"

"Am I only a dream, then, *ma mie?*"

It was the Demoiselle Lucie's voice—a bit piteous, the golden tones shaken.

"I must get back," he groaned—although at her question his heart seemed to die within him. "Let me wake!"

"Am *I* a dream?" Now the voice was angry; the demoiselle drew close. "Am I not *real?*"

A little foot stamped furiously on his, a little hand darted out, pinched him viciously close above his elbow. He felt the sting of the pain and rubbed it, gazing at her stupidly.

"Am I a dream, think you?" she murmured, and, raising her palms, set them on his temples, bringing down his head until his eyes looked straight into hers.

Laveller gazed—gazed down, down deep into their depths, lost himself in them. Her warm, sweet breath fanned his cheek; whatever this was, wherever he was—*she* was no dream!

"But I must return—get back to my trench!" The soldier in him clung to the necessity.

"My son—" it was the mother speaking now—"my son, you *are* in your trench."

Laveller gazed at her, bewildered. His eyes swept the lovely scene about him. When he turned to her again it was with the look of a sorely perplexed child. She smiled.

"Have no fear," she said. "Everything is well. You are in your trench—but your trench centuries ago; yes, twice a hundred years ago, counting time as you do—and as once we did."

A chill ran through him. Were they mad? Was he mad? His arm slipped down over a soft shoulder; the touch steadied him, then he was able to go on.

"And you?" he forced himself to ask.

He caught a swift glance between the two, and in answer to some unspoken question the mother nodded. The Demoiselle Lucie pressed soft hands against Peter's face, looked again into his eyes.

"Ma mie," she said gently, "we have been—" she hesitated—"what you call—dead—to your world these two hundred years!"

But before she had spoken the words Laveller, I think, had sensed what was coming. And if for a fleeting instant he had felt a touch of ice in every vein, it vanished beneath the exaltation that raced through him, vanished as frost beneath a mist-scattering sun. For if this were true—why, then there was no such thing as death! And it was true!

It was true! He knew it with a shining certainty that had upon it not the shadow of a shadow—but how much his desire to believe entered into this certainty who can tell?

He looked at the château. Of course! It was that whose ruins loomed out of the darkness when the flares split the night—in whose cellars he had longed to sleep. Death—oh, the foolish, fearful hearts of men!—this death? This glorious place of peace and beauty?

And this wondrous girl whose brown eyes were the keys of heart's desire! Death—he laughed and laughed again.

Another thought struck him, swept through him like a torrent. He must get back to the trenches and tell them this great truth he had found. Why, he was like a traveler from a dying world who unwittingly stumbles upon a secret to turn that world dead to hope into a living heaven!

There was no longer need for men to fear the splintering shell, the fire that seared them, the bullets, or the shining steel. What did they matter when this —*this*—was the truth? He must get back and tell them. Even those two Scots would lie still on the wires when he whispered this to them.

But he forgot—*they* knew now. But they could not return to tell—as he could. He was wild with joy, exultant, lifted up to the skies, a demigod—the bearer of a truth that would free the devil-ridden world from its demons; a new Prometheus who bore back to mankind a more precious flame than had the old.

"I must go!" he cried. "I must tell them! Show me how to return— swiftly!"

A doubt assailed him; he pondered it.

"But they may not believe me," he whispered. "No. I must show them proof. I must carry something back to prove this to them."

The Lady of Tocquelain smiled. She lifted a little knife from the table, and, reaching over to a rose-tree, cut from it a cluster of buds; thrust it toward his eager hand.

Before he could grasp it the maid had taken it.

"Wait!" she murmured. "I will give you another message."

There was a quill and ink upon the table, and Peter wondered how they had come; he had not seen them before—but with so many wonders, what was this small one? There was a slip of paper in the Demoiselle Lucie's hand, too. She bent her little, dusky head and wrote; blew upon the paper, waved it in the air to dry it; sighed, smiled at Peter, and wrapped it about the stem of the rosebud cluster; placed it on the table, and waved back Peter's questing hand.

"Your coat," she said. "You will need it, for now you must go back."

She thrust his arms into the garment. She was laughing—but there were tears in the great, brown eyes; the red mouth was very wistful.

Now the older woman arose, stretched out her hand again; Laveller bent over it, kissed it.

"We shall be here waiting for you, my son," she said softly. "When it is time for you to—come back."

He reached for the roses with the paper wrapped about their stems. The maid darted a hand over his, lifted them before he could touch them.

"You must not read it until you have gone," she said—and again the rose flame burned throat and cheeks.

Hand in hand, like children, they sped over the greensward to where Peter had first met her. They stopped there, regarding each other gravely—and then that other miracle which had happened to Laveller and that he had forgotten in the shock of his wider realization called for utterance.

"I love you!" whispered Peter Laveller to this living, long-dead Demoiselle de Tocquelain.

She sighed, and was in his arms.

"Oh, I know you do!" she cried. "I know you do, dear one—but I was so afraid you would go without telling me so."

She raised her sweet lips, pressed them long to his; drew back.

"I loved you from the moment I saw you standing here," she told him, "and I will be here waiting for you when you return. And now you must go, dear love of mine; but wait—"

He felt a hand steal into the pocket of his tunic, press something over his heart.

"The messages," she said. "Take them. And remember—I will wait. I promise, I, Lucie de Tocquelain—"

There was a singing in his head. He opened his eyes. He was back in his trench, and in his ears still rang the name of the *demoiselle,* and over his heart he felt still the pressure of her hand. His head was half turned toward three men who were regarding him.

One of them had a watch in his hand; it was the surgeon. Why was he looking at his watch. Had he been gone long? he wondered.

Well, what did it matter, when he was the bearer of such a message? His weariness had gone; he was transformed, jubilant; his soul was shouting pae-ans. Forgetting discipline, he sprang toward the three.

"There is no such thing as death!" he cried. "We must send this message along the lines—at once! At once, do you understand? Tell it to the world—I have proof—"

He stammered and choked in his eagerness. The three glanced at each other. His major lifted his electric flash, clicked it in Peter's face, started oddly—then quietly walked over and stood between the lad and his rifle.

"Just get your breath a moment, my boy, and then tell us about it," he said.

They were devilishly unconcerned, were they now? Well, wait till they had heard what he *had* to tell them!

And tell them Peter did, leaving out only what had passed between him and the *demoiselle*—for, after all, wasn't that his own personal affair? And gravely and silently they listened to him. But always the trouble deepened in his major's eyes as Laveller poured forth the story.

"And then—I came back, came back as quickly as I could, to help us all; to lift us out of all this—" his hands swept out in a wide gesture of disgust—"for none of it matters! When we die—we live!" he ended.

Upon the face of the man of science rested profound satisfaction.

"A perfect demonstration; better than I could ever have hoped!" he spoke over Laveller's head to the major. "Great, how great is the imagination of man!"

There was a tinge of awe in his voice.

Imagination? Peter was cut to the sensitive, vibrant soul of him:

They didn't believe him! He would show them!

"But I have proof!" he cried.

He threw open his greatcoat, ran his hand into his tunic-pocket; his fingers closed over a bit of paper wrapped around a stem. Ah—now he would show them!

He drew it out, thrust it toward them.

"Look!" His voice was like a triumphant trumpet-call.

What was the matter with them? Could they not see? Why did their eyes search his face instead of realizing what he was offering them? He looked at what he held—then, incredulous, brought it close to his own eyes—gazed and gazed, with a sound in his ears as though the universe were slipping away behind him, with a heart that seemed to have forgotten to beat. For in his hand, stem wrapped in paper, was no fresh and fragrant rosebud cluster his brown-eyed *demoiselle's* mother had clipped for him in the garden.

No—there was but a sprig of artificial buds, worn and torn and stained, faded and old!

A great numbness crept over Peter.

Dumbly he looked at the surgeon, at his captain, at the major whose face was now troubled indeed and somewhat stern.

"What does it mean?" he muttered.

Had it all been a dream? Was there no radiant Lucie—save in his own mind —no brown-eyed maid who loved him and whom he loved?

The scientist stepped forward, took the worn little sprig from the relaxed grip. The bit of paper slipped off, remained in Peter's fingers.

"You certainly deserve to know just what you've been through, my boy," the urbane, capable voice beat upon his dulled hearing, "after such a reaction as you have provided to our little experiment." He laughed pleasantly.

Experiment? Experiment? A dull rage began to grow in Peter—vicious, slowly rising.

"Messieur!" called the major appealingly, somewhat warningly, it seemed, to his distinguished visitor.

"Oh, by your leave, major," went on the great man, "here is a lad of high intelligence—of education, you could know that by the way he expressed himself—he will understand."

The major was not a scientist—he was a Frenchman, human, and with an imagination of his own. He shrugged; but he moved a little closer to the resting rifle.

"We had been discussing, your officers and I," the capable voice went on, "dreams that are the half-awakened mind's effort to explain some touch, some unfamiliar sound, or whatnot that has aroused it from its sleep. One is slumbering, say, and a window nearby is broken. The sleeper hears, the consciousness endeavors to learn—but it has given over its control to the subconscious. And this rises accommodatingly to its mate's assistance. But it is irresponsible, and it can express itself only in pictures.

★   ★   ★

"It takes the sound and—well weaves a little romance around it. It does its best to explain—alas! Its best is only a more or less fantastic lie—recognized as such by the consciousness the moment it becomes awake.

"And the movement of the subconsciousness in this picture production is inconceivably rapid. It can depict in the fraction of a second a series of incidents that if actually lived would take hours—yes, days—of time. You follow me, do you now? Perhaps you recognize the experience I outline? You certainly should."

Laveller nodded. The bitter, consuming rage was mounting within him steadily. But he was outwardly calm, all alert. He would hear what this self-satisfied devil had done to him, and then—

"Your officers disagreed with some of my conclusions. I saw you here, weary, concentrated upon the duty at hand, half in hypnosis from the strain and the steady flaring and dying of the lights. You offered a perfect clinical subject, a laboratory test unexcelled—"

Could he keep his hands from his throat until he had finished? Laveller wondered. Lucie, his Lucie, a fantastic lie—

"Steady, *mon vieux*—" it was his major whispering. Ah, when he struck, he must do it quickly, his officer was too close, too close. Still—he must keep his watch for him through the slit. He would be peering there perhaps, when he, Peter, leaped.

"And so—" the surgeon's tones were in his best student-clinic manner— "and so I took a little sprig of artificial flowers that I had found pressed between the leaves of an old missal I had picked up in the ruins of the château yonder. On a slip of paper I wrote a line of French—for then I thought you a French soldier. It was a simple line from the ballad of Aucassin and Nicolette—

And there she waits to greet him when all his days are run.

"Also, there was a name written on the title-page of the missal, the name, no doubt, of its long-dead owner—'Lucie de Tocquelain'—"

Lucie! Peter's rage and hatred were beaten back by a great surge of longing—rushed back stronger than ever.

"So I passed the sprig of flowers before your unseeing eyes; consciously unseeing, I mean, for it was certain your subconsciousness would take note of them. I showed you the line of writing—your subconsciousness absorbed this, too, with its suggestion of a love troth, a separation, an awaiting. I wrapped it about the stem of the sprig, I thrust them both into your pocket, and called the name of Lucie de Tocquelain into your ear.

"The problem was what your other self would make of those four things—

the ancient cluster, the suggestion in the line of writing, the touch, and the name—a fascinating problem, indeed!

"And hardly had I withdrawn my hand, almost before my lips closed on the word I had whispered—you had turned to us shouting that there was no such thing as death, and pouring out, like one inspired, that remarkable story of yours—all, all built by your imagination from—"

But he got no further. The searing rage in Laveller had burst all bounds, had flared forth murderously, had hurled him silently at the surgeon's throat. There were flashes of flame before his eyes—red, sparkling sheets of flame. He would die for it, but he would kill this cold-blooded fiend who could take a man out of hell, open up to him heaven, and then thrust him back into hell grown now a hundred times more cruel, with all hope dead in him for eternity.

Before he could strike, strong hands gripped him, held him back. The scarlet curtain flared before his eyes, faded away. He thought he heard a tender, golden voice whispering to him:

"It is nothing! It is nothing! See as I do!"

He was standing between his officers, who held him fast on each side. They were silent, looking at the now white-faced surgeon with more than somewhat of cold, unfriendly sternness in their eyes.

"My boy, my boy—" that scientist's poise was gone; his voice trembling, agitated. "I did not understand—I am sorry—I never thought you would take it so seriously."

Laveller spoke to his officers—quietly. "It is over, sirs. You need not hold me."

They looked at him, released him, patted him on the shoulder, fixed again their visitor with that same cold scrutiny.

Laveller turned stumblingly to the parapet. His eyes were full of tears. Brain and heart and soul were nothing but a blind desolation, a waste utterly barren of hope or of even the ghost of the wish to hope. That message of his, the sacred truth that was to set the feet of a tormented world on the path of paradise—a dream.

His Lucie, his brown-eyed *demoiselle* who had murmured her love for him —a thing compounded of a word, a touch, a writing, and an artificial flower!

He could not, would not believe it. Why, he could still feel the touch of her soft lips on his, her warm body quivering in his arms. And she had said he would come back—and promised to wait for him.

What was that in his hand? It was the paper that had wrapped the rosebuds —the cursed paper with which that cold devil had experimented with him.

Laveller crumpled it savagely—raised it to hurl it at his feet.

Someone seemed to stay his hand.

Slowly he opened it.

The three men watching him saw a glory steal over his face, a radiance like that of a soul redeemed from endless torture. All its sorrow, its agony, was wiped out, leaving it a boy's once more.

He stood, wide-eyed, dreaming.

The major stepped forward, gently drew the paper from Laveller.

There were many star-shells floating on high now, the trench was filled with their glare, and in their light he scanned the fragment.

On his face when he raised it there was a great awe—and as they took it from him and read this same awe dropped down upon the others like a veil.

For over the line the surgeon had written were now three other lines—in old French—

> *Nor grieve, dear heart, nor fear the seeming—*
> *Here is waking after dreaming.*
> *She who loves you,*   *Lucie*

That was McAndrews's story, and it was Hawtry who finally broke the silence that followed his telling of it.

"The lines had been on the paper, of course," he said; "they were probably faint, and your surgeon had not noticed them. It was drizzling, and the dampness brought them out."

"No," answered McAndrews; "they had not been there."

"But how can you be so sure?" remonstrated the psychologist.

"Because *I* was the surgeon," said McAndrews quietly. "The paper was a page torn from my notebook. When I wrapped it about the sprig it was blank—except for the line I myself had written there.

"But there was one more bit of—well, shall we call it evidence, John? The handwriting in Laveller's message was the same as that found in the missive enclosing the flowers. And the signature 'Lucie' was that same signature, curve for curve and quaint, old-fashioned angle for angle."

A longer silence fell, broken once more by Hawtry, abruptly.

"What became of the paper?" he asked. "Was the ink analyzed? Didn't you even attempt to—"

"As we stood there wondering," interrupted McAndrews, "a squall swept down upon the trench. It tore the paper from my hand—carried it away. Laveller watched it go; he made no effort to go after it.

" 'It does not matter. I know now,' he said—and smiled at me, the forgiving, happy smile of a joyous boy. 'I apologize to you, doctor. You're the best friend I ever had. I thought at first you had done *to* me what no other man would do to another—I see now that you have done *for* me what no other man could.'

"And that is all. He went through the war neither seeking death nor avoiding it. I loved him like a son. He would have died after that Mount Kemmel affair had it not been for me. He wanted to live long enough to bid his father and sister goodby, and I—patched him up. He did it, and then set forth for the trench beneath the shadow of the ruined old château where his brown-eyed demoiselle had found him."

"Why?" asked Hawtry.

"Because he thought that from there he could—go back—to her more quickly."

"To me an absolutely unwarranted conclusion," said the psychologist, wholly irritated, half angry. "There is some simple, natural explanation of it all."

"Of course, John," answered McAndrews soothingly—"of course there is. Tell us it, can't you."

But Hawtry, it seemed, could not offer any particulars.

BEYOND THE DOOR

J. PAUL SUTER

You haven't told me yet how it happened," I said to Mrs. Malkin.
She set her lips and eyed me, sharply.
"Didn't you talk with the coroner, sir?"
"Yes, of course," I admitted; "but as I understand you found my uncle, I thought—"
"Well, I wouldn't care to say anything about it," she interrupted, with decision.

This housekeeper of my uncle's was somewhat taller than I, and much heavier—two physical preponderances which afford any woman possessing them an advantage over the inferior male. She appeared a subject for diplomacy rather than argument.

Noting her ample jaw, her breadth of cheek, the unsentimental glint of her eye, I decided on conciliation. I placed a chair for her, there in my Uncle Godfrey's study, and dropped into another, myself.

"At least, before we go over the other parts of the house, suppose we rest a little," I suggested, in my most unctuous manner. "The place rather gets on one's nerves—don't you think so?"

It was sheer luck—I claim no credit for it. My chance reflection found the weak spot in her fortifications. She replied to it with an undoubted smack of satisfaction:

"It's more than seven years that I've been doing for Mr. Sarston, sir. Bringing him his meals regular as clockwork, keeping the house clean—as clean as he'd let me—and sleeping at my own home, o' nights; and in all that time I've said, over and over, there ain't a house in New York the equal of this for queerness."

"Nor anywhere else," I encouraged her, with a laugh; and her confidences opened another notch:

"You're likely right in that, too, sir. As I've said to poor Mr. Sarston, many a time, 'It's all well enough,' says I, 'to have bugs for a hobby. You can afford it; and being a bachelor and by yourself, you don't have to consider other people's likes and dislikes. And it's all well enough if you want to, says I, to keep thousands and thousands o' them in cabinets, all over the place, the way you do. But when it comes to pinnin' them on the walls in regular armies,' I says, 'and on the ceiling of your own study; and even on different parts of the furniture, so that a body don't know what awful things she's agoin' to find under her hand of a sudden when she does the dusting; why then,' I says to him, 'it's drivin' a decent woman too far.' "

"And did he never try to reform his ways when you told him that?" I asked, smiling.

"To be frank with you, Mr. Robinson when I talked like that to him, he generally raised my pay. And what was a body to do then?"

"I can't see how Lucy Lawton stood the place as long as she did," I observed, watching Mrs. Malkin's red face very closely.

She swallowed the bait, and leaned forward, hands on knees.

"Poor girl, it got on her nerves. But she was the quiet kind. You never saw her, sir?"

I shook my head.

"One of them slim, faded girls, with light hair, and hardly a word to say for herself. I don't believe she got to know the nextdoor neighbor in the whole year she lived with your uncle. She was an orphan, wasn't she, sir?"

"Yes," I said. "Godfrey Sarston and I were her only living relatives. That was why she came from Australia to stay with him, after her father's death."

Mrs. Malkin nodded. I was hoping that, putting a check on my eagerness, I could lead her on to a number of things I greatly desired to know. Up to the time I had induced the housekeeper to show me through this strange house of my Uncle Godfrey's, the whole affair had been a mystery of lips which closed and faces which were averted at my approach. Even the coroner seemed unwilling to tell me just how my uncle had died.

"Did you understand she was going to live with him, sir?" asked Mrs. Malkin, looking hard at me.

I confirmed myself to a nod.

"Well, so did I. Yet, after a year, back she went."

"She went suddenly?" I suggested.

"So suddenly that I never knew a thing about it till after she was gone. I came to do my chores one day, and she was here. I came the next, and she had started back to Australia. That's how sudden she went."

"They must have had a falling out," I conjectured. "I suppose it was because of the house."

"Maybe it was and maybe it wasn't."

"You know of other reasons?"

"I have eyes in my head," she said. "But I'm not going to talk about it. Shall we be getting on now, sir?"

I tried another lead:

"I hadn't seen my uncle in five years, you know. He seemed terribly changed. He was not an old man, by any means, yet when I saw him at the funeral—" I paused, expectantly.

To my relief, she responded readily:

"He looked that way for the last few months, especially that last week, I spoke to him about it, two days before—before it happened, sir—and told him he'd do well to see the doctor again. But he cut me off short. My sister took sick the same day, and I was called out of town. The next time I saw him, he was—"

She paused, and then went on, sobbing:

"To think of him lyin' there in that awful place, and callin' and callin' for me, as I know he must, and me not around to hear him!"

As she stopped again, suddenly, and threw a suspicious glance at me, I hastened to insert a matter-of-fact question:

"Did he appear ill on that last day?"

"Not so much ill, as—"

"Yes?" I prompted.

She was silent a long time, while I waited, afraid that some word of mine had brought back her former attitude of hostility. Then she seemed to make up her mind.

"I oughtn't to say another word. I've said too much, already. But you've been liberal with me, sir, and I know somethin' you've a right to be told, which I'm thinkin' no one else is agoin' to tell you. Look at the bottom of his study door a minute, sir."

I followed her direction.

What I saw led me to drop to my hands and knees the better to examine it.

"Why should he put a rubber strip on the bottom of his door?" I asked, getting up.

She replied with another enigmatical suggestion:

"Look at these, if you will, sir. "You'll remember that he slept in this study. That was his bed, over there in the alcove."

"Bolts!" I exclaimed. And I reinforced sight with touch by shooting one of them back and forth a few times. "Double bolts on the inside of this bedroom door! An upstairs room, at that. What was the idea?"

Mrs. Malkin portentously shook her head and sighed, as one unburdening her mind.

"Only this can I say, sir; he was afraid of something—terribly afraid, sir. Something that came in the night."

"What was it?" I demanded.

"I don't know, sir."

"It was in the night that—it happened?" I asked.

She nodded; then, as if the prologue were over, as if she had prepared my mind sufficiently, she produced something from under her apron. She must have been holding it there all the time.

"It's his diary, sir. It was lying here on the floor. I saved it for you, before the police could get their hands on it."

I opened the little book. One of the sheets near the back was crumpled, and I glanced at it, idly.

What I read there impelled me to slap the cover shut again.

"Did you read this?" I demanded.

She met my gaze, frankly.

"I looked into it, sir, just as you did—only just looked into it. Not for worlds would I do even that again!"

"I noticed some reference here to a slab in the cellar. What slab is that?"

"It covers an old, dried-up well, sir."

"Will you show it to me?"

"You can find it for yourself, sir, if you wish. I'm not goin' down there," she said, decidedly.

"Ah, well, I've seen enough for today," I told her. "I'll take the diary back to my hotel and read it."

I did not return to my hotel, however. In my one brief glance into the little book, I had seen something which had bitten into my soul, only a few words, but they had brought me very near to that queer, solitary man who had been my uncle.

I dismissed Mrs. Malkin, and remained in the study. There was the fitting place to read the diary he had left behind him.

His personality lingered like a vapor in that study. I settled into his deep morris chair, and turned it to catch the light from the single, narrow window —the light, doubtless, by which he had written much of his work on entomology.

That same struggling illumination played shadowy tricks with hosts of wall-crucified insects, which seemed engaged in a united effort to crawl upward in sinuous lines. Some of their number, impaled to the ceiling itself, peered quiveringly down on the aspiring multitude. The whole house, with its crisp dead, rustling in any vagrant breeze, brought back to my mind the hand that had pinned them, one by one, on wall and ceiling and furniture. A kindly hand, I reflected, though eccentric; one not to be turned aside from its single hobby.

When quiet, peering Uncle Godfrey went, there passed out another of those scientific enthusiasts, whose passion for exact truth in some one direction has extended the bounds of human knowledge. Could not his unquestioned merits have been balanced against his sin? Was it necessary to even-handed justice that he die face-to-face with Horror, struggling with the thing he most feared? I ponder the question still, though his body—strangely bruised—has been long at rest.

The entries in the little book began with the fifteenth of June. Everything before that date had been torn out. There, in the room where it had been written, I read my Uncle Godfrey's diary.

"It is done. I am trembling so that the words will hardly form under my pen, but my mind is collected. My course was for the best. Suppose I had married her? She would have been unwilling to live in this house. At the outset, her wishes would have come between me and my work, and that would have been only the beginning.

"As a married man, I could not have concentrated properly, I could not have surrounded myself with the atmosphere indispensable to the writing of my book. My scientific message would never have been delivered. As it is, though my heart is sore, I shall stifle these memories in work.

"I wish I had been more gentle with her, especially when she sank to her knees before me, tonight. She kissed my hand. I should not have repulsed her so roughly. In particular, my words could have been better chosen. I said to her, bitterly: 'Get up, and don't nuzzle my hand like a dog.' She rose, without a word, and left me. How was I to know that, within an hour—

"I am largely to blame. Yet, had I taken any other course afterward than the one I did, the authorities would have misunderstood."

Again, there followed a space from which the sheets had been torn; but from the sixteenth of July, all the pages were intact. Something had come over the writing, too. It was still precise and clear—my Uncle Godfrey's characteristic hand—but the letters were less firm. As the entries approached the end, this difference became still more marked.

Here follows, then, the whole of his story; or as much of it as will ever be known. I shall let his words speak for him, without further interruption:

"My nerves are becoming more seriously affected. If certain annoyances do not shortly cease, I shall be obliged to procure medical advice. To be more specific, I find myself, at times, obsessed by an almost uncontrollable desire to descend to the cellar and lift the slab over the old well.

"I never have yielded to the impulse, but it had persisted for minutes together with such intensity that I have had to put work aside, and literally hold myself down in my chair. This insane desire comes only in the dead of night, when its disquieting effect is heightened by the various noises peculiar to the house.

"For instance, there often is a draft of air along the hallways, which causes a rustling among the specimens impaled on the walls. Lately, too, there have been other nocturnal sounds, strongly suggestive of the busy clamor of rats and mice. This calls for investigation. I have been at considerable expense to make the house proof against rodents, which might destroy some of my best specimens. If some structural defect has opened a way for them, the situation must be corrected at once."

"July 17th. The foundations and cellar were examined today by a workman. He states positively that there is no place of ingress for rodents. He contented himself with looking at the slab over the old well, without lifting it."

"July 19th. While I was sitting in this chair, late last night, writing, the impulse to descend to the cellar suddenly came upon me with tremendous insistence. I yielded—which, perhaps, was as well. For at least I satisfied myself that the disquiet which possesses me has no external cause.

"The long journey through the hallways was difficult. Several times, I was keenly aware of the same sounds (perhaps I should say, the same IMPRESSIONS of sounds) that I had erroneously laid to rats. I am convinced now that they are more symptoms of my nervous condition. Further indications of this came in the fact that, as I opened the cellar door, the small noises abruptly ceased. There was no final scamper of tiny footfalls to suggest rats disturbed at their occupations.

"Indeed, I was conscious of a certain impression of expectant silence—as if the thing behind the noises, whatever it was, had paused to watch me enter its domain. Throughout my time in the cellar, I seemed surrounded by this same atmosphere. Sheer 'nerves,' of course.

"In the main, I held myself well under control. As I was about to leave the cellar, however, I unguardedly glanced back over my shoulder at the stone slab covering the old well. At that, a violent tremor came over me, and, losing all command, I rushed back up the cellar stairs, thence to this study. My nerves are playing me sorry tricks."

"July 30th. For more than a week, all has been well. The tone of my nerves seems distinctly better. Mrs. Malkin, who has remarked several times lately upon my paleness, expressed the conviction this afternoon that I am nearly my old self again. This is encouraging. I was beginning to fear that the severe strain of the past few months had left an indelible mark upon me.

"With continued health, I shall be able to finish my book by spring."

"July 31st. Mrs. Malkin remained rather late tonight in connection with some item of housework, and it was quite dark when I returned to my study from bolting the street door after her. The blackness of the upper hall, which the former owner of the house inexplicably failed to wire for electricity, was profound. As I came to the top of the second flight of stairs, something clutched at my foot, and, for an instant, almost pulled me back. I freed myself and ran to the study."

"August 3rd. Again the awful insistence. I sit here, with this diary upon my knee, and it seems that fingers of iron are tearing at me. I WILL NOT go! My nerves may be utterly unstrung again (I fear they are), but I am still their master."

"August 4th. I did not yield, last night. After a bitter struggle, which must have lasted nearly an hour, the desire to go to the cellar suddenly departed. I must not give in at any time."

"August 5th. Tonight, the rat noises (I shall call them that for want of a more appropriate term) are very noticeable. I went to the length of unbolting my door and stepping into the hallway to listen. After a few minutes, I seemed to be aware of something large and gray watching me from the darkness at the end of the passage. This is a bizarre statement, of course, but it exactly describes my impression. I withdrew hastily into the study, and bolted the door.

"Now that my nerves' condition is so palpably affecting the optic nerve, I must not much longer delay seeing a specialist. But—how much shall I tell him?"

"August 8th. Several times, tonight, while sitting here at my work, I have seemed to hear soft footsteps, in the passage. 'Nerves' again, of course, or else some new trick of the wind among the specimens on the walls."

"August 9th. By my watch it is four o'clock in the morning. My mind is made up to record the experience I have passed through. Calmness may come that way.

"Feeling rather fatigued last night, from the strain of a weary day of research, I retired early. My sleep was more refreshing than usual, as it is likely to be when one is genuinely tired. I awakened, however (it must have been about an hour ago), with a start of tremendous violence.

"There was moonlight in the room. My nerves were on edge, but for a moment, I saw nothing unusual. Then, glancing toward the door, I perceived what appeared to be thin, white fingers, thrust under it—exactly as if some one outside the door were trying to attract my attention in that manner. I rose and turned on the light, but the fingers were gone.

"Needless to say, I did not open the door. I write the occurrence down, just as it took place, or as it seemed; but I can not trust myself to comment upon it."

"August 10th. Have fastened heavy rubber strips on the bottom of my bedroom door."

"August 15th. All quiet, for several nights. I am hoping that the rubber strips, being something definite and tangible, have had a salutary effect upon my nerves. Perhaps I shall not need to see a doctor."

"August 17th. Once more, I have been aroused from sleep. The interruptions seem to come always at the same hour—about three o'clock in the morning. I had been dreaming of the well in the cellar—the same dream, over and over—everything black except the slab, and a figure with bowed head and averted face sitting there. Also, I had vague dreams about a dog. Can it be that my last words to her have impressed that on my mind? I must pull myself together. In particular, I must not, under any pressure, yield, and visit the cellar after nightfall."

"August 18th. Am feeling much more hopeful. Mrs. Malkin remarked on it, while serving dinner. This improvement is due largely to a consultation I have had with Dr. Sartwell, the distinguished specialist in nervous diseases. I went into full details with him, excepting certain reservations. He scouted the idea that my experiences could be other than purely mental.

"When he recommended a change of scene (which I had been expecting), I told him positively that it was out of the question. He said then that, with the aid of a tonic and an occasional sleeping draft, I am likely to progress well enough at home. This is distinctly encouraging. I erred in not going to him at the start. Without doubt, most, if not all, of my hallucinations could have been averted.

"I have been suffering a needless penalty from my nerves for an action I took solely in the interests of science. I have no disposition to tolerate it further. From today, I shall report regularly to Dr. Sartwell."

"August 19th. Used the sleeping draft last night, with gratifying results. The doctor says I must repeat the dose for several nights, until my nerves are well under control again."

"August 21st. All well. It seems that I have found the way out—a very simple and prosaic way. I might have avoided much needless annoyance by seeking expert advice at the beginning. Before retiring, last night, I unbolted my study door and took a turn up and down the passage. I felt no trepidation. The place was as it used to be, before these fancies assailed me. A visit to the cellar after nightfall will be the test for my complete recovery, but I am not yet quite ready for that. Patience!"

★　★　★

"August 22nd. I have just read yesterday's entry, thinking to steady myself. It is cheerful—almost gay; and there are other entries like it in preceding pages. I am a mouse, in the grip of a cat. Let me have freedom for ever so short a time, and I begin to rejoice at my escape. Then the paw descends again.

"It is four in the morning—the usual hour. I retired rather late, last night, after administering the draft. Instead of the dreamless sleep, which heretofore has followed the use of the drug, the slumber into which I fell was punctuated by recurrent visions of the slab, with the bowed figure upon it. Also, I had one poignant dream in which the dog was involved.

"At length, I awakened, and reached mechanically for the light switch beside my bed. When my hand encountered nothing, I suddenly realized the truth. I was standing in my study, with my other hand upon the doorknob. It required only a moment, of course, to find the light and switch it on. I saw then that the bolt had been drawn back.

"The door was quite unlocked. My awakening must have interrupted me in the very act of opening it. I could hear something moving restlessly in the passage outside the door."

"August 23rd. I must beware of sleeping at night. Without confiding the fact to Dr. Sartwell, I have begun to take the drug in the daytime. At first, Mrs. Malkin's views on the subject were pronounced, but my explanations of 'doctor's orders' has silenced her. I am awake for breakfast and supper, and sleep in the hours between. She is leaving me, each evening, a cold lunch to be eaten at midnight."

"August 26th. Several times, I have caught myself nodding in my chair. The last time, I am sure that, on arousing, I perceived the rubber strip under the door bent inward, as if something were pushing it from the other side. I must not, under any circumstances, permit myself to fall asleep."

"September 2nd. Mrs. Malkin is to be away, because of her sister's illness. I can not help dreading her absence. Though she is here only in the daytime, even that companionship is very welcome."

"September 3rd. Let me put this into writing. The mere labor of composition has a soothing influence upon me. God knows, I need such an influence now, as never before!

"In spite of all my watchfulness, I fell asleep, tonight—across my bed. I must have been utterly exhausted. The dream I had was the one about the dog. I was patting the creature's head, over and over.

"I awoke, at last, to find myself in darkness, and in a standing position. There was a suggestion of chill and earthiness in the air. While I was drowsily trying to get my bearings, I became aware that something was muzzling my hand, as a dog might do.

"Still saturated with my dream, I was not greatly astonished. I extended my hand, to pat the dog's head. That brought me to my senses. I was standing in the cellar.

"THE THING BEFORE ME WAS NOT A DOG!

"I can not tell how I fled back up the cellar stairs. I know, however, that, as I turned, the slab was visible, in spite of the darkness, with something sitting upon it. All the way up the stairs, hands snatched at my feet. . . ."

This entry seemed to finish this diary, for blank pages followed it; but I remembered the crumpled sheet, near the back of the book. It was partly torn out, as if a hand had clutched it, convulsively. The writing on it, too, was markedly in contrast to the precise, albeit nervous penmanship of even the last entry I had perused. I was forced to hold the scrawl up to the light to decipher it. This is what I read:

"My hand keeps on writing, in spite of myself. What is this? I do not wish to write, but it compels me. Yes, yes, I will tell the truth, I will tell the truth."

A heavy blot followed, partly covering the writing. With difficulty, I made it out:

"The guilt is mine—mine, only. I loved her too well, yet I was unwilling to marry, though she entreated me on her knees—though she kissed my hand. I told her my scientific work came first. She did it, herself. I was not expecting that—I swear I was not expecting it. But I was afraid the authorities would misunderstand. So I took what seemed the best course. She had no friends here who would inquire.

"It is waiting outside my door. I FEEL it. It compels me, through my thoughts. My hand keeps on writing. I must not fall asleep. I must think only of what I am writing. I must—"

Then came the words I had seen when Mrs. Malkin had handed me the book. They were written very large. In places, the pen had dug through the paper. Though they were scrawled, I read them at a glance:

"Not the slab in the cellar! Not that! Oh, my God, anything but that! Anything—"

By what strange compulsion was the hand forced to write down what was in the brain; even to the ultimate thoughts; even to those final words?

The gray light from outside, slanting down through two dull little windows, sank into the sodden hole near the inner wall. The coroner and I stood in the cellar, but not too near the hole.

A small, demonstrative, dark man—the chief of detectives—stood a little apart from us, his eyes intent, his natural animation suppressed. We were watching the stooped shoulders of a police constable, who was angling in the well.

"See anything, Walters?" inquired the detective, raspingly.

The policeman shook his head.

The little man turned his questioning to me.

"You're quite sure?" he demanded.

"Ask the coroner. He saw the diary," I told him.

"I'm afraid there can be no doubt," the coroner confirmed, in his heavy, tired voice.

He was an old man, with lacklustre eyes. It had seemed best to me, on the whole, that he should read my uncle's diary. His position entitled him to all the available facts. What we were seeking in the well might especially concern him.

He looked at me opaquely now, while the policeman bent double again. Then he spoke—like one who reluctantly and at last does his duty. He nodded toward the slab of gray stone, which lay in the shadow to the left of the well.

"It doesn't seem very heavy, does it?" he suggested, in an undertone.

I shook my head. "Still, it's stone," I demurred. "A man would have to be rather strong to lift it."

"To lift it—yes." He glanced about the cellar. "Ah, I forgot," he said, abruptly. "It is in my office, as part of the evidence." He went on, half to himself: "A man—even though not very strong—could take a stick—for instance, the stick that is now in my office—and prop up the slab. If he wished to look into the well," he whispered.

The policeman interrupted, straightening again with a groan, and laying his electric torch beside the well.

"It's breaking my back," he complained. "There's dirt down there. It seems loose, but I can't get through it. Somebody'll have to go down."

The detective cut in:

"I'm lighter than you, Walters."

"I'm not afraid, sir."

"I didn't say you were," the little man snapped. "There's nothing down there, anyway—though we'll have to prove that, I suppose." He glanced truculently at me, but went on talking to the constable: "Rig the rope around me, and don't bungle the knot. I've no intention of falling into the place."

"There is something there," whispered the coroner, slowly, to me. His eyes left the little detective and the policeman, carefully tying and testing knots, and turned again to the square slab of stone.

"Suppose—while a man was looking into that hole—with the stone propped up—he should accidentally knock the prop away?" He was still whispering.

"A stone so light that he could prop it up wouldn't be heavy enough to kill him," I objected.

"No." He laid a hand on my shoulder. "Not to kill him—to paralyze him —if it struck the spine in a certain way. To render him helpless, but not unconscious. The post mortem would disclose that, through the bruises on the body."

The policeman and the detective had adjusted the knots to their satisfaction. They were bickering now as to the details of the descent.

"Would that cause death?" I whispered.

"You must remember that the housekeeper was absent for two days. In two days, even that pressure—" He stared at me hard, to make sure that I understood—"with the head down—"

Again the policeman interrupted:

"I'll stand at the well, if you gentlemen will grab the rope behind me. It won't be much of a pull. I'll take the brunt of it."

We let the little man down, with the electric torch strapped to his waist, and some sort of implement—a trowel or a small spade—in his hand. It seemed a long time before his voice, curiously hollow, directed us to stop. The hole must have been deep.

We braced ourselves. I was second, the coroner, last. The policeman relieved his strain somewhat by snagging the rope against the edge of the well.

A noise like muffled scratching reached us from below. Occasionally, the rope shook and shifted slightly at the edge of the hole. At last, the detective's hollow voice spoke.

"What does he say?" the coroner demanded.

The policeman turned his square, dogged face toward us.

"I think he's found something," he explained.

The rope jerked and shifted again. Some sort of struggle seemed to be going on below. The weight suddenly increased, and as suddenly lessened, as if something had been grasped, then had managed to elude the grasp and slip away. I could catch the detective's rapid breathing now; also the sound of inarticulate speech in his hollow voice.

The next words I caught came more clearly. They were a command to pull up. At the same moment, the weight on the rope grew heavier, and remained so.

The policeman's big shoulders began straining, rhythmically.

"All together," he directed. "Take it easy. Pull when I do."

Slowly, the rope passed through our hands. Then it tightened suddenly, and there was an ejaculation from below—just below. Still holding fast, the policeman contrived to stoop over and look. He translated the ejaculation for us.

"Let down a little. He's struck with it against the side."

We slackened the rope, until the detective's voice gave us the word again. The rhythmic tugging continued. Something dark appeared, quite abruptly, at the top of the hole. My nerves leapt in spite of me, but it was merely the top of the detective's head—his dark hair. Something white came next—his pale face, with staring eyes. Then his shoulders, bowed forward, the better to support what was in his arms. Then—

I looked away; but, as he laid his burden down at the side of the well, the detective whispered to us:

"He had her covered up with dirt—covered up . . ."

He began to laugh—a little, high cackle, like a child's—until the coroner took him by the shoulders and deliberately shook him. Then the policeman led him out of the cellar.

It was not then, but afterward, that I put my question to the coroner.

"Tell me," I demanded. "People pass there at all hours. Why didn't my uncle call for help?"

"I have thought of that," he replied. "I believe he did call. I think, probably, he screamed. But his head was down, and he couldn't raise it. His screams must have been swallowed up in the well."

"You are sure he didn't murder her?" He had given me that assurance before but I wished it again.

"Almost sure," he declared. "Though it was on his account, undoubtedly, that she killed herself. Few of us are punished as accurately for our sins as he was."

One should be thankful, even for crumbs of comfort. I am thankful.

But there are times when my uncle's face rises before me. After all, we were the same blood, our sympathies had much in common; under any given circumstances, our thoughts and feelings must have been largely the same. I seem to see him in that final death march along the unlighted passageway—obeying an imperative summons—going on, step by step—down the stairway to the first floor, down the cellar stairs—at last, lifting the slab.

I try not to think of the final expiation. Yet was it final? I wonder. Did the last Door of all, when it opened, find him willing to pass through? Or was something waiting beyond that Door?

THE SHADOWS

HENRY S. WHITEHEAD

I did not begin to see the shadows until I had lived in Old Morris' house for more than a week. Old Morris, dead and gone these many years, had been the scion of a still earlier Irish settler in Santa Cruz, of a family which had come into the island when the Danes, failing to colonize its rich acres, had opened it, in the middle of the Eighteenth Century, to colonists; and younger sons of Irish, Scottish, and English gentry had taken up sugar estates and commenced that baronial life which lasted for a century and which declined after the abolition of slavery and the German bounty on beet sugar had started the long process of West Indian commercial decadence. Mr. Morris' youth had been spent in the French islands.

The shadows were at first so vague that I attributed them wholly to the slight weakness which began to affect my eyes in early childhood, and which, while never materially interfering with the enjoyment of life in general, had necessitated the use of glasses when I used my eyes to read or write. My first experience of them was about one o'clock in the morning. I had been at a "Gentlemen's Party" at Hacker's house, "Emerald," as some poetic-minded ancestor of Hacker's had named the family estate three miles out of Christiansted, the northerly town, built on the site of the ancient abandoned French town of Bassin.

I had come home from the party and was undressing in my bedroom, which is one of two rooms on the westerly side of the house which stands at the edge of the old "Sunday Market." These two bedrooms open on the market-place, and I had chosen them, rather than the more airy rooms on the other side, because of the space outside. I like to look out on trees in the early mornings, whenever possible, and the ancient market-place is overshadowed with the foliage of hundred-year-old mahogany trees, and a few gnarled "otaheites" and Chinese-bean trees.

I had nearly finished undressing, had noted that my servant had let down and properly fastened the mosquito netting, and had stepped into the other bedroom to open the jalousies so that I might get as much of the night-breeze as possible circulating through the house. I was coming back through the doorway between the two bedrooms, and taking off my dressing gown at the moment when the first faint perception of what I have called "the shadows" made itself apparent. It was very dark, just after switching off the electric light in that front bedroom. I had, in fact, to feel for the doorway. In this I experienced some difficulty, and my eyes had not fully adjusted themselves to the thin starlight seeping in through the slanted jalousies of my own room when I passed through the doorway and groped my way toward the great mahogany four-poster in which I was about to lie down for my belated rest.

I saw the nearest post looming before me, closer than I had expected. Putting out my hand, I grasped—nothing. I winked in some surprise, and peered through the slightly increasing light, as my eyes adjusted themselves to the sudden change. Yes, surely,—there was the corner of the bedstead just in front of my face! By now my eyes were sufficiently attuned to the amount of light from outside to see a little plainer. I was puzzled. The bed was not where I had supposed it to be. What could have happened? That the servants should have moved my bed without orders to do so was incredible. Besides, I had undressed, in full electric light in that room, not more than a few minutes ago, and then the bed was standing exactly where it had been since I had had it moved into that room a week before. I kicked gently, before me with a slippered foot, against the place where that bedpost appeared to be standing— and my foot met no resistance.

I stepped over to the light in my own room, and snapped the button. In the sudden glare, everything, readjusted itself to normal. There stood my bed, and here in their accustomed places about the room were ranged the chairs, the polished wardrobe (we do not use cupboards in the West India Islands), the mahogany dressing table,—even my clothes which I had hung over a chair where Albertina my servant would find them in the morning and put them (they were of white drill) into the soiled-clothes bag in the morning.

I shook my head. Light and shadow in these islands seem, somehow, different from what they are at home in the United States! The tricks they play are different tricks, somehow.

I snapped off the light again, and in the ensuing dead blackness, I crawled in under the loose edge of the mosquito netting, tucked it along under the edge of the mattress on that side, adjusted my pillows and the sheets, and settled myself for a good sleep. Even to a moderate man, these gentlemen's parties are rather wearing sometimes. They invariably last too long. I closed my eyes and was asleep before I could have put these last ideas into words.

In the morning the recollection of the experience with the bed-being-in-the-wrong-place was gone. I jumped out of bed and into my shower bath at half-past six, for I had promised O'Brien, captain of the U.S. Marines, to go out with him to the rifle range at La Grande Princesse that morning and look over the butts with him. I like O'Brien, and I am not uninterested in the efficiency of Uncle Sam's Marines, but my chief objective was to watch the pelicans. Out there on the glorious beach of Estate Grande Princesse ("Big Princess" as the Black People call it), a colony of pelicans make their home, and it is a never-ending source of amusement to me to watch them fish. A Caribbean pelican is probably the most graceful flier we have in these latitudes,—barring not even the hurricane bird, that describer of noble arcs and parabolas,—and the most insanely, absurdly awkward creature on land that Providence has cared in a light-hearted moment to create!

I expressed my interest in Captain O'Brien's latest improvements, and while he was talking shop to one of his lieutenants and half a dozen enlisted men he has camped out there, I slipped down to the beach to watch the pelicans fish. Three or four of them were describing curves and turns of indescribable complexity and perfect grace over the green water of the reef-enclosed white beach. Ever and again one would stop short in the air, fold himself up like a jackknife, turn head downward, his great pouched bill extended like the head of a cruel spear, and drop like a plummet into the water, emerging an instant later with the pouch distended with a fish.

I stayed a trifle too long,—for my eyes. Driving back I observed that I had picked up several sun-spots, and when I arrived home I polished a set of yellowish sun-spectacles I keep for such emergencies and put them on.

The east side of the house had been shaded against the pouring morning sunlight, and in this double shade I looked to see my eyes clear up. The sun-spots persisted, however, in that annoying, recurrent way they have,—almost disappearing and then returning in undiminished kaleidoscopic grotesqueness,—those strange blocks and parcels of pure color changing as one winks from indigo to brown and from brown to orange and then to a blinding turquoise-blue, according to some eery natural law of physics, within the fluids of the eye itself.

The sun-spots were so persistent that morning that I decided to keep my eyes closed for some considerable time and see if that would allow them to run their course and wear themselves out. Blue and mauve grotesques of the vague, general shape of diving pelicans swam and jumped inside my eyes. It was very annoying. I called to Albertina.

"Albertina," said I, when she had come to the door, "please go into my bedroom and close all the jalousies tight. Keep out all the light you can, please."

"Ahl roight, sir," replied the obedient Albertina, and I heard her slapping the jalousie-blinds together with sharp little clicks.

"De jalousie ahl close, sir," reported Albertina. I thanked her, and proceeded with half-shut eyes into the bedroom, which, not yet invaded with afternoon's sunlight and closely shuttered, offered an appearance of deep twilight. I lay, face down, across the bed, a pillow under my face, and my eyes buried in darkness.

Very gradually, the diving pelican faded out, to a cube, to a dim, recurrent blur, to nothingness. I raised my head and rolled over on my side, placing the pillow back where it belonged. And as I opened my eyes on the dim room, there stood, in faint, shadowy outline, in the opposite corner of the room, away from the outside wall on the market-place side, the huge, Danish bedstead I had vaguely noted the night before, or rather, early that morning.

It was the most curious sensation, looking at that bed in the dimness of the room. I was reminded of those fourth-dimensional tales which are so popular nowadays, for the bed impinged, spatially, on my large bureau, and the curious thing was that I could see the bureau at the same time! I rubbed my eyes, a little unwisely, but not enough to bring back the pelican sun-spots into them, for I remembered and desisted pretty promptly. I looked, fixedly, at the great bed, and it blurred and dimmed and faded out of my vision.

Again, I was greatly puzzled, and I went over to where it seemed to stand and walked through it,—it being no longer visible to my now restored vision, free of the effects of the sun-spots,—and then I went out into the "hall"—a West Indian drawing room is called "the hall"—and sat down to think over this strange phenomenon. I could not account for it. If it had been poor Prentice, now! Prentice attended all the "gentlemen's parties" to which he was invited with a kind of religious regularity, and had to be helped into his car with a similar regularity, a regularity which was verging on the monotonous nowadays, as the invitations became more and more strained. No,—in my case it was, if there was anything certain about it, assuredly not the effects of strong liquors, for barring an occasional sociable swizzle I retained here in my West Indian residence my American convictions that moderation in such matters was a reasonable virtue. I reasoned out the matter of the phantom bedstead,—for so I was already thinking of it,—as far as I was able. That it was a phantom of defective eyesight I had no reasonable doubt. I had had my eyes examined in New York three months before, and the oculist had pleased me greatly by assuring me that there were no visible indications of deterioration. In fact, Dr. Jusserand had said at that time that my eyes were stronger, sounder, than when he had made his last examination six months before.

Perhaps this conviction,—that the appearance was due to my own physical shortcoming—accounts for the fact that I was not (what shall I say?) *disturbed,* by what I saw, or thought I saw. Confront the most thoroughgoing materialist with a ghost, and he will act precisely like anyone else; like any normal human being who believes in the material world as the outward and visible sign of something which animates it. All normal human beings, it seems to me, are sacramentalists!

I was, for this reason, able to think clearly about the phenomenon. My mind was not clouded and bemused with fear, and its known physiological effects. I can, quite easily, record what I "saw" in the course of the next few days. The bed was clearer to my vision and apprehension than it had been. It seemed to have grown in visibility; in a kind of substantialness, if there is such a word! It appeared more *material* than it had before, less shadowy.

I looked about the room and saw other furniture: a huge, old-fashioned mahogany bureau with men's heads carved on the knuckles of the front legs, Danish fashion. There is precisely such carving on pieces in the museum in Copenhagen, they tell me, those who have seen my drawing of it. I was actually able to do that, and had completed a kind of plan-picture of the room, putting in all the shadow-furniture, and leaving my own, actual furniture out. Thank the God in whom I devoutly believe,—and know to be more powerful than the Powers of Evil,—I was able to finish that rather elaborate drawing before . . . Well, I must not "run ahead of my story."

That night when I was ready to retire, and had once more opened up the jalousies of the front bedroom, and had switched off the light, I looked, naturally enough under the circumstances, for the outlines of that ghostly furniture. They were much clearer now. I studied them with a certain sense of almost "scientific" detachment. It was, even then, apparent to me that no weakness of the strange complexity which is the human eye could reasonably account for the presence of a well-defined set of mahogany furniture in a room already furnished with real furniture! But I was by now sufficiently accustomed to it to be able to examine it all without that always-disturbing element of fear,—strangeness. I looked at the bedstead and the "roll-back" chairs, and the great bureau, and a ghostly, huge, and quaintly carved wardrobe, studying their outlines, noting their relative positions. It was on that occasion that it occurred to me that it would be of interest to make some kind of drawing of them. I looked the harder after that, fixing the details and the relations of them all in my mind, and then I went into the hall and got some paper and a pencil and set to work.

It was hard work, this of reproducing something which I was well aware was some kind of an "apparition," especially after looking at the furniture in the dark bedroom, switching on the light in another room and then trying to reproduce. I could not, of course, make a direct comparison. I mean it was impossible to look at my drawing and then look at the furniture. There was always a necessary interval between the two processes. I persisted through several evenings, and even for a couple of evenings fell into the custom of going into my bedroom in the evening's darkness, looking at what was there, and then attempting to reproduce it. After five or six days, I had a fair plan, in considerable detail, of the arrangement of this strange furniture in my bedroom,—a plan or drawing which would be recognizable if there were anyone now alive who remembered such an arrangement of such furniture. It will be apparent that a story had been growing up in my mind, or, at least, that I had come to some kind of conviction that what I "saw" was a reproduction of something that had once existed in that same detail and that precise order!

On the seventh night, there came an interruption.

I had, by that time, finished my work, pretty well. I had drawn the room as it would have looked with that furniture in it, and had gone over the whole with India ink, very carefully. As a drawing, the thing was finished, so far as my indifferent skill as a draftsman would permit.

That seventh evening, I was looking over the appearance of the room, such qualms as the eeriness of the situation might have otherwise produced reduced to next-to-nothing partly by my interest, in part by having become accustomed to it all. I was making, this evening, as careful a comparison as possible between my remembered work on paper and the detailed appearance of the room. By now, the furniture stood out clearly, in a kind of light of its own which I can roughly compare only to "phosphorescence." It was not, quite, that. But that will serve, lame as it is, and trite perhaps, to indicate what I mean. I suppose the appearance of the room was something like what a cat "sees" when she arches her back,—as Algernon Blackwood has pointed out, in *John Silence,*—and rubs against the imaginary legs of some personage entirely invisible to the man in the armchair who idly wonders what has taken possession of his house-pet.

I was, as I say, studying the detail. I could not find that I had left out anything salient. The detail was, too, quite clear now. There were no blurred outlines as there had been on the first few nights. My own, material furniture had, so to speak, sunk back into invisibility, which was sensible enough, seeing that I had put the room in as nearly perfect darkness as I could, and there was no moon to interfere, those nights.

I had run my eyes all around it, up and down the twisted legs of the great bureau, along the carved ornamentation of the top of the wardrobe, along the lines of the chairs, and had come back to the bed. It was at this point of my checking-up that I got what I must describe as the first "shock" of the entire experience.

Something moved, beside the bed.

I peered, carefully, straining my eyes to catch what it might be. It had been something bulky, a slow-moving object, on the far side of the bed, blurred, somewhat, just as the original outlines had been blurred in the beginning of my week's experience. The now strong and clear outlines of the bed, and what I might describe as its ethereal substance, stood between me and it. Besides, the vision of the slow-moving mass was further obscured by a ghostly mosquito-net, which had been one of the last of the details to come into the scope of my strange night-vision.

Those folds of the mosquito-netting moved,—waved, before my eyes.

Someone, it might almost be imagined, was getting into that bed!

I sat, petrified. This was a bit too much for me. I could feel the little chills run up and down my spine. My scalp prickled. I put my hands on my knees, and pressed hard. I drew several deep breaths. "All-overish" is an old New England expression, once much used by spinsters, I believe, resident in that intellectual section of the United States. Whatever the precise connotation of the term, that was the way I felt. I could feel the reactive sensation, I mean, of that particular portion of the whole experience, in every part of my being,—body, mind, and soul! It was,—paralyzing. I reached up a hand that was trembling violently,—I could barely control it, and the fingers, when they touched the hard-rubber button, felt numb,—and switched on the bedroom light, and spent the next ten minutes recovering.

That night, when I came to retire, I dreaded,—actually dreaded,—what might come to my vision when I snapped off the light. This, however, I managed to reason out with myself. I used several arguments—nothing had so far occurred to annoy or injure me; if this were to be a cumulative experience, if something were to be "revealed" to me by this deliberate process of slow materialization which had been progressing for the last week or so, then it might as well be for some good and useful purpose. I might be, in a sense, the agent of Providence! If it were otherwise; if it were the evil work of some discarnate spirit, or something of the sort, well, every Sunday since my childhood, in church, I had recited the Creed, and so admitted, along with the clergy and the rest of the congregation, that God our Father had created all things,—visible *and invisible!* If it were this part of His creation at work, for *any* purpose, then He was stronger than they. I said a brief prayer before turning off that light, and put my trust in Him. It may appear to some a bit old-fashioned,—even Victorian! But He does not change along with the current fashions of human thought about Him, and this "human thought," and "the modern mind," and all the rest of it, does not mean the vast, the overwhelming majority of people. It involves only a few dozen prideful "intellectuals" at best, or worst!

I switched off the light, and, already clearer, I saw what must have been Old Morris, getting into bed.

I had interviewed old Mr. Bonesteel, the chief government surveyor, a gentleman of parts and much experience, a West Indian born on this island.

Mr. Bonesteel, in response to my guarded enquiries,—for I had, of course, already suspected Old Morris; was not my house still called his?—had stated that he remembered Old Morris well, in his own remote youth. His description of that personage and this apparition tallied. This, undoubtedly, was Old Morris. That it was *someone,* was apparent. I felt, somehow, rather relieved to realize that it was he. I knew something about him, you see. Mr. Bonesteel had given me a good description and many anecdotes, quite freely, and as though he enjoyed being called on for information about one of the old-timers like Morris. He had been more reticent, guarded, in fact, when I pressed him for details of Morris' end. That there had been some obscurity, —intentional or otherwise, I could never ascertain,—about the old man, I had already known. Such casual enquiries as I had made on other occasions through natural interest in the person whose name still clung to my house sixty years or more since he had lived in it, had never got me anywhere. I had only gathered what Mr. Bonesteel's more ample account corroborated: that Morris had been eccentric, in some ways, amusingly so. That he had been extraordinarily well-to-do. That he gave occasional large parties, which, contrary to the custom of the hospitable island of St. Croix, were always required to come to a conclusion well before midnight. Why, there was a story of Old Morris almost literally getting rid of a few reluctant guests, by one device or another, from these parties, a circumstance on which hinged several of the amusing anecdotes of that eccentric person!

Old Morris, as I knew, had not always lived on St. Croix. His youth had been spent in Martinique, in the then smaller and less important town of Fort-de-France. That, of course, was many years before the terrific calamity of the destruction of St. Pierre had taken place, by the eruption of Mt. Pelée. Old Morris, coming to St. Croix in young middle age,—forty-five or thereabouts,—had already been accounted a rich man. He had been engaged in no business. He was not a planter, not a storekeeper, had no profession. Where he produced his affluence was one of the local mysteries. His age, it seemed, was the other.

"I suppose," Mr. Bonesteel had said, "that Morris was nearer a hundred than ninety, when he,—ah,—died. I was a child of about eight at that time. I shall be seventy next August-month. That, you see, would be about sixty-two years ago, about 1861, or about the time your Civil War was beginning. Now my father has told me,—he died when I was nineteen,—that Old Morris looked exactly the same when he was a boy! Extraordinary. The Black People used to say—" Mr. Bonesteel fell silent, and his eyes had an old man's dim, far-away look.

"The Black People have some very strange beliefs, Mr. Bonesteel," said I, attempting to prompt him. "A good many of them I have heard about myself, and they interest me very much. What particular—"

Mr. Bonesteel turned his mild, blue eyes upon me, reflectively.

"You must drop in at my house one of these days, Mr. Stewart," said he, mildly. "I have some rare old rum that I'd be glad to have you sample, sir! There's not much of it on the island these days, since Uncle Sam turned his prohibition laws loose on us in 1922."

"Thank you very much indeed, Mr. Bonesteel," I replied. "I shall take the first occasion to do so, sir; not that I care especially for 'old rum' except a spoonful in a cup of tea, or in pudding sauce, perhaps; but the pleasure of your company, sir, is always an inducement."

Mr. Bonesteel bowed to me gravely, and I returned his bow from where I sat in his airy office in Government House.

"Would you object to mentioning what that 'belief' was, sir?"

A slightly pained expression replaced my old friend's look of hospitality.

"All that is a lot of foolishness!" said he, with something like asperity. He looked at me, contemplatively.

"Not that I believe in such things, you must understand. Still, a man sees a good many things in these islands, in a lifetime, you know! Well, the Black People—" Mr. Bonesteel looked apprehensively about him, as though reluctant to have one of his clerks overhear what he was about to say, and leaned toward me from his chair, lowering his voice to a whisper.

"They said,—it was a remark here and a kind of hint there, you must understand; nothing definite,—that Morris had interfered, down there in Martinique, with some of their queer doings—offended the Zombi, something of the kind; that Morris had made some kind of conditions—oh, it was very vague, and probably all mixed up!—you know, whereby he was to have a long life and all the money he wanted,—something like that,—and afterward . . .

"Well, Mr. Stewart, you just ask somebody, sometime about Morris' death."

Not another word about Old Morris could I extract out of Mr. Bonesteel.

But of course he had me aroused. I tried Despard, who lives on the other end of the island, a man educated at the Sorbonne, and who knows, it is said, everything there is to know about the island and its affairs.

It was much the same with Mr. Despard, who is an entirely different kind of person; younger, for one thing, than my old friend the government surveyor.

Mr. Despard smiled, a kind of wry smile. "Old Morris!" said he, reflectively, and paused.

"Might I venture to ask—no offense, my dear sir!—why you wish to rake up such an old matter as Old Morris' death?"

I was a bit nonplussed, I confess. Mr. Despard had been perfectly courteous, as he always is, but, somehow, I had not expected such an intervention on his part.

"Why," said I, "I should find it hard to tell you, precisely, Mr. Despard. It is not that I am averse to being frank in the face of such an enquiry as yours, sir. I was not aware that there was anything important,—serious, as your tone implies,—about that matter. Put it down to mere curiosity if you will, and answer or not, as you wish, sir."

I was, perhaps, a little nettled at this unexpected, and as it then seemed to me, finicky obstruction being placed in my way. What could there be in such a case for this formal reticence,—these verbal safe-guards? If it were a "jumbee" story, there was no importance to it. If otherwise, well, I might be regarded by Despard as a person of reasonable discretion. Perhaps Despard was some relative of Old Morris, and there was something a bit off-color about his death. That, too, might account for Mr. Bonesteel's reticence.

"By the way," I enquired, noting Despard's reticence, "might I ask another question, Mr. Despard?"

"Certainly, Mr. Stewart."

"I do not wish to impress you as idly or unduly curious, but—are you and Mr. Bonesteel related in any way?"

"No, sir. We are not related in any way at all, sir."

"Thank you, Mr. Despard," said I, and, bowing to each other after the fashion set here by the Danes, we parted.

I had not learned a thing about Old Morris' death.

I went in to see Mrs. Heidenklang. Here, if anywhere, I should find out what was intriguing me.

Mrs. Heidenklang is an ancient Creole lady, relict of a prosperous storekeeper, who lives, surrounded by a certain state of her own, propped up in bed in an environment of a stupendous quantity of lacy things and gauzy ruffles. I did not intend to mention Old Morris to her, but only to get some information about the Zombi, if that should be possible.

I found the old lady, surrounded by her ruffles and lace things, in one of her good days. Her health has been precarious for twenty years!

It was not difficult to get her talking about the Zombi.

"Yes," said Mrs. Heidenklang, "it is extraordinary how the old beliefs and the old words cling in their minds! Why, Mr. Stewart, I was hearing about a trial in the police court a few days ago. One old Black woman had summoned another for abusive language. On the witness stand the complaining old woman said: 'She cahl me a wuthless ole Cartagene, sir!' Now, think of that! Carthage was destroyed 'way back in the days of Cato the Elder, you know, Mr. Stewart! The greatest town of all Africa. To be a Carthaginian meant to be a sea-robber,—a pirate; that is, a thief. One old woman on this island, more than two thousand years afterward, wishes to call another a thief, and the word 'Cartagene' is the word she naturally uses! I suppose that has persisted on the West Coast and throughout all those village dialects in Africa without a break, all these centuries! The Zombi of the French islands? Yes, Mr. Stewart. There are some extraordinary beliefs. Why, perhaps you've heard mention made of Old Morris, Mr. Stewart. He used to live in your house, you know?"

I held my breath. Here was a possible trove. I nodded my head. I did not dare to speak!

"Well, Old Morris, you see, lived most of his earlier days in Martinique, and, it is said, he had a somewhat adventurous life there, Mr. Stewart. Just what he did or how he got himself involved, seems never to have been made clear, but—in some way, Mr. Stewart, the Black People believe, Morris got himself involved with a very powerful 'Jumbee,' and that is where what I said about the persistence of ancient beliefs comes in. Look on that table there, among those photographs, Mr. Stewart. There! that's the place. I wish I were able to get up and assist you. These maids! Everything askew, I have no doubt! Do you observe a kind of fish-headed thing, about as big as the palm of your hand? Yes! that is it!"

I found the "fish-headed thing" and carried it over to Mrs. Heidenklang, She took it in her hand and looked at it. It lacked a nose, but otherwise it was intact, a strange, uncouth-looking little godling, made of anciently polished volcanic stone, with huge, protruding eyes, small, humanlike ears, and what must have been a nose like a Tortola jackfish, or a black witch-bird, with its parrot beak.

"Now that," continued Mrs. Heidenklang, "is one of the very ancient household gods of the aborigines of Martinique, and you will observe the likeness in the idea to the *Lares* and *Penates* of your school-Latin days. Whether this is a *lar* or a *penate,* I can not tell," and the old lady paused to smile at her little joke, "but at any rate he is a representation of something very powerful,—a fish-god of the Caribs. There's something Egyptian about the idea, too, I've always suspected; and, Mr. Stewart, a Carib or an Arawak Indian,—there were both in these islands, you know,—looked much like an ancient Egyptian; perhaps half like your Zuñi or Aztec Indians, and half Egyptian, would be a fair statement of his appearance. These fish-gods had men's bodies, you see, precisely like the hawk-headed and jackal-headed deities of ancient Egypt.

"It was one of those, the Black People say, with which Mr. Morris got himself mixed up,—'Gahd knows' as they say—how! And, Mr. Stewart, they say, his death was terrible! The particulars I've never heard, but my father knew, and he was sick for several days, after seeing Mr. Morris' body. Extraordinary, isn't it? And when are you coming this way again, Mr. Stewart? Do drop in and call on an old lady."

I felt that I was progressing.

The next time I saw Mr. Bonesteel, which was that very evening, I stopped him on the street and asked for a word with him.

"What was the date, or the approximate date, Mr. Bonesteel, of Mr. Morris' death? Could you recall that, sir?"

Mr. Bonesteel paused and considered.

"It was just before Christmas," said he. "I remember it not so much by Christmas as by the races, which always take place the day after Christmas. Morris had entered his sorrel mare Santurce, and, as he left no heirs, there was no one who 'owned' Santurce, and she had to be withdrawn from the races. It affected the betting very materially and a good many persons were annoyed about it, but there wasn't anything that could be done."

I thanked Mr. Bonesteel, and not without reason, for his answer had fitted into something that had been growing in my mind. Christmas was only eight days off. This drama of the furniture and Old Morris getting into bed, I had thought (and not unnaturally, it seems to me), might be a kind of re-enactment of the tragedy of his death. If I had the courage to watch, night after night, I might be relieved of the necessity of asking any questions. I might witness whatever had occurred, in some weird reproduction, engineered, God knows how!

For three nights now, I had seen the phenomenon of Old Morris getting into bed repeated, and each time it was clearer. I had sketched him into my drawing, a short, squat figure, rather stooped and fat, but possessed of a strange gorillalike energy. His movements, as he walked toward the bed, seized the edge of the mosquito-netting and climbed in, were, somehow, full of *power,* which was the more apparent since these were ordinary motions. One could not help imagining that Old Morris would have been a tough customer to tackle, for all his alleged age!

This evening, at the hour when this phenomenon was accustomed to enact itself, that is, about eleven o'clock, I watched again. The scene was very much clearer, and I observed something I had not noticed before. Old Morris' *simulacrum* paused just before seizing the edge of the netting, raised its eyes, and began, with its right hand, a motion precisely like one who is about to sign himself with the cross. The motion was abruptly arrested, however, only the first of the four touches on the body being made.

I saw, too, something of the expression of the face that night, for the first time. At the moment of making the arrested sign, it was one of despairing horror. Immediately afterward, as this motion appeared to be abandoned for the abrupt clutching of the lower edge of the mosquito-net, it changed into a look of ferocious stubbornness, of almost savage self-confidence. I lost the facial expression as the appearance sank down upon the bed and pulled the ghostly bedclothes over itself.

Three nights later, when all this had become as greatly intensified as had the clearing-up process that had affected the furniture, I observed another motion, or what might be taken for the faint foreshadowing of another motion. This was not on the part of Old Morris. It made itself apparent as lightly and elusively as the swift flight of a moth across the reflection of a lamp, over near the bedroom door (the doors in my house are more than ten feet high, in fourteen-foot-high-walls), a mere flicker of something,—something entering the room. I looked, and peered at that corner, straining my eyes, but nothing could I see save what I might describe as an intensification of the black shadow in that corner near the door, vaguely formed like a slim human figure, though grossly out of all human proportion. The vague shadow looked purple against the black. It was about ten feet high, and otherwise as though cast by an incredibly tall, thin human being.

I made nothing of it then; and again, despite all this cumulative experience with the strange shadows of my bedroom, attributed this last phenomenon to my eyes. It was too vague to be at that time accounted otherwise than as a mere subjective effect.

But the night following, I watched for it at the proper moment in the sequence of Old Morris' movements as he got into bed, and this time it was distinctly clearer. The shadow, it was, of some monstrous shape, ten feet tall, long, angular, of vaguely human appearance, though even in its merely shadowed form, somehow cruelly, strangely inhuman! I can not describe the cold horror of its realization. The head-part was, relatively to the proportions of the body, short and broad, like a pumpkin head of a "man" made of sticks by boys, to frighten passers-by on Hallowe'en.

The next evening I was out again to an entertainment at the residence of one of my hospitable friends, and arrived home after midnight. There stood the ghostly furniture, there on the bed was the form of the apparently sleeping Old Morris, and there in the corner stood the shadow, little changed from last night's appearance.

The next night would be pretty close to the date of Old Morris' death. It would be that night, or the next at latest, according to Mr. Bonesteel's statement. The next day I could not avoid the sensation of something impending!

I entered my room and turned off the light a little before eleven, seated myself, and waited.

The furniture tonight was, to my vision, absolutely indistinguishable from reality. This statement may sound somewhat strange, for it will be remembered that I was sitting in the dark. Approximating terms again, I may say, however, that the furniture was visible in a light of its own, a kind of "phosphorescence," which apparently emanated from it. Certainly there was no natural source of light. Perhaps I may express the matter thus: that light and darkness were *reversed* in the case of this ghostly bed, bureau, wardrobe, and chairs. When actual light was turned on, they disappeared. In darkness, which, of course, is the absence of physical light, they emerged. That is the nearest I can get to it. At any rate, tonight the furniture was entirely, perfectly, visible to me.

Old Morris came in at the usual time. I could see him with a clarity exactly comparable to what I have said about the furniture. He made his slight pause, his arrested motion of the right hand, and then, as usual, cast from him, according to his expression, the desire for that protective gesture, and reached a hard-looking, gnarled fist out to take hold of the mosquito-netting.

As he did so, a fearful thing leaped upon him, a thing out of the corner by the high doorway,—the dreadful, purplish shadow-thing. I had not been looking in that direction, and while I had not forgotten this newest of the strange items in this fantasmagoria which had been repeating itself before my eyes for many nights, I was wholly unprepared for its sudden appearance and malignant activity.

I have said the shadow was purplish against black. Now that it had taken form, as the furniture and Old Morris himself had taken form, I observed that this purplish coloration was actual. It was a glistening, humanlike, almost metallic-appearing thing, certainly ten feet high, completely covered with great, iridescent fish-scales, each perhaps four square inches in area, which shimmered as it leaped across the room. I saw it for only a matter of a second or two. I saw it clutch surely and with a deadly malignity, the hunched body of Old Morris, from behind, just, you will remember, as the old man was about to climb into his bed. The dreadful thing turned him about as a wasp turns a fly, in great, flail-like, glistening arms, and never, to the day of my death, do I ever expect to be free of the look on Old Morris' face—a look of a lost soul who knows that there is no hope for him in this world or the next, —as the great, squat, rounded head, a head precisely like that of Mrs. Heidenklang's little fish-jumbee, descended, revealing to my horrified sight one glimpse of a huge, scythelike parrot-beak which it used, with a nodding motion of the ugly head, to plunge into its writhing victim's breast, with a tearing motion like the barracuda when it attacks and tears. . . .

I fainted then, for that was the last of the fearful picture which I can remember.

I awakened a little after one o'clock, in a dark and empty room, peopled by no ghosts, and with my own, more commonplace, mahogany furniture thinly outlined in the faint light of the new moon which was shining cleanly in a starry sky. The fresh night-wind stirred the netting of my bed. I rose, shakily, and went and leaned out of the window, and lit and puffed rapidly at a cigarette, which perhaps did something to settle my jangling nerves.

The next morning, with a feeling of loathing which has gradually worn itself out in the course of the months which have now elapsed since my dreadful experience, I took up my drawing again, and added as well as I could the fearful scene I had witnessed. The completed picture was a horror, crude as is my work in this direction. I wanted to destroy it, but I did not, and I laid it away under some unused clothing in one of the large drawers of my bedroom wardrobe.

Three days later, just after Christmas, I observed Mr. Despard's car driving through the streets, the driver being alone. I stopped the boy and asked him where Mr. Despard was at the moment. The driver told me Mr. Despard was having breakfast,—the West Indian midday meal,—with Mr. Bonesteel at that gentleman's house on the Prince's Cross Street. I thanked him and went home. I took out the drawing, folded it, and placed it in the inside breast pocket of my coat, and started for Bonesteel's house.

I arrived fifteen minutes or so before the breakfast hour, and was pleasantly received by my old friend and his guest. Mr. Bonesteel pressed me to join them at breakfast, but I declined.

Mr. Bonesteel brought in a swizzle, compounded of his very old rum, and after partaking of this in ceremonious fashion, I engaged the attention of both gentlemen.

"Gentlemen," said I, "I trust that you will not regard me as too much of a bore, but I have, I believe, a legitimate reason for asking you if you will tell me the manner in which the gentleman known as Old Morris, who once occupied my house, met his death."

I stopped there, and immediately discovered that I had thrown my kind old host into a state of embarrassed confusion. Glancing at Mr. Despard, I saw at once that if I had not actually offended him, I had, by my question, at least put him "on his dignity." He was looking at me severely, rather, and I confess that for a moment I felt a bit like a schoolboy. Mr. Bonesteel caught something of this atmosphere, and looked helplessly at Despard. Both men shifted uneasily in their chairs; each waited for the other to speak.

Despard, at last, cleared his throat.

"You will excuse me, Mr. Stewart," said he, slowly, "but you have asked a question which for certain reasons, no one, aware of the circumstances, would desire to answer. The reasons are, briefly, that Mr. Morris, in certain respects, was—what shall I say, not to do the matter an injustice?—well, perhaps I might say he was abnormal. I do not mean that he was crazy. He was, though, eccentric. His end was such that stating it would open up a considerable argument, one which agitated this island for a long time after he was found dead. By a kind of general consent, that matter is taboo on the island. That will explain to you why no one wishes to answer your question. I am free to say that Mr. Bonesteel here, in considerable distress, told me that you had asked it of him. You also asked me about it not long ago. I can add only that the manner of Mr. Morris' end was such that—" Mr. Despard hesitated, and looked down, a frown on his brow, at his shoe, which he tapped nervously on the tiled floor of the gallery where we were seated.

"Old Morris, Mr. Stewart," he resumed, after a moment's reflection, in which, I imagined, he was carefully choosing his words, "was, to put it plainly, murdered! There was much discussion over the identity of the murderer, but the most of it, the unpleasant part of the discussion, was rather whether he was killed by human agency or not! Perhaps you will see now, sir, the difficulty of the matter. To admit that he was murdered by an ordinary murderer is, to my mind, an impossibility. To assert that some other agency, something abhuman, killed him, opens up the question of one's belief, one's credulity. 'Magic' and occult agencies are, as you are aware, strongly intrenched in the minds of the ignorant people of these islands. None of us cares to admit a similar belief. Does that satisfy you, Mr. Stewart, and will you let the matter rest there, sir?"

I drew out the picture, and, without unfolding it, laid it across my knees. I nodded to Mr. Despard, and, turning to our host, asked:

"As a child, Mr. Bonesteel, were you familiar with the arrangement of Mr. Morris' bedroom?"

"Yes, sir," replied Mr. Bonesteel, and added: "Everybody was! Persons who had never been in the old man's house, crowded in when—" I intercepted a kind of warning look passing from Despard to the speaker. Mr. Bonesteel, looking much embarrassed, looked at me in that helpless fashion I have already mentioned, and remarked that it was hot weather these days!

"Then," said I, "perhaps you will recognize its arrangement and even some of the details of its furnishing," and I unfolded the picture and handed it to Mr. Bonesteel.

If I had anticipated its effect upon the old man, I would have been more discreet, but I confess I was nettled by their attitude. By handing it to Mr. Bonesteel (I could not give it to both of them at once) I did the natural thing, for he was our host. The old man looked at what I had handed him, and (this is the only way I can describe what happened) became, suddenly, as though petrified. His eyes bulged out of his head, his lower jaw dropped and hung open. The paper slipped from his nerveless grasp and fluttered and zigzagged to the floor, landing at Despard's feet. Despard stooped and picked it up, ostensibly to restore it to me, but in doing so, he glanced at it, and had *his* reaction. He leaped frantically to his feet, and positively goggled at the picture, then at me. Oh, I was having my little revenge for their reticence, right enough!

"My God!" shouted Despard. "My God, Mr. Stewart, where did you get such a thing?"

Mr. Bonesteel drew in a deep breath, the first, it seemed, for sixty seconds, and added his word.

"Oh my God!" muttered the old man, shakily. "Mr. Stewart, Mr. Stewart! what is it, what is it? where—"

"It is a Martinique fish-zombie, what is known to professional occult investigators like Elliott O'Donnell and William Hope Hodgson as an 'elemental,' " I explained, calmly. "It is a representation of how poor Mr. Morris actually met his death; until now, as I understood it, a purely conjectural matter. Christiansted is built on the ruins of French Bassin, you will remember," I added. "It is a very likely spot for an 'elemental'!"

"But, but," almost shouted Mr. Despard, "Mr. Stewart, where did you get this, its—"

"I made it," said I, quietly, folding up the picture and placing it back in my inside pocket.

"But how—?" this from both Despard and Bonesteel, speaking in unison.

"I saw it happen, you see," I replied, taking my hat, bowing formally to both gentlemen, and murmuring my regret at not being able to remain for breakfast, I departed.

And as I reached the bottom of Mr. Bonesteel's gallery steps and turned along the street in the direction of Old Morris' house, where I live, I could hear their voices speaking together:

"But how, how—?" This was Bonesteel.

"Why, why—?" And that was Despard.

THE BLACK STONE

ROBERT E. HOWARD

THEY SAY FOUL BEINGS OF OLD TIMES STILL LURK
IN DARK FORGOTTEN CORNERS OF THE WORLD,
AND GATES STILL GAPE TO LOOSE, ON CERTAIN NIGHTS,
SHAPES PENT IN HELL.
—JUSTIN GEOFFREY

I read of it first in the strange book of Von Junzt, the German eccentric who lived so curiously and died in such grisly and mysterious fashion. It was my fortune to have access to his *Nameless Cults* in the original edition, the so-called Black Book, published in Düsseldorf in 1839, shortly before a hounding doom overtook the author. Collectors of rare literature are familiar with *Nameless Cults* mainly through the cheap and faulty translation which was pirated in London by Bridewell in 1845, and the carefully expurgated edition put out by the Golden Goblin Press of New York in 1909. But the volume I stumbled upon was one of the unexpurgated German copies, with heavy leather covers and rusty iron hasps. I doubt if there are more than half a dozen such volumes in the entire world today, for the quantity issued was not great, and when the manner of the author's demise was bruited about, many possessors of the book burned their volumes in panic.

Von Junzt spent his entire life (1795–1840) delving into forbidden subjects; he traveled in all parts of the world, gained entrance into innumerable secret societies, and read countless little known and esoteric books and manuscripts in the original; and in the chapters of the Black Book, which range from startling clarity of exposition to murky ambiguity, there are statements and hints to freeze the blood of a thinking man. Reading what Von Junzt *dared* put in print arouses uneasy speculations as to what it was that he dared *not* tell. What dark matters, for instance, were contained in those closely written pages that formed the unpublished manuscript on which he worked unceasingly for months before his death, and which lay torn and scattered all over the floor of the locked and bolted chamber in which Von Junzt was found dead with the marks of taloned fingers on his throat? It will never be known, for the author's closest friend, the Frenchman Alexis Ladeau, after having spent a whole night piecing the fragments together and reading what was written, burnt them to ashes and cut his own throat with a razor.

But the contents of the published matter are shuddersome enough, even if one accepts the general view that they but represent the ravings of a madman. There among many strange things I found mention of the Black Stone, that curious, sinister monolith that broods among the mountains of Hungary, and about which so many dark legends cluster. Von Junzt did not devote much space to it—the bulk of his grim work concerns cults and objects of dark worship which he maintained existed in his day, and it would seem that the Black Stone represents some order or being lost and forgotten centuries ago. But he spoke of it as one of the *keys*—a phrase used many times by him, in various relations, and constituting one of the obscurities of his work. And he hinted briefly at curious sights to be seen about the monolith on midsummer's night. He mentioned Otto Dostmann's theory that this monolith was a remnant of the Hunnish invasion and had been erected to commemorate a victory of Attila over the Goths. Von Junzt contradicted this assertion without giving any refutatory facts, merely remarking that to attribute the origin of the Black Stone to the Huns was as logical as assuming that William the Conqueror reared Stonehenge.

This implication of enormous antiquity piqued my interest immensely, and after some difficulty I succeeded in locating a rat-eaten and moldering copy of Dostmann's *Remnants of Lost Empires* (Berlin, 1809, "Der Drachenhaus" Press). I was disappointed to find that Dostmann referred to the Black Stone even more briefly than had Von Junzt, dismissing it with a few lines as an artifact comparatively modern in contrast with the Greco-Roman ruins of Asia Minor which were his pet theme. He admitted his inability to make out the defaced characters on the monolith but pronounced them unmistakably Mongoloid. However, little as I learned from Dostmann, he did mention the name of the village adjacent to the Black Stone—Stregoicavar—an ominous name, meaning something like Witch-Town.

A close scrutiny of guide-books and travel articles gave me no further information—Stregoicavar, not on any map that I could find, lay in a wild, little-frequented region, out of the path of casual tourists. But I did find subject for thought in Dornly's *Magyar Folklore*. In his chapter on "Dream Myths" he mentions the Black Stone and tells of some curious superstitions regarding it—especially the belief that if anyone sleeps in the vicinity of the monolith, that person will be haunted by monstrous nightmares forever after;

and he cited tales of the peasants regarding too-curious people who ventured to visit the Stone on Midsummer Night and who died raving mad because of *something* they saw there.

That was all I could glean from Dornly, but my interest was even more intensely roused as I sensed a distinctly sinister aura about the Stone. The suggestion of dark antiquity, the recurrent hint of unnatural events on Midsummer Night, touched some slumbering instinct in my being, as one senses, rather than hears, the flowing of some dark subterranean river in the night.

And I suddenly saw a connection between this Stone and a certain weird and fantastic poem written by the mad poet, Justin Geoffrey: "The People of the Monolith." Inquiries led to the information that Geoffrey had indeed written that poem while traveling in Hungary, and I could not doubt that the Black Stone was the very monolith to which he referred in his strange verse. Reading his stanzas again, I felt once more the strange dim stirrings of subconscious promptings that I had noticed when first reading of the Stone.

I had been casting about for a place to spend a short vacation and I made up my mind. I went to Stregoicavar. A train of obsolete style carried me from Temesvár to within striking distance, at least, of my objective, and a three days' ride in a jouncing coach brought me to the little village which lay in a fertile valley high up in the fir-clad mountains. The journey itself was uneventful, but during the first day we passed the old battlefield of Schomvaal where the brave Polish-Hungarian knight, Count Boris Vladinoff, made his gallant and futile stand against the victorious hosts of Suleiman the Magnificent, when the Grand Turk swept over eastern Europe in 1526.

The driver of the coach pointed out to me a great heap of crumbling stones on a hill nearby, under which, he said, the bones of the brave Count lay. I remembered a passage from Larson's *Turkish Wars*: "After the skirmish" (in which the Count with his small army had beaten back the Turkish advance-guard) "the Count was standing beneath the half-ruined walls of the old castle on the hill, giving orders as to the disposition of his forces, when an aide brought to him a small lacquered case which had been taken from the body of the famous Turkish scribe and historian, Selim Bahadur, who had fallen in the fight. The Count took therefrom a roll of parchment and began to read, but he had not read far before he turned very pale and, without saying a word, replaced the parchment in the case and thrust the case into his cloak. At that very instant a hidden Turkish battery suddenly opened fire, and the balls striking the old castle, the Hungarians were horrified to see the walls crash down in ruin, completely covering the brave Count. Without a leader the gallant little army was cut to pieces, and in the war-swept years that followed, the bones of the nobleman were never recovered. Today the natives point out a huge and moldering pile of ruins near Schomvaal beneath which, they say, still rests all that the centuries have left of Count Boris Vladinoff."

I found the village of Stregoicavar a dreamy, drowsy little village that apparently belied its sinister cognomen—a forgotten back-eddy that Progress had passed by. The quaint houses and the quainter dress and manners of the people were those of an earlier century. They were friendly, mildly curious but not inquisitive, though visitors from the outside world were extremely rare.

"Ten years ago another American came here and stayed a few days in the village," said the owner of the tavern where I had put up, "a young fellow and queer-acting—mumbled to himself—a poet, I think."

I knew he must mean Justin Geoffrey.

"Yes, he was a poet," I answered, "and he wrote a poem about a bit of scenery near this very village."

"Indeed?" Mine host's interest was aroused. "Then, since all great poets are strange in their speech and actions, he must have achieved great fame, for his actions and conversations were the strangest of any man I ever knew."

"As is usual with artists," I answered, "most of his recognition has come since his death."

"He is dead, then?"

"He died screaming in a madhouse five years ago."

"Too bad, too bad," sighed mine host sympathetically. "Poor lad—he looked too long at the Black Stone."

My heart gave a leap, but I masked my keen interest and said casually: "I have heard something of this Black Stone; somewhere near this village, is it not?"

"Nearer than Christian folk wish," he responded. "Look!" He drew me to a latticed window and pointed up at the fir-clad slopes of the brooding blue mountains. "There beyond where you see the bare face of that jutting cliff stands that accursed Stone. Would that it were ground to powder and the powder flung into the Danube to be carried to the deepest ocean! Once men tried to destroy the thing, but each man who laid hammer or maul against it came to an evil end. So now the people shun it."

"What is there so evil about it?" I asked curiously.

"It is a demon-haunted thing," he answered uneasily and with the suggestion of a shudder. "In my childhood I knew a young man who came up from below and laughed at our traditions—in his foolhardiness he went to the Stone one Midsummer Night and at dawn stumbled into the village again, stricken dumb and mad. Something had shattered his brain and sealed his lips, for until the day of his death, which came soon after, he spoke only to utter terrible blasphemies or to slaver gibberish.

"My own nephew when very small was lost in the mountains and slept in the woods near the Stone, and now in his manhood he is tortured by foul dreams, so that at times he makes the night hideous with his screams and wakes with cold sweat upon him.

"But let us talk of something else, *Herr;* it is not good to dwell upon such things."

I remarked on the evident age of the tavern, and he answered with pride: "The foundations are more than four hundred years old; the original house was the only one in the village which was not burned to the ground when Suleiman's devils swept through the mountains. Here, in the house that then stood on these same foundations, it is said, the scribe Selim Bahadur had his headquarters while ravaging the country hereabouts."

I learned then that the present inhabitants of Stregoicavar are not descendants of the people who dwelt there before the Turkish raid of 1526. The victorious Moslems left no living human in the village or the vicinity hereabouts when they passed over. Men, women, and children they wiped out in one red holocaust of murder, leaving a vast stretch of country silent and utterly deserted. The present people of Stregoicavar are descended from hardy settlers from the lower valleys who came into the upper levels and rebuilt the ruined village after the Turk was thrust back.

Mine host did not speak of the extermination of the original inhabitants with any great resentment, and I learned that his ancestors in the lower levels had looked on the mountaineers with even more hatred and aversion than they regarded the Turks. He was rather vague regarding the causes of this feud, but said that the original inhabitants of Stregoicavar had been in the habit of making stealthy raids on the lowlands and stealing girls and children. Moreover, he said that they were not exactly of the same blood as his own people; the sturdy, original Magyar-Slavic stock had mixed and intermarried with a degraded aboriginal race until the breeds had blended, producing an unsavory amalgamation. Who these aborigines were, he had not the slightest idea, but maintained that they were "pagans" and had dwelt in the mountains since time immemorial, before the coming of the conquering peoples.

I attached little importance to this tale; seeing in it merely a parallel to the amalgamation of Celtic tribes with Mediterranean aborigines in the Galloway hills, with the resultant mixed race which, as Picts, has such an extensive part in Scotch legendry. Time has a curiously foreshortening effect on folklore, and just as tales of the Picts became intertwined with legends of an older Mongoloid race, so eventually to the Picts was ascribed the repulsive appearance of the squat primitives, whose individuality merged, in the telling, into

Pictish tales, and was forgotten; so, I felt, the supposed inhuman attributes of the first villagers of Stregoicavar could be traced to older, outworn myths with invading Huns and Mongols.

The morning after my arrival I received directions from my host, who gave them worriedly, and set out to find the Black Stone. A few hours' tramp up the fir-covered slopes brought me to the face of the rugged, solid stone cliff which jutted boldly from the mountainside. A narrow trail wound up it, and mounting this, I looked out over the peaceful valley of Stregoicavar, which seemed to drowse, guarded on either hand by the great blue mountains. No huts or any sign of human tenancy showed between the cliffs whereon I stood and the village. I saw numbers of scattering farms in the valley but all lay on the other side of Stregoicavar, which itself seemed to shrink from the brooding slopes which masked the Black Stone.

The summit of the cliffs proved to be a sort of thickly wooded plateau. I made my way through the dense growth for a short distance and came into a wide glade; and in the center of the glade reared a gaunt figure of black stone.

It was octagonal in shape, some sixteen feet in height and about a foot and a half thick. It had once evidently been highly polished, but now the surface was thickly dinted as if savage efforts had been made to demolish it; but the hammers had done little more than to flake off small bits of stone and mutilate the characters which once had evidently marched in a spiraling line round and round the shaft to the top. Up to ten feet from the base these characters were almost completely blotted out, so that it was very difficult to trace their direction. Higher up they were plainer, and I managed to squirm part of the way up the shaft and scan them at close range. All were more or less defaced, but I was positive that they symbolized no language now remembered on the face of the earth. I am fairly familiar with all hieroglyphics known to researchers and philologists, and I can say with certainty that those characters were like nothing of which I have ever read or heard. The nearest approach to them that I ever saw were some crude scratches on a gigantic and strangely symmetrical rock in a lost valley of Yucatán. I remember that when I pointed out these marks to the archeologist who was my companion, he maintained that they either represented natural weathering or the idle scratching of some Indian. To my theory that the rock was really the base of a long-vanished column, he merely laughed, calling my attention to the dimensions of it, which suggested, if it were built with any natural rules of architectural symmetry, a column a thousand feet high. But I was not convinced.

I will not say that the characters on the Black Stone were similar to those on the colossal rock in Yucatán; but one suggested the other. As to the substance of the monolith, again I was baffled. The stone of which it was composed was a dully gleaming black, whose surface, where it was not dinted and roughened, created a curious illusion of semi-transparency.

I spent most of the morning there and came away baffled. No connection of the Stone with any other artifact in the world suggested itself to me. It was as if the monolith had been reared by alien hands, in an age distant and apart from human ken.

I returned to the village with my interest in no way abated. Now that I had seen the curious thing, my desire was still more keenly whetted to investigate the matter further and seek to learn by what strange hands and for what strange purpose the Black Stone had been reared in the long ago.

I sought out the tavern-keeper's nephew and questioned him in regard to his dreams, but he was vague, though willing to oblige. He did not mind discussing them, but was unable to describe them with any clarity. Though he dreamed the same dreams repeatedly, and though they were hideously vivid at the time, they left no distinct impression on his waking mind. He remembered them only as chaotic nightmares through which huge whirling fires shot lurid tongues of flame and a black drum bellowed incessantly. One thing only he clearly remembered—in one dream he had seen the Black Stone, not on a mountain slope but set like a spire on a colossal black castle.

As for the rest of the villagers I found them not inclined to talk about the Stone, with the exception of the schoolmaster, a man of surprising education, who spent much more of his time out in the world than any of the rest.

He was much interested in what I told him of Von Junzt's remarks about the Stone, and warmly agreed with the German author in the alleged age of the monolith. He believed that a coven had once existed in the vicinity and that possibly all of the original villagers had been members of that fertility cult which once threatened to undermine European civilization and gave rise to the tales of witchcraft. He cited the very name of the village to prove his point; it had not been originally named Stregoicavar, he said; according to legends the builders had called it Xuthltan, which was the aboriginal name of the site on which the village had been built many centuries ago.

This fact roused again an indescribable feeling of uneasiness. The barbarous name did not suggest connection with any Scythic, Slavic, or Mongolian race to which an aboriginal people of these mountains would, under natural circumstances, have belonged.

That the Magyars and Slavs of the lower valleys believed the original inhabitants of the village to be members of the witchcraft cult was evident, the schoolmaster said, by the name they gave it, which name continued to be used even after the older settlers had been massacred by the Turks, and the village rebuilt by a cleaner and more wholesome breed.

He did not believe that the members of the cult erected the monolith, but he did believe that they used it as a center of their activities, and repeating vague legends which had been handed down since before the Turkish invasion, he advanced the theory that the degenerate villagers had used it as a sort of altar on which they offered human sacrifices, using as victims the girls and babies stolen from his own ancestors in the lower valleys.

He discounted the myths of weird events on Midsummer Night, as well as a curious legend of a strange deity which the witch-people of Xuthltan were said to have invoked with chants and wild rituals of flagellation and slaughter.

He had never visited the Stone on Midsummer Night, he said, but he would not fear to do so; whatever *had* existed or taken place there in the past, had been long engulfed in the mists of time and oblivion. The Black Stone had lost its meaning save as a link to a dead and dusty past.

It was while returning from a visit with this schoolmaster one night about a week after my arrival at Stregoicavar that a sudden recollection struck me— it was Midsummer Night! The very time that the legends linked with grisly implications to the Black Stone. I turned away from the tavern and strode swiftly through the village. Stregoicavar lay silent; the villagers retired early. I saw no one as I passed rapidly out of the village and up into the firs which masked the mountain slopes in a weird light and etched the shadows blackly. No wind blew through the firs, but a mysterious, intangible rustling and whispering was abroad. Surely on such nights in past centuries, my whimsical imagination told me, naked witches astride magic broomsticks had flown across this valley, pursued by jeering demoniac familiars.

I came to the cliffs and was somewhat disquieted to note that the illusive moonlight lent them a subtle appearance I had not noticed before—in the weird light they appeared less like natural cliffs and more like the ruins of cyclopean and Titan-reared battlements jutting from the mountain slope.

Shaking off this hallucination with difficulty, I came upon the plateau and hesitated a moment before I plunged into the brooding darkness of the woods. A sort of breathless tenseness hung over the shadows, like an unseen monster holding its breath lest it scare away its prey.

I shook off the sensation—a natural one, considering the eeriness of the place and its evil reputation—and made my way through the wood, experiencing a most unpleasant sensation that I was being followed, and halting once, sure that something clammy and unstable had brushed against my face in the darkness.

I came out into the glade and saw the tall monolith rearing its gaunt height above the sward. At the edge of the woods on the side toward the cliff was a stone which formed a sort of natural seat. I sat down, reflecting that it was probably while there that the mad poet, Justin Geoffrey, had written his fantastic "People of the Monolith." Mine host thought that it was the Stone which had caused Geoffrey's insanity, but the seeds of madness had been sown in the poet's brain long before he ever came to Stregoicavar.

A glance at my watch showed that the hour of midnight was close at hand. I leaned back, waiting whatever ghostly demonstration might appear. A thin night wind started up among the branches of the firs, with an uncanny suggestion of faint, unseen pipes whispering an eerie and evil tune. The monotony of the sound and my steady gazing at the monolith produced a sort of self-hypnosis upon me; I grew drowsy. I fought this feeling, but sleep stole on me in spite of myself; the monolith seemed to sway and dance, strangely distorted to my gaze, and then I slept.

I opened my eyes and sought to rise, but lay still, as if an icy hand gripped me helpless. Cold terror stole over me. The glade was no longer deserted. It was thronged by a silent crowd of strange people, and my distended eyes took in strange barbaric details of costume which my reason told me were archaic and forgotten even in this backward land. Surely, I thought, these are villagers who have come here to hold some fantastic conclave—but another glance told me that these people were not of the folk of Stregoicavar. They were a shorter, more squat race, whose brows were lower, whose faces were broader and duller. Some had Slavic or Magyar features, but those features were degraded as from a mixture of some baser, alien strain I could not classify. Many wore the hides of wild beasts, and their whole appearance, both men and women, was one of sensual brutishness. They terrified and repelled me, but they gave me no heed. They formed in a vast half-circle in front of the monolith and began a sort of chant, flinging their arms in unison and weaving their bodies rhythmically from the waist upward. All eyes were fixed on the top of the Stone, which they seemed to be invoking. But the strangest of all was the dimness of their voices; not fifty yards from me hundreds of men and women were unmistakably lifting their voices in a wild chant, yet those voices came to me as a faint indistinguishable murmur as if from across vast leagues of Space—or *time*.

Before the monolith stood a sort of brazier from which a vile, nauseous yellow smoke billowed upward, curling curiously in an undulating spiral around the black shaft, like a vast unstable serpent.

On one side of this brazier lay two figures—a young girl, stark naked and bound hand and foot, and an infant, apparently only a few months old. On the other side of the brazier squatted a hideous old hag with a queer sort of black drum on her lap; this drum she beat with slow, light blows of her open palms, but I could not hear the sound.

The rhythm of the swaying bodies grew faster, and into the space between the people and the monolith sprang a naked young woman, her eyes blazing, her long black hair flying loose. Spinning dizzily on her toes, she whirled across the open space and fell prostrate before the Stone, where she lay motionless. The next instant a fantastic figure followed her—a man from whose waist hung a goatskin, and whose features were entirely hidden by a sort of mask made from a huge wolf's head, so that he looked like a monstrous, nightmare being, horribly compounded of elements both human and bestial. In his hand he held a bunch of long fir switches bound together at the larger ends, and the moonlight glinted on a chain of heavy gold looped about his neck. A smaller chain depending from it suggested a pendant of some sort, but this was missing.

The people tossed their arms violently and seemed to redouble their shouts as this grotesque creature loped across the open space with many a fantastic leap and caper. Coming to the woman who lay before the monolith, he began to lash her with the switches he bore, and she leaped up and spun into the wild mazes of the most incredible dance I have ever seen. And her tormentor danced with her, keeping the wild rhythm, matching her every whirl and bound, while incessantly raining cruel blows on her naked body. And at every blow he shouted a single word, over and over, and all the people shouted it back. I could see the working of their lips, and now the faint far-off murmur of their voices merged and blended into one distant shout, repeated over and over with slobbering ecstasy. But what that one word was, I could not make out.

In dizzy whirls spun the wild dancers, while the lookers-on, standing still in their tracks, followed the rhythm of their dance with swaying bodies and weaving arms. Madness grew in the eyes of the capering votaress and was reflected in the eyes of the watchers. Wilder and more extravagant grew the whirling frenzy of that mad dance—it became a bestial and obscene thing, while the old hag howled and battered the drum like a crazy woman, and the switches cracked out a devil's tune.

Blood trickled down the dancer's limbs, but she seemed not to feel the lashing save as a stimulus for further enormities of outrageous motion; bounding into the midst of the yellow smoke which now spread out tenuous tentacles to embrace both flying figures, she seemed to merge with that foul fog and veil herself with it. Then emerging into plain view, closely followed by the beast-thing that flogged her, she shot into an indescribable, explosive burst of dynamic mad motion, and on the very crest of that mad wave, she dropped suddenly to the sward, quivering and panting as if completely overcome by her frenzied exertions. The lashing continued with unabated violence and intensity, and she began to wriggle toward the monolith on her belly. The priest—or such I will call him—followed, lashing her unprotected body with all the power of his arm as she writhed along, leaving a heavy track of blood on the trampled earth. She reached the monolith and, gasping and panting, flung both arms about it and covered the cold stone with fierce hot kisses, as in frenzied and unholy adoration.

The fantastic priest bounded high in the air, flinging away the red-dabbled switches, and the worshippers, howling and foaming at the mouths, turned on each other with tooth and nail, rending one another's garments and flesh in a blind passion of bestiality. The priest swept up the infant with a long arm, and shouting again that Name, whirled the wailing babe high in the air and dashed its brains out against the monolith, leaving a ghastly stain on the black surface. Cold with horror, I saw him rip the tiny body open with his bare brutish fingers and fling handfuls of blood on the shaft, then toss the red and torn shape into the brazier, extinguishing flame and smoke in a crimson rain, while the maddened brutes behind him howled over and over that Name. Then suddenly they all fell prostrate, writhing like snakes, while the priest flung wide his gory hands as in triumph. I opened my mouth to scream my horror and loathing, but only a dry rattle sounded; a huge monstrous toad-like *thing* squatted on the top of the monolith!

I saw its bloated, repulsive, and unstable outline against the moonlight, and set in what would have been the face of a natural creature, its huge, blinking eyes which reflected all the lust, abysmal greed, obscene cruelty, and monstrous evil that has stalked the sons of men since their ancestors moved blind and hairless in the tree-tops. In those grisly eyes mirrored all the unholy things and vile secrets that sleep in the cities under the sea, and that skulk from the light of day in the blackness of primordial caverns. And so that ghastly thing that the unhallowed ritual of cruelty and sadism and blood had evoked from the silence of the hills, leered and blinked down on its bestial worshippers, who groveled in abhorrent abasement before it.

Now the beast-masked priest lifted the bound and weakly writhing girl in his brutish hands and held her up toward that horror on the monolith. And as that monstrosity sucked in its breath, lustfully and slobberingly, something snapped in my brain and I fell into a merciful faint.

I opened my eyes on a still white dawn. All the events of the night rushed back on me and I sprang up, then stared about me in amazement. The monolith brooded gaunt and silent above the sward which waved, green and untrampled, in the morning breeze. A few quick strides took me across the glade; here had the dancers leaped and bounded until the ground should have been trampled bare, and here had the votaress wriggled her painful way to the Stone, streaming blood on the earth. But no drop of crimson showed on the uncrushed sward. I looked, shudderingly, at the side of the monolith against which the bestial priest had brained the stolen baby—but no dark stain or grisly clot showed there.

A dream! It had been a wild nightmare—or else—I shrugged my shoulders. What vivid clarity for a dream!

I returned quietly to the village and entered the inn without being seen. And there I sat meditating over the strange events of the night. More and more was I prone to discard the dream-theory. That what I had seen was illusion and without material substance, was evident. But I believed that I had looked on the mirrored shadow of a deed perpetrated in ghastly actuality in bygone days. But how was I to know? What proof to show that my vision had been a gathering of foul specters rather than a mere nightmare originating in my own brain?

As if for answer a name flashed into my mind—Selim Bahadur! According to legend this man, who had been a soldier as well as a scribe, had commanded that part of Suleiman's army which had devastated Stregoicavar. It seemed logical enough; and if so, he had gone straight from the blotted-out countryside to the bloody field of Schomvaal, and his doom. I sprang up with a sudden shout—that manuscript which was taken from the Turk's body, and which Count Boris shuddered over—might it not contain some narration of what the conquering Turks found in Stregoicavar? What else could have shaken the iron nerves of the Polish adventurer? And since the bones of the Count had never been recovered, what more certain than that lacquered case, with its mysterious contents, still lay hidden beneath the ruins that covered Boris Vladinoff? I began packing my bag with fierce haste.

Three days later found me ensconced in a little village a few miles from the old battlefield, and when the moon rose I was working with savage intensity on the great pile of crumbling stone that crowned the hill. It was backbreaking toil—looking back now I cannot see how I accomplished it, though I labored without a pause from moonrise to dawn. Just as the sun was coming up I tore aside the last tangle of stones and looked on all that was mortal of Count Boris Vladinoff—only a few pitiful fragments of crumbling bone—and among them, crushed out of all original shape, lay a case whose lacquered surface had kept it from complete decay through the centuries.

I seized it with frenzied eagerness, and piling back some of the stones on the bones I hurried away; for I did not care to be discovered by the suspicious peasants in an act of apparent desecration.

Back in my tavern chamber I opened the case and found the parchment comparatively intact; and there was something else in the case—a small squat object wrapped in silk. I was wild to plumb the secrets of those yellowed pages, but weariness forbade me. Since leaving Stregoicavar I had hardly slept at all, and the terrific exertions of the previous night combined to overcome me. In spite of myself I was forced to stretch myself down on my bed, nor did I awake until sundown.

I snatched a hasty supper, and then in the light of a flickering candle, I set myself to read the neat Turkish characters that covered the parchment. It was difficult work, for I am not deeply versed in the language and the archaic style of the narrative baffled me. But as I toiled through it, a word or phrase here and there leaped at me and a dimly growing horror shook me in its grip. I bent my energies fiercely to the task, and as the tale grew clearer and took more tangible form my blood chilled in my veins, my hair stood up, and my tongue clove to my mouth. All external things partook of the grisly madness of that infernal manuscript until the night sounds of insects and creatures in the woods took the form of ghastly murmurings and stealthy treadings of ghoulish horrors and the sighing of the night wind changed to tittering obscene gloating of evil over the souls of men.

At last when gray dawn was stealing through the latticed window, I laid down the manuscript and took up and unwrapped the thing in the bit of silk. Staring at it with haggard eyes I knew the truth of the matter was clinched, even had it been possible to doubt the veracity of that terrible manuscript.

And I replaced both obscene things in the case, nor did I rest or sleep or eat until that case containing them had been weighted with stones and flung into the deepest current of the Danube which, God grant, carried them back into the Hell from which they came.

It was no dream I dreamed on Midsummer Midnight in the hills above Stregoicavar. Well for Justin Geoffrey that he tarried there only in the sunlight and went his way, for had he gazed upon that ghastly conclave, his mad brain would have snapped before it did. How my own reason held, I do not know.

No—it was no dream—I gazed upon a foul rite of votaries long dead, come up from Hell to worship as of old; ghosts that bowed before a ghost. For Hell has long claimed their hideous god. Long, long he dwelt among the hills, a brain-shattering vestige of an outworn age, but no longer his obscene talons clutch for the souls of living men, and his kingdom is a dead kingdom, peopled only by the ghosts of those who served him in his lifetime and theirs.

By what foul alchemy or godless sorcery the Gates of Hell are opened on that one eerie night I do not know, but mine own eyes have seen. And I know I looked on no living thing that night, for the manuscript written in the careful hand of Selim Bahadur narrated at length what he and his raiders found in the valley of Stregoicavar; and I read, set down in detail, the blasphemous obscenities that torture wrung from the lips of screaming worshippers;

and I read, too, of the lost, grim black cavern high in the hills where the horrified Turks hemmed a monstrous, bloated, wallowing toadlike being and slew it with flame and ancient steel blessed in old times by Muhammad, and with incantations that were old when Arabia was young. And even staunch old Selim's hand shook as he recorded the cataclysmic, earth-shaking death-howls of the monstrosity which died not alone; for a half-score of his slayers perished with him, in ways that Selim would not or could not describe.

And that squat idol carved of gold and wrapped in silk was an image of *himself,* and Selim tore it from the golden chain that looped the neck of the slain high priest of the mask.

Well that the Turks swept that foul valley with torch and cleanly steel! Such sights as those brooding mountains have looked on belong to the darkness and abysses of lost eons. No—it is not fear of the toad-thing that makes me shudder in the night. He is made fast in Hell with his nauseous horde, freed only for an hour on the most weird night of the year, as I have seen. And of his worshippers, none remains.

But it is the realization that such things once crouched beast-like above the souls of men which brings cold sweat to my brow; and I fear to peer again into the leaves of Von Junzt's abomination. For now I understand his repeated phrase of *keys!*—age! Keys to Outer Doors—links with an abhorrent past and —who knows?—of abhorrent spheres of the *present.* And I understand why the cliffs look like battlements in the moonlight and why the tavern-keeper's nightmare-haunted nephew saw in his dream, the Black Stone like a spire on a cyclopean black castle. If men ever excavate among those mountains, they may find incredible things below those masking slopes. For the cave wherein the Turks trapped the—*thing*—was not truly a cavern, and I shudder to con-template the gigantic gulf of eons which must stretch between this age and the time when the earth shook herself and reared up, like a wave, those blue mountains that, rising, enveloped unthinkable things. May no man ever seek to uproot that ghastly spire men call the Black Stone!

A Key! Aye, it is a Key, symbol of a forgotten horror. That horror had faded into the limbo from which it crawled, loathsomely, in the black dawn of the earth. But what of the other fiendish possibilities hinted at by Von Junzt—what of the monstrous hand which strangled out his life? Since read-ing what Selim Bahadur wrote, I can no longer doubt anything in the Black Book. Man was not always master of the earth—*and is he now?*

And the thought recurs to me—if such a monstrous entity as the Master of the Monolith somehow survived its own unspeakably distant epoch so long— *what nameless shapes may even now lurk in the dark places of the world?*

UBBO-SATHLA

CLARK ASHTON SMITH

FOR UBBO-SATHLA IS THE SOURCE AND THE END. BEFORE THE COMING OF ZHOTHAQQUAH OR YOK-ZOTHOTH OR KTHULHUT FROM THE STARS, UBBO-SATHLA DWELT IN THE STEAMING FENS OF THE NEW-MADE EARTH: A MASS WITHOUT HEAD OR MEMBERS, SPAWNING THE GREY, FORMLESS EFTS OF THE PRIME AND THE GRISLY PROTOTYPES OF TERRENE LIFE . . . AND ALL EARTHLY LIFE, IT IS TOLD, SHALL GO BACK AT LAST THROUGH THE GREAT CIRCLE OF TIME TO UBBO-SATHLA.
—*THE BOOK OF EIBON*

Paul Tregardis found the milky crystal in a litter of oddments from many lands and eras. He had entered the shop of the curio-dealer through an aimless impulse, with no object in mind, other than the idle distraction of eyeing and fingering a miscellany of far-gathered things. Looking desultorily about, his attention had been drawn by a dull glimmering on one of the tables; and he had extricated the queer orb-like stone from its shadowy, crowded position between an ugly little Aztec idol, the fossil egg of a dinornis, and an obscene fetish of black wood from the Niger.

The thing was about the size of a small orange and was slightly flattened at the ends, like a planet at its poles. It puzzled Tregardis, for it was not like an ordinary crystal, being cloudy and changeable, with an intermittent glowing in its heart, as if it were alternately illumed and darkened from within. Holding it to the wintry window, he studied it for a while without being able to determine the secret of this singular and regular alternation. His puzzlement was soon complicated by a dawning sense of vague and irrecognizable familiarity, as if he had seen the thing before under circumstances that were now wholly forgotten.

He appealed to the curio-dealer, a dwarfish Hebrew with an air of dusty

antiquity, who gave the impression of being lost to commercial consider-
ations in some web of cabbalistic reverie.

"Can you tell me anything about this?"

The dealer gave an indescribable, simultaneous shrug of his shoulders and
his eyebrows.

"It is very old—palaeogean, one might say. I cannot tell you much, for
little is known. A geologist found it in Greenland, beneath glacial ice, in the
Miocene strata. Who knows? It may have belonged to some sorcerer of
primeval Thule. Greenland was a warm, fertile region beneath the sun of
Miocene times. No doubt it is a magic crystal; and a man might behold
strange visions in its heart, if he looked long enough."

Tregardis was quite startled; for the dealer's apparently fantastic suggestion
had brought to mind his own delvings in a branch of obscure lore; and, in
particular, had recalled the *Book of Eibon*, that strangest and rarest of occult
forgotten volumes, which is said to have come down through a series of
manifold translations from a prehistoric original written in the lost language
of Hyperborea. Tregardis, with much difficulty, had obtained the mediaeval
French version—a copy that had been owned by many generations of sorcerers and Satanists—but had never been able to find the Greek manuscript from
which the version was derived.

The remote, fabulous original was supposed to have been the work of a
great Hyperborean wizard, from whom it had taken its name. It was a collection of dark and baleful myths; of liturgies, rituals, and incantations both evil
and esoteric. Not without shudders, in the course of studies that the average
person would have considered more than singular, Tregardis had collated the
French volume with the frightful *Necronomicon* of the mad Arab, Abdul Alhazred. He had found many correspondences of the blackest and most appalling significance, together with much forbidden data that was either unknown
to the Arab or omitted by him . . . or by his translators.

Was this what he had been trying to recall, Tregardis wondered—the brief,
casual reference, in the *Book of Eibon*, to a cloudy crystal that had been owned
by the wizard Zon Mezzamalech, in Mhu Thulan? Of course, it was all too
fantastic, too hypothetic, too incredible—but Mhu Thulan, that northern
portion of ancient Hyperborea, was supposed to have corresponded roughly
with modern Greenland, which had formerly been joined as a peninsula to
the main continent. Could the stone in his hand, by some fabulous fortuity,
be the crystal of Zon Mezzamalech?

Tregardis smiled at himself with inward irony for even conceiving the
absurd notion. Such things did not occur—at least, not in present-day London; and in all likelihood, the *Book of Eibon* was sheer superstitious fantasy,
anyway. Nevertheless, there was something about the crystal that continued

to tease and inveigle him. He ended by purchasing it, at a fairly moderate price. The sum was named by the seller and paid by the buyer without bargaining.

With the crystal in his pocket, Paul Tregardis hastened back to his lodgings instead of resuming his leisurely saunter. He installed the milky globe on his writing-table, where it stood firmly enough on one of its oblate ends. Then, still smiling at his own absurdity, he took down the yellow parchment manuscript of the *Book of Eibon* from its place in a somewhat inclusive collection of recherché literature. He opened the vermiculated leather cover with hasps of tarnished steel, and read over to himself, translating from the archaic French as he read, the paragraph that referred to Zon Mezzamalech:

"This wizard, who was mighty among sorcerers, had found a cloudy stone, orb-like and somewhat flattened at the ends, in which he could behold many visions of the terrene past, even to the Earth's beginning, when Ubbo-Sathla, the unbegotten source, lay vast and swollen and yeasty amid the vaporing slime. . . . But of that which he beheld, Zon Mezzamalech left little record; and people say that he vanished presently, in a way that is not known; and after him the cloudy crystal was lost."

Paul Tregardis laid the manuscript aside. Again there was something that tantalized and beguiled him, like a lost dream or a memory forfeit to oblivion. Impelled by a feeling which he did not scrutinize or question, he sat down before the table and began to stare intently into the cold, nebulous orb. He felt an expectation which, somehow, was so familiar, so permeative a part of his consciousness, that he did not even name it to himself.

Minute by minute he sat, and watched the alternate glimmering and fading of the mysterious light in the heart of the crystal. By imperceptible degrees, there stole upon him a sense of dream-like duality, both in respect to his person and his surroundings. He was still Paul Tregardis—and yet he was someone else; the room was his London apartment—and chamber in some foreign but well-known place. And in both milieus he peered steadfastly into the same crystal.

After an interim, without surprise on the part of Tregardis, the process of re-identification became complete. He knew that he was Zon Mezzamalech, a sorcerer of Mhu Thulan, and a student of all lore anterior to his own epoch. Wise with dreadful secrets that were not known to Paul Tregardis, amateur of anthropology and the occult sciences in latter-day London, he sought by means of the milky crystal to attain an even older and more fearful knowledge.

He had acquired the stone in dubitable ways, from a more than sinister source. It was unique and without fellow in any land or time. In its depths, all former years, all things that had ever been, were supposedly mirrored, and would reveal themselves to the patient visionary. And through the crystal,

Zon Mezzamalech had dreamt to recover the wisdom of the gods who died before the Earth was born. They had passed to the lightless void, leaving their lore inscribed upon tablets of ultra-stellar stone; and the tablets were guarded in the primal mire by the formless, idiotic demiurge, Ubbo-Sathla. Only by means of the crystal could he hope to find and read the tablets.

For the first time, he was making trial of the globe's reputed virtues. About him an ivory-panelled chamber, filled with his magic books and paraphernalia, was fading slowly from his consciousness. Before him, on a table of some dark Hyperborean wood that had been graven with grotesque ciphers, the crystal appeared to swell and deepen, and in its filmy depth he beheld a swift and broken swirling of dim scenes, fleeting like the bubbles of a mill-race. As if he looked upon an actual world, cities, forests, mountains, seas, and meadows flowed beneath him, lightening and darkening as with the passage of days and nights in some weirdly accelerated stream of time.

Zon Mezzamalech had forgotten Paul Tregardis—had lost the remembrance of his own entity and his own surroundings in Mhu Thulan. Moment by moment, the flowing vision in the crystal became more definite and distinct, and the orb itself deepened till he grew giddy, as if he were peering from an insecure height into some never-fathomed abyss. He knew that time was racing backward in the crystal, was unrolling for him the pageant of all past days; but a strange alarm had seized him, and he feared to gaze longer. Like one who has nearly fallen from a precipice, he caught himself with a violent start and drew back from the mystic orb.

Again, to his gaze, the enormous whirling world into which he had peered was a small and cloudy crystal on his rune-wrought table in Mhu Thulan. Then, by degrees, it seemed that the great room with sculptured panels of mammoth ivory was narrowing to another and dingier place; and Zon Mez-zamalech, losing his preternatural wisdom and sorcerous power, went back by a weird regression into Paul Tregardis.

And yet not wholly, it seemed, was he able to return. Tregardis, dazed and wondering, found himself before the writing-table on which he had set the oblate sphere. He felt the confusion of one who has dreamt and has not yet fully awakened from the dream. The room puzzled him vaguely, as if something were wrong with its size and furnishings; and his remembrance of purchasing the crystal from a curio-dealer was oddly and discrepantly mingled with an impression that he had acquired it in a very different manner.

He felt that something very strange had happened to him when he peered into the crystal; but just what it was he could not seem to recollect. It had left him in the sort of psychic muddlement that follows a debauch of hashish. He assured himself that he was Paul Tregardis, that he lived on a certain street in London, that the year was 1933; but such commonplace verities had somehow lost their meaning and their validity; and everything about him was shadowlike and insubstantial. The very walls seemed to waver like smoke; the people in the streets were phantoms of phantoms; and he himself was a lost shadow, a wandering echo of something long forgot.

He resolved that he would not repeat his experiment of crystal-gazing. The effects were too unpleasant and equivocal. But the very next day, by an unreasoning impulse to which he yielded almost mechanically, without reluctation, he found himself seated before the misty orb. Again he became the sorcerer Zon Mezzamalech in Mhu Thulan; again he dreamt to retrieve the wisdom of the ante-mundane gods; again he drew back from the deepening crystal with the terror of one who fears to fall; and once more—but doubtfully and dimly, like a failing wraith—he was Paul Tregardis.

Three times did Tregardis repeat the experience on successive days; and each time his own person and the world about him became more tenuous and confused than before. His sensations were those of a dreamer who is on the verge of waking; and London itself was unreal as the lands that slip from the dreamer's ken, receding in filmy mist and cloudy light. Beyond it all, he felt the looming and crowding of vast imageries, alien but half familiar. It was as if the phantasmagoria of time and space were dissolving about him, to reveal some veritable reality—or another dream of space and time.

There came, at last, the day when he sat down before the crystal—and did not return as Paul Tregardis. It was the day when Zon Mezzamalech, boldly disregarding certain evil and portentous warnings, resolved to overcome his curious fear of falling bodily into the visionary world that he beheld—a fear that had hitherto prevented him from following the backward stream of time for any distance. He must, he assured himself, conquer his fear if he were ever to see and read the lost tablets of the gods. He had beheld nothing more than a few fragments of the years of Mhu Thulan immediately posterior to the present—the years of his own lifetime; and there were inestimable cycles between these years and the Beginning.

Again, to his gaze, the crystal deepened immeasurably, with scenes and happenings that flowed in a retrograde stream. Again the magic ciphers of the dark table faded from his ken, and the sorcerously carven walls of his chamber melted into less than dream. Once more he grew giddy with an awful vertigo as he bent above the swirling and milling of the terrible gulfs of time in the world-like orb. Fearfully, in spite of his resolution, he would have drawn away; but he had looked and leaned too long. There was a sense of abysmal falling, a suction as of ineluctable winds, of maelstroms that bore him down through fleet unstable visions of his own past life into antenatal years and dimensions. He seemed to endure the pangs of an inverse dissolution; and then he was no longer Zon Mezzamalech, the wise and learned watcher of the crystal, but an actual part of the weirdly racing stream that ran back to reattain the Beginning.

He seemed to live unnumbered lives, to die myriad deaths, forgetting each time the death and life that had gone before. He fought as a warrior in half-legendary battles; he was a child playing in the ruins of some olden city of Mhu Thulan; he was the king who had reigned when the city was in its prime, the prophet who had foretold its building and its doom. A woman, he wept for the bygone dead in necropoli long-crumbled; an antique wizard, he muttered the rude spells of earlier sorcery; a priest of some prehuman god, he wielded the sacrificial knife in cave-temples of pillared basalt. Life by life, era by era, he retraced the long and groping cycles through which Hyperborea had risen from savagery to a high civilization.

He became a barbarian of some troglodytic tribe, fleeing from the slow, turreted ice of a former glacial age into lands illumed by the ruddy flare of perpetual volcanoes. Then, after incomputable years, he was no longer man but a man-like beast, roving in forests of giant fern and calamite, or building an uncouth nest in the boughs of mighty cycads.

Through aeons of anterior sensation, of crude lust and hunger, of aboriginal terror and madness, there was someone—or something—that went ever backward in time. Death became birth, and birth was death. In a slow vision of reverse change, the Earth appeared to melt away, to slough off the hills and mountains of its latter strata. Always the sun grew larger and hotter above the fuming swamps that teemed with a crasser life, with a more fulsome vegetation. And the thing that had been Paul Tregardis, that had been Zon Mezzamalech, was a part of all the monstrous devolution. It flew with the claw-tipped wings of a pterodactyl, it swam in tepid seas with the vast, winding bulk of an ichthyosaurus, it bellowed uncouthly with the armored throat of some forgotten behemoth to the huge moon that burned through Liassic mists.

At length, after aeons of immemorial brutehood, it became one of the lost serpent-men who reared their cities of black gneiss and fought their venomous wars in the world's first continent. It walked undulously in antehuman streets, in strange crooked vaults; it peered at primeval stars from high, Babelian towers; it bowed with hissing litanies to great serpent-idols. Through years and ages of the ophidian era it returned, and was a thing that crawled in the ooze, that had not yet learned to think and dream and build. And the time came when there was no longer a continent, but only a vast, chaotic marsh, a sea of slime, without limit or horizon, that seethed with a blind writhing of amorphous vapors.

There, in the grey beginning of Earth, the formless mass that was Ubbo-Sathla reposed amid the slime and the vapors. Headless, without organs or members, it sloughed from its oozy sides, in a slow, ceaseless wave, the amoebic forms that were the archetypes of earthly life. Horrible it was, if there had been aught to apprehend the horror; and loathsome, if there had been any to feel loathing. About it, prone or tilted in the mire, there lay the mighty tablets of star-quarried stone that were writ with the inconceivable wisdom of the pre-mundane gods.

And there, to the goal of a forgotten search, was drawn the thing that had been—or would sometime be—Paul Tregardis and Zon Mezzamalech. Becoming a shapeless eft of the prime, it crawled sluggishly and obliviously across the fallen tablets of the gods, and fought and ravened blindly with the other spawn of Ubbo-Sathla.

Of Zon Mezzamalech and his vanishing, there is no mention anywhere, save the brief passage in the *Book of Eibon*. Concerning Paul Tregardis, who also disappeared, there was a curt notice in several London papers. No one seems to have known anything about him: he is gone as if he had never been; and the crystal, presumably, is gone too. At least, no one has found it.

The Watcher in the Green Room

Hugh B. Cave

The plump, stumpy man in the double-breasted gray coat was quite obviously drunk. He walked with an exaggerated shuffle which carried him perilously close to the edge of the high curbing, whereupon he stopped short, drew his fat hands from their respective pockets, and gravely regarded the drooling gutter beneath him. Proceeding sluggishly in this manner, he successfully navigated three blocks of gleaming sidewalk, turned left into Peterboro Street, and arrived before a red-brick apartment building whose square front frowned down upon him with disapproving solemnity.

He stood staring, apparently unaware that the hour was midnight and that the rain which had fallen steadily since early evening had made of him a drenched, dishevelled street-walker. Before him, as he stood thus contemplating the wide entrance, the door opened and a man and a woman descended the stone steps. They gazed at him queerly. The man spoke.

"Drunk again, Kolitt?"

"Still," the drunken one replied, grinning.

"You'd better let Frank help you," the woman advised. "You'll be invading the wrong apartment again."

The plump man raised one hand up and out in a clumsy salute.

"A camel," he said, "never forgets."

The man and woman hesitated. In an undertone the man muttered:

"Poor devil! It's too bad. I suppose it's the easiest way to forget."

The drunken one did not hear. He grinned idiotically as the man and woman went their way, leaving him to ascend the steps alone. In the lobby he groped in the pockets of his coat and produced a key-ring. Mechanically he thrust two fingers into the brass mail-box marked ANTHONY KOLITT. Then, opening the heavy inner door with a key proportionately large, he marched down the corridor, climbed two flights of rubber-carpeted stairs, and let himself into apartment number thirty-one.

"Five days gone," he mumbled, closing the door behind him. "If they haven't found out by now, they never will."

The thought sobered him, but he was still drunk enough to fumble awkwardly for the light-switch. The bright light blinded him. Blinking, he groped down the short hall to the living-room and lowered himself heavily, coat and all, into an overstuffed chair close to the radio. Reaching out, he lit the lamp on the end-table beside him; then he stretched himself, relaxed, and gazed intently at a large gray photograph which stared at him serenely from atop the radio.

The photograph was of a woman—attractive, straight-haired, somber-eyed, perhaps thirty years of age. It stood formally in a square silver frame, bare of ornamentation or inscription. The plump man studied it without emotion, as if he had studied it precisely the same way a great many times before. Presently he rose, removed his wet garments and shoes, and walked near-naked into the adjoining room. When he returned, he held a bottle and glass in his hands. He filled the glass, raised it toward the photograph, and said quietly:

"Pleasant dreams."

Then he turned out the light and paced unsteadily into the bedroom.

The bedroom was small and square, boasting a wooden three-quarter bed, a squat table, a massive old-fashioned bureau, and a single yellow-curtained window. The plump man sat on the bed and removed his socks. He stared at the bureau, grinned cruelly, and said:

"Too big, eh? Old style, is it? Well, it's a good thing it *was* big; otherwise you'd be kind of cramped for room, sweetheart. For once you won't complain, eh?"

The bed was unmade. He climbed into it and shaped the pillow with his fists, then lay on his back and gazed at the ceiling. The room was not quite dark. Its single window was high above the street outside and level with the roof of a building across the way. The wet window-pane exuded a green glow, reflecting the pale glare of a neon sign on the near-by roof. The glow was pleasant; the plump man enjoyed looking at it. It made fantastic, green-edged shapes on the walls of the room and transformed the huge bureau in the corner into a monstrous four-legged beast. He liked the beast. It was something to talk to.

"So you got her at last, eh?" he said drunkenly. "Ate her right up and swallowed her." His laugh was a low gurgle. "Serves her right, that does, for getting silly notions. She'd have found fault with anything, *she* would! I'm glad you got her—glad your insides were big enough to hold her. Yes, sir, that's poetic justice."

The bureau was half in shadow. Even the visible portions of it were shadowed, ill-defined, so that no separate details were distinct. It was more massive than usual tonight, because the green light was dimmed by the drizzling rain. Last night, when there had been no rain, the hulk had been a huge, staring hound. The night before that it had been a fantastic horse with many malformed heads. Well, there was nothing strange about that. Almost any object of furniture could assume changing shapes in semidarkness. The extent of the shapes depended entirely on the strength of the observer's imagination.

The plump man chuckled to himself. *He* had a good enough imagination. It had come in handy, too, not so very long ago. And right now it was a blessing. It kept him from thinking too much about certain unpleasant things which had occurred recently.

He studied the bureau lazily. It had assumed a different shape tonight, probably because of the rain. It had eyes, several of them—they were the protruding knobs on the drawers. It had thick, misshapen legs, too, and a bloated torso. What would Bellini, the goggled-eyed chap downstairs, say to that? Most likely he'd look with wide eyes, and shudder, and whisper warnings in his thin, womanish voice. Bellini was like a lot of other superstitious fools; he made too much out of nothing. Sentimental idiot! If he *knew* what the bureau contained, he'd run screaming back to his stuffy apartment at the back of the building, and hide himself there!

"Well, he won't know," the plump man said indifferently. "That's our secret, eh, old boy? When we move out of here in a few days more, we'll take it with us. *Then* let 'em learn the truth, if they can!"

Still drunk, he saluted the bulging shape in the corner. Then he dragged the bedclothes around him and hunched his knees into his stomach, and went to sleep.

Pale sunlight was streaking the walls of the room when he woke. He lay motionless many minutes, aware that his mouth was dry and swollen and his head aching. Some day, he reflected wearily, somebody would discover a way to take the hangover out of hard liquor.

He put both hands to his forehead and pressed hard, then rubbed his eyes with the heels of his palms. What time was it? About ten o'clock, probably; it was hard to tell, because the sunlight in the room was so feeble.

Stiffly he climbed out of bed and groped for a pair of slippers, then scuffed noisily into the kitchenette and opened the ice-box door. While he was thumbing the cork out of a gin bottle, the door at the end of the hall rattled. Scowling, he paced back along the corridor and fumbled with the knob.

"Who is it?"

"Me. Welks," said the man outside.

The plump man opened the door slowly and stood there with the gin bottle dangling in his fist. The other man—the same who had offered to assist him last night—said hesitantly:

"Thought I'd see if everything was all right, Kolitt. You were in pretty bad shape last night."

"I was drunk, eh?"

"You weren't exactly sober."

The plump one scowled, then stepped aside, grinning.

"Come in. Have a drink," he said. "'Scuse the attire. I just got up."

He closed the door and led his visitor down the hall, then motioned the man to a chair and went into the kitchen for two glasses. Returning, he said:

"I guess your wife was shocked, eh?"

"Not at all." The other man accepted the full glass and turned it idly in his fingers. He seemed unsure of himself. "She knows what you're going through. We all do. Can't blame a chap for hitting the bottle under such circumstances." He hesitated, stared at the plump man's bleary eyes. "But aren't you overdoing it, Kolitt? What'll your wife say when she does come back?"

"She won't come back."

"Why so sure?"

"I'm no fool." He upended the glass in his mouth and swallowed noisily. "When a man's wife walks out on him, Welks, there's a reason. She doesn't just go for a hike."

"You mean there's another man?"

"If there is, good luck to him."

"You're taking it hard, old boy."

"I'm no fool," Anthony Kolitt repeated. "When a man comes home and finds his wife's clothes and her bags gone, and the house empty, and a good-bye note on the bureau . . . You asked me yesterday why I didn't notify the police and have them find her. That's why."

The man named Welks put down his glass and stood erect.

"Sorry, old man," he said. "I didn't know."

He paced into the hall, stopped, turned again.

"Anything I can do——" he mumbled.

He closed the hall door after him.

Anthony Kolitt poured himself another drink. A little while later he put on a lavender dressing-gown and paced to the door. Stooping, he picked up the morning paper, then returned to the living-room, sat in the overstuffed chair, placed the gin bottle, a glass, and a pack of cigarettes within reach on the smoke-stand, and leisurely began to read the sporting pages.

He was quite drunk again when Mr. Cesare Bellini, from downstairs, called upon him two hours later; so drunk, in fact, that he shook Bellini's hand warmly and said with a large grin:

"Well, well! Come right in!"

Mr. Bellini was not usually welcome. He was a tall, painfully slender young man with ascetic features and untrimmed raven hair. He was a student —though what particular kind of student he was, Anthony Kolitt had never troubled to find out. Mr. Bellini was one of those "queer, artistic" chaps. It was believed that he gave readings, or something of the sort, to people who came professionally to see him.

"I have come to see if there is anything, no matter how insignificant, I can do for you," he said jerkily.

He sat stiffly in a straight-backed chair, leaning forward toward Anthony Kolitt with his lean hands flat upon his knees. His trousers needed pressing, Mr. Kolitt observed. He also needed instructions on how to knot a necktie. The one acceptable thing about him was the pale blue silk handkerchief protruding from his breast pocket; it gave him an almost feminine air of daintiness.

"What do you mean?" Mr. Kolitt shrugged. "You think you can find *her* for me?"

"If I could," Bellini murmured, "I would."

"Well, why can't you? You're a spiritualist or something, aren't you?"

"A spiritualist? No, no. I am not that, Mr. Kolitt."

"Well, what about the people who come to see you? They come to get readings, and that sort of business, don't they?"

"No. You are mistaken. They come for advice. They come with troubles in their hearts. Me, I look in their minds and tell them what they should do."

"Oh. You're a psychologist, eh?" Mr. Kolitt grinned.

"Psychopathist, rather, Mr. Kolitt."

"Well," Mr. Kolitt said drunkenly, "go ahead. Do your stuff. I'm drunk; I ought to be easy."

"It is a strange thing, drink," Bellini murmured, moving his head sideways over its protruding Adam's apple. "Some men, they drink to celebrate. They are happy; they wish to be happier. Others drink like you, to forget a sadness. You are lonely, no?"

"Oh, I got a pal," Mr. Kolitt declared warmly.

"A pal? Here?"

"Right in the next room, young feller. Come along." He stood up, swaying in an attempt to balance himself. "I'll show you."

Bellini did not understand. He frowned, and the frown darkened his already dark eyes and bunched his brows together over his hooked nose. He suspected apparently, that Mr. Kolitt's pal was an ephemeral being born of gin fumes. Silently he followed Mr. Kolitt into the bedroom.

"There," said Mr. Kolitt, pointing.

"But I see nothing."

"Not now you don't. Of course not. It's only there at night."

"At night?" Bellini frowned. "I am afraid I do not——"

"Then le' me explain, and you *will* understand."

Mr. Kolitt sat importantly on the unmade bed and hooked the heels of his slippers on the wooden bed-frame. Folding his arms around his upthrust knees, he grinned into his guest's face and hiccuped noisily. Then, without haste, he slyly proceeded to inform the thin young man of the nightly visitor which, created by a combination of green light, shadow, and applied imagination, emanated from the massive bureau in the corner. And, having finished this prolonged dissertation, he released his knees and sprawled back up on the bed, expecting to be amused no end by Bellini's outburst of horror.

The outburst was not forthcoming. Bellini peered at him thoughtfully a moment, as if wondering how much of the speech could justly be attributed to a belly full of liquor. He then turned and studied the window, the bureau, and the respective arrangement of each to the other. Finally he said, frowning:

"That is a most dangerous game, my friend."

Mr. Kolitt was disappointed. Obviously so. He sat up, blinking. He said petulantly:

"Eh? Dangerous?"

"You are—how do you say it?—flirting with fire," Bellini declared.

"You mean I'll be scaring myself?"

"Perhaps. But it is not so simple. This thing which you are making out of nothing—this monster which is one night a large dog, and another night a many-headed horse, and another night a horrific portent unlike any named beast—it is, perhaps, only a thing of lights and shadows, as you have told me. But you are playing foolishly with profound metaphysics, my friend. With ontology. With the essence of all being. You are a blind man, walking treacherous ways of darkness."

"Eh?" Mr. Kolitt said again. "I'm what?"

"You are a fool," Bellini said simply. "You do not comprehend. The imagination, it is a powerful force. It is a productive faculty, seeking everywhere for truth. If there is no truth, it creates truth. This thing you are creating for your amusement, it is unreal, perhaps. But if you are too persistent, you will make it real."

"Sure," Mr. Kolitt agreed pleasantly. "Then I could get it drunk, like me, eh? We'd be pals."

"Very well. It is good to joke, my friend. It is good to be unafraid. That is because you do not understand. Yesterday a woman came to me and said: 'I had a dream, and in my dream my son came to me and bent over me and spoke to me. How is that? He is dead. Can the dead return? And I said to her: 'Yes, the dead do sometimes return. But the man who came to you was a real man. You created him by thinking of him. He spoke the words you, yourself, put into his mouth. If you had willed him to kiss you, he would have kissed you.' That is what I told her, and it is true. The same is true with you. When you create this strange portent in your mind, it is a reality. It is what you make it. It does what you will it."

"Suppose I willed it to get me a drink," Mr. Kolitt murmured gently.

"Very well. You are making a fool of me. I will go. But *you* are the fool, my friend. You are toying with the very essence of life. I hope you are not so drunk one night that you mistake life for death."

Apparently it was not difficult to anger Bellini's Latin temperament. His dark eyes burned. He turned deliberately and stared at the huge bureau.

"If I were you," he said bluntly, "I would move that where lights and shadows and your fertile imagination"—he spoke the word with significant emphasis—"would no longer transform it into something other than what it is. Good day, my friend."

Mr. Kolitt swayed forward, protesting.

"Now wait a minute. I didn't mean to poke fun at you. I——"

"Good day," Bellini repeated coldly. "I do not enjoy being made the idiot. To a man so drunk as you, all wisdom is a waste of time. I will come again, perhaps, when you are more sober."

The hall door clicked shut behind him.

Mr. Kolitt sat on the bed, blinked foolishly at the bureau a moment, and said gravely.

"Now see what you've done. You've scared the nice man away."

Mr. Kolitt was neither drunk nor quite sober when he let himself into his apartment that night. He had spent most of the evening at the theater around the corner, and the offering there had been unpleasantly sinister. The silver screen, reflected Mr. Kolitt, was a peril sadly in need of censorship. It should be against the law to show certain pictures to certain people. Tonight's presentation had made him shudder.

He did not recall the name of the picture, but the majority of its scenes had been of a strikingly weird nature. One in particular was so vivid in his mind, even now, that it made him uneasy.

"Ugh!" he grunted. "I can see it yet, that damned thing!"

The thing which bothered him had been a monster; a manufactured monster, to be sure—created by experts out of immense sheets of rubberized cloth and animated by internal gears and levers—but horrible, nevertheless. He had visions of it advancing toward him, as it had advanced upon the unfortunate villain in the picture. Such things, he decided, should be outlawed.

The hour, now, was eleven o'clock. After leaving the theater, he had visited the Business Men's Club and vainly attempted to drive away his morbidity by batting a small white ping-pong ball across a table in the gameroom. Tiring of that, he had won seven dollars playing poker, and had spent the seven dollars on a quart of excellent rye whisky. He needed the whisky. It would steady his nerves. For the past several days his nerves had needed constant attention and lubrication.

He took the bottle from his pocket and placed it gently on the radio, beside his wife's photograph. Methodically he removed his tie, shirt, trousers, and shoes, and went to the bedroom for his dressing-gown. Then he turned on the radio and sat in the overstuffed chair, with a book in his lap.

He opened the book. It was a mystery story. He liked mystery stories. This one would take his mind off his own troubles and make him forget himself. He reached for the bottle and looked about for a glass. Finding none, he shrugged his hunched-up shoulders and upended the bottle in his mouth, drinking noisily. Then, grinning, he began to read.

Reading, he became aware presently that the dance music emanating from the radio had become something less pleasant. Voices rasped at him. He listened a moment, scowling, then leaned forward abruptly to turn the dial; but instead of turning it, he listened again. It was one of those things you just had to listen to. There was a sound of wind howling, and rain beating eerily against shut windows. There were voices whispering. The voices ceased. Into the strange silence came the ominous tread of slow footsteps: clump . . . clump . . . clump. . . .

Mr. Kolitt grunted and turned the radio off. He leaned back in his chair, trembling. For a while he stared with wide eyes at the photograph of his wife; then, with an obvious effort, he focused his attention on the book in his lap. Before he had read half a page more, he snapped the book shut and dropped it on the floor.

"Damnation!" he said. "Everywhere I turn there's murder and horror! There ought to be a law against such things! It's uncivilized!"

He stood up and drank deeply from the bottle. Snarling, he strode into the bedroom and switched on the light. His gaze wandered to the bureau in the corner. He said viciously:

"Blast him and his big talk! It's his fault. He's the one who started this business!"

He was thinking of Bellini. Bellini's smoldering eyes and deliberate words plagued him.

The single window was again wet with rain, and its drooling glass winked with many green eyes, derisively. The glass was pretty, Mr. Kolitt thought. It was like a large, moving tray in a jeweler's store. Each green-edged drop of water was a tiny precious emerald.

"And I suppose if I sat down and imagined 'em to be emeralds," he grunted, "they'd *be* emeralds. Yes they would not!"

He smiled crookedly then, as if relieved at thus finding a flaw in Bellini's reasoning. Quietly he removed the rest of his clothes and went to the bureau. Opening the top drawer, he took out clean pajamas; then he looked down at the lower drawers and tapped the bottom one with his naked foot.

"Comfortable?" he said quietly.

He unfolded the pajamas. They were green, with white stripes. Methodically he got into them and stood idly before the bureau, his elbows angling outward as he buttoned the green jacket-front. The room was warm. Frowning, he walked to the radiator and turned the small handle on the side of it. Then he stood at the window, looking out. Across the way, the green neon sign was like giant handwriting in the drizzle.

"Tonight's the last night I'll be looking at you," he said. "We're moving out of here tomorrow—me and the hope chest here." He turned his head drunkenly to peer at the bureau. "Yep. It's safe enough for us to clear out now. The neighbors won't be suspicious. They'll think I'm just a poor lonely devil trying to forget."

He was aware suddenly that the odor of his own breath, tainted with liquor fumes, was not the only odor in the room. There was another smell, less pleasant and more significant—a sour emanation suggesting decay, as of spoiled meat. Eyes narrowed and lips puckered slightly, he strode quickly to the bureau and stooped to bring his nostrils close to the lower drawers. When he straightened again he stood staring, his hands pressing hard against his hips.

"We'll be leaving tomorrow, all right," he muttered. "It won't be too soon, at that. I'll have to burn incense in here before the moving-men come."

He went into the living-room, then, and took the bottle he had left there on the smoke-stand. Quietly he turned out the light, and the hall light, too, and paced back to the bedroom. He opened the window six inches at the bottom, to let out that offensive odor. Then he went to bed.

He did not sleep. The room was too warm, and that unpleasant smell of pollution was too much in evidence. He lay with his thoughts, and they were morbid thoughts, parading rapidly across the bed. First marched the memories of that night not so long ago, when he had knelt on the floor of this very room, with a keen-edged kitchen-knife in one hand and a hacksaw . . . but it was better to forget those things. Then came the neighbors, finding him drunk, asking him questions, offering their sympathies. "Oh, but she'll come back, Mr. Kolitt! Women are strange creatures. They do strange things, but they are just women after all. She'll come back." And again: "Don't worry, old boy. She hasn't walked out on you for good. We all have our little family troubles. You and she—well, you've been going it pretty hot and heavy for quite a while. We've all known it. But she'll get over it."

And then Bellini. Damn Bellini!

Mr. Kolitt drained the contents of his bottle and leaned over to place the empty container on the floor. He lay back, enjoying the pleasant sensation of warmth that crept through him as the liquor found its way into his internals. Bellini was a superstitious young idiot, nothing else! His ideas were soap-bubbles filled with hot air. How could you bring something to life just by imagining it?

He turned suddenly on his side and peered at the bureau. The room was darker than usual, because the rain outside was a cold rain, and the combination of cold outside and warmth inside had fogged the window-pane. The huge bureau in the corner was a mastodonic shape of gloom, cloaked at one end in a winding-sheet of changing green light. It was neither hound nor horse tonight, Mr. Kolitt reflected. It was merely a swollen hulk with protruding eyes. What would Bellini say to that?

"Well, I won't look at the damned thing," he thought drunkenly. "I'll pack off to sleep and forget it."

But he looked, because the thing was fixed firmly in his mind, and his eyes refused to remain closed. Again and again he cursed himself for looking; but when he was not looking he was wondering what new shape the thing in the corner had assumed, and then his eyes opened again to find out.

This was foolish, too, because the thing had not changed shape since he had first peered at it. It was still a huge, bloated monstrosity with short, stumpy protuberances for legs, and a balloon-like excrescence for a head. "Like the thing in the movies tonight," he thought suddenly and shuddered.

The thing in the movies had been a gigantic abhorrence supposedly called into being by obscene incantations. In the end, it had deliberately and awfully devoured its creator. Recalling those things, Mr. Kolitt gazed with renewed interest at the similar monster in his own room; then he shut his eyes and mumbled aloud:

"Ugh! I'll be giving myself D.T.s!"

For a while, this time, he succeeded in keeping his eyes closed, but he did not sleep. His thoughts were too vivid and his mind too alert to permit sleep. He wanted a drink, but was secretly glad that the bottle was empty. He had already drunk too much. The liquor was keeping him awake instead of making him drowsy. It was keeping alive the unpleasant parade of thoughts which persisted in marching through his mind. Especially was it keeping alive that annoying vision of Bellini, and the words that went with it.

Again Mr. Kolitt looked at the monster, and again shuddered violently.

"My God!" he muttered aloud. "I'd hate to bring *you* to life!"

The thought, expressed thus in blunt syllables, alarmed him infinitely more than when he had kept it to himself. He wanted all at once to recall it, lest the monster should take it seriously and heed the suggestion. He wanted, too, to get out of bed and turn on the light, thereby transforming the monster into its original form. But the light-switch was terrifyingly far away, and to reach it he would have to pass within a yard of the beast's bloated head.

There were several other things he wanted to do, too. He wanted to shriek at the thing to stop glaring at him, and he wanted to go into the next room and look at the clock, to see how long it would be before daylight filtered through the green-glowing window. Fearfully he considered the wisdom of tiptoeing to the window and drawing the shade, to shut out that green glare; but if he did that, the room would be in total darkness, and the horror would still be there even though invisible.

He no longer thought about Bellini, or about the other thing which lay in the bureau's lower drawers. He thought only of himself, and of his increasing terror. It was foolish terror, he knew. It was the result of going to the wrong kind of a movie, and listening to a mystery play on the radio, and reading a weird detective story, and guzzling too much liquor. But those things were done now, and could not be amended. And the monster was here, threatening him.

"But it's only wood," he mumbled. "It's not real."

If he got up and walked toward it, and touched it, his fear would be gone and he would be laughing at himself for being a drunken fool. That would be the end of *that,* and he could turn on the light and go to sleep in security. But if the thing *were* real—if it were not made of wood—and he walked toward it——

Another thought came then, and caused him to cringe back into the wall. *She* had sent it. She had created it, just as the man in the movies had created *his* monster. The thing hated him for what he had done to her. It meant to kill him.

He lay rigid, staring at it. Yes, it was moving, and it was moving of its own accord—not because of the mist on the window-pane. Its hideous head was swaying from side to side, not much, but enough to be noticeable. Its small eyes were glaring maliciously. It was getting ready to attack him.

The blood ebbed from Mr. Kolitt's face. Slowly, with caution born of the fear which ate voraciously into him, he drew aside, inch by inch, the bed-clothes which covered him. Fearfully he wormed his legs toward the edge of the bed, and lowered them until his bare feet touched the floor. Not once did his wide eyes blink or his fixed gaze leave the greenish shape in the corner. If he could reach the threshold and slam the door shut behind him, there might be a possibility of escape. The hall door was but a few strides distant, and once in the hall he could run with all his might, shouting for help.

Warily he rose to a sitting position and put his hands behind him, pushing himself up. An eternity passed while his trembling body straightened and stood erect. Then he hesitated again, stifling the groan that welled to his lips.

The thing was eyeing him malevolently. It was not a creature of his imagination. It was real; he knew it was real. Its horrible head had stopped swaying; its bloated, swollen body was slowly expanding and contracting. It was waiting—waiting for him to make the first move. If he attempted to escape, if he took a single forward step, it would fall upon him.

Frantically he wrenched his gaze away from it and glanced toward the doorway. The door was open. His only chance lay in that direction. If he waited any longer——

He hurled himself forward. Three steps he took, and on the fourth he stood rigid, paralyzed by the sucking, scraping sound which rose behind him. He turned, terrified, and the thing seized him as he recoiled from it. The impact flung him to the floor. For a single horrific instant he stared up into the loathsome, undulating countenance above him. A scream jangled from his throat. Then his eyes and nose and mouth were smothered under an emanation of putrescent vileness, and that cavernous maw engulfed him.

Eight hours later the janitor discovered him there. The janitor, a red-faced, large-stomached Swede of more than middle age, shuffled past Mr. Kolitt's door with a garbage pail in his one hand and a mound of newspapers in his other. He had reached the mid-point in his daily round of collections. He wondered why Mr. Kolitt had failed to put out a wastebasket. Then he became aware of a most unpleasant and nauseating odor which filled the corridor. And, because the stench seemed to emanate from Mr. Kolitt's apartment, he knocked on Mr. Kolitt's door.

A moment later he let himself in with his own key.

He found Mr. Kolitt in the bedroom, midway between bed and doorway. Mr. Kolitt was dead. His legs and torso lay in a pool of dark red blood, and the entire upper portion of his plump body had been devoured. Those parts of him which remained were shapeless and unrecognizable beneath a pall of viscous green slime; and this foul excrescence, whose unbearable stench had first attracted the janitor's attention, extended from Mr. Kolitt's mutilated body to the bedroom window, where the sill was likewise coated with it.

These things the janitor saw and at first failed to assimilate. Unable to comprehend such horror, he merely stood staring. Then, believing his eyes at last, he shouted incoherent words in a guttural voice and leaned back against the wall, retching.

Later, a sober-faced Frenchwoman, who was a modiste, sat in Mr. Kolitt's living-room and said to the policemen who were questioning her:

"I have told you all I know. There I was, sitting in my apartment across the court from this one, and I heard a man screaming. I put down my needle and thread and hurried to the window, and I saw the thing coming out of this man's window. I do not know what it was. There was rain falling, and I saw only what the green light from the advertising sign showed me. It was large and it was greenish; that is all I am sure of. So large was it that it seemed to fold together as it flowed over his window-sill, and then stretched itself out like a big fat slug when it crawled over the edge of the roof up above. That is all I know."

"But what in thunder *was* it?" one of the policemen demanded irritably.

Mr. Bellini, the ascetic-faced young man from downstairs, said quietly: "If you will come again into the bedroom, gentlemen, I will show you what it was." And when they had followed him there, he pointed unemotionally to the huge bureau in the corner, and said: "It was a monster he made out of this. It destroyed him because he learned somehow to fear it, and, fearing it, he willed it to do what it did."

"Huh?" mumbled one policeman. "Feared it? Why?"

"That I do not know."

"Well, we'll damned soon find out," the policeman snapped. "Give me a hand here, Jenkins."

Beginning with the top drawer, the two policemen removed the bureau's contents. They did so carefully, inspecting each item before dropping it to the floor. In the third drawer from the bottom they found, wedged far back and buried beneath heavy articles of wearing-apparel, a woman's arm, wrapped in an oblong of torn sheeting which was caked with congealed blood.

In the next drawer they found four more blood-caked packages, which they unwrapped with increasing horror. In the last drawer of all they found a single large bundle which contained a woman's head.

Mr. Bellini, standing as near them as they would permit, gazed calmly into the woman's rigid features and said without emotion:

"It is his wife."

THE LADY IN GRAY

DONALD WANDREI

During the whole of my life, the hours from sunset to sunrise, when other people sleep, have been oppressive with fear. Since early childhood, I have been subject to terrifying dreams, from which neither physicians nor psychologists have been able to offer me the slightest relief. Doctors could find no organic derangement save for a few minor troubles such as are common to all men. My life has been singularly free of accidents, shocks, tragedies, and misfortunes. Financial worries have never beset me. I have pursued my career, at which success came steadily. Psychiatrists have devoted months to analyzing me, probing my life, my emotional development, my conscious and subconscious minds, hypnotizing me, making innumerable tests, and searching for secret fears or obsessions that might account for my nightmares, but in vain. Sedatives, opiates, dieting, travel, rest: these have been urged upon me at one time or another, and I have tried them without success. To doctors, I am a healthy man of thirty-four. To psychiatrists, I am a mentally sound, normal, and balanced person whose extraordinary dreams they either discount or discredit.

This is no comfort for me. I have come to dread the hours when night approaches. I would gladly expend my fortune if I could be relieved of the visions that possess my nocturnal mind, but the great diagnosticians of America and the foremost psychiatrists of Europe have alike labored in vain.

As I sit here now, writing these last words, a calm and a despair burden me, though my head seems clear as seldom before, despite the horror, the loathing, the terror, the revulsion, and the fear that combined in the first, and I believe final, profound shock which annihilated only a few minutes ago, and in full daylight, what hopes I had of fulfilling my life. That dreadful thing is at my elbow while I write; and when I have written, I shall destroy.

Let me go back for many years. I have been, I repeat, subject since early childhood to hideous dreams. Disembodied heads that rolled after me; cities of colossal and alien statuary; fire that burned and beasts that leaped; falls downward from titanic precipices; falls skyward up from pits of ancient evil; the old ones, waiting and waiting; flights through eternal blackness from nothing or something I only sensed; the grind of infernal torture machines against my flesh; monsters all of flowers and animals, fish and birds and stones, wood and metal and gas united incredibly; the pale avengers; descent into necrophilic regions; the leering of a bodiless eye in the midst of vast and forlorn plains; a corpse that rose and turned upon me the visage of a friend, with tentacles and ribbons of tattered black flesh writhing outward as though blown by gusts of wind; the little ones who pattered toward me with strange supplications; sunlight upon an oak-covered hill, sunlight whose malignance, nameless color, pulse, and odor instilled in me the unreasoning hate that is allied with madness; orchids lifting blooms like children's faces, and sipping blood; the dead ones who came, and came again; that awful moment when I drowned, and a fat thing swam out of the sea-depths to nibble; mewing blades of grass which purred avidly as my feet trod upon them; these and countless other such nightmares, inflicted through slumber as far back as I can remember, bred in me a deep and rooted aversion to sleep. Yet sleep I must, like all mortal men. And what shall I say of those darker dreams, those fantasmal processions that did not and do not correspond with any knowledge I possess? What of the city beneath the sea, all of vermilion marble and corroded bronze, in whose queerly curved geometry rest the glowing configurations of things that earth never bore? What of the whisperer in darkness, and the call of Cthulhu? I saw the seven deaths of Commoriom, and the twenty-three sleepers where Hali raises its black spires in Carcosa. Who else has witnessed the dead titans waken, or the color out of space, or the ichor of stone gods?

These, these tormented me and wakened me to fever and to sweat in the hours past midnight, and the silence before the gray of dawn. But they were small things, old dreams, compared with those of late.

I can not now narrate the events leading up to my acquaintance with Miriam, nor the brief but boundless love that we enjoyed, the eternal marriage we planned, and her tragic death when the airplane in which she was nearing the city from a visit to her parents fell upon the eve of our wedding. Perhaps the shock of that waking nightmare completed the slow devastation to which sleeping nightmares had almost brought my mind. I am not the one to say. Miriam was dead, all her strange beauty, the gray of her eyes, the gray and subdued mood of her personality, the pallor of her cheeks, the haunted and roving spirit prisoned within her, gone. I thought of her as the lady in gray, as she lay in her bier, like a woman from Poe, or an eery creature out of

The Turn of the Screw. So lovely, so unreal, so alien, and yet so eerily sweet. Dead, and not for me. Even the day was gray, that wild, autumnal afternoon, and the leaves that the wind blew rustled with a dry, sad sound, until the rain began falling later, and the world turned to a duller gray where the noise of slashing drops rivalled the sodden howl of gusts, and I was alone with my loneliness.

In the sanctuary of my chamber that night, I dreamed a dream. I dreamed that Miriam came to me, and took my hand, and led me forth. Now we came to a great and slimy sea, whose frightful color appalled me more than its stench. The blackness of the sea, its viscidity, and the universal atmosphere of decay, made me sick before ever she led me into it, so that the touch of that fluid brought a double horror. Far out in the sea, as I struggled with choking lungs, the lady in gray, who floated luminous above its surface, turned without reason or warning, and guided me back.

I could not account, in the morning, for the awful stuff that coated me, or the mephitic smell in my chamber. Only after arduous labors was I able to remove it from my person, and I was compelled to burn every article that the slimy, sticky, nauseating stuff had stained.

That night, I dreamed merely of skies of flame, and lands whose sinister red masses of rock soared from sere valleys where nothing lived and no plant flourished toward a cyclopean metropolis suspended in the heavens; and thus, for many nights, my old dreams recurred, until there came a time when I visioned again the lady in gray; and in my sleep, she took me by the hand, and raised me from my bed. We walked across plains of dusty gray, and she led me to a pillar. Now there dwelt in this pillar a great white worm, yet not a worm; a fat thing, like a slug, all gray, and with the face, if I may call the hideous thing such, of a rational creature; a horned visage whose red, white and gray pulp sickened me; but Miriam commanded, and I obeyed. I strode to the pillar, and lo, it fell apart. Out of those shards rose the loathly worm, and I gathered it in my arms. It curled. Then my lady in gray led me across that tremendous and desolate plain to my chamber, where she left me, committing to my care the dweller of the pillar. Over me she bent, and the gray thing kissed the gray woman with its beaked mouth; and then she leaned above me and caressed my lips, and she drifted upon her way, like a fog, soundless, and without visible steps.

I was frightened in the morning when I discovered that huge and horrible slug beside me. As I remember, I leaped from bed and with the tongs from my fireplace I beat and crushed it to a froth. Then I wrapped the pulp in the stained sheets, and burned it in the furnace. Then I bathed. Then I found the gray dust on my shoes, as I was dressing, and fear came to me anew.

There is, indeed, in Afterglow Cemetery, where they had buried Miriam, a kind of ashy soil; and though the grass grows green, and tall grow the wild flowers, they have never conquered the soil; so that in spring the gray shows through, and in autumn the dust lies lightly upon dead leaf and dying blade.

But I would not go there to find my tracks; for if I found my prints, I would have the horror of somnambulism added to my delirium; and if I did not find my footsteps, I would have a more poignant fear. *Where had I been? Whence came the gigantic worm?*

Thereafter, for many nights, so many nights that the loss of Miriam became a dull ache partly obliterated in time and memory, I dreamed the old dreams, of falling and fleeing and cities beneath the sea; of torture, of unknown beasts, and of unsocketed eyes.

Then the lady in gray came again one night in early winter, when I was beginning to forget, as much as I could. That night was yesternight. All the day, the snow had been falling, and the northwest wind, with a prolonged wail, had driven it onward, and whipped it into drifts, while the branches of naked trees ground and soughed mournfully together, so that, as the bleakness of evening drew near, I became a prey to melancholy, and depressed by thoughts of Miriam, who was dead. The frozen scream of the wind shrilled higher, and to that far-away cry I fell asleep. And when I slept, she came to me, to lead me forth.

Through the desolate plains she led me, and into the shadows of a forest, whither we penetrated deeper and deeper with the boles of tremendous trees rising ever taller around us; and thus we reached the cavern that she entered; and I followed after, striving to approach her, yet unable to close by one inch the distance between us. Now a strange thing happened, for the cavern swept sharply downward, until it became vertical, plunging toward the bowels of earth; and now a stranger thing happened, for we sank, as though falling gently, and yet we must make an effort, as though we were walking normally, but the horizontal had become the vertical. And slowly I drew closer at last to Miriam, until after age-long falling, we came to rest far, far, incredibly far beneath the surface of earth. And now I found us in the midst of a vault whose ceiling swept onward in arches of ever vaster scope and huger curves, while the walls receded like the naves of a cosmic and buried cathedral; and so I followed her down the aisle of that spacious edifice; and ghostly tapers, rising like giant torches beside our way, cast, in the little damp gusts of wind which fretfully stirred them, grotesque and wavering shadows upon the floor; and the gray robes of Miriam, the gray death-garments, fluttered behind her, streaming almost to my face as the distance between us lessened. Thus we came to the blackwood door, which swung wide and silent upon its great hinges as we approached; and the lady in gray drifted within, and I followed. Now I found myself within a crypt, whose three red tapers, guttering to their end, cast a somber and sinister glow; one at her head, and one at her feet, and one dripping scarlet drops upon her breast. For there lay Miriam, my lady in gray, in repose upon everlasting marble. At her head, a bowl of the slime of the black sea; at her feet, the white worm resurrected; and in her hands, folded across her breast, one the taper, and one a gardenia, whose fragrance, spicy and virginal, overpowered the odor of the chamber of death.

Now in my dream, with the queer logic of dreams, I thought this natural and had no fear; so I went to my lady in gray, and lo, at my coming, the bowl spilled over, but I brushed it aside, and the great worm rose, but I trampled it under, while the candles guttered out, and the gardenia glowed weirdly phosphorescent. By that luminescence, faint as it was, I saw that Miriam stirred, and a sigh passed across her, and I lifted her in my arms. Now the gardenia palely lighted my way, and through the rustling darkness I carried her, and the gray of her robes swept downward and around my ankles as I walked; until I came to the gusty corridor, and the tapers that flared, and the stately march of arches in cathedralesque tiers. So, with the curious illogic of dreams, the vertical corridor disappeared, and I walked onward through the vast chamber, until I emerged upon the plain. The gray dust rose, but the gray robes of Miriam fell about me, and the dust passed away. The heavens were empty of stars. In blackness I walked, save for the single flower whose scent sweetened the air, and whose glow lighted a path. Thus I clung to Miriam, and carried my lady in gray to my chamber.

Only a little ago, I wakened from my dream.

I stared and stared for all eternity, with cycles of oppressive and wildly swirling circles of frozen blackness alternating with red holocausts of flame to shatter the tranquility of my mind, and for ever. Not again for me the ways of man, or the mortal habitations of earth, or the transitory and ephemeral uncertainties of life. I have written, and now I shall die, of my own hand, and by my own choice.

For, when I wakened, I wakened to see the lady in gray seated beside my bed. In her face were the rotting vestiges of the grave, and her robes hung tattered and moldy; but these three things corrupted me from being: the fresh gardenia in her hands; her finger-nails, long and yellow, as only the fingernails of those dead and buried six months or more have ever grown; *and the dreadful way in which her hands were twirling the flower, while her black, liquescent eyes centered upon me!*

Scarlet Dream

C. L. Moore

ONE

Northwest Smith bought the shawl in the Lakkmanda Markets of Mars. It was one of his chiefest joys to wander through the stalls and stands of that greatest of market-places whose wares are drawn from all the planets of the solar system, and beyond. So many songs have been sung and so many tales written of that fascinating chaos called the Lakkmanda Markets that there is little need to detail it here. He shouldered his way through the colorful cosmopolitan throng, the speech of a thousand races beating in his ears, the mingled odors of perfume and sweat and spice and food and the thousand nameless smells of the place assailing his nostrils. Vendors cried their wares in the tongues of a score of worlds.

As he strolled through the thick of the crowd, savoring the confusion and the odors and the sights from lands beyond counting, his eye was caught by a flash of that peculiar geranium scarlet that seems to lift itself bodily from its background and smite the eye with all but physical violence. It came from a shawl thrown carelessly across a carved chest, typically Martian drylander work by the exquisite detail of that carving, so oddly at variance with the characteristics of the harsh dryland race. He recognized the Venusian origin of the brass tray on the shawl, and knew the heap of carved ivory beasts that the tray held as the work of one of the least-known races on Jupiter's largest moon, but from all his wide experience he could draw no remembrance of any such woven work as that of the shawl. Idly curious, he paused at the booth and asked of its attendant,

"How much for the scarf?"

The man—he was a canal Martian—glanced over his shoulder and said carelessly, "Oh, that. You can have it for half a *cris*—gives me a headache to look at the thing."

Smith grinned and said, "I'll give you five dollars."

"Ten."

"Six and a half, and that's my last offer."

"Oh, take the thing." The Martian smiled and lifted the tray of ivory beasts from the chest.

Smith drew out the shawl. It clung to his hands like a live thing, softer and lighter than Martian "lamb's-wool." He felt sure it was woven from the hair of some beast rather than from vegetable fiber, for the electric clinging of it sparkled with life. And the crazy pattern dazzled him with its utter strangeness. Unlike any pattern he had seen in all the years of his far wanderings, the wild, leaping scarlet threaded its nameless design in one continuous, tangled line through the twilight blue of the background. That dim blue was clouded exquisitely with violet and green—sleepy evening colors against which the staring scarlet flamed like something more sinister and alive than color. He felt that he could almost put his hand between the color and the cloth, so vividly did it start up from its background.

"Where in the universe did this come from?" he demanded of the attendant.

The man shrugged.

"Who knows? It came in with a bale of scrap cloth from New York. I was a little curious about it myself, and called the market-master there to trace it. He says it was sold for scrap by a down-and-out Venusian who claimed he'd found it in a derelict ship floating around one of the asteroids. He didn't know what nationality the ship had been—a very early model, he said, probably one of the first space-ships, made before the identification symbols were adopted. I've wondered why he sold the thing for scrap. He could have got double the price, anyhow, if he'd made any effort."

"Funny." Smith stared down at the dizzy pattern writhing through the cloth in his hands. "Well, it's warm and light enough. If it doesn't drive me crazy trying to follow the pattern, I'll sleep warm at night."

He crumpled it in one hand, the whole six-foot square of it folding easily into his palm, and stuffed the silky bundle into his pocket—and thereupon forgot it until after his return to his quarters that evening.

He had taken one of the cubicle steel rooms in the great steel lodging-houses the Martian government offers for a very nominal rent to transients. The original purpose was to house those motley hordes of spacemen that swarm every port city of the civilized planets, offering them accommodations cheap and satisfactory enough so that they will not seek the black byways of the town and there fall in with the denizens of the Martian underworld whose lawlessness is a byword among space sailors.

The great steel building that housed Smith and countless others was not entirely free from the influences of Martian byways, and if the police had

actually searched the place with any degree of thoroughness a large percent-
age of its dwellers might have been transferred to the Emperor's prisons—
Smith almost certainly among them, for his activities were rarely within the
law and though he could not recall at the moment any particularly flagrant
sins committed in Lakkdarol, a charge could certainly have been found
against him by the most half-hearted searcher. However, the likelihood of a
police raid was very remote, and Smith, as he went in under the steel portals
of the great door, rubbed shoulders with smugglers and pirates and fugitives
and sinners of all the sins that keep the spaceways thronged.

In his little cubicle he switched on the light and saw a dozen blurred
replicas of himself, reflected dimly in the steel walls, spring into being with
the sudden glow. In that curious company he moved forward to a chair and
pulled out the crumpled shawl. Shaking it in the mirror-walled room produced a sudden wild writhing of scarlet patterns over walls and floor and
ceiling, and for an instant the room whirled in an inexplicable kaleidoscope
and he had the impression that the four-dimensional walls had opened suddenly to undreamed-of vastnesses where living scarlet in wild, unruly patterns
shivered through the void.

Then in a moment the walls closed in again and the dim reflections quieted and became only the images of a tall, brown man with pale eyes, holding
a curious shawl in his hands. There was a strange, sensuous pleasure in the
clinging of the silky wool to his fingers, the lightness of it, the warmth. He
spread it out on the table and traced the screaming scarlet pattern with his
finger, trying to follow that one writhing line through the intricacies of its
path, and the more he stared the more irritatingly clear it became to him that
there must be a purpose in that whirl of color, that if he stared long enough,
surely he must trace it out. . . .

When he slept that night he spread the bright shawl across his bed, and the
brilliance of it colored his dreams fantastically. . . .

That threading scarlet was a labyrinthin path down which he stumbled
blindly, and at every turn he looked back and saw himself in myriad replicas,
always wandering lost and alone through the pattern of the path. Sometimes
it shook itself under his feet, and whenever he thought he saw the end it
would writhe into fresh intricacies. . . .

The sky was a great shawl threaded with scarlet lightning that shivered and
squirmed as he watched, then wound itself into the familiar, dizzy pattern
that became one mighty Word in a nameless writing, whose meaning he
shuddered on the verge of understanding, and woke in icy terror just before
the significance of it broke upon his brain. . . .

He slept again, and saw the shawl hanging in a blue dusk the color of its background, stared and stared until the square of it melted imperceptibly into the dimness and the scarlet was a pattern incised lividly upon a gate . . . a gate of strange outline in a high wall, half seen through that curious, cloudy twilight blurred with exquisite patches of green and violet, so that it seemed no mortal twilight, but some strange and lovely evening in a land where the air was suffused with colored mists, and no winds blew. He felt himself moving forward without effort, and the gate opened before him. . . .

He was mounting a long flight of steps. In one of the metamorphoses of dreams it did not surprise him that the gate had vanished, or that he had no remembrance of having climbed the long flight stretching away behind him. The lovely colored twilight still veiled the air, so that he could see but dimly the steps rising before him and melting into the mist.

And now, suddenly, he was aware of a stirring in the dimness, and a girl came flying down the stairs in a headlong, stumbling terror. He could see the shadow of it on her face, and her long, bright-colored hair streamed out behind her, and from head to foot she was dabbled with blood. In her blind flight she must not have seen him, for she came plunging downward three steps at a time and blundered full into him as he stood undecided, watching. The impact all but unbalanced him, but his arms closed instinctively about her and for a moment she hung in his embrace, utterly spent, gasping against his broad leather breast and too breathless even to wonder who had stopped her. The smell of fresh blood rose to his nostrils from her dreadfully spattered garments.

Finally she lifted her head and raised a flushed, creamy-brown face to him, gulping in air through lips the color of holly berries. Her dabbled hair, so fantastically golden that it might have been almost orange, shivered about her face as she clung to him with lifted, lovely face. In that dizzy moment he saw that her eyes were sherry-brown with tints of red, and the fantastic, colored beauty of her face had a wild tinge of something utterly at odds with anything he had ever known before. It might have been the look in her eyes. . . .

"Oh!" she gasped. "It—it has her! Let me go! . . . Let me——"

Smith shook her gently.

"What has her?" he demanded. "Who? Listen to me! You're covered with blood, do you know it? Are you hurt?"

She shook her head wildly.

"No—no—let me go! I must—not my blood—hers. . . ."

She sobbed on the last word, and suddenly collapsed in his arms, weeping with a violent intensity that shook her from head to foot. Smith gazed helplessly about over the orange head, then gathered the shaking girl in his arms and went on up the stairs through the violet gloaming.

★ ★ ★

He must have climbed for all of five minutes before the twilight thinned a little and he saw that the stairs ended at the head of a long hallway, high-arched like a cathedral aisle. A row of low doors ran down one side of the hall, and he turned aside at random into the nearest. It gave upon a gallery whose arches opened into blue space. A low bench ran along the wall under the gallery windows, and he crossed toward it, gently setting down the sobbing girl and supporting her against his shoulder.

"My sister," she wept. "It has her—oh, my sister!"

"Don't cry, don't cry," Smith heard his own voice saying, surprisingly. "It's all a dream, you know. Don't cry—there never was any sister—you don't exist at all—don't cry so."

She jerked her head up at that, startled out of her sobs for a moment, and stared at him with sherry-brown eyes drowned in tears. Her lashes clung together in wet, starry points. She stared with searching eyes, taking in the leather-brownness of him, his spaceman's suit, his scarred dark face and eyes paler than steel. And then a look of infinite pity softened the strangeness of her face, and she said gently,

"Oh . . . you come from—from—you still believe that you dream!"

"I *know* I'm dreaming," persisted Smith childishly. "I'm lying asleep in Lakkdarol and dreaming of you, and all this, and when I wake——"

She shook her head sadly.

"You will never wake. You have come into a more deadly dream than you could ever guess. There is no waking from this land."

"What do you mean? Why not?" A little absurd panic was starting up in his mind at the sorrow and pity in her voice, the sureness of her words. Yet this was one of those rare dreams wherein he knew quite definitely that he dreamed. He could not be mistaken. . . .

"There are many dream countries," she said, "many nebulous, unreal half-lands where the souls of sleepers wander, places that have an actual, tenuous existence, if one knows the way. . . . But here—it has happened before, you see—one may not blunder without passing a door that opens one way only. And he who has the key to open it may come through, but he can never find the way into his own waking land again. Tell me—what key opened the door to you?"

"The shawl," Smith murmured. "The shawl . . . of course. That damnable red pattern, dizzy——"

He passed a hand across his eyes, for the memory of it, writhing, alive, searingly scarlet, burned behind his eyelids.

"What was it?" she demanded, breathlessly, he thought, as if a half-hopeless eagerness forced the question from her lips. "Can you remember?"

"A red pattern," he said slowly, "a thread of bright scarlet woven into a blue shawl—nightmare pattern—painted on the gate I came by . . . but it's only a dream, of course. In a few minutes I'll wake. . . ."

She clutched his knee excitedly.

"Can you remember?" she demanded. "The pattern—the red pattern? The Word?"

"Word?" he wondered stupidly. "Word—in the sky? No—no, I don't want to remember—crazy pattern, you know. Can't forget it—but no, I couldn't tell you what it was, or trace it for you. Never was anything like it—thank God. It was on that shawl. . . ."

"Woven on a shawl," she murmured to herself. "Yes, of course. But how you ever came by it, in your world—when it—when *it*—oh!"

Memory of whatever tragedy had sent her flying down the stairs swept back in a flood, and her face crumpled into tears again. "My sister!"

"Tell me what happened." Smith woke from his daze at the sound of her sob. "Can't I help? Please let me try—tell me about it."

"My sister," she said faintly. "It caught her in the hall—caught her before my eyes—spattered me with her blood. Oh! . . ."

"It?" puzzled Smith. "What? Is there danger?" and his hand moved instinctively toward his gun.

She caught the gesture and smiled a little scornfully through her tears.

"It," she said. "The—the Thing. No gun can harm it, no man can fight it —It came, and that was all."

"But what is it? What does it look like? Is it near?"

"It's everywhere. One never knows—until the mist begins to thicken and the pulse of red shows through—and then it's too late. We do not fight it, or think of it overmuch—life would be unbearable. For it hungers and must be fed, and we who feed it strive to live as happily as we may before the Thing comes for us. But one can never know."

"Where did it come from? What is it?"

"No one knows—it has always been here—always will be . . . too nebulous to die or be killed—a Thing out of some alien place we couldn't understand, I suppose—somewhere so long ago, or in some such unthinkable dimension that we will never have any knowledge of its origin. But as I say, we try not to think."

"If it eats flesh," said Smith stubbornly, "it must be vulnerable—and I have my gun."

"Try if you like," she shrugged. "Others have tried—and it still comes. It dwells here, we believe, if it dwells anywhere. We are—taken—more often in these halls than elsewhere. When you are weary of life you might bring your gun and wait under this roof. You may not have long to wait."

"I'm not ready to try the experiment just yet," Smith grinned. "If the Thing lives here, why do you come?"

She shrugged again, apathetically. "If we do not, it will come after us when it hungers. And we come here for—for our food." She shot him a curious glance from under lowered lids. "You wouldn't understand. But as you say, it's a dangerous place. We'd best go now—you will come with me, won't you? I shall be lonely, now." And her eyes brimmed again.

"Of course. I'm sorry, my dear. I'll do what I can for you—until I wake." He grinned at the fantastic sound of this.

"You will not wake," she said quietly. "Better not to hope, I think. You are trapped here with the rest of us and here you must stay until you die." He rose and held out his hand.

"Let's go, then," he said. "Maybe you're right, but—well, come on."

She took his hand and jumped up. The orange hair, too fantastically colored for anything outside a dream, swung about her brilliantly. He saw now that she wore a single white garment, brief and belted, over the creamy brownness of her body. It was torn now, and hideously stained. She made a picture of strange and vivid loveliness, all white and gold and bloody, in the misted twilight of the gallery.

"Where are we going?" she asked Smith. "Out there?" And he nodded toward the blueness beyond the windows.

She drew her shoulders together in a little shudder of distaste.

"Oh, no," she said.

"What is it?"

"Listen." She took him by the arms and lifted a serious face to his. "If you must stay here—and you must, for there is only one way out save death, and that is a worse way even than dying—you must learn to ask no questions about the—the Temple. This is the Temple. Here it dwells. Here we—feed.

"There are halls we know, and we keep to them. It is wiser. You saved my life when you stopped me on those stairs—no one has ever gone down into that mist and darkness, and returned. I should have known, seeing you climb them, that you were not of us . . . for whatever lies beyond, wherever that stairway leads—it is better not to know. It is better not to look out the windows of this place. We have learned that, too. For from the outside the Temple looks strange enough, but from the inside, looking out, one is liable to see things it is better not to see. . . . What that blue space is, on which this gallery opens, I do not know—I have no wish to know. There are windows here opening on stranger things than this—but we turn our eyes away when we pass them. You will learn. . . ."

She took his hand, smiling a little.

"Come with me, now."

And in silence they left the gallery opening on space and went down the hall where the blue mist floated so beautifully with its clouds of violet and green confusing the eye, and a great stillness all about.

The hallway led straight, as nearly as he could see, for the floating clouds veiled it, toward the great portals of the Temple. In the form of a mighty triple arch it opened out of the clouded twilight up on a shining day like no day he had ever seen on any planet. The light came from no visible source, and there was a lucid quality about it, nebulous but unmistakable, as if one were looking through the depths of a crystal, or through clear water that trembled a little now and then. It was diffused through the translucent day from a sky as shining and unfamiliar as everything else in this amazing dreamland.

They stood under the great arch of the Temple, looking out over the shining land beyond. Afterward he could never quite remember what had made it so unutterably strange, so indefinably dreadful. There were trees, feathery masses of green and bronze above the bronze-green grass; the bright air shimmered, and through the leaves he caught the glimmer of water not far away. At first glance it seemed a perfectly normal scene—yet tiny details caught his eye that sent ripples of coldness down his back. The grass, for instance. . . .

When they stepped down upon it and began to cross the meadow toward the trees beyond which water gleamed, he saw that the blades were short and soft as fur, and they seemed to cling to his companion's bare feet as she walked. As he looked out over the meadow he saw that long waves of it, from every direction, were rippling toward them as if the wind blew from all sides at once toward the common center that was themselves. Yet no wind blew.

"It—it's alive," he stammered, startled. "The grass!"

"Yes, of course," she said indifferently.

And then he realized that though the feathery fronds of the trees waved now and then, gracefully together, there was no wind. And they did not sway in one direction only, but by twos and threes in many ways, dipping and rising with a secret, contained life of their own.

When they reached the belt of woodland he looked up curiously and heard the whisper and rustle of leaves above him, bending down as if in curiosity as the two passed beneath. They never bent far enough to touch them, but a sinister air of watchfulness, of aliveness, brooded over the whole uncannily alive landscape, and the ripples of the grass followed them wherever they went.

The lake, like that twilight in the Temple, was a sleepy blue clouded with violet and green, not like real water, for the colored blurs did not diffuse or change as it rippled.

On the shore, a little above the water line, stood a tiny, shrine-like building of some creamy stone, its walls no more than a series of arches open to the blue, translucent day. The girl led him to the doorway and gestured within negligently.

"I live here," she said.

Smith stared. It was quite empty save for two low couches with a blue coverlet thrown across each. Very classic it looked, with its whiteness and austerity, the arches opening on a vista of woodland and grass beyond.

"Doesn't it ever get cold?" he asked. "Where do you eat? Where are your books and food and clothes?"

"I have some spare tunics under my couch," she said. "That's all. No books, no other clothing, no food. We feed at the Temple. And it is never any colder or warmer than this."

"But what do you do?"

"Do? Oh, swim in the lake, sleep and rest and wander through the woods. Time passes very quickly."

"Idyllic," murmured Smith, "but rather tiresome, I should think."

"When one knows," she said, "that the next moment may be one's last, life is savored to the full. One stretches the hours out as long as possible. No, for us it is not tiresome."

"But have you no cities? Where are the other people?"

"It is best not to collect in crowds. Somehow they seem to draw—it. We live in twos and threes—sometimes alone. We have no cities. We do nothing —what purpose in beginning anything when we know we shall not live to end it? Why even think too long of one thing? Come down to the lake."

She took his hand and led him across the clinging grass to the sandy brink of the water, and they sank in silence on the narrow beach. Smith looked out over the lake where vague colors misted the blue, trying not to think of the fantastic things that were happening to him. Indeed, it was hard to do much thinking, here, in the midst of the blueness and the silence, the very air dreamy about them . . . the cloudy water lapping the shore with tiny, soft sounds like the breathing of a sleeper. The place was heavy with the stillness and the dreamy colors, and Smith was never sure, afterward, whether in his dream he did not sleep for a while; for presently he heard a stir at his side and the girl reseated herself, clad in a fresh tunic, all the blood washed away. He could not remember her having left, but it did not trouble him.

The light had for some time been sinking and blurring, and imperceptibly a cloudy blue twilight closed about them, seeming somehow to rise from the blurring lake, for it partook of that same dreamy blueness clouded with vague colors. Smith thought that he would be content never to rise again from that cool sand, to sit here forever in the blurring twilight and the silence of his dream. How long he did sit there he never knew. The blue peace enfolded him utterly, until he was stepped in its misty evening colors and permeated through and through with the tranced quiet.

The darkness had deepened until he could no longer see any more than the nearest wavelets lapping the sand. Beyond, and all about, the dream-world melted into the violet-misted blueness of the twilight. He was not aware that he had turned his head, but presently he found himself looking down on the girl beside him. She was lying on the pale sand, her hair a fan of darkness to frame the pallor of her face. In the twilight her mouth was dark too, and from the darkness under her lashes he slowly became aware that she was watching him unwinkingly.

For a long while he sat there, gazing down, meeting the half-hooded eyes in silence. And presently, with the effortless detachment of one who moves in a dream, he bent down to meet her lifting arms. The sand was cool and sweet, and her mouth tasted faintly of blood.

TWO

There was no sunrise in that land. Lucid day brightened slowly over the breathing landscape, and grass and trees stirred with wakening awareness, rather horribly in the beauty of the morning. When Smith woke, he saw the girl coming up from the lake, shaking blue water from her orange hair. Blue droplets clung to the creaminess of her skin, and she was laughing and flushed from head to foot in the glowing dawn.

Smith sat up on his couch and pushed back the blue coverlet.

"I'm hungry," he said. "When and what do we eat?"

The laughter vanished from her face in a breath. She gave her hair a troubled shake and said doubtfully,

"Hungry?"

"Yes, starved? Didn't you say you get your food at the Temple? Let's go up there."

She sent him a sidelong, enigmatic glance from under her lashes as she turned aside.

"Very well," she said.

"Anything wrong?" He reached out as she passed and pulled her to his knee, kissing the troubled mouth lightly. And again he tasted blood.

"Oh, no." She ruffled his hair and rose. "I'll be ready in a moment, and then we'll go."

And so again they passed the belt of woods where the trees bent down to watch, and crossed the rippling grassland. From all directions long waves of it came blowing toward them as before, and the fur-like blades clung to their feet. Smith tried not to notice. Everywhere, he was seeing this morning, an undercurrent of nameless unpleasantness ran beneath the surface of this lovely land.

As they crossed the live grass a memory suddenly returned to him, and he said, "What did you mean, yesterday, when you said that there was a way— out—other than death?"

She did not meet his eyes as she answered, in that troubled voice, "Worse than dying, I said. A way out we do not speak of here."

"But if there's any way at all, I must know of it," he persisted. "Tell me."

She swept the orange hair like a veil between them, bending her head and saying indistinctly, "A way out you could not take. A way too costly. And— and I do not wish you to go, now. . . ."

"I must know," said Smith relentlessly.

She paused then, and stood looking up at him, her sherry-colored eyes disturbed.

"By the way you came," she said at last. "By virtue of the Word. But that gate is impassable."

"Why?"

"It is death to pronounce the Word. Literally. I do not know it now, could not speak it if I would. But in the Temple there is one room where the Word is graven in scarlet on the wall, and its power is so great that the echoes of it ring forever round and round that room. If one stands before the graven symbol and lets the force of it beat upon his brain he will hear, and know— and shriek the awful syllables aloud—and so die. It is a word from some tongue so alien to all our being that the spoken sound of it, echoing in the throat of a living man, is disrupting enough to rip the very fibers of the human body apart—to blast its atoms asunder, to destroy body and mind as utterly as if they had never been. And because the sound is so disruptive it somehow blasts open for an instant the door between your world and mine. But the danger is dreadful, for it may open the door to other worlds too, and let things through more terrible than we can dream of. Some say it was thus that the Thing gained access to our land eons ago. And if you are not standing exactly where the door opens, on the one spot in the room that is protected, as the center of a whirlwind is quiet, and if you do not pass instantly out of the sound of the Word, it will blast you asunder as it does the one who has pronounced it for you. So you see how impos——" Here she broke off with a little scream and glanced down in half-laughing annoyance, then took two or three little running steps and turned.

"The grass," she explained ruefully, pointing to her feet. The brown bareness of them was dotted with scores of tiny blood-spots. "If one stands too long in one place, barefoot, it will pierce the skin and drink—stupid of me to forget. But come."

Smith went on at her side, looking round with new eyes upon the lovely pellucid land, too beautiful and frightening for anything outside a dream. All about them the hungry grass came hurrying in long, converging waves as they advanced. Were the trees, then, flesh-eating too? Cannibal trees and vampire grass—he shuddered a little and looked ahead.

The Temple stood tall before them, a building of some nameless material as mistily blue as far-off mountains on the Earth. The mistiness did not condense or clarify as they approached, and the outlines of the place were mysteriously hard to fix in mind—he could never understand, afterward, just why. When he tried too hard to concentrate on one particular corner or tower or window it blurred before his eyes as if the focus were at fault—as if the whole strange, veiled building stood just on the borderland of another dimension.

From the immense triple arch of the doorway, as they approached—a triple arch like nothing he had ever seen before, so irritatingly hard to focus upon that he could not be sure just wherein its difference lay—a pale blue mist issued smokily. And when they stepped within they walked into that twilight dimness he was coming to know so well.

The great hall lay straight and veiled before them, but after a few steps the girl drew him aside and under another archway, into a long gallery through whose drifting haze he could see rows of men and women kneeling against the wall with bowed heads, as if in prayer. She led him down the line to the end, and he saw then that they knelt before small spigots curving up from the wall at regular intervals. She dropped to her knees before one and, motioning him to follow, bent her head and laid her lips to the up-curved spout. Dubiously he followed her example.

Instantly with the touch of his mouth on the nameless substance of the spigot something hot and, strangely, at once salty and sweet flowed into his mouth. There was an acridity about it that gave a curious tang, and the more he drank the more avid he became. Hauntingly delicious it was, and warmth flowed through him more strongly with every draft. Yet somewhere deep within him memory stirred unpleasantly . . . somewhere, somehow, he had known this hot, acrid, salty taste before, and—suddenly suspicions struck him like a bludgeon, and he perked his lips from the spout as if burnt. A tiny thread of scarlet trickled from the wall. He passed the back of one hand across his lips and brought it away red. He knew that odor, then.

The girl knelt beside him with closed eyes, rapt avidity in every line of her.

When he seized her shoulder she twitched away and opened protesting eyes, but did not lift her lips from the spigot. Smith gestured violently, and with one last long draft she rose and turned a half-angry face to his, but he laid a finger on her reddened lips.

He followed her in silence past the kneeling lines again. When they reached the hall outside he swung upon her and gripped her shoulders angrily.

"What was that?" he demanded.

Her eyes slid away. She shrugged.

"What were you expecting? We feed as we must, here. You'll learn to drink without a qualm—if it does not come for you too soon."

A moment longer he stared angrily down into her evasive, strangely lovely face. Then he turned without a word and strode down the hallway through the drifting mists toward the door. He heard her bare feet pattering along behind hurriedly, but he did not look back. Not until he had come out into the glowing day and half crossed the grasslands did he relent enough to glance around. She paced at his heels with bowed head, the orange hair swinging about her face and unhappiness eloquent in every motion. The submission of her touched him suddenly, and he paused for her to catch up, smiling down half reluctantly on the bent orange head.

She lifted a tragic face to his, and there were tears in the sherry eyes. So he had no choice but to laugh and lift her up against his leather-clad breast and kiss the drooping mouth into smiles again. But he understood, now, the faintly acrid bitterness of her kisses.

"Still," he said, when they had reached the little white shrine among the trees, "there must be some other food than—that. Does no grain grow? Isn't there any wild life in the woods? Haven't the trees fruit?

She gave him another sidelong look from under dropped lashes, warily.

"No," she said. "Nothing but the grass grows here. No living thing dwells in this land but man—and it. And as for the fruit of the trees—give thanks that they bloom but once in a lifetime."

"Why?"

"Better not to speak of it," she said.

The phrase, the constant evasion, was beginning to wear on Smith's nerves. He said nothing of it then, but he turned from her and went down to the beach, dropping to the sand and striving to recapture last night's languor and peace. His hunger was curiously satisfied, even from the few swallows he had taken, and gradually the drowsy content of the day before began to flow over him in deepening waves. After all, it was a lovely land. . . .

That day drew dreamily to a close, and darkness rose in a mist from the misty lake, and he came to find in kisses that tasted of blood a certain tang that but pointed their sweetness. And in the morning he woke to the slowly brightening day, swam with the girl in the blue, tingling waters of the lake—and reluctantly went up through the woods and across the ravenous grass to the Temple, driven by a hunger greater than his repugnance. He went up with a slight nausea rising within him, and yet strangely eager. . . .

Once more the Temple rose veiled and indefinite under the glowing sky, and once more he plunged into the eternal twilight of its corridors, turned aside as one who knows the way, knelt of his own accord in the line of drinkers along the wall. . . .

With the first draft that nausea rose within him almost overwhelmingly, but when the warmth of the drink had spread through him the nausea died and nothing was left but hunger and eagerness, and he drank blindly until the girl's hand on his shoulder roused him.

A sort of intoxication had wakened within him with the burning of that hot, salt drink in his veins, and he went back across the hurrying grass in a half-daze. Through most of the pellucid day it lasted, and the slow dark was rising from the lake before clearness returned to him.

THREE

And so life resolved itself into a very simple thing. The days glowed by and the blurred darknesses came and went. Life held little any more but the bright clarity of the day and the dimness of the dark, morning journeys to drink at the Temple fountain and the bitter kisses of the girl with the orange hair. Time had ceased for him. Slow day followed slow day, and the same round of living circled over and over, and the only change—perhaps he did not see it then—was the deepening look in the girl's eyes when they rested upon him, her growing silences.

One evening just as the first faint dimness was clouding the air, and the lake smoked hazily, he happened to glance off across its surface and thought he saw through the rising mists the outline of very far mountains, and he asked curiously,

"What lies beyond the lake? Aren't those mountains over there?"

The girl turned her head quickly and her sherry-brown eyes darkened with something like dread.

"I don't know," she said. "We believe it best not to wonder what lies—beyond."

And suddenly Smith's irritation with the old evasions woke and he said violently,

"Damn your beliefs! I'm sick of that answer to every question I ask! Don't you ever wonder about anything? Are you all so thoroughly cowed by this dread of something unseen that every spark of your spirit is dead?"

She turned the sorrowful, sherry gaze upon him.

"We learn by experience," she said. "Those who wonder—those who investigate—die. We live in a land alive with danger, incomprehensible, intangible, terrible. Life is bearable only if we do not look too closely—only if we accept conditions and make the most of them. You must not ask questions if you would live.

"As for the mountains beyond, and all the unknown country that lies over the horizons—they are as unreachable as a mirage. For in a land where no food grows, where we must visit the Temple daily or starve, how could an explorer provision himself for a journey? No, we are bound here by unbreakable bonds, and we must live here until we die."

Smith shrugged. The languor of the evening was coming upon him, and the brief flare of irritation had died as swiftly as it rose.

Yet from that outburst dated the beginning of his discontent. Somehow, despite the lovely languor of the place, despite the sweet bitterness of the Temple fountains and the sweeter bitterness of the kisses that were his for the asking, he could not drive from his mind the vision of those far mountains veiled in rising haze. Unrest had wakened within him, and like some sleeper arising from a lotus-dream his mind turned more and more frequently to the desire for action, adventure, some other use for his danger-hardened body than the exigencies of sleep and food and love.

On all sides stretched the moving, restless woods, farther than the eye could reach. The grasslands rippled, and over the dim horizon the far mountains beckoned him. Even the mystery of the Temple and its endless twilight began to torment his waking moments. He dallied with the idea of exploring those hallways which the dwellers in this lotus-land avoided, of gazing from the strange windows that opened upon inexplicable blue. Surely life, even here, must hold some more fervent meaning than that he followed now. What lay beyond the wood and grasslands? What mysterious country did those mountains wall?

He began to harry his companion with questions that woke more and more often the look of dread behind her eyes, but he gained little satisfaction. She belonged to a people without history, without ambition, their lives bent wholly toward wringing from each moment its full sweetness in anticipation of the terror to come. Evasion was the keynote of their existence, perhaps with reason. Perhaps all the adventurous spirits among them had followed their curiosity into danger and death, and the only ones left were the submissive souls who led their bucolically voluptuous lives in this Elysium so shadowed with horror.

In this colored lotus-land, memories of the world he had left grew upon him more and more vividly: he remembered the hurrying crowds of the planets' capitals, the lights, the noise, the laughter. He saw space-ships cleaving the night sky with flame, flashing from world to world through the star-flecked darkness. He remembered sudden brawls in saloons and space-sailor dives when the air was alive with shouts and tumult, and heat-guns slashed their blue-hot flame and the smell of burnt flesh hung heavy. Life marched in pageant past his remembering eyes, violent, vivid, shoulder to shoulder with death. And nostalgia wrenched at him for the lovely, terribly, brawling worlds he had left behind.

Daily the unrest grew upon him. The girl made pathetic little attempts to find some sort of entertainment that would occupy his ranging mind. She led him on timid excursions into the living woods, even conquered her horror of the Temple enough to follow him on timorous tiptoe as he explored a little way down the corridors which did not arouse in her too anguished a terror. But she must have known from the first that it was hopeless.

One day as they lay on the sand watching the lake ripple bluely under a crystal sky, Smith's eyes, dwelling on the faint shadow of the mountains, half unseeingly, suddenly narrowed into a hardness as bright and pale as steel. Muscle ridged his abruptly set jaw and he sat upright with a jerk, pushing away the girl who had been leaning on his shoulder.

"I'm through," he said harshly, and rose.

"What—what is it?" The girl stumbled to her feet.

"I'm going away—anywhere. To those mountains, I think. I'm leaving now!"

"But—you wish to die, then?"

"Better the real thing than a living death like this," he said. "At least I'll have a little more excitement first."

"But, what of your food? There's nothing to keep you alive, even if you escape the greater dangers. Why, you'll dare not even lie down on the grass at night—it would eat you alive! You have no chance at all to live if you leave this grove—and me."

"If I must die, I shall," he said. "I've been thinking it over, and I've made up my mind. I could explore the Temple and so come on *it* and die. But do *something* I must, and it seems to me my best chance is in trying to reach some country where food grows before I starve. It's worth trying. I can't go on like this."

She looked at him miserably, tears brimming her sherry eyes. He opened his mouth to speak, but before he could say a word her eyes strayed beyond his shoulder and suddenly she smiled, a dreadful frozen little smile.

"You will not go," she said. "Death has come for us now."

She said it so calmly, so unafraid that he did not understand until she pointed beyond him. He turned.

The air between them and the shrine was curiously agitated. As he watched, it began to resolve itself into a nebulous blue mist that thickened and darkened . . . blurry tinges of violet and green began to blow through it vaguely, and then by imperceptible degrees a flush of rose appeared in the mist—deepened, thickened, contracted into burning scarlet that seared his eyes, pulsed alively—and he knew that it had come.

An aura of menace seemed to radiate from it, strengthening as the mist strengthened, reaching out in hunger toward his mind. He felt it as tangibly as he saw it—cloudy danger reaching out avidly for them both.

The girl was not afraid. Somehow he knew this, though he dared not turn, dared not wrench his eyes from that hypnotically pulsing scarlet. . . . She whispered very softly from behind him,

"So I die with you, I am content." And the sound of her voice freed him from the snare of the crimson pulse.

He barked a wolfish laugh, abruptly—welcoming even this diversion from the eternal idyl he had been living—and the gun leaping to his hand spurted a long blue flame so instantly that the girl behind him caught her breath. The steel-blue dazzle illumined the gathering mist lividly, passed through it without obstruction and charred the ground beyond. Smith set his teeth and swung a figure-eight pattern of flame through and through the mist, lacing it with blue heat. And when that finger of fire crossed the scarlet pulse the impact jarred the whole nebulous cloud violently, so that its outlines wavered and shrank, and the pulse of crimson sizzled under the heat—shriveled—began to fade in desperate haste.

Smith swept the ray back and forth along the redness, tracing its pattern with destruction, but it faded too swiftly for him. In little more than an instant it had paled and disembodied and vanished save for a fading flush of rose, and the blue-hot blade of his flame sizzled harmlessly through the disappearing mist to sear the ground beyond. He switched off the heat, then, and stood breathing a little unevenly as the death-cloud thinned and paled and vanished before his eyes, until no trace of it was left and the air glowed lucid and transparent once more.

The unmistakable odor of burning flesh caught at his nostrils, and he wondered for a moment if the Thing had indeed materialized a nucleus of matter, and then he saw that the smell came from the seared grass his flame had struck. The tiny, furry blades were all writhing away from the burnt spot, straining at their roots as if a wind blew them back, and from the blackened area a thick smoke rose, reeking with the odor of burnt meat. Smith, remembering their vampire habits, turned away, half nauseated.

The girl had sunk to the sand behind him, trembling now that the danger was gone.

"Is—it dead?" she breathed, when she could master her quivering mouth.

"I don't know. No way of telling. Probably not."

"What will—will you do now?"

He slid the heat-gun back into its holster and settled the belt purposefully.

"What I started out to do."

The girl scrambled up in desperate haste.

"Wait!" she gasped, "wait!" and clutched at his arm to steady herself. And he waited until the trembling had passed. Then she went on, "Come up to the Temple once more before you go."

"All right. Not a bad idea. It may be a long time before my next—meal."

And so again they crossed the fur-soft grass that bore down upon them in long ripples from every part of the meadow.

The Temple rose dim and unreal before them, and as they entered blue twilight folded them dreamily about. Smith turned by habit toward the gallery of drinkers, but the girl laid upon his arm a hand that shook a little, and murmured,

"Come this way."

He followed in growing surprise down the hallway through the drifting mists and away from the gallery he knew so well. It seemed to him that the mist thickened as they advanced, and in the uncertain light he could never be sure that the walls did not waver as nebulously as the blurring air. He felt a curious impulse to step through their intangible barriers and out of the hall into—what?

Presently steps rose under his feet, almost imperceptibly, and after a while the pressure on his arm drew him aside. They went in under a low, heavy arch of stone and entered the strangest room he had ever seen. It appeared to be seven-sided, as nearly as he could judge through the drifting mist, and curious, converging lines were graven deep in the floor.

It seemed to him that forces outside his comprehension were beating violently against the seven walls, circling like hurricanes through the dimness until the whole room was a maelstrom of invisible tumult.

When he lifted his eyes to the wall, he knew where he was. Blazoned on the dim stone, burning through the twilight like some other-dimensional fire, the scarlet pattern writhed across the wall.

The sight of it, somehow, set up a commotion in his brain, and it was with whirling head and stumbling feet that he answered to the pressure on his arm.

Dimly he realized that he stood at the very center of those strange, converging lines, feeling forces beyond reason coursing through him along paths outside any knowledge he possessed.

Then for one moment arms clasped his neck and a warm, fragrant body pressed against him, and a voice sobbed in his ear.

"If you must leave me, then go back through the Door, beloved—life without you—more dreadful even than a death like this. . . ." A kiss that stung of blood clung to his lips for an instant; then the clasp loosened and he stood alone.

Through the twilight he saw her dimly outlined against the Word. And he thought as she stood there that it was as if the invisible currents beat bodily against her, so that she swayed and wavered before him, her outlines blurring and forming again as the forces from which he was so mystically protected buffeted her mercilessly.

And he saw knowledge dawning terribly upon her face, as the meaning of the Word seeped slowly into her mind. The sweet brown face twisted hideously, the blood-red lips writhed apart to shriek a Word—in a moment of clarity he actually saw her tongue twisting incredibly to form the syllables of the unspeakable thing never meant for human lips to frame. Her mouth opened into an impossible shape . . . she gasped in the blurry mist and shrieked aloud. . . .

FOUR

Smith was walking along a twisting path so scarlet that he could not bear to look down, a path that wound and unwound and shook itself under his feet so that he stumbled at every step. He was groping through a blinding mist clouded with violet and green, and in his ears a dreadful whisper rang—the first syllable of an unutterable Word. . . . Whenever he neared the end of the path, it shook itself under him and doubled back, and weariness like a drug was sinking into his brain, and the sleepy twilight colors of the mist lulled him, and——

"He's waking up!" said an exultant voice in his ear.

Smith lifted heavy eyelids upon a room without walls—a room wherein multiple figures extending into infinity moved to and fro in countless hosts. . . .

"Smith! N. W.! Wake up!" urged that familiar voice from somewhere near.

He blinked. The myriad diminishing figures resolved themselves into the reflections of two men in a steel-walled room, bending over him. The friendly, anxious face of his partner, Yarol the Venusian, leaned above the bed.

"By Pharol, N. W.," said the well-remembered, ribald voice, "you've been asleep for a week! We thought you'd never come out of it—must have been an awful brand of whiskey!"

Smith managed a feeble grin—amazing how weak he felt—and turned an inquiring gaze upon the other figure.

"I'm a doctor," said that individual meeting the questing stare. "Your friend called me in three days ago and I've been working on you ever since. It must have been all of five or six days since you fell into this coma—have you any idea what caused it?"

Smith's pale eyes roved the room. He did not find what he sought, and though his weak murmur answered the doctor's question, the man was never to know it.

"Shawl?"

"I threw the damned thing away," confessed Yarol. "Stood it for three days and then gave up. That red pattern gave me the worst headache I've had since we found that case of black wine on the asteroid. Remember?"

"Where——?"

"Gave it to a space-rat checking out for Venus. Sorry. Did you really want it? I'll buy you another."

Smith did not answer. The weakness was rushing up about him in gray waves. He closed his eyes, hearing the echoes of that first dreadful syllable whispering through his head . . . whisper from a dream. . . . Yarol heard him murmur softly,

"And—I never even knew—her name. . . ."

THE DREAMS IN THE WITCH HOUSE

H. P. LOVECRAFT

Whether the dreams brought on the fever or the fever brought on the dreams Walter Gilman did not know. Behind everything crouched the brooding, festering horror of the ancient town, and of the mouldy, unhallowed garret gable where he wrote and studied and wrestled with figures and formulae when he was not tossing on the meagre iron bed. His ears were growing sensitive to a preternatural and intolerable degree, and he had long ago stopped the cheap mantel clock whose ticking had come to seem like a thunder of artillery. At night the subtle stirring of the black city outside, the sinister scurrying of rats in the wormy partitions, and the creaking of hidden timbers in the centuried house, were enough to give him a sense of strident pandemonium. The darkness always teemed with unexplained sound—and yet he sometimes shook with fear lest the noises he heard should subside and allow him to hear certain other, fainter, noises which he suspected were lurking behind them.

He was in the changeless, legend-haunted city of Arkham, with its clustering gambrel roofs that sway and sag over attics where witches hid from the King's men in the dark, olden days of the Province. Nor was any spot in that city more steeped in macabre memory than the gable room which harboured him—for it was this house and this room which had likewise harboured old Keziah Mason, whose flight from Salem Gaol at the last no one was ever able to explain. That was in 1692—the gaoler had gone mad and babbled of a small, white-fanged furry thing which scuttled out of Keziah's cell, and not even Cotton Mather could explain the curves and angles smeared on the grey stone walls with some red, sticky fluid.

Possibly Gilman ought not to have studied so hard. Non-Euclidean calculus and quantum physics are enough to stretch any brain; and when one mixes them with folklore, and tries to trace a strange background of multidimensional reality behind the ghoulish hints of the Gothic tales and the wild whispers of the chimney-corner, one can hardly expect to be wholly free from mental tension. Gilman came from Haverhill, but it was only after he had entered college in Arkham that he began to connect his mathematics with the fantastic legends of elder magic. Something in the air of the hoary town worked obscurely on his imagination. The professors at Miskatonic had urged him to slacken up, and had voluntarily cut down his course at several points. Moreover, they had stopped him from consulting the dubious old books on forbidden secrets that were kept under lock and key in a vault at the university library. But all these precautions came late in the day, so that Gilman had some terrible hints from the dreaded *Necronomicon* of Abdul Alhazred, the fragmentary *Book of Eibon,* and the suppressed *Unaussprechlichen Kulten* of von Junzt to correlate with his abstract formulae on the properties of space and the linkage of dimensions known and unknown.

He knew his room was in the old Witch House—that, indeed, was why he had taken it. There was much in the Essex County records about Keziah Mason's trial, and what she had admitted under pressure to the Court of Oyer and Terminer had fascinated Gilman beyond all reason. She had told Judge Hathorne of lines and curves that could be made to point out directions leading through the walls of space to other spaces beyond, and had implied that such lines and curves were frequently used at certain midnight. meetings in the dark valley of the white stone beyond Meadow Hill and on the unpeopled island in the river. She had spoken also of the Black Man, of her oath, and of her new secret name of Nahab. Then she had drawn those devices on the walls of her cell and vanished.

Gilman believed strange things about Keziah, and had felt a queer thrill on learning that her dwelling was still standing after more than 235 years. When he heard the hushed Arkham whispers about Keziah's persistent presence in the old house and the narrow streets, about the irregular human tooth-marks left on certain sleepers in that and other houses, about the childish cries heard near May-Eve, and Hallowmass, about the stench often noted in the old house's attic just after those dreaded seasons, and about the small, furry, sharp-toothed thing which haunted the mouldering structure and the town and nuzzled people curiously in the black hours before dawn, he resolved to live in the place at any cost. A room was easy to secure; for the house was unpopular, hard to rent, and long given over to cheap lodgings. Gilman could not have told what he expected to find there, but he knew he wanted to be in the building where some circumstance had more or less suddenly given a mediocre old woman of the seventeenth century an insight into mathematical depths perhaps beyond the utmost modern delvings of Planck, Heisenberg, Einstein, and de Sitter.

He studied the timber and plaster walls for traces of cryptic designs at every accessible spot where the paper had peeled, and within a week managed to get the eastern attic room where Keziah was held to have practiced her spells. It had been vacant from the first—for no one had ever been willing to stay there long—but the Polish landlord had grown wary about renting it. Yet nothing whatever happened to Gilman till about the time of the fever. No ghostly Keziah flitted through the sombre halls and chambers, no small furry thing crept into his dismal eyrie to nuzzle him, and no record of the witch's incantations rewarded his constant search. Sometimes he would take walks through shadowy tangles of unpaved musty-smelling lanes where eldritch brown houses of unknown age leaned and tottered and leered mockingly through narrow, small-paned windows. Here he knew strange things had happened once, and there was a faint suggestion behind the surface that everything of that monstrous past might not—at least in the darkest, narrowest, and most intricately crooked alleys—have utterly perished. He also rowed out twice to the ill-regarded island in the river, and made a sketch of the singular angles described by the moss-grown rows of grey standing stones whose origin was so obscure and immemorial.

Gilman's room was of good size but queerly irregular shape; the north wall slanting perceptibly inward from the outer to the inner end, while the low ceiling slanted gently downward in the same direction. Aside from an obvious rat-hole and the signs of other stopped-up ones, there was no access—nor any appearance of a former avenue of access—to the space which must have existed between the slanting wall and the straight outer wall on the house's north side, though a view from the exterior shewed where a window had been boarded up at a very remote date. The loft above the ceiling—which must have had a slanting floor—was likewise inaccessible. When Gilman climbed up a ladder to the cobwebbed level loft above the rest of the attic he found vestiges of a bygone aperture tightly and heavily covered with ancient planking and secured by the stout wooden pegs common in colonial carpentry. No amount of persuasion, however, could induce the stolid landlord to let him investigate either of these two closed spaces.

As time wore along, his absorption in the irregular wall and ceiling of his room increased; for he began to read into the odd angles a mathematical significance which seemed to offer vague clues regarding their purpose. Old Keziah, he reflected, might have had excellent reasons for living in a room with peculiar angles; for was it not through certain angles that she claimed to have gone outside the boundaries of the world of space we know? His interest gradually veered away from the unplumbed voids beyond the slanting surfaces, since it now appeared that the purpose of those surfaces concerned the side he was already on.

The touch of brain-fever and the dreams began early in February. For some time, apparently, the curious angles of Gilman's room had been having a strange, almost hypnotic effect on him; and as the bleak winter advanced he had found himself staring more and more intently at the corner where the down-slanting ceiling met the inward-slanting wall. About this period his inability to concentrate on his formal studies worried him considerably, his apprehensions about the mid-year examinations being very acute. But the exaggerated sense of hearing was scarcely less annoying. Life had become an insistent and almost unendurable cacophony, and there was that constant, terrifying impression of *other* sounds—perhaps from regions beyond life—trembling on the very brink of audibility. So far as concrete noises went, the rats in the ancient partitions were the worst. Sometimes their scratching seemed not only furtive, but deliberate. When it came from beyond the slanting north wall it was mixed with a sort of dry rattling—and when it came from the century-closed loft above the slanting ceiling Gilman always braced himself as if expecting some horror which only bided its time before descending to engulf him utterly.

The dreams were wholly beyond the pale of sanity, and Gilman felt that they must be a result, jointly, of his studies in mathematics and in folklore. He had been thinking too much about the vague regions which his formulae told him must lie beyond the three dimensions we know, and about the possibility that old Keziah Mason—guided by some influence past all conjecture—had actually found the gate to those regions. The yellowed county records containing her testimony and that of her accusers were so damnably suggestive of things beyond human experience—and the descriptions of the darting little furry object which served as her familiar were so painfully realistic despite their incredible details.

That object—no larger than a good-sized rat and quaintly called by the townspeople "Brown Jenkin"—seemed to have been the fruit of a remarkable case of sympathetic herd-delusion, for in 1692 no less than eleven persons had testified to glimpsing it. There were recent rumours, too, with a baffling and disconcerting amount of agreement. Witnesses said it had long hair and the shape of a rat, but that its sharp-toothed, bearded face was evilly human while its paws were like tiny human hands. It took messages betwixt old Keziah and the devil, and was nursed on the witch's blood—which it sucked like a vampire. Its voice was a kind of loathsome titter, and it could speak all languages. Of all the bizarre monstrosities in Gilman's dreams, nothing filled him with greater panic and nausea than this blasphemous and diminutive hybrid, whose image flitted across his vision in a form a thousandfold more hateful than anything his waking mind had deduced from the ancient records and the modern whispers.

Gilman's dreams consisted largely in plunges through limitless abysses of inexplicably coloured twilight and baffingly disordered sound; abysses whose material and gravitational properties, and whose relation to his own entity, he could not even begin to explain. He did not walk or climb, fly or swim, crawl or wriggle; yet always experienced a mode of motion partly voluntary and partly involuntary. Of his own condition he could not well judge, for sight of his arms, legs, and torso seemed always cut off by some odd disarrangement of perspective; but he felt that his physical organization and faculties were somehow marvellously transmuted and obliquely projected—though not without a certain grotesque relationship to his normal proportions and properties.

The abysses were by no means vacant, being crowded with indescribably angled masses of alien-hued substance, some of which appeared to be organic while others seemed inorganic. A few of the organic objects tended to awake vague memories in the back of his mind, though he could form no conscious idea of what they mockingly resembled or suggested. In the later dreams he began to distinguish separate categories into which the organic objects appeared to be divided, and which seemed to involve in each case a radically different species of conduct-pattern and basic motivation. Of these categories one seemed to him to include objects slightly less illogical and irrelevant in their motions than the members of the other categories.

All the objects—organic and inorganic alike—were totally beyond description or even comprehension. Gilman sometimes compared the inorganic masses to prisms, labyrinths, clusters of cubes and planes, and Cyclopean buildings; and the organic things struck him variously as groups of bubbles, octopi, centipedes, living Hindoo idols, and intricate Arabesques roused into a kind of ophidian animation. Everything he saw was unspeakably menacing and horrible; and whenever one of the organic entities appeared by its motions to be noticing him, he felt a stark, hideous fright which generally jolted him awake. Of how the organic entities moved, he could tell no more than of how he moved himself. In time he observed a further mystery—the tendency of certain entities to appear suddenly out of empty space, or to disappear totally with equal suddenness. The shrieking, roaring confusion of sound which permeated the abysses was past all analysis as to pitch, timbre, or rhythm; but seemed to be synchronous with vague visual changes in all the indefinite objects, organic and inorganic alike. Gilman had a constant sense of dread that it might rise to some unbearable degree of intensity during one or another of its obscure, relentlessly inevitable fluctuations.

But it was not in these vortices of complete alienage that he saw Brown Jenkin. That shocking little horror was reserved for certain lighter, sharper dreams which assailed him just before he dropped into the fullest depths of sleep. He would be lying in the dark fighting to keep awake when a faint lambent glow would seem to shimmer around the centuried room, shewing in a violet mist the convergence of angled planes which had seized his brain so insidiously. The horror would appear to pop out of the rat-hole in the corner and patter toward him over the sagging, wide-planked floor with evil expectancy in its tiny, bearded human face—but mercifully, this dream always melted away before the object got close enough to nuzzle him. It had hellishly long, sharp, canine teeth. Gilman tried to stop up the rat-hole every day, but each night the real tenants of the partitions would gnaw away the obstruction, whatever it might be. Once he had the landlord nail tin over it, but the next night the rats gnawed a fresh hole—in making which they pushed or dragged out into the room a curious little fragment of bone.

Gilman did not report his fever to the doctor, for he knew he could not pass the examinations if ordered to the college infirmary when every moment was needed for cramming. As it was, he failed in Calculus D and Advanced General Psychology, though not without hope of making up lost ground before the end of the term. It was in March when the fresh element entered his lighter preliminary dreaming, and the nightmare shape of Brown Jenkin began to be companioned by the nebulous blur which grew more and more to resemble a bent old woman. This addition disturbed him more than he could account for, but finally he decided that it was like an ancient crone whom he had twice actually encountered in the dark tangle of lanes near the abandoned wharves. On those occasions the evil, sardonic, and seemingly unmotivated stare of the beldame had set him almost shivering—especially the first time, when an overgrown rat darting across the shadowed mouth of a neighbouring alley had made him think irrationally of Brown Jenkin. Now, he reflected, those nervous fears were being mirrored in his disordered dreams.

That the influence of the old house was unwholesome, he could not deny; but traces of his early morbid interest still held him there. He argued that the fever alone was responsible for his nightly phantasies, and that when the touch abated he would be free from the monstrous visions. Those visions, however, were of abhorrent vividness and convincingness, and whenever he awaked he retained a vague sense of having undergone much more than he remembered. He was hideously sure that in unrecalled dreams he had talked with both Brown Jenkin and the old woman, and that they had been urging him to go somewhere with them and to meet a third being of greater potency.

Toward the end of March he began to pick up in his mathematics, though other studies bothered him increasingly. He was getting an intuitive knack for solving Riemannian equations, and astonished Professor Upham by his comprehension of fourth-dimensional and other problems which had floored all the rest of the class. One afternoon there was a discussion of possible freakish curvatures in space, and of theoretical points of approach or even contact between our part of the cosmos and various other regions as distant as the farthest stars or the trans-galactic gulfs themselves—or even as fabulously remote as the tentatively conceivable cosmic units beyond the whole Einsteinian space-time continuum. Gilman's handling of this theme filled everyone with admiration, even though some of his hypothetical illustrations caused an increase in the always plentiful gossip about his nervous and solitary eccentricity. What made the students shake their heads was his sober theory that a man might—given mathematical knowledge admittedly beyond all likelihood of human acquirement—step deliberately from the earth to any other celestial body which might lie at one of an infinity of specific points in the cosmic pattern.

Such a step, he said, would require only two stages; first, a passage out of the three-dimensional sphere we know, and second, a passage back to the three-dimensional sphere at another point, perhaps one of infinite remoteness. That this could be accomplished without loss of life was in many cases conceivable. Any being from any part of three-dimensional space could probably survive in the fourth dimension; and its survival of the second stage would depend upon what alien part of three-dimensional space it might select for its re-entry. Denizens of some planets might be able to live on certain others—even planets belonging to other galaxies, or to similar-dimensional phases of other space-time continua—though of course there must be vast numbers of mutually uninhabitable even though mathematically juxtaposed bodies or zones of space.

It was also possible that the inhabitants of a given dimensional realm could survive entry to many unknown and incomprehensible realms of additional or indefinitely multiplied dimensions—be they within or outside the given space-time continuum—and that the converse would be likewise true. This was a matter for speculation, though one could be fairly certain that the type of mutation involved in a passage from any given dimensional plane to the next higher plane would not be destructive of biological integrity as we understand it. Gilman could not be very clear about his reasons for this last assumption, but his haziness here was more than overbalanced by his clearness on other complex points. Professor Upham especially liked his demonstration of the kinship of higher mathematics to certain phases of magical lore transmitted down the ages from an ineffable antiquity—human or pre-human—whose knowledge of the cosmos and its laws was greater than ours.

Around the first of April Gilman worried considerably because his slow fever did not abate. He was also troubled by what some of his fellow-lodgers said about his sleep-walking. It seemed that he was often absent from his bed, and that the creaking of his floor at certain hours of the night was remarked by the man in the room below. This fellow also spoke of hearing the tread of shod feet in the night; but Gilman was sure he must have been mistaken in this, since shoes as well as other apparel were always precisely in place in the morning. One could develop all sorts of aural delusions in this morbid old house—for did not Gilman himself, even in daylight, now feel certain that noises other than rat-scratchings came from the black voids beyond the slanting wall and above the slanting ceiling? His pathologically sensitive ears began to listen for faint footfalls in the immemorially sealed loft overhead, and sometimes the illusion of such things was agonisingly realistic.

However, he knew that he had actually become a somnambulist; for twice at night his room had been found vacant, though with all his clothing in place. Of this he had been assured by Frank Elwood, the one fellow-student whose poverty forced him to room in this squalid and unpopular house. Elwood had been studying in the small hours and had come up for help on a differential equation, only to find Gilman absent. It had been rather presumptuous of him to open the unlocked door after knocking had failed to rouse a response, but he had needed the help very badly and thought that his host would not mind a gentle prodding awake. On neither occasion, though, had Gilman been there—and when told of the matter he wondered where he could have been wandering, barefoot and with only his night-clothes on. He resolved to investigate the matter if reports of his sleep-walking continued, and thought of sprinkling flour on the floor of the corridor to see where his footsteps might lead. The door was the only conceivable egress, for there was no possible foothold outside the narrow window.

As April advanced Gilman's fever-sharpened ears were disturbed by the whining prayers of a superstitious loomfixer named Joe Mazurewicz, who had a room on the ground floor. Mazurewicz had told long, rambling stories about the ghost of old Keziah and the furry, sharp-fanged, nuzzling thing, and had said he was so badly haunted at times that only his silver crucifix—given him for the purpose by Father Iwanicki of St. Stanislaus' Church—could bring him relief. Now he was praying because the Witches' Sabbath was drawing near. May-Eve was Walpurgis-Night, when hell's blackest evil roamed the earth and all the slaves of Satan gathered for nameless rites and deeds. It was always a very bad time in Arkham, even though the fine folks up in Miskatonic Avenue and High and Saltonstall Streets pretended to know nothing about it. There would be bad doings—and a child or two would probably be missing. Joe knew about such things, for his grandmother in the old country had heard tales from her grandmother. It was wise to pray and count one's beads at this season. For three months Keziah and Brown Jenkin had not been near Joe's room, nor near Paul Choynski's room, nor anywhere else—and it meant no good when they held off like that. They must be up to something.

Gilman dropped in at a doctor's office on the 16th of the month, and was surprised to find his temperature was not as high as he had feared. The physician questioned him sharply, and advised him to see a nerve specialist. On reflection, he was glad he had not consulted the still more inquisitive college doctor. Old Waldron, who had curtailed his activities before, would have made him take a rest—an impossible thing now that he was so close to great results in his equations. He was certainly near the boundary between the known universe and the fourth dimension, and who could say how much farther he might go?

But even as these thoughts came to him he wondered at the source of his strange confidence. Did all of this perilous sense of imminence come from the formulae on the sheets he covered day by day? The soft, stealthy, imaginary footsteps in the sealed loft above were unnerving. And now, too, there was a growing feeling that somebody was constantly persuading him to do something terrible which he could not do. How about the somnambulism? Where did he go sometimes in the night? And what was that faint suggestion of sound which once in a while seemed to trickle through the maddening confusion of identifiable sounds even in broad daylight and full wakefulness? Its rhythm did not correspond to anything on earth, unless perhaps to the cadence of one or two unmentionable Sabbat-chants, and sometimes he feared it corresponded to certain attributes of the vague shrieking or roaring in those wholly alien abysses of dream.

The dreams were meanwhile getting to be atrocious. In the lighter preliminary phase the evil old woman was now of fiendish distinctness, and Gilman knew she was the one who had frightened him in the slums. Her bent back, long nose, and shrivelled chin were unmistakable, and her shapeless brown garments were like those he remembered. The expression on her face was one of hideous malevolence and exultation, and when he awaked he could recall a croaking voice that persuaded and threatened. He must meet the Black Man, and go with them all to the throne of Azathoth at the centre of ultimate Chaos. That was what she said. He must sign in his own blood the book of Azathoth and take a new secret name now that his independent delvings had gone so far. What kept him from going with her and Brown Jenkin and the other to the throne of Chaos where the thin flutes pipe mindlessly was the fact that he had seen the name "Azathoth" in the *Necronomicon,* and knew it stood for a primal evil too horrible for description.

The old woman always appeared out of thin air near the corner where the downward slant met the inward slant. She seemed to crystallise at a point closer to the ceiling than to the floor, and every night she was a little nearer and more distinct before the dream shifted. Brown Jenkin, too, was always a little nearer at the last, and its yellowish-white fangs glistened shockingly in that unearthly violet phosphorescence. Its shrill loathsome tittering stuck more and more in Gilman's head, and he could remember in the morning how it had pronounced the words "Azathoth" and "Nyarlathotep".

In the deeper dreams everything was likewise more distinct, and Gilman felt that the twilight abysses around him were those of the fourth dimension. Those organic entities whose motions seemed least flagrantly irrelevant and unmotivated were probably projections of life-forms from our own planet, including human beings. What the others were in their own dimensional sphere or spheres he dared not try to think. Two of the less irrelevantly moving things—a rather large congeries of iridescent, prolately spheroidal bubbles and a very much smaller polyhedron of unknown colours and rapidly shifting surface angles—seemed to take notice of him and follow him about or float ahead as he changed position among the titan prisms, labyrinths, cube-and-plane clusters, and quasi-buildings; and all the while the vague shrieking and roaring waxed louder and louder, as if approaching some monstrous climax of utterly unendurable intensity.

During the night of April 19–20 the new development occurred. Gilman was half-involuntarily moving about in the twilight abysses with the bubble-mass and the small polyhedron floating ahead, when he noticed the peculiarly regular angles formed by the edges of some gigantic neighbouring prism-clusters. In another second he was out of the abyss and standing tremulously on a rocky hillside bathed in intense, diffused green light. He was barefooted and in his night-clothes, and when he tried to walk discovered that he could scarcely lift his feet. A swirling vapour hid everything but the immediate sloping terrain from sight, and he shrank from the thought of the sounds that might surge out of that vapour.

Then he saw the two shapes laboriously crawling toward him—the old woman and the little furry thing. The crone strained up to her knees and managed to cross her arms in a singular fashion, while Brown Jenkin pointed in a certain direction with a horribly anthropoid fore paw which it raised with evident difficulty. Spurred by an impulse he did not originate, Gilman dragged himself forward along a course determined by the angle of the old woman's arms and the direction of the small monstrosity's paw, and before he had shuffled three steps he was back in the twilight abysses. Geometrical shapes seethed around him, and he fell dizzily and interminably. At last he woke in his bed in the crazily angled garret of the eldritch old house.

He was good for nothing that morning, and stayed away from all his classes. Some unknown attraction was pulling his eyes in a seemingly irrelevant direction, for he could not help staring at a certain vacant spot on the floor. As the day advanced the focus of his unseeing eyes changed position, and by noon he had conquered the impulse to stare at vacancy. About two o'clock he went out for lunch, and as he threaded the narrow lanes of the city he found himself turning always to the southeast. Only an effort halted him at a cafeteria in Church Street, and after the meal he felt the unknown pull still more strongly.

He would have to consult a nerve specialist after all—perhaps there was a connexion with his somnambulism—but meanwhile he might at least try to break the morbid spell himself. Undoubtedly he could still manage to walk away from the pull; so with great resolution he headed against it and dragged himself deliberately north along Garrison Street. By the time he had reached the bridge over the Miskatonic he was in a cold perspiration, and he clutched at the iron railing as he gazed upstream at the ill-regarded island whose regular lines of ancient standing stones brooded sullenly in the afternoon sunlight.

Then he gave a start. For there was a clearly visible living figure on that desolate island, and a second glance told him it was certainly the strange old woman whose sinister aspect had worked itself so disastrously into his dreams. The tall grass near her was moving, too, as if some other living thing were crawling close to the ground. When the old woman began to turn toward him he fled precipitately off the bridge and into the shelter of the town's labyrinthine waterfront alleys. Distant though the island was, he felt that a monstrous and invincible evil could flow from the sardonic stare of that bent, ancient figure in brown.

The southeastward pull still held, and only with tremendous resolution could Gilman drag himself into the old house and up the rickety stairs. For hours he sat silent and aimless, with his eyes shifting gradually westward. About six o'clock his sharpened ears caught the whining prayers of Joe Mazurewicz two floors below, and in desperation he seized his hat and walked out into the sunset-golden streets, letting the now directly southward pull carry him where it might. An hour later darkness found him in the open fields beyond Hangman's Brook, with the glimmering spring stars shining ahead. The urge to walk was gradually changing to an urge to leap mystically into space, and suddenly he realised just where the source of the pull lay.

It was in the sky. A definite point among the stars had a claim on him and was calling him. Apparently it was a point somewhere between Hydra and Argo Navis, and he knew that he had been urged toward it ever since he had awaked soon after dawn. In the morning it had been underfoot; afternoon found it rising in the southeast, and now it was roughly south but wheeling toward the west. What was the meaning of this new thing? Was he going mad? How long would it last? Again mustering his resolution, Gilman turned and dragged himself back to the sinister old house.

Mazurewicz was waiting for him at the door, and seemed both anxious and reluctant to whisper some fresh bit of superstition. It was about the witch light. Joe had been out celebrating the night before—it was Patriots' Day in Massachusetts—and had come home after midnight. Looking up at the house from outside, he had thought at first that Gilman's window was dark; but then he had seen the faint violet glow within. He wanted to warn the gentleman about that glow, for everybody in Arkham knew it was Keziah's witch light which played near Brown Jenkin and the ghost of the old crone herself. He had not mentioned this before, but now he must tell about it because it meant that Keziah and her long-toothed familiar were haunting the young gentleman. Sometimes he and Paul Choynski and Landlord Dombrowski thought they saw that light seeping out of cracks in the sealed loft above the young gentleman's room, but they had all agreed not to talk about that. However, it would be better for the gentleman to take another room and get a crucifix from some good priest like Father Iwanicki.

As the man rambled on Gilman felt a nameless panic clutch at his throat. He knew that Joe must have been half drunk when he came home the night before, yet this mention of a violet light in the garret window was of frightful import. It was a lambent glow of this sort which always played about the old woman and the small furry thing in those lighter, sharper dreams which prefaced his plunge into unknown abysses, and the thought that a wakeful second person could see the dream-luminance was utterly beyond sane harbourage. Yet where had the fellow got such an odd notion? Had he himself talked as well as walked around the house in his sleep? No, Joe said, he had not—but he must check up on this. Perhaps Frank Elwood could tell him something, though he hated to ask.

Fever—wild dreams—somnambulism—illusions of sounds—a pull toward a point in the sky—and now a suspicion of insane sleep-talking! He must stop studying, see a nerve specialist, and take himself in hand. When he climbed to the second story he paused at Elwood's door but saw that the other youth was out. Reluctantly he continued up to his garret room and sat down in the dark. His gaze was still pulled to the southwest, but he also found himself listening intently for some sound in the closed loft above, and half imagining that an evil violet light seeped down through an infinitesimal crack in the low, slanting ceiling.

That night as Gilman slept the violet light broke upon him with heightened intensity, and the old witch and small furry thing—getting closer than ever before—mocked him with inhuman squeals and devilish gestures. He was glad to sink into the vaguely roaring twilight abysses, though the pursuit of that iridescent bubble-congeries and that kaleidoscopic little polyhedron was menacing and irritating. Then came the shift as vast converging planes of a slippery-looking substance loomed above and below him—a shift which ended in a flash of delirium and a blaze of unknown, alien light in which yellow, carmine, and indigo were madly and inextricably blended.

He was half lying on a high, fantastically balustraded terrace above a boundless jungle of outlandish, incredible peaks, balanced planes, domes, minarets, horizontal discs poised on pinnacles, and numberless forms of still greater wildness—some of stone and some of metal—which glittered gorgeously in the mixed, almost blistering glare from a polychromatic sky. Looking upward he saw three stupendous discs of flame, each of a different hue, and at a different height above an infinitely distant curving horizon of low mountains. Behind him tiers of higher terraces towered aloft as far as he could see. The city below stretched away to the limits of vision, and he hoped that no sound would well up from it.

The pavement from which he easily raised himself was of a veined, polished stone beyond his power to identify, and the tiles were cut in bizarre-angled shapes which struck him as less asymmetrical than based on some unearthly symmetry whose laws he could not comprehend. The balustrade was chest-high, delicate, and fantastically wrought, while along the rail were ranged at short intervals little figures of grotesque design and exquisite workmanship. They, like the whole balustrade, seemed to be made of some sort of shining metal whose colour could not be guessed in this chaos of mixed effulgences; and their nature utterly defied conjecture. They represented some ridged, barrel-shaped object with thin horizontal arms radiating spoke-like from a central ring, and with vertical knobs or bulbs projecting from the head and base of the barrel. Each of these knobs was the hub of a system of five long, flat, triangularly tapering arms arranged around it like the arms of a starfish—nearly horizontal, but curving slightly away from the central barrel. The base of the bottom knob was fused to the long railing with so delicate a point of contact that several figures had been broken off and were missing. The figures were about four and a half inches in height, while the spiky arms gave them a maximum diameter of about two and a half inches.

When Gilman stood up the tiles felt hot to his bare feet. He was wholly alone, and his first act was to walk to the balustrade and look dizzily down at the endless, Cyclopean city almost two thousand feet below. As he listened he thought a rhythmic confusion of faint musical pipings covering a wide tonal range welled up from the narrow streets beneath, and he wished he might discern the denizens of the place. The sight turned him giddy after a while, so that he would have fallen to the pavement had he not clutched instinctively at the lustrous balustrade. His right hand fell on one of the projecting figures, the touch seeming to steady him slightly. It was too much, however, for the exotic delicacy of the metal-work, and the spiky figure snapped off under his grasp. Still half-dazed, he continued to clutch it as his other hand seized a vacant space on the smooth railing.

But now his oversensitive ears caught something behind him, and he looked back across the level terrace. Approaching him softly though without apparent furtiveness were five figures, two of which were the sinister old woman and the fanged, furry little animal. The other three were what sent him unconscious—for they were living entities about eight feet high, shaped precisely like the spiky images on the balustrade, and propelling themselves by a spider-like wriggling of their lower set of starfish-arms.

Gilman awaked in his bed, drenched by a cold perspiration and with a smarting sensation in his face, hands, and feet. Springing to the floor, he washed and dressed in frantic haste, as if it were necessary for him to get out of the house as quickly as possible. He did not know where he wished to go, but felt that once more he would have to sacrifice his classes. The odd pull toward that spot in the sky between Hydra and Argo had abated, but another of even greater strength had taken its place. Now he felt that he must go north—infinitely north. He dreaded to cross the bridge that gave a view of the desolate island in the Miskatonic, so went over the Peabody Avenue bridge. Very often he stumbled, for his eyes and ears were chained to an extremely lofty point in the blank blue sky.

After about an hour he got himself under better control, and saw that he was far from the city. All around him stretched the bleak emptiness of salt marshes, while the narrow road ahead led to Innsmouth—that ancient, half-deserted town which Arkham people were so curiously unwilling to visit. Though the northward pull had not diminished, he resisted it as he had resisted the other pull, and finally found that he could almost balance the one against the other. Plodding back to town and getting some coffee at a soda fountain, he dragged himself into the public library and browsed aimlessly among the lighter magazines. Once he met some friends who remarked how oddly sunburned he looked, but he did not tell them of his walk. At three o'clock he took some lunch at a restaurant, noting meanwhile that the pull had either lessened or divided itself. After that he killed the time at a cheap cinema show, seeing the inane performance over and over again without paying any attention to it.

About nine at night he drifted homeward and stumbled into the ancient house. Joe Mazurewicz was whining unintelligible prayers, and Gilman hastened up to his own garret chamber without pausing to see if Elwood was in. It was when he turned on the feeble electric light that the shock came. At once he saw there was something on the table which did not belong there, and a second look left no room for doubt. Lying on its side—for it could not stand up alone—was the exotic spiky figure which in his monstrous dream he had broken off the fantastic balustrade. No detail was missing. The ridged, barrel-shaped centre, the thin, radiating arms, the knobs at each end, and the flat, slightly outward-curving starfish-arms spreading from those knobs—all were there. In the electric light the colour seemed to be a kind of iridescent grey veined with green, and Gilman could see amidst his horror and bewilderment that one of the knobs ended in a jagged break corresponding to its former point of attachment to the dream-railing.

Only his tendency toward a dazed stupor prevented him from screaming aloud. This fusion of dream and reality was too much to bear. Still dazed, he clutched at the spiky thing and staggered downstairs to Landlord Dombrowski's quarters. The whining prayers of the superstitious loomfixer were still sounding through the mouldy halls, but Gilman did not mind them now. The landlord was in, and greeted him pleasantly. No, he had not seen that thing before and did not know anything about it. But his wife had said she found a funny tin thing in one of the beds when she fixed the rooms at noon, and maybe that was it. Dombrowski called her, and she waddled in. Yes, that was the thing. She had found it in the young gentleman's bed—on the side next the wall. It had looked very queer to her, but of course the young gentleman had lots of queer things in his room—books and curios and pictures and markings on paper. She certainly knew nothing about it.

So Gilman climbed upstairs again in a mental turmoil, convinced that he was either still dreaming or that his somnambulism had run to incredible extremes and led him to depredations in unknown places. Where had he got this outré thing? He did not recall seeing it in any museum in Arkham. It must have been somewhere, though; and the sight of it as he snatched it in his sleep must have caused the odd dream-picture of the balustraded terrace. Next day he would make some very guarded inquiries—and perhaps see the nerve specialist.

Meanwhile he would try to keep track of his somnambulism. As he went upstairs and across the garret hall he sprinkled about some flour which he had borrowed—with a frank admission as to its purpose—from the landlord. He had stopped at Elwood's door on the way, but had found all dark within. Entering his room, he placed the spiky thing on the table, and lay down in complete mental and physical exhaustion without pausing to undress. From the closed loft above the slanting ceiling he thought he heard a faint scratching and padding, but he was too disorganised even to mind it. That cryptical pull from the north was getting very strong again, though it seemed now to come from a lower place in the sky.

In the dazzling violet light of dream the old woman and the fanged, furry thing came again and with a greater distinctness than on any former occasion. This time they actually reached him, and he felt the crone's withered claws clutching at him. He was pulled out of bed and into empty space, and for a moment he heard a rhythmic roaring and saw the twilight amorphousness of the vague abysses seething around him. But that moment was very brief, for presently he was in a crude, windowless little space with rough beams and planks rising to a peak just above his head, and with a curious slanting floor underfoot. Propped level on that floor were low cases full of books of every degree of antiquity and disintegration, and in the centre were a table and bench, both apparently fastened in place. Small objects of unknown shape and nature were ranged on the tops of the cases, and in the flaming violet light. Gilman thought he saw a counterpart of the spiky image which had puzzled him so horribly. On the left the floor fell abruptly away, leaving a black triangular gulf out of which, after a second's dry rattling, there presently climbed the hateful little furry thing with the yellow fangs and bearded human face.

The evilly grinning beldame still clutched him, and beyond the table stood a figure he had never seen before—a tall, lean man of dead black colouration but without the slightest sign of negroid features; wholly devoid of either hair or beard, and wearing as his only garment a shapeless robe of some heavy black fabric. His feet were indistinguishable because of the table and bench, but he must have been shod, since there was a clicking whenever he changed position. The man did not speak, and bore no trace of expression on his small, regular features. He merely pointed to a book of prodigious size which lay open on the table, while the beldame thrust a huge grey quill into Gilman's right hand. Over everything was a pall of intensely maddening fear, and the climax was reached when the furry thing ran up the dreamer's clothing to his shoulders and then down his left arm, finally biting him sharply in the wrist just below his cuff. As the blood spurted from this wound Gilman lapsed into a faint.

He awaked on the morning of the 22nd with a pain in his left wrist, and saw that his cuff was brown with dried blood. His recollections were very confused, but the scene with the black man in the unknown space stood out vividly. The rats must have bitten him as he slept, giving rise to the climax of that frightful dream. Opening the door, he saw that the flour on the corridor floor was undisturbed except for the huge prints of the loutish fellow who roomed at the other end of the garret. So he had not been sleep-walking this time. But something would have to be done about those rats. He would speak to the landlord about them. Again he tried to stop up the hole at the base of the slanting wall, wedging in a candlestick which seemed of about the right size. His ears were ringing horribly, as if with the residual echoes of some horrible noise heard in dreams.

As he bathed and changed clothes he tried to recall what he had dreamed after the scene in the violet-litten space, but nothing definite would crystallise in his mind. That scene itself must have corresponded to the sealed loft overhead, which had begun to attack his imagination so violently, but later impressions were faint and hazy. There were suggestions of the vague, twilight abysses, and of still vaster, blacker abysses beyond them—abysses in which all fixed suggestions of form were absent. He had been taken there by the bubble-congeries and the little polyhedron which always dogged him; but they, like himself, had changed to wisps of milky, barely luminous mist in this farther void of ultimate blackness. Something else had gone on ahead—a larger wisp which now and then condensed into nameless approximations of form—and he thought that their progress had not been in a straight line, but rather along the alien curves and spirals of some ethereal vortex which obeyed laws unknown to the physics and mathematics of any conceivable cosmos. Eventually there had been a hint of vast, leaping shadows, of a monstrous, half-acoustic pulsing, and of the thin, monotonous piping of an unseen flute—but that was all. Gilman decided he had picked up that last conception from what he had read in the *Necronomicon* about the mindless entity Azathoth, which rules all time and space from a curiously environed black throne at the centre of Chaos.

When the blood was washed away the wrist wound proved very slight, and Gilman puzzled over the location of the two tiny punctures. It occurred to him that there was no blood on the bedspread where he had lain—which was very curious in view of the amount on his skin and cuff. Had he been sleep-walking within his room, and had the rat bitten him as he sat in some chair or paused in some less rational position? He looked in every corner for brownish drops or stains, but did not find any. He had better, he thought, sprinkle flour within the room as well as outside the door—though after all no further proof of his sleep-walking was needed. He knew he did walk—and the thing to do now was to stop it. He must ask Frank Elwood for help. This morning the strange pulls from space seemed lessened, though they were replaced by another sensation even more inexplicable. It was a vague, insistent impulse to fly away from his present situation, but held not a hint of the specific direction in which he wished to fly. As he picked up the strange spiky image on the table he thought the older northward pull grew a trifle stronger; but even so, it was wholly overruled by the newer and more bewildering urge.

He took the spiky image down to Elwood's room, steeling himself against the whines of the loomfixer which welled up from the ground floor. Elwood was in, thank heaven, and appeared to be stirring about. There was time for a little conversation before leaving for breakfast and college, so Gilman hurriedly poured forth an account of his recent dreams and fears. His host was very sympathetic, and agreed that something ought to be done. He was shocked by his guest's drawn, haggard aspect, and noticed the queer, abnormal-looking sunburn which others had remarked during the past week. There was not much, though, that he could say. He had not seen Gilman on any sleep-walking expedition, and had no idea what the curious image could be. He had, though, heard the French-Canadian who lodged just under Gilman talking to Mazurewicz one evening. They were telling each other how badly they dreaded the coming of Walpurgis-Night, now only a few days off; and were exchanging pitying comments about the poor, doomed young gentleman. Desrochers, the fellow under Gilman's room, had spoken of nocturnal footsteps both shod and unshod, and of the violet light he saw one night when he had stolen fearfully up to peer through Gilman's keyhole. He had not dared to peer, he told Mazurewicz, after he had glimpsed that light through the cracks around the door. There had been soft talking, too— and as he began to describe it his voice had sunk to an inaudible whisper.

Elwood could not imagine what had set these superstitious creatures gossiping, but supposed their imaginations had been roused by Gilman's late hours and somnolent walking and talking on the one hand, and by the nearness of traditionally feared May-Eve on the other hand. That Gilman talked in his sleep was plain, and it was obviously from Desrochers' keyhole-listenings that the delusive notion of the violet dream-light had got abroad. These simple people were quick to imagine they had seen any odd thing they had heard about. As for a plan of action—Gilman had better move down to Elwood's room and avoid sleeping alone. Elwood would, if awake, rouse him whenever he began to talk or rise in his sleep. Very soon, too, he must see the specialist. Meanwhile they would take the spiky image around to the various museums and to certain professors; seeking identification and stating that it had been found in a public rubbish-can. Also, Dombrowski must attend to the poisoning of those rats in the walls.

Braced up by Elwood's companionship, Gilman attended classes that day. Strange urges still tugged at him, but he could sidetrack them with considerable success. During a free period he shewed the queer image to several professors, all of whom were intensely interested, though none of them could shed any light upon its nature or origin. That night he slept on a couch which Elwood had had the landlord bring to the second-story room, and for the first time in weeks was wholly free from disquieting dreams. But the feverishness still hung on, and the whines of the loomfixer were an unnerving influence.

During the next few days Gilman enjoyed an almost perfect immunity from morbid manifestations. He had, Elwood said, shewed no tendency to talk or rise in his sleep; and meanwhile the landlord was putting rat-poison everywhere. The only disturbing element was the talk among the superstitious foreigners, whose imaginations had become highly excited. Mazurewicz was always trying to make him get a crucifix, and finally forced one upon him which he said had been blessed by the good Father Iwanicki. Desrochers, too, had something to say—in fact, he insisted that cautious steps had sounded in the now vacant room above him on the first and second nights of Gilman's absence from it. Paul Choynski thought he heard sounds in the halls and on the stairs at night, and claimed that his door had been softly tried, while Mrs. Dombrowski vowed she had seen Brown Jenkin for the first time since All-Hallows. But such naive reports could mean very little, and Gilman let the cheap metal crucifix hang idly from a knob on his host's dresser.

For three days Gilman and Elwood canvassed the local museums in an effort to identify the strange spiky image, but always without success. In every quarter, however, interest was intense; for the utter alienage of the thing was a tremendous challenge to scientific curiosity. One of the small radiating arms was broken off and subjected to chemical analysis, and the result is still talked about in college circles. Professor Ellery found platinum, iron, and tellurium in the strange alloy; but mixed with these were at least three other apparent elements of high atomic weight which chemistry was absolutely powerless to classify. Not only did they fail to correspond with any known element, but they did not even fit the vacant places reserved for probable elements in the periodic system. The mystery remains unsolved to this day, though the image is on exhibition at the museum of Miskatonic University.

On the morning of April 27 a fresh rat-hole appeared in the room where Gilman was a guest, but Dombrowski tinned it up during the day. The poison was not having much effect, for scratchings and scurryings in the walls were virtually undiminished. Elwood was out late that night, and Gilman waited up for him. He did not wish to go to sleep in a room alone— especially since he thought he had glimpsed in the evening twilight the repellent old woman whose image had become so horribly transferred to his dreams. He wondered who she was, and what had been near her rattling the tin can in a rubbish-heap at the mouth of a squalid courtyard. The crone had seemed to notice him and leer evilly at him—though perhaps this was merely his imagination.

The next day both youths felt very tired, and knew they would sleep like logs when night came. In the evening they drowsily discussed the mathematical studies which had so completely and perhaps harmfully engrossed Gilman, and speculated about the linkage with ancient magic and folklore which seemed so darkly probable. They spoke of old Keziah Mason, and Elwood agreed that Gilman had good scientific grounds for thinking she might have stumbled on strange and significant information. The hidden cults to which these witches belonged often guarded and handed down surprising secrets from elder, forgotten aeons; and it was by no means impossible that Keziah had actually mastered the art of passing through dimensional gates. Tradition emphasises the uselessness of material barriers in halting a witch's motions; and who can say what underlies the old tales of broomstick rides through the night?

Whether a modern student could ever gain similar powers from mathematical research alone, was still to be seen. Success, Gilman added, might lead to dangerous and unthinkable situations; for who could foretell the conditions pervading an adjacent but normally inaccessible dimension? On the other hand, the picturesque possibilities were enormous. Time could not exist in certain belts of space, and by entering and remaining in such a belt one might preserve one's life and age indefinitely; never suffering organic metabolism or deterioration except for slight amounts incurred during visits to one's own or similar planes. One might, for example, pass into a timeless dimension and emerge at some remote period of the earth's history as young as before.

Whether anybody had ever managed to do this, one could hardly conjecture with any degree of authority. Old legends are hazy and ambiguous, and in historic times all attempts at crossing forbidden gaps seem complicated by strange and terrible alliances with beings and messengers from outside. There was the immemorial figure of the deputy or messenger of hidden and terrible powers—the "Black Man" of the witch-cult, and the "Nyarlathotep" of the *Necronomicon*. There was, too, the baffling problem of the lesser messengers or intermediaries—the quasi-animals and queer hybrids which legend depicts as witches' familiars. As Gilman and Elwood retired, too sleepy to argue further, they heard Joe Mazurewicz reel into the house half-drunk, and shuddered at the desperate wildness of his whining prayers.

That night Gilman saw the violet light again. In his dream he had heard a scratching and gnawing in the partitions, and thought that someone fumbled clumsily at the latch. Then he saw the old woman and the small furry thing advancing toward him over the carpeted floor. The beldame's face was alight with inhuman exultation, and the little yellow-toothed morbidity tittered mockingly as it pointed at the heavily sleeping form of Elwood on the other couch across the room. A paralysis of fear stifled all attempts to cry out. As once before, the hideous crone seized Gilman by the shoulders, yanking him out of bed and into empty space. Again the infinitude of the shrieking twilight abysses flashed past him, but in another second he thought he was in a dark, muddy, unknown alley of foetid odours, with the rotting walls of ancient houses towering up on every hand.

Ahead was the robed black man he had seen in the peaked space in the other dream, while from a lesser distance the old woman was beckoning and grimacing imperiously. Brown Jenkin was rubbing itself with a kind of affectionate playfulness around the ankles of the black man, which the deep mud largely concealed. There was a dark open doorway on the right, to which the black man silently pointed. Into this the grimacing crone started, dragging Gilman after her by his pajama sleeve. There were evil-smelling staircases which creaked ominously, and on which the old woman seemed to radiate a faint violet light; and finally a door leading off a landing. The crone fumbled with the latch and pushed the door open, motioning to Gilman to wait and disappearing inside the black aperture.

The youth's oversensitive ears caught a hideous strangled cry, and presently the beldame came out of the room bearing a small, senseless form which she thrust at the dreamer as if ordering him to carry it. The sight of this form, and the expression on its face, broke the spell. Still too dazed to cry out, he plunged recklessly down the noisome staircase and into the mud outside; halting only when seized and choked by the waiting black man. As consciousness departed he heard the faint, shrill tittering of the fanged, rat-like abnormality.

On the morning of the 29th Gilman awaked into a maelstrom of horror. The instant he opened his eyes he knew something was terribly wrong, for he was back in his old garret room with the slanting wall and ceiling, sprawled on the now unmade bed. His throat was aching inexplicably, and as he struggled to a sitting posture he saw with growing fright that his feet and pajama-bottoms were brown with caked mud. For the moment his recollections were hopelessly hazy, but he knew at least that he must have been sleepwalking. Elwood had been lost too deeply in slumber to hear and stop him. On the floor were confused muddy prints, but oddly enough they did not extend all the way to the door. The more Gilman looked at them, the more peculiar they seemed; for in addition to those he could recognise as his there were some smaller, almost round markings—such as the legs of a large chair or table might make, except that most of them tended to be divided into halves. There were also some curious muddy rat-tracks leading out of a fresh hole and back into it again. Utter bewilderment and the fear of madness racked Gilman as he staggered to the door and saw that there were no muddy prints outside. The more he remembered of his hideous dream the more terrified he felt, and it added to his desperation to hear Joe Mazurewicz chanting mournfully two floors below.

Descending to Elwood's room he roused his still-sleeping host and began telling of how he had found himself, but Elwood could form no idea of what might really have happened. Where Gilman could have been, how he got back to his room without making tracks in the hall, and how the muddy, furniture-like prints came to be mixed with his in the garret chamber, were wholly beyond conjecture. Then there were those dark, livid marks on his throat, as if he had tried to strangle himself. He put his hands up to them, but found that they did not even approximately fit. While they were talking Desrochers dropped in to say that he had heard a terrific clattering overhead in the dark small hours. No, there had been no one on the stairs after midnight—though just before midnight he had heard faint footfalls in the garret, and cautiously descending steps he did not like. It was, he added, a very bad time of year for Arkham. The young gentleman had better be sure to wear the crucifix Joe Mazurewicz had given him. Even the daytime was not safe, for after dawn there had been strange sounds in the house—especially a thin, childish wail hastily choked off.

Gilman mechanically attended classes that morning, but was wholly unable to fix his mind on his studies. A mood of hideous apprehension and expectancy had seized him, and he seemed to be awaiting the fall of some annihilating blow. At noon he lunched at the University Spa, picking up a paper from the next seat as he waited for dessert. But he never ate that dessert; for an item on the paper's first page left him limp, wild-eyed, and able only to pay his check and stagger back to Elwood's room.

There had been a strange kidnapping the night before in Orne's Gangway, and the two-year-old child of a clod-like laundry worker named Anastasia Wolejko had completely vanished from sight. The mother, it appeared, had feared the event for some time; but the reasons she assigned for her fear were so grotesque that no one took them seriously. She had, she said, seen Brown Jenkin about the place now and then ever since early in March, and knew from its grimaces and titterings that little Ladislas must be marked for sacrifice at the awful Sabbat on Walpurgis-Night. She had asked her neighbour Mary Czanek to sleep in the room and try to protect the child, but Mary had not dared. She could not tell the police, for they never believed such things. Children had been taken that way every year ever since she could remember. And her friend Pete Stowacki would not help because he wanted the child out of the way anyhow.

But what threw Gilman into a cold perspiration was the report of a pair of revellers who had been walking past the mouth of the gangway just after midnight. They admitted they had been drunk, but both vowed they had seen a crazily dressed trio furtively entering the dark passageway. There had, they said, been a huge robed negro, a little old woman in rags, and a young white man in his night-clothes. The old woman had been dragging the youth, while around the feet of the negro a tame rat was rubbing and weaving in the brown mud.

Gilman sat in a daze all the afternoon, and Elwood—who had meanwhile seen the papers and formed terrible conjectures from them—found him thus when he came home. This time neither could doubt but that something hideously serious was closing in around them. Between the phantasms of nightmare and the realities of the objective world a monstrous and unthinkable relationship was crystallising, and only stupendous vigilance could avert still more direful developments. Gilman must see a specialist sooner or later, but not just now, when all the papers were full of this kidnapping business.

Just what had really happened was maddeningly obscure, and for a moment both Gilman and Elwood exchanged whispered theories of the wildest kind. Had Gilman unconsciously succeeded better than he knew in his studies of space and its dimensions? Had he actually slipped outside our sphere to points unguessed and unimaginable? Where—if anywhere—had he been on those nights of daemoniac alienage? The roaring twilight abysses—the green hillside—the blistering terrace—the pulls from the stars—the ultimate black vortex—the black man—the muddy alley and the stairs—the old witch and the fanged, furry horror—the bubble-congeries and the little polyhedron— the strange sunburn—the wrist wound—the unexplained image—the muddy feet—the throat-marks—the tales and fears of the superstitious foreigners— what did all this mean? To what extent could the laws of sanity apply to such a case?

There was no sleep for either of them that night, but next day they both cut classes and drowsed. This was April 30th, and with the dusk would come the hellish Sabbat-time which all the foreigners and the superstitious old folk feared. Mazurewicz came home at six o'clock and said people at the mill were whispering that the Walpurgis-revels would be held in the dark ravine beyond Meadow Hill where the old white stone stands in a place queerly void of all plant-life. Some of them had even told the police and advised them to look there for the missing Wolejko child, but they did not believe anything would be done. Joe insisted that the poor young gentleman wear his nickel-chained crucifix, and Gilman put it on and dropped it inside his shirt to humour the fellow.

Late at night the two youths sat drowsing in their chairs, lulled by the rhythmical praying of the loomfixer on the floor below. Gilman listened as he nodded, his preternaturally sharpened hearing seeming to strain for some subtle, dreaded murmur beyond the noises in the ancient house. Unwholesome recollections of things in the *Necronomicon* and the Black Book welled up, and he found himself swaying to infandous rhythms said to pertain to the blackest ceremonies of the Sabbat and to have an origin outside the time and space we comprehend.

Presently he realised what he was listening for—the hellish chant of the celebrants in the distant black valley. How did he know so much about what they expected? How did he know the time when Nahab and her acolyte were due to bear the brimming bowl which would follow the black cock and the black goat? He saw that Elwood had dropped asleep, and tried to call out and waken him. Something, however, closed his throat. He was not his own master. Had he signed the black man's book after all?

Then his fevered, abnormal hearing caught the distant, wind-borne notes. Over miles of hill and field and alley they came, but he recognised them none the less. The fires must be lit, and the dancers must be starting in. How could he keep himself from going? What was it that had enmeshed him? Mathematics—folklore—the house—old Keziah—Brown Jenkin . . . and now he saw that there was a fresh rat-hole in the wall near his couch. Above the distant chanting and the nearer praying of Joe Mazurewicz came another sound—a stealthy, determined scratching in the partitions. He hoped the electric lights would not go out. Then he saw the fanged, bearded little face in the rat-hole —the accursed little face which he at last realised bore such a shocking, mocking resemblance to old Keziah's—and heard the faint fumbling at the door.

The screaming twilight abysses flashed before him, and he felt himself helpless in the formless grasp of the iridescent bubble-congeries. Ahead raced the small, kaleidoscopic polyhedron, and all through the churning void there was a heightening and acceleration of the vague tonal pattern which seemed to foreshadow some unutterable and unendurable climax. He seemed to know what was coming—the monstrous burst of Walpurgis-rhythm in whose cosmic timbre would be concentrated all the primal, ultimate space-time seethings which lie behind the massed spheres of matter and sometimes break forth in measured reverberations that penetrate faintly to every layer of entity and give hideous significance throughout the worlds to certain dreaded periods.

But all this vanished in a second. He was again in the cramped, violet-litten peaked space with the slanting floor, the low cases of ancient books, the bench and table, the queer objects, and the triangular gulf at one side. On the table lay a small white figure—an infant boy, unclothed and unconscious— while on the other side stood the monstrous, leering old woman with a gleaming, grotesque-hafted knife in her right hand, and a queerly proportioned pale metal bowl covered with curiously chased designs and having delicate lateral handles in her left. She was intoning some croaking ritual in a language which Gilman could not understand, but which seemed like something guardedly quoted in the *Necronomicon*.

As the scene grew clear he saw the ancient crone bend forward and extend the empty bowl across the table—and unable to control his own motions, he reached far forward and took it in both hands, noticing as he did so its comparative lightness. At the same moment the disgusting form of Brown Jenkin scrambled up over the brink of the triangular black gulf on his left. The crone now motioned him to hold the bowl in a certain position while she raised the huge, grotesque knife above the small white victim as high as her right hand could reach. The fanged, furry thing began tittering a continuation of the unknown ritual, while the witch croaked loathsome responses. Gilman felt a gnawing, poignant abhorrence shoot through his mental and emotional paralysis, and the light metal bowl shook in his grasp. A second later the downward motion of the knife broke the spell completely, and he dropped the bowl with a resounding bell-like clangour while his hands darted out frantically to stop the monstrous deed.

In an instant he had edged up the slanting floor around the end of the table and wrenched the knife from the old woman's claws; sending it clattering over the brink of the narrow triangular gulf. In another instant, however, matters were reversed; for those murderous claws had locked themselves tightly around his own throat, while the wrinkled face was twisted with insane fury. He felt the chain of the cheap crucifix grinding into his neck, and in his peril wondered how the sight of the object itself would affect the evil creature. Her strength was altogether superhuman, but as she continued her choking he reached feebly in his shirt and drew out the metal symbol, snapping the chain and pulling it free.

At sight of the device the witch seemed struck with panic, and her grip relaxed long enough to give Gilman a chance to break it entirely. He pulled the steel-like claws from his neck, and would have dragged the beldame over the edge of the gulf had not the claws received a fresh access of strength and closed in again. This time he resolved to reply in kind, and his own hands reached out for the creature's throat. Before she saw what he was doing he had the chain of the crucifix twisted about her neck, and a moment later he had tightened it enough to cut off her breath. During her last struggle he felt something bite at his ankle, and saw that Brown Jenkin had come to her aid. With one savage kick he sent the morbidity over the edge of the gulf and heard it whimper on some level far below.

Whether he had killed the ancient crone he did not know, but he let her rest on the floor where she had fallen. Then, as he turned away, he saw on the table a sight which nearly snapped the last thread of his reason. Brown Jenkin, tough of sinew and with four tiny hands of daemoniac dexterity, had been busy while the witch was throttling him, and his efforts had been in vain. What he had prevented the knife from doing to the victim's chest, the yellow fangs of the furry blasphemy had done to a wrist—and the bowl so lately on the floor stood full beside the small lifeless body.

In his dream-delirium Gilman heard the hellish, alien-rhythmed chant of the Sabbat coming from an infinite distance, and knew the black man must be there. Confused memories mixed themselves with his mathematics, and he believed his subconscious mind held the *angles* which he needed to guide him back to the normal world—alone and unaided for the first time. He felt sure he was in the immemorially sealed loft above his own room, but whether he could ever escape through the slanting floor or the long-stopped egress he doubted greatly. Besides, would not an escape from a dream-loft bring him merely into a dream-house—an abnormal projection of the actual place he sought? He was wholly bewildered as to the relation betwixt dream and reality in all his experiences.

The passage through the vague abysses would be frightful, for the Walpurgis-rhythm would be vibrating, and at last he would have to hear that hitherto veiled cosmic pulsing which he so mortally dreaded. Even now he could detect a low, monstrous shaking whose tempo he suspected all too well. At Sabbat-time it always mounted and reached through to the worlds to summon the initiate to nameless rites. Half the chants of the Sabbat were patterned on this faintly overheard pulsing which no earthly ear could endure in its unveiled spatial fulness. Gilman wondered, too, whether he could trust his instinct to take him back to the right part of space. How could he be sure he would not land on that green-litten hillside of a far planet, on the tessellated terrace above the city of tentacled monsters somewhere beyond the galaxy, or in the spiral black vortices of that ultimate void of Chaos wherein reigns the mindless daemon-sultan Azathoth?

Just before he made the plunge the violet light went out and left him in utter blackness. The witch—old Keziah—Nahab—that must have meant her death. And mixed with the distant chant of the Sabbat and the whimpers of Brown Jenkin in the gulf below he thought he heard another and wilder whine from unknown depths. Joe Mazurewicz—the prayers against the Crawling Chaos now turning to an inexplicably triumphant shriek—worlds of sardonic actuality impinging on vortices of febrile dream—Iä! Shub-Niggurath! The Goat with a Thousand Young. . . .

They found Gilman on the floor of his queerly angled old garret room long before dawn, for the terrible cry had brought Desrochers and Choynski and Dombrowski and Mazurewicz at once, and had even wakened the soundly sleeping Elwood in his chair. He was alive, and with open, staring eyes, but seemed largely unconscious. On his throat were the marks of murderous hands, and on his left ankle was a distressing rat-bite. His clothing was badly rumpled, and Joe's crucifix was missing. Elwood trembled, afraid even to speculate on what new form his friend's sleep-walking had taken. Mazurewicz seemed half-dazed because of a "sign" he said he had had in response to his prayers, and he crossed himself frantically when the squealing and whimpering of a rat sounded from beyond the slanting partition.

When the dreamer was settled on his couch in Elwood's room they sent for Dr. Malkowski—a local practitioner who would repeat no tales where they might prove embarrassing—and he gave Gilman two hypodermic injections which caused him to relax in something like natural drowsiness. During the day the patient regained consciousness at times and whispered his newest dream disjointedly to Elwood. It was a painful process, and at its very start brought out a fresh and disconcerting fact.

Gilman—whose ears had so lately possessed an abnormal sensitiveness— was now stone deaf. Dr. Malkowski, summoned again in haste, told Elwood that both ear-drums were ruptured, as if by the impact of some stupendous sound intense beyond all human conception or endurance. How such a sound could have been heard in the last few hours without arousing all the Miskatonic Valley was more than the honest physician could say.

Elwood wrote his part of the colloquy on paper, so that a fairly easy communication was maintained. Neither knew what to make of the whole chaotic business, and decided it would be better if they thought as little as possible about it. Both, though, agreed that they must leave this ancient and accursed house as soon as it could be arranged. Evening papers spoke of a police raid on some curious revellers in a ravine beyond Meadow Hill just before dawn, and mentioned that the white stone there was an object of age-long superstitious regard. Nobody had been caught, but among the scattering fugitives had been glimpsed a huge negro. In another column it was stated that no trace of the missing child Ladislas Wolejko had been found.

The crowning horror came that very night. Elwood will never forget it, and was forced to stay out of college the rest of the term because of the resulting nervous breakdown. He had thought he heard rats in the partitions all the evening, but paid little attention to them. Then, long after both he and Gilman had retired, the atrocious shrieking began. Elwood jumped up, turned on the lights, and rushed over to his guest's couch. The occupant was emitting sounds of veritably inhuman nature, as if racked by some torment beyond description. He was writhing under the bedclothes, and a great red stain was beginning to appear on the blankets.

Elwood scarcely dared to touch him, but gradually the screaming and writhing subsided. By this time Dombrowski, Choynski, Desrochers, Mazurewicz, and the top-floor lodger were all crowding into the doorway, and the landlord had sent his wife back to telephone for Dr. Malkowski. Everybody shrieked when a large rat-like form suddenly jumped out from beneath the ensanguined bedclothes and scuttled across the floor to a fresh, open hole close by. When the doctor arrived and began to pull down those frightful covers Walter Gilman was dead.

It would be barbarous to do more than suggest what had killed Gilman. There had been virtually a tunnel through his body—something had eaten his heart out. Dombrowski, frantic at the failure of his constant rat-poisoning efforts, cast aside all thought of his lease and within a week had moved with all his older lodgers to a dingy but less ancient house in Walnut Street. The worst thing for a while was keeping Joe Mazurewicz quiet; for the brooding loomfixer would never stay sober, and was constantly whining and muttering about spectral and terrible things.

It seems that on that last hideous night Joe had stooped to look at the crimson rat-tracks which led from Gilman's couch to the nearby hole. On the carpet they were very indistinct, but a piece of open flooring intervened between the carpet's edge and the base-board. There Mazurewicz had found something monstrous—or thought he had, for no one else could quite agree with him despite the undeniable queerness of the prints. The tracks on the flooring were certainly vastly unlike the average prints of a rat, but even Choynski and Desrochers would not admit that they were like the prints of four tiny human hands.

The house was never rented again. As soon as Dombrowski left it the pall of its final desolation began to descend, for people shunned it both on account of its old reputation and because of the new foetid odour. Perhaps the ex-landlord's rat-poison had worked after all, for not long after his departure the place became a neighbourhood nuisance. Health officials traced the smell to the closed spaces above and beside the eastern garret room, and agreed that the number of dead rats must be enormous. They decided, however, that it was not worth their while to hew open and disinfect the long sealed spaces; for the foetor would soon be over, and the locality was not one which encouraged fastidious standards. Indeed, there were always vague local tales of unexplained stenches upstairs in the Witch House just after May-Eve and Hallowmass. The neighbours grumblingly acquiesced in the inertia—but the foetor none the less formed an additional count against the place. Toward the last the house was condemned as an habitation by the building inspector.

Gilman's dreams and their attendant circumstances have never been explained. Elwood, whose thoughts on the entire episode are sometimes almost maddening, came back to college the next autumn and graduated in the following June. He found the spectral gossip of the town much diminished, and it is indeed a fact that—notwithstanding certain reports of a ghostly

tittering in the deserted house which lasted almost as long as that edifice itself
—no fresh appearances either of old Keziah or of Brown Jenkin have been
muttered of since Gilman's death. It is rather fortunate that Elwood was not
in Arkham in that later year when certain events abruptly renewed the local
whispers about elder horrors. Of course he heard about the matter afterward
and suffered untold torments of black and bewildered speculation; but even
that was not as bad as actual nearness and several possible sights would have
been.

In March, 1931, a gale wrecked the roof and great chimney of the vacant
Witch House, so that a chaos of crumbling bricks, blackened, moss-grown
shingles, and rotting planks and timbers crashed down into the loft and broke
through the floor beneath. The whole attic story was choked with debris
from above, but no one took the trouble to touch the mess before the inevitable razing of the decrepit structure. That ultimate step came in the following
December, and it was when Gilman's old room was cleared out by reluctant,
apprehensive workmen that the gossip began.

Among the rubbish which had crashed through the ancient slanting ceiling
were several things which made the workmen pause and call in the police.
Later the police in turn called in the coroner and several professors from the
university. There were bones—badly crushed and splintered, but clearly rec-
ognisable as human—whose manifestly modern date conflicted puzzlingly
with the remote period at which their only possible lurking-place, the low,
slant-floored loft overhead, had supposedly been sealed from all human access. The coroner's physician decided that some belonged to a small child,
while certain others—found mixed with shreds of rotten brownish cloth—
belonged to a rather undersized, bent female of advanced years. Careful sift-
ing of debris also disclosed many tiny bones of rats caught in the collapse, as
well as older ratbones gnawed by small fangs in a fashion now and then highly
productive of controversy and reflection.

Other objects found included the mingled fragments of many books and
papers, together with a yellowish dust left from the total disintegration of still
older books and papers. All, without exception, appeared to deal with black
magic in its most advanced and horrible forms; and the evidently recent date
of certain items is still a mystery as unsolved as that of the modern human
bones. An even greater mystery is the absolute homogeneity of the crabbed,
archaic writing found on a wide range of papers whose conditions and water-
marks suggest age differences of at least 150 to 200 years. To some, though,
the greatest mystery of all is the variety of utterly inexplicable objects—
objects whose shapes, materials, types of workmanship, and purposes baffle all
conjecture—found scattered amidst the wreckage in evidently diverse states
of injury. One of these things—which excited several Miskatonic professors

profoundly—is a badly damaged monstrosity plainly resembling the strange image which Gilman gave to the college museum, save that it is larger, wrought of some peculiar bluish stone instead of metal, and possessed of a singularly angled pedestal with undecipherable hieroglyphics.

Archaeologists and anthropologists are still trying to explain the bizarre designs chased on a crushed bowl of light metal whose inner side bore ominous brownish stains when found. Foreigners and credulous grandmothers are equally garrulous about the modern nickel crucifix with broken chain mixed in the rubbish and shiveringly identified by Joe Mazurewicz as that which he had given poor Gilman many years before. Some believe this crucifix was dragged up to the sealed loft by rats, while others think it must have been on the floor in some corner of Gilman's old room all the time. Still others, including Joe himself, have theories too wild and fantastic for sober credence.

When the slanting wall of Gilman's room was torn out, the once sealed triangular space between the partition and the house's north wall was found to contain much less structural debris, even in proportion to its size, than the room itself, though it had a ghastly layer of older materials which paralysed the wreckers with horror. In brief, the floor was a veritable ossuary of the bones of small children—some fairly modern, but others extending back in infinite gradations to a period so remote that crumbling was almost complete. On this deep bony layer rested a knife of great size, obvious antiquity, and grotesque, ornate, and exotic design—above which the debris was piled.

In the midst of this debris, wedged between a fallen plank and a cluster of cemented bricks from the ruined chimney, was an object destined to cause more bafflement, veiled fright, and openly superstitious talk in Arkham than anything else discovered in the haunted and accursed building. This object was the partly crushed skeleton of a huge, diseased rat, whose abnormalities of form are still a topic of debate and source of singular reticence among the members of Miskatonic's department of comparative anatomy. Very little concerning this skeleton has leaked out, but the workmen who found it whisper in shocked tones about the long, brownish hairs with which it was associated.

The bones of the tiny paws, it is rumoured, imply prehensile characteristics more typical of a diminutive monkey than of a rat; while the small skull with its savage yellow fangs is of the utmost anomalousness, appearing from certain angles like a miniature, monstrously degraded parody of a human skull. The workmen crossed themselves in fright when they came upon this blasphemy, but later burned candles of gratitude in St. Stanislaus' Church because of the shrill, ghostly tittering they felt they would never hear again.

THE ISLE
OF THE SLEEPER

EDMOND HAMILTON

Garrison lay face down on the life-raft and felt the sun slowly cooking his brain. After four days, his only sensations were of heat and thirst; he was too dizzily sick to feel hunger any more. The little raft rose and sank on the long, lazy Pacific swells, and each time it fell, the blue water gently smacked his face.

He knew dimly that he would not last much longer. It was only a matter of hours now until he would give way and gulp up the blue water that slapped so invitingly at his face, and then he would die rather horribly. Of course a sane man wouldn't drink sea-water, but then a man who has been floating in mid-Pacific four days without food or drink is not quite sane.

He thought bitterly again that the others were the lucky ones, those who had gone to swift death when the explosion sank the *Mary D.* Those others of the crew, all of them, were at peace now, gently drifting and bumping down in the cool shadowed ooze of the bottom. It was only he, jumping instinctively from the freighter deck as the explosion ripped it, who had been unfortunate enough to live.

Garrison began thinking of water again. He knew that was only hastening the end, but he couldn't keep his weakened mind from doing it. Greedy visions floated through his brain, of silver brooks running over brown stones, of bubbling springs and placid rivers and blue lakes. He saw crystal tumblers of ice-water, beaded with frost. He sobbed, his face crushed against the hot, salt-crusted canvas.

Hours had become eternities for him. He did not realize the sun had gone down, until the furnace-blast scorching him eased a little. Then he raised his head, opened bleared, red-rimmed eyes. It was night, and the raft drifted on dark, lulling waters, the sky a jungle thick with stars. Garrison let his face fall again.

How many eternities later was it that a new, startlingly unfamiliar sound impinged on his dimmed consciousness? A dull rasping and grinding, close to his ears. It began and ceased in roughly regular rhythm. Rasp, rasp—then silence. And then the rasp, rasp. . . .

The unfamiliarity of the sound roused in his deadened brain a vague desire to investigate. He raised himself, as slowly and stiffly as a corpse coming alive, upon his elbows. He stared numbly. Two feet in front of his face was solid land.

The life-raft had drifted onto the sandy beach of a dark island, and lay now with one end grinding and rasping into the sand. There was no other sound but the sucking of the surf. The wheeling companies of stars looked solemnly down. The island stretched in front of Garrison, a dark, unguessable mass.

"It's land," he heard a dry voice croak.

Then Garrison realized that the voice was his own. He was conscious that somehow he had staggered to his feet.

"Land," his salt-crusted lips whispered again.

Garrison stepped off the raft, and went to his knees on the sand. He hitched himself up by a miracle of drunken effort, and unsteadily he started forward in a blind, directionless run.

He ran in a clumsy, stooping posture, head sagging, thin hands hanging nervelessly. His dazed eyes could make out nothing in the darkness. He was like a blinded, maddened animal, moving by instinct rather than intelligence.

He slipped in loose sand, and tripped over rocks, but went reeling on. Then he tripped again and fell. And this time he did not get up. His tired body relaxed gratefully, luxuriously. His mind darkened, slipped into a shadowy dusk. He was aware only of the holy, dusky calm taking possession of his mind. This, then, was death? He slipped into darkness with the sigh of a tired child.

But later, Garrison awoke. That was a strange thing, he thought as consciousness first revived, to awake from death. But he knew suddenly that he was not dead. For fierce thirst still burned his throat, and how can a dead man feel thirst? He wrenched open his gummed, swollen eyelids—to the dazzling splash of bright sunshine.

By convulsive effort, he got to a sitting position. Then with numbed, wild gaze he stared about him. His mind was too dazed to appreciate the full impact of the surprise, and he felt only a vague wonder at what he saw.

Around him rose a thick forest of unearthly beauty. Huge, black-trunked trees towered high above him, shutting out the sky with great masses of silvery foliage. Their interlacing branches were twined with dark, arboring vines. And on the vines grew enormous, orchid-like blooms, wonderful, tender-hued flowers that cascaded in spilled beauty toward the green turf.

Brilliant macaws and parrots flashed screeching through the flowers, and liquid notes of bird-song tinkled sweetly. In the long, hushed silences, a soft wind wandered whispering through the trees, laden with strange, spicy scents and haunting undertones of exquisite perfume.

Garrison stared dazedly. Then through the trees he saw a shining thread of water, a tiny, fern-fringed brook singing through the woods. The crazed longing of four days burst into raging life within him. He ran weakly forward, with an inarticulate cry. A minute later he was lying flat, crushing the ferns, his face buried in the cool crystal stream.

It took all his will to force himself to stop drinking. He was trembling when he raised his head from the water, and his parched mouth and withered tongue seemed slowly expanding. Tears twitched his eyelids.

"I'm saved," he sobbed hoarsely. "Saved!"

Garrison forced himself to get up and stumble away from the stream. He felt even yet no hunger, but he knew that he needed food.

Close by he found it, a tall tree heavy with round red fruit. The fruit looked and tasted like an apple but had a hard, stone-like core. When he had eaten some of it, he felt a little stronger. And he saw now that he was in no danger of starving, for there were many trees with fruit.

Also, there was plenty of life evident in this hushed, faery forest. Brown hares bolted through the ferns, and flying squirrels shot in dizzy arcs from branch to branch, and monkeys chattered in the distance.

"Lucky, to stumble on this island," he mumbled. "Most islands in this part of the Pacific are just bare rock. Probably isn't very big—and doesn't look inhabited at all."

He started in an unsteady tramp toward the distant boom of the surf. He was astounded, as he went, by the variety of life he glimpsed. Two spotted leopards, bounding up a distant tree. Grunting wild pigs rooting in thickets. He heard a hyena somewhere near him, barking in the brush. Deer in large number, swift and beautiful. It seemed incredible to find such life on a small Pacific island.

Then he emerged from the thick woods onto a narrow, sandy beach. The white blob of the life-raft lay on the sand where the tide had left it. Sweeping his gaze along the shore, Garrison saw that the island was five miles long, and two across. It was all blanketed by the thick forest, a green isle sleeping on the vast bosom of the sea. There were no signs whatever that humans had ever been here.

Garrison started trudging along the shore, for it was easier going on the beach than in the forest. He had gone less than a half-mile when out of the woods beside him suddenly stepped the girl. She appeared so startlingly that he stood frozen, staring at her.

"Lord above!" he exclaimed. "Where did *you* come from?"

She smiled. "My name is Myrrha," she said.

She was a white girl—he saw that first. Then his stunned brain perceived that this girl was young and lovely. He doubted if she was more than seventeen. Her dress was queer—a scanty tunic of soft white cloth, belted with a jeweled girdle. Her ivory shoulders were left bare by it, and its skirt stopped short of her rounded knees.

Her eyes were steady on his face. They were soft, wistfully tender black eyes, in which doubt mixed with glad eagerness. Her red-ripe lips were parted a little in excitement. Black silky hair was combed back in a soft mass from her broad, low brow.

"Myrrha?" Garrison repeated dazedly.

"From in the forest, I saw you here," she said, with a quick gesture of slim fingers. Excitement was eager in her eyes as she added, "I was so glad that at last there is somebody else."

"You mean that you and I are the only people on the island?" Garrison cried. "That you've been here alone?"

Myrrha nodded. "Yes, except for the Sleeper, of course."

"The Sleeper?" Garrison could not comprehend her. He cried, "How long have you been on the island?"

"Ever since I can remember, of course," she said, looking at him wonderingly.

"But how did you get here?" he exclaimed.

"I don't understand you," Myrrha said perplexedly. "I have been here from the first. I am part of the dream, the same as you and everything else here."

"Part of the dream?" Garrison echoed. "What in the world do you mean by that?"

Myrrha's puzzlement increased. She looked at him with astonished wonder in her clear eyes.

"You mean, you don't understand it?" she asked. "Why, that is strange—I understood it all from the first. Though I don't know just *how* I did——"

"Will you quit talking riddles and explain?" Garrison demanded. Then he saw the hurt in her child-like eyes and awkwardly tempered his speech. "I'm sorry. I'm just excited, impatient. What did you mean by saying you were part of the dream?"

Her answer stunned him.

"Everything here is just a dream," Myrrha said, with the eager quickness of a child trying to explain something. "This island is really just barren rock, and the forest and animals and you and I are only a dream. They all seem real to us, of course, since we too are part of the dream."

"Why—you're crazy!" Garrison exploded. "This forest—the animals—you—a dream? And I, too?"

"Of course," Myrrha said earnestly. "You are part of the dream, the same as I am."

Garrison repressed a strong desire to swear. Then he felt pity for the girl. She believed what she was saying, he saw. She must, he thought, have grown up here alone, and somehow evolved this wild theory.

"Whose dream is it we're part of, Myrrha?" he asked, humoring her. "Who dreamt us?"

"The Sleeper, of course," she said instantly.

Garrison felt a strong desire to laugh. This was, surely, the most insane adventure he had ever had.

"And who is the Sleeper?" he asked.

Myrrha's soft face sobered with a touch of awe. "He is just—the Sleeper. He lies in the depths of the forest, sleeping, never waking. And whatever he dreams has reality on this island. The Sleeper dreamed the forests and brooks you see around you. He dreamed the animals, and the birds. He dreamed *me* —and I was suddenly here. Since I have been here, he has dreamed many other animals, but no other people until you. I am glad he dreamed you. I was lonely!"

And Myrrha's dark eyes broke into a dancing smile of pleasure. Her soft, bare arm hooked through Garrison's with confident affection.

"So the Sleeper dreamed me, did he?" Garrison said amusedly. "I'd like to see this Sleeper."

The awe came back on Myrrha's face and she answered slowly.

"I can take you to see him. But you must promise not to go near him."

And quite simply, she started to lead the way off the beach into the woods, following an invisible trail of her own that led deviously toward the center of the forested island.

Parrots and monkeys scolded them as they trod the green turf between aisles of giant, flower-decked trees. The soft wind swept them with spicy, perfumed breath. In the air hummed a myriad of gorgeous insects.

Myrrha was like a gay little woodnymph at his side, laughing up at the scolding birds, plucking a great blue bloom from a vine to thrust in her black hair, dancing along on little bare white feet. But once she held Garrison suddenly back, and he saw the dangerously beautiful shape of a leopard fade into the foliage ahead.

"I could wish that the Sleeper hadn't dreamed *them,*" Garrison said dryly.

"Those are only his bad dreams," Myrrha said earnestly. "He has dreamed many beautiful things here, but sometimes he dreams too of evil things."

"Logical enough," Garrison laughed. "How did you figure all that out?"

Myrrha smiled back as she shook her head. "I don't know. It was in my mind, somehow, when the Sleeper dreamed me."

They had threaded through more than a mile of the faery forest, and now entered a long glade of tall, tremendous trees, a natural cathedral of green gloom and hushed silence. Myrrha pressed against Garrison a little timidly as they went on.

"We are near the Sleeper," she whispered. "Make no loud sound. All life on the island fears to go near him, and even I—I am afraid."

Curiosity stirred in Garrison as they went forward. Then as they stopped in a moment, sharp wonder replaced it.

They stood at the edge of a perfectly circular clear space in the hushed green glade. Grass covered it like an emerald carpet. Out there in the center of the circle, in the sunlight there was inset in the grass a low, square dais of dazzling crystal.

On the crystal dais stood a low copper couch, with strangely carved sides. And on the couch, wrapped in a robe of golden cloth ornamented with black figures, lay the motionless figure of a man.

He lay quite unmoving, upon his side, one bare arm flung across his downturned head. As Garrison went closer, Myrrha fearfully trying to keep him back, he saw that the man's hair was dark, his skin white. Nothing else could be seen, shrouded as he was in the golden robe.

"The Sleeper," whispered Myrrha. She had halted him with plucking fingers, a dozen feet from the crystal dais. Her dark eyes were wide with awe as she stared at the recumbent figure.

"Good Lord, this must be a corpse laid here for burial by some unknown race, long ago!" Garrison exclaimed. "But how it has been preserved perfectly for so long, lying here in the open——"

"No, he is not dead, only sleeping," murmured Myrrha. "Speak not so loudly, lest you awaken him."

"I'm going to examine that body," Garrison muttered with intense interest, starting forward.

But Myrrha held him, clinging frantically, her face chalk-white with terror.

"No, you must not! If you awaken the Sleeper, his dream will end—we and everything else he has dreamed into being on the island will perish!"

"Nonsense," he said, but she held to him.

"Remember, you promised you would not go near him!" There was frantic horror and heartbreak in her voice.

Garrison softened at sight of the girl's terrified emotion.

"All right," he told her. "I'll let him alone."

Myrrha drew him fearfully back out of the sunlit clearing into the glade. She led hastily back the way they had come, looking apprehensively behind her.

"Had you awakened him, you would have destroyed us all," she told him, a catch in her voice. "That is why all the animals, even, do not go near the Sleeper—somehow they sense that."

Garrison felt he understood all this. There must once have been a civilized race on this unknown island, one that had embalmed the dead man so perfectly that he had lain indefinitely on his copper couch, unchanged. The animals, fearing the dead, would avoid him.

And it was natural that Myrrha, growing up alone on the island, would think the corpse a sleeper and evolve her weird belief that everything on the island was the Sleeper's dream. For Garrison had no doubt now that Myrrha was a castaway like himself, grown up here from childhood.

She was happy now with child-like relief as they left the glade of the Sleeper behind them.

"I take you now to my home, Gair'-son," she said, trying to repeat his name as he had told it to her.

Garrison looked back thoughtfully and said, "I'd like to have a closer look at that body sometime."

Instantly the panic flashed back on Myrrha's face. She clung to him, desperate entreaty in her eyes.

"Gair'son, you must never touch the Sleeper! It is as I said—if he ever awakes, we who are only his dream will meet our end. Promise me you'll never touch him!"

He could feel her heart hammer with terror. "All right, Myrrha," he said soothingly. "I promise not to touch him."

They came soon to Myrrha's home. It was on a wooded slope at the north end of the island, amid great trees. A foaming little stream rushed down there, and right beside it snuggled a dainty bower of twisted green withes, thatched with velvety moss.

Myrrha showed him how she had made a door of boughs that could be closed at night against the animals. And she showed him fruit and nuts she had collected for food, and the soft couch she had made of fragrant ferns.

"It will not be lonely now, with you here, Gair'son," she said fondly.

"But I can't live in this too," he objected.

"Why not?" Myrrha asked, clear eyes puzzled. "It is big enough for both of us."

Garrison tried awkwardly to explain.

Her eyes filled with tears and her soft mouth quivered. "You do not like me, Gair'son."

Hastily, he tried to soothe her. And as he held her, he was suddenly conscious of the appeal of her soft beauty, of her rounded ivory body and graceful limbs that the scanty tunic scarcely concealed, of the pure forehead and wide, hurt dark eyes beneath her silky black hair.

"Myrrha," he muttered.

And somehow then he was holding her tighter, fragrant red lips against his own hungry ones, silkiest of perfumed black hair against his hand. "Myrrha —Myrrha——"

So began Garrison's life with Myrrha on the island. It was a fantastic life, and yet it was more real to him in the next few days than all his past life in the busy, bustling world.

It was Myrrha who made it so warmly real for him. It seemed to him that he had never known what love was until he met this girl, so child-like in her utter simplicity of mind, so wonderfully womanly in her soft loveliness and devotion to him.

He wondered much how Myrrha had come to the island, how she had survived and grown here. And she was able to tell him but little. Her notions of time were vague. She had been on the island just as now, she said, ever since the Sleeper dreamed her.

And when Myrrha talked so earnestly of the Sleeper, Garrison would smile and draw her fondly closer. He made no more attempts to disillusion her of her belief, for he saw that nothing could shake her queer faith. But Garrison wondered much about that lifeless form on the copper couch.

On the third morning, Garrison and Myrrha went down the wooded slope from the bower—and stopped in surprize. A small lake had appeared at the foot of the hill—a blue, shining little lake that had not been there the night before.

Myrrha clapped her hands in glee. "Gair'son, look! The Sleeper has dreamed a lake!"

"You think the Sleeper dreamed this lake, too?" Garrison said, though he was himself surprized.

"Of course," she said confidently.

He laughed. "Something happened to dam up that little stream during the night—that's what did it."

"It is not so," Myrrha asserted. "It was the Sleeper's dream."

"'We are such stuff as dreams are made on,'" quoted Garrison, smiling. "No matter how it came here, it looks like a good place to swim. Come on!"

But in the next few days, there were things that Garrison found harder to explain than the lake.

There were the elephants, for instance. Garrison saw them one afternoon, two huge, humped gray shapes pushing ponderously through the distant forest. He stood rooted in amazement.

"Why didn't you tell me there were elephants on the island?" Garrison exclaimed to the girl.

Myrrha shook her head. "There never were any until now, Gair'son. The Sleeper must have just dreamed them."

"Rubbish," he said impatiently. "They've been here—you just didn't happen to see them before."

Yet he had inward doubts. He and Myrrha had been over all the island in the last few days, and had seen no elephants or tracks of any. Yet the great beasts were here now, beyond doubt.

It was the same with the giant, three-foot blue butterflies he saw the next day, and the seals that appeared in the lake a day later. They had not been there before—they were there now. And Myrrha said quite simply the Sleeper had dreamed them too.

"Sleeper, my eye!" Garrison said impatiently. He told her, "I'm going and look at that body again."

"You will not go too near the Sleeper—will not touch him?" Myrrha pleaded anxiously. "Remember, you promised me——"

"I'll keep my promise," he reassured her.

"I will go with you," Myrrha declared.

"Don't quite trust me, eh?" he smiled.

"It is not that, Gair'son," she said earnestly. "But we have been so happy —I fear lest something you do might awake the Sleeper, and bring an end to us and everything else here."

This time his arm was about her waist as they went through the forest, and into that hushed and solemn glade of green gloom where no life seemed ever to venture. And he could feel her heart pounding as they came to that silent, circular space of sunlight.

In its center still dazzled the crystal dais, and upon it still stood the copper couch on which rested the body of the Sleeper. He lay as before, wrapped in the shrouding golden robe, one arm across his down-turned head.

"A miracle of preservation, that body," Garrison muttered, staring. "Archeologists would go crazy to examine——"

He stopped, for Myrrha had shuddered wildly beside him. The girl gasped, "Look—the Sleeper stirs, and sighs!"

For a moment, Garrison almost thought he *did* see a faint movement of the body under the golden shroud, almost thought he heard a low, singing groan. Then he dismissed the fantastic idea.

"It was just the wind sighing, and stirring the robe, Myrrha," he said. But her face was aghast with fear.

"Gair'son, let us leave here, quickly! The Sleeper is having bad dreams— and that means evil on the island!"

As she led him frantically back through the glade, the girl was quivering with terror.

"I am afraid, Gair'son! The Sleeper groaned and that means his dream was evil."

He held her trembling softness close to him. "Don't be afraid, Myrrha."

But that night, fear came to Garrison himself, for there came—the beast-men. He awoke in the little bower, Myrrha still sleeping in his arms, and heard strange, heavy foot-steps outside, snuffling grunts, a clumsy clawing at the door.

Then the rude door was torn open, and against the starlit sky he saw the dark silhouettes of the creatures outside. Hunched, huge, hairy shapes of men nearer the animal than the human, with bowed, gorilla-like limbs and bestial snouted faces out of which green eyes blazed through the darkness at the frozen Garrison.

"The things of evil that the Sleeper dreamed!" screamed Myrrha, awakening at that moment.

The bestial figures started to enter, unloosing a babel of chattering and grunting as they heard the girl's voice. Their hairy hands reached in the dark —and then Garrison broke from the trance that had held him, and went mad with terror and loathing.

He smashed wild blows against the hairy bodies, yelling his horror. The creatures recoiled out of the dark hut, running swiftly back on hunched legs into the trees.

"Myrrha, we've got to get out of here before they come back!" Garrison cried unsteadily. "Come on!"

He was half carrying her as he plunged out of the bower, and ran into the dark forest. In a moment they heard the raging, chattering uproar of the beastmen, tearing the bower apart.

Garrison's horror-clouded mind recovered itself only minutes later. His frantic flight had brought Myrrha and him into a dark thicket of tall bushes.

"Gair'son, *they* are what the Sleeper dreamed today as we watched!" cried Myrrha, shuddering wildly. "I knew his dreams were evil."

"Listen!" Garrison suddenly exclaimed. And they both heard an angry, chattering uproar drawing closer in the forest.

"God, they're trailing us!" cried Garrison, aghast. "They want—they want *you*, Myrrha."

He wrenched a great branch from a tree, and with the rude club in his hand, stumbled blindly on through the woods with Myrrha. And after them, veering to follow them, came the pursuit.

Hour after hour they dodged and fled through the nighted forest, and always the chattering, unclean horde pursued. The paling dawn found them at the southern end of the island, Myrrha exhausted and clinging pitiably to him.

"We can't run from them for ever," Garrison said hoarsely. "Sooner or later, they'll catch up to us."

Then sudden hope lit his haggard face. "Maybe they wouldn't follow us to that clearing where the Sleeper lies! None of the animals on the island ever go there."

"No, let us not go there!" Myrrha cried.

But he overrode her protests, stumbled desperately with her through the woods to the hushed, solemn glade that lay silent as ever in the rising sun.

He carried the fainting girl to within a dozen feet of the crystal dais. On his couch, the Sleeper's dark, down-turned head was still immobile under his upflung arm and golden robe.

"I am afraid," Myrrha whispered, looking fearfully at the motionless form.

"We're safe here, I think," Garrison panted. "They won't follow——"

"*Gair'son!*"

Out of the glade into the clearing had burst the unclean, hairy horde—the beastmen!

Myrrha's scream catapulted Garrison fiercely forward to meet them, to hold them from her. His heavy club swung in raging blows that crushed the skulls of two of the creatures like eggshells.

But the others came at him, with shrill yells of animal rage, bestial, snouted faces slavering their rage, reaching for him with incredibly powerful hands. He slammed the club wildly against their faces, crushing bone and muscle. Then Myrrha screamed again.

Garrison turned for a split second, and cried out hoarsely. Three of the beastmen had left the attack on him, had circled past him and had seized the girl. Ivory body struggling in the grip of hairy arms—Garrison's blood froze at the sight. And before he could turn back, hands gripped him, too.

"Myrrha!" he cried madly, struggling to smash aside his own attackers, to reach her side.

He glimpsed her white face, her horror-dilated eyes. He heard her frantic cry.

"Gair'son—wake the Sleeper! It's better for us all, for everything here to perish, than for us to die like this——"

He couldn't reach her. The clawing, hairy hands held him back, would have him down in a moment.

"Wake the Sleeper, Gair'son! End everything——"

The beast-men had him to his knees, by now. His red-lit, tortured soul knew that there was no hope of saving Myrrha, no hope except the wild one that her cry had voiced. If he woke the Sleeper—if that did end Myrrha, everything—better for her to end that way.

Garrison made a last effort against the clutching, tearing claws. He swung his club wildly around his head, and threw it straight at the motionless form on the copper couch. He saw the club strike the Sleeper's bare shoulder, saw blood flow from the bruising wound. And then he glimpsed the Sleeper stirring wildly, starting up to a sitting position. . . .

A sudden mistiness came over everything. The trees, the grass, the dais and couch, Myrrha's white body and the hairy beast-men—all seemed suddenly fading, vanishing. And Garrison was aware that his own body, too, was vanishing, fading.

Through dimming sight, as his own body disappeared, he saw the Sleeper sitting up, opening his eyes. And in the final moment before his body vanished, before everything vanished, Garrison saw and recognized the Sleeper's face.

It was his own face! He, Garrison, was vanishing like everything else—but the Sleeper was Garrison, too, and the Sleeper had awakened.

With that incredible realization, his consciousness whirled into darkness. And then instantly he was conscious again. And he found himself sitting stiffly and alone in the sunlight, Myrrha and the beast-men and all else gone. He, the Sleeper, had awakened.

Wildly, Garrison stared. He had been lying on bare rock, and around him stretched a lifeless, barren island of rock without one spot of life, one speck of green. And Garrison sobbed aloud as he realized.

He, who had stumbled ashore and fallen into exhausted slumber here, had been the Sleeper. And his dream had created the forest and animals and Myrrha, and had even created a dream-Garrison like himself who had lived and loved in this domain of dream. And when he had awakened, the dream had failed and vanished.

Something made him turn his sagging head to the sea. The black speck of a ship was out there, heading for the island. . . .

★   ★   ★

The captain of the tanker felt sympathetic toward this castaway he had rescued, and who lay now in the berth of his lamplit cabin. He felt glad that his search for survivors of the *Mary D.*, that he had begun on receiving the doomed freighter's interrupted distress call, had saved at least this one man. But the grayhaired seaman's kindly face was troubled, now, and he spoke reluctantly.

"I don't doubt you had a wild dream of some kind," he said. "Lying delirious on that rocky island—who wouldn't?"

"It wasn't just a delirious dream—this dream was a *reality!*" Garrison cried. "Those things I dreamed, the forest and beasts and the girl and the other me —they all had real existence, somehow, as long as I lay dreaming them."

"Oh, come now," the captain told him. "You're too intelligent to believe that."

"I do believe it, though," Garrison said. And his eyes glimmered with tears. "I believe that I met the only girl I'll ever love in a dream that was real and solid while it lasted.

"How was the dream made real? I don't know—I don't know. Maybe some queer force impregnating that island, attuned to the mental force of the subconscious mind. Whatever caused it, I know that it all *was* real. I know— by this."

And he rolled up his sleeve, baring his shoulder. There was a fresh, angry wound on it.

"That is the wound the other Garrison, the dream Garrison, made in the Sleeper's shoulder when he threw the club. I didn't have that wound when I fell asleep on the island. I had it when I awoke."

PRESCIENCE

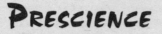

NELSON S. BOND

His visitor said fearfully, "It's that way whenever I'm in a crowded room, doctor. Or if I walk down a street at noon hour. Sometimes I want to scream and kick and fight my way clear of the throng that binds me in—"

Dr. Barton said, "Yes. Yes, I quite understand." But his tone was not entirely sympathetic. It was brusque, hurried, impatient. He said, "Mr. Peebles, I am going to give you these tablets. Keep them on your person. Whenever you feel one of these . . . er . . . nervous attacks coming on, take a tablet."

"I . . . I'm afraid you don't quite understand, doctor. I don't need sedatives. There's nothing wrong with me physically. I've been examined thoroughly by expert diagnosticians. And I—"

"My *dear* Mr. Peebles!" Dr. Barton rose. "Believe me when I say I understand your case perfectly. If you will just confide your fears to my keeping—"

He let his words dwindle off. The patient colored, impressed. He scraped his chair backward, picked up the tablets and faltered toward the door.

"Yes, doctor. I didn't mean to offend you. If you think I'll be all right—"

"Of course, Mr. Peebles. Now, you may return Thursday, if you will. Good day, sir."

The visitor ducked out. Dr. Barton's eyes filmed, mirroring the distaste he felt. For a lingering moment he continued to stare at the door panel. Then he dropped into his chair, muttering petulantly.

Dr. Barton was quite fed up with neurotics. And that was particularly awkward because he—Dr. Homer Barton—was numbered among the town's most eminent and accomplished psychiatrists.

Into his soothing, apple-green walled office, during the past twelve years, had crept a steady stream of patients suffering an infinitude of mental ailments. He had seen, and spoken with, and treated all kinds from mild claustrophobiacs to weeping persecutionists.

Oftimes his quiet, competent manner had brought about cures. At other times he had succeeded in arresting partly developed cases. He had known failure, too. The big, white hospital on the Hill held some of them; held them in thickly padded rooms, behind doors barred with steel.

But Dr. Barton was utterly fed up with neurotic people. He voiced his grievance, now, to the nurse who had opened the door and was silently waiting his attention.

"Fools, Miss Allen!" he snapped. "They're fools—the whole lot of them! Neuroses—bah! Phobias and complexes—bah! Fundamentally, there is but one thing that bothers all of them. Fear!"

Miss Allen said, "Yes, doctor. There is a—"

"Fear!" repeated Dr. Barton bitterly. "And do you know *what* it is they fear, Miss Allen? I do. It is not open or closed spaces. Animals or sharp points or height. Heat or cold or any of those multitudinous things they whine and complain to me about. Those are but substitutes; manifestations of the one basic fear that possesses all of them.

"They fear, Miss Allen—death! Twelve years in this horrible occupation has convinced me that there is but one factor underlying all the complexes and phobias of my patients. They are afraid to die. And since their puny minds refuse to acknowledge the cause of their fear, their subconscious gives them a palliative. A secondary fear to supplant the real one they dare not name, even to themselves!"

Miss Allen nodded understandingly. She said, "Then that should make their cure even more simple, doctor. Or am I too optimistic?"

"Barring physiological defects," continued Barton, musing, "little children are completely sane. Why? Because they do not fear death. There is relatively little insanity among aborigines; the so-called 'backward' or 'pagan' people. Nor among the laboring classes of our race.

"*I* would never become a mental case, Miss Allen, because I am a fundamentalist. I do not needlessly torture myself with vain ponderings on my after life. I accept, calmly and as a matter of fact, the credo that the real 'I' is everlasting; imperishable.

"With this comfort, with the assurance that death holds no horrors for me, my mind is balanced."

He looked at her as if seeing her for the first time.

"Excuse me," he said. "I did not mean to bother you with my annoyance, but I am so everlastingly weary of soothing frightened people—"

Nurse Allen knew her employer's moods perfectly.

"Yes, doctor," she said. "There is a Mrs. Williams waiting. Shall I show her in?"

"Not today," said Barton. "Ask her to come back tomorrow, I'm tired."

"But if you'll excuse me, doctor, she's been waiting more than an hour—"

Barton shrugged. After all, this *was* his business. A business which paid him handsomely.

"Oh, very well!" he said resignedly. "Show her in."

"Yes, sir." The nurse vanished. When the door opened softly, a few seconds later, Dr. Barton's ire had completely disappeared. He was a living model of complacency; a twentieth century soothsayer sitting behind a soft, rubbed walnut desk, hands folded before him with the smooth quietude of reflecting Buddha. He rose as his patient entered.

"Mrs. Williams? Please be seated."

She was a drab little woman. For a moment he could not help wondering where she had heard of him, or even if he had been wise in admitting her. Her clothes were definitely not Fifth Avenue. Her hands were work-coarsened and red. A shopgirl, possibly, or somebody's cook. She could never afford to pay Dr. Barton's prices if this were so—

"I came to see you, doctor," she said, "because I could not stay away any longer. And my employer, Mrs. Rand, said you were wonderful at solving troubles of the—mind?"

"Mrs. Rand?" Dr. Barton remembered her dimly. An elderly woman with nervous indigestion. Her trouble, treated by a general practitioner, was late hours and overrich food. Dr. Barton had given it a fancy name—he had long since learned the layman's love for polysyllables—and suggested a course in Yoga. The Yoga concept had given Mrs. Rand something to think about. The enforced rigidity of diet had effected a cure.

"Yes, Mrs. Williams. And your trouble—?"

The little woman twisted a handkerchief nervously.

"I . . . I see things, doctor. I see them before they actually happen."

Dr. Barton's face remained placid, but he yawned mentally. There were no variations in this job. Only the same recurrent themes, over and over again. But he said politely, "Yes? Go on, please."

"It is something with which I have been gifted—or cursed—ever since I was a little girl. But lately it has happened with such frequency, almost every time I go to bed, as a matter of fact, that it . . . it frightens me.

"I have dreams—but they are not dreams. For within a few weeks, or a few days, that scene which is so clear to me in my dream actually *happens!*"

She looked at him hopefully. "Did you ever hear of anything like that before?"

Dr. Barton avoided answering. Of course he had. Everyone had. But he said, noncommittally, "Please go on."

"Three nights ago, for instance, I dreamed that I was in a strange room. A room I had never seen before in my life. It was the drawing room of a large house, and somehow I was aware that I had come after something.

"As I was wondering what this thing was, a strange lady appeared in the doorway. She held out to me an oblong box.

" 'Can you identify this?' she asked.

" 'I'll try, ma'am,' I said. I opened the box. In it lay a pair of white evening gloves which belonged to my mistress, Mrs. Rand.

" 'Yes, ma'am,' I said in my dream. 'These belong to Mrs. Rand.'

" 'Then you may take them to her,' said the strange lady. 'And here's a little gift for your trouble.' And she gave me a dollar bill. I remember it particularly because it had—Here, I'll show you!"

Mrs. Williams dug into a worn handbag; brought out a dollar bill which she passed across the desk to the doctor. Barton looked at it.

"That red ink blot," said Mrs. Williams. "That was the identifying mark on the dollar bill the lady gave me in my dream."

Barton handed back the bill. He said, "But you got this bill where, Mrs. Williams?"

"This morning," said the little woman, "Mrs. Rand was very excited. Last night at the opera she mislaid her evening gloves. She telephoned an advertisement to the newspapers at once.

"Early this afternoon, she received a call from a lady in Westchester. A perfect stranger. And since Thomas, the chauffeur, had driven Mr. Rand downtown, Mrs. Rand asked *me* to go out after the gloves."

"And then—?"

"When I got there," said Mrs. Williams, "into that house, I knew *instantly* it was the one I had visited in my dream two nights before. I even knew what was going to happen. But I couldn't do anything about it.

"It was a dreadful feeling. I felt captive; bound by a chain too strong for breaking. I saw the lady, strange no longer, appear in the doorway. I watched her lips open as if fascinated. I knew she was going to say, 'Can you identify this?'—and she did. I knew what I was going to say. And I tried to stop myself; to say something different. Somehow I had an idea if I could only change the words, something important would come about—"

"Well?" said Barton.

Mrs. Williams shook her head miserably. "It was no use. The words came from my lips and I couldn't stop them. I said, 'Yes, ma'am. These belong to Mrs. Rand—' "

Dr. Barton tried hard not to frown. He was more than ever disgusted with his occupation. The same old groove, over and over again. Escape mechanisms! A drab little woman, dissatisfied with her lot, knowing that she would soon leave this earth. Who subconsciously projected her servile present into the past, attributing to herself strange powers—

"Is it . . . does it mean anything, doctor?" asked the little woman fearfully.

Dr. Barton's impatience rose suddenly. After all, this was no wealthy patient who must be cajoled and deferred to and handled with kid gloves. He said:

"Mrs. Williams, yours is not at all an unusual case. The phenomenon which troubles you is as old as the history of mankind, has been studied and discussed since the days of the first doctors.

"I think I should tell you that, despite what you may think, you did *not* dream this first, then have the event happen to you. Actually, you experienced what the philosopher, Henri Bergson, calls 'the memory of the present.'

"*This* is what happened. You entered a strange house. You were a trifle tired, or hungry, or affected by a touch of the sun. Possibly excited by an unaccustomed responsibility. However that may be, your nervous system suffered a momentary synapse—a breaking of the nervous current, as an electrical current may be disturbed by a bolt of lightning.

"That brief fraction of a second sufficed to erase from your mind, completely, all which had gone before. Thus, when you . . . er . . . snapped out of your mental hiatus, it seemed to you that you had 'been through this scene before.' While actually, it was the *first* time you had ever witnessed it."

The little woman wrung her handkerchief annoyingly.

"But . . . but, doctor," she cried. "The dollar bill? I remembered it from the dream."

Dr. Barton said, "Nonsense! The human mind remembers, consciously, that which it wishes to remember. You say you have this experience often. Has it ever occurred to you to rise from your sleep and write down one of these episodes? So that later you might check the dream against a happening?"

"No, sir. I never remember the dream until the scene is presented—"

"Exactly! In other words, it is just what I told you it was." Dr. Barton rose. "If you will take my advice, Mrs. Williams, it would be well for you to stop worrying."

"Worrying, doctor?" Mrs. Williams rose uncertainly. "But I'm not worrying about anything. I have sufficient money for my needs. I have no children. I—"

"I strongly suspect, madam," said Barton caustically, "you are worrying about the salvation of your soul. You fear the afterworld. Therein lies your reason for dreaming these strange daydreams. Good day, Mrs. Williams."

The little woman flushed. She scrabbled in her old handbag. There were tears in her eyes; Dr. Barton saw them not with compassion but with annoyance.

"There is no charge, Mrs. Williams," he said gruffly. "It has been a pleasure to be able to tell someone the cold truth for a change. The truth that most people are cowards."

"Yes, doctor," said the little woman humbly. Then, halfway to the door, "But if I have one of these experiences again——? Is there anything I should do?"

"There is nothing. You must not——"

Dr. Barton stopped suddenly. Never had his exasperation been so great. Now a great thought came to him. He had no wealthy client in this patient. Why not use her as a guinea pig? At one time allay her fears for evermore— and prove his own theory. His brow cleared. He smiled.

"Mrs. Williams?" he said.

The woman turned hopefully. "Yes, doctor?"

"You say you have these dreams frequently?"

"Yes, sir."

"Good. Then come with me. I think I can cure your case."

It was to his smaller office that he led her. There he had a small cot for invalid patients; a number of impressive machines used in treating those whose cases demanded imposing paraphernalia.

"Lie down, Mrs. Williams," he said. Gone was Dr. Barton's impatience now. He was once again the suave psychiatrist, handling with smooth deftness a nerve-wracked victim of strain. "Right here. That's right.

"Now—relax. Stretch if you want to. Ease all your muscles. There—that's right. Look up, now, please——"

He snapped a switch. In the quiet gloom of the room one tiny light began to flicker. A many-faceted globe in the machine which was suspended just over the patient's head. It swirled into motion. The facets caught the light, shifted them into dancing colors.

"Don't look away, Mrs. Williams. Look at the light. There—that's right. See how soothing it is? So pleasant. So relaxing. And you are tired . . . tired . . . terribly tired——"

There was no sound save the somewhat heavier breathing of the patient. The distant hum of the machine. Dr. Barton spoke again in a whisper.

"Now you are sleeping . . . sleeping. Aren't you, Mrs. Williams?"

The little woman's voice was like a wisp from far away.

"I . . . am sleeping——"

Dr. Barton smiled sardonically. There was no problem here. She was more susceptible than most to hypnotism. That indicated a receptive will. No wonder she had been prey to these repetitive dreams.

He said, "Are you dreaming now, Mrs. Williams. Tell me your dream?"

"I am . . . dreaming . . . doctor."

"Tell me."

The woman's voice was slow, faltering, unaccented.

"I am . . . in a room. It is night . . . I think . . . because the lights are on. But not . . . for long. I am . . . getting ready for bed . . . now I am turning off the lights—"

There was a long silence. Dr. Barton said, "And now, Mrs. Williams?"

"It is dark . . . but there is a light from the street lamp outside. I am . . . shifting . . . turning. I am restless. It seems there is something . . . I am trying to remember . . . something important. But I cannot quite . . . remember what it is—"

Again silence. Barton smiled. He persisted, "Yes?"

"I do not know . . . I am asleep . . . now—"

Barton almost laughed aloud. Asleep! That should amuse his fellow psychiatrists. He had hypnotized a woman into believing she was asleep! Sleep within sleep—

Despite himself, he started. For suddenly from Mrs. Williams' throat had burst a gasp; a startled cry. Swiftly he touched her pulse. It was strong; almost too strong. It was pounding as though from panic.

"Yes, Mrs. Williams?" he purred excitedly. "A dream has come to you?"

"No! No! I am awake again! There is redness . . . in my room. It is . . . fire! I can . . . feel the heat!" Her voice rose. "I am . . . climbing out of my bed. I . . . run to the door . . . but the panels are . . . too hot. I dare not . . . open it—

"Now I am . . . running to the window. I . . . throw it . . . open. I climb out. The fire escape . . . is cold against . . . my bare feet—"

Dr. Barton nodded silently. Strange how detailed these fear dreams were. Fire, now. That was a convincing proof of his theory. Had not mankind, from time immemorable, conjoined thoughts of heat and flame with their dread of the afterworld? Like the others, this little woman feared death. And with that fear in her subconscious, she dreamed such dreams as this—

Her voice went on; harsh with horror.

"I hear . . . the wailing of sirens . . . and the screams . . . of people in the streets . . . below. I am . . . climbing down the . . . fire escape now. A burst of flame . . . licks from one of the windows . . . and scorches my . . . hands.

"But I am nearing . . . safety. . . . The crackling of fire . . . sounds in my ears . . . and I am panting . . . Just a few more . . . steps—"

* * *

Dr. Barton frowned. He saw, now, what he must do. He must teach this woman, once and for all, that dreams are not harmful things. That this fire, this flame, this awful heat and the fear of impending death lived only in her mind. He spoke curtly.

"Do you hear me, Mrs. Williams?"

"The house is crumbling . . . into ruin—" A pause; a shifting of the head as though hearing a far-away sound. "I . . . hear you . . . doctor—"

"You must not avoid this fire," said Barton crisply. "It cannot hurt you. It is but a dream; a hallucination. I tell you, you are lying in your bed, asleep. This is only a dream."

"A . . . dream?"

"Yes. Only a dream, Mrs. Williams. Now you must go back into the house. Is there a window near you?"

"There is . . . a window . . . but from it leap . . . red tongues of . . . flame. The heat burns me . . . even as I wait—"

"You must go in the window!" said Barton firmly. "I command you to go into the window. The fire will turn cool before you. You will not be harmed! Go in!"

Before him, the little woman's body twisted as if in an agony of indecision.

"I . . . cannot . . . doctor."

"You must! Enter the window!"

"Yes . . . doctor." A brief silence. Then, "I am . . . entering . . . the window. But it is hot . . . now the fire . . . the great flames— *Ooooh!*"

Her scream shattered the throbbing silence of the room into tattered fragments of sound. Despite himself, Barton felt a shudder course coldly through him. There was stark agony in that scream. Torment and fear and anguish. But he steeled himself to speak.

"You see, Mrs. Williams? There was nothing to fear. You are safe. You are all right now?"

Only the faint humming of the machine. The distant sound of the woman's labored breathing. Dr. Barton spoke again, sharply.

"You are all right now?"

And then the answer. In a dreary voice. A toneless voice. "I am . . . all right . . . now."

"Good. There is no heat?"

"There is . . . no heat."

"Now you will return to your room. Find your bed, lie down in it. Sleep once more."

Brief silence. Then, "I cannot find . . . my room. I cannot find . . . my bed—"

"Then you are still dreaming, Mrs. Williams. What is your dream now? What do you see?"

"There is . . . no heat. I cannot find . . . my room. It is dark. I am still dreaming. I see nothing . . . in my dream . . . but writhing darkness. I stand alone . . . on a vast, empty plain. But I am not alone. Mists surround me. And out of the mists—"

Dr. Barton was startled at what happened then, so unexpected was it. The woman's voice changed suddenly; her throat was torn with a wild and terrifying scream. Then came laughter. A wild cacophony of sound like that which sometimes echoed from the cells of the great, white building on the Hill.

Words began tumbling from her lips. Madly. Wildly. Gloatingly. As she told what she saw. Told it in its every revolting detail. Every intricate little movement and meaning. Words, thoughts, ideas of evil older than Earth itself poured from her.

For stark seconds, Barton listened, horrified. It was incredible that the mind of a demure little woman like this should be host to such thoughts; that from her lips could spill such a repugnant stream. The things she told were such that even Dr. Barton, experienced psychiatrist as he was, tasted the weak bile of disgust on his lips.

The creatures she envisioned in her dreaming were the embodiment of sheer horror; her hateful words swept all the cleanliness and good from the thing called Man, made him a stinking creature asquat in a mire of abomination!

With a swift motion, Dr. Barton touched the ray switch, flicked it off. The humming ceased. The light ended its flickering. Dr. Barton called, "Mrs. Williams—waken! I command you to wake!"

The body on the cot stirred, opened its eyes. Mrs. Williams, meek, humble again, rose to a sitting posture.

"Yes, doctor. What is it you want me to do?"

"It is already done, Mrs. Williams." Dr. Barton could scarcely realize that from this quiet creature's lips, a moment ago, had flooded words and thoughts unspeakable in their vileness. "Our experiment is finished."

"And did you . . . I mean, is everything—?"

"You will be all right now," promised Barton. "You will dream no more, I believe."

He did not tell her about the final stage of her dreaming. It was enough that he had allayed her fears. He felt certain, did Dr. Barton, that there would be in the future no more prescient dreams—

* * *

Dr. Barton saw no more patients that afternoon. He found time for a round of golf before sundown; after that he had dinner at the club and enjoyed a movie in the evening. He went home and slept soundly. His mind was untroubled, for Dr. Barton was prey to no personal neuroses, phobias, or complexes. His code of living was simple. His philosophy of life admitted no hindering fear of an afterworld. And on such fear, he knew, was based all of mankind's mental ailments.

The next morning he arrived at his office ready for a new day's work. Miss Allen was already there. She had an open newspaper on the desk before her. She greeted him with excitement and horror.

"—a most *dreadful* thing last night, doctor!" she said. "I can hardly believe it. You remember that little Mrs. Williams who came here yesterday afternoon?"

"Yes, of course. Why?"

"Oh, it's terrible! Last night a fire broke out in Mrs. Rand's home, and—"

"What!" Dr. Barton's face paled. "Let me see!" He clutched the newspaper, found the account.

—firemen had the conflagration under control and all members of the Rand family were rescued. The housekeeper, a Mrs. Williams, was the only victim. She was seen to climb from her bedroom window to the fire escape and make her way down to within a few steps of safety.

Then, apparently overcome by the heat, she stopped and deliberately stepped back into the heart of the fire, into a dining-room window. Observers believe she must have died instantly—

Died instantly! That scream! That sudden change in manner!

"What is it, Dr. Barton?" cried Miss Allen. "Oh, Dr. Barton, what *is* it?"

But Dr. Barton, philosopher and scientist, did not hear. He did not even know that his trembling hands had dropped the paper, that his eyes were bleak and staring, nor that from his throat there bubbled such mad, inchoate laughter as often echoed from the cells of the big, white building on the Hill—

The Dreams
of Albert Moreland

Fritz Leiber, Jr.

I think of the autumn of 1939, not as the beginning of the Second World War, but as the period in which Albert Moreland dreamed the dream. The two events—the war and the dream—are not, however, divorced in my mind. Indeed, I sometimes fear that there is a connection between them, but it is a connection which no sane person will consider seriously, if he is wise.

Albert Moreland was, and perhaps still is, a professional chess-player. That fact has an important bearing on the dream, or dreams. He made most of his scant income at a games arcade in Lower Manhattan, taking on all comers—the enthusiast who gets a kick out of trying to beat an expert, the lonely man who turns to chess as to a drug, or the down-and-outer tempted into purchasing a half hour of intellectual dignity for a quarter.

After I got to know Moreland, I often wandered into the arcade and watched him playing as many as three or four games simultaneously, oblivious to the clicking and whirring of the pinball games and the intermittent reports from the shooting gallery. He got fifteen cents for every win; the house took the extra dime. When he lost, neither got anything.

Eventually I found out that he was a much better player than he needed to be for his arcade job. He had won casual games from internationally famous masters. A couple of Manhattan clubs had wanted to groom him for the big tournaments, but lack of ambition kept him drifting along in obscurity. I got the impression that he thought chess too trivial a business to warrant serious consideration, although he was perfectly willing to dribble his life away at the arcade, waiting for something really important to come along, if it ever did. Once in a while he eked out his income by playing on a club team, getting as much as five dollars.

I met him at the old brownstone house where we both had rooms on the same floor, and it was there that he first told me about the dream.

We had just finished a game of chess, and I was idly watching the battle-scarred pieces slide off the board and pile up in a fold of the blanket on his cot. Outside a fretful wind eddied the dry grit. There was a surge of traffic noises, and the buzz of a defective neon sign. I had just lost, but I was glad that Moreland never let me win, as he occasionally did with the players at the arcade, to encourage them. Indeed, I thought myself fortunate in being able to play with Moreland at all, not knowing then that I was probably the best friend he had.

I was saying something obvious about chess.

"You think it a complicated game?" he inquired, peering at me with quizzical intentness, his dark eyes like round windows pushed up under heavy eaves. "Well, perhaps it is. But I play a game a thousand times more complex every night in my dreams. And the queer thing is that the game goes on night after night. The same game. I never really sleep. Only dream about the game."

Then he told me, speaking with a mixture of facetious jest and uncomfortable seriousness that was to characterize many of our conversations.

The images of his dream, as he described them, were impressively simple, without any of the usual merging and incongruity. A board so vast he sometimes had to walk out on it to move his pieces. A great many more squares than in chess and arranged in patches of different colors, the power of the pieces varying according to the color of the square on which they stood. Above and to each side of the board only blackness, but a blackness that suggested starless infinity, as if, as he put it, the scene were laid on the very top of the universe.

When he was awake he could not quite remember all the rules of the game, although he recalled a great many isolated points, including the interesting fact that—quite unlike chess—his pieces and those of his adversary did not duplicate each other. Yet he was convinced that he not only understood the game perfectly while dreaming, but also was able to play it in the highly strategic manner of the master chess player. It was, he said, as though his night mind had many more dimensions of thought than his waking mind, and were able to grasp intuitively complex series of moves that would ordinarily have to be reasoned out step by step.

"A feeling of increased mental power is a very ordinary dream-delusion, isn't it?" he added, peering at me sharply. "And so I suppose you might say it's a very ordinary dream."

I did not know quite how to take that last remark, so I prodded him with a question.

"What do the pieces look like?"

It turned out that they were similar to those of chess in that they were considerably stylized and yet suggested the original forms—architectural, animal, ornamental—which had served as their inspiration. But there the similarity ended. The inspiring forms, so far as he could guess at them, were grotesque in the extreme. There were terraced towers subtly distorted out of the perpendicular, strangely asymmetric polygons that made him think of temples and tombs, vegetable-animal shapes which defied classification and whose formalized limbs and external organs suggested a variety of unknown functions. The more powerful pieces seemed to be modeled after life forms, for they carried stylized weapons and other implements, and wore things similar to crowns and tiaras—a little like the king, queen and bishop in chess —while the carving indicated voluminous robes and hoods. But they were in no other sense anthropomorphic. Moreland sought in vain for earthly analogies, mentioning Hindu idols, prehistoric reptiles, futurist sculpture, squids bearing daggers in their tentacles, and huge ants and mantes and other insects with fantastically adapted end organs.

"I think you would have to search the whole universe—every planet and every dead sun—before you could find the original models," he said, frowning. "Remember, there is nothing cloudy or vague about the pieces themselves in my dream. They are as tangible as this rook." He picked up the piece, clenched his fist around it for a moment, and then held it out toward me on his open palm. "It is only in what they suggest that the vagueness lies."

It was strange, but his words seemed to open some dream-eye in my own mind, so that I could almost see the things he described. I asked him if he experienced fear during his dreams.

He replied that the pieces one and all filled him with repugnance—those based on higher life forms usually to a greater degree than the architectural ones. He hated to have to touch or handle them. There was one piece in particular which had an intensely morbid fascination for his dream-self. He identified it as "the archer" because the stylized weapon it bore gave the impression of being able to hurt at a distance; but like the rest it was quite inhuman. He described it as representing a kind of intermediate, warped life form which had achieved more than human intellectual power without losing —but rather gaining—in brute cruelty and malignity. It was one of the opposing pieces for which there was no duplicate among his own. The mingled fear and loathing it inspired in him sometimes became so great that they interfered with his strategic grasp of the whole dream-game, and he was afraid his feeling toward it would sometime rise to such a pitch that he would be forced to capture it just to get it off the board, even though such a capture might compromise his whole position.

"God knows how my mind ever cooked up such a hideous entity," he finished, with a quick grin. "Five hundred years ago I'd have said the Devil put it there."

"Speaking of the Devil," I asked, immediately feeling my flippancy was silly, "whom do you play against in your dream?"

Again he frowned. "I don't know. The opposing pieces move by themselves. I will have made a move, and then, after waiting for what seems like an eon, all on edge as in chess, one of the opposing pieces will begin to shake a little and then to wobble back and forth. Gradually the movement increases in extent until the piece gets off balance and begins to rock and career across the board, like a water tumbler on a pitching ship, until it reaches the proper square. Then, slowly, as it began, the movement subsides. I don't know, but it always makes me think of some huge, invisible, senile creature—crafty, selfish, cruel. You've watched that trembly old man at the arcade? The one who always drags the pieces across the board without lifting them, his hand constantly shaking? It's a little like that."

I nodded. His description made it very vivid. For the first time I began to think of how unpleasant such a dream might be.

"And it goes on night after night?" I asked.

"Night after night!" he affirmed with sudden fierceness. "And always the same game. It has been more than a month now, and my forces are just beginning to grapple with the enemy. It's draining off my mental energy. I wish it would stop. I'm getting so that I hate to go to sleep." He paused and turned away. "It seems queer," he said after a moment in a softer voice, smiling apologetically, "It seems queer to get so worked up over a dream. But if you've had bad ones, you know how they can cloud your thoughts all day. And I haven't really managed to get over to you the sort of feeling that grips me while I'm dreaming, and while my brain is working at the game and plotting move-sequence after move-sequence and weighing a thousand complex possibilities. There's repugnance, yes, and fear. I've told you that. But the dominant feeling is one of responsibility. I must not lose the game. More than my own personal welfare depends upon it. There are some terrible stakes involved, though I am never quite sure what they are.

"When you were a little child, did you ever worry tremendously about something, with that complete lack of proportion characteristic of childhood? Did you ever feel that everything, literally everything, depended upon your performing some trivial action, some unimportant duty, in just the right way? Well, while I dream, I have the feeling that I'm playing for some stake as big as the fate of mankind. One wrong move may plunge the universe into unending night. Sometimes, in my dream, I feel sure of it."

His voice trailed off and he stared at the chessmen. I made some remarks and started to tell about an air-raid nightmare I had just had, but it didn't seem very important. And I gave him some vague advice about changing his sleeping habits, which did not seem very important either, although he accepted it with good grace. As I started back to my room he said, "Amusing to think, isn't it, that I'll be playing the game again as soon as my head hits the pillow?" He grinned and added lightly, "Perhaps it will be over sooner than I expect. Lately I've had the feeling that my adversary is about to unleash a surprise attack, although he pretends to be on the defensive." He grinned again and shut the door.

As I waited for sleep, staring at the wavy churning darkness that is more in the eyes than outside them, I began to wonder whether Moreland did not stand in greater need of psychiatric treatment than most chess-players. Certainly a person without family, friends, or proper occupation is liable to mental aberrations. Yet he seemed sane enough. Perhaps the dream was a compensation for his failure to use anything like the full potentialities of his highly talented mind, even at chessplaying. Certainly it was a satisfyingly grandiose vision, with its unearthly background and its implications of stupendous mental skill.

There floated into my mind the lines from the *Rubaiyat* about the cosmic chess-player who, "Hither and thither moves and checks, and slays, And one by one back in the Closet lays."

Then I thought of the emotional atmosphere of his dreams, and the feelings of terror and boundless responsibility, of tremendous duties and cataclysmic consequences—feelings I recognized from my own dreams—and I compared them with the mad, dismal state of the world (for it was October, and sense of utter catastrophe had not yet been dulled) and I thought of the million drifting Morelands suddenly shocked into a realization of the desperate plight of things and of priceless chances lost forever in the past and of their own ill-defined but certain complicity in the disaster. I began to see Moreland's dream as the symbol of a last-ditch, too-late struggle against the implacable forces of fate and chance. And my night thoughts began to revolve around the fancy that some cosmic beings, neither gods nor men, had created human life long ago as a jest or experiment or artistic form, and had now decided to base the fate of their creation on the result of a game of skill played against one of their creatures.

Suddenly I realized that I was wide awake and that the darkness was no longer restful. I snapped on the light and impulsively decided to see if Moreland was still up.

The hall was as shadowy and funereal as that of most boarding houses late at night, and I tried to minimize the inevitable dry creakings. I waited for a few moments in front of Moreland's door, but heard nothing, so instead of knocking, I presumed upon our familiarity and edged open the door, quietly, in order not to disturb him if he were abed.

It was then that I heard his voice, and so certain was my impression that the sound came from a considerable distance that I immediately walked back to the stair-well and called, "Moreland, are you down there?"

Only then did I realize what he had said. Perhaps it was the peculiarity of the words that caused them first to register on my mind as merely a series of sounds.

The words were, "My spider-thing seizes your armor-bearer. I threaten." It instantly occurred to me that the words were similar in general form to any one of a number of conventional expressions in chess, such as, "My rook captures your bishop. I give check." But there are no such pieces as "spider-things" or "armor-bearers" in chess or any other game I know of.

I automatically walked back towards his room, though I still doubted he was there. The voice had sounded much too far away—outside the building or at least in a remote section of it.

But he was lying on the cot, his upturned face revealed by the light of a distant electric advertisement, which blinked on and off at regular intervals. The traffic sounds, which had been almost inaudible in the hall, made the half-darkness restless and irritably alive. The defective neon sign still buzzed and droned insectlike as it had earlier in the evening.

I tiptoed over and looked down at him. His face, more pale than it should have been because of some quality of the intermittent light, was set in an expression of painfully intense concentration—forehead vertically furrowed, muscles around the eye contracted, lips pursed to a line. I wondered if I ought to awaken him. I was acutely aware of the impersonally murmuring city all around us—block on block of shuttling, routined, aloof existence—and the contrast made his sleeping face seem all the more sensitive and vividly individual and unguarded, like some soft though purposefully tense organism which has lost its protective shell.

As I waited uncertainly, the tight lips opened a little without losing any of their tautness. He spoke, and for a second time the impression of distance was so compelling that I involuntarily looked over my shoulder and out the dustily glowing window. Then I began to tremble.

"My coiled-thing writhes to the thirteenth square of the green ruler's domain," was what he said, but I can only suggest the quality of the voice. Some inconceivable sort of distance had drained it of all richness and throati-ness and overtones so that it was hollow and flat and faint and disturbingly mournful, as voices sometimes sound in open country, or from up on a high roof, or when there is a bad telephone connection. I felt I was the victim of some gruesome deception, and yet I knew that ventriloquism is a matter of motionless lips and clever suggestion rather than any really convincing change in the quality of the voice itself. Without volition there rose in my mind visions of infinite space, unending darkness. I felt as if I were being wrenched up and away from the world, so that Manhattan lay below me like a black asymmetric spearhead outlined by leaden waters, and then still farther outward at increasing speed until earth and sun and stars and galaxies were all lost and I was beyond the universe. To such a degree did the quality of Moreland's voice affect me.

I do not know how long I stood there waiting for him to speak again, with the noises of Manhattan flowing around yet not quite touching me, and the electric sign blinking on and off unalterably like the ticking of a clock. I could only think about the game that was being played, and wonder whether Moreland's adversary had yet made an answering move, and whether things were going for or against Moreland. There was no telling from his face; its intensity of concentration did not change. During those moments or minutes I stood there, I believed implicitly in the reality of the game. As if I myself were somehow dreaming, I could not question the rationality of my belief or break the spell which bound me.

When finally his lips parted a little and I experienced again that impression of impossible, eerie ventriloquism—the words this time being, "My horned-creature vaults over the twisted tower, challenging the archer"—my fear broke loose from whatever controlled it and I stumbled toward the door.

Then came what was, in an oblique way, the strangest part of the whole episode. In the time it took me to walk the length of the corridor back to my room, most of my fear and most of the feeling of complete alienage and otherworldliness which had dominated me while I was watching Moreland's face, receded so swiftly that I even forgot, for the time being, how great they had been. I do not know why that happened. Perhaps it was because the unwholesome realm of Moreland's dream was so grotesquely dissimilar to anything in the real world. Whatever the cause, by the time I opened the door to my room I was thinking, "Such nightmares can't be wholesome. Perhaps he should see a psychiatrist. Yet it's only a dream," and so on. I felt tired and stupid. Very soon I was asleep.

But some wraith of the original emotions must have lingered, for I awoke next morning with the fear that something had happened to Moreland. Dressing hurriedly, I knocked at his door, but found the room empty, the bedclothes still rumpled. I inquired of the landlady, and she said he had gone out at eight-fifteen as usual. The bald statement did not quite satisfy my vague anxiety. But since my job-hunting that day happened to lie in the direction of the arcade, I had an excuse to wander in. Moreland was stolidly pushing pieces around with an abstracted, tousle-haired fellow of Slavic features, and casually conducting two rapid-fire checker games on the side. Reassured, I went on without bothering him.

That evening we had a long talk about dreams in general, and I found him surprisingly well-read on the subject and scientifically cautious in his attitudes. Rather to my chagrin, it was I who introduced such dubious topics as clairvoyance, mental telepathy, and the possibility of strange telescopings and other distortions of time and space during dream states. Some foolish reticence about admitting I had pushed my way into his room last night kept me from telling him what I had heard and seen, but he freely told me he had had another installment of the usual dream. He seemed to take a more philosophical attitude now that he had shared his experiences with someone. Together we speculated as to the possible daytime sources of his dream. It was after twelve when we said goodnight.

I went away with the feeling of having been let down—vaguely unsatisfied. I think the fear I had experienced the previous night and then almost forgotten must have been gnawing at me obscurely.

And the following evening it found an avenue of return. Thinking Moreland must be tired of talking about dreams, I coaxed him into a game of chess. But in the middle of the game he put back a piece he was about to move, and said, "You know, that damned dream of mine is getting very bothersome."

It turned out that his dream adversary had finally loosed the long-threatened attack, and that the dream itself had turned into a kind of nightmare. "It's very much like what happens to you in a game of chess," he explained. "You go along confident that you have a strong position and that the game is taking the right direction. Every move your opponent makes is one you have foreseen. You get to feeling almost omniscient. Suddenly he makes a totally unexpected attacking move. For a moment you think it must be a stupid blunder on his part. Then you look a little more closely and realize that you have totally overlooked something and that his attack is a sound one. Then you begin to sweat.

"Of course, I've always experienced fear and anxiety and a sense of overpowering responsibility during the dream. But my pieces were like a wall, protecting me. Now I can see only the cracks in that wall. At any one of a hundred weak points it might conceivably be broken. Whenever one of the opposing pieces begins to wobble and shake, I wonder whether, when its move is completed, there will flash into my mind the unalterable and unavoidable combination of moves leading to my defeat. Last night I thought I saw such a move, and the terror was so great that everything swirled and I seemed to drop through millions of miles of emptiness in an instant. Yet just in that instant of waking I realized I had miscalculated, and that my position, though perilous, was still secure. It was so vivid that I almost carried with me into my waking thoughts the reason why, but then some of the steps in the train of dream-reasoning dropped out, as if my waking mind were not big enough to hold them all."

He also told me that his fixation on "the archer" was becoming increasingly troublesome. It filled him with a special kind of terror, different in quality, but perhaps higher in pitch than that engendered in him by the dream as a whole: a crazy morbid terror, characterized by intense repugnance, nerve-twisting exasperation, and reckless suicidal impulses.

"I can't get rid of the feeling," he said, "that the beastly thing will in some unfair and underhanded manner be the means of my defeat."

He looked very tired to me, although his face was of the compact, tough-skinned sort that does not readily show fatigue, and I felt concern for his physical and nervous welfare. I suggested that he consult a doctor (I did not like to say psychiatrist) and pointed out that sleeping tablets might be of some help.

"But in a deeper sleep the dream might be even more vivid and real," he answered, grimacing sardonically. "No, I'd rather play out the game under the present conditions."

I was glad to find that he still viewed the dream as an interesting and temporary psychological phenomenon (what else he could have viewed it as, I did not stop to analyze). Even while admitting to me the exceptional intensity of his emotions, he maintained something of a jesting air. Once he compared his dream to a paranoid's delusions of persecution, and asked whether I didn't think it was good enough to get him admitted to an asylum.

"Then I could forget the arcade and devote all my time to dream-chess," he said, laughing sharply as soon as he saw I was beginning to wonder whether he had not meant the remark half-seriously.

But some part of my mind was not convinced by his protestations, and when later I tossed in the dark, my imagination perversely kept picturing the universe as a great arena in which each creature is doomed to engage in a losing game of skill against demoniac mentalities which, however long they may play cat and mouse, are always assured of final mastery—or almost assured, so that it would be a miracle if they were beaten. I found myself comparing them to certain chess-players, who if they cannot beat an opponent by superior skill, will capitalize on unpleasant personal mannerisms in order to exasperate him and break down the lucidity of his thinking.

This mood colored my own nebulous dreams and persisted into the next day. As I walked the streets I felt myself inundated by an omnipresent anxiety, and I sensed taut, nervous misery in each passing face. For once I seemed able to look behind the mask which every person wears and which is so characteristically pronounced in a congested city, and see what lay behind—the egotistical sensitivity, the smouldering irritation, the thwarted longing, the defeat . . . and, above all, the anxiety, too ill-defined and lacking in definite object to be called fear, but nonetheless infecting every thought and action, and making trivial things terrible. And it seemed to me that social, economic, and physiological factors, even Death and the War, were insufficient to explain such anxiety, and that it was in reality an upwelling from something dubious and horrible in the very constitution of the universe.

That evening I found myself at the arcade. Here too I sensed a difference in things, for Moreland's abstraction was not the calculating boredom with which I was familiar, and his tiredness was shockingly apparent. One of his three opponents, after shifting around restlessly, called his attention to a move, and Moreland jerked his head as if he had been dozing. He immediately made an answering move, and quickly lost his queen and the game by a trap that was very obvious even to me. A little later he lost another game by an equally elementary oversight. The boss of the arcade, a big beefy man, ambled over and stood behind Moreland, his heavy-jowled face impassive, seeming to study the position of the pieces in the last game. Moreland lost that too.

"Who won?" asked the boss.

Moreland indicated his opponent. The boss grunted noncommittally and walked off.

No one else sat down to play. It was near closing time. I was not sure whether Moreland had noticed me, but after a while he stood up and nodded at me, and got his hat and coat. We walked the long stretch back to the rooming house. He hardly spoke a word, and my sensation of morbid insight into the world around persisted and kept me silent. He walked as usual with long, slightly stiff-kneed strides, hands in his pockets, hat pulled low, frowning at the pavement a dozen feet ahead.

When we reached the room he sat down without taking off his coat and said, "Of course, it was the dream that made me lose those games. When I woke this morning it was terribly vivid, and I almost remembered the exact position and all the rules. I started to make a diagram. . . ."

He indicated a piece of wrapping paper on the table. Hasty criss-crossed lines, incomplete, represented what seemed to be the corner of an indefinitely larger pattern. There were about five hundred squares. On various squares were marks and names standing for pieces, and there were arrows radiating out from the pieces to show their power of movement.

"I got that far. Then I began to forget," he said tiredly, staring at the floor.

"But I'm still very close to it. Like a mathematical puzzle you've not quite solved. Parts of the board kept flashing into my mind all day, so that I felt with a little more effort I would be able to grasp the whole. Yet I can't."

His voice changed. "I'm going to lose, you know. It's that piece I call 'the archer.' Last night I couldn't concentrate on the board; it kept drawing my eyes. The worst thing is that it's the spearhead of my adversary's attack. I ache to capture it. But I must not, for it's a kind of catspaw too, the bait of the strategic trap my adversary is laying. If I capture it, I will expose myself to defeat. So I must watch it coming closer and closer—it has an ugly, double-angled sort of hopping move—knowing that my only chance is to sit tight until my adversary overreaches himself and I can counterattack. But I won't be able to. Soon, perhaps tonight, my nerve will crack and I will capture it."

I was studying the diagram with great interest, and only half heard the rest —a description of the actual appearance of "the archer." I heard him say something about "a five-lobed head . . . the head almost hidden by a hood . . . appendages, each with four joints, appearing from under the robe . . . an eight-pronged weapon with wheels and levers about it, and little bag-shaped receptacles, as though for poison . . . posture suggesting it is lifting the weapon to aim it . . . all intricately carved in some lustrous red stone, speckled with violet . . . an expression of bestial, supernatural malevolence. . . ."

Just then all my attention focused suddenly on the diagram, and I felt a tightening shiver of excitement, for I recognized two familiar names, which I had never heard Moreland mention while awake. "Spider-thing" and "green ruler."

Without pausing to think, I told him of how I had listened to his sleep-talking three nights before, and about the peculiar phrases he had spoken which tallied so well with the entries on the diagram. I poured out my account with melodramatic haste. My discovery of the entries on the diagram, nothing exceptionally amazing in itself, probably made such a great impression on me because I had hitherto strangely forgotten or repressed the intense fear I had experienced when I had watched Moreland sleeping.

Before I was finished, however, I noticed the growing anxiety of his expression, and abruptly realized that what I was saying might not have the best effect on him. So I minimized my recollection of the unwholesome quality of his voice—the overpowering impression of distance—and the fear it engendered in me.

Even so, it was obvious that he had received a severe shock. For a little while he seemed to be on the verge of some serious nervous derangement, walking up and down with fierce, jerky movements, throwing out crazy statements, coming back again and again to the diabolical convincingness of the dream—which my revelation seemed to have intensified for him—and finally breaking down into vague appeals for help.

Those appeals had an immediate effect on me, making me forget any wild thoughts of my own and putting everything on a personal level. All my instincts were now to aid Moreland, and I once again saw the whole matter as something for a psychiatrist to handle. Our roles had changed. I was no longer the half-awed listener, but the steadying friend to whom he turned for advice. That, more than anything, gave me a feeling of confidence and made my previous speculations seem childish and unhealthy. I felt contemptuous of myself for having encouraged his delusive trains of imagination, and I did as much as I could to make up for it.

After a while my repeated reassurances seemed to take effect. He grew calm and our talk became reasonable once more, though every now and then he would appeal to me about some particular point that worried him. I discovered for the first time the extent to which he had taken the dream seriously. During his lonely broodings, he told me, he had sometimes become convinced that his mind left his body while he slept and traveled immeasurable distances to some transcosmic realm where the game was played. He had the illusion, he said, of getting perilously close to the innermost secrets of the universe and finding they were rotten and evil and sardonic. At times he had been terribly afraid that the pathway between his mind and the realm of the game would "open up" to such a degree that he would be "sucked up bodily from the world," as he put it. His belief that loss of the game would doom the world itself had been much stronger than he had ever admitted to me previously. He had traced a frightening relationship between the progress of the game and of the War, and had begun to believe that the ultimate issue of the War—though not necessarily the victory of either side—hung on the outcome of the game.

At times it had got so bad, he revealed, that his only relief had been in the thought that, no matter what happened, he could never convince others of the reality of his dream. They would always be able to view it as a manifestation of insanity or overwrought imagination. No matter how vivid it became to him he would never have concrete, objective proof.

"It's this way," he said. "You saw me sleeping, didn't you? Right here on this cot. You heard me talk in my sleep, didn't you? About the game. Well, that absolutely proves to you that it's all just a dream, doesn't it? You couldn't rightly believe anything else, could you?"

I do not know why those last ambiguous questions of his should have had such a reassuring effect on me of all people, who had only three nights ago trembled at the indescribable quality of his voice as he talked from his dream.

But they did. They seemed like the final seal on an agreement between us to the effect that the dream was only a dream and meant nothing. I began to feel rather buoyant and self-satisfied, like a doctor who has just pulled his patient through a dangerous crisis. I talked to Moreland in what I now realize was almost a pompously sympathetic way, without noticing how dispirited were his obedient nods of agreement. He said little after those last questions.

I even persuaded him to go out to a nearby lunchroom for a midnight snack, as if—God help me!—I were celebrating my victory over the dream. As we sat at the not-too-dirty counter, smoking our cigarettes and sipping burningly hot coffee, I noticed that he had begun to smile again, which added to my satisfaction. I was blind to the ultimate dejection and submissive hopelessness that lay behind those smiles. As I left him at the door of his room, he suddenly caught hold of my hand and said, "I want to tell you how grateful I am for the way you've worked to pull me out of this mess," I made a deprecating gesture. "No, wait," he continued, "It does mean a lot. Well, anyway, thanks."

I went away with a contented, almost virtuous feeling. I had no apprehensions whatever. I only mused, in a heavily philosophic way, over the strange forms fear and anxiety can assume in our pitiably tangled civilization.

As soon as I was dressed next morning, I rapped briskly at his door and impulsively pushed in without waiting for an answer. For once sunlight was pouring through the dusty window.

Then I saw it, and everything else receded.

It was lying on the crumpled bedclothes, half hidden by a fold of blanket, a thing perhaps ten inches high, as solid as any statuette, and as undeniably real. But from the first glance I knew that its form bore no relation to any earthly creature. This fact would have been as apparent to someone who knew nothing of art as to an expert. I also knew that the red, violet-flecked substance from which it had been carved or cast had no classification among the earthly gems and minerals. Every detail was there. The five-lobed head, almost hidden by a hood. The appendages, each with four joints, appearing from under the robe. The eight-pronged weapon with wheels and levers about it, and the little bag-shaped receptacles, as though for poison. Posture suggesting it was lifting the weapon to aim it. An expression of bestial, supernatural malevolence.

Beyond doubting, it was the thing of which Moreland had dreamed. The thing which had horrified and fascinated him, as it now did me, which had rasped unendurably on his nerves, as it now began to rasp on mine. The thing which had been the spearhead and catspaw of his adversary's attack, and whose capture—and it now seemed evident that it had been captured—

meant the probable loss of the game. The thing which had somehow been sucked back along an ever-opening path across unimaginable distances from a realm of madness ruling the universe.

Beyond doubting, it was "the archer."

The Unspeakable Betrothal

Robert Bloch

Not far thence is the secret garden in which grow like strange flowers the kinds of sleep, so different one from the other . . . the sleep induced by datura, by the multiple extracts of ether, the sleep of belladonna, of opium, of valerian; flowers whose petals remain shut until the day when the pre-destined visitor shall come and, touching them, bid them open, and for long hours inhale the aroma of their peculiar dreams into a marvelling and bewildered being.

——*Proust:* Remembrance of Things Past

Avis knew she wasn't really as sick as Doctor Clegg had said. She was merely bored with living. The death-impulse, perhaps; then again, it might have been nothing more than her distaste for clever young men who persisted in addressing her as *"O rara Avis."*

She felt better now, though. The fever had settled until it was no more than one of the white blankets which covered her—something she could toss aside with a gesture, if it weren't so pleasant just to burrow into it, to snuggle deeply within its confining warmth.

Avis smiled as she realized the truth; monotony was the one thing that didn't bore her. The sterility of excitement was the really jading routine, after all. This quiet, uneventful feeling of restfulness seemed rich and fertile by comparison. Rich and fertile—creative—womb.

The words linked. Back to the womb. Dark room, warm bed, lying doubled up in the restful, nourishing lethargy of fever . . .

It wasn't the womb, exactly; she hadn't gone back that far, she knew. But it did remind her of the days when she was a little girl. Just a little girl with big round eyes, mirroring the curiosity that lay behind them. Just a little girl, living all alone in a huge old house, like a fairy princess in an enchanted castle.

Of course her aunt and uncle had lived here too, and it wasn't a really truly castle, and nobody else knew that she was a princess. Except Marvin Mason, that is.

Marvin had lived next door and sometimes he'd come over and play with her. They would come up to her room and look out of the high window— the little round window that bordered on the sky.

Marvin knew that she was a sure enough princess, and he knew that her room was an ivory tower. The window was an enchanted window, and when they stood on a chair and peeked out they could see the world behind the sky.

Sometimes she wasn't quite sure if Marvin Mason honest and truly saw the world beyond the window; maybe he just said he did because he was stuck on her.

But he listened very quietly while she told him stories about that world. Sometimes she told him stories she had read in books, and other times she made them up out of her very own head. It was only later that the dreams came, and she told him *those* stories, too.

That is, she always started to, but somehow the words would go wrong. She didn't always know the words for what she saw in those dreams. They were very special dreams; they came only on those nights when Aunt May left the window open, and there was no moon. She would lie in the bed, all curled up in a little ball, and wait for the wind to come through the high, round window. It came quietly, and she would feel it on her forehead and neck, like fingers stroking. Cool, soft fingers, stroking her face; soothing fingers that made her uncurl and stretch out so that the shadows could cover her body.

Even then she slept in the big bed, and the shadows would pour down from the window in a path. She wasn't asleep when the shadows came, so she knew they were real. They came on the breeze, from the window, and covered her up. Maybe it was the shadows that were cool and not the wind; maybe the shadows stroked her hair until she fell asleep.

But she would sleep then, and the dreams always came. They followed the same path as the wind and the shadows; they poured down from the sky, through the window. There were voices she heard but could not understand; colors she saw but could not name; shapes she glimpsed but which never seemed to resemble any figures she found in picture books.

Sometimes the same voices and colors and shapes came again and again, until she learned to recognize them, in a way. There was the deep, buzzing voice that seemed to come from right inside her own head, although she knew it really issued from the black, shiny pyramid-thing that had the arms with eyes in it. It didn't look slimy or nasty, and there was nothing to be afraid of—Avis could never understand why Marvin Mason made her shut up when she started telling about those dreams.

But he was only a little boy, and he got scared and ran home to his Mommy. Avis didn't have any Mommy, only Aunt May; but she would never tell Aunt May such things. Besides, why should she? The dreams didn't frighten her, and they were so very real and interesting. Sometimes, on gray, rainy days when there was nothing to do but play with dolls or cut out pictures to paste in her album, she wished that night would hurry up and come. Then she could dream and make everything real again.

She got so she liked to stay in bed, and would pretend to have a cold so she didn't have to go to school. Avis would look up at the window and wait for the dreams to come—but they never came in the daytime; only at night.

Often she wondered what it was like *up there*.

The dreams must come from the sky; she knew that. The voices and shapes *lived* way up, somewhere beyond the window. Aunt May said that dreams came from tummy-aches, but she knew that wasn't so.

Aunt May was always worried about tummy-aches, and she scolded Avis for not going outside to play, said she was getting pale and puny.

But Avis felt fine, and she had her secret to think of. Now she scarcely ever saw Marvin Mason any more, and she didn't bother to read. It wasn't much fun to pretend she was a princess, either. Because the dreams were ever so much realer, and she could talk to the voices and ask them to take her with them when they went away.

She got so she could almost understand what they were saying. The shiny thing that just hung through the window now—the one that looked like it had so much more to it she couldn't see—it made music inside her head that she recognized. Not a real tune; more like words in a rhyme. In her dreams she asked it to take her away. She would crawl up on its back and let it fly with her up over the stars. That was funny, asking it to fly; but she knew that the part beyond the window had wings. Wings as big as the world.

She begged and pleaded, but the voices made her understand that they couldn't take little girls back with them. That is, not entirely. Because it was too cold and too far, and something would change her.

She said she didn't care how she changed; she wanted to go. She would let them do anything they wanted if only they would take her: It would be nice to be able to talk to them all the time and feel that cool softness; to dream forever.

One night they came to her and there were more things than she had ever seen before. They hung through the window and in the air all over the room —they were so funny, some of them; you could see through them and sometimes one was partly inside another. She knew she giggled in her sleep, but she couldn't help it. Then she was quiet and listening to them.

They told her it was all right. They would carry her away. Only she mustn't tell anyone and she mustn't be frightened; they would come for her soon. They couldn't take her as she was, and she must be willing to change.

Avis said yes, and they all hummed a sort of music together, and went away.

The next morning Avis was really and truly sick and didn't want to get up. She could hardly breathe, she was so warm—and when Aunt May brought in a tray she wouldn't eat a bite.

That night she didn't dream. Her head ached, and she tossed all night long. But there was a moon out, so the dreams couldn't get through anyway. She knew they would come back when the moon was gone again, so she waited. Besides, she hurt so that she didn't really care. She had to feel better before she was ready to go anywhere.

The next day Dr. Clegg came to see her. Dr. Clegg was a good friend of Aunt May's and he was always visiting her because he was her guardian.

Dr. Clegg held her hand and asked her what seemed to be the matter with his young lady today?

Avis was too smart to say anything, and besides there was a shiny thing in her mouth. Dr. Clegg took it out and looked at it and shook his head. After a while he went away and then Aunt May and Uncle Roscoe came in. They made her swallow some medicine that tasted just awful.

By this time it was getting dark and there was a storm coming outside. Avis wasn't able to talk much, and when they shut the round window she couldn't ask them to please leave it open tonight because there was no moon and they were coming for her.

But everything kept going round and round, and when Aunt May walked past the bed she seemed to flatten out like a shadow, or one of the things, only she made a loud noise which was really the thunder outside and now she was sleeping really and truly even though she heard the thunder but the thunder wasn't real nothing was real except the things that was it nothing was real any more but the things.

And they came through the window it wasn't closed after all because she opened it and she was crawling out high up there where she had never crawled before but it was easy without a body and soon she would have a new body they wanted the old one because they carried it but she didn't care because she didn't need it and now they would carry her *ulnagr Yuggoth farnomi ilyaa. . . .*

That was when Aunt Mary and Uncle Roscoe found her and pulled her

down from the window. They said later she had screamed at the top of her
voice, or else she would have gone over without anyone noticing.

After that Dr. Clegg took her away to the hospital where there were no
high windows and they came in to see her all night long. The dreams
stopped.

When at last she was well enough to go back home, she found that the
window was gone, too.

Aunt May and Uncle Roscoe had boarded it up, because she was a somnambulist. She didn't know what a somnambulist was, but guessed it had
something to do with her being sick and the dreams not coming any more.

For the dreams stopped, then. There was no way of making them come
back, and she really didn't want them any more. It was fun to play outside
with Marvin Mason now, and she went back to school when the new semester began.

Now, without the window to look at, she just slept at night. Aunt May
and Uncle Roscoe were glad, and Dr. Clegg said she was turning out to be a
mighty fine little specimen.

Avis could remember it all now as though it were yesterday. Or today. Or
tomorrow.

How she grew up. How Marvin Mason fell in love with her. How she
went to college and they became engaged. How she felt the night Aunt May
and Uncle Roscoe were killed in the crash at Leedsville. That was a bad time.

An even worse time was when Marvin Mason had gone away. He was in
service now, overseas. She had stayed on all alone in the house, for it was her
house now.

Reba came in days to do the housework, and Dr. Clegg dropped around,
even after she turned 21 and officially inherited her estate.

He didn't seem to approve of her present mode of living. He asked her
several times why she didn't shut up the house and move into a small apartment downtown. He was concerned because she showed no desire to keep
up the friendships she had made in college; Avis was curiously reminded of
the solicitude he had exhibited during her childhood.

But Avis was no longer a child. She proved that by removing what had
always seemed to her a symbol of adult domination; she had the high round
window in her room unboarded once more.

It was a silly gesture. She knew it at the time, but somehow it held a
curious significance for her. For one thing it re-established a linkage with her
childhood, and more and more childhood came to epitomize happiness for
her.

With Marvin Mason gone, and Aunt May and Uncle Roscoe dead, there
was little enough to fill the present. Avis would sit up in her bedroom and

pore over the scrapbooks she had so assiduously pasted up as a girl. She had kept her dolls and the old fairy tale books; she spent drowsy afternoons examining them.

It was almost possible to lose one's time-sense in such pastimes. Her surroundings were unchanged. Of course, Avis was larger now and the bed wasn't quite as massive nor the window as high.

But both were there, waiting for the little girl that she became when, at nightfall, she curled up into a ball and snuggled under the sheets—snuggled and stared up at the high, round window that bordered the sky.

Avis wanted to dream again.

At first, she *couldn't*.

After all, she was a grown woman, engaged to be married; she wasn't a character out of *Peter Ibbetson*. And those dreams of her childhood had been silly.

But they were *nice*. Yes, even when she had been ill and nearly fallen out of the window that time, it had been pleasant to dream. Of course those voices and shapes were nothing but Freudian fantasies—everyone knew that.

Or did they?

Suppose it was all real? Suppose dreams are not just subconscious manifestations; caused by indigestion and gas pressure.

What if dreams are really a product of electronic impulse—or planetary radiations—attuned to the wave-length of the sleeping mind? Thought is an electrical impulse. Life itself is an electrical impulse. Perhaps a dreamer is like a spiritualist medium; placed in a receptive state during sleep. Instead of ghosts, the creatures of another world or another dimension can come through, if the sleeper is granted the rare gift of acting as a *filter*. What if the dreams feed on the dreamer for substance, just as spirits attain ectoplasmic being by draining the medium of energy?

Avis thought and thought about it, and when she had evolved this theory, everything seemed to fit. Not that she would ever tell anyone about her attitude. Dr. Clegg would only laugh at her, or still worse, shake his head. Marvin Mason didn't approve either. Nobody wanted her to dream. They still treated her like a little girl.

Very well, she would be a little girl; a little girl who could do as she pleased, now. She would dream.

It was shortly after reaching this decision that the dreams began again; almost as though they had been waiting until she would fully accept them in terms of their own reality.

Yes, they came back, slowly, a bit at a time. Avis found that it helped to concentrate on the past during the day; to strive to remember her childhood. To this end she spent more and more time in her room, leaving Reba to tend to housework downstairs. As for fresh air, she always could look out of her window. It was high and small, but she would climb on a stool and gaze up at the sky through the round aperture; watching the clouds that veiled the blue beyond, and waiting for night to come.

Then she would sleep in the big bed and wait for the wind. The wind soothed and the darkness slithered, and soon she could hear the buzzing, burring voices. At first only the voices came back, and they were faint and far away. Gradually they increased in intensity and once more she was able to discriminate, to recognize individual intonations.

Timidly, hesitantly, the figures re-emerged. Each night they grew stronger. Avis Long (little girl with big round eyes in big bed below round window) welcomed their presence.

She wasn't alone any more. No need to see her friends, or talk to that silly old Dr. Clegg. No need to waste much time gossiping with Reba, or fussing over meals. No need to dress or venture out. There was the window by day and the dreams by night.

Then all at once she was curiously weak, and this illness came. But it was all false, somehow; this physical change.

Her mind was untouched. She knew that. No matter how often Dr. Clegg pursed his lips and hinted about calling in a "specialist", she wasn't afraid. Of course Avis knew he really wanted her to see a psychiatrist. The doddering fool was filled with glib patter about "retreat from reality" and "escape mechanisms".

But he didn't understand about the dreams. She wouldn't tell him, either. He'd never know the richness, the fullness, the sense of completion that came from experiencing contact with other worlds.

Avis knew *that* now. The voices and shapes that came in the window were from other worlds. As a naive child she had invited them by her very unsophistication. Now, striving consciously to return to the childlike attitude, she again admitted them.

They were from other worlds; worlds of wonder and splendor. Now they could meet only on the plane of dreams, but someday; someday soon, she would bridge the gap.

They whispered about her body. Something about the trip, making the "change". It couldn't be explained in *their* words. But she trusted them, and after all, a physical change was of slight importance contrasted with the opportunity.

Soon she would be well again, strong again. Strong enough to say "yes." And then they would come for her when the moon was right. Until then, she could strengthen the determination, and the dream.

Avis Long lay in the great bed and basked in the blackness; the blackness that poured palpably through the open window. The shapes filtered down, wriggling through the warps, feeding upon the night; growing, pulsing, encompassing all.

They reassured her about the body but she didn't care and she told them she didn't care because the body was unimportant and yes, she would gladly consider it an exchange if only she could go and she knew she belonged.

Not beyond the rim of the stars but between it and amongst substance dwells that which is blackness in blackness for Yuggoth is only a symbol no that is wrong there are no symbols for all is reality and only perception is limited ch'yar ul'nyar shaggornyth . . .

It is hard for us to make you understand but I do understand *you can not fight it* I will not fight it *they will try to stop you* nothing shall stop me for I belong *yes you belong* will it be soon *yes it will be soon* very soon *yes very soon* . . .

Marvin Mason was unprepared for this sort of reception. Of course, Avis hadn't written, and she wasn't at the station to meet him—but the possibility of her being seriously ill had never occurred to him.

He had come out to the house at once, and it was a shock when Dr. Clegg met him at the door.

The old man's face was grim, and the tenor of his opening remarks still grimmer.

They faced each other in the library downstairs; Mason self-consciously diffident in khaki, the older man a bit too professionally brusque.

"Just what is it, Doctor?" Mason asked.

"I don't know. Slight, recurrent fever. Listlessness. I've checked everything. No TB, no trace of lowgrade infection. Her trouble isn't—organic."

"You mean something's wrong with her mind?"

Dr. Clegg slumped into an armchair and lowered his head.

"Mason, I could say many things to you; about the psychosomatic theory of medicine, about the benefits of psychiatry, about—but never mind. It would be sheer hypocrisy.

"I've talked to Avis; rather, I've tried to talk to her. She won't say much, but what she does say disturbs me. Her actions disturb me even more.

"You can guess what I'm driving at, I think, when I tell you that she is leading the life of an eight-year-old girl. The life she *did* lead at that age."

Mason scowled. "Don't tell me she sits in her room again and looks out of that window?"

Dr. Clegg nodded.

"But I thought it was boarded up long ago, because she's a somnambulist and—"

"She had it unboarded, several months ago. And she is not, never was, a somnambulist."

"What do you mean?"

"Avis Long never walked in her sleep. I remember the night she was found on that window's edge; not ledge, for there is no ledge. She was perched on the edge of the open window, already halfway out; a little tyke hanging through a high window.

"But there was no chair beneath her, no ladder. No way for her to climb up. She was simply *there*."

Dr. Clegg looked away before continuing.

"Don't ask me what it means. I can't explain, and I wouldn't want to. I'd have to talk about the things she talks about—the dreams, and the presences that come to her; the presences that want her to go *away*.

"Mason, it's up to you. I can't honestly move to have her committed on the basis of material evidence. Confinement means nothing to *them;* you can't build a wall to keep out dreams.

"But you love her. You can save her. You can make her well, make her take an interest in reality. Oh, I know it sounds mawkish and stupid, just as the other sounds wild and fantastic.

"Yet it's true. It's happening right now, to her. She's asleep up in her room at this very moment. She's hearing the voices—I know that much. Let her hear your voice."

Mason walked out of the room and started up the stairs.

"But what do you mean, you can't marry me?"

Mason stared at the huddled figure in the swirl of bedclothes. He tried to avoid the direct stare of Avis Long's curiously childlike eyes; just as he avoided gazing up at the black, ominous aperture of the round window.

"I can't, that's all," Avis answered. Even her voice seemed to hold a childlike quality. The high, piercing tones might well have emanated from the throat of a little girl; a tired little girl, half-asleep and a bit petulant about being abruptly awakened.

"But our plans—your letters—"

"I'm sorry, dear. I can't talk about it. You know I haven't been well. Dr. Clegg is downstairs, he must have told you."

"But you're getting better," Mason pleaded. "You'll be up and around again in a few days."

Avis shook her head. A smile—the secret smile of a naughty child—clung to the corners of her mouth.

"You can't understand, Marvin. You never *could* understand. That's because you belong here." A gesture indicated the room. "I belong somewhere else." Her finger stabbed, unconsciously, towards the window.

Marvin looked at the window now. He couldn't help it. The round black hole that led to nothingness. Or—something. The sky outside was dark, moonless. A cold wind curled about the bed.

"Let me close the window for you, dear," he said, striving to keep his voice even and gentle.

"No."

"But you're ill—you'll catch cold."

"That isn't why you want to close it." Even in accusation, the voice was curiously piping. Avis sat bolt upright and confronted him.

"You're jealous, Marvin. Jealous of me. Jealous of *them*. You would never let me dream. You would never let me go. And I want to go. They're coming for me.

"I know why Dr. Clegg sent you up here. He wants you to persuade me to go away. He'd like to shut me up, just as he wants to shut the window. He wants to keep me here because he's afraid. You're all afraid of what lies—out there.

"Well, it's no use. You can't stop me. You can't stop *them!*"

"Take it easy, darling—"

"Never mind. Do you think I care what they do to me, if only I can go? I'm not afraid. I know I can't go as I am now. I know they must alter me.

"There are certain parts they want for reasons of their own. You'd be frightened if I told you. But I'm not afraid. You say I'm sick and insane; don't deny it. Yet I'm healthy enough, sane enough to face them and their world. It's you who are too morbid to endure it all."

Avis Long was wailing now; a thin, high-pitched wail of a little girl in a tantrum.

"You and I are leaving this house tomorrow," Mason said. "We're going away. We'll be married and live happily ever after—in good old storybook style. The trouble with you, young lady, is that you've never had to grow up. All this nonsense about goblins and other worlds—"

Avis screamed.

Mason ignored her.

"Right now I'm going to shut that window," he declared.

Avis continued to scream. The shrill ululation echoed on a sustained note as Mason reached up and closed the round pane of glass over the black aperture. The wind resisted his efforts, but he shut the window and secured the latch.

Then her fingers were digging into his throat from the rear, and her scream was pouring down his ear.

"I'll kill you!" she wailed. It was the wail of an enraged child.

But there was nothing of the child, or the invalid, in the strength behind her clawing fingers. He fought her off, panting.

Then, suddenly, Dr. Clegg was in the room. A hypodermic needle flashed and gleamed in an arc of plunging silver.

They carried her back to the bed, tucked her in. The blankets nestled about the weary face of a child in sleep.

The window was closed tightly now.

Everything was in order as the two men turned out the light and tiptoed from the room.

Neither of them said a word until they stood downstairs once again.

Facing the fireplace, Mason sighed.

"Somehow I'll get her out of here tomorrow," he promised. "Perhaps it was too abrupt—my coming back tonight and waking her. I wasn't very tactful.

"But something about her; something about that room, frightened me."

Dr. Clegg lit his pipe. "I know," he said. "That's why I couldn't pretend to you that I completely understand. There's more to it than mere hallucination."

"I'm going to sit up here tonight," Mason continued. "Just in case something might happen."

"She'll sleep," Dr. Clegg assured him. "No need to worry."

"I'll feel better if I stay. I'm beginning to get a theory about all this talk—other worlds, and changes in her body before a trip. It ties in with the window, somehow. And it sounds like a fantasy on suicide."

"The death-impulse? Perhaps. I should have thought of that possibility. Dreams foreshadowing death—on second thought, Mason, I may stay with you. We can make ourselves comfortable here before the fire, I suppose."

Silence settled.

It must have been well after midnight before either of them moved from their place before the fire.

Then a sharp splinter of sound crashed from above. Before the tinkling echo died away, both men were on their feet and moving towards the stairway.

There was no further noise from above, and neither of them exchanged a single word. Only the thud of their running footsteps on the stairs broke the silence. And as they paused outside Avis Long's room, the silence seemed to deepen in intensity. It was a silence palpable, complete, accomplished.

Dr. Clegg's hand darted to the doorknob, wrenched it ineffectually.

"Locked!" he muttered. "She must have gotten up and locked it."

Mason scowled.

"The window—do you think she could have—?"

Dr. Clegg refused to meet his glance. Instead he turned and put his massive shoulder to the door panel. A bulge of muscle ridged his neck.

Then the panel splintered and gave way. Mason reached around and opened the door from inside.

They entered the darkened room, Dr. Clegg, in the lead, fumbling for the light-switch. The harsh, electric glare flooded the scene.

It was a tribute to the power of suggestion that both men glanced, not at the patient in the bed, but at the round window high up on the wall.

Cold night air streamed through a jagged aperture, where the glass had been shattered, as though by the blow of a gigantic fist.

Fragments of glass littered the floor beneath, but there was no trace of any missile. And obviously, the glass had been broken from the outer side of the pane.

"The wind," Mason murmured, weakly, but he could not look at Dr. Clegg as he spoke. For there was no wind, only the cold, soft breeze that billowed ever so gently from the nighted sky above. Only the cold, soft breeze, rustling the curtains and prompting a sarabande of shadows on the wall; shadows that danced in silence over the great bed in the corner.

The breeze and the silence and the shadows enveloped them as they stared now at the bed.

Avis Long's head was turned towards them on the pillow. They could see her face quite plainly, and Dr. Clegg realized on the basis of experience what Mason knew instinctively—Avis Long's eyes were closed in death.

But that is not what made Mason gasp and shudder—nor did the sight of death alone cause Dr. Clegg to scream aloud.

There was nothing whatsoever to frighten the beholder of the placid countenance turned towards them in death. They did not scream at the sight of Avis Long's face.

Lying on the pillow of the huge bed, Avis Long's face bore a look of perfect peace.

But Avis Long's body was . . . gone.

Lover
When You're Near Me

Richard Matheson

The silvery welded ship came rushing backwards through the veils of broken cloud, tobogganing down the atmosphere of Station Four. Fires of deceleration jetted red from the reactor ports, roaring their hurricane thrust against the clutch of gravity.

Air thickened; the glittering rocket speck slid easier, settling itself downward like a parachuting missile. Sunlight splashed its metal sides with light and the blue ocean waters billowed wide to swallow it. The ship dipped in a wide arc and backed down toward the reddish-green clad land.

Inside its tiny cabin, the three men lay strapped and waiting for the shock of contact. Their eyes were closed, their hands tight and blood-drained. Muscle blocks struggled against the drag.

The earth swept up and blocked its way; the ship settled hard on its rear braces, trembling. Then, in an instant, it stood motionless and silent, successfully navigated through a thousand billion miles of vacuumed night.

A quarter mile away were the warehouse, the village and the house.

Critical. That was the official record. It was supposed to be secret but David Lindell knew it; all the Wentner men had known it. Station Four The Birds and the Three-Moon Psycho Ward. That was scuttlebutt and to be taken with a fistful of salt. Lindell knew that too.

But it all meant something; the laughter, the ribbing, the silence from upstairs. They put a man on other stations for two years at a clip. Here on Four it was only for six months. That meant something. It adds up, they used to say in the briefing room on Earth. *Wentner's Interstellar Trading Company* doesn't break its heart for nothing. And Lindell believed it.

"But like I always say," he said, "it's no use worrying myself."

He said it to Martin, the ship's co-pilot as the two of them trudged across the wide meadow toward the distant compound carrying Lindell's luggage.

"You have the right idea," said Martin. "Don't worry yourself."

"That's what I always say," said Lindell.

After a while they passed the silent gargantuan warehouse. The sliding doors were half open and, inside, Lindell could see the concrete floor empty and sunlight filtering through the skylight. Martin told him the cargo ship had emptied it out a few weeks before. Lindell grunted and shifted his luggage.

"Where are the workers?" he asked.

Martin gestured his helmeted head toward the workers' village about three hundred yards away. There was no sound from the low-slung white dwellings methodically arranged to form three sides of a rectangle. The windows blinked fiercely in the sunlight.

"Guess they're sacked out," Martin judged. "They sleep a lot when work is done. You'll see them tomorrow when shipments start coming in again."

"Got their families with them?" Lindell asked.

"Nope."

"Thought it was company policy."

"Not here. The Gnees don't have much family life. Too few men and they're all pretty dumb."

"Great," Lindell said. "Dandy." He shrugged. "Well, it's no use worrying myself about it."

While they were on the stairs to the hallway of the house, he asked Martin where Corrigan was.

"He went home with the cargo ship," Martin said. "They do that once in a while. There's nothing here to do anyway after the goods are picked up."

"Oh," said Lindell. "What's this door?" He kicked it open and looked in at the combination living room-library.

"All the comforts of," he said.

"More," said Martin, looking over Lindell's shoulder. "Over there you have a movie projector and a tape recorder."

"Swell," Lindell said. "I can talk to myself legal." Then he grimaced. "Let's dump these bags. My arms are falling off."

They shuffled down the hall and Lindell glanced into the small kitchen as they passed. It was porcelain paneled and well kept.

"Can this Gnee woman cook?" he asked.

"From what I hear," said Martin, "you'll be packing it in like a king."

"Glad to hear it. Say, incidentally, you got any idea why they call this joint the Three-Moon Psycho Ward?"

"Who calls it?"

"The boys back on Earth."

"The boys are all wet. You'll like it here."

"But why is it only a six month stint?"

"Here's your bedroom," Martin said.

As they entered, she was making the bed, her back turned to the door. They thumped down the bags and she turned.

Lindell's hands twitched. Oh well, he rallied, I've seen worse in my day.

She wore a heavy robe fastened at the neck and falling to the floor like a truncated cone of cloth. All he could see was her head.

It was a squat, coarsely-grained head, pink and hairless. Like the mottled belly of an expecting bitch, he decided. For ears there were cavities on the sides of her flat, chinless face. Her nose was a stub, single nostriled. Her lips were thick and monkey-like, outlining a small circle of mouth. Hello Beautiful, Lindell decided not to say.

She came across the room quietly and he blinked at her eyes. Then she placed a moist, spongy hand in his.

"Hi," he said.

"She can't hear," Martin said. "Telepathic."

"That's right, I forgot." *Hello,* he thought, and *Hello* came back the answering welcome. *It is good to have you.*

"Thanks," he said. She seemed a decent kid, he thought to himself; weird but homey. A question touched his brain like a timid hand.

"Yeah, sure," he said. *Yes,* he added in his mind.

"What's that?" Martin asked.

"She asked if she should unpack, I think." Lindell slumped down on the bed. "Ahhh," he said. "This I like." He pushed exploring fingers into the mattress.

"Say, how do you know it's a she?" he asked when he and Martin were walking back down the hall while the Gnee woman unpacked.

"The robe. The males don't wear robes."

"That's all?"

Martin grinned. "A few other things of absolutely no interest to you."

They moved into the living room and Lindell tried out the easy chair for size. He leaned back and stroked the arms with satisfied fingers.

"Critical or no," he said, "this station has 'em all beat for comfort."

He sat there, momentarily reflecting on her eyes. They were huge eyes, covering a full third of her face; like big glass saucers with dark cup rings for pupils. And they were moist; bowls of liquid. He shrugged and let it go. So what, he thought, it's nothing.

"Hah? What?" he asked, hearing Martin's voice.

"I said—be careful." Martin was holding up a shiny gas pistol. "This is loaded," he warned.

"Who needs it?"

"You won't. Just standard equipment." Martin put it back in the desk drawer and shoved the drawer back in. "And you know where all your books are," he said. "The warehouse office is set up like all the other station offices." Lindell nodded.

Martin glanced at his watch. "Well, I have to be going."

"Let's see," he continued as he and Lindell started for the door. "Anything else to tell you? You know the rule about not harming the people, of course?"

"Who's gonna harm—whoops!"

They'd almost knocked her over as they exited from the room. She jumped back one more bouncy step and stared at them, eyes wide and frightened.

"Take it easy, kiddo," Lindell soothed. "What's up?"

Eat? The thought cringed before him like a beggar at the back door of his mind. He pursed his lips and nodded. "You took the words right out of my head."

He looked at her and concentrated. *I'll be back as soon as I walk the co-pilot back to his ship. Make something good.*

She nodded violently and rushed toward the kitchen.

"Where's she off to like a bat?" Martin asked as they turned for the stairs and Lindell told him.

"That's what I call service deluxe," he said, chuckling, as they descended. "This telepathy is okay. At the other stations it was either learn half the language to get a ham sandwich or try and teach 'em English so I wouldn't starve. Either way I really had to sweat for my supper until things got settled."

He looked pleased. "This is hot," he said.

Their heavy boots crushed down the tall crisp blue grass as they approached the upright ship. Martin held out his hand. "Take it easy, Lindell. See you in six."

"Right enough. Give old man Wentner a kick in the pants for me."

"Will do."

He watched the co-pilot dwindle in size ascending the metal ladder to the hatchway. A midget Martin pulled himself into the ship and clanged the metal port shut behind himself. Lindell waved back at the tiny figure at the port and then turned and ran away to escape the blast.

He stood on a hill underneath the heavy scarlet foliage of a tree. Inside the ship's belly he heard a liquid cough, a rush of exploding gasses. He watched the ship hang for a moment on its flaming exhaust and then flash up into the

green-blue sky, leaving scorched plant life in its wake. In a moment it was
gone.

He walked in lazy strides back toward the house, gazing appreciatively at
the profusion of livid plants and flowers in the meadow around him, bulbous
insects hanging over them.

He took off his jacket and let it hang from one hand as he walked. The sun
felt good on his lean back.

"Boys," he said to the fragrant air. "You're all wet."

The great blazing sun was almost gone, spraying the sky with the blood of
its cyclic dying. Soon the three moons would rise; guaranteed to drive insane
a man looking for a shadow to call his own.

Lindell sat at the living room window gazing out over the countryside.
You couldn't beat it, he thought; for air or climate or all the things that grew
in Earth's paling technicolor. Nature had outdone herself in this tucked away
corner of the galaxy. He sighed and stretched, wondering about supper.

Drink?

He started, chopping a yawn in half, and drew his fingers together so fast
that the knuckle bones crackled.

He saw her standing at his side, proffering a tray with a glass on it. He
reached for it, feeling his heart placate itself after the initial jolt.

"I'd knock or something," he suggested. The big eyes were elliptical now.
They stared at him without comprehension.

"Well, let it go," he said, after a sip of the warm tangy liquid. He smacked
his lips and took another sip, a long one.

"Damn good," he said. "Thanks, Lover."

He blinked at himself. That brings a guy up short, he decided. *Lover?* Of
all the unlikely names in the universe— He glanced at her with a chuckle
bubbling up in his throat.

She hadn't moved. Her face was screwed up into what he assumed was a
smile. But her mouth wasn't designed for smiling.

"Hey, when are we eating?" he asked, feeling an edge uncomfortable
under the unmoving gaze of her watery eye globes.

She turned and hurried to the door. There she turned.

All ready already, he got the message.

He grinned, downed the drink, got up and followed her eager shuffle
down the dim hallway.

He pushed away the plate with a sigh and leaned back in the chair.

"That's what I call good," he said.

Like a hidden spring, he felt her pleasure well up in his mind. *Lover thanks you.* She certainly picked up the name fast, he thought. She looked at him, eyes wide. Was she trying to smile again, he wondered? To him the expression looked like all her others; the facial poses of an idiot. He thought she was smiling though because of the thoughts that accompanied the expression.

Then he found his eyes watering in empathy and he turned his head, blinking. A trifle nervously, he dumped a teaspoon of sugar in his coffee and stirred. He could feel her eyes on him. A twinge of displeasure marred his thoughts and she turned away abruptly. That's better, he thought, and felt all right again.

"Hey, tell me Lover," he started to say. Well, might as well get used to it, he figured. *You have a husband?* Her returned thoughts were confused.

A mate? he reworded.

Oh, yes.

In the workers' village?

They have no mates, she answered and he thought he sensed a note of hauteur in her reply.

He shrugged and took a sip of coffee. "Well," he said to himself, "one satisfied worker would drive the rest of 'em crazy anyway. They'd be biting their nails if they had nails. And on that note, good night."

In bed he sat writing in his much-used diary. Between its beat-up covers were inscribed the sparse comments he had made on half a dozen different planets. This was his seventh selection. *My lucky number,* he paragraphed in blue ink.

Again no sound. *To sleep?* His pen skidded and spit out three fat blots. He looked up and saw her with the tray again.

"Yeah," he said. *Yeah. Thanks, Lover. But, look, will you just let me know when you. . . .*

He stopped, seeing it was hopeless.

"This will make me sleep?" he asked. *Oh, yes,* was the reply.

He took a sip, looking down at the ink-blotted page. Just started it anyway, he thought, no loss of priceless literature. He ripped out the page and crumpled it in one hand.

"This is good stuff," he said, nodding his head toward the glass. He held up the paper. *Throw it away, haah? Throw away?* she asked.

"That's right," he said. "Now clear out. What in 'ell are you doing in a gent's boudoir anyway?"

She scuttled across the floor and he grinned as she closed the door quietly behind herself.

Finishing the drink, he set the glass down on the bedside table and turned off the lamp. He settled back on the soft pillow with a sigh. Some critter, he thought in drowsy satisfaction.

Good night.

He opened his heavy-lidded eyes and looked around. There was no one in the room. He sank back.

Good night.

He raised up on one elbow, squinting into the darkness.

Good night. "Oh," he said. "Good night yourself." The thoughts abated. He fell back again and made his mouth a tooth-edged cave with yawning.

"How 'bout that?" he muttered, thickly, turning on his side. "Absolutely no mirrors. See? Nothin' up my sleeves. Howboutha—"

He had a dream. The dream covered him with sweat.

After breakfast, he left the house with her farewells tugging at his brain and headed across for the warehouse. Already, he saw, the Gnee men were formed in a moving line, carrying bundles on their heads. They marched into the warehouse, deposited their burden on the concrete and had it checked off by a Gnee foreman who stood in the center of the floor holding a clipboard thick with tissue-thin vouchers.

As Lindell approached, the men all bowed and looked more subservient as they continued on their rounds. He noticed that their heads were flatter than Lover's, a little more darkly tinted with smaller eyes. Their bodies were broad and thick-muscled. They *do* look stupid, he thought.

As he came up to the man who was doing the checking and sent out an unanswered thought, he saw that they weren't telepathic either; or didn't want to be.

"How doody," said the man in a squeaky voice. "I check. You check?"

"That's okay," Lindell said, pushing back the clipboard. "Just bring it into the office when the first batch is all in."

"What, haah?" said the man. Jeez, are you a case, Lindell thought.

"Bring *this,"* he said, tapping the clipped sheaf of paper. "Bring to office." He pointed again. "Bring to me—*me*. When goods all in."

The man's splotchy face lit up with a look of vibrant stupidity and he nodded sharply. Lindell patted his shoulder. Good boy, rasped his mind, I bet you're dynamite in a crisis. He headed for the office, gritting his teeth.

Inside, he shut the plastiglass door behind him and looked around the office. It was the same as he remembered from other stations. Except for the cot in one corner. Don't tell me I have to sleep out here nights?—he thought with a groan.

He moved closer. On the flat soil-cased pillow was the imprint of a head. He picked up a light brown hair. And what the hell is this? he wondered.

Under the cot he found a buckleless belt. On the wall by the cot there were violent scratches as though a man in fever had tried to get out of the office the hard way. He stared at them.

"This joint is haunted," he concluded with a vague shake of his head. Then he turned away with a shrug. No use worrying myself, he thought. I got six months to go and nothing's going to get *me* down.

He sat down quickly before the desk and dragged the heavy station log before himself. With a shrug he flipped open the heavy cover and started reading from the beginning.

The first entries were twenty years dry. They were signed *Jefferson Winters,* or, a little later, a hasty *Jeff.* At the end of six months and fifty-two closely packed pages, Lindell found page 53 covered with a floridly penned message —*Station Four, goodbye forever! Jeff* didn't seem to have had any difficulties adjusting to the life there.

Lindell shifted back in the creaking chair and pulled the heavy book on his lap with a sigh of boredom.

It was after the first replacement's second month that the entries started to get ragged. There were blurred words, hurried scrawling, mistakes deleted and re-done. Some of the errors apparently had been corrected much later by still another replacement.

It was that way through the next four hundred or so sleep-inducing pages; a sorry chain of flaws and eventual corrections. Lindell flipped through them wearily, without the slightest interest in their content.

Then he reached entries signed *Bill Corrigan* and, with a blinking yawn, he straightened himself up, propped the book on the desk and paid closer attention.

They were the same as in every case before, excluding the first one; efficient beginnings declining markedly to increased wildness, the penmanship erring more extravagantly with each month until, at last, it became almost illegible. He found a few blatantly miscalculated additions which he corrected in his careful hand.

Corrigan's writing, he noted, broke off in the middle of a word one afternoon. And, for the last month and a half of Corrigan's stay, there were nothing but blank pages. He thumbed through them carelessly, shaking his head slowly. Have to admit it, he thought, I don't get it.

Sitting in the living room through twilight, and later at supper, he began to get the sensation that Lover's thoughts were, somehow, alive; like microscopic insects crawling in and out among the fissures of his brain. Sometimes they barely moved; other times they leaped excitedly. Once, when he became a little irritated with her staring, the thoughts were like invisible suppliants pawing clumsily at his mind.

What was worse, he realized later while reading in bed, the sensation occurred even when she wasn't in the same room with him. It was disconcerting enough to feel an endless stream of thoughts flowing into him while she was close; this remote control business was just a little too much for his taste.

Hey, how about it? he tried to reason her away good naturedly. But all he got back was the picture of her looking at him wide-eyed and uncomprehending.

"Aah, nuts," he muttered and tossed his book on the bedside table. Maybe that's it, he thought, settling down for the night. This telepathy gimmick, maybe that was what got the other men. Well, not me, he vowed. I just won't worry myself about it. And he turned out the lamp, said good night to the air and went to sleep.

"Sleep," he muttered, unaware, only half conscious. It wasn't sleep; not deep enough by half. A cloudy haze submerged his mind and filled it with the same detailed scene. It telescoped and sank away in a burst. It magnified, welling up and swallowing him and everything.

Lover. Lover. Echo of a shriek in a long black corridor. The robe fluttering close by. He saw her pale features. No, he said, stay away. Far—close—beyond—upon. He cried out. No. *No.* NO!

He jolted up in the darkness with a choking grunt, eyes full open. He stared groggily around the empty bedroom, his thoughts roiling.

He reached out in the darkness and flicked on the lamp. Hurriedly he stuck a cigarette between his lips and lay slumped against the headboard blowing out clouds of curling smoke. He raised his hand and saw that it shook. He muttered words without sense.

Then his nostrils twitched and his lips drew back in revulsion. What the hell died? he thought. There was a heavy saccharine odor in the air, getting worse every second. He tossed off the covers.

At the foot of the bed he found them; a thick pile of livid purple flowers arranged there.

He looked at them a moment and then bent over to pick them up and throw them away. He drew back gasping as a thorn punctured his right thumb.

He pressed out fat blood drops and sucked the wound, his brain assailed by the thickening smell.

It's very nice of you, he sent her the message, *but no more flowers.*
She looked at him. She doesn't get it, he knew.
"Do you understand?" he asked.
Floods of affection gurgled over the layers of his brain like syrup. He

stirred his coffee restlessly and the transfer eased as though she were determined not to offend him. The kitchen was silent except for the clink of his silver on the breakfast dishes and the slight whispering rustle of her robe.

He gulped down coffee and stood to leave. *I'll eat lunch around* . . .

I know. Her thought cut into his, mildly commanding. He grinned a little to himself as he headed down the hall. Her telepathied message had come with an almost mother-like chiding.

Then, crossing the grounds, he recalled the dream again and the departing grin emptied his features of amusement.

All morning he wondered irritably what made the Gnee men so stupid. If they dropped a bundle it was a project to pick it up again. They're like brainless cows, he thought, watching them through the office windows as they plodded through their tasks, eyes dull and unblinking, their thick shoulders sloping inward.

He knew definitely now that they weren't telepathic. He'd tried several times to give them orders with his mind alone and there was no receipt of message. They only reacted to loudly repeated words of two, or preferably less, syllables. And they reacted moronically at that.

In the middle of the morning he looked up from the backlog of paper work that Corrigan had left and realized, with some shock, that her thoughts were reaching him all the way from the house.

And yet they weren't thoughts he could translate into words. They were sensations, amorphously present. He got the feeling that she was checking, sending out exploratory beams now and again to see if all were well with him.

The first few times it did no worse than amuse him. He chuckled softly and went back to his work.

But then the proddings assumed an annoyingly regular time pattern and he began to squirm in his chair. He found himself becoming rigidly erect and anticipating seconds before they came.

By late morning he was repulsing them consciously; tossing his pen on the desk and ordering her angrily to leave him alone when he worked. Her thoughts would break off penitently. And soon come back again, like creeping things that stole upon him, insinuating and beyond insult.

His nerves began to fray a little. He left the office and prowled the warehouse floor, tearing open bundles and checking goods with impatient fingers. The thoughts followed him around faithfully. "How doody," said the Gnee foreman every time Lindell passed, making him angrier yet.

Once he straightened up suddenly over a bundle and said loudly, *"Go away!"*

The foreman jumped a foot in the air, his pencil and clipboard went flying and he hid behind a pillar and looked fearfully at Lindell. Lindell pretended not to notice.

Later, back in the office, he sat thinking, the open log book before him. No wonder the Gnee men didn't telepathize, he thought. They knew what was good for them.

Then he looked out the window at the plodding line of workers.

What if they weren't just *avoiding* telepathy? What if they were incapable of it; had once held the ability and, because of it, had been broken to their present state of hopeless stolidity.

He thought of what Martin had said about the women outnumbering the men. And a phrase entered his mind—*matriarchy by mind*. The phrase offended him but he was suddenly afraid it might be true. It would explain why the other men had cracked. For, if the women were in control, it might well be that, in their inherent lust for dominance, they made no distinction between their own men and the men from Earth. A man is a man is a man. He twisted angrily at the idea of possibly being considered on a level with the dolts who lived in the village.

He stood up abruptly. I'm not hungry, he thought, not at all. But I'm going back to the house and order her to make me lunch and let her know I'm not hungry either. I'll make her used to being dominated herself and then she'll get no chance to pick at me. No bug-eyed Gnee woman, by God, is going to get *me* down.

Then he blinked and turned away quickly when he realized that he was staring at the wild pattern of scratches on the far office wall. And the belt without a buckle that still curled limply underneath the cot.

The dream again. It tore at his brain tissues with claws of razor. Sweat covering him. He tossed on the bed with a groan and was suddenly awake, staring into the darkness.

He thought he saw something at the foot of the bed. He closed his eyes and shook his head and looked again. The room was empty. He felt mind-drenching thoughts recede like some alien tide.

His fists contracted angrily. She's been at me while I slept, he thought, Goddamn her hide, she'd been at me.

He pushed aside the covers and crawled to the foot of the bed nervously.

He couldn't see them. But the cloying fumes undulated up from the floor like erected serpents slithering into his nostrils. Gagging, he slumped down on the mattress, his stomach wrenched. Why? his brain mumbled over and over.

My God, *why?*

★   ★   ★

Angrily, he threw the flowers away in her sight and the thoughts pleaded and showered over him like raindrops.

"I said *no*, didn't I?" he yelled at her.

Then he sat down at the table and controlled himself as well as he could. I've a long way to go, he told his will, ease off, ease off.

Now he was sure he knew why it was only six months. That would be more than enough. But I won't crack. He commanded himself. It's a cinch she isn't going to crack so conserve yourself. *She's too stupid to crack,* he thought deliberately, hoping she'd pick it up.

She apparently did for her shoulders slumped dejectedly all of a sudden. And during breakfast, she circled him like a timorous wraith, keeping her face averted and her thoughts aloof. He found himself almost sorry for her then. It probably wasn't her fault, he thought, it was just an inborn trait among Gnee women to dominate men.

Then he realized that her thoughts were at him again, tender and gratefully maudlin. He tried to neutralize himself and ignore them as they sought to break through his apathy like honeyed picks.

All day he worked hard and made payments in spices and grain to the Gnee foreman to be forwarded to the workers. He wondered if the payments would go eventually to the women. Wherever they were.

"I'm taping my voice," he dictated later that night. "I want to hear myself talking so I can forget her. There's no one else to talk to so I'll have to talk to myself. A sad case. Well, here goes.

"Here I am on Station Four, folks, having a wonderful time and wish you were here instead of me. Oh, it's not *that* bad, don't get me wrong. But I guess I know what knocked out Corrigan and the poor bastards before him. It was Lover and her cannibal mind eating them up. But I'll tell you this; it's not going to eat *me* up. That much you can put bets on. Lover isn't going to . . .

"No, I didn't call you! Come on, get out of my life, will ya? Go to a movie or something. Yeah, yeah, I know. Well, go to bed then. Just leave me alone." *Alone.*

"There. That's for her. She'll have to go some to get me clawing at the walls."

But he carefully locked the door to his room when he went to bed. And he groaned in his sleep because of the same nightmare and his limbs thrashed and all peace and rest were crowded out.

He twisted into wakefulness in mid-morning and stumbled up to check the door. He fumbled at the lock with heavy fingers. Finally his thickened brain divined the fact that the door was still locked and he went back to bed in a weaving line and fell on it into a stupored sleep.

When he woke up in the morning there were flowers at the foot of his bed, luxuriantly purple and foul-smelling and the door was locked.

He couldn't ask her about it because he left the kitchen in revulsion when she called him *dear*.

No more flowers! I'll promise! cried her pursuing thoughts. He locked himself in the living room and sat at the desk, feeling sick. Get hold of yourself!—he ordered his system, clasping his hands tightly and holding his teeth firmly clenched.

Eat?

She was outside the door; he knew it. He closed his eyes. *Go away, leave me alone,* he told her.

I'm sorry, dear, she said.

"Stop calling me 'dear'!" he shouted, slamming his fist on the desk surface. As he twisted in the chair, his belt buckle caught on the drawer handle and it jerked out. He found himself staring down at the shiny gas pistol. Almost unconsciously he reached down and touched its slick barrel.

He shoved in the drawer with a convulsive movement. None of that! he swore.

He looked around suddenly, feeling alone and free. He got up and hurried to the window. Down below, he saw her hurrying across the grounds with a basket on her arm. She's going for vegetables, he thought. But what made her leave so suddenly?

Of course. The pistol. She must have gotten his thoughts of violent intent.

He sighed and calmed down a little, feeling as if his brain had been drained of thick, noxious fluids.

I've still got cards in my hand, he soothed himself.

While she was out he decided to look in her room and see if he could find the shifting panel that enabled her to enter his room with the flowers. He hurried down the hall and pushed open the door to her barely furnished little chamber.

His brain was immediately attacked by the odor of a reeking pile of the purple flowers in one corner. He held a hand over his mouth and nose as he looked down in distaste at the living and dead blossoms.

What did they represent?—he wondered. An offering of thoughtfulness? His throat contracted. Or was it more than thoughtfulness? He grimaced at the thought and remembered that first evening when he'd dubbed her Lover. What had possessed him to choose that name from the infinity of possible names? He hoped he didn't know.

On the couch he found a small pile of odds and ends. There was a button, a pair of broken shoe laces, the piece of crumpled paper he had told her to throw away. And a belt buckle with the initials W. C. stamped on it.

There were no secret panels.

He sat in the kitchen staring into an untouched cup of coffee. No way she could get in his room. W. C.—William Corrigan. He had to fight it, keep fighting it.

Time passed. And suddenly, he realized that she was back in the house again. There was no sound; it was like the return of a ghost. But he knew it. A cloud of feeling preceded her, came plunging through the rooms like an excited puppy, searching. Thoughts swirled. *You are well? You are not angry? Lover is back*—all hastily and eagerly clutching at him.

She swept into the room so quickly that his hands twitched and he upset the cup. The hot liquid splashed over his shirt and trousers as he jumped back, knocking over the chair.

She put down the basket and got a towel as she patted the stains dry. She'd never been so close to him. She'd never actually touched him before except for that first handshake.

There was an aroma about her. It made his chest heave painfully. And all the time, her thoughts caressed his mind as her hands seemed to be caressing his body.

There. There . . . I am here with you.

David dear.

Almost in horror, he stared at her spongy pink skin, her huge eyes, her tiny wound of a mouth.

And, in the office that morning, he made three straight mistakes in the log book and tore out a whole page and hurled it across the room with a choking cry of rage.

Avoid her. No point in remonstration. He tried to raze his mental ground so that her thoughts could not find domicile there. If he relaxed his mind enough, her thoughts flowed through and out. Perhaps taking part of his will as they left but he'd have to risk that.

And if he worked hard and crowded his head with stodgy banks of figures, it kept her at a distance and his hands did not tremble so badly.

Maybe I should sleep in the office, he thought. Then he found Corrigan's note.

It was on a white slip of paper stuck away in the log book, hidden white on white. He only found it because he was going through the pages one at a time, reciting the dates in a loud voice to keep his mind filled.

God help me, read the note, black and jagged-lettered, *Lover comes through the walls!*

Lindell stared. *I saw it myself,* attested the words, *I'm going out of my mind. Always that damn animal mind tugging and tearing at me. And now I can't even shut away her body. I slept out here but she came anyway. And I . . .*

Lindell read it again and it was a wind fanning the fires of terror. *Through the walls.* The words agonized him. Was it possible?

And it was Corrigan then who had named her Lover. From the very start, the relationship had been on her terms. Lindell had had nothing to say about it.

"Lover," he muttered and her thoughts enveloped him suddenly like a carrion's wings swooping down from the sky. He flung up his arms and cried out—"Leave me alone!"

And, as her phantom mind slipped off, he had the sense that it was with less timidity, with the patience such as a man knowing his own great strength can afford to display.

He sank back on the chair, exhausted, suddenly, depleted with fighting it. He crumpled the note in his right hand, thinking of the scratches on the wall behind him.

And he saw in his mind: Corrigan tossing on the cot, burning with fever, rearing up with a shriek of horror to see her standing before him. But then. *Then?* The scene was dark.

He rubbed a shaking hand over his face. Don't crack, he said to himself. But it was more a frightened entreaty than a command. Wasting fogs of premonition flooded over him in chilling waves. *She comes through the walls.*

That night again, he poured the potion she made down his bathroom sink. He locked the door and, in the lightless room, he squatted in one corner, peering and waiting, lungs bellowing in spasmodic bursts.

The thermostat lowered the heat. The floorboards got icy and his teeth started chattering. I'm not going to bed, he vowed angrily. He didn't know why it was that suddenly the bed frightened him. I don't know, he forced the words through his brain because he felt vaguely that he *did* know and he didn't want to admit it, even for a second.

But after hours of futile waiting, he had to straighten up with a snapping of joints and stumble back to bed. There, he crawled under the blankets and lay trembling, trying to stay awake. She'll come while I'm asleep, he thought, I mustn't sleep.

When he woke up in the morning there were the flowers on the floor for him. And that was another day before a mass of days that sank crushed into the lump of months.

* * *

You can get used to horror, he thought. When it has lost immediacy and is no longer pungent and has become a steady diet. When it has degraded to a chain of mind-numbing events. When shocks are like scalpels picking and jabbing at delicate ganglia until they have lost all feeling.

Yet, though it was no longer terror, it was worse. For his nerves were raw and bleeding a hemophilia of rage. He fought his battles to the dregs of seconds, gaunt willed, shouting her off, firing lances of hate from his jaded mind; tortured by her surrenders that were her victories. She always came back. Like an enraging cat, rubbing endless sycophantic sides against him, filling him with thoughts of—*yes, admit it!*—he screamed to himself through midnight struggles . . .

Thoughts of *love*.

And there was the undercurrent, the promise of new shock that would topple his already shaking edifice. It needed only that—an added push, another stab of the blade, one more drop of the shattering hammer.

The shapeless threat hung over him. He waited for it, poised for it a hundred times an hour, especially at night. Wait. Waiting. And, sometimes, when he thought he knew what he was waiting for, the shock of admission made him shudder and made him want to claw at walls and break things and run until the blackness swallowed him.

If he could only forget her, he thought. Yes, if you could forget her for a while, just a little while, it would be all right.

He mumbled that to himself as he set up the movie projector in the living room.

She begged from the kitchen—*Can I see?*

"No!"

Now all his replies, worded or thought, were like the snapping retorts of a jangled old man. If only the six months would end. That was the problem. The months weren't moving fast enough. And time was like her—not to be reasoned with or intimidated.

There were many reels on the wall shelf. But his hand reached out without hesitation and picked out one. He didn't notice it; his mind was calloused to suggestion.

He adjusted the reel on the spindle and turned out the lights. He sat down with a tired groan as the flickering milky cone of light shot out from the lens, throwing pictures on the screen.

A lean, dark-bearded man was posing, arms crossed, white teeth showing in an artificial smile. He came closer to the camera. The sun flashed, blurring the film a second. Black screen. Title: *Picture of me.*

The man, high cheek-boned, bright-eyed, stood laughing soundlessly out from the screen. He pointed to the side and the camera swung around. Lindell sat up sharply.

It was the station.

Apparently it was autumn. For, as the camera swung past the house, the village, jerking a moment as though changing hands, he saw the trees surrounded by heaps of dead leaves. He sat there shivering, waiting for something, he didn't know what.

The screen blacked. Another title roughly etched in white. *Jeff In the Office*. The man peered at the camera, an idiotic smile on his face, white skin accentuated by the immaculate black outline of his beard.

Fadeout—in. The man doing a jig around the empty warehouse floor, hands poised delicately in the air, his dark hair bouncing wildly on his skull.

Another title flashing on the screen. Lindell stiffened in his seat, his breath cut off abruptly.

Title: *Lover*.

There was her face horribly repellent in black and white. She was standing by his bedroom window, her face a mask of delight. He could tell now it was delight. Once he would have said she looked like a maniac, her mouth twisted like a living scar, her grotesque eyes staring.

She spun and her robe swirled out. He saw her puffy ankles and his stomach grew rock taut.

She approached the camera; he saw filmy eyelids slide down over her eyes. His hands began to tremble violently. It was his dream. It made him sick. It was his dream to the detail. Then it had never been a dream—not from his own mind.

A sob tore at his throat. She was undoing the robe. *Here it is!* he screamed in his panic-stricken mind. He whimpered and reached out shakily to turn off the projector.

No.

It was a cold command in the darkness. *Watch me,* she ordered. He sat bound in a vise of terror, staring in sick fascination as the robe slid from her neck, pulled down over her round shoulders. She twisted sensuously. The robe sank into a heavy, swirling heap on the floor.

He screamed.

He flung out an arm and it swept into the burning projector. It crashed down on the floor. The room was night. He struggled up and lurched across the room. *Nice? Nice?* The word dug at him mercilessly as he fumbled for the door. He found it, rushed into the hall. Her door opened and she stood in the half light, the robe hanging from one smooth shoulder.

He jolted to a halt. "Get out of here!" he yelled.

No.

He made a convulsive move for her, hands out like rigid claws. The sight of her pink, dewy flesh spun him away. *Yes?* her mind suggested. It seemed as if he heard it spoken in a slyly rising voice . . .

"Listen!" he cried, reaching out for the door to his room. "Listen, you have to go, do you understand? Go to your mate!"

He twisted back in utter horror.

I am with him now—her message had said.

The thought paralyzed him. He stared, open-mouthed, heart pounding in slow, gigantic beats as the robe slipped over her shoulders and started down her arms.

He whirled with a cry and slammed the door behind him. His fingers shook on the lock. Her thoughts were a wailing in his mind. He whimpered in fright and sickness and knew it was no good because he couldn't lock her out.

There were monkeys chattering in his brain. They lay on their backs in a circle and kicked at the inside of his skull. They grabbed juicy blobs of grey in their dirty paws and they squeezed.

He rolled on his side with a groan. I'll go crazy, he thought. Like Corrigan, like all of them but the first one; that slimy one who started it all; who added a new and hideous warp to the corrugation of her dominating Gnee mind; who had named her Lover because he meant it.

Suddenly he sat up with a gasp of terror, staring at the foot of the bed. *She comes through the walls!*—howled his brain. Nothing there, his eyes saw. His fingers clutched at the sheets. He felt sweat dripping off his brow and rolling down the embankment of his nose.

He lay down. Up again! He whimpered like a frightened child. A cloud of blackness was falling over him. Her. Her. He groaned. "No." In the blackness. No use.

He whined. Sleep. Sleep. The word throbbed, swelled and depressed in his brain. This is the time. He knew it, knew it, knew. . . .

The blade falling, sanity decapitated and twitching bloody in the basket.

No! He tried to push himself up but he couldn't. Sleep. A black tide of night hovering, tracking.

Sleep.

He fell back on the pillow, pushed up weakly on one elbow.

"No." His lungs were crusted. "No."

He struggled. It was too much. He screamed a thick, bubbling scream. She threw his will aside, snapped and futile. She was using all her strength now and he was enervated, beaten. He thudded back on the pillow, glassy-eyed

and limp. He moaned weakly and his eyes shut—opened—shut—opened—
shut. . . .

The dream again. Insane. Not a dream.

When he woke up there were no flowers. The courtship was ended. He
gaped blankly and unbelievingly at the imprint of a body beside him on the
bed.

It was still warm and moist.

He laughed out loud. He wrote curse words in his diary. He wrote them
in tall black letters, holding the pencil like a knife. He wrote them in the log
book too. He tore up vouchers if they weren't the right color. His entries
were crooked lines of figures like wavy-numbered tendrils. Sometimes he
didn't care about that. Mostly he didn't notice.

He prowled the filled warehouse behind locked doors, red-eyed and muttering. He clambered up on the bundles and stared out through the skylight
at the empty sky. He was lighter by fifteen pounds, unwashed. His face was
black with wiry growth. He was going to have an immaculate beard. She
wanted it. She didn't want him to wash or shave or be healthy. She called him
Jeff.

You can't fight that, he told himself. You can't win because you lose. If
you advance you are retreating because, when you are too tired to fight, she
comes back and takes your city and your soul.

That's why he whispered to the warehouse so no one would hear, "There
is a thing to do."

That's why, late at night, he sneaked to the living room and put the gas
pistol in his pocket. Never harm the Gnees. Well, that was wrong. It was kill
or be killed. That's why I'm taking the pistol to bed with me. That's why I'm
stroking it as I stare up at the ceiling. Yes, this is it. This is my rock to rest on
through the daynights.

And he turned over plans as an animal snuffles over flat stones to find bugs
for supper.

Days. Days. Days. He whispered, "Kill her."

He nodded and smiled to himself and patted the cool metal. You're my
friend, he said, you're my only friend. She has to die, we all know that.

He made lots of plans and they were all the same one. He killed her a
million times in his mind—in secret chambers of his mind that he had discovered and opened; where he could crouch clever and undisturbed while he
made his plans.

Animals. He walked and looked at the workers' village. Animals. I'm not
going to end up like you. I'm not going to I'm not going to I'm not going to
I'm. . . .

★ ★ ★

He lurched up from his office desk, eyes wide, slaver running over his lips. He held the pistol tight in his palsied hand.

He flung open the office door and staggered over the concrete, through the lanes between roof-high stacks. His mouth was a line. He held the pistol pointing.

He flung up the catch and dragged back one heavy door. He plunged into the pouring sunlight and broke into a run. Wisps of terror licked out from the house. He reveled in them. He ran faster. He fell down because his legs were weak. The pistol went flying. He crawled to it and brushed off the dust. Now we'll see, he promised the monkeys in his head, *now*.

He stood up dizzily. He started to hobble for the house.

He heard a rushing in the air, a flicker of light dashed over his cheeks and eyes. He looked up and blinked and saw the cargo ship.

Six months.

He dropped the pistol and slumped down beside it and plucked at blue grass stupidly. He stared at the ship dumbly as it came down and stopped and the hatches opened and men climbed out.

"Why," he said, "that's cutting it too thin for me."

And his voice was quite normal except that he broke into giggling and sobbing and had a fist fight with the air.

"You'll be all right," they told him on the way back to Earth. And they shot more sedative to his shrieking nerves to make him forget.

But he never did.

PERCHANCE TO DREAM

CHARLES BEAUMONT

lease sit down," the psychiatrist said, indicating a somewhat worn leather couch.

Automatically, Hall sat down. Instinctively, he leaned back. Dizziness flooded through him, his eyelids fell like sashweights, the blackness came. He jumped up quickly and slapped his right cheek, then he slapped his left cheek, hard.

"I'm sorry, Doctor," he said.

The psychiatrist, who was tall and young and not in the least Viennese nodded. "You prefer to stand?" he asked, gently.

"Prefer?" Hall threw his head back and laughed. "That's good," he said. *"Prefer!"*

"I'm afraid I don't quite understand."

"Neither do I, Doctor." He pinched the flesh of his left hand until it hurt. "No, no: that isn't true. I do understand. That's the whole trouble. I do."

"You—want to tell me about it?"

"Yes. No." It's silly, he thought. You can't help me. No one can. I'm alone! "Forget it," he said and started for the door.

The psychiatrist said, "Wait a minute." His voice was friendly, concerned; but not patronizing. "Running away won't do you much good, will it?"

Hall hesitated.

"Forgive the cliché. Actually, running away is often the best answer. But I don't know yet that yours is that sort of problem."

"Did Dr. Jackson tell you about me?"

"No. Jim said he was sending you over, but he thought you'd do a better job on the details. I only know that your name is Philip Hall, you're thirty-one, and you haven't been able to sleep for a long time."

"Yes. A long time . . ." To be exact, seventy-two hours, Hall thought, glancing at the clock. Seventy-two horrible hours . . .

The psychiatrist tapped out a cigarette. "Aren't you—" he began.

"Tired? God yes. I'm the tiredest man on Earth! I could sleep forever. But that's just it, you see: I would. I'd never wake up."

"Please," the psychiatrist said.

Hall bit his lip. There wasn't, he supposed, much point to it. But, after all, what *else* was there for him to do? Where would he go? "You mind if I pace?"

"Stand on your head, if you like."

"Okay. I'll take one of your cigarettes." He drew the smoke into his lungs and walked over to the window. Fourteen floors below, the toy people and the toy cars moved. He watched them and thought, this guy's all right. Sharp. Intelligent. Nothing like what I expected. Who can say—*maybe* it'll do some good. "I'm not sure where to begin."

"It doesn't matter. The beginning might be easier for you."

Hall shook his head, violently. The beginning, he thought. Was there such a thing?

"Just take it easy."

After a lengthy pause, Hall said: "I first found out about the power of the human mind when I was ten. Close to that time, anyway. We had a tapestry in the bedroom. It was a great big thing, the size of a rug, with fringe on the edges. It showed a group of soldiers—Napoleonic soldiers—on horses. They were at the brink of some kind of cliff, and the first horse was reared up. My mother told me something. She told me that if I stared at the tapestry long enough, the horses would start to move. They'd go right over the cliff, she said. I tried it, but nothing happened. She said, 'You've got to take time. You've got to *think* about it.' So, every night, before I went to bed, I'd sit up and stare at that damn tapestry. And, finally, it happened. Over they went, all the horses, all the men, over the edge of the cliff . . ." Hall stubbed out the cigarette and began to pace. "Scared hell out of me," he said. "When I looked again, they were all back. It got to be a game with me. Later on, I tried it with pictures in magazines, and pretty soon I was able to move locomotives and send balloons flying and make dogs open their mouths: everything, anything I wanted."

He paused, ran a hand through his hair. "Not too unusual, you're thinking," he said. "Every kid does it. Like standing in a closet and shining a flashlight through your finger, or sewing up the heel of your palm . . . common stuff?"

The psychiatrist shrugged.

"There was a difference," Hall said. "One day it got out of control. I was looking at a coloring book. One of the pictures showed a knight and a dragon fighting. For fun I decided to make the knight drop his lance. He did. The dragon started after him, breathing fire. In another second the dragon's mouth was open and he was getting ready to eat the knight. I blinked and shook my head, like always, only—nothing happened. I mean, the picture didn't go back. Not even when I closed the book and opened it again. But I didn't think too much about it, even then."

He walked to the desk and took another cigarette. It slipped from his hands.

"You've been on Dexedrine," the psychiatrist said, watching as Hall tried to pick up the cigarette.

"Yes."

"How many grains a day?"

"Thirty, thirty-five, I don't know."

"Potent. Knocks out your co-ordination. I suppose Jim warned you?"

"Yes, he warned me."

"Well, let's get along. What happened then?"

"Nothing." Hall allowed the psychiatrist to light his cigarette. "For a while, I forgot about the 'game' almost completely. Then, when I turned thirteen, I got sick. Rheumatic heart—"

The psychiatrist leaned forward and frowned. "And Jim let you have thirty-five—"

"Don't interrupt!" He decided not to mention that he had gotten the drug from his aunt, that Dr. Jackson knew nothing about it. "I had to stay in bed a lot. No activity; might kill me. So I read books and listened to the radio. One night I heard a ghost story. 'Hermit's Cave' it was called. All about a man who gets drowned and comes back to haunt his wife. My parents were gone, at a movie. I was alone. And I kept thinking about that story, imagining the ghost. Maybe, I thought to myself, he's in that closet. I knew he wasn't; I knew there wasn't any such thing as a ghost, really. But there was a little part of my mind that kept saying, 'Look at the closet. Watch the door. He's in there, Philip, and he's going to come out.' I picked up a book and tried to read, but I couldn't help glancing at the closet door. It was open a crack. Everything dark behind it. Everything dark and quiet."

"And the door moved."

"That's right."

"You understand that there's nothing terribly unusual in anything you've said so far?"

"I know," Hall said. "It was my imagination. It *was,* and I realized it even then. But—I got just as scared. Just as scared as if a ghost actually *had* opened that door! And that's the whole point. The mind, Doctor. It's everything. If you *think* you have a pain in your arm and there's no physical reason for it, you don't hurt any less . . . My mother died because she thought she had a fatal disease. The autopsy showed malnutrition, nothing else. But she died just the same!"

"I won't dispute the point."

"All right. I just don't want you to tell me it's all in my mind. I *know* it is."

"Go on."

"They told me I'd never really get well, I'd have to take it easy the rest of my life. Because of the heart. No strenuous exercises, no stairs, no long walks. No shocks. Shock produces excessive adrenalin, they said. Bad. So that's the way it was. When I got out of school, I grabbed a soft desk job. Unexciting: numbers, adding numbers, that's all. Things went okay for a few years. Then it started again. I read about where some woman got into her car at night and happened to check for something in the back seat and found a man hidden there. Waiting. It stuck with me; I started dreaming about it. So every night, when I got into my car, I automatically patted the rear seat and floorboards. It satisfied me for a while, until I started thinking, 'What if I forget to check?' Or, 'What if there's something back there that isn't human?' I had to drive across Laurel Canyon to get home, and you know how twisty that stretch is. Thirty-fifty-foot drops, straight down. I'd get this feeling halfway across. 'There's someone . . . something . . . in the back of the car!' Hidden, in darkness. Fat and shiny. I'll look in the rear-view mirror and I'll see his hands ready to circle my throat . . . Again, Doctor: understand me. *I knew it was my imagination.* I had no doubt at all that the back seat was empty—hell, I kept the car locked and I double-checked! But, I told myself, you keep thinking this way, Hall, and you'll see those hands. It'll be a reflection, or somebody's headlights, or nothing at all—but you'll see them! Finally, one night, I did see them! The car lurched a couple of times and went down the embankment."

The psychiatrist said, "Wait a minute," rose, and switched the tape on a small machine.

"I knew how powerful the mind was, then," Hall continued. "I know that ghosts and demons did exist, they did, if you only thought about them long enough and hard enough. After all, one of them almost killed me!" He pressed the lighted end of the cigarette against his flesh; the fog lifted instantly. "Dr. Jackson told me afterwards that one more serious shock like that would finish me. And that's when I started having the dream."

There was a silence in the room, compounded of distant automobile horns, the ticking of the ship's-wheel clock, the insectival tapping of the receptionist's typewriter. Hall's own tortured breathing.

"They say dreams last only a couple of seconds," he said. "I don't know whether that's true or not. It doesn't matter. They *seem* to last longer. Sometimes I've dreamed a whole lifetime; sometimes generations have passed.

Once in a while, time stops completely; it's a frozen moment, lasting forever. When I was a kid I saw the Flash Gordon serials; you remember? I loved them, and when the last episode was over, I went home and started dreaming more. Each night, another episode. They were vivid, too, and I remembered them when I woke up. I even wrote them down, to make sure I wouldn't forget. Crazy?"

"No," said the psychiatrist.

"I did, anyway. The same thing happened with the Oz books and the Burroughs books. I'd keep them going. But after the age of fifteen, or so, I didn't dream much. Only once in a while. Then, a week ago—" Hall stopped talking. He asked the location of the bathroom and went there and splashed cold water on his face. Then he returned and stood by the window.

"A week ago?" the psychiatrist said, flipping the tape machine back on.

"I went to bed around eleven-thirty. I wasn't too tired, but I needed the rest, on account of my heart. Right away the dream started. I was walking along Venice Pier. It was close to midnight. The place was crowded, people everywhere; you know the kind they used to get there. Sailors, dumpy looking dames, kids in leather jackets. The pitchmen were going through their routines. You could hear the roller coasters thundering along the tracks, the people inside the roller coasters, screaming; you could hear the bells and the guns cracking and the crazy songs they play on calliopes. And, far away, the ocean, moving. Everything was bright and gaudy and cheap. I walked for a while, stepping on gum and candy apples, wondering why I was there."

Hall's eyes closed. He opened them quickly and rubbed them. "Halfway to the end, passing the penny arcade, I saw a girl. She was about twenty-two or -three. White dress, very thin and tight, and a funny white hat. Her legs were bare, nicely muscled and tan. She was alone. I stopped and watched her, and I remember thinking, "She *must* have a boy friend. He *must* be here somewhere." But she didn't seem to be waiting for anyone, or looking. Unconsciously, I began to follow her. At a distance.

"She walked past a couple of concessions, then she stopped at one called 'The Whip' and strolled in and went for a ride. The air was hot. It caught her dress as she went around and sent it whirling. It didn't bother her at all. She just held onto the bar and closed her eyes, and—I don't know, a kind of ecstasy seemed to come over her. She began to laugh. A high-pitched, musical sound. I stood by the fence and watched her, wondering why such a beautiful girl should be laughing in a cheap carnival ride, in the middle of the night, all by herself. Then my hands froze on the fence, because suddenly I saw that she was looking at me. Every time the car would whip around, she'd be looking. And there was something that said, Don't go away, don't leave, don't move . . .

"The ride stopped and she got out and walked over to me. As naturally as if we'd known each other for years, she put her arm in mine, and said, 'We've been expecting you, Mr. Hall.' Her voice was deep and soft, and her face, close up, was even more beautiful than it had seemed. Full, rich lips, a little wet; dark, flashing eyes; a warm gleam to her flesh. I didn't answer. She laughed again and tugged at my sleeve. 'Come on, darling,' she said. 'We haven't much time.' And we walked, almost running, to The Silver Flash—a roller coaster, the highest on the pier. I knew I shouldn't go on it because of my heart condition, but she wouldn't listen. She said I had to, for her. So we bought our tickets and got into the first seat of the car . . ."

Hall held his breath for a moment, then let it out, slowly. As he relived the episode, he found that it was easier to stay awake. Much easier.

"That," he said, "was the end of the first dream. I woke up sweating and trembling, and thought about it most of the day, wondering where it had all come from. I'd only been to Venice Pier once in my life, with my mother. Years ago. But that night, just as it'd happened with the serials, the dream picked up exactly where it had left off. We were settling into the seat. Rough leather, cracked and peeling, I recall. The grab bar iron, painted black, the paint rubbed away in the center.

"I tried to get out, thinking. Now's the time to do it; do it now or you'll be too late! But the girl held me, and whispered to me. We'd be together, she said. Close together. If I'd do this one thing for her, she'd belong to me. 'Please! Please!' Then the car started. A little jerk; the kids beginning to yell and scream; the *clack-clack* of the chain pulling up; and up, slowly, too late now, too late for anything, up the steep wooden hill . . .

"A third of the way to the top, with her holding me, pressing herself against me, I woke up again. Next night, we went up a little farther. Foot by foot, slowly, up the hill. At the half-way point, the girl began kissing me. And laughing. 'Look down!' she told me. 'Look down, Philip!' And I did and saw little people and little cars and everything tiny and unreal.

"Finally we were within a few feet of the crest. The night was black and the wind was fast and cold now, and I was scared, so scared that I couldn't move. The girl laughed louder than ever, and a strange expression came into her eyes. I remembered then how no one else had noticed her. How the ticket-taker had taken the two stubs and looked around questioningly.

" 'Who are you?' " I screamed. And she said, 'Don't you know?' And she stood up and pulled the grab-bar out of my hands. I leaned forward to get it.

"Then we reached the top. And I saw her face and I knew what she was going to do, instantly: I knew. I tried to get back in the seat, but I felt her hands on me then and I heard her voice, laughing, high, laughing and shrieking with delight, and—"

Hall smashed his fist against the wall, stopped and waited for calm to return.

When it did, he said, "That's the whole thing, Doctor. Now you know why I don't care to go to sleep. When I do—and I'll have to, eventually; I realize that!—the dream will go on. And my heart won't take it!"

The psychiatrist pressed a button on his desk.

"Whoever she is," Hall went on, "she'll push me. And I'll fall. Hundreds of feet. I'll see the cement rushing up in a blur to meet me and I'll feel the first horrible pain of contact—"

There was a click.

The office door opened.

A girl walked in.

"Miss Thomas," the psychiatrist began, "I'd like you to—"

Philip Hall screamed. He stared at the girl in the white nurse's uniform and took a step backward. "Oh, Christ! No!"

"Mr. Hall, this is my receptionist, Miss Thomas."

"No," Hall cried. "It's her. It is. And I know who she is now, God save me! I know who she is!"

The girl in the white uniform took a tentative step into the room.

Hall screamed again, threw his hands over his face, turned and tried to run.

A voice called, "Stop him!"

Hall felt the sharp pain of the sill against his knee, realized in one hideous moment what was happening. Blindly he reached out, grasping. But it was too late. As if drawn by a giant force, he tumbled through the open window, out into the cold clean air.

"Hall!"

All the way down, all the long and endless way down past the thirteen floors to the gray, unyielding, hard concrete, his mind worked; and his eyes never closed . . .

"I'm afraid he's dead," the psychiatrist said, removing his fingers from Hall's wrist.

The girl in the white uniform made a little gasping sound. "But," she said, "only a minute ago, I saw him and he was—"

"I know. It's funny; when he came in, I told him to sit down. He did. And in less than two seconds he was asleep. Then he gave that yell you heard and . . ."

"Heart attack?"

"Yes." The psychiatrist rubbed his cheek thoughtfully. "Well," he said. "I guess there are worse ways to go. At least he died peacefully."

THE RIVER
OF NIGHT'S DREAMING

KARL EDWARD WAGNER

Everywhere: greyness and rain.

The activities bus with its uniformed occupants. The wet pavement that crawled along the crest of the high bluff. The storm-fretted waters of the bay far below. The night itself, gauzy with grey mist and traceries of rain, feebly probed by the wan headlights of the bus.

Greyness and rain merged in a slither of skidding rubber, and a protesting bawl of brakes and tearing metal.

For an instant the activities bus paused upon the broken guard rail, hung half swallowed by the greyness and rain upon the edge of the precipice. Then, with thirty voices swelling a chorus to the screams of rubber and steel, the bus plunged over the edge.

Halfway down it struck glancingly against the limestone face, shearing off wheels amidst a shower of glass and bits of metal, its plunge unchecked. Another carom, and the bus began to break apart, tearing open before its final impact onto the wave-frothed jumble of boulders far below. Water and sound surged upward into the night, as metal crumpled and split open, scattering bits of humanity like seeds flung from a bursting melon.

Briefly those trapped within the submerging bus made despairing noises—in the night they were no more than the cries of kittens, tied in a sack and thrown into the river. Then the waters closed over the tangle of wreckage, and greyness and rain silenced the torrent of sound.

She struggled to the surface and dragged air into her lungs in a shuddering spasm. Treading water, she stared about her—her actions still automatic, for the crushing impact into the dark waters had all but knocked her unconscious. Perhaps for a moment she *had* lost consciousness; she was too dazed to remember anything very clearly. Anything.

Fragments of memory returned. The rain and the night, the activities bus carrying them back to their prison. Then the plunge into darkness, the terror of her companions, metal bursting apart. Alone in another instant, flung helplessly into the night, and the stunning embrace of the waves.

Her thoughts were clearing now. She worked her feet out of her tennis shoes and tugged damp hair away from her face, trying to see where she was. The body of the bus had torn open, she vaguely realized, and she had been thrown out of the wreckage and into the bay. She could see the darker bulk of the cliff looming out of the greyness not far from her, and dimly came the moans and cries of other survivors. She could not see them, but she could imagine their presence, huddled upon the rocks between the water and the vertical bluff.

Soon the failure of the activities bus to return would cause alarm. The gap in the guard rail would be noticed. Rescuers would come, with lights and ropes and stretchers, to pluck them off the rocks and hurry them away in ambulances to the prison's medical ward.

She stopped herself. Without thought, she had begun to swim toward the other survivors. But why? She took stock of her situation. As well as she could judge, she had escaped injury. She could easily join the others where they clung to the rocks, await rescue—and once the doctors were satisfied she was whole and hearty, she would be back on her locked ward again. A prisoner, perhaps until the end of her days.

Far across the bay, she could barely make out the phantom glimmering of the lights of the city. The distance was great—in miles, two? three? more?—for the prison was a long drive beyond the outskirts of the city and around the sparsely settled shore of the bay. But she was athletically trim and a strong swimmer—she exercised regularly to help pass the long days. How many days, she could not remember. She only knew she would not let them take her back to that place.

The rescue workers would soon be here. Once they'd taken care of those who clung to the shoreline, they'd send divers to raise the bus—and when they didn't find her body among those in the wreckage, they'd assume she was drowned, her body washed away. There would surely be others who were missing, others whose bodies even now drifted beneath the bay. Divers and boatmen with drag hooks would search for them. Some they might never find.

Her they would never find.

She turned her back to the cliff and began to swim out into the bay. Slow, patient strokes—she must conserve her strength. This was a dangerous act, she knew, but then they would be all the slower to suspect when they discovered she was missing. The rashness of her decision only meant that the chances of escape were all the better. Certainly, they would search along the shoreline close by the wreck—perhaps use dogs to hunt down any who might have tried to escape along the desolate stretch of high cliffs. But they would not believe that one of their prisoners would attempt to swim across to the distant city—and once she reached the city, no bloodhounds could seek her out there.

The black rise of rock vanished into the grey rain behind her, and with it dwindled the sobbing wails of her fellow prisoners. No longer her fellows. She had turned her back on that existence. Beyond, where lights smeared the distant greyness, she would find a new existence for herself.

For a while she swam a breaststroke, switching to a backstroke whenever she began to tire. The rain fell heavily onto her upturned face; choppy waves spilled into her mouth, forcing her to abandon the backstroke each time before she was fully rested. Just take it slow, take your time, she told herself. Only the distant lights gave any direction to the greyness now. If she tried to turn back, she might swim aimlessly through the darkness, until . . .

Her dress, a drab prison smock, was weighing her down. She hesitated a moment—she would need clothing when she reached the shore, but so encumbered she would never reach the city. She could not waste strength in agonizing over her dilemma. There was no choice. She tugged at the buttons. A quick struggle, and she was able to wrench the wet dress over her head and pull it free. She flung the shapeless garment away from her, and it sank into the night. Another struggle, and her socks followed.

She struck out again for the faraway lights. Her bra and panties were no more drag than a swimsuit, and she moved through the water cleanly— berating herself for not having done this earlier. In the rain and the darkness it was impossible to judge how far she had swum. At least halfway, she fervently hoped. The adrenaline that had coursed through her earlier with its glib assurances of strength was beginning to fade, and she became increasingly aware of bruises and wrenched muscles suffered in the wreck.

The lights never appeared to come any closer, and by now she had lost track of time as well. She wondered whether the flow of the current might not be carrying her away from her destination whenever she rested, and that fear sent new power into her strokes. The brassiere straps chafed her shoulders, but this irritation was scarcely noticed against the gnawing ache of fatigue. She fought down her growing panic, concentrating her entire being upon the phantom lights in the distance.

The lights seemed no closer than the stars might have been—only the stars were already lost in the greyness and rain. At times the city lights vanished as well, blotted out as she labored through a swell. She was cut off from everything in those moments, cut off from space and from time and from reality.

There was only the greyness and the rain, pressing her deeper against the dark water. Memories of her past faded—she had always heard that a drowning victim's life flashed before her, but she could scarcely remember any fragment of her life before they had shut her away. Perhaps that memory would return when at last her straining muscles failed, and the water closed over her face in an unrelinquished kiss.

But then the lights *were* closer—she was certain of it this time. True, the lights were fewer than she had remembered, but she knew it must be far into the night after her seemingly endless swim. Hope sped renewed energy into limbs that had moved like a mechanical toy, slowly winding down. There was a current here, she sensed, seeking to drive her away from the lights and back into the limitless expanse she had struggled to escape.

As she fought against the current, she found she could at last make out the shoreline before her. Now she felt a new rush of fear. Sheer walls of stone awaited her. The city had been built along a bluff. She might reach the shore, but she could never climb its rock face.

She had fought too hard to surrender to despair now. Grimly she attacked the current, working her way along the shoreline. It was all but impossible to see anything—only the looming wall of blackness that cruelly barred her from the city invisible upon its heights. Then, beyond her in the night, the blackness seemed to recede somewhat. Scarcely daring to hope, she swam toward this break in the wall. The current steadily increased. Her muscles stabbed with fatigue, but now she had to swim all the harder to keep from being swept away.

The bluff was indeed lower here, but as a defense against the floods, they had built a wall where the natural barrier fell away. She clutched at the mossy stones in desperation—her clawing fingers finding no purchase. The current dragged her back, denying her a moment's respite.

She sobbed a curse. The heavy rains had driven the water to highest levels, leaving no rim of shoreline beneath cliff or dike. But since there was no escape for her along the direction she had come, she forced her aching limbs to fight on against the current. The line of the dike seemed to be curving inward, and she thought surely she could see a break in the barrier of blackness not far ahead.

She made painful progress against the increasing current, and at length was able to understand where she was. The seawall rose above a river that flowed through the city and into the bay. The city's storm sewers swelling its stream, the river rushed in full flood against the man-made bulwark. Its force was almost more than she could swim against now. Again and again she clutched at the slippery face of the wall, striving to gain a hold. Each time the current dragged her back again.

Storm sewers, some of them submerged now, poured into the river from the wall—their cross currents creating whirling eddies that shielded her one moment, tore at her the next, but allowed her to make desperate headway against the river itself. Bits of debris, caught up by the flood, struck at her invisibly. Rats, swimming frenziedly from the flooded sewers, struggled past her, sought to crawl onto her shoulders and face. She hit out at them, heedless of their bites, too intent on fighting the current herself to feel new horror.

A sudden eddy spun her against a recess in the seawall, and in the next instant her legs bruised against a submerged ledge. She half swam, half crawled forward, her fingers clawing slime-carpeted steps. Her breath sobbing in relief, she dragged herself out of the water and onto a flight of stone steps set out from the face of the wall.

For a long while she was contented to press herself against the wet stone, her aching limbs no longer straining to keep her afloat, her chest hammering in exhaustion. The flood washed against her feet, its level still rising, and a sodden rat clawed onto her leg—finding refuge as she had done. She crawled higher onto the steps, becoming aware of her surroundings once more.

So. She had made it. She smiled shakily and looked back toward the direction she had come. Rain and darkness and distance made an impenetrable barrier, but she imagined the rescue workers must be checking off the names of those they had found. There would be no checkmark beside her name.

She hugged her bare ribs. The night was chill, and she had no protection from the rain. She remembered now that she was almost naked. What would anyone think who saw her like this? Perhaps in the darkness her panties and bra would pass for a bikini—but what would a bather be doing out at this hour and in this place? She might explain that she had been sunbathing, had fallen asleep, taken refuge from the storm, and had then been forced to flee from the rising waters. But when news of the bus wreck spread, anyone who saw her would remember.

She must find shelter and clothing—somewhere. Her chance to escape had been born of the moment; she had not had time yet to think matters through. She only knew she could not let them recapture her now. Whatever the odds against her, she would face them.

She stood up, leaning against the face of the wall until she felt her legs would hold her upright. The flight of steps ran diagonally down from the top of the seawall. There was no railing on the outward face, and the stone was treacherous with slime and streaming water. Painfully she edged her way upward, trying not to think about the rushing waters below her. If she slipped, there was no way she could check her fall; she would tumble down into the black torrent, and this time there would be no escape.

The climb seemed as difficult as had her long swim, and her aching muscles seemed to rebel against the task of bearing her up the slippery steps, but at length she gained the upper landing and stumbled onto the stormwashed pavement atop the seawall. She blinked her eyes uncertainly, drawing a long breath. The rain pressed her black hair to her neck and shoulders, sluiced away the muck and filth from her skin.

There were no lights to be seen along here. A balustrade guarded the edge of the seawall, with a gap to give access to the stairs. A street, barren of any traffic at this hour, ran along the top of the wall, and, across the empty street, rows of brick buildings made a second barrier. Evidently she had come upon a district of warehouses and such—and, from all appearances, this section was considerably rundown. There were no streetlights here, but even in the darkness she could sense the disused aspect of the row of buildings with their boarded-over windows and filthy fronts, the brick street with its humped and broken paving.

She shivered. It was doubly fortunate that none were here to mark her sudden appearance. In a section like this, and dressed as she was, it was unlikely that anyone she might encounter would be of Good Samaritan inclinations.

Clothing. She had to find clothing. Any sort of clothing. She darted across the uneven paving and into the deeper shadow of the building fronts. Her best bet would be to find a shop: perhaps some sordid second-hand place such as this street might well harbor, a place without elaborate burglar alarms, if possible. She could break in, or at worst find a window display and try her luck at smash and grab. Just a simple raincoat would make her far less vulnerable. Eventually she would need money, shelter, and food, until she could leave the city for someplace far away.

As she crept along the deserted street, she found herself wondering whether she could find anything at all here. Doorways were padlocked and boarded over; behind rusted gratings, windows showed rotting planks and dirty shards of glass. The waterfront street seemed to be completely abandoned—a deserted row of ancient buildings enclosing forgotten wares, cheaper to let rot than to haul away, even as it was cheaper to let these brick hulks stand than to pull them down. Even the expected winos and derelicts seemed to have deserted this section of the city. She began to wish she might encounter at least a passing car.

The street had not been deserted by the rats. Probably they had been driven into the night by the rising waters. Once she began to notice them, she realized there were more and more of them—creeping boldly along the street. Huge, knowing brutes; some of them large as cats. They didn't seem afraid of her, and at times she thought they might be gathering in a pack to follow her. She had heard of rats attacking children and invalids, but surely . . . She wished she were out of this district.

The street plunged on atop the riverside, and still there were no lights or signs of human activity. The rain continued to pour down from the drowned night skies. She began to think about crawling into one of the dark warehouses to wait for morning, then thought of being alone in a dark, abandoned building with a closing pack of rats. She walked faster.

Some of the empty buildings showed signs of former grandeur, and she hoped she was coming toward a better section of the river-front. Elaborate entranceways of fluted columns and marble steps gave onto the street. Grotesque Victorian façades and misshapen statuary presented imposing fronts to buildings filled with the same musty decay as the brick warehouses. She must be reaching the old merchants' district of the city, although these structures as well appeared long abandoned, waiting only for the wrecking ball of urban renewal. She wished she could escape this street, for there seemed to be more rats in the darkness behind her than she could safely ignore.

Perhaps she might find an alleyway between buildings that would let her flee this waterfront section and enter some inhabited neighborhood—for it became increasingly evident that this street had long been derelict. She peered closely at each building, but never could she find a gap between them. Without a light, she dared not enter blindly and try to find her way through some ramshackle building.

She paused for a moment and listened. For some while she had heard a scramble of wet claws and fretful squealings from the darkness behind her. Now she heard only the rain. Were the rats silently closing about her?

She stood before a columned portico—a bank or church?—and gazed into the darker shadow, wondering whether she might seek shelter. A statue—she supposed it was of an angel or some symbolic figure—stood before one of the marble columns. She could discern little of its features, only that it must have been malformed—presumably by vandalism—for it was hunched over and appeared to be supported against the column by thick cables or ropes. She could not see its face.

Not liking the silence, she hurried on again. Once past the portico, she turned quickly and looked back—to see if the rats were creeping after her. She saw no rats. She could see the row of columns. The misshapen figure was no longer there.

She began to run then. Blindly, not thinking where her panic drove her.

To her right, there was only the balustrade, marking the edge of the wall, and the rushing waters below. To her left, the unbroken row of derelict buildings. Behind her, the night and the rain, and something whose presence had driven away the pursuing rats. And ahead of her—she was close enough to see it now—the street made a dead end against a rock wall.

Stumbling toward it, for she dared not turn back the way she had run, she saw that the wall was not unbroken—that a stairway climbed steeply to a terrace up above. Here the bluff rose high against the river once again, so that the seawall ended against the rising stone. There were buildings crowded against the height, fronted upon the terrace a level above. In one of the windows, a light shone through the rain.

Her breath shook in ragged gasps and her legs were rubbery, but she forced herself to half run, half clamber up the rain-slick steps to the terrace above. Here, again a level of brick paving and a balustrade to guard the edge. Boarded windows and desolate façades greeted her from a row of decrepit houses, shouldered together on the rise. The light had been to her right, out above the river.

She could see it clearly now. It beckoned from the last house on the terrace—a looming Victorian pile built over the bluff. A casement window, level with the far end of the terrace, opened onto a neglected garden. She climbed over the low wall that separated the house from the terrace, and crouched outside the curtained window.

Inside, a comfortable-looking sitting room with old-fashioned appointments. An older woman was crocheting, while in a chair beside her a young woman, dressed in a maid's costume, was reading aloud from a book. Across the corner room, another casement window looked out over the black water far below.

Had her fear and exhaustion been less consuming, she might have taken a less reckless course, might have paused to consider what effect her appearance would make. But she remembered a certain shuffling sound she had heard as she scrambled up onto the terrace, and the way the darkness had seemed to gather upon the top of the stairway when she glanced back a moment gone. With no thought but to escape the night, she tapped her knuckles sharply against the casement window.

At the tapping at the window, the older woman looked up from her work, the maid let the yellow-bound volume drop onto her white apron. They stared at the casement, not so much frightened as if uncertain of what they had heard. The curtain inside veiled her presence from them.

Please! she prayed, without voice to cry out. She tapped more insistently, pressing herself against the glass. They would see that she was only a girl, see her distress.

They were standing now, the older woman speaking too quickly for her to catch the words. The maid darted to the window, fumbled with its latch.

Another second, and the casement swung open and she tumbled into the room.

She knelt in a huddle on the floor, too exhausted to move any farther. Her body shook and water dripped from her bare flesh. She felt like some half-drowned kitten, plucked from the storm to shelter. Vaguely she could hear their startled queries, the protective clash as the casement latch closed out the rain and the curtain swept across the night.

The maid had brought a coverlet and was furiously toweling her dry. The maid's attentions reminded her that she must offer some sort of account of herself—before her benefactors summoned the police, whose investigation would put a quick end to her freedom.

"I'm all right now," she told them shakily. "Just let me get my breath back, get warm."

"What's your name, child?" the older woman inquired solicitously. "Camilla, bring some hot tea."

She groped for a name to tell them. "Cassilda." The maid's name had put this in mind, and it was suited to her surroundings. "Cassilda Archer." Dr. Archer would indeed be interested in *that* appropriation.

"You poor child! How did you come here? Were you . . . attacked?"

Her thoughts worked quickly. Satisfy their curiosity, but don't make them suspicious. Justify your predicament, but don't alarm them.

"I was hitchhiking." She spoke in uncertain bursts. "A man picked me up. He took me to a deserted section near the river. He made me take off my clothes. He was going to . . ." She didn't need to feign her shudder.

"Here's the tea, Mrs. Castaigne. I've added a touch of brandy."

"Thank you, Camilla. Drink some of this, dear."

She used the interruption to collect her thoughts. The two women were alone here, or else any others would have been summoned.

"When he started to pull down his trousers . . . I hurt him. Then I jumped out and ran as hard as I could. I don't think he came after me, but then I was wandering lost in the rain. I couldn't find anyone to help me. I didn't have anything with me except my underwear. I think a tramp was following me. Then I saw your light and ran toward it.

"Please, don't call the police!" She forestalled their obvious next move. "I'm not hurt. I know I couldn't face the shame of a rape investigation. Besides, they'd never be able to catch that man by now."

"But surely you must want me to contact someone for you."

"There's no one who would care. I'm on my own. That man has my pack and the few bucks in my handbag. If you could please let me stay here for the

rest of the night, lend me some clothes just for tomorrow, and in the morning I'll phone a friend who can wire me some money."

Mrs. Castaigne hugged her protectively. "You poor child! What you've
been through! Of course you'll stay with us for the night—and don't fret
about having to relive your terrible ordeal for a lot of leering policemen!
Tomorrow there'll be plenty of time for you to decide what you'd like to do.

"Camilla, draw a nice hot bath for Cassilda. She's to sleep in Constance's
room, so see that there's a warm comforter, and lay out a gown for her. And
you, Cassilda, must drink another cup of this tea. As badly chilled as you are,
child, you'll be fortunate indeed to escape your death of pneumonia!"

Over the rim of her cup, the girl examined the room and its occupants
more closely. The sitting room was distinctly old-fashioned—furnished like a
parlor in an old photograph, or like a set from some movie that was supposed
to be taking place at the turn of the century. Even the lights were either gas
or kerosene. Probably this house hadn't changed much since years ago before
the neighborhood had begun to decay. Anyone would have to be a little
eccentric to keep staying on here, although probably this place was all Mrs.
Castaigne had, and Mr. Castaigne wasn't in evidence. The house and property couldn't be worth much in this neighborhood, although the furnishings
might fetch a little money as antiques—she was no judge of that, but everything looked to be carefully preserved.

Mrs. Castaigne seemed well fitted to this room and its furnishings. Hers
was a face that might belong to a woman of forty or of sixty—well featured
but too stern for a younger woman, yet without the lines and age marks of an
elderly lady. Her figure was still very good, and she wore a tight-waisted,
ankle-length dress that seemed to belong to the period of the house. The
hands that stroked her bare shoulders were strong and white and unblem-
ished, and the hair she wore piled atop her head was as black as the girl's own.

It occurred to her that Mrs. Castaigne must surely be too young for this
house. Probably she was a daughter or more likely a granddaughter of its
original owners—a widow who lived alone with her young maid. And who
might Constance be, whose room she was to sleep in?

"Your bath is ready now, Miss Archer." Camilla reappeared. Wrapped in
the coverlet, the girl followed her. Mrs. Castaigne helped support her, for her
legs had barely strength to stand, and she felt ready to pass out from fatigue.

The bathroom was spacious—steamy from the vast claw-footed tub and
smelling of bath salts. Its plumbing and fixtures were no more modern than
the rest of the house. Camilla entered with her and, to her surprise, helped
her remove her scant clothing and assisted her into the tub. She was too tired
to feel ill at ease at this unaccustomed show of attention, and when the maid
began to rub her back with scented soap, she sighed at the luxury.

"Who else lives here?" she asked casually.

"Only Mrs. Castaigne and myself, Miss Archer."

"Mrs. Castaigne mentioned someone—Constance?—whose room I am to have."

"Miss Castaigne is no longer with us, Miss Archer."

"Please call me Cassilda. I don't like to be so formal."

"If that's what you wish to be called, of course . . . Cassilda."

Camilla couldn't be very far from her own age, she guessed. Despite the old-fashioned maid's outfit—black dress and stockings, with frilled white apron and cap—the other girl was probably no more than in her early twenties. The maid wore her long blonde hair in an upswept topknot like her mistress's, and the girl supposed the maid only followed Mrs. Castaigne's preferences. Camilla's figure was full—much more buxom than her own boyish slenderness—and her cinch-waisted costume accented this. Her eyes were bright blue, shining above a straight nose and wide-mouthed face.

"You've hurt yourself." Camilla ran her fingers tenderly along the bruises that marred the girl's ribs and legs.

"There was a struggle. And I fell in the darkness—I don't know how many times."

"And you've cut yourself." Camilla lifted the other girl's black hair away from her neck. "Here on your shoulders and throat. But I don't believe it's anything to worry about." Her fingers carefully touched the livid scrapes.

"Are you certain there isn't someone whom we should let know of your safe whereabouts?"

"There is no one who would care. I am alone."

"Poor Cassilda."

"All I want is to sleep," she murmured. The warm bath was easing the ache from her flesh, leaving her deliciously sleepy.

Camilla left her, to return with large towels. The maid helped her from the tub, wrapping her in one towel as she dried her with another. She felt faint with drowsiness, allowed herself to relax against the blonde girl. Camilla was very strong, supporting the girl easily as she toweled her small breasts. Camilla's fingers found the parting of her thighs, lingered, then returned again in a less than casual touch.

Her dark eyes were wide as she stared into Camilla's luminous blue gaze, but she felt too pleasurably relaxed to object when the maid's touch became more intimate. Her breath caught, and held.

"You're very warm, Cassilda."

"Hurry, Camilla." Mrs. Castaigne spoke from the doorway. "The poor child is about to drop. Help her into her nightdress."

Past wondering, the girl lifted her arms to let Camilla drape the beribboned lawn nightdress over her head and to her ankles. In another moment she was being ushered into a bedroom, furnished in the fashion of the rest of the house, and to an ornate brass bed whose mattress swallowed her up like a wave of foam. She felt the quilts drawn over her, sensed their presence hovering over her, and then she slipped into a deep sleep of utter exhaustion.

"Is there no one?"

"Nothing at all."

"Of course. How else could she be here? She is ours."

Her dreams were troubled by formless fears—deeply disturbing as experienced, yet their substance was already forgotten when she awoke at length on the echo of her outcry. She stared about her anxiously, uncertain where she was. Her disorientation was the same as when she awakened after receiving shock, only this place wasn't a ward, and the woman who entered the room wasn't one of her wardens.

"Good morning, Cassilda." The maid drew back the curtains to let long shadows streak across the room. "I should say, good evening, as it's almost that time. You've slept throughout the day, poor dear."

Cassilda? Yes, that was she. Memory came tumbling back in a confused jumble. She raised herself from her pillows and looked about the bedchamber she had been too tired to examine before. It was distinctly a woman's room— a young woman's—and she remembered that it had been Mrs. Castaigne's daughter's room. It scarcely seemed to have been unused for very long: the brass bed was brightly polished, the walnut of the wardrobe, the chests of drawers and the dressing table made a rich glow, and the gay pastels of the curtains and wallpaper offset the gravity of the high tinned ceiling and parquetry floor. Small oriental rugs and pillows upon the chairs and chaise lounge made bright points of color. Again she thought of a movie set, for the room was altogether lacking in anything modern. She knew very little about antiques, but she guessed that the style of furnishings must go back before the First World War.

Camilla was arranging a single red rose in a crystal bud vase upon the dressing table. She caught the girl's gaze in the mirror. "Did you sleep well, Cassilda? I thought I heard you cry out, just as I knocked."

"A bad dream, I suppose. But I slept well. I don't, usually." They had made her take pills to sleep.

"Are you awake, Cassilda? I thought I heard your voice." Mrs. Castaigne smiled from the doorway and crossed to her bed. She was dressed much the same as the night before.

"I didn't mean to sleep so long," she apologized.

"Poor child! I shouldn't wonder that you slept so, after your dreadful ordeal. Do you feel strong enough to take a little soup?"

"I really must be going. I can't impose any further."

"I won't hear any more of that, my dear. Of course you'll stay with us until you're feeling stronger." Mrs. Castaigne sat beside her on the bed, placed a cold hand against her brow. "Why, Cassilda, your face is simply aglow. I do hope you haven't taken a fever. Look, your hands are positively trembling!"

"I feel all right." In fact, she did not. She did feel as if she were running a fever, and her muscles were so sore that she wasn't sure she could walk. The trembling didn't concern her: the injections they gave her every two weeks made her shake, so they gave her little pills to stop the shaking. Now she didn't have those pills, but since it was time again for another shot, the injection and its side effects would soon wear off.

"I'm going to bring you some tonic, dear. And Camilla will bring you some good nourishing soup, which you must try to take. Poor Cassilda, if we don't nurse you carefully, I'm afraid you may fall dangerously ill."

"But I can't be such a nuisance to you," she protested as a matter of form. "I really must be going."

"Where to, dear child?" Mrs. Castaigne held her hands gravely. "Have you someplace else to go? Is there someone you wish us to inform of your safety?"

"No," she admitted, trying to make everything sound right. "I've no place to go; there's no one who matters. I was on my way down the coast, hoping to find a job during the resort season. I know one or two old girlfriends who could put me up until I get settled."

"See there. Then there's no earthly reason why you can't just stay here until you're feeling strong again. Why, perhaps I might find a position for you myself. But we shall discuss these things later when you're feeling well. For the moment, just settle back on your pillow and let us help you get well."

Mrs. Castaigne bent over her, kissed her on the forehead. Her lips were cool. "How lovely you are, Cassilda." She smiled, patting her hand.

The girl smiled back, and returned the woman's firm grip. She'd seen no sign of a TV or radio here, and an old eccentric like Mrs. Castaigne probably didn't even read the papers. Even if Mrs. Castaigne had heard about the bus wreck, she plainly was too overjoyed at having a visitor to break her lonely routine to concern herself with a possible escapee—assuming they hadn't just listed her as drowned. She couldn't have hoped for a better place to hide out until things cooled off.

★ ★ ★

The tonic had a bitter licorice taste and made her drowsy, so that she fell asleep not long after Camilla carried away her tray. Despite her long sleep throughout that day, fever and exhaustion drew her back down again—although her previous sleep robbed this one of restful oblivion. Again came troubled dreams, this time cutting more harshly into her consciousness.

She dreamed of Dr. Archer—her stern face and mannish shoulders craning over the bed. The girl's wrists and ankles were fixed to each corner of the bed by padded leather cuffs. Dr. Archer was speaking to her in a scolding tone, while her wardens were pulling up her skirt, dragging down her panties. A syringe gleamed in Dr. Archer's hand, and there was a sharp stinging in her buttock.

She was struggling again, but to no avail. Dr. Archer was shouting at her, and a stout nurse was tightening the last few buckles of the straitjacket that bound her arms to her chest in a loveless hug. The straps were so tight she could hardly draw a breath, and while she could not understand what Dr. Archer was saying she recognized the spurting needle that Dr. Archer thrust into her.

She was strapped tightly to the narrow bed, her eyes staring at the grey ceiling as they wheeled her through the corridors to Dr. Archer's special room. Then they stopped; they were there, and Dr. Archer was bending over her again. Then came the sting to her arm as they penetrated her veins, the helpless headlong rush of the drug—and Dr. Archer smiles and turns to her machine, and the current blasts into her tightly strapped skull and her body arches and strains against the restraints and her scream strangles against the rubber gag clenched in her teeth.

But the face that looks into hers now is not Dr. Archer's, and the hands that shake her are not cruel.

"Cassilda! Cassilda! Wake up! It's only a nightmare!"

Camilla's blonde and blue-eyed face finally focused into her awakening vision.

"Only a nightmare," Camilla reassured her. "Poor darling." The hands that held her shoulders lifted to smooth her black hair from her eyes, to cup her face. Camilla bent over her, kissed her gently on her dry lips.

"What is it?" Mrs. Castaigne, wearing her nightdress and carrying a candle, came anxiously into the room.

"Poor Cassilda has had bad dreams," Camilla told her. "And her face feels ever so warm."

"Dear child!" Mrs. Castaigne set down her candlestick. "She must take some more tonic at once. Perhaps you should sit with her, Camilla, to see that her sleep is untroubled."

"Certainly, madame. I'll just fetch the tonic."

"Please, don't bother . . ." But the room became a vertiginous blur as she tried to sit up. She slumped back and closed her eyes tightly for a moment. Her body *did* feel feverish, her mouth dry, and the trembling when she moved her hand to take the medicine glass was so obvious that Camilla shook her head and held the glass to her lips herself. She swallowed dutifully, wondering how much of this was a reaction to the Prolixin still in her flesh. The injection would soon be wearing off, she knew, for when she smiled back at her nurses, the sharp edges of color were beginning to show once again through the haze the medication drew over her perception.

"I'll be all right soon," she promised them.

"Then do try to sleep, darling." Mrs. Castaigne patted her arm. "You must regain your strength. Camilla will be here to watch over you.

"Be certain that the curtains are drawn against any night vapors," she directed her maid. "Call me, if necessary."

"Of course, madame. I'll not leave her side."

She was dreaming again—or dreaming still.

Darkness surrounded her like a black leather mask, and her body shook with uncontrollable spasms. Her naked flesh was slick with chill sweat, although her mouth was burning dry. She moaned and tossed—striving to awaken order from out of the damp blackness, but the blackness only embraced her with smothering tenacity.

Cold lips were crushing her own, thrusting a cold tongue into her feverish mouth, bruising the skin of her throat. Fingers, slender and strong, caressed her breasts, held her nipples to hungry lips. Her hands thrashed about, touched smooth flesh. It came to her that her eyes were indeed wide open, that the darkness was so profound she could no more than sense the presence of other shapes close beside her.

Her own movements were languid, dreamlike. Through the spasms that racked her flesh, she became aware of a perverse thrill of ecstasy. Her fingers brushed somnolently against the cool flesh that crouched over her, with no more purpose or strength than the drifting limbs of a drowning victim.

A compelling lassitude bound her, even as the blackness blinded her. She seemed to be drifting away, apart from her body, apart from her dream, into deeper ever deeper darkness. The sensual arousal that lashed her lost reality against the lethargy and fever that held her physically, and rising out of the eroticism of her delirium shrilled whispers of underlying revulsion and terror.

One pair of lips imprisoned her mouth and throat now, sucking at her breath, while other lips crept down across her breasts, hovered upon her navel, then pounced upon the opening of her thighs. Her breath caught in a shudder, was sucked away by the lips that held her mouth, as the coldness began to creep into her burning flesh.

She felt herself smothering, unable to draw breath, so that her body arched in panic, her limbs thrashed aimlessly. Her efforts to break away were as ineffectual as her struggle to awaken. The lips that stole her breath released her, but only for a moment. In the darkness she felt other flesh pinion her tossing body, move against her with cool strength. Chill fire tormented her loins, and as she opened her mouth to cry out, or to sigh, smooth thighs pressed down onto her cheeks and the coldness gripped her breath. Mutely, she obeyed the needs that commanded her, that overwhelmed her, and through the darkness blindly flowed her silent scream of ecstasy and of horror.

Cassilda awoke.

Sunlight spiked into her room—the colored panes creating a false prism effect. Camilla, who had been adjusting the curtains, turned and smiled at the sound of her movement.

"Good morning, Cassilda. Are you feeling better this morning?"

"A great deal better." Cassilda returned her smile. "I feel as if I'd slept for days." She frowned slightly, suddenly uncertain.

Camilla touched her forehead. "Your fever has left you; Mrs. Castaigne will be delighted to learn that. You've slept away most of yesterday and all through last night. Shall I bring your breakfast tray now?"

"Please—I'm famished. But I really think I should be getting up."

"After breakfast, if you wish. And now I'll inform madame that you're feeling much better."

Mrs. Castaigne appeared as the maid was clearing away the breakfast things. "How very much better you look today, Cassilda. Camilla tells me you feel well enough to sit up."

"I really can't play the invalid and continue to impose upon your hospitality any longer. Would it be possible that you might lend me some clothing? My own garments . . ." Cassilda frowned, trying to remember why she had burst in upon her benefactress virtually naked.

"Certainly, my dear." Mrs. Castaigne squeezed her shoulder. "You must see if some of my daughter's garments won't fit you. You cannot be very far from Constance, I'm certain. Camilla will assist you."

She was lightheaded when first she tried to stand, but Cassilda clung to the brass bedposts until her legs felt strong enough to hold her. The maid was busying herself at the chest of drawers, removing items of clothing from beneath neat coverings of tissue paper. A faint odor of dried rose petals drifted from a sachet beneath the folded garments.

"I do hope you'll overlook it if these are not of the latest mode," Mrs.

Castaigne was saying. "It has been some time since Constance was with us here."

"Your daughter is . . . ?"

"Away."

Cassilda declined to intrude further. There was a dressing screen behind which she retired, while Mrs. Castaigne waited upon the chaise lounge. Trailing a scent of dried roses from the garments she carried, Camilla joined her behind the screen and helped her out of her nightdress.

There were undergarments of fine silk, airy lace and gauzy pastels. Cassilda found herself puzzled, both from their unfamiliarity and at the same time their familiarity, and while her thoughts struggled with the mystery, her hands seemed to dress her body with practiced movements. First the chemise, knee-length and trimmed with light lace and ribbons. Seated upon a chair, she drew on pale stockings of patterned silk, held at mid-thigh by beribboned garters. Then silk knickers, open front and back and tied at the waist, trimmed with lace and ruching where they flared below her stocking tops. A frilled petticoat fell almost to her ankles.

"I won't need that," Cassilda protested. Camilla had presented her with a bone corset of white and sky broché.

"Nonsense, my dear," Mrs. Castaigne directed, coming around the dressing screen to oversee. "You may think of me as old-fashioned, but I insist that you not ruin your figure."

Cassilda submitted, suddenly wondering why she had thought anything out of the ordinary about it. She hooked the straight busk together in front, while Camilla gathered the laces at the back. The maid tugged sharply at the laces, squeezing out her breath. Cassilda bent forward and steadied herself against the back of the chair, as Camilla braced a knee against the small of her back, pulling the laces as tight as possible before tying them. Once her corset was secured, she drew over it a camisole of white cotton lace and trimmed with ribbon, matching her petticoat. Somewhat dizzy, Cassilda sat stiffly before the dressing table, while the maid brushed out her long black hair and gathered it in a loose knot atop her head, pinning it in place with tortoise-shell combs. Opening the wardrobe, Camilla found her a pair of shoes, with high heels that mushroomed outward at the bottom, which fit her easily.

"How lovely, Cassilda!" Mrs. Castaigne approved. "One would scarcely recognize you as the poor drowned thing that came out of the night!"

Cassilda stood up and examined herself in the full length dressing mirror. It was as if she looked upon a stranger, and yet she knew she looked upon herself. The corset constricted her waist and forced her slight figure into an "S" curve—hips back, bust forward—imparting an unexpected opulence, further enhanced by the gauzy profusion of lace and silk. Her face, dark-eyed and finely boned, returned her gaze watchfully from beneath a lustrous pile of black hair. She touched herself, almost in wonder, almost believing that the reflection in the mirror was a photograph of someone else.

Camilla selected for her a long-sleeved linen shirtwaist, buttoned at the cuffs and all the way to her throat, then helped her into a skirt of some darker material that fell away from her cinched waist to her ankles. Cassilda studied herself in the mirror, while the maid fussed about her.

I look like someone in an old illustration—a Gibson girl, she thought, then puzzled at her thought.

Through the open window she could hear the vague noises of the city, and for the first time she realized that intermingled with these familiar sounds was the clatter of horses' hooves upon the brick pavement.

"You simply must not say anything more about leaving us, Cassilda," Mrs. Castaigne insisted, laying a hand upon the girl's knee as she leaned toward her confidentially.

Beside her on the settee, Cassilda felt the pressure of her touch through the rustling layers of petticoat. It haunted her, this flowing whisper of sound that came with her every movement, for it seemed at once strange and again familiar—a shivery sigh of silk against silk, like the whisk of dry snow sliding across stone. She smiled, holding her teacup with automatic poise, and wondered that such little, commonplace sensations should seem at all out of the ordinary to her. Even the rigid embrace of her corset seemed quite familiar to her now, so that she sat gracefully at ease, listening to her benefactress, while a part of her thoughts stirred in uneasy wonder.

"You have said yourself that you have no immediate prospects," Mrs. Castaigne continued. "I shouldn't have to remind you of the dangers the city holds for unattached young women. You were extremely fortunate in your escape from those white slavers who had abducted you. Without family or friends to question your disappearance—well, I shan't suggest what horrible fate awaited you."

Cassilda shivered at the memory of her escape—a memory as formless and uncertain, beyond her *need* to escape, as that of her life prior to her abduction. She had made only vague replies to Mrs. Castaigne's gentle questioning, nor was she at all certain which fragments of her story were half-truths or lies.

Of one thing she was certain beyond all doubt: the danger from which she had fled awaited her beyond the shelter of this house.

"It has been so lonely here since Constance went away," Mrs. Castaigne was saying. "Camilla is a great comfort to me, but nonetheless she has her household duties to occupy her, and I have often considered engaging a companion. I should be only too happy if you would consent to remain with us in this position—at least for the present time."

"You're much too kind! Of course I'll stay."

"I promise you that your duties shall be no more onerous than to provide amusements for a rather old-fashioned lady of retiring disposition. I hope it won't prove too dull for you, my dear."

"It suits my temperament perfectly," Cassilda assured her. "I am thoroughly content to follow quiet pursuits within doors."

"Wonderful!" Mrs. Castaigne took her hands. "Then it's settled. I know Camilla will be delighted to have another young spirit about the place. And you may relieve her of some of her tasks."

"What shall I do?" Cassilda begged her, overjoyed at her good fortune.

"Would you read to me, please, my dear? I find it so relaxing to the body and so stimulating to the mind. I've taken up far too much of Camilla's time from her chores, having her read to me for hours on end."

"Of course." Cassilda returned Camilla's smile as she entered the sitting room to collect the tea things. From her delight, it was evident that the maid had been listening from the hallway. "What would you like for me to read to you?"

"That book over there beneath the lamp." Mrs. Castaigne indicated a volume bound in yellow cloth. "It is a recent drama—and a most curious work, as you shall quickly see. Camilla was reading it to me on the night you came to us."

Taking up the book, Cassilda again experienced a strange sense of unaccountable *déjà vu,* and she wondered where she might previously have read *The King in Yellow,* if indeed she ever had.

"I believe we are ready to begin the second act," Mrs. Castaigne told her.

Cassilda was reading in bed when Camilla knocked tentatively at her door. She set aside her book with an almost furtive movement. *"Entrez vous."*

"I was afraid you might already be asleep," the maid explained, "but then I saw light beneath your door. I'd forgotten to bring you your tonic before retiring."

Camilla, *en déshabillé,* carried in the medicine glass on a silver tray. Her fluttering lace and pastels seemed a pretty contrast to the black maid's uniform she ordinarily wore.

"I wasn't able to go to sleep just yet," Cassilda confessed, sitting up in bed. "I was reading."

Camilla handed her the tonic. "Let me see. Ah, yes. What a thoroughly wicked book to be reading in bed!"

"Have you read *The King in Yellow?"*

"I have read it through aloud to madame, and more than once. It is a favorite of hers."

"It is sinful and more than sinful to imbue such decadence with so compelling a fascination. I cannot imagine that anyone could have allowed it to be published. The author must have been mad to pen such thoughts."

"And yet, you read it."

Cassilda made a place for her on the edge of the bed. "Its fascination is too great a temptation to resist. I wanted to read further after Mrs. Castaigne bade me good-night."

"It was Constance's book." Camilla huddled close beside her against the pillows. "Perhaps that is why madame cherishes it so."

Cassilda opened the yellow-bound volume to the page she had been reading. Camilla craned her blonde head over her shoulder to read with her. She had removed her corset, and her ample figure swelled against her beribboned chemise. Cassilda in her nightdress felt almost scrawny as she compared her own small bosom to the other girl's.

"Is it not strange?" she remarked. "Here in this decadent drama we read of Cassilda and Camilla."

"I wonder if we two are very much like them," Camilla laughed.

"They are such very dear friends."

"And so are we, are we not?"

"I do so want us to be."

"But you haven't read beyond the second act, dear Cassilda. How can you know what may their fate be?"

"Oh, Camilla!" Cassilda leaned her face back against Camilla's perfumed breasts. "Don't tease me so!"

The blonde girl hugged her fiercely, stroking her back. "Poor, lost Cassilda."

Cassilda nestled against her, listening to the heartbeat beneath her cheek. She was feeling warm and sleepy, for all that the book had disturbed her. The tonic always carried her to dreamy oblivion, and it was pleasant to drift to sleep in Camilla's soft embrace.

"Were you and Constance friends?" she wondered.

"We were the very dearest of friends."

"You must miss her very much."

"No longer."

Cassilda sat at the escritoire in her room, writing in a journal she had found there. Her petticoats crowded against the legs of the writing table as she leaned forward to reach the inkwell. From time to time she paused to stare pensively past the open curtains of her window, upon the deepening blue of the evening sky as it met the angled rooftops of the buildings along the waterfront below.

"I think I should feel content here," she wrote. "Mrs. Castaigne is strict in her demands, but I am certain she takes a sincere interest in my own well-being, and that she has only the kindliest regard for me. My duties during the day are of the lightest nature and consist primarily of reading to Mrs. Castaigne or of singing at the piano while she occupies herself with her needlework, and in all other ways making myself companionable to her in our simple amusements.

"I have offered to assist Camilla at her chores, but Mrs. Castaigne will not have it that I perform other than the lightest household tasks. Camilla is a very dear friend to me, and her sweet attentions easily distract me from what might otherwise become a tedium of sitting about the house day to day. Nonetheless, I have no desire to leave my situation here, nor to adventure into the streets outside the house. We are not in an especially attractive section of the city here, being at some remove from the shops and in a district given over to waterfront warehouses and commercial establishments. We receive no visitors, other than the tradesmen who supply our needs, nor is Mrs. Castaigne of a disposition to wish to seek out the society of others.

"Withal, my instincts suggest that Mrs. Castaigne has sought the existence of a recluse out of some very great emotional distress which has robbed life of its interests for her. It is evident from the attention and instruction she has bestowed upon me that she sees in me a reflection of her daughter, and I am convinced that it is in the loss of Constance where lies the dark secret of her self-imposed withdrawal from the world. I am sensible of the pain Mrs. Castaigne harbors within her breast, for the subject of her daughter's absence is never brought into our conversations, and for this reason I have felt loath to question her, although I am certain that this is the key to the mystery that holds us in this house."

Cassilda concluded her entry with the date: June 7th, 189—

She frowned in an instant's consternation. What *was* the date? How silly. She referred to a previous day's entry, then completed the date. For a moment she turned idly back through her journal, smiling faintly at the many pages of entries that filled the diary, each progressively dated, each penned in the same neat hand as the entry she had just completed.

Cassilda sat at her dressing table in her room. It was night, and she had removed her outer clothing preparatory to retiring. She gazed at her reflection—the gauzy paleness of her chemise, stockings and knickers was framed against Camilla's black maid's uniform, as the blonde girl stood behind her, brushing out her dark hair.

Upon the dressing table she had spread out the contents of a tin box she had found in one of the drawers, and she and Camilla had been looking over them as she prepared for bed. There were paper dolls, valentines and greeting cards, illustrations clipped from magazines, a lovely cut-out of a swan. She also found a crystal ball that rested upon an ebony cradle. Within the crystal sphere was a tiny house, covered with snow, with trees and a frozen lake and a young girl playing. When Cassilda picked it up, the snow stirred faintly in the transparent fluid that filled the globe. She turned the crystal sphere upside down for a moment, then quickly righted it, and a snowstorm drifted down about the tiny house.

"How wonderful it would be to dwell forever in a crystal fairyland just like the people in this little house," Cassilda remarked, peering into the crystal ball.

Something else seemed to stir within the swirling snowflakes, she thought; but when the snow had settled once more, the tableau was unchanged. No: there was a small mound there beside the child at play, that she was certain she had not seen before. Cassilda overturned the crystal globe once again, and peered more closely. There it was. Another tiny figure spinning amidst the snowflakes. A second girl. She must have broken loose from the tableau. The tiny figure drifted to rest upon the frozen lake, and the snowflakes once more covered her from view.

"Where is Constance Castaigne?" Cassilda asked.

"Constance . . . became quite ill," Camilla told her carefully. "She was always subject to nervous attacks. One night she suffered one of her fits, and she . . ."

"Camilla!" Mrs. Castaigne's voice from the doorway was stern. "You know how I despise gossip—especially idle gossip concerning another's misfortunes."

The maid's face was downcast. "I'm very sorry, madame. I meant no mischief."

The older woman scowled as she crossed the room. Cassilda wondered if she meant to strike the maid. "Being sorry does not pardon the offense of a wagging tongue. Perhaps a lesson in behavior will improve your manners in the future. Go at once to your room."

"Please, madame . . ."

"Your insolence begins to annoy me, Camilla."

"Please, don't be harsh with her!" Cassilda begged, as the maid hurried from the room. "She was only answering my question."

Standing behind the seated girl, Mrs. Castaigne placed her hands upon her shoulders and smiled down at her. "An innocent question, my dear. However, the subject is extremely painful to me, and Camilla well knows the distress it causes me to hear it brought up. I shall tell you this now, and that shall end the matter. My daughter suffered a severe attack of brain fever. She is confined in a mental sanitarium."

Cassilda crossed her arms over her breasts to place her hands upon the older woman's wrists. "I'm terribly sorry."

"I'm certain you can appreciate how sorely this subject distresses me." Mrs. Castaigne smiled, meeting her eyes in the mirror.

"I shan't mention it again."

"Of course not. And now, my dear, you must hurry and make yourself ready for bed. Too much exertion so soon after your illness will certainly bring about a relapse. Hurry along now, while I fetch your tonic."

"I'm sure I don't need any more medicine. Sometimes I think it must bring on evil dreams."

"Now don't argue, Cassilda dear." The fingers on her shoulders tightened their grip. "You must do as you're told. You can't very well perform your duties as companion if you lie about ill all day, now can you? And you *do* want to stay."

"Certainly!" Cassilda thought this last had not been voiced as a question. "I want to do whatever you ask."

"I know you do, Cassilda. And I only want to make you into a perfect young lady. Now let me help you into your night things."

Cassilda opened her eyes into complete darkness that swirled about her in an invisible current. She sat upright in her bed, fighting back the vertigo that she had decided must come from the tonic they gave her nightly. Something had wakened her. Another bad dream? She knew she often suffered them. Was she about to be sick? She was certain that the tonic made her feel drugged.

Her wide eyes stared sleeplessly at the darkness. She knew sleep would not return easily, for she feared to lapse again into the wicked dreams that disturbed her rest and left her lethargic throughout the next day. She could not even be certain that this now might not be another of those dreams.

In the absolute silence of the house, she could hear her heart pulse, her breath stir anxiously.

There was another sound, more distant, and of almost the same monotonous regularity. She thought she heard a woman's muffled sobbing.

Mrs. Castaigne, she thought. The talk of her daughter had upset her terribly. Underscoring the sobbing came a sharp, rhythmic crack, as if a rocker sounded against a loose board.

Cassilda felt upon the nightstand beside her bed. Her fingers found matches. Striking one, she lit the candle that was there—her actions entirely automatic. Stepping down out of her bed, she caught up the candlestick and moved cautiously out of her room.

In the hallway, she listened for the direction of the sound. Her candle forced a small nimbus of light against the enveloping darkness of the old house. Cassilda shivered and drew her nightdress closer about her throat; its gauzy lace and ribbons were no barrier to the cold darkness that swirled about her island of candlelight.

The sobbing seemed no louder as she crept down the hallway toward Mrs. Castaigne's bedroom. There, the bedroom door was open, and within was only silent darkness.

"Mrs. Castaigne?" Cassilda called softly, without answer.

The sound of muffled sobbing continued, and now seemed to come from overhead. Cassilda followed its sound to the end of the hallway, where a flight of stairs led to the maid's quarters in the attic. Cassilda paused fearfully at the foot of the stairway, thrusting her candle without effect against the darkness above. She could still hear the sobbing, but the other sharp sound had ceased. Her head seemed to float in the darkness as she listened, but despite her dreamlike lethargy, she knew her thoughts raced too wildly now for sleep. Catching up the hem of her nightdress, Cassilda cautiously ascended the stairs.

Once she gained the landing above, she could see the blade of yellow light that shone beneath the door to Camilla's room, and from within came the sounds that had summoned her. Quickly Cassilda crossed to the maid's room and knocked softly upon the door.

"Camilla? It's Cassilda. Are you all right?"

Again no answer, although she sensed movement within. The muffled sobs continued.

Cassilda tried the doorknob, found it was not locked. She pushed the door open and stepped inside, dazzled a moment by the bright glare of the oil lamp.

Camilla, dressed only in her corset and undergarments, stood bent over the foot of her bed. Her ankles were lashed to the base of either post, her wrists tied together and stretched forward by a rope fixed to the headboard. Exposed by the open-style knickers, her buttocks were criss-crossed with red welts. She turned her head to look at Cassilda, and the other girl saw that Camilla's cries were gagged by a complicated leather bridle strapped about her head.

"Come in, Cassilda, since you wish to join us," said Mrs. Castaigne from behind her. Cassilda heard her close the door and lock it, before the girl had courage enough to turn around. Mrs. Castaigne wore no more clothing than did Camilla, and she switched her riding crop anticipatorially. Looking from mistress to maid, Cassilda saw that both pairs of eyes glowed alike with the lusts of unholy pleasure.

For a long interval Cassilda resisted awakening, hovering in a languor of unformed dreaming despite the rising awareness that she still slept. When she opened her eyes at last, she stared at the candlestick on her nightstand, observing without comprehension that the candle had burned down to a misshapen nub of cold wax. Confused memories came to her, slipping away again as her mind sought to grasp them. She had dreamed . . .

Her mouth seemed bruised and sour with a chemical taste that was not the usual anisette aftertaste of the tonic, and her limbs ached as if sore from too strenuous exercise the day before. Cassilda hoped she was not going to have a relapse of the fever that had stricken her after she had fled the convent that stormy night so many weeks ago.

She struggled for a moment with that memory. The sisters in black robes and white aprons had intended to wall her up alive in her cell because she had yielded to the temptation of certain unspeakable desires . . . The memory clouded and eluded her, like a fragment of some incompletely remembered book.

There were too many elusive memories, memories that died unheard . . . Had she not read that? *The King in Yellow* lay open upon her nightstand. Had she been reading, then fallen asleep to such dreams of depravity? But dreams, like memories, faded mirage-like whenever she touched them, leaving only tempting images to beguile her.

Forcing her cramped muscles to obey her, Cassilda climbed from her bed. Camilla was late with her tray this morning, and she might as well get dressed to make herself forget the dreams. As she slipped out of her nightdress, she looked at her reflection in the full length dressing mirror.

The marks were beginning to fade now, but the still painful welts made red streaks across the white flesh of her shoulders, back and thighs. Fragments of repressed nightmare returned as she stared in growing fear. She reached out her hands, touching the reflection in wonder. There were bruises on her wrists, and unbidden came a memory of her weight straining against the cords that bound her wrists to a hook from the attic rafter.

Behind her, in the mirror, Mrs. Castaigne ran the tip of her tongue along her smiling lips.

"Up and about already, Cassilda? I hope you've made up your mind to be a better young lady today. You were most unruly last night."

Her brain reeling under the onrush of memories, Cassilda stared mutely. Camilla, obsequious in her maid's costume, her smile a cynical sneer, entered carrying a complex leather harness of many straps and buckles.

"I think we must do something more to improve your posture, Cassilda," Mrs. Castaigne purred. "You may think me a bit old-fashioned, but I insist that a young lady's figure must be properly trained if she is to look her best."

"What are you doing to me?" Cassilda wondered, feeling panic.

"Only giving you the instruction a young lady must have if she is to serve as my companion. And you *do* want to be a proper young lady, don't you, Cassilda."

"I'm leaving this house. Right now."

"We both know why you can't. Besides, you don't really want to go. You quite enjoy our cozy little *ménage à trois.*"

"You're deranged."

"And you're one to talk, dear Cassilda." Mrs. Castaigne's smile was far more menacing than any threatened blow. "I think, Camilla, the scold's bridle will teach this silly girl to mind that wicked tongue."

A crash of thunder broke her out of her stupor. Out of reflex, she tried to dislodge the hard rubber ball that filled her mouth, choked on saliva when she failed. Half strangled by the gag strapped over her face, she strained in panic to sit up. Her wrists and ankles were held fast, and, as her eyes dilated in unreasoning fear, a flash of lightning beyond the window rippled down upon her spreadeagled body, held to the brass bedposts by padded leather cuffs.

Images, too chaotic and incomprehensible to form coherent memory, exploded in bright shards from her shattered mind.

She was being forced into a straitjacket, flung into a padded cell, and they were bricking up the door . . . no, it was some bizarre corset device, forcing her neck back, crushing her abdomen, arms laced painfully into a single glove at her back . . . Camilla was helping her into a gown of satin and velvet and lace, and then into a hood of padded leather that they buckled over her head as they led her to the gallows . . . and the nurses held her down while Dr. Archer penetrated her with a grotesque syringe of vile poison, and Mrs. Castaigne forced the yellow tonic down her throat as she pinned her face between her thighs . . . and Camilla's lips dripped blood as she rose from her kiss, and her fangs were hypodermic needles, injecting poison, sucking life . . . they were wheeling her into the torture chamber, where Dr. Archer awaited her ("It's only a frontal lobotomy, just to relieve the pressure on these two diseased lobes.") and plunges the bloody scalpel deep between her thighs . . . and they were strapping her into the metal chair in the death cell, shoving the rubber gag between her teeth and blinding her with the leather hood, and Dr. Archer grasps the thick black handle of the switch and pulls it down and sends the current ripping through her nerves . . . she stands naked in shackles before the black-masked judges, and Dr.

Archer gloatingly exposes the giant needle ("Just an injection of my elixir, and she's quite safe for two more weeks.") . . . and the nurses in rubber aprons hold her writhing upon the altar, while Dr. Archer adjusts the hangman's mask and thrusts the electrodes into her breast . . . ("Just a shot of my Prolixin, and she's quite sane for two more weeks.") . . . then the judge in wig and mask and black robe smacks down the braided whip and screams, "She must be locked away forever!" . . . she tears away the mask and Dr. Archer screams, "She must be locked inside forever!" . . . she tears away the mask and Mrs. Castaigne screams, "She must be locked in here forever!" . . . she tears away the mask and her own face screams, "She must be locked in you forever!" . . . then Camilla and Mrs. Castaigne lead her back into her cell, and they strap her to her bed and force the rubber gag between her teeth, and Mrs. Castaigne adjusts her surgeon's mask while Camilla clamps the electrodes to her nipples, and the current rips into her and her brain screams and screams unheard . . . "I think she no longer needs to be drugged." Mrs. Castaigne smiles and her lips are bright with blood. "She's one of us now. She always has been one with us." . . . and they leave her alone in darkness on the promise, "We'll begin again tomorrow," and the echo "She'll be good for two more weeks."

She moaned and writhed upon the soiled sheets, struggling to escape the images that spurted like fetid purulence from her tortured brain. With the next explosive burst of lightning, her naked body lifted in a convulsive arc from the mattress, and her scream against the gag was like the first agonized outcry of the newborn.

The spasm passed. She dropped back limply onto the sodden mattress. Slippery with sweat and blood, her relaxed hand slid the rest of the way out of the padded cuff. Quietly in the darkness, she considered her free hand—suddenly calm, for she knew she had slipped wrist restraints any number of times before this.

Beneath the press of the storm, the huge house lay in darkness and silence. With her free hand she unbuckled the other wrist cuff, then the straps that held the gag in place, and the restraints that pinned her ankles. Her tread no louder than a phantom's, she glided from bed and crossed the room. A flicker of lightning revealed shabby furnishings and a disordered array of fetishist garments and paraphernalia, but she threw open the window and looked down upon the black waters of the lake and saw the cloud waves breaking upon the base of the cliff, and when she turned away from that vision her eyes knew what they beheld and her smile was that of a lamia.

Wraith-like she drifted through the dark house, passing along the silent rooms and hallways and stairs, and when she reached the kitchen she found what she knew was the key to unlock the dark mystery that bound her here. She closed her hand upon it, and her fingers remembered its feel.

Camilla's face was tight with sudden fear as she awakened at the clasp of fingers closed upon her lips, but she made no struggle as she stared at the carving knife that almost touched her eyes.

"What happened to Constance?" The fingers relaxed to let her whisper, but the knife did not waver.

"She had a secret lover. One night she crept through the sitting room window and ran away with him. Mrs. Castaigne showed her no mercy."

"Sleep now," she told Camilla, and kissed her tenderly as she freed her with a swift motion that her hand remembered.

In the darkness of Mrs. Castaigne's room she paused beside the motionless figure on the bed.

"Mother?"

"Yes, Constance?"

"I've come home."

"You're dead."

"I remembered the way back."

And she showed her the key and opened the way.

It only remained for her to go. She could no longer find shelter in this house. She must leave as she had entered.

She left the knife. That key had served its purpose. Through the hallways she returned, in the darkness her bare feet sometimes treading upon rich carpets, sometimes dust and fallen plaster. Her naked flesh tingled with the blood that had freed her soul.

She reached the sitting room and looked upon the storm that lashed the night beyond. For one gleam of lightning the room seemed festooned with torn wallpaper; empty wine bottles littered the floor and dingy furnishings. The flickering mirage passed, and she saw that the room was exactly as she remembered. She must leave by the window.

There was a tapping at the window.

She started, then recoiled in horror as another repressed memory escaped into consciousness.

The figure that had pursued her through the darkness on that night she had sought refuge here. It waited for her now at the window. Half-glimpsed before, it now was fully revealed in the glare of the lightning.

Moisture glistened darkly upon its rippling and exaggerated musculature. Its uncouth head and shoulders hunched forward bullishly; its face was distorted with insensate lust and drooling madness. A grotesque phallus swung between its misshapen legs—serpentine, possessed of its own life and volition. Like an obscene worm, it stretched blindly toward her, blood oozing from its toothless maw.

She raised her hands to ward it off, and the monstrosity pawed at the window, mocking her every terrified movement as it waited there on the other side of the rainslick glass.

The horror was beyond enduring. There was another casement window to the corner sitting room, the one that overlooked the waters of the river. She spun about and lunged toward it—noticing from the corner of her eye that the creature outside also whirled about, sensing her intent, flung itself toward the far window to forestall her.

The glass of the casement shattered, even as the creature's blubbery hands stretched out toward her. There was no pain in that release, only a dreamlike vertigo as she plunged into the greyness and the rain. Then the water and the darkness received her falling body, and she set out again into the night, letting the current carry her, she knew not where.

"A few personal effects remain to be officially disposed of, Dr. Archer— since there's no one to claim them. It's been long enough now since the bus accident, and we'd like to be able to close the files on this catastrophe."

"Let's have a look." The psychiatrist opened the box of personal belongings. There wasn't much; there never was in such cases, and had there been anything worth stealing, it was already unofficially disposed of.

"They still haven't found a body," the ward superintendent wondered. "Do you suppose . . . ?"

"Callous as it sounds, I rather hope not," Dr. Archer confided. "This patient was a paranoid schizophrenic—and dangerous."

"Seemed quiet enough on the ward."

"Thanks to a lot of ECT—and to depot phenothiazines. Without regular therapy, the delusional system would quickly regain control, and the patient would become frankly murderous."

There were a few toiletry items and some articles of clothing, a brassiere and pantyhose. "I guess send this over to Social Services. These shouldn't be allowed on a locked ward," the psychiatrist pointed to the nylons, "nor these smut magazines."

"They always find some way to smuggle the stuff in," the ward superintendent sighed, "and I've been working here at Coastal State since back before the War. What about these other books?"

Dr. Archer considered the stack of dog-eared gothic romance novels. "Just return these to the Patients' Library. What's this one?"

Beneath the paperbacks lay a small hardcover volume, bound in yellow cloth, somewhat soiled from age.

"Out of the Patients' Library too, I suppose. People have donated all sorts of books over the years, and if the patients don't tear them up, they just stay on the shelves forever."

"The King in Yellow," Dr. Archer read from the spine, opening the book. On the flyleaf a name was penned in a graceful script: *Constance Castaigne.*

"Perhaps the name of a patient who left it here," the superintendent suggested. "Around the turn of the century this was a private sanitarium. Somehow, though, the name seems to ring a distant bell."

"Let's just be sure this isn't vintage porno."

"I can't be sure—maybe something the oldtimers talked about when I first started here. I seem to remember there was some famous scandal involving one of the wealthy families in the city. A murderess, was it? And something about a suicide, or was it an escape? I can't recall . . ."

"Harmless nineteenth century romantic nonsense," Dr. Archer concluded. "Send it back to the library."

The psychiatrist glanced at a last few lines before closing the book:

Cassilda. I tell you, I am lost! Utterly lost!

Camilla. (terrified herself.) You have seen the King . . . ?

Cassilda. And he has taken from me the power to direct or to escape my dreams.

THE DEPTHS

RAMSEY CAMPBELL

As Miles emerged, a woman and a pink-eyed dog stumped by. She glanced at the house; then, humming tunelessly, she aimed the same contemptuous look at Miles. As if the lead was a remote control, the dog began to growl. They thought Miles was the same as the house.

He almost wished that were true; at least it would have been a kind of contact. He strolled through West Derby village and groped in his mind for ideas. Pastels drained from the evening sky. Wood pigeons paraded in a tree-lined close. A mother was crying 'Don't you dare go out of this garden again.' A woman was brushing her driveway and singing that she was glad she was Bugs Bunny. Beyond a brace of cars, in a living-room that displayed a bar complete with beer-pumps, a couple listened to Beethoven's Greatest Hits.

Miles sat drinking beer at a table behind the Crown, at the edge of the bowling green. Apart from the click of bowls the summer evening seemed as blank as his mind. Yet the idea had promised to be exactly what he and his publisher needed: no more days of drinking tea until his head swam, of glaring at the sheet of paper in the typewriter while it glared an unanswerable challenge back at him. He hadn't realized until now how untrustworthy inspirations were.

Perhaps he ought to have foreseen the problem. The owners had told him that there was nothing wrong with the house—nothing except the aloofness and silent disgust of their neighbours. If they had known what had happened there they would never have bought the house; why should they be treated as though by living there they had taken on the guilt?

Still, that was no more unreasonable than the crime itself. The previous owner had been a bank manager, as relaxed as a man could be in his job; his wife had owned a small boutique. They'd seemed entirely at peace with each other. Nobody who had known them could believe what he had done to her. Everyone Miles approached had refused to discuss it, as though by keeping quiet about it they might prevent it from having taken place at all.

The deserted green was smudged with darkness. 'We're closing now,' the barmaid said, surprised that anyone was still outside. Miles lifted the faint sketch of a tankard and gulped a throatful of beer, grimacing. The more he researched the book, the weaker it seemed to be.

To make things worse, he'd told the television interviewer that it was near completion. At least the programme wouldn't be broadcast for months, by which time he might be well into a book about the locations of murder—but it wasn't the book he had promised his publisher, and he wasn't sure that it would have the same appeal.

Long dark houses slumbered beyond an archway between cottages, lit windows hovered in the arch. A signboard reserved a weedy patch of ground for a library. A grey figure was caged by the pillars of the village cross. On the roof of a pub extension gargoyles began barking, for they were dogs. A cottage claimed to be a sawmill, but the smell seemed to be of manure. Though his brain was taking notes, it wouldn't stop nagging.

He gazed across Lord Sefton's estate towards the tower blocks of Cantril Farm. Their windows were broken ranks of small bright perforations in the night. For a moment, as his mind wobbled on the edge of exhaustion, the unstable patterns of light seemed a code which he needed to break to solve his problems. But how could they have anything to do with it? Such a murder in Cantril Farm, in the concrete barracks among which Liverpool communities had been scattered, he might have understood; here in West Derby it didn't make sense.

As he entered the deserted close, he heard movements beneath eaves. It must be nesting birds, but it was as though the sedate house had secret thoughts. He was grinning as he pushed open his gate, until his hand recoiled. The white gate was stickily red.

It was paint. Someone had written SADIST in an ungainly dripping scrawl. The neighbours could erase that—he wouldn't be here much longer. He let himself into the house.

For a moment he hesitated, listening to the dark. Nothing fled as he switched on the lights. The hall was just a hall, surmounted by a concertina of stairs; the metal and vinyl of the kitchen gleamed like an Ideal Home display; the corduroy suite sat plump and smug on the dark green pelt of the living-room. He felt as though he was lodging in a show house, without even the company of a shelf of his books.

Yet it was here, from the kitchen to the living-room, that everything had happened—here that the bank manager had systematically rendered his wife unrecognizable as a human being. Miles stood in the empty room and tried to

imagine the scene. Had her mind collapsed, or had she been unable to withdraw from what was being done to her? Had her husband known what he
was doing, right up to the moment when he'd dug the carving-knife into his
throat and run headlong at the wall?

It was no good: here at the scene of the crime, Miles found the whole
thing literally unimaginable. For an uneasy moment he suspected that might
have been true of the killer and his victim. As Miles went upstairs, he was
planning the compromise to offer his publisher: *Murderers' Houses? Dark Places
of the World?* Perhaps it mightn't be such a bad book after all.

When he switched off the lights, darkness came upstairs from the hall. He
lay in bed and watched the shadows of the curtains furling and unfurling
above him. He was touching the gate, which felt like flesh; it split open, and
his hand plunged in. Though the image was unpleasant it seemed remote,
drawing him down into sleep.

The room appeared to have grown much darker when he woke in the grip
of utter panic.

He didn't dare move, not until he knew what was wrong. The shadows
were frozen above him, the curtains hung like sheets of lead. His mouth
tasted metallic, and made him think of blood. He was sure that he wasn't
alone in the dark. The worst of it was that there was something he mustn't do
—but he had no idea what it was.

He'd begun to search his mind desperately when he realized that was
exactly what he ought not to have done. The thought which welled up was
so atrocious that his head began to shudder. He was trying to shake out the
thought, to deny that it was his. He grabbed the light-cord, to scare it back
into the dark.

Was the light failing? The room looked steeped in dimness, a grimy fluid
whose sediment clung to his eyes. If anything the light had made him worse,
for another thought came welling up like bile, and another. They were worse
than the atrocities which the house had seen. He had to get out of the house.

He slammed his suitcase—thank God he'd lived out of it, rather than use
the wardrobe—and dragged it onto the landing. He was halfway down, and
the thuds of the case on the stairs were making his scalp crawl, when he
realized that he'd left a notebook in the living-room.

He faltered in the hallway. He mustn't be fully awake: the carpet felt moist
underfoot. His skull felt soft and porous, no protection at all for his mind. He
had to have the notebook. Shouldering the door aside, he strode blindly into
the room.

The light which dangled spider-like from the central plaster flower showed
him the notebook on a fat armchair. Had the chairs soaked up all that had
been done here? If he touched them, what might well up? But there was

worse in his head, which was seething. He grabbed the notebook and ran
into the hall, gasping for air.

His car sounded harsh as a saw among the sleeping houses. He felt as
though the neat hygienic facades had cast him out. At least he had to concentrate on his driving, and was deaf to the rest of his mind. The road through
Liverpool was unnaturally bright as a playing-field. When the Mersey Tunnel
closed overhead he felt that an insubstantial but suffocating burden had settled
on his scalp. At last he emerged, only to plunge into darkness.

Though his sleep was free of nightmares, they were waiting whenever he
jerked awake. It was as if he kept struggling out of a dark pit, having repeatedly forgotten what was at the top. Sunlight blazed through the curtains as
though they were tissue paper, but couldn't reach inside his head. Eventually,
when he couldn't bear another such awakening, he stumbled to the bathroom.

When he'd washed and shaved he still felt grimy. It must be the lack of
sleep. He sat gazing over his desk. The pebbledashed houses of Neston blazed
like the cloudless sky; their outlines were knife-edged. Next door's drain
sounded like someone bubbling the last of a drink through a straw. All this
was less vivid than his thoughts—but wasn't that as it should be?

An hour later he still hadn't written a word. The nightmares were crowding everything else out of his mind. Even to think required an effort that
made his skin feel infested, swarming.

A random insight saved him. Mightn't it solve both his problems if he
wrote the nightmares down? Since he'd had them in the house in West Derby
—since he felt they had somehow been produced by the house—couldn't he
discuss them in his book?

He scribbled them out until his tired eyes closed. When he reread what
he'd written he grew feverishly ashamed. How could he imagine such things?
If anything was obscene, they were. Nothing could have made him write
down the idea which he'd left until last. Though he was tempted to tear up
the notebook, he stuffed it out of sight at the back of a drawer and hurried
out to forget.

He sat on the edge of the promenade and gazed across the Dee marshes.
Heat-haze made the Welsh hills look like piles of smoke. Families strolled as
though this were still a watering-place; children played carefully, inhibited by
parents. The children seemed wary of Miles; perhaps they sensed his tension,
saw how his fingers were digging into his thighs. He must write the book
soon, to prove that he could.

Ranks of pebbledashed houses, street after street of identical Siamese twins,
marched him home. They reminded him of cells in a single organism. He
wouldn't starve if he didn't write—not for a while, at any rate—but he felt

uneasy whenever he had to dip into his savings; their unobtrusive growth was reassuring, a talisman of success. He missed his street and had to walk back. Even then he had to peer twice at the street name before he was sure it was his.

He sat in the living-room, too exhausted to make himself dinner. Van Gogh landscapes, frozen in the instant before they became unbearably intense, throbbed on the walls. Shelves of Miles's novels reminded him of how he'd lost momentum. The last nightmare was still demanding to be written, until he forced it into the depths of his mind. He would rather have no ideas than that.

When he woke, the nightmare had left him. He felt enervated but clean. He lit up his watch and found he'd slept for hours. It was time for the Book Programme. He'd switched on the television and was turning on the light when he heard his voice at the far end of the room, in the dark.

He was on television, but that was hardly reassuring; his one television interview wasn't due to be broadcast for months. It was as though he'd slept that time away. His face floated up from the grey of the screen as he sat down, cursing. By the time his book was published, nobody would remember this interview.

The linkman and the editing had invoked another writer now. Good God, was that all they were using of Miles? He remembered the cameras following him into the West Derby house, the neighbours glaring, shaking their heads. It was as though they'd managed to censor him, after all.

No, here he was again. 'Jonathan Miles is a crime novelist who feels he can no longer rely on his imagination. Desperate for new ideas, he lived for several weeks in a house where, last year, a murder was committed.' Miles was already losing his temper, but there was worse to come: they'd used none of his observations about the creative process, only the sequence in which he ushered the camera about the house like Hitchcock in the *Psycho* trailer. 'Viewers who find this distasteful,' the linkman said unctuously, 'may be reassured to hear that the murder in question is not so topical or popular as Mr Miles seems to think.'

Miles glared at the screen while the programme came to an end, while an announcer explained that *Where Do You Get Your Ideas?* had been broadcast ahead of schedule because of an industrial dispute. And now here was the news, all of it as bad as Miles felt. A child had been murdered, said a headline; a Chief Constable had described it as the worst case of his career. Miles felt guiltily resentful; no doubt it would help distract people from his book.

Then he sat forward, gaping. Surely he must have misheard; perhaps his insomnia was talking. The newsreader looked unreal as a talking bust, but his voice went on, measured, concerned, inexorable. 'The baby was found in a microwave oven. Neighbours broke into the house on hearing the cries, but were unable to locate it in time.' Even worse than the scene he was describing was the fact that it was the last of Miles's nightmares, the one he had refused to write down.

Couldn't it have been coincidence? Coincidence, coincidence, the train chattered, and seemed likely to do so all the way to London. If he had somehow been able to predict what was going to happen, he didn't want to know—especially not now, when he could sense new nightmares forming.

He suppressed them before they grew clear. He needed to keep his mind uncluttered for the meeting with his publisher; he gazed out of the window, to relax. Trees turned as they passed, unravelling beneath foliage. On a platform a chorus line of commuters bent to their luggage, one by one. The train drew the sun after it through clouds, like a balloon.

Once out of Euston Station and its random patterns of swarming, he strolled to the publishers. Buildings glared like blocks of salt, which seemed to have drained all moisture from the air. He felt hot and grimy, anxious both to face the worst and to delay. Hugo Burgess had been ominously casual: 'If you happen to be in London soon we might have a chat about things . . .'

A receptionist on a dais that overlooked the foyer kept Miles waiting until he began to sweat. Eventually a lift produced Hugo, smiling apologetically. Was he apologizing in advance for what he had to say? 'I suppose you saw yourself on television,' he said when they reached his office.

'Yes, I'm afraid so.'

'I shouldn't give it another thought. The telly people are envious buggers. They begrudge every second they give to discussing books. Sometimes I think they resent the competition and get their own back by being patronizing.' He was pawing through the heaps of books and papers on his desk, apparently in search of the phone. 'It did occur to me that it would be nice to publish fairly soon,' he murmured.

Miles hadn't realized that sweat could break out in so many places at once. 'I've run into some problems.'

Burgess was peering at items he had rediscovered in the heaps. 'Yes?' he said without looking up.

Miles summarized his new idea clumsily. Should he have written to Burgess in advance? 'I found there simply wasn't enough material in the West Derby case,' he pleaded.

'Well, we certainly don't want padding.' When Burgess eventually glanced up he looked encouraging. 'The more facts we can offer the better. I think the public is outgrowing fantasy, now that we're well and truly in the scientific age. People want to feel informed. Writing needs to be as accurate as any other science, don't you think?' He hauled a glossy pamphlet out of one of the piles. 'Yes, here it is. I'd call this the last gasp of fantasy.'

It was a painting, lovingly detailed and photographically realistic, of a girl who was being simultaneously mutilated and raped. It proved to be the cover of a new magazine, *Ghastly*. Within the pamphlet the editor promised 'a quarterly that will wipe out the old horror pulps—everything they didn't dare to be.'

'It won't last,' Burgess said. 'Most people are embarrassed to admit to reading fantasy now, and that will only make more so. The book you're planning is more what they want—something they know is true. That way they don't feel they're indulging themselves.' He disinterred the phone at last. 'Just let me call a car and we'll go into the West End for lunch.'

Afterwards they continued drinking in Hugo's club. Miles thought Hugo was trying to midwife the book. Later he dined alone, then lingered for a while in the hotel bar; his spotlessly impersonal room had made him feel isolated. Over the incessant trickle of muzak he kept hearing Burgess: 'I wonder how soon you'll be able to let me have sample chapters . . .'

Next morning he was surprised how refreshed he felt, especially once he'd taken a shower. Over lunch he unburdened himself to his agent. 'I don't know how much research may be involved.'

'Now look, you mustn't worry about Hugo. I'll speak to him. I know he won't mind waiting if he knows it's for the good of the book.' Susie Barker patted his hand; her bangles sounded like silver castanets. 'Now here's an idea for you. Why don't you do up a sample chapter or two on the West Derby case? That way we'll keep Hugo happy, and I'll do my best to sell it as an article.'

When they'd kissed goodbye Miles strolled along the Charing Cross Road, composing the chapter in his head and looking for himself in bookshop displays. Miles, Miles, books said in a window stacked with crime novels. NIGHT OF ATROCITIES, headlines cried on an adjacent newspaper stand.

He dodged into Foyles. That was better: he occupied half a shelf, though his earliest titles looked faded and dusty. When he emerged he was content to drift with the rushhour crowds—until a newsvendor's placard stopped him. BRITAIN'S NIGHT OF HORROR, it said.

It didn't matter, it had nothing to do with him. In that case, why couldn't he find out what had happened? He didn't need to buy a paper, he could read the report as the newsvendor snatched the top copy to reveal the same beneath. 'Last night was Britain's worst night of murders in living memory . . .'

Before he'd read halfway down the column the noise of the crowd seemed to close in, to grow incomprehensible and menacing. The newsprint was snatched away again and again like a macabre card trick. He sidled away from the news-stand as though from the scene of a crime, but already he'd recognized every detail. If he hadn't repressed them on the way to London he could have written the reports himself. He even knew what the newspaper had omitted to report: that one of the victims had been forced to eat parts of herself.

Weeks later the newspapers were still in an uproar. Though the moderates pointed out that the murders had been unrelated and unmotivated, committed by people with no previous history of violence or of any kind of crime, for most of the papers that only made it worse. They used the most unpleasant photographs of the criminals that they could find, and presented the crimes as evidence of the impotence of the law, of a total collapse of standards. Opinion polls declared that the majority was in favour of an immediate return of the death penalty. 'MEN LIKE THESE MUST NOT GO UNPUNISHED', a headline said, pretending it was quoting. Miles grew hot with frustration and guilt—for he felt he could have prevented the crimes.

All too soon after he'd come back from London, the nightmares had returned. His mind had already felt raw from brooding, and he had been unable to resist; he'd known only that he must get rid of them somehow. They were worse than the others: more urgent, more appalling.

He'd scribbled them out as though he was inspired, then he'd glared blindly at the blackened page. It hadn't been enough. The seething in his head, the crawling of his scalp, had not been relieved even slightly. This time he had to develop the ideas, imagine them fully, or they would cling and fester in his mind.

He'd spent the day and half the night writing, drinking tea until he hardly knew what he was doing. He'd invented character after character, building them like Frankenstein out of fragments of people, only to subject them to gloatingly prolonged atrocities, both the victims and the perpetrators.

When he'd finished, his head felt like an empty rusty can. He might have vomited if he had been able to stand. His gaze had fallen on a paragraph he'd written, and he'd swept the pages onto the floor, snarling with disgust. 'Next morning he couldn't remember what he'd done—but when he reached in his pocket and touched the soft object his hand came out covered with blood . . .'

He'd stumbled across the landing to his bedroom, desperate to forget his ravings. When he'd woken next morning he had been astonished to find that he'd fallen asleep as soon as he had gone to bed. As he'd lain there, feeling purged, an insight so powerful it was impossible to doubt had seized him. If he hadn't written out these things they would have happened in reality.

But he had written them out: they were no longer part of him. In fact they had never been so, however they had felt. That made him feel cleaner, absolved him of responsibility. He stuffed the sloganeering newspapers into the wastebasket and arranged his desk for work.

By God, there was nothing so enjoyable as feeling ready to write. While a pot of tea brewed he strolled about the house and revelled in the sunlight, his release from the nightmares, his surge of energy. Next door a man with a beard of shaving foam dodged out of sight, like a timid Santa Claus.

Miles had composed the first paragraph before he sat down to write, a trick that always helped him write more fluently—but a week later he was still struggling to get the chapter into publishable shape. All that he found crucial about his research—the idea that by staying in the West Derby house he had trapped a source of utter madness, which had probably caused the original murder—he'd had to suppress. Why, if he said any of that in print they would think he was mad himself. Indeed, once he'd thought of writing it, it no longer seemed convincing.

When he could no longer bear the sight of the article, he typed a fresh copy and sent it to Susie. She called the following day, which seemed encouragingly quick. Had he been so aware of what he was failing to write that he hadn't noticed what he'd achieved?

'Well, Jonathan, I have to say this,' she said as soon as she'd greeted him. 'It isn't up to your standard. Frankly, I think you ought to scrap it and start again.'

'Oh.' After a considerable pause he could think of nothing to say except, 'All right.'

'You sound exhausted. Perhaps that's the trouble.' When he didn't answer she said, 'You listen to your Auntie Susie. Forget the whole thing for a fortnight and go away on holiday. You've been driving yourself too hard— you looked tired the last time I saw you. I'll explain to Hugo, and I'll see if I can't talk up the article you're going to write when you come back.'

She chatted reassuringly for a while, then left him staring at the phone. He was realizing how much he'd counted on selling the article. Apart from royalties, which never amounted to as much as he expected, when had he last had the reassurance of a cheque? He couldn't go on holiday, for he would feel he hadn't earned it; if he spent the time worrying about the extravagance, that would be no holiday at all.

But he turned the idea over gingerly in his mind, as though something might crawl out from beneath—but really, he could see no arguments against it. Writing out the nightmares had drained them of power; they were just stories now. As he dialled Hugo's number, to ask him for the address of the magazine, he was already thinking up a pseudonym for himself.

For a fortnight he walked around Anglesey. Everything was hallucinatorily intense: beyond cracks in the island's grassy coastline, the sea glittered as though crystallizing and shattering; across the sea, Welsh hills and mist appeared to be creating each other. Beaches were composed of rocks like brown crusty loaves decorated with shells. Anemones unfurled deep in glassy pools. When night fell he lay on a slab of rock and watched the stars begin to swarm.

As he strolled he was improving the chapters in his mind, now that the first version had clarified his themes. He wrote the article in three days, and was sure it was publishable. Not only was it the fullest description yet of the murder, but he'd managed to explain the way the neighbours had behaved: they'd needed to dramatize their repudiation of all that had been done in the house, they'd used him as a scapegoat to cast out, to proclaim that it had nothing to do with them.

When he'd sent the manuscript to Susie he felt pleasantly tired. The houses of Neston grew silver in the evening, the horizon was turning to ash. Once the room was so dark that he couldn't read, he went to bed. As he drifted towards sleep he heard next door's drain bubbling to itself.

But what was causing bubbles to form in the greyish substance that resembled fluid less than flesh? They were slower and thicker than tar, and took longer to form. Their source was rushing upward to confront him face to face. The surface was quivering, ready to erupt, when he awoke.

He felt hot and grimy, and somehow ashamed. The dream had been a distortion of the last thing he'd heard, that was all; surely it wouldn't prevent him from sleeping. A moment later he was clinging to it desperately; its dreaminess was comforting, and it was preferable by far to the ideas that were crowding into his mind. He knew now why he felt grimy.

He couldn't lose himself in sleep; the nightmares were embedded there, minute, precise and appalling. When he switched on the light it seemed to isolate him. Night had bricked up all the windows. He couldn't bear to be alone with the nightmares—but there was only one way to be rid of them.

The following night he woke having fallen asleep at his desk. His last line met his eyes: 'Hours later he sat back on his haunches, still chewing doggedly . . .' When he gulped the lukewarm tea it tasted rusty as blood. His surroundings seemed remote, and he could regain them only by purging his mind. His task wasn't even half finished. His eyes felt like dusty pebbles. The pen jerked in his hand, spattering the page.

Next morning Susie rang, wrenching him awake at his desk. 'Your article is tremendous. I'm sure we'll do well with it. Now I wonder if you can let me have a chapter breakdown of the rest of the book to show Hugo?'

Miles was fully awake now, and appalled by what had happened in his mind while he had been sleeping. 'No,' he muttered.

'Are there any problems you'd like to tell me about?'

If only he could! But he couldn't tell her that while he had been asleep, having nearly discharged his task, a new crowd of nightmares had gathered in his mind and were clamouring to be written. Perhaps now they would never end.

'Come and see me if it would help,' Susie said.

How could he, when his mind was screaming to be purged? But if he didn't force himself to leave his desk, perhaps he never would. 'All right,' he said dully. 'I'll come down tomorrow.'

When tomorrow came it meant only that he could switch off his desk-lamp; he was nowhere near finishing. He barely managed to find a seat on the train, which was crowded with football fans. Opened beercans spat; the air grew rusty with the smell of beer. The train emerged roaring from a tunnel, but Miles was still in his own, which was far darker and more oppressive. Around him they were chanting football songs, which sounded distant as a waveband buried in static. He wrote under cover of his briefcase, so that nobody would glimpse what he was writing.

Though he still hadn't finished when he reach London, he no longer cared. The chatter of the wheels, the incessant chanting, the pounding of blood and nightmares in his skull had numbed him. He sat for a while in Euston. The white tiles glared like ice, a huge voice loomed above him.

As soon as she saw him Susie demanded, 'Have you seen a doctor?'

Even a psychiatrist couldn't help him. 'I'll be all right,' he said, hiding behind a bright false smile.

'I've thought of some possibilities for your book,' she said over lunch. 'What about that house in Edinburgh where almost the same murder was committed twice, fifty years apart? The man who did the second always said he hadn't known about the first . . .' She obviously hoped to revive him with ideas—but the nightmare which was replaying itself, endless as a loop of film, would let nothing else into his skull. The victim had managed to tear one hand free and was trying to protect herself.

'And isn't there the lady in Sutton who collected bricks from the scenes of crimes? She was meaning to use them to build a miniature Black Museum. She ought to be worth tracing,' Susie said as the man seized the flailing hand by its wrist. 'And then if you want to extend the scope of the book there's the mother of the Meathook Murder victims, who still gets letters pretending to be from her children.'

The man had captured the wrist now. Slowly and deliberately, with a grin that looked pale as a crack in clay, he—Miles was barely able to swallow; his head, and every sound in the restaurant, was pounding. 'They sound like good ideas,' he mumbled, to shut Susie up.

Back at her office, a royalty fee had arrived. She wrote him a cheque at once, as though that might cure him. As he slipped it into his briefcase, she caught sight of the notebooks in which he'd written on the train. 'Are they something I can look at?' she said.

His surge of guilt was so intense that it was panic. 'No, it's nothing, it's just something, no,' he stammered.

Hours later he was walking. Men loitered behind boys playing pinball; the machines flashed like fireworks, splashing the men's masks. Addicts were gathering outside the all-night chemist's on Piccadilly; in the subterranean Gents', a starved youth washed blood from a syringe. Off Regent Street, Soho glared like an amusement arcade. On Oxford Street figures in expensive dresses, their bald heads gleaming, gestured broken-wristed in windows.

He had no idea why he was walking. Was he hoping the crowds would distract him? Was that why he peered at their faces, more and more desperately? Nobody looked at all reassuring. Women were perfect as corpses, men seemed to glow with concealed aggression; some were dragons, their mouths full of smoke.

He'd walked past the girl before he reacted. Gasping, he struggled through a knot of people on the corner of Dean Street and dashed across, against the lights. In the moments before he realized that he'd dodged ahead of her and was staring, he saw her bright quick eyes, the delicate web of veins beneath them, the freckles that peppered the bridge of her nose, the pulsing of blood in her neck. She was so intensely present to him that it was appalling.

Then she stepped aside, annoyed by him, whatever he was. He reached out, but couldn't quite seize her arm. He had to stop her somehow. 'Don't,' he cried.

At that, she fled. He'd started after her when two policemen blocked his path. Perhaps they hadn't noticed him, perhaps they wouldn't grab him—but it was too late; she was lost in the Oxford Street crowd. He turned and ran, fleeing back to his hotel.

As soon as he reached his room he began writing. His head felt stuffed with hot ash. He was scribbling so fast that he hardly knew what he was saying. How much time did he have? His hand was cramped and shaking, his writing was surrounded by a spittle of ink.

He was halfway through a sentence when, quite without warning, his mind went blank. His pen was clawing spasmodically at the page, but the urgency had gone; the nightmare had left him. He lay in the anonymous bed in the dark, hoping he was wrong.

In the morning he went down to the lobby as late as he could bear. The face of the girl he'd seen in Oxford Street stared up at him from a newspaper. In the photograph her eyes looked dull and reproachful, though perhaps they seemed so only to him. He fled upstairs without reading the report. He already knew more than the newspaper would have been able to tell.

Eventually he went home Neston. It didn't matter where he went; the nightmares would find him. He was an outcast from surrounding reality. He was focused inward on his raw wound of a mind, waiting for the next outbreak of horrors to infest him.

Next day he sat at his desk. The sunlit houses opposite glared back like empty pages. Even to think of writing made his skin prickle. He went walking, but it was no good: beyond the marshes, factories coughed into the sky; grass-blades whipped the air like razors; birds swooped, shrieking knives with wings. The sunlight seemed violent and pitiless, vampirizing the landscape.

There seemed no reason why the nightmares should ever stop. Either he would be forced to write them out, to involve himself more and more deeply in them, or they would be acted out in reality. In any case he was at their mercy; there was nothing he could do.

But wasn't he avoiding the truth? It hadn't been coincidence that had given him the chance he'd missed in Oxford Street. Perhaps he had been capable of intervention all along, if he had only known. However dismaying the responsibility was, surely it was preferable to helplessness. His glimpse in Oxford Street had made all the victims unbearably human.

He sat waiting. Pale waves snaked across the surface of the grass; in the heat-haze they looked as though water was welling up from the marshes. His scalp felt shrunken, but that was only nervousness and the storm that was clotting overhead. When eventually the clouds moved on, unbroken, they left a sediment of twilight that clung to him as he trudged home.

No, it was more than that. His skin felt grimy, unclean. The nightmares were close. He hurried to let his car out of the garage, then he sat like a private detective in the driver's seat outside his house. His hands clenched on the steering wheel. His head began to crawl, to swarm.

He mustn't be trapped into self-disgust. He reminded himself that the nightmares weren't coming from him, and forced his mind to grasp them, to be guided by them. Shame made him feel coated in hot grease. When at last the car coasted forward, was it acting out his urge to flee? Should he follow that street sign, or that one?

Just as the signs grew meaningless because he'd stared too long, he knew which way to go. His instincts had been waiting to take hold, and they were urgent now. He drove through the lampless streets, where lit curtains cut rectangles from the night, and out into the larger dark.

He found he was heading for Chester. Trees beside the road were giant scarecrows, brandishing tattered foliage. Grey clouds crawled grub-like across the sky; he could hardly distinguish them from the crawling in his skull. He was desperate to purge his mind.

Roman walls loomed between the timber buildings of Chester, which were black and white as the moon. A few couples were window-shopping along the enclosed rows above the streets. On the bridge that crossed the main street, a clock perched like a moon-faced bird. Miles remembered a day when he'd walked by the river, boats passing slowly as clouds, a brass band on a small bandstand playing 'Blow the Wind Southerly'. How could the nightmare take place here?

It could, for it was urging him deeper into the city. He was driving so fast through the spotless streets that he almost missed the police station. Its blue sign drew him aside. That was where he must go. Somehow he had to persuade them that he knew where a crime was taking place.

He was still yards away from the police station when his foot faltered on the accelerator. The car shuddered and tried to jerk forward, but that was no use. The nearer he came to the police station, the weaker his instinct became. Was it being suppressed by his nervousness? Whatever the reason, he could guide nobody except himself.

As soon as he turned the car the urgency seized him. It was agonizing now. It rushed him out of the centre of Chester, into streets of small houses and shops that looked dusty as furniture shoved out of sight in an attic. They were deserted except for a man in an ankle-length overcoat, who limped by like a sack with a head.

Miles stamped on the brake as the car passed the mouth of an alley. Snatching the keys, he slammed the door and ran into the alley, between two shops whose posters looked ancient and faded as Victorian photographs. The walls of the alley were chunks of spiky darkness above which cramped windows peered, but he didn't need to see to know where he was going.

He was shocked to find how slowly he had to run, how out of condition he was. His lungs seemed to be filling with lumps of rust, his throat was scraped raw. He was less running than staggering forward. Amid the uproar of his senses, it took him a while to feel that he was too late.

He halted as best he could. His feet slithered on the uneven flagstones, his hands clawed at the walls. As soon as he began to listen he wished he had not. Ahead in the dark, there was a faint incessant shriek that seemed to be trying to emerge from more than one mouth. He knew there was only one victim.

Before long he made out a dark object further down the alley. In fact it was two objects, one of which lay on the flagstones while the other rose to its feet, a dull gleam in its hand. A moment later the figure with the gleam was fleeing, its footsteps flapping like wings between the close walls.

The shrieking had stopped. The dark object lay still. Miles forced himself forward, to see what he'd failed to prevent. As soon as he'd glimpsed it he staggered away, choking back a scream.

He'd achieved nothing except to delay writing out the rest of the horrors. They were breeding faster in his skull, which felt as though it was cracking. He drove home blindly. The hedgerows and the night had merged into a dark mass that spilled towards the road, smudging its edges. Perhaps he might crash —but he wasn't allowed that relief, for the nightmares were herding him back to his desk.

The scratching of his pen, and a low half-articulate moaning which he recognized sometimes as his voice, kept him company. Next day the snap of the letter-box made him drop his pen; otherwise he might not have been able to force himself away from the desk.

The package contained the first issue of *Ghastly*. 'Hope you like it,' the editor gushed. 'It's already been banned in some areas, which has helped sales no end. You'll see we announce your stories as coming attractions, and we look forward to publishing them.' On the cover the girl was still writhing, but the contents were far worse. Miles had read only a paragraph when he tore the glossy pages into shreds.

How could anyone enjoy reading that? The pebbledashed houses of Neston gleamed innocently back at him. Who knew what his neighbours read behind their locked doors? Perhaps in time some of them would gloat over his pornographic horrors, reassuring themselves that this was only horror fiction, not pornography at all: just as he'd reassured himself that they were only stories now, nothing to do with reality—certainly nothing to do with him, self-confident and bland: they looked as convinced of their innocence as he was trying to feel—and all at once he knew where the nightmares were coming from.

He couldn't see how that would help him. Before he'd begun to suffer from his writer's block, there had been occasions when a story had surged up from his unconscious and demanded to be written. Those stories had been products of his own mind, yet he couldn't shake them off except by writing —but now he was suffering nightmares on behalf of the world.

No wonder they were so terrible, or that they were growing worse. If material repressed into the unconscious was bound to erupt in some less manageable form, how much more powerful that must be when the unconscious was collective! Precisely because people were unable to come to terms with the crimes, repudiated them as utterly inhuman or simply unimaginable, the horrors would reappear in a worse form and possess whoever they pleased. He remembered thinking that the patterns of life in the tower blocks had something to do with the West Derby murder. They had, of course. Everything had.

And now the repressions were focused in him. There was no reason why they should ever leave him; on the contrary, they seemed likely to grow more numerous and more peremptory. Was he releasing them by writing them out, or was the writing another form of repudiation?

One was still left in his brain. It felt like a boil in his skull. Suddenly he knew that he wasn't equal to writing it out, whatever else might happen. Had his imagination burned out at last? He would be content never to write another word. It occurred to him that the book he'd discussed with Hugo was just another form of rejection: knowing you were reading about real people reassured you they were other than yourself.

He slumped at his desk. He was a burden of flesh that felt encrusted with grit. Nothing moved except the festering nightmare in his head. Unless he got rid of it somehow, it felt as though it would never go away. He'd failed twice to intervene in reality, but need he fail again? If he succeeded, was it possible that might change things for good?

He was at the front door when the phone rang. Was it Susie? If she knew what was filling his head, she would never want to speak to him again. He left the phone ringing in the dark house and fled to his car.

The pain in his skull urged him through the dimming fields and villages to Birkenhead, where it seemed to abandon him. Not that it had faded—his mind felt like an abscessed tooth—but it was no longer able to guide him. Was something anxious to prevent him from reaching his goal?

The bare streets of warehouses and factories and terraces went on for miles, brick-red slabs pierced far too seldom by windows. At the peak hour the town centre grew black with swarms of people, the Mersey Tunnel drew in endless sluggish segments of cars. He drove jerkily, staring at faces.

Eventually he left the car in Hamilton Square, overlooked by insurance offices caged by railings, and trudged towards the docks. Except for his footsteps, the streets were deserted. Perhaps the agony would be cured before he arrived wherever he was going. He was beyond caring what that implied.

It was dark now. At the end of rows of houses whose doors opened onto cracked pavements he saw docked ships, glaring metal mansions. Beneath the iron mesh of swing bridges, a scum of neon light floated on the oily water. Sunken rails snagged his feet. In pubs on street corners he heard tribes of dockers, a sullen wordless roar that sounded like a warning. Out here the moan of a ship on the Irish Sea was the only voice he heard.

When at last he halted, he had no idea where he was. The pavement on which he was walking was eaten away by rubbly ground; he could smell collapsed buildings. A roofless house stood like a rotten tooth, lit by a single street lamp harsh as lightning. Streets still led from the opposite pavement, and despite the ache—which had aborted nearly all his thoughts—he knew that the street directly opposite was where he must go.

There was silence. Everything was yet to happen. The lull seemed to give him a brief chance to think. Suppose he managed to prevent it? Repressing the ideas of the crimes only made them erupt in a worse form—how much worse might it be to repress the crimes themselves?

Nevertheless he stepped forward. Something had to cure him of his agony. He stayed on the treacherous pavement of the side street, for the roadway was skinless, a mass of bricks and mud. Houses pressed close to him, almost forcing him into the road. Where their doors and windows ought to be were patches of new brick. The far end of the street was impenetrably dark.

When he reached it, he saw why. A wall at least ten feet high was built flush against the last houses. Peering upward, he made out the glint of broken glass. He was closed in by the wall and the plugged houses, in the midst of desolation.

Without warning—quite irrelevantly, it seemed—he remembered something he'd read about years ago while researching a novel: the Mosaic ritual of the Day of Atonement. They'd driven out the scapegoat, burdened with all the sins of the people, into the wilderness. Another goat had been sacrificed. The images chafed together in his head; he couldn't grasp their meaning—and then he realized why there was so much room for them in his mind. The aching nightmare was fading.

At once he was unable to turn away from the wall, for he was atrociously afraid. He knew why this nightmare could not have been acted out without him. Along the bricked-up street he heard footsteps approaching.

When he risked a glance over his shoulder, he saw that there were two figures. Their faces were blacked out by the darkness, but the glints in their hands were sharp. He was trying to claw his way up the wall, though already his lungs were labouring. Everything was over—the sleepless nights, the poison in his brain, the nightmare of responsibility—but he knew that while he would soon not be able to scream, it would take him much longer to die.

Dream
of a Mannikin

Thomas Ligotti

Once upon a Wednesday afternoon, promptly at two o'clock, a girl stepped into my office. It was her first session, and she introduced herself as Amy Locher. (And didn't you once tell me that long ago you had a doll with this same first name?) Under the present circumstances I don't think it too gross a violation of professional ethics to use the subject's real name in describing her case to you. Certainly there's something more than simple ethics between us, *ma chère amie*. Besides, I understood from Miss Locher that you recommended me to her. This didn't seem necessarily ominous at first; perhaps, I speculated, your relationship with the girl was such that made it awkward for you to take her on as one of your own patients. Actually it's still not clear to me, my love, just how deeply you can be implicated in the overall experience I had with the petite Miss L. So you'll have to forgive any stupidities of mine which may crudely crop up in the body of this correspondence.

My first impression of Miss Locher, as she positioned herself almost sidesaddle in a leather chair before me, was that of a tense and disturbed but basically efficient and selfseeking young woman. She was dressed and accessoried, I noticed, in much the classic style which you normally favor. I won't go into our first visit preliminaries here (though we can discuss these and other matters at dinner this Saturday if only you are willing). After a brief chat we zeroed in on the girl's immediate impetus for consulting me. This involved, as you may or may not know, a distressing dream she had recently suffered. What will follow, as I have composed them from my tape of the September 10th session, are the events of that dream.

In the dream our subject has entered into a new life, at least to the extent that she holds down a different job from her waking one. She had already informed me that for some five years she has worked as a secretary for a tool and die firm. (And could this possibly be *your* delicate touch? Tooling into oblivion.) However, her working day in the dream finds her as a long-time employee of a fashionable clothes shop. Like those state witnesses the government wishes to protect with new identities, she has been out-fitted by the dream with what seems to be a mostly tacit but somehow complete biography; a marvelous trick of the mind, this. It appears that the duties of her new job require her to change the clothes of the mannikins in the front window, this according to some mysterious schedule. She in fact feels as if her entire existence is slavishly given over to dressing and undressing these dummies. She is profoundly dissatisfied with her lot, and the mannikins become the focal point of her animus.

Such is the general background pre-supposed by the dream, which now begins in proper. On a particularly gloomy day in her era of thralldom, our dummy dresser approaches her work. She is resentful and frightened, the latter emotion an irrational "given" at this point in the dream. An awesome load of new clothes is waiting to attire a windowful of naked mannikins. Their unwarm, uncold bodies repel her touch. (Note this rare awareness of temperature in a dream, albeit neutral.) She bitterly surveys the ranks of these puttyfaced creatures and then says: "Time to stop dancing and get dressed, sleeping beauties." These words are spoken without spontaneity, as if ritually uttered to inaugurate each dressing session. But the dream changes before the dresser is able to put one stitch on the dummies, who stare at nothing with "anticipating" eyes.

The working day is now finished. She has returned to her small apartment, where she retires to bed . . . and has a dream. (This dream is that of the mannikin dresser and not hers, she emphatically pointed out!)

The mannikin dresser dreams she is in her bedroom. But what she now thinks of as her "bedroom" is to all appearances actually an archaically furnished hall with the dimensions of a small theater. The room is dimly lit by some jeweled lamps along the walls, the lights shining "with a strange glaziness" upon an intricately patterned carpet and upon the massive pieces of antique furniture around the room. She perceives the objects of the scene more as pure ideas than material phenomena, for details are blurry and there are many shadows. There is something, however, which she visualizes quite clearly: one of the walls of this lofty room is missing, and beyond this great gap is a view of star-clustered blackness which, irrationally, may in truth represent the depths of a colossal mirror. In any case, this maze of stars and blackness appears as an enormous mural and suggests an uncertain location for a room formerly thought to be nestled at the cozy crossroads of well-known coordinates. Now it is truly just a lost point within the unfathomable universe of sleep.

The dreamer is positioned on the other side of the room from the brink of the starry abyss. Sitting on the edge of an armless, backless couch of complex brocade, she stares and waits "without breath or heartbeat," these functions being quite unnecessary to her dream self. Everything is in silence. This silence, however, is somehow charged with strange currents of force which she can't really explain, an insane physics electrifying the atmosphere with demonic powers lurking just beyond the threshold of sensory perception. All is perceived with elusive dream senses.

Then a new feeling enters the dream, one slightly more tangible. There seems to be an iciness drifting in from that dazzling starscape across the room. Suddenly our dreamer experiences a premonitory dread of something unknown. Without moving from her place on that uncomfortable couch, she visually searches the room for clues to the source of her terror. Many areas are inaccessible to her sight—like a picture that has been scribbled out in places —but she sees nothing particularly frightening and is relieved for a moment. Then her anxiety begins anew when she realizes for the first time that she hasn't looked behind her, and indeed she seems physically unable to do so.

Something is back there. She feels this to be a horrible truth. She *almost* knows what the thing is, but, afflicted with some kind of oneiric aphasia, she cannot find the word for the thing she fears. She can only wait, hoping that sudden shock will soon bring her out of the dream, for she is now aware that "she is dreaming," thinking of herself in the third person.

The words "she is dreaming" somehow form a ubiquitous motif for the present situation: as a legend written somewhere at the bottom of the dream, as echoing voices bouncing here and there around the room, as a motto printed upon fortune cookie-like strips of paper and hidden in bureau drawers, and as a broken record repeating itself on an ancient victrola inside the dreamer's head. Then all the words of this monotonous slogan gather from their divers places and like an alighting flock of birds settle in the area behind the dreamer's back. There they twitter for a moment, as upon the frozen shoulders of a statue in a park. This is actually the way it seems to the dreamer, including the statue comparison. Something of a statuesque nature is back there, approaching her. Something that is radiating a searing field of tension, coming closer, its great shadow falling across and enlarging her own upon the floor. Still she cannot turn around, cannot move her body, which is stiff-jointed and rigid. Perhaps she can scream, she thinks, and makes an attempt to do so. But this fails, because by then there is already a firm and tepid hand that has covered her mouth from behind. The fingers on her lips feel like thick, naked crayons. Then she sees a long slim arm extending itself over her left shoulder, and a hand that is holding some filthy rags before her eyes and shaking them, "making them dance." And at that moment a dry sibilant voice whispers into her ear: "It's time to get dressed, little dolling."

She tries to look away, her eyes being the only things she can move. Now, for the first time, she notices that all around the room—in the shadowed places—are people dressed as dolls. Their forms are collapsed, their mouths opened wide. They do not look as if they are still alive. Some of them have actually become dolls, their flesh no longer supple and their eyes having lost the appearance of teary moistness. Others are at various intermediate stages between humanness and dollhood. With horror, the dreamer now becomes aware that her own mouth is opened wide and will not close.

But at last, through the power of her fear, she is able to turn around and face the menacing agent. The dream now reaches a shattering crescendo and she awakes. She does not, however, awake in the bed of the mannikin dresser in her dream within a dream, but instead finds herself directly transported into the tangled, though real, bedcovers of her secretary self. Not exactly sure where or who she is for a moment, her first impulse on awaking is to complete the movement she began in the dream; that is, turning around to look behind her. (The hypnopompic hallucination that followed served as a "strong motivating factor" in her decision to seek the powers of a psychiatrist.) What she saw, upon pivoting about, was more than just a simple headboard with a blank wall above. For projecting out of that moon-whitened wall was the face of a female mannikin. And what particularly disturbed her about this illusion (and here we go deeper into already dubious realms) was that the face didn't melt away into the background of the wall the way postdream projections usually do. It seems, rather, that this protruding visage, in one smooth movement, *withdrew* back into the wall. Her screams summoned more than a few concerned persons from neighboring apartments.

End of dream and related experiences.

Now, my darling, you can probably imagine my reaction to the above psychic yarn. Every loose skein I followed led me back to you. The character of Miss Locher's dream is strongly reminiscent, in both mood and scenario, of matters you have been exploring for some years now. I'm referring, of course, to the all-around astral ambiance of Miss Locher's dream and how eerily it relates to certain notions (very well, *theories*) that in my opinion have become altogether too central to your *oeuvre* as well as to your *vie*. Above all, I refer to those "otherworlds" you say you've detected through a combination of occult studies and depth analysis.

Let me digress for a brief lecture apropos of the preceding.

It's not that I object to your delving into speculative models of reality, sweetheart, but why this particular one? Why posit these "little zones," as

I've heard you call them, having such hideous attributes, or should I say *anti*-attributes (to keep up with your theoretical lingo)? To whimsically joke about such bizarrerie with phrases like "pockets of interference" and "cosmic static," belies your talents as a thoughtful member of our profession. And the rest of it: the hyperuncanniness, the warped relationships that are supposed to obtain in these places, the "games with reality," and all the other transcendent nonsense. I realize that psychology has charted some awfully weird areas in its maps of the mind, but you've gone so far into the ultra-mental hinterlands of metaphysics that I fear you will not return (at least not with your reputation intact).

To speak of your ideas with regard to Miss Locher's dream, you can see the connections, especially in the tortuous plot of her narrative. But I'll tell you when these connections really struck me with a hammerblow. It was just after she had related her dream to me. She was now riding the saddle of her chair in the normal position, and she made a few remarks obviously intended to convey the full extent of her distress. I'm sure she thought it de rigueur to tell me that after her dream episode she began entertaining doubts concerning who she really was. Secretary? Attirer of mannikins? Other? Other other? She knew, of course, the identity of her genuine, factual self; it was just some "new sense of unreality" that undermined complete assurance in this matter.

Surely you can see how the above identity tricks fit in with those "harassments of the self" that you say are one of the characteristic happenings in these zones of yours. And just what are the boundaries of the self? Is there a secret communion of seemingly separate things? How do animate and inanimate relate? Very boring, m'dear . . . zzzzz.

It all reminds me of that trite little fable of the Chinese (Chuang Tzu?) who dreamed he was a butterfly but upon waking affected not to know whether he was a man who'd dreamed he was a butterfly or a butterfly now dreaming . . . you get the idea. The question is: "Do things like butterflies dream?" (Ans.:no. Recall the lab studies in this field, if you will for once.) The issue is ended right there. However—as I'm sure you would contest—suppose the dreamer is not a man or butterfly, but both . . . or neither, something else altogether. Or suppose . . . really we could go on and on like this, and we have. Possibly the most repellent concept you've developed is that which you call "divine masochism," or the doctrine of a Bigger Self terrorizing its little splinter selves, precisely that Something Else Altogether scarifying the man-butterfly with uncanny suspicions that there's a game going on over its collective head.

The trouble with all this, my beloved, is the way you're so adamant about its objective reality, and how you sometimes manage to infect others with your peculiar convictions. Me, for instance. After hearing Miss Locher tell her dream story, I found myself unconsciously analyzing it much as you might have. Her multiplication of roles (including the role reversal with the mannikin) really did put me in mind of some divine being that was splintering and scarring itself to relieve its cosmic ennui, as indeed a few of the well-reputed gods of world religion supposedly do. I also thought of your "divinity of the dream," that thing which is all-powerful in its own realm. Contemplating the realm of Miss Locher's dream, I came to deeply feel that old truism of a solipsistic dream deity commanding all it sees, all of which is only itself. And a corollary to solipsism even occurred to me: if, in any dream of a universe, one has to *always* allow that there is another, waking universe, then the problem becomes, as with our Chinese sleepyhead, knowing when one is actually dreaming and what form the waking self may have; and this one can *never* know. The fact that the overwhelming majority of thinkers rejects any doctrine of solipsism suggests the basic horror and disgusting unreality of its implications. And after all, the horrific feeling of unreality is much more prevalent (to certain people) in what we call human "reality" than in human dreams, where everything is absolutely real.

See what you've done to me! For reasons that you well know, I always try to argue your case, my love. I can't help myself. But I don't think it's right to be exerting your influence upon innocents like Miss Locher. I should tell you that I hypnotized the girl. Her unconscious testimony seems very much to incriminate you. She almost demanded the hypnosis, feeling this to be an easy way of unveiling the source of her problems. And because of her frantic demands, I obliged her. A serendipitous discovery ensued.

She was an excellent subject. In hypnosis we restricted ourselves to penetrating the mysteries of her dream. I had her recount the events of this nightmare with the more accurate memory of her hypnotized state. Her earlier version was amazingly factual, with the exception of one important datum which I'll get to in a moment. I asked her to elaborate on her feelings in the dream and any sense of meaning she experienced. Her responses to these questions were sometimes given in the incoherent language of delirium and dream. She said some quite horrible things about life and lies and "this dream of flesh." I don't think I need expand on the chilling nonsense she uttered, for I've heard you say much the same in one of your "states." (Really, it's appalling the way you dwell both on and in your zones of the metaphysically flayed self.)

That little thing which Miss Locher mentioned only under hypnosis, and which I temporarily omitted above, was a very telling piece of info. It told on you. For when my patient first described the scenes of her dream drama to me, she had forgotten—or just neglected to mention—the presence of another character hidden in the background. This character was the proprietor of the nameless clothing store, a domineering boss who was played by a certain lady psychoanalyst. Not that you were ever on stage, even in a cameo appearance. But the hypnotized Miss Locher did remark in passing on the identity of the employer of that oneiric working girl, this being one of the many underlying suppositions of the dream. So you, my dear, were present in Miss Locher's hypnotic statement in more than just spirit.

I found this revelation immensely helpful in coordinating the separate items of evidence against you. The nature of the evidence, however, was such that I could not rule out the possibility of a conspiracy between you and Miss Locher. So I refrained from asking my new patient anything about her relationship with you, and I didn't inform her of what she disclosed under hypnosis. My assumption was that she was guilty until proven otherwise.

Alternatives did occur to me, though, especially when I realized Miss Locher's extraordinary susceptibility to hypnosis. Isn't it just possible, sweet love, that Miss Locher's incredible dream was induced by one of those post-hypnotic suggestions at which you're so well practised? I know that lab experiments in this area are sometimes eerily successful; and eeriness is, without argument, your specialty. Still another possibility involves the study of dream telepathy, in which you have no small interest. So what were you doing the night Miss Locher underwent her dream ordeal? (You weren't with me, I know that!) And how many of those eidola on my poor patient's mental screen were images projected from an outside source? These are just some of the bizarre questions which lately seem so necessary to ask.

But the answers to such questions would still only establish your means in this crime. What about your motive? On this point I need not exert my psychic resources. It seems there is nothing you won't do to impose your ideas upon common humanity—deplorably on your patients, obnoxiously on your colleagues, and affectionately (I hope) on me. I know it must be hard for a lonely visionary like yourself to remain mute and ignored, but you've chosen such an eccentric path to follow that I fear there are few spirits brave enough to accompany you into those zones of deception and pain, at least not voluntarily.

Which brings us back to Miss Locher. By the end of our first, and only, session I still wasn't sure whether she was a willing or unwilling agent of yours; hence, I kept mum, very mum, about anything concerning you. Nor did she happen to speak of you in any significant way, except of course unconsciously in hypnosis. At any rate, she certainly appeared to be a genuinely disturbed young lady, and she asked me to prescribe for her. As Dr. Bovary tried to assuage the oppressive dreams of his wife with a prescription of valerian and camphor baths, I supplied Miss Locher with a program for serenity that included valium and companionship (the latter of which I also recommend for us, dolling). Then we made a date for the following Wednesday at the same time. Miss Locher seemed most grateful, though not enough, according to my secretary, to pay up what she owed. And wait till you find out where she wanted us to send the bill.

The following week Miss Locher did not appear for her appointment. This did not really alarm me, for as you know many patients—armed with a script for tranquilizers and a single experience of therapy—decide they don't need any more help. But by then I had developed such a personal interest in Miss Locher's case that I was seriously disappointed at the prospect of not being able to pursue it further.

After fifteen patientless minutes had elapsed, I had my secretary call Miss Locher at the number she gave us. (With my former secretary—poor thing! —this would have been done automatically; so the new girl is not as good as you said she was, doctor. I shouldn't have let you insinuate her into my employ . . . but that's my fault, isn't it?) Maggie came into my office a few minutes later, presumably after she'd tried to reach Miss Locher. With rather cryptic impudence she suggested I dial the number myself, giving me the form containing all the information on our new patient. Then she left the room without saying another word. The nerve of that soon-to-be-unemployed girl.

I called the number—which incidentally plays the song about Mary's lamb on the push-button phone in my office—and it rang twice before someone answered. This someone had the voice of a young woman but was not our Miss Locher. In any case, the way this person answered the phone told me I had a wrong number (the right wrong number). Nevertheless, I asked if a Miss Locher could be reached at that number or any of its possible extensions; but the answering voice expressed total ignorance regarding the existence of any person by that name. I thanked her and hung up.

You will have to forgive me, my lovely, if by this time I began to feel like the victim of a hoax, your hoax to be exact. "Maggie," I intercommed, "how many more appointments for this afternoon?" "Just one," she immediately answered, and then without being asked, said: "But I can cancel it if you'd like." I said I would like, that I would be gone for the rest of the afternoon.

My intention was to call on Miss Locher at the, probably also phony, address on her new patient form. I had the suspicion that the address would lead to the same geographical spot as had the electronic nexus of the false phone number. Of course I could have easily verified this without leaving my office; but knowing you, sweet one, I thought that a personal visit was warranted. And I was right.

The address was an hour's drive away. It was in a fashionable suburb on the

other side of town from that fashionable suburb in which I have my office.
(And I wish you would remove your own place of business from its present
location, unless for some reason you need to be near a skid-row source that
broadcasts on frequencies of chaos and squalor, which you'd probably claim.)
I parked my big black car down the block from the street number I was
seeking, which turned out to be located in the middle of the suburb's shopping district.

This was last Wednesday, and if you'll recall it was quite an unusual day (an
accomplishment I do *not* list among all your orchestrated connivings of my
adventure). It was dim and moody most of the morning, and so prematurely
dark by late afternoon that there were stars seemingly visible in the sky. A
storm was imminent and the air was appropriately galvanized with a pre-
deluge feeling of suspense. Display windows were softly glowing, and one
jewelry store I passed twinkled with electric glory in the corner of my eye. In
the stillness I strolled beside a row of trees, each of their slender trunks
planted in a complex mosaic along the sidewalk, all of their tiny leaves fluttering.

Of course, there's no further need to describe the atmosphere of a place
you've visited many times, dear love. But I just wanted to show how sensitive
I was to a certain kind of portentous mood, and how ripe I'd become for the
staged antics to follow. Very good, doctor!

Distancewise, I only had to walk a few gloomy steps before arriving at the
place purported to be the home of our Miss L. By then it was quite clear
what I would find. There were no surprises so far. When I looked up at the
neon-inscribed name of the shop, I heard a young woman's telephone voice
whispering the words into my ear: Mademoiselle Fashions. A fake French
accent here, S.V.P. And this is the store—no?—where it seems you acquire
so many of your own lovely ensembles. But I'm jumping ahead with my
expectations.

What I did not expect were the sheer *lengths* to which you would go in
order to arouse my sense of strange revelation. Was this, I pray, done to bring
us closer in the divine bonds of unreality? Anyway, I saw what you wanted
me to see, or what I thought you wanted me to see, in the window of Mlle
Fashions. The thing was even dressed in the same plaid-skirted outfit that I
recall Miss Locher was wearing on her only visit to my office. And I have to
admit that I was a bit shocked—perhaps attributable in part to the unstable
climatic conditions of the day—when I focused on the frozen face of the
mannikin. Then again, perhaps I was subliminally looking for a resemblance
between Miss Locher (your fellow conspirator, whether she knows it or not)
and the figure in the window. You can probably guess what I noticed, or

thought I noticed, about its eyes—what you would have me perceive as a certain *moistness* in their fixed gaze. Oh, woe is this Wednesday's child!

Unfortunately, I was unable to linger long enough to positively confirm the above perception, for a medium-intensity shower began to descend at that point. The rain sent me running to a nearby phone booth, where I had some business to conduct anyway. Retrieving the number of the clothes store from my memory, I phoned them for the second time that afternoon. That was easy. What was not quite as easy was imitating your voice, my high-pitched love, and asking if the store's accounting department had mailed out a bill that month for my, I mean your, charge account. My impersonation of you must have been adequate, for the voice on the phone reminded me that I'd already taken care of all my recent expenditures. You thanked the salesgirl for this information, apologizing for your forgetfulness, and then said goodbye. Perhaps I should have asked the girl if she was the one who helped rig up that mannikin to look like Miss Locher, if indeed the situation was not the other way around, with Miss Locher following the fashion of display-window dummies. In any case, I did establish a definite link between you and the clothes store. It seemed you might have accomplices anywhere, and to tell you the truth I was beginning to feel a bit paranoid standing in that little phone booth.

The rain was coming down even harder as I made a mad dash back to my black sedan. A bit soaked, I sat in the car for a few moments wiping off my rain-spotted glasses with a handkerchief. I said that I felt a slight case of paranoia coming on, and what follows proves it. While sitting there with my glasses off, I thought I saw something move in the rearview mirror. My visual vulnerability, combined with the claustrophobic sensation of being in a car with rain-blinded windows, together added up to a momentary but very definite panic on my part. Of course I quickly put on my glasses and found that there was nothing whatever in the back seat. But the point is that I was forced to physically verify this fact in order to relieve my spasm of anxiety. You succeeded, my love, in getting me to experience a moment of self-terror, and in that moment I, too, became your accomplice against myself. Brava!

You have indeed succeeded—assuming all my inferences thus far are for the most part true—perhaps more than you know or ever intended. Having confessed this much, I can now get to the *real* focus and "motivating factor" of my appeal to you. This has far less to do with A. Locher than it does with us, dearest. Please try to be sympathetic and, above all, patient.

I have not been well lately, and you know the reason why. This business with Miss Locher, far from bringing us to a more intimate understanding of each other, has only made the situation worse. Horrible nightmares have been plaguing me every night. Me, of all people! And they are directly due to the well-intentioned (I think) influence of you and Miss L. Let me describe one of these nightmares for you, and thereby describe them all. This will be the last dream story, I promise.

In the dream I am in my bedroom, sitting upon my unmade bed and wearing my pajamas (Oh, will you never see them?). The room is partially illuminated by beams from a streetlight shining through the window. And it also seems to me that a whole galaxy of constellations, although not actually witnessed firsthand, are contributing their light to the scene, a ghastly glowing which unnaturally blanches the entire upstairs of the house. I have to use the bathroom and walk sleepily out to the hallway . . . where I get the shock of my life.

In the whitened hallway—I cannot say *brightened,* because it is almost as if a very fine and luminous powder coats everything—are these things lying up and down the floor, at the top of the stairway, and even upon the stairs themselves as they disappear into the darker regions below. These things are people dressed as dolls, or else dolls made up to look like people. I remember being confused about which it was.

Their heads are turned in all directions as I emerge from the bedroom, and their eyes shine in the white darkness. Paralyzed—yes!—with terror, I merely return a fixed gaze, wondering if my eyes are shining the same as theirs. Then one of the doll people, slouching against the wall on my left, turns its head haltingly upon a stiff little neck and looks into my eyes. Worse, it talks. And its voice is an horrific cackling parody of speech. Even more horrible are its words, as it says: "Become as we are, sweetie. Die *into* us." Suddenly I begin to feel very weak, as if my life were being drained out of me. Summoning all my powers of movement, I manage to rush back to my bed to end the dream.

After I awake, screaming, my heart pounds like a mad prisoner inside me and doesn't let up until morning. This is very disturbing, for there's truth in those studies relating nightmares to cardiac arrest. For some poor souls, that imaginary incubus squatting upon their sleeping forms can do real medical harm. And I do not want to become one of these cases.

You can help me, sweetheart. I know you didn't intend things to turn out this way, but that elaborate joke you perpetrated with the help of Miss Locher has really gotten to me. Consciously, of course, I still uphold the criticism I've already expressed about the basic absurdity of your work. Unconsciously, however, you seem to have awakened me to a stratum (*zone,* I know you would say) of uncanny terror in my mind-soul. I will at least admit that your ideas form a powerful psychic metaphor, though no more than that. Which is quite enough, isn't it? It's certainly quite enough to inspire the writing of this letter, in which I plead for your attention, since I've failed to attract it in any other way. I can't go on like this! You have strange powers over me, as if you didn't already know it. Please release me from your spell, and let's begin a normal romance. Who really gives a damn about the metaphysics of invisible realms anyway? It's only emotions, not abstractions, that count. Love and terror are the true realities, whatever the unknowable mechanics are that turn their wheels, and our own.

In Miss Locher I believe you sent me the embodiment of your deepest convictions. But suppose I start admitting weird things about Miss L? Suppose I admit that she was somehow just a dream. (Then she must have been my secretary's dream too, for she saw her.) Suppose I even admit that Miss Locher was not a girl but actually a multi-selved *thing*—part Man, part mannikin—and with your assistance dreamed itself for a time into existence, reproduced itself in human form just as we reproduce ourselves as an infinite variety of images and shapes, all those impersonations of our flesh? You would like to have me think of things like this. You would like to have me think of all the mysterious connections among the things of this world, and of other worlds. So what if there are? I don't care anymore.

Forget other selves. Forget the third (fourth, nth) person view of life; only first and second persons are important (I and thou). And by all means forget dreams. I, for one, know I'm not a dream. I am real, Dr. —— (There, how do you like being anonymized?) So please be so kind as to acknowledge my existence.

It is now after midnight, and I dread going to sleep and having another of those nightmares. You can save me from this fate, if only you can find it in your heart to do so. But you must hurry. Time is running out for us, my love, just as these last few waking moments are now running out for me. Tell me it is still not too late for our love. Please don't destroy everything for us. You will only hurt yourself. And despite your high-flown theory of masochism, there is really nothing divine about it. So no more of your strange psychic deceptions. Be simple, be nice. Oh, I am so tired. I must say good night, then, but not good.

Bye, my foolish love. Hear me now. Sleep your singular sleep and dream of the many, the others. They are also part of you, part of us. Die into them and leave me in peace. I will come for you later, and then you can always be with me in a special corner all your own, just as my little Amy once was. This is what you've wanted, and this you shall have. Die into them. Yes, die into them, you simple soul, you silly dolling. Die with a nice bright gleam in your eyes.

Never Visit Venice

Robert Aickman

Travel is a good thing; it stimulates the imagination. Everything else is a snare and a delusion. Our own journey is entirely imaginative. Therein lies its strength.
—Louis-Ferdinand Céline

Henry Fern was neither successful in the world's eyes nor unsuccessful; partly because he lived in a world society in which to be either requires considerable craft. Fern was not good at material scheming. His job stood far below his theoretical capacities, but he had a very clear idea of his own defects, and was inclined inwardly to believe that but for one or two strokes of sheer good fortune, he would have been a mere social derelict. He did not sufficiently understand that it has been made almost impossible to be a social derelict.

Not that Fern was adapted to that status any better than to the status of tycoon. Like most introverts, he was very dependent upon small, minute-to-minute comforts, no matter whence they came. Fern's gaze upon life was very decisively inwards. He read much. He reflected much. One of his purest pleasures was an entire day in bed; all by himself, in excellent health. He lived in a quite pleasant suburban flat, with a view over a park. Unfortunately, the park, for the most part, was more beautiful when Fern was not there; because when he was there, it tended to fill with raucous loiterers and tiny piercing radios.

Fern was an only child. His parents were far off and in poorer circumstances than when he had been a boy. He had much difficulty, not perhaps in making friends, but in keeping up an interest in them. There seemed to be something in him which made him different from most of the people he encountered in the office or in the train or in the park or at the houses of others. He could not succeed in defining what this difference was, and he simultaneously congratulated and despised himself for having it. He would sincerely have liked to be rid of it, but at the same time was pretty sure it was the best thing about him. If only others were interested in the best!

One thing it plainly did was hold Fern back in what people called his career. Here it did damage in several different ways. That it disconnected him from the network of favour and promotion was only the most obvious. Much worse was that it made favour and promotion seem to Fern doubtfully worth while. Worse still was that it made him see through the work he had to do: see that, like so much that is called work, it was little more than protective colouration; but see also that the blank disclosure of this fact would destroy not merely the work itself and his own income, but the hopes of the many who were committed to at least a half-belief in its importance, even when they chafed against it. Worst of all probably was the simple fact that this passionate division inside him ate up his energy and sent it to waste. Fern would have liked to be an artist, but seemed to himself to have little creative talent. He soon realized that it has become a difficult world for those who possibly are artists only in living. There is so little scope for practice and rehearsal.

Nor could Fern find a woman who seemed to feel in the least as he did. Having heard and read often that it is useless to seek for one's ideal woman, that the very fancy of an ideal woman is an absurdity, he at first made up his mind to concentrate upon the good qualities that were actually to be found, which were undoubtedly many, at least by accepted standards. He even became engaged to be married on two occasions; but the more he saw of each fiancée, despite her beauty and charm of character, the more he felt himself an alien and an imposter. Unable to dissemble any more, he had himself broken off the engagement. He had felt much anguish, but it was not, he felt, anguish of the right kind. Even in that he seemed isolated. The women must have realized something of the truth, because though both, when he spoke, expressed aggressive dismay, since marriage is so much sought after for itself, they soon went quietly, and were heard of by Fern no more. Now he was nearing forty: not, he thought, unhappy, when all was considered; but he could not do so much considering every day, and often he felt puzzled and sadly lonely. Things could be so very much worse, and that very easily, as none knew better than Fern; but this reflection, well justified though it was, did not prevent Fern from thinking, not infrequently, of suicide, or from letting the back of his mind dwell pleasurably and recurrently upon the thought of Death's warm, white, and loving arms.

One thing about which Fern felt true anguish was the problem of travel, or, as others put it, his "holidays."

Here the shortage of money really mattered. "Why do I not go out for more?" he asked himself.

He had no difficulty in answering himself. Apart from the obvious doubt as to whether it was a good bargain to sell himself further into slavery in order to receive in return perhaps seven more days each year for travel and enough extra money to travel a little (a very little) more comfortably, he saw well that even these rewards might be vitiated by the extra care that would probably travel with the recipient of them. He realized early that, except for a few natural bohemians, travel can be of value only when based upon private resources: hence the almost universal adulteration of travel into organized tourism, an art into a science, so that the shrinking surface of the earth, in its physical aspect as in its way of life, becomes a single place, not worth leaving home to see. Fern saw this very clearly, but it was considerably too wide and theoretical a consideration to deter one so truly a traveller but who had yet travelled so little as Fern. What really held Fern back from travel, as from much else, was the lack of a fellow-traveller; remembering always that this fellow-traveller had to comply pretty nearly with an ideal which Fern could by no means define, but could only sense and serve, present or (as almost always) absent beyond reasonable hope.

He had shared a holiday with both his fiancées—one holiday in each case. Much the same things had happened each time; doubtless because men notoriously involve themselves (even when they do it half-heartedly) with the same woman in different shapes, or, perhaps, as Lord Chesterfield says, because women are so much more alike than are men. On each occasion, it had been two or three weeks of differing objectives, conscious and unconscious, at all levels, and, especially, of utterly different responses to everything encountered; but a matter also of determined and scrupulous effort on both sides not only to understand but to act upon and make allowances for the other's point of view. All these things had made of the holiday a reproduction or extension of common life, which was not at all what Fern had in mind. Both parties had, in the American formula, "worked at" the relationship, worked as hard as slaves under an overseer; but the product was unmarketable. "You're too soulful about everything," complained one of the girls. She spoke quite affectionately, and truly for his own good, as the world goes, and as Fern perceived. None the less, he came to surmise that for him travel might be a mystical undertaking. He had some time read of Renan's concept that for each man there is an individual "means to salvation": for some the ascent to Monsalvat, for some alcohol or laudanum, for some wenching and whoring, for some even the common business of day-to-day life. For Fern salvation might lie in travel; but surely not in solitary travel. And how much more difficult than ever this new consideration would make finding a companion! Almost, how impossible! Fern felt his soul (as the girl had called it) shrink when he first clearly sensed the hopeless conflict between deepest need and inevitable absence of response; the conflict which makes even men and women who are capable of better things live as they do. He and the girl were on a public seat in Bruges at the time; among the trees along the Dyver, looking at the swans on the canal.

At least politeness had been maintained on these trips; from first to last. It was something by no means to be despised. Moreover, when Fern had travelled with others, with a man friend, or with a party, he had fared considerably worse. Then there had been little in the way of manners and no obligation even to essay mutuality. In the longer run, therefore, Fern had travelled little and enjoyed less. This in no way modified his unworldly attitude to travel. He knew that few people do enjoy it, despite the ever-increasing number who set forth; and resented the fact that actual experience of travel had seemed, for practical purposes, to put him among the majority—of them, but not with them, as usual. Nor could he see even the possibility of a solution. Not enough money. Not enough time. And no intimates, let alone initiates. It had been quite bad enough even when he had only been twenty-five.

Fern began to have a dream. Foreshadowings or intimations came to him first; thereafter, at irregular intervals, the whole experience (in so far as it could be described as a whole), or bits or scraps of it, portions or distortions. There seemed to be no system in its total or partial recurrence. As far as Fern was concerned, it merely did not come often enough. He felt that it would be unlucky (by which he meant destructive) to note too precisely the dates of the dream's reappearances. But Fern was soon musing about the content of the dream during waking hours; sometimes even by policy and on purpose. To the infrequent dream of the night, he added an increasing habit of deliberate daydreaming; a pastime so disapproved of by the experts.

Fern's dream, though glowing, was simple.

He dreamed that he was in Venice, where he had never been. He was drifting in a gondola across an expanse of water he had read about, called the Lagoon. Lying in his embrace at the bottom of the boat was a woman in evening dress or party dress or gay dress of some kind. He did not know how he had met her: whether in Venice or in London. Conceivably, even, he knew her already, outside the dream; had long known her, or at least set eyes on her. When he awoke, he could never remember her face with sufficient clarity; or perhaps could remember only for a moment or two after waking, in the manner of dreams. It was a serious frustration, because the woman was very desirable, and because between Fern and her, and between them only as far as Fern was concerned, was understanding and affinity. Such understanding could not last, Fern realized even in the dream: it might not last beyond that one night; or it might last as long as six or seven days. Fern could always remember the woman's dress: but it was not always the same dress; it was sometimes white, sometimes black, sometimes crimson, sometimes mottled like a fish. Above the boat, were always stars, and always the sky was a peculiarly deep lilac, which lingered with Fern and which he had never seen in the world exterior to the dream. There was never a moon, but behind the gondola, along some kind of waterfront, sparkled the raffish, immemorial, and evocative lights of Fern's hypothetical Venice. Ahead, in contrast, lay a long, dark reef, with occasional and solitary lights only. There were tiny waves lapping round the gondola, and Fern was in some way aware of bigger waves beating slowly on the far side of the reef. He never knew where the two of them were going, but they were going somewhere, because journeys without destination are as work without product: the product may disappoint, but is indispensible and has to be borne. Fern wished that he could enter the dream at an earlier point, so that he might have some idea of how he had met the woman, but always when awareness began, the pair of them were a long way out across the water with the string of gaudy lights far behind. For some reason, Fern had an idea that he had met the woman by eager but slightly furtive arrangement, outside an enormous hotel, very fashionable and luxurious. The gondolier was always vague: Fern had read and been told that, since the advent of powered craft, gondoliers were costly and difficult. (None the less, this one seemed, whatever the explanation, to be devoted and amenable.)

The beginning and the end of the dream were lost in the lilac night. The beginning, Fern thought, the beginning of the whole, wonderful experience might have been only a few hours earlier. The end he hesitated to speculate about. Nor could he even, upon waking, remember anything that he and the woman had said to one another. A curious, disembodied feeling came back with him, however, and remained with him until the demands of the day ahead dragged him within minutes into full consciousness. He felt that his personal identity had been in partial dissolution, and that in some measure he had been also the night, the gondola, and even the woman with him. This sense of disembodiment he could even sometimes recapture in his daydreams, when circumstances permitted sufficient concentration. Above all, the dream, possibly more tender than passionate, brought a boundless feeling of plain and simple relief. Fern could not conceive of the world's cares ever diminishing to permit so intense a relief in waking life.

By day, more and more often, Fern saw himself in Venice. By night—on *those* nights—he was in Venice.

It had begun happening years ago, and he had still never been to Venice. The impact of Fern's dream upon waking existence seemed confined to the fact that when men and women spoke of their goals in life, as men and women occasionally do, referring to a sales managership or a partnership or a nice little cottage in the country or a family of four boys and four girls, Fern at once saw that lilac sky, heard the lapping of those tiny waves, felt a deep, obscure pain, and sensed an even greater isolation than usual.

He supposed that the dream was fragile. If thought about too practically, if analysed too closely, it might well cease to recur. The dream was probably best left in the back of the mind, at the edges of the mind; within that mental area which comes into its own between waking and sleeping—and, less happily, between sleeping and waking.

Possibly, therefore, the dream had the effect of actually deterring Fern from looking out much more practical knowledge about Venice. All he knew about the place was scrappy, unco-ordinated stuff ingathered from before the time when the dream had first visited him: for example, he had read a steam-rollered abridgement of Arthur Machen's Casanova translation, and, long before that, a costumed legend of Venice in the Renaissance by Rafael Sabatini, which belonged to his mother. Fern fully realized that, even geographically, the real Venice could hardly be much like his dream. And it scarcely needs adding that the woman in the dream seemed outside the bounds of possibility, let alone the money to pay for her and the gondola. Just as the real Venice could not resemble the dream Venice, so real life could not resemble life in the dream.

For years, then, Fern teetered along the tightrope between content and discontent; between mild self-congratulation and black frustration; between the gritty disillusionments of human intimacy and travel (for Fern the two became more and more inseparable), and the truth and power of his dream. It might be a twilight tightrope, but twilight was not an hour which Fern despised.

So when trouble was added unto Fern in the end, he failed for a long time to be aware of it. Then one spring day, and what was more, in the office, he suddenly realized that his dream had not returned for a long time. He thought that it must have been months since it had last visited him; perhaps more than a year. And, in consequence, he perceived that the dream of the day, always so much paler, of course, but normally, and given even reasonably right circumstances, almost summonable at will, had become totally bloodless and faintly hysterical. Instead of advancing to meet him half-way when he felt the need of it, it was more and more requiring to be conjured, even compelled. It had become much like an aspirin: an anodyne strictly exterior, and so a deceiver. Fern soon came to see that for months he had been standing naked against life's stones and spears without knowing it.

Even though it was the spring, always the most difficult season of the year, he looked himself over, confirmed that he was surviving, and seemed to inaugurate an inner change. This was perhaps the moment, which comes to so many, when Fern simultaneously matured and withered. He became more practical, as people call it; less demanding of life.

He was sincerely astonished when during that same summer he was given significant promotion in his work. In due course, he was equally surprised to find that the additional responsibilities of his new position by no means outweighed the advantage of the greater pay, as he had always supposed they would; the truth being that the tendency is for all to carry the same responsibility, so that soon all will receive the same reward, if reward will any longer be the word. People felt vaguely but approvingly that Fern had taken more of a grip on himself. Fern, cheated of his dream, sometimes even felt something of the kind himself. Two or three years passed, while the land steadily receded beneath Fern's tightrope.

When the dream snapped off (as seemed to Fern to have happened, so abrupt had been his discovery), its place was taken in the back and at the edges of Fern's mind by the sentiment of death. "God!" he had thought earlier, feeling pierced by a sword through the stomach, as, at that moment, we all do; "God! I am going to have to die." But in those days, with the rest of us, he had thought of it only occasionally. Now the thought was no longer an infrequent, stabbing shock. It was a softfooted, never-absent familiar; neither quite an enemy to him nor quite a friend. The thought was steadily making Fern dusty, mangy, less visible; all in the midst of his perceptibly greater successfulness.

And it was almost as if it were these two things in conjunction, the new practicality and the faint, ever-spinning sentiment of death, that brought about Fern's ultimate decision actually to see Venice; as if he had abruptly said out loud, "After all, a man should visit Venice before he dies." With departure in sight, and upon the advice of an older man, he read the Prince of Lampedusa's *Gattopardo* in an English paperback. "It happens to be about Sicily," observed Fern's friend, "but it applies to the whole of Italy, and it's concerned with the only thing that matters there, unless you're an actual archaeologist." Fern gathered that the only thing which mattered was that Italy had undergone a great change.

TWO

Despite his ruminations and his hopes, Fern had never before travelled beyond France, the Low Countries, and Scandinavia, to all of which regions he considered himself comparatively acclimatized and much attached. By the time he found himself, as will shortly be seen, thinking once more about his dream, he had been in and around Venice for seventeen days, and they had been days of surprise, horror, fantasy, and conflict.

He could find kinship with no one. There was something terrifyingly insane about the total breakdown of the place: the utter discrepancy between the majesty and mystery of the monuments and the tininess of all who dwelt around them or came supposedly to gaze upon them. Fern looked upon these mighty works and despaired. Now he sat on an eighteenth-century stone bollard at the tip of the Punta di Salute, and summed it all up.

Many times Fern had read or been told that the great trouble with Venice was the swarm of visitors. You could hardly see the real people, he had always been informed. Indeed, the real people were often said to be dying out.

But by now it was the visitors who seemed to him a mere mist: a flutter of small, anxious sparrows, endlessly twittering, whether rich or poor, about "currency" (Fern could fully understand only those who twittered in English); endlessly pecked and gashed by the local hawks; endlessly keeping up with neighbours at home, who were as unqualified to visit Venice as themselves. All visitors had at once too little time and too much. As he wandered down a *calle* or through a palazzo, he perceived that very few indeed of the visitors visited anything beyond the cathedral and the seat of the former rulers; or saw much even of these, if only because of the crowd inside and the shouting of the guides, as mechanical and stereotyped as the swift mutterings of the priests.

The visitors sat about the Piazza San Marco, proclaimed by so many wise voices, as the world's most beautiful work of man (though infested with pigeons, shot or mutilated elsewhere in Italy), in a constant stew, rich or poor, about the prices: a preoccupation which was thoroughly justified. The women took off their shoes because they had walked a few hundred yards. They stuck out their poor legs, and, to do them justice, endeavoured intermittently but with pathetic unproficiency, to catch at life as it passed, to utter the right cries. If life, their faces enquired, could not be caught in Venice, where could it be caught? For a few, right back at home. Fern felt; for the majority, no longer anywhere. Of the men, most were past even making the attempt. They sat looking foolish, fretful, bored, insufficiently occupied, and, above all, out of place. Nor could Fern but agree it was hard that one could not buy an aniseed or a cup of coffee in a place so beautiful without the beauty being tarnished by the price—a price probably unavoidable from the caterer's point of view, because of forces as uncontrollable by him as by Fern. . . . And, of course, there were other visitors, mainly English, who despised the great and ancient monuments, structures on so different a scale from themselves, and spent their time poking their noses into what they conceived to be the "real living and working conditions" of the Venetians.

It was not so much the visitors, with their fleeting passage, their phantom foreign money, that startled Fern, but these same Venetians. So far from the place being half empty, as he had been led to expect, it was swarming from edge to edge; and it swarmed with sentimental, self-satisfied philistines, more identical and mass-produced than he would have thought possible, inescapable except inside the faded, ill-kept palazzi where one had to pay to enter. Those among the Venetians who were not leeching on the visitors seemed to be industrial workers from the vast plants lined up across the water at Mestre; labour force to the war machines of a new invader holding the city under siege of modernity and required merely to await the inevitable self-induced collapse, much as the Turks waited for Byzantium to destroy itself.

The human din in Venice cancelled the quiet which might have been expected from the absence of Motor Moloch. It continued throughout the twenty-four hours, merely becoming after midnight more sinister, shrill, and unpredictable. Every night, gangs of youths screamed their way through the alleys. Folding iron shutters crashed like cannon through the early watches. Altercations, sexual or political, continued fortissimi in male voices for fifty minutes at a time. Fern, in his pension attic, would look at his watch and see it was two o'clock, three o'clock, four o'clock. The noise would diminish, he would fall asleep, and then there would be more screaming boys, more clanging shutters. It was a highly traditional uproar perhaps, but Venice seemed to have an unhappy aptitude for combining only the worst of past society with the society of today. What might once have been falcons, had become hawks, and were now carrion crows.

Fern went to hear *Rigoletto* at the Fenice and to hear a concert with a famous conductor and a famous soloist: Both occasions were more than half empty, and such people as were there were either elderly Americans doing their duty by a dead ideal (often at the behest of their hotel porters) and intermittently slumbering, or dubious Italian youths, palpably with free seats and very concerned to make clear that fact to the fools who had paid. The performances in themselves seemed to Fern good, but that only made it worse. They seemed to be provided for a bygone generation, a bygone species of man, a world that had been laughed out of life and replaced by nothing.

Fern wandered through the shouting, pushing crowds, more and more sick at heart. As, at the concert, the beauty of the performance only made more poignant the entire absence of an audience, so, in the city at large, the incomparable magnificence and grace of the structures only made more dispiriting the entire absence of these qualities in the beholders. The stripped palaces, indifferently maintained even when a few rooms were "open to the public," failed even to evoke their past. They would appeal only to those ultimate playboys who positively prefer their roses or their canals to be dead.

Fern found only one place that satisfied when regarded even as a ghost, and as thus offering life of a kind and in a degree. This was a suite of comparatively small bedrooms and dressing rooms and powder rooms high up in one of the remoter palaces, all fragile woodwork in faded green, red, and gold, with elaborate Murano looking-glasses; tender, canopied beds; and flowery dressing tables. These small, fastidious, flirtatious rooms, alone in all Venice, vouchsafed that frisson which is history. Obviously, few came near them, other than an occasional perfunctory cleaner, from year's end to year's end. This might spare the delightful rooms for their proper wraiths, but it also pointed to an insoluble dilemma.

In most of the palazzi, Fern could spend a morning or afternoon and see only a handful of his kind in the whole building, and all of them rushing through in twenty minutes. Nor could this be sensibly objected to: with the destruction of their owners the palazzi had been destroyed also. It was offensive to pretend that these corpses still lived; odious to seek profit from their corruption.

Between the beauty of Venice and the people there was no link: not even of ignorant awe; perhaps that least of all. Much as the folk had pillaged the Roman villas, so Venice was being pillaged now; and Fern sensed that the very fact of the pillage being often called preservation implied that total dissolution was in sight. Venice was rotted with the world's new littleness. To many her beauty was actually antagonistic, as imposing upon them a demand to which they were unable to rise. Soon the Lagoon would be "reclaimed" and the Venetian dream submitted to a new law of values; a puritan law antithetical to the law of pleasure that had prevailed there for so long; the terrain applied to the uses of the post-Garibaldian mass, existing only in its own expansion. Mestre and multiplication would compel unconditional surrender. The state of affairs that Fern now looked upon was more of a pretence, more of a masquerade than anything even in Venice's past. It was perhaps proper that Venice should end with a divertissement, but Fern felt that the fires of dawn were visible through the holes in the scenery; the decapitation overdue.

The Venetian dream?

Perched on his bollard, Fern realized with a start that he had been in Venice seventeen days, and not given a thought to his own dream.

During those seventeen days, he had not spoken to a single person except in the ways of triviality and cross-purposes. He never struck up acquaintence easily, but the conflictual impact of Venice, at once so lovely and so appalling, had transfixed him into even more of a trance than usual. He had wandered with a set stare; lost in a dream of another kind, a seemingly impersonal dream in which the dreamer had been the shadow. Big ships were passing quite frequently along the Canale della Giudecca to his left, into and out from the docks renewed by Mussolini. Unlike so much else, the ships were beautiful and alive at the same time. The scale of things contracted to the problems of one dreamer. Fern felt very lonely.

A manifest Englishman landed with an Italian youth from the *traghetto* at Fern's rear. He was bald and barrel-shaped. His large moustache and fringe of hair were ginger. He wore a brown tweed jacket buttoned across his stomach, dingy grey trousers, and an untidy shirt with a club tie. One might see him presiding knowledgeably over a weekend rally of motor cars in Surrey or Hampshire.

He walked out to the end of the stone promontory, dragging the Italian boy (in open white shirt and tight, bright trousers) by the hand. The Italian boy was making a girlish show of reluctance. The Englishman, a few feet away from Fern's bollard, pointed with his free hand to some object in the distance; something about which it was inconceivable to him that no one else should care, let alone a person for whom he himself cared so much. All the same, the boy did not care at all. He was no longer going through the motions of petulance, but stood quite still, looking blank, bored, resistant of new knowledge, and professionally handsome.

"Damn it!" said the Englishman. "You might show some interest."

The boy said nothing. An expression of dreadful disappointment and wild rage transfigured the Englishman's unremarkable face. He said something in Italian which Fern took to be at once bitter and obscene. At the same time, he threw away the boy's hand as if it had turned glutinous in his grasp. He then strutted off by himself towards the Zattere.

The Italian still stood looking fixedly at the paving stones. Then he thrust one hand into the back pocket of his trousers and produced a neat pocketbook: possibly a gift from the Englishman. After examining the contents with almost comic care, he returned the pocketbook to its place and strolled off. In pursuit, Fern imagined; though he did not turn round to see. Judging from many experiences since his arrival, he thought that were he to do so, the next approach might be to him. He had found it a situation that put him at a loss in all its aspects. He simply could not live up to what was expected of a lone Englishman in Italy.

By now he felt so alone that he almost wished that he could. Hitherto in Venice he had been neither happy nor unhappy but simply amazed; on occasion aghast. Now the recollection of his dream had coincided with the rapid dissolution of the perambulating philosopher in him. Acclimatization to Venice had set in with a rush. The September breeze blew gently up the Canale di San Marco in Fern's face; sweet and cool, as it sighed for the slow sickness of Venice's stifling summer. The flashy motor-boats cackled and yelped around him, driving the gondolas to their death. Fern, thrust back upon his own life, passed his hand over his legs, his arms, his shoulders. He felt a pain he had almost forgotten during the years he had walked his tightrope.

What could Venice do for him but sadden him further? Fern decided to go home next day; if the owner of the pension would permit him to depart ahead of his time. He rose, extended and contracted his legs, stumped up and down a bit, gazed for the last time upon one particularly incomparable Venetian prospect, and felt quite equal to weeping, had it not been for the self-consciousness of solitude in a foreign land.

He walked away.

THREE

That evening, Fern pushed his way along the Molo. He wanted no more unsettled business in his heart.

The owner of the pension had indicated that for a room in modern Venice, as for so much else, there is always a queue. He tried to charge Fern up to the end of the week, but did not try to keep him. Fern had already suspected that in the campaign between the visitors and the Venetians there are few clear-cut victories on either side.

Fern had even an excuse for his promenade. It was to be his last night in Venice, and, as he might have put it in his manly and practical aspect, "You can't leave Venice without ever having been in a gondola." Gondolas may not last much longer, nor may people. But gondolas, being no longer very functional, are not much good without someone to love on the journey.

On the Molo, Americans stood about, japing one another uneasily or over-confidently; wondering how to fill in before flying on to Athens or back to Paris the next morning; questing for highballs or local vintages on the rocks. Uncontrolled Italian children and their plump, doting parents effortlessly dominated the prospect. Away to the south, over towards Chioggia, single lights gleamed romantically. The sky was turning to deep lilac and filling with festive, silvery stars.

Fern turned leftwards up an alley, where it was quieter, then wound about through dark courts and passages, like a beetle through a tome. Immediately he was alone, or almost so, among the great dark buildings, his mind returned to those small, elegant bedrooms and boudoirs at the top of the palazzo he had visited. The recollection of them made him shiver with the pathos of something so hopelessly irrecoverable that was still so hopelessly necessary. Thinking about them, feeling still the intensity of their atmosphere, he could smell the perfume of the Venetian decadence; that long century when the lion drowsed, awaiting Napoleon, the city fell irrevocably to pieces, and all the fashionable wore curious, enveloping masks, so that they looked partly like strange animals, partly like comedians, and partly like ravishers and ravished.

There was such a figure standing before him; dark and motionless against the rail along the side of a canal, which edged the small piazzetta Fern had entered; neither quite in the light from the one lamp in the piazzetta, nor quite out of it. Fern slipped into a shadowy doorway and stared, silent and listening to his heartbeat.

On the other side of the canal loomed a formless stone structure, from all the windows of which seemed to shine an even, pale light, something between pink and blue; and Fern, whose hearing was at all times excessively acute, thought he could detect the faint echo of music and revelry seeping through the thick walls and closed casements. Then he realized that the pale light was the reflection of the late evening sky on the glass, and that the sound was no more than the general cry of Venice. He drew himself together.

Almost in silence down the canal came a gondola. Fern, however sharp his ears, could hear only the softest plash, plash, plash. Then the *ferro* came into view, and the gondola stopped by the figure against the railing. The gondolier seemed to be dressed in black. But Fern's attention was concentrated upon the equally dark passenger; the person for whom the gondola had come.

At first, and in the most curious way, nothing more seemed to happen. The gondola just lay there in the faintly coloured dusk; with the gondolier almost invisible, and the presumed passenger still apparently waiting for someone or something, certainly making no motion to step aboard, indeed making no motion of any kind. Two middle-aged men, both dressed in light colours, crossed the piazzetta from the opposite corner, and proceeded in the direction from which Fern had come. They were talking loudly and simultaneously, in the usual way, and gave no sign of noticing the gondola and the figure by the railing. Of course, there was no reason why they should notice them. All the same, Fern felt that two or three minutes must have passed while the group remained motionless in dim outline against the vast stone building on the other side of the canal.

At least that length of time passed before it occurred to Fern that it might be for him they waited. He had set forth to destroy his dream (even though he had not expressed it quite like that) and thereby, as so often, might have wound up the mechanism for making it come true; because life goes ever crabwise, as that great Venetian, Baron Corvo, constantly proclaimed. Fern shrank back into his dark doorway. He feared lest the whiteness of his face give him away.

The strange set piece lingered for a few more moments. Then Fern realized that the figure which had been standing by the railing was now somehow in the gondola, and that the gondola was once more coming towards him. It glided down the side of the piazzetta, making only the ghost of a sound; the plash, plash, plash of the paddle might have been the wings of a night bird, or the trembling of Fern's own heart muscles. Five or six gay little children ran across the piazzetta in the line of the two men in grey. They were heavily preoccupied with abusing and hitting one another.

Peeping out, Fern saw that the passenger was still standing in the gondola, somewhat towards the bow. The whole course of events was too fanciful, so that Fern's only resolution was to withdraw. He was waiting until the disappearance of the gondola should make this possible. The gondola could hardly have taken more than a minute to pass, but before it had departed from Fern's view, as he hid in his doorway, the standing passenger made a slight movement; from within the dark hooded cloak a woman looked straight into Fern's pale face, and seemed to smile in welcome. In an instant, the gondola was gone.

A narrow *fondamenta* continued alongside the canal from out of the piazzetta. Fern ran to the corner and hastened after the vanishing boat, which seemed now to be travelling very much faster. As he sped on, his shoes clattering on the stones, he wondered if insidious Venice had promoted an insanity in him, a mad confusion between dream and dread. He was pretty sure that, if he should run at all, he should by rights run in the opposite direction. But having started to run, having begun such a disturbance of the night, he had to run on. He nearly managed to overtake the boat just as it was passing under the next bridge. One would have been convinced that the gondolier at least must have heard him and seen him, but the gondola slid on undeflected. Fern realized that beyond the bridge the *fondamenta* did not continue. He stood on the crest of the arch and watched. He did not care, had no title, to call after. The stones of Venice closed softly over the departing shadow.

And then, only twenty or thirty minutes later, something happened which explained these small but singular events.

Deep in thought, and troubled in soul, Fern strolled back to the wide promenade which faces the Canale di San Marco and is the principal waterfront of the city. The distance from the piazzetta of the odd events was not great, but in Venice, for better or for worse, one can seldom walk straight ahead and unobstructed for more than a few paces, and Fern, his mind in any case on other things, lost himself in a small way at least twice. In the end, he emerged on the Riva degli Schiavoni. Everything was brightly illuminated, the sky was perfect, and Fern reflected that, after all, Venice did look rather festive, even a trifle exalted, as she should do. But his mind was on his own loneliness, and on his dream: if, at this late hour, he had, after all, made a tiny concession to Venice, he wanted someone with whom to join hands on it, wanted that person badly. Even so, he stood still, uncertain whether to turn leftwards where it would be quieter, or rightwards where adventure was more likely. Now that the chance had gone, he very positively wished that he had spoken to the woman in the piazzetta. It could hardly have been a matter of life or death. Fern trembled slightly. He was indeed an irresolute creature. By now, reason told him, it could hardly matter less which way he turned.

He simply lacked the heart, the energy, the curiosity to wander off towards the darker area to the left; to take a brisk solitary constitutional along the front, safe except perhaps from cutpurses, as his father would certainly do, and think nothing of it, indeed be all the better for it. Fern turned towards Danieli's (a line of American women leaned like beautiful wasting candles over the rail of the roof-garden, high above); towards the Piazza; towards life, in the commercial or Thomas Cook connotation of the word.

Within a minute or two, he thought he saw again the woman whose face he had seen so momentarily in the gondola.

She was standing by herself in much the same way at the edge of the canal, though this time it was the Canale di San Marco, almost the sea. She was still wearing the hooded black cloak, as in a picture by one of the Longhis, but was no longer so muffled in it. It looked to Fern that beneath it she was wearing a spreading, period dress. Despite the crowd, which had by no means ceased to push and bawl in his ears, he was really frightened. He did not put the thought into words within his head, but his thought was that this was an apparition, and that he was having a breakdown. The figure stood there so motionless, so detached from all those vulgar people, so spectrally apparelled; and, of course, so recurrent. As in the piazzetta, he stood and stared; not unlike a ghost himself. Everything faded but that single figure.

Then she walked steadily towards him, twenty or twenty-five yards, and spoke.

"English?"

She really was dressed in an eighteenth-century style, and beneath her hood Fern could see piled-up hair.

"Yes," said Fern. "English."

"The city of Venice would like to invite you for a gondola trip."

Here indeed was an explanation: at least within limits. She was connected with "publicity" and was merely dressing the part. It was an explanation all too consistent with what Fern had seen of the place. He laughed a little too brashly, a little too brusquely.

But no doubt she was accustomed professionally to all gradations of oafishness.

"Complimentary, of course," she said.

That, thought Fern, was less like the Venice he had so far seen.

The woman was an Italian and did not speak words such as *complimentary* with ease.

"Are you alone?" asked the woman.

"Yes," said Fern. "Quite alone. You must invite someone else. I don't qualify."

"But you do qualify," said the woman. "The city of Venice wants to help lonely visitors."

It sounded ghastly, but the woman spoke with an aspect of sincerity that at least made it possible to reply with reasonable self-respect.

"Tell me more," said Fern.

"We go in a gondola," explained the woman, speaking carefully, in the way of professional guides, as if to a backward child, "along the Grand Canal and across the Lagoon."

It was not the manner in which Fern had visualized the realization of his dream, but no doubt it was the dream which controlled the situation, and not he. Just then he could hardly be expected to think it all out.

"We?" enquired Fern. "How many will there be?"

"Just you and I." She said it with the dignity that certain Italian women can bring to statements that many other women can utter only with a blush and giggle or excessive explanation.

"And, of course, the gondolier," she added with a beautiful smile.

"I shall be very pleased," said Fern. "Thank you." He managed to accept with some degree of the same simplicity.

"There you are," she said, using perhaps not quite the right idiom, and pointing to a gondola. Fern, even though apprehensive of capsizing the unknown craft, managed to hand her in as if to the manner born. They settled side by side on the cushions. Her cloak and wide skirt beneath spread themselves over his legs. She had neither spoken to the gondolier nor, as far as Fern had noticed, even looked at him. He cast off in silence, and they were out on the canal, with the other side, the Isola di San Giorgio Maggiore looking disproportionately nearer almost on the instant. Fern tried to squint backwards in order to examine the gondolier, but it was difficult to see more than his shoes.

Fern squinted backwards a second time. They were not shoes. They were black feet.

But now there was nothing to worry about: indeed, when things were rightly conceived, there never had been anything to worry about. "I think I saw you earlier this evening," said Fern conversationally. "On one of the narrower canals."

"People often see me, but it is only a few that I can call," she replied in her not quite perfect idiom.

She began to describe the sights they were passing. Fern knew most of them already, and more about them than the very basic information deemed appropriate for Anglo-Saxon visitors. All the same, he liked listening to her deep voice and was often charmed by the way she put things. The effect of her simple tale was quite different when one was alone with her, he felt, than it would have been if she had been speaking to a crowd of tourists. They entered the Grand Canal. Just visible across the water to the left was the bollard on which that same afternoon Fern had summed up his conflictual condemnation; had sentenced Venice to depart from his life the next morning.

Fern continued listening respectfully, but by now he could feel the warmth of her body, and the spreading of her stiff skirt over his legs was delightful. It was difficult to listen indefinitely to such topographical platitudes when there was so much else that might be said, and doubtless a limit on the time.

He must have conveyed something of discontent to her because it seemed to him that her flow of facts (not all of them facts, either, he rather thought) began to falter. As they were traversing the few seconds of darkness under the Ponte dell'Accademia, she said, "Perhaps you know Venice as well as I do?" Her tone was not peevish but friendly and solicitous, and Fern decided at once that it was a most unusual thing for a professional guide, always fearful of losing all justification for existence if any real knowledge on the part of the visitor is admitted. Fern's heart warmed to her further.

"I'm sure not," he said. "I've been here just over two weeks. Just long enough to know that two months are needed or perhaps two years."

"If I go beyond the obvious things, I get into what you call deep waters."

"I can well imagine," replied Fern, not necessarily imagining very clearly. "Let's stick to the obvious things."

Fern, when he thought about it, could see and hear that the Canal Grande, most beautiful thoroughfare in the world (as so many have said), was its usual horrible self, loaded with roaring power-craft, congested with idiot tourists, lined with darkened palaces that should have been alive with lights; but he found that for once he was hardly thinking about it at all. He even reflected that he was glad the power-craft made his own progress slower; though it was, as ever in modern Venice, hard on the black gondolier.

"It was all so beautiful once."

Fern could hardly believe his ears. He had so far found it a point of honour among Venetians not to admit that things had ever been better than they were now. He believed, indeed, that most of them were quite sincerely unaware of the fact.

Fern took his companion's hand. It seemed a very soft and unprofessional hand, and she let it lay in his undisturbed.

She spoke again. "There is a rich American woman further back who has collected all the ugliest things in the world. You could never believe how ugly and how many. She keeps them in a half-built palazzo, which she never finishes. I could not bring myself to spoil so nice an evening by pointing it out."

"I know about her," smiled Fern. "I've been there."

"Can such a woman be capable of love?"

They were slowly passing the Palazzo Rezzonico.

"Never the time and the place and the one capable of love, said the English poet." Fern was rather surprised by himself.

A speed-boat full of white-shirted youths whizzed across their bows, almost capsizing them.

"It will be better out on the Lagoon," said Fern's companion, drawing up her feet. "Less interference and more real danger."

Fern could not be sure what exactly she meant, but she seemed to find the prospect pleasurable, because her eyes gleamed for a second inside her hood as she spoke.

"Why danger?"

"At night there is always some danger out on the Lagoon." She said it placidly, perhaps with a faint potentiality of contempt. Fern did not risk making the potential actual.

However curious Fern was about her, he asked no personal questions. He probably felt that they could elicit only inappropriate answers, but more important was the fact that he found the relationship easy and delightful, just as it was. Particularly unwise would have been any reference to the many others with whom she must have made this excursion; "lonely people": Fern knew it was an odious cliché. It had never before occurred to Fern as possible that what was, after all, companionship on a business basis could so touch his real feelings. Least of all was it the way in which he had dreamed it.

But now she seemed to have shrunk away into the blackness. Fern still held her hand, but he felt that the racket around them, the emptiness of the palaces, spread a paralysing infection of disillusionment. He too began to long for the Lagoon.

He decided that sincerity was best.

"I really didn't mean to stop you talking. I was enjoying it."

"I have nothing to tell which you do not know already." Her voice was muffled by the black garment into which she had withdrawn.

"I used to have a dream," said Fern in something of a rush. "For years I dreamt that I was doing—exactly what I am doing now."

"Venice is everyone's dream," she replied. "Venice *is* a dream."

"With no reality?"

"The reality is what you call a nightmare."

They were within two or three hundred yards of the Rialto bridge, high and wide with the marble bowers of ancient jewellers and poisonsellers. Here the scene on both sides of the canal was more animated: people sat at waterside café tables; a barge ploughed up and down bearing massed singers of "O Sole Mio" and "Torna a Surriento." Many people were at least attempting to enjoy themselves.

"The city fathers would hardly approve of your calling Venice a nightmare," said Fern, pressing her hand.

"The city fathers, as you call them, are all dead. Everyone in Venice is dead. It is a dead city. Do you need to be told?"

Then Fern got it out; put it into words. "I need you to love me."

Amid the glare of the café lights, and the booming of the drum, he lifted himself on to his elbow and looked down at her elusive face, cased in its dark hood.

She said nothing.

"Make my dream come true. Love me."

She still did not speak. Now they were actually abreast of the man with the vast drum. He shouted something light-hearted and scatological as the gondola toiled past in the broken water. Boom, boom, boom, boom.

"Make my life worth while. Redeem me."

From the depths of her black cloak she looked into his eyes.

"You said you dreamed no longer. Do you know why?"

"I think I began to despair of the dream coming true."

"The dream stopped when you decided to visit Venice. Never visit Venice."

She stirred, withdrew her hand, and kissed him softly with cool lips.

"Set me free," said Fern, "Give me peace."

In the long darkness beneath the Ponte di Rialto, he put his hand on the tight bodice over her breast. When they emerged, his arms were so fast around her that nothing could ever part them. The sorters in the Post Office on the Fondamenta dei Tedeschi perceived this and called shrilly. It was rare to see anyone in a gondola except the elderly and exhausted, with death making a busy third at the paddle.

There was no more for Fern to say except endearments. On and up past the dark palaces went the gondola, ploughing and labouring, tilting and rocking, as powered craft, large and small, shot past like squibs and rockets. The very extremity and eccentricity of the consequent, artificial motion added to the isolation as Fern made love on the deep, velvety cushions. Their black gondolier must have had the tirelessness of a demiurge, so regular and relentless was their advance.

"You are the moon and the stars," said Fern. "You are the apples on the tree, the gold of the morning, the desire of the evening. You are good, you are lovely, you are life. You are my heart's delight."

The Palazzo Vendramin-Calergi came into sight.

"Isolde!" said Fern tenderly.

He had found a travelling companion.

"Tristan!" she replied, entering into the spirit of it.

"Perhaps that was when Venice died?" suggested Fern. "When *Tristan and Isolde* was composed here."

"If Venice ever really lived!" she retorted.

But the gondolier changed the subject for them by turning off the Grand Canal on to the Rio di San Felice. They were bound for the wide waters of the Lagoon.

In the Sacca della Misericordia, the almost square bay on the Venetian north shore, all was silent. There are no footways and in the buildings was only an occasional dim light, suggesting a rogue tenant, even now up to no good.

"Is this where the danger begins?" asked Fern.

She made no reply, but drew even closer. Beneath the dim, lilac amphora of the sky, she was all black or white, like Pierrot. The gondolier, with strokes as strong and regular as if he were swinging a scythe, swept them forward to their consummation.

Here, to the north of Venice, the Lagoon was incandescent. It seemed to Fern, who had never seen it like this before, a nearer word than phosphorescent, because the light which gleamed from the water, faintly around the gondola, but in distant patches quite brightly, was multicoloured, blue, green, white, yellow, pink; and always with lilac in it too, from the infusion of the sky. There were small glittering waves, and vast, indefinite areas of coloured froth or scum, like torn lace. Already it was a little colder.

They approached an island. Fern saw the white shape of a Renaissance church and, extending from it along the entire shore, a high wall, as of a prison or asylum. Ranged in the small piazzetta before the church door was a line of figures, indistinct in respect of age, sex, or costume, but each bearing a lighted Venetian lantern, a decorated light on a decorated pole, a device, here, now, and always one of the distinctive splendours of Venice. The figures seemed to agitate the lanterns almost frenziedly, in welcome to Fern and his companion, but from the group Fern could hear no sound, though by now they were less than a hundred yards away, and the whiteness of the church behind them was luminous as a leper's face.

"Isn't it San Michele?" whispered Fern. "The cemetery island, where at night no one stays?"

"The dead stay. By this time, no one knows how many of them. All who permit themselves to be taken from their beds, dressed in the streets, and buried." She pressed her soft cool lips on his to dismiss the thought.

When Fern looked up once more, they were almost past the island. The line of figures with the gorgeous lanterns lay far astern, though the lanterns were still tilting at odd, wild angles. It occurred to Fern that the figures were not expecting the gondola to stop, but had come out in order to speed it on its way, as it might be the barge of Bianca Capello. He saw that the lights were now higher in the air, as the poles were lifted joyously to their full length. But there was still no sound beyond the sounds of night and the sea.

Out here, while the small, scattered navigation lights flickered and bickered, Fern could see that, in places, the water was not merely faintly radiant but transparent right down to the wrack and garbage settled on the bottom from earliest times. In other places, it was opaque, sometimes as if great volumes of powder had been dissolved in it, and sometimes as if it were effervescent and gaseous. Every now and then Fern could see bones, human or animal, arranged in dead seaweed, or a hideous pile of discarded domestic-ities, or a small, vague underwater mountain, not quite mineral, not quite vegetable, not quite animal, but riddled and crawling with life of a kind, notwithstanding. Big lumpy fish and pale grey or pale pink serpentine crea-tures, elaborately devious in structure, glided in and out of the clear patches, sometimes seeming almost to gambol round the gondola, occasionally break-ing surface for a second, with a gasp and croak. Everywhere was an entangle-ment of seadrift, rotted but constantly self-renewing. The north shore of Venice, always the dark side of the city, was now a necklace of single lamps round the throat of the night: the different floors of the buildings were levelled off by distance and amalgamated with the public lamp posts of the Fondamenta Nuove. Over on the left of the gondola, the ancient glassworks of Murano, working day and night to produce brittle joys for visitors, thrust quick swords of fire into the encroaching blackness.

Further than Murano it seemed impossible for even this gondolier to con-tinue with so much power; but there was no sign of flagging.

"He is a strong man," said Fern.

"Here there is a current," replied his companion. "Here the struggle ends."

Fern perceived that they had indeed changed direction. Ahead lay a long dark shore, as in his dream. But he knew quite well what it was. It was the Litorale; the long, narrow, reef strengthened and sustained through the ages to prevent the high seas of the Adriatic from entering the Lagoon and eroding Venice; a reef penetrated by three gaps or *porti,* through which shipping passed, one of which, Fern knew, must be somewhere ahead, the Porto di Lido, standing at the north of that notorious wilderness of pleasure. He realized now where their journey would end. Where else could an official tour of Venice terminate but at Lido?

"We leave the Laguna Morta and enter the Laguna Viva," said his guide.

Fern was not sure that this was exactly accurate; but it did not really matter, because the next thing she said was, "This is the moment of love," and because of that, for some little time, was what it proved to be.

After so many mortal years, Fern's dream was proving more than true. Fern was proving himself right and the rest of the world wrong.

Now the sky was at last completely black, the stars gave little light, and the effulgent Lagoon was becoming the sombre sea. Upon all the black gondolier must have looked down, with more time to stare, now that his work was lighter, but about him it did not seem to Fern the moment to concern himself. To Fern, life had become an affair of moments only; a present without past, without future.

How long had passed by the hands of Fern's watch, he never knew, because when, somewhat later, he looked at his watch, he found that it had stopped.

FOUR

When first he stirred, he realized that a fairly stiff breeze was blowing round the little craft. The gondola was tossing and plunging quite seriously.

Fern drew himself up and looked round. There were biggish waves, and the scanty lighting at the northern, garrison end of Lido, instead of lying ahead, was distinctly to the leftward, the garish glow of the pleasure grounds completely out of sight: to all intents and purposes, Fern realized with a shock, the lights of the Lido pleasure area were *behind* them. It was somewhere in this watery region that on the Festa de Sensa the Doge at the prow of the *Bucentaur,* loveliest vessel in the world, each year married the sea. It startled him that his own strange marriage had found its culmination just there. This was when Fern looked at his watch.

Then he twisted right round, for the first time since he had entered the boat, and, kneeling on the keel, looked straight back at the gondolier. Then he had his third and greatest shock. There was no one there at all. The gondola was merely being swept out to sea on the current. It came to Fern that, even though there are said to be but small tides or no tides in the Mediterranean, yet the very expression *Laguna Morta* referred to areas "under water only at high tides"; and that now the Lagoon was emptying, pouring out through the relatively narrow breach ahead.

When Fern first roused himself after the moment of love, he had left his companion remuffled in her black cloak, soft, small, and silent. Now he turned to where she lay beside him. He could not decide what first to say. It seemed terrible to speak at once of the mere practical circumstances, and worse if the circumstances were of danger, as he could not doubt they were. He was appalled by the surmise that the gondolier, strong as he was, had been somehow swept from the boat, while the two of them had been lost in passion and the spell of the night. Gently, he put out his hand and drew away the black hood. Then, in the solitude of the sea and against the rising wind, Fern screamed out loud. Inside the black hood was a white skull; and an instantaneous throwing back of the entire black cloak, revealed inside it only an entire white skeleton.

FIVE

At the Porto di Lido, the main entrance to the harbour of Venice, two very long stone breakwaters run far out to sea. There was no question for Fern of a storm having arisen, or of any serious change at all in the weather. The change was merely that brought about by leaving a more or less still and dead pool for the living, unpredictable ocean. Even the wind which so alarmed Fern was little more than the breeze encountered in almost all regions when one embarks seriously upon open waters. Between the Porto di Lido breakwaters, therefore, vessels passed in and out in fair numbers, hardly sentient of the racing ebb which for a single gondola was so formidable.

Fern, in fact, passed no fewer than four incoming ships; and two others overtook him. Some of them came far too close to his uncontrolled cockleshell, but his wild shouting and waving reached never a soul aboard any of them, so black was the night, so black his craft, in accordance with the decree of 1562. Between the long breakwaters, the passing ships were the obvious danger: it was certainly not rough, though it was reasonably unpleasant for a man pitching about in a vessel so small as a gondola. The possibility of the gondola, instead of being run down, sinking beneath him, did not, therefore, seriously occur to him until the real sea was drawing quite near.

He shrank forward to the peak of the vessel, so as to separate himself from his now terrible companion, and squatted before the tall iron ferro, only a few inches ahead. The ferro would surely drag the boat down all the faster when the moment came.

At the very end of the leftward or San Erasmo breakwater, the shorter of the two, Fern could just make out a large inscription daubed by supporters of the previous Italian regime, and never obliterated owing to difficulty of access —and perhaps other things. It was to the effect that a simple hour as a lion is to be preferred to a lifetime as an ass.

And now there was only the Lido breakwater and, afterwards, the turbulent, nocturnal Adriatic. The gondola sped on like a black leaf on a millstream.

Fern had proved his resolution to leave Venice before the morrow night.

THE DREAM
OF THE WOLF

SCOTT BRADFIELD

*WITHOUT THE DREAM ONE WOULD HAVE FOUND NO OCCASION FOR A DIVISION
OF THE WORLD.*
—NIETZSCHE

*L*ast night I dreamed I was *Canis lupus tundrarum,* the Alaskan tundra
wolf," Larry Chambers said, confronted by hot Cream O' Wheat,
one jelly donut, black coffee with sugar. "I was surrounded by a vast
white plain and sparse gray patches of vegetation. I loped along at a
brisk pace, quickening the hot pulse of my blood. I felt extraordinarily swift,
hungry, powerful. . . ." Larry gripped his donut; red jelly squirted across his
knuckles. "My jaws were enormous, my paws heavy and callused." He took a
bite, chewed with his mouth open. "My pelt was thick and white and warm.
The cold breeze carried aromas of fox, rabbit, caribou, rodent, fowl, mol-
lusc. . . ."

"Caroline!" Sherryl Chambers reached for the damp dishcloth. "Eat over
the table, *please.* Just look at this. You've dripped cereal all over your new
shoes."

Caroline gazed up intently at her father, her chin propped against the table
edge. Her fist gripped a grainy spoon.

"I heard a noise behind me and I turned." Larry warmed his palms against
the white coffee cup. "The mouse hesitated—just for a moment—and then
quickly I pounced, pinned him beneath my paw. His eyes were wide with
panic, his tiny heart fluttered wildly. His fear blossomed in the air like pol-
len—"

"What did you do, Daddy? What did you do to the mouse?"

Larry observed the clock radio. *KRQQ helicopter watch for a Monday, March twenty-third,* the radio said. *An overturned tanker truck has traffic backed up all the way to the Civic Center. . . .*

"I ate him," Larry said. The time was eight-fifteen.

"Caroline. Finish your cereal before it gets cold."

"But Daddy's a wolf again, Mommy. He caught a mouse and he *ate* it."

"I'm practically certain it was the *tundrarum,*" Larry said, and pulled on his sport coat.

"Please, Caroline. I won't ask you again."

"But I want the rest of Daddy's donut."

"Finish your cereal. *Then* we'll discuss Daddy's donut."

"I think I'll stop by the library again tonight." Larry got up from the table. His spoon remained gripped by the thickening cereal like a fossil in La Brea.

"Sure, honey. And pick up some milk on the way home, will you? *Try* and remember."

"I will," Larry said, "I'll try," recalling the brilliant white ice, the warm easy taste of the blood.

"And here—bend over." Sherryl moistened the tip of a napkin with her lips. "There's jelly all over your face."

"It's the blood, Daddy. It's the mouse's blood."

"Thanks," Larry said, and went into the living room.

Caroline watched the kitchen door swing shut. After a few moments she heard the front door open and close.

"Daddy forgot to kiss me goodbye," she said.

Sherryl spilled pots and pans into the sink. "Daddy's a little preoccupied this morning, dear."

Caroline thought for a moment. The bitten jelly donut sat in the middle of the table like a promise.

"Daddy ate a mouse," she said finally, and made a proud little flourish in the air with her spoon.

Canis lupus youngi, canis lupus crassodon, canis niger rufus, Larry thought, and boarded the RTD at Beverly and Fairfax. The wolf, he thought. The wolf of the dream, the wolf of the world. He showed the driver his pass. Wolves in Utah, Northern Mexico, Baffin Island, even Hollywood. Wolves secretly everywhere, Larry thought, and moved down the crowded aisle. Elderly women jostled fitfully in their seats like birds on a wire.

"Larry! Hey—Spaceman!"

Andrew Prytowsky waved his *Wall Street Journal.* "Sit here." He removed his briefcase from the window seat and placed it in his lap. "Rest that frazzled brain of yours. You may need it later."

"Thanks," Larry said, squeezed into the vacant seat and recalled an exotic afternoon nap. *Canis lupus chanco,* Tibetan spring, crepuscular hour. His pack downed a goat. Blood spattered the gray dust like droplets of quivering mercury.

"That's earnings, Larry. *That's* reliable income. *That's* retirement security, a summer cottage, a sporty new car." Andrew shook the American Exchange Index at him, as if reproving an unhousebroken puppy. "Fifteen points in two weeks, just like I promised. Did you hear me? *Fifteen* points. Consolidated Plastics Ink. Plastic bullets, the weapon of the future. Cheap, easy to manufacture, minimal production overhead. You could have cut yourself a piece of that, Larry. I certainly gave you every opportunity. But then *my* word's not good enough for you, is it? You've already got your savings account, your fixed interest, your automatic teller, your free promotional albums. You've got yourself a coffin—*that's* what you've got. Fixed interest is going to bury you. Listen to me, pal. I can help. Let's talk taxfree municipal bonds for just one second—"

Larry sighed and gazed out the smudged window. Outside the Natural History Museum sidewalk vendors sold hot dogs, lemonade and pretzels while behind them ancient bones surfaced occasionally from the bubbling tar pit.

". . . in the long run we're not just talking safety. We're talking variable income *and* easy liquidity." Prytowsky slapped Larry's chest with the rolled-up newspaper. "Get *with* it, Spaceman. What are you now? Late thirties, early forties? You want to spend the rest of your life with your head in the clouds? Or do you want to come back down to earth and enjoy a little of the *good* life? Your little girl—Carol, Karen, whatever. She may be four or five now, pal, but college is *tomorrow. Tomorrow,* Spaceman. And you want your little girl to go to college, don't you? Well, *don't* you? Of *course* you do! Of *course!"*

The traffic light turned green, the RTD's clutch connected with a sudden sledgehammer sound. Oily gray smoke swirled outside the window.

"And what about that devilish little wife of yours? Take it from me, Spaceman. A woman's eye is *always* looking out for those greener pastures. It's not their *fault,* Spaceman—it's just their *nature.* . . . Hey, *Larry."* The rolled-up newspaper jabbed Larry's side. "You even listening to me or what?"

"Sure," Larry said, and the bus entered Beverly Hills. Exorbitant hood ornaments flashed in the sun like grails. "Easy liquidity, interest variations. I'll think about it. I really will. It's just I have a lot on my mind right now, that's all. I mean, I'll get back to you on all this. I really will." *Canis lupus arabs, pallipes, baileyi, nubilis, monstrabilis,* he thought. The wolves of the dream, the wolves of the world.

"Still having those nutty dreams of yours, Spaceman? Your wife told my wife. You dream you're a dog or something?"

"A wolf. *Canis lupus*. It's not even the same subspecies as a dog."

"Oh." Andrew discarded his newspaper under his seat. "Sure."

"Wolves are far more intelligent than any dog. They're fiercer hunters, loyaler mates. Their social organization alone—"

"Yeah—right, Spaceman. I stand corrected. I'll bet in your dreams you really raise hell with those stupid dogs—hey, Larry, old pal?" Andrew said, and disboarded with his briefcase at Westwood Boulevard.

As the bus approached 27th Avenue Larry moved back through the crowd of passengers who stood and sat about with newspapers, magazines and detached expressions as they vacantly chewed Certs, peanuts from a bag, impassive bubble gum, like a herd of grazing buffalo while the wolf, the wolf of Larry's mind, roamed casually among them, searching out the weak, the sickly, the injured, the ones who always betrayed themselves with brief and anxious glances—the elderly woman with the aluminum walker, the gawky adolescent with the bad complexion and crooked teeth. Wolves in Tibet, Montana, South America, Micronesia, Larry thought, disembarked at 25th Avenue and entered Tower Tire and Rubber Company. He showed his pass to the security guard, then rode the humming elevator to the twelfth floor. When Larry stepped into the foyer the secretaries, gathered around the receptionist's desk, exchanged quick significant glances like secret memoranda. Larry heard them giggling as he disappeared into the maze of high white paritions that organized office cubicles like discrete cells in an ant farm.

Larry entered his office.

"Ready for Monday?" Marty Cabrillo asked.

Larry hung his coat on the rack, turned.

The marketing supervisor stood in front of Larry's aluminum bookshelf, gazing aimlessly at the spines of large gray Acco-Grip binders. "Frankly," Marty said, "I'd rather be in Shasta. How was your weekend?"

"Fine, just fine," Larry said, sat down at his desk and opened the top desk drawer.

"I thought I'd drop by and see if the Orange County sales figures were in yet. Didn't mean to barge in, you know."

"Certainly. Help yourself." Larry gestured equivocally with his right hand, rummaged in the desk drawer with his left.

"Ed Conklin called from Costa Mesa and said he still hasn't received the Goodyear flyers. I told him no problem—you'd get right back to him. All right?"

"Right." Larry slammed shut one drawer and pulled open another. "No problem. Here we are . . ." He removed a large faded-green hardcover book. One of the book's corners was bloated with dog-eared pages. Larry wiped off dust and bits of paper against his trousers. *The Wolves of North America: Part 1, Classification of Wolves.*

Marty propped one hand casually in his pocket. "I hope you don't take this the wrong way or anything, Larry . . . I mean, I'm not trying to pull rank on you or anything. But maybe you could try being just a little bit more careful around here the next few weeks or so. Think of it as a friendly warning, okay?"

Larry looked up from his book.

"It's not me, Larry." Marty placed his hand emphatically over his heart. "You know me, right? But district managers are starting to complain. Late orders, unitemized bills, stuff like that. *Harmless* stuff, really. Nothing I couldn't cover for you. But the guys upstairs aren't so patient—that's all I'm trying to say. I'm just trying to say it's my job, too. All right?"

Finally Larry located the *tundrarum's* subspecies guide. *Type locality: Point Barrow, Alaska. Type Specimen: No. 16748, probably female, skull only. U.S. National Museum; collected by Lt. P. H. Ray . . .*

"But for God's sake don't take any of this personal or anything. It's not really serious. Everybody has their off days—it's just the way things go. People get, well, *distracted.*"

"I knew it." Larry pointed at the page. "Just what I thought. Look—*tundrarum* is 'closely allied to *pambisileus.*' Exactly as I suspected. The dentition was a dead giveaway."

Marty fumbled for a cigarette from his shirt pocket, a Bic lighter from his slacks. "Well," he said, and took a long drag from his Kool. Then, after a moment, "You know, Larry, Beatrice and I have always been interested in this ecology stuff ourselves. You should visit our cabin in Shasta sometime. There's nothing like it—clean air, trees, privacy. We even joined the Sierra Club last year. . . . But look, I could talk about this stuff all day, but we've *both* got to get back to work, right?" Marty paused outside the cubicle. "We'll get together and talk about it over lunch sometime, okay? And maybe you could drop the sales figures by my office later? Before noon, maybe?"

That night Larry returned home after the dinner dishes had been washed. He glanced into Caroline's room. She was asleep. Stuffed wolves, cubs and one incongruous unicorn lay toppled around her on the bed like dominoes. He found Sherryl in the master bedroom, applying Insta-Curls to her hair and balancing a black rectangular apparatus in her lap.

Larry sat on the edge of the bed, glimpsed himself in the vanity mirror. He had forgotten to shave that morning. His eyes were dark, sunken, feral. (The lone wolf lopes across an empty plain. Late afternoon, clear blue sky. The pale crescent moon appears on the horizon like a specter. Other wolves howl in the distance.)

Larry turned to his wife. "I went all the way out to the UCLA Research Library, then found out the school's between quarters. The library closed at five."

"That's too bad, dear. Would you plug that in for me?"

Sherryl pulled a plastic cap over her head. Two coiled black wires attached the cap to the black rectangular box. Larry connected the plug to the wall socket and the black box began to hum. Gradually the plastic cap inflated. "Larry, I wish I knew how to phrase this a bit more delicately, but it's been on my mind a lot lately." Sherryl turned the page of a K Mart Sweepstakes Sale brochure. "You may not believe this, Larry, but there are actually people in this world who like to talk about some things besides *wolves* every once in a blue moon."

Larry turned again to his reflection. He had forgotten to finish Cabrillo's sales figures. Tomorrow, he assured himself. First thing.

"I remember when we had decent conversations. We went out occasionally. We went to movies, or even dancing. Do you remember the last time we went out together—I mean, just out of the *house?* It was that horrid PTA meeting last fall, with that dreadful woman—the hunchback with the butterfly glasses, you remember? Something about a rummage sale and new tether poles? Do you *know* how long ago that was? And frankly, Larry, I wouldn't call that much of a night *out.*"

Larry ran his hand lightly along the smooth edge of the humming black box. "Look, honey. I know I get a little out of hand sometimes . . . I *know* that. Especially lately." He placed his hand on his forehead. A soft pressure seemed to be increasing inside his skull, like an inflating plastic cap. "I've been forgetful . . . and I realize I must seem a little nutty at times. . . ." The wolves, he thought, trying to strengthen himself. The call of the pack, the track of the moon, the hot quick pulse of the blood. But the wolves abruptly seemed very far away. "I know you don't understand. *I* don't really understand. . . . But these aren't just dreams. When I'm a wolf, I'm *real.* The places I see, the feelings I feel—they're *real.* As real as I am now, talking to you. As real as this bed." He grasped the king-size silk comforter. "I'm not making all this up. . . . And I'll *try* to be a little more thoughtful. We'll go out to dinner this weekend, I promise. But try putting up with me a little longer. Give me a little credit, that's all . . ."

Sherryl glanced up. She took the humming black box from his hand.

"Did you say something, hon?" She patted the plastic cap. "Hold on and

I'll be finished in a minute." She turned another page of the brochure. Then, with a heavy red felt marker, she circled the sale price of Handi-Wipes.

Larry walked into the bathroom and brushed his gleaming white teeth.

"Last night I dreamed of the Pleistocene."

"Where is that, Daddy?"

"It's not a place, honey. It's a time. A long time ago."

"You mean dinosaurs, Daddy? Did you dream you were a *dinosaur?*"

"No, darling. The dinosaurs were all gone by then. I was *canis dirus,* I think. I'll check on it. The tundra was far colder and more desolate than before. The sky was filled with this weird, reddish glow I've never seen before, like the atmosphere of some alien planet. Ice was everywhere. Three of us remained in the pack. My mate had died the previous night beneath a shelf of ice while the rest of us huddled around to keep her warm. Dominant, I led the others across the white ice, my tail slightly erect. We were terribly cold, tired, hungry . . ."

"Weren't there any mice, Daddy? Or any snails?"

"No. We had traveled for days. We had discovered no spoor. Except one."

"Was it a deer, Daddy? Did you kill the deer and eat it?"

"No. It was Man's spoor. We were seeking an encampment of men." He turned. Sherryl was beating eggs into a bowl and watching David Hartman on the portable television. "Sherryl, that was the strangest part. I've read about it, anthropologists have suggested it—a prehistoric, communal bond between man and wolf. We weren't afraid. We sought shelter with them, food, companionship, allies in the hunt."

Larry watched his wife. After a moment she said, "That's nice, dear."

David Hartman said, "Later in this half hour we'll be meeting Lorna Backus to discuss her new hit album, and then take an idyllic trip up the coast to scenic New Hampshire, the Granite State, as part of our 'States of the Union' series. Please stay with us."

"I've always wanted to live in New Hampshire," Sherryl said.

Every day on his way home from work Larry stopped at the Fairfax branch library. Many of the books he needed he had to request through interlibrary loan. He read Lopez's *Of Wolves and Men,* Fox's *The Soul of the Wolf,* Mech's *The Wolf: The Ecology and Behavior of an Endangered Species,* Pimlott's *The World of the Wolf,* Mowat's *Never Cry Wolf,* Ewer's *The Carnivores,* and the pertinent articles and symposiums published in *American Zoologist, American Scientist, Journal of Zoology, Journal of Mammalogy* and *The Canadian Field Naturalist.* Sherryl pulled the blankets off the bed one day and three books came loose, thudding onto the floor. "I'd really appreciate it, Larry, if you could start picking up after yourself. It's bad enough with Caroline. And just look —this one's almost a month overdue." Larry returned them to the library that night, checked out three more, and xeroxed the "Canids" essay in *Grzimek's Animal Life Encyclopedia.*

On the way out the door he noticed a three-by-five file card tacked to the Community Billboard. *Spiritual Counseling, Dream Analysis, Budget Rates, Free Parking.* Her name was Anita Louise. She lived on the top floor of a faded Sunset Boulevard brownstone, and claimed to be circuitously related to Tina Louise, the former star of *Gilligan's Island.* Her living room was furnished with tattered green lawn chairs and orange-crate bookshelves. She required a personal item; Larry handed her his watch. She closed her eyes. "I can see the wolf now," she said. Her fingers smudged the watch's crystal face, wound the stem, tested the flexible metal band. "While he leads you through the forest of life, he warns you of the thorny paths. When the time comes, he will lead you into Paradise."

"The wolf doesn't guide me," Larry said. "I *am* the wolf. Sometimes I am the guide, the leader of my pack."

"The ways of the spirit world are often baffling to those unlearned in its ways," Anita told him. "I take Visa and MasterCard. I take personal checks, but I need to see at least two pieces of I.D."

Before he left, Larry reminded her about his watch.

"I don't know, Evelyn. I really just don't know. I mean, I *love* Larry and all, but you can't imagine how difficult life's been around here lately—especially the last few months." Sherryl held the telephone receiver with her left hand, a cold coffee cup with her right. She listened for a moment. "No, Evelyn, I don't think *you* understand. This isn't a hobby. It's not as if Larry was collecting stamps, or a *bowler* or something. I could understand that. *That* would be understandable. But all Larry talks about anymore is wolves. Wolves this and wolves that. Wolves at the dinner table, wolves in bed, wolves even when we're driving to the market. Wolves are everywhere, he keeps saying. And honestly, Evelyn, sometimes I almost believe him. I start looking over my shoulder. I hear a dog bark and I make sure the door's bolted. . . . Well, of *course* I try to be understanding. I'm trying to tell you that. But I have to worry about Caroline too, you know. . . . Well, listen for a minute and I'll tell you what happened yesterday. We're sitting at breakfast, you see, and Larry starts telling Caroline—a four-year-old girl, remember—how he's off in the woods somewhere, God only knows *where,* and he meets this female dog and, well, I can't go on. . . . No, I simply can't. It's too embarrassing. . . . No, Evelyn. You've completely missed the point. It's mating season, get it? And Larry starts going into explicit detail. . . . Well, maybe. But that's not even the worst part. . . . Hold *on* for one second and I'll tell you. They, well, I don't know how to phrase this delicately. They get *stuck*. . . . No, Evelyn. Honestly, sometimes I don't think you're even listening to me. They get stuck *together*. Can you believe that? What am I supposed to say? Caroline's not going to outgrow a trauma like this, though. I can promise you that." Sherryl heard the kitchen door opening behind her. "Hold on, Evelyn," she said, and turned.

Caroline blocked the door open with her foot. "What are you talking about?" Her hand gripped the plastic Pez dispenser. Wylie Coyote's head was propped back by her thumb, and a small pink lozenge extruded from his throat.

"It's Evelyn, dear. We're just talking."

Caroline's lips were flushed and purple; purple stains speckled her white dress. She thought for a moment, took the candy with her teeth and chewed. Finally she said, "I think somebody may have spilled grape juice on one of Daddy's wolf books."

Larry read Guy Endore's *The Werewolf of Paris,* Hesse's *Steppenwolf,* Rowland's *Animals With Human Faces,* Pollard's *Wolves and Werewolves,* Lane's *The Wild Boy of Aveyron,* Malson's *Wolf Children and the Problem of Human Nature.* Marty gave him the card of a Jungian in Topanga Canyon who sat Larry in a plush chair, said "archetype" a few times, informed him that *everyone* is fascinated with evil, sadism, pain ("It's perfectly normal, perfectly *human*"), recommended Robert Eisler's *Man into Wolf,* charged seventy-five dollars and offered him a Valium prescription with refill. "But when I'm a wolf, I never know evil," Larry said as he was ushered out the door by a blond receptionist. "When I'm a wolf, I know only peace."

"I don't know, Larry. It just gives me the creeps," Sherryl said that night after Caroline was in bed. "It's *weird,* that's what it is. Bullying defenseless little mice and deer that never hurt anybody. Talking about killing, and blood, and ice—and particularly at *breakfast.*"

Larry was awake until 2:00 a.m. watching *The Wolf Man* on Channel Five. Claude Raines said, "There's good and evil in every man's soul. In this case, the evil takes the shape of a wolf." No, Larry thought, and read Freud's *The Case of the Wolf-Man,* the first chapter of Mack's *Nightmares and Human Conflict.* No. Then he went to bed and dreamed of the wolves.

"The wolf spirit has always been considered very *wakan,*" Hungry Bear said, his feet propped on his desk. He poked out his cigarette against the rim of the metal wastebasket, then prepared to light another. "Most tribes believe the wolf's howl portends bad things. The Lakota say, 'The man who dreams of the wolf is not really on his guard, but the man haughtily closes his eyes, for he is very much on his guard.' I don't know what that means, exactly, but I read it somewhere." Hungry Bear refilled his Dixie Cup with vin rosé. His grimy T-shirt was taut against his large stomach; a band of pale skin bordered his belt. He wore a plaid Irish derby atop his braided hair. "I try to do a good deal of reading," he said, and fumbled in his diminished pack of Salems.

"So do I," Larry said. "Maybe you could recommend—"

"I don't think the wolf was ever recognized as any sort of deity, but I could be wrong." Hungry Bear was watching the smoke unravel from his cigarette. "But still, you shouldn't be too worried. It's very common for animal spirits to possess a man. They use his body when he's asleep. When he awakes, he can't remember anything . . . oh, but wait. That's not quite right, is it? You said you *remember* your dreams? Well, again, I could be wrong. I guess you *could* remember. Sure, I don't see why not," Hungry Bear said, and poured more vin rosé.

"*I* inhabit the body of the *wolf,*" Larry said, beginning to lose interest, and glanced around the cluttered office. The venetian blinds were cracked and dusty, the floors littered with tattered men's magazines, empty wine bottles and crumpled cigarette packs. After a moment he added, "I don't even know what I should call you. *Mister* Bear?"

"No, of course not." Hungry Bear waved away the notion, dispersing smoke. "Call me Jim. That's my real name. Jim Prideux. I took Hungry Bear for business purposes. If you remember, Hungry Bear was the brand name of a terrific canned chili. It was discontinued after the war, though, I'm afraid." He checked his shirt pocket. "Do you see a pack of cigarettes over there? Seems I'm running short."

"You're not Indian?" Larry asked.

"Sure. Of course I'm Indian. One-eighth pure Shoshone. My great-grandmother was a Shoshone princess. Well, maybe not a princess, exactly. But *her* father was an authentic medicine man. I've inherited the gift." Jim Prideux rummaged through the papers on his desk. "Are you sure you don't see them? I'm sure I bought a pack less than an hour ago."

"This is very nice," Sherryl said, and swallowed her last bite of red snapper. She touched her lips delicately with the napkin. "It's *so* nice to get out of the house for a change. You wouldn't know how much."

"Sure I would, darling," Andrew Prytowsky said, and poured more Chenin Blanc.

"No, I don't think you would, Andy. Your wife, Danielle, is *normal*. You

wouldn't know what it's like living with someone as . . . . well, as *unstable* as
Larry's been acting lately."

"I'm sure it's been very difficult for you."

"Marty Cabrillo, Larry's boss at work, got Larry in touch with a doctor, a
good doctor. Larry visits him *once* and then tells me he isn't going anymore. I
say to Larry, don't you think he can help you? And Larry says no, he can't, he
can't help him at all. He says the doctor is *stupid.* Can you believe that? I say
to Larry, this man has a *Ph.D.* I don't think you can just call a man with a
Ph.D. *stupid.* And so then Larry says *I* don't know what *I'm* talking about,
either. Larry thinks he knows more than a man with a Ph.D. That's what
Larry thinks."

"Here. Why don't you finish it?" Andrew put down the empty bottle and
flagged the waiter with his upraised MasterCard.

"I'm sorry, Andy." Sherryl dabbed her eyes with the napkin. "It's just I'm
so shook up lately. All I ever asked for was a normal life. That's not too
much, is it? A nice home, a normal husband. Someone who could give me a
little help and support. Is that too much to ask? Is it?"

"Of course not." Andrew signed the check. After the waiter left he said,
"I'm glad we could do this."

Sherryl folded her napkin and replaced it on the table. "I'm glad you
called. This was very nice."

"We'll do it again."

"Yes," Sherryl said. "We should."

Two weeks later Larry returned home from work and found the letter on
the kitchen table.

Dear Larry,
I know you're going to take this the wrong way and I only hope you realize
Caroline and I still care about you but I've thought about this a lot and even
sought professional counseling on one occasion and I think it's the only solution
right now at this moment in our lives. Especially for Caroline who is at a very
tender age. Please don't try calling because I told my mother not to tell you where
we are for a while. Please realize I don't want to hurt you and this will probably
be better for both of us in the long run, and I hope you make it through your
difficulties and I'll think good thoughts for you often.

                                                        SHERRYL

"You can't just keep moping around, Larry. Things'll get better, just you
wait. I sense big improvements coming in your life. But first you've *got* to
start being more careful around the office." Marty sat on the edge of Larry's

desk. He pulled a string of magnetized paper clips in and out of a clear plastic dispenser. "Did I tell you Henderson asked about you yesterday? Asked about you *by name*. Now, I'm not trying to make you paranoid or anything, but if Henderson asked about you, then you can bet your socks the *rest* of the guys in Management have been tossing your name around. And Henderson's not a bad guy, Larry. I'm not suggesting that. But there's been a sincere . . . a sincere *concern* about your performance around here lately. And don't think I don't understand. Really, Larry, I'm very sensitive to your position. Beatrice and I came close to breaking up a couple times ourselves—and I don't know *what* I'd do without Betty and the kids. But you've got to keep your chin up, buddy. Plow straight ahead. And remember—I'm on *your* side."

At his desk, Larry made careful, persistent marks on a sheet of graph paper. The frequency of dreams had increased over the past few weeks: the line on the graph swooped upward. Often three, even four times a night he started awake in bed, clicked on the reading lamp and reached for a pen and notepad from the end table, quickly jotting down terrain and subspecies characteristics while the aromas of forest, desert and tundra were displaced by the close, stale odors of grimy bedsheets, leftover Swanson frozen dinner entrées, and Johnson's Chlorophyll-Scented Home Deodorizer.

"I'm really sincere about this, Larry. I can't keep covering for you. I need some assurances, I need to start seeing some real *effort* on your part. You're going to start seeing Dave Boudreau on the third floor. He's our employee stress counselor—but that doesn't mean he's like a shrink or anything, Larry. I know how you feel about *them*. Dave Boudreau's just a regular guy like you and me who happens to have a lot of experience with these sorts of problems. You and Sherryl, I mean. All right, Larry? Does that sound fair to you?"

"Sure, Marty," Larry said, "I appreciate your help, I really do," and peeled another sheet from the Thrifty pad. Abscissa, he thought: real time. Ordinate: dream time. At the top of the page he scribbled *Pleistocene*.

"I'm dreaming now more than ever," Larry told Dave Boudreau the following Thursday. "Sometimes half a dozen times each night. Look, I've kept a record—" Larry opened a large red loose-leaf binder, flipped through a sheaf of papers and unclamped a sheet of graph paper. "There, that's last Friday. Six times." He held the sheet of paper over the desk, pointing at it. "And Sunday—*seven* times. And that's not even the significant part. I haven't even got to *that* part yet."

Dave Boudreau sat behind his desk and rocked slightly in a swivel chair. He glanced politely at the statistical chart. Then his abstract gaze returned to Tahitian surf in a framed travel poster. He heard the binder clamp click again.

Larry pulled up his chair until the armrests knocked the edge of the desk.

"Increasingly I dream of the Pleistocene, the Ice Age. The Great Hunt, when man and wolf hunted together, bound by one pack, responsible to one community, seeking their common prey across the cold ice, beneath the cold sun. Is *that* something? Is that one hell of an archetype or what?"

Casually Boudreau opened the manila folder on his desk.

CHAMBERS, LAWRENCE
SUPPLIES AND SERVICES DEPARTMENT
BORN: 3-6-45   EYES: BLUE

"And don't get me wrong. I'm just kidding about that archetype stuff. That's not even close, that's not even in the same ballpark. These aren't memories, for chrissakes. When I dream of the wolf, I *am* the wolf. I've been wolves in New York, Montana and Beirut. It's as if time and space, dream and reality, have just *opened up,* joined me with everything, everything *real.* I'm living the *one life,* understand? The life of the hunter and the prey, the dream and the world, the blood and the spirit. It's really spectacular, don't you think? Have you ever heard anything like it?"

In the space reserved for Counselor's Comments Boudreau scribbled "wolf nut," and underlined it three times.

When Larry arrived at work the following Monday the security guard took his I.D. card and, after consulting his log, asked him to please wait one moment. The guard picked up his phone and asked the operator for Personnel Management. "This is station six. Mr. Lawrence Chambers has just arrived." The guard listened quietly to the voice at the other end. He snapped his pencil against the desk in four-four time.

Finally he put down the phone and said, "I'm sorry. I'll have to keep your card. Would you please follow me?"

They walked down the hall to Payroll. Larry was given his final paycheck and, in a separate envelope, another check for employee minimum compensation.

By the time Larry returned home it was still only 10:00 a.m. He cleared the old newspapers from the stoop, unbound and opened the whitest, most recent one. He read for a few minutes, then refolded the paper and placed it with the others beside the fireplace. He picked up Harrington and Paquet's *Wolves of the World* and put it down again. He got up and walked to the kitchen. Dishes piled high in the sink, four full bags of trash. The few remaining dishes in the dishwasher were swirled with white mineral deposits. In the refrigerator he found a garlic bulb with long green shoots, an empty bottle of Worcestershire sauce and an egg. He drank stale apple juice from the plastic green pitcher, then continued making his rounds. In the bathroom: toothpaste, toothbrush, comb, water glass, eye drops, Mercurochrome, a stray bandage, Sherryl's pH-balanced Spring Mountain shampoo, his electric razor. All the clothes and toys were gone from Caroline's room. Over the bed the poster of a wolf gazed down at him, its eyes sharp, canny, primitively alert.

He tried to watch television. People won sailboats and trash compactors on game shows, cheated one another and plotted financial coups on soap operas. After a while he got up again and returned to the bathroom, opened the medicine cabinet. Johnson's Baby Aspirin, an old stiffened toothbrush, mouthwash, a bobby pin. High on the top shelf he found Sherryl's Seconal in a childproof bottle. He took two. Then he got into bed.

Sometime after dawn he dreamed again of the wolves, but this time the dream was fragmentary and detached. He viewed the wolves from very far away. From atop a high bluff, perhaps, or hidden behind some bushes like Jane Goodall. The wolves moved down into the gully and paused before a small stream, drinking. Two cubs splashed and chased one another through the puddles. The other wolves observed them dispassionately. The sun was going down. Larry woke up. It was just past 6:00 a.m.

He stayed indoors throughout the day. In the evening he might walk to the corner Liquor Mart to cash a check and purchase milk, scotch, Stouffer's frozen dinners. Sometimes, remembering Sherryl and Caroline, he turned the television up louder. It wasn't their physical presence he missed (he could hardly recall their faces anymore) but rather their noise: the clatter of dishes, the inconstant whir and jingle of mechanical toys. Soundless, the air seemed thinner, staler, more oppressive, as if he were sealed inside an airtight crystal vault. The silence invested everything—the walls, the furniture, the diminishing vial of Seconal, the large empty bedrooms, even the mindless chatter of the Flintstones on television. He drank his beer beside the front window and watched the dust swirl soundlessly in the soundless shafts of light, recalling the wolves and the soundless expanse of white ice where not only the noise but even the aromas and textures of the landscape seemed to be leaking from the dreamlike atmosphere, as if from the cracks in some domed underwater city. In the mornings, now, he hardly recalled his dreams at all anymore. Sporadic glimpses of wolf, prey, sky, moon, interspliced meaninglessly like the frames of some surrealist montage. He smoked three packs of cigarettes a day, just to give his hands something to do. The scotch and Seconal compelled him to take so many naps during the day that he couldn't sleep at night. Wolves, he thought. Wolves in Utah, Baffin Island, Tibet, even Hollywood. Wolves secretly everywhere . . . Eventually the dreams disappeared entirely. Sleep became a dark visionless place where nothing ever happened.

The Seconal, he thought one morning, and departed for the library. He squinted at the sunlight, staggered occasionally. People looked at him. A book entitled *Sleep* by Gay Gaer Luce and Julius Siegal confirmed his suspicions. Alcohol and barbiturates suppressed the dream stage of sleep. He returned home and poured the scotch down the sink, the remaining Seconal down the toilet. He lay in bed throughout the afternoon, night and following morning. He tossed and turned. He couldn't keep his eyes closed more than a minute. His heart palpitated disconcertingly. He tried to remember the wolf's image, and remembered only pictures in books. He tried to recall the prey's hot, steaming blood, and tasted only yesterday's Chicken McNuggets. He wanted the map of the sky, and found only the close, humid rectangle of the bedroom. He got up and went into the living room. It was night again. In order to dream, he must sleep. In order to regain the real, he must dispel the illusion: newspapers, furniture, unswept carpets, Sherryl's letter, Caroline's toys, easy liquidity, magazines and books. He realized then that evil was not the wolf, but rather the wolf's disavowal. Violence wasn't something in nature, but rather something in nature's systematic repression. Madness isn't the dream, but rather the world deprived of the dream, he thought, selected a stale pretzel from the bowl, chewed and gazed out the window at the dim, empty streets below, where occasional streetlamps illuminated silent, unoccupied cars parked along the curbs. The moon made a faint impression against the high screen of fog. A distant siren wailed, a dog barked and in their homes the population slept fitfully, often aided by Seconal and Valium, descending through soft penetrable stages of sleep, seeking that fugitive half-world in which they struggled to dream beneath the repressive shadows of the real.

A few weeks after signing Larry Chambers's termination notice, Marty Cabrillo took his wife to Shasta. "Two weeks alone," he promised her. "We'll leave the kids with your mother. Just the two of us, the trees, candlelight dinners again, just like I always said it would be." But Marty said nothing during the long drive. Beatrice put her arm around him and he shrugged at her. "Please," he said. "I can't get comfortable." At the cabin they sat out on the sun deck. Marty held paperbacks and turned the pages. Beatrice read *People* magazine. After only a few days they returned home. "I'm sorry, honey," Marty said to her. "I'll make it up to you. I promise."

"What's the matter with you lately?"

"Nothing. Just things on my mind."

"Work?"

"Sort of."

After a while Beatrice said, "Larry," folded her arms and gazed out the window at Ventura car lots.

The following Sunday Marty drove to Ralph's in Fairfax, loaded four bags of groceries into his Toyota station wagon and drove to Larry's house on Clifton Boulevard. The front yard was brown and overgrown. Aluminum garbage cans, streaked with rust, lay overturned in the alley. Dormant snails studded the front of the house, their slick intricate trails glistening in the sunlight. Marty knocked, rang the bell a few times. The door was ajar and he pushed it open. A pyramid of bundled newspapers blocked the door, permitting him just to squeeze through. In the living room, torn magazines and moldy dishes lay strewn across the sofa, chairs and floor. The telephone receiver was off the hook, wailing faintly like a distant, premonitory siren. At first the room seemed oddly disproportionate, as if the furniture had all been rearranged. Then he noticed Larry asleep on the middle of the floor, his head propped by a sofa cushion, his arm wrapped around a leg of the coffee table. "He must've lost eighty, ninety pounds," Marty told Beatrice later that night. "His clothes stank, he hadn't shaved or washed in I don't know how long. And all I could think looking at him there was it's all *my* fault. *I* was responsible. Me, Marty Cabrillo."

Marty followed the ambulance to St. John's, wishing they would run the siren. "Dehydration," the doctor told him, while Marty paid the deposit on a private room. Larry lay in a stiff, geometric white bed, a glucose bottle hanging beside him, a white tube connected to his arm by white adhesive tape. Every so often the glucose bubbled. "We'll bring him along slow, have him eating solid food in a couple days. I think he'll be all right," the doctor said, and handed Marty another form to sign.

"It's all my fault," Marty said when Larry regained consciousness the following morning. "Look, I brought you some books to read. And the flowers—they're from Sherryl. Beatrice got in touch with her last night and she's on her way here right now. The worst is over, pal. The worst is all behind you."

Later Sherryl told him, "We missed you. Caroline missed you. *I* missed you. Oh, Larry. You just look so *aw*ful." Sherryl laid her head in Larry's lap and cried, hugging him. Silently Larry stroked her long blond hair. Sherryl had been staying with her sister in Burbank, working as a secretary at one of the studios. Her boss was a flushed, obese little man who put his hand on her knee while she took dictation, or snuck up behind her every once in a while and gave her a sharp pinch. "Loosen up, relax. Life's short," he told her. Caroline hated her new nursery school and cried nearly every day. Sherryl's sister had begun bringing the classified pages home, pointing out to her the best bets on her own apartment. Andy had promised to help out, but every time she called his office his secretary said he was still out of town on business. And then one of the Volvo's tires went flat, and in all the rush of moving she realized she had misplaced her triple-A card, and so she just started crying, right there on the side of the freeway, because it seemed as if nothing, nothing ever went right for her anymore.

"We need you, Larry," Sherryl said. "You need us. I'm sorry what happened, but I always loved you. It wasn't because I didn't love you. And Marty thinks he can get your old job back—"

Marty leaned forward, whispered something.

"He says he's certain. He's certain he can get it back. Did you hear, honey? Everything's going to be all right. We're all going to be happy again, just like before."

Sherryl brought Caroline home a month later.

"Is Daddy home?" Caroline asked.

"He's at work now, honey. But he'll be back soon. He's missed you."

Caroline waited to be unbuckled, climbed out of the car. The front yard was green and delicate, the house repainted yellow. The place seemed only dimly familiar, like the photograph Mommy showed her of where she lived when she was born.

"All your toys are in your room, sweetheart. Be good and play for a while. Mommy'll fix dinner."

Caroline's room had been repainted too. Over her bed hung a bright new Yosemite Sam poster. She opened the oak toy chest. The toys were boxed and neatly arranged, just like on shelves at the store. She went into the bedroom and looked at Daddy's bookcase. The large picture books were gone, along with their photographs of wolves and deer and rabbits and forests and men with rifles and hairy, misshapen primitive men. Bent paperbacks had replaced them. The covers depicted beautiful men and women, Nazi insignia, secret dossiers, demonic children, cowboys on horses, murder weapons.

She heard the front door open. "Hi, honey. Sorry I'm late. I ran into Andy Prytowsky on the bus—remember him? I introduced you at a party last year. Anyway, I told him I'd drop by his office tomorrow. I figure it's time we started some sort of college fund for Caroline. I'm pretty excited about it. Andy says he can work us a nice little tax break, too. Oh, and look what else. I bought us some wine. For later."

Caroline walked halfway down the hall. Mommy and Daddy stood at the door, kissing.

"There she is. There's my little girl."

Daddy picked her up high in the air. His face seemed strange and unfamiliar, like the front of the house.

"So how have you been, sweetheart?" Daddy put her down.

"I'll finish dinner," Sherryl said.

"Come and sit down." Daddy led her to the sofa. "Tell me what you've been up to. Did you have fun at Aunt Judy's?"

Caroline picked at a scab on her knee. "I guess."

"What do you want to do? I thought we'd go to a movie later. Would you like that?"

Caroline clasped her hands in her lap. Here is the church, and here is the steeple. When you open the doors you see all the people.

"What should we do right now? Do you want to play a game? Do you want me to read you one of your Dr. Seuss books?"

Caroline thought for a while. Daddy's large, rough hand ran through her hair, snagging it. Delicately, she pushed his hand away.

"I want to watch television," she said after a while.

Three nights each week Larry went to the YMCA with Marty. Sherryl began subscribing to *Sunset Magazine,* and over dinner they discussed a new home, or at least improvements on their present one. Finally Marty suggested they buy into his Shasta property. "Betty and I don't make it up there more than three or four times a year. The rest of the time it'd be all yours." Larry took out a second mortgage, paid Marty a lump sum and began sharing the monthly payments. The first few months they drove up nearly every weekend. Then Larry received a promotion which required him to make weekly trips to the Bakersfield office. "I'm really bushed from all this driving," he told Sherryl. "We'll try and make Shasta *next* weekend." Caroline started grade school in the fall. Sherryl joined an ERA support group and was gone two nights a week. Occasionally Larry spent the night in Bakersfield, and drove from there directly to work the next morning.

"All I told Conklin was I've got a merchandise deficit from his store three months in a row. It wasn't like I called him a thief or anything. I just wanted an explanation. I'm entitled to that much, don't you think? It's my job, right?"

"I'm sure he didn't mean it, Larry. He was probably just upset." Sherryl sat on the sofa, smoking a cigarette.

"I'm sure he *was* upset. I'm sure he *was.*" Larry sat at the dining room table. The table was covered with inventories, company billing statements and large gray Acco-Grip binders. His briefcase sat open on the chair beside him. "And now *I'm* a little upset, all right? Is that all right with you?"

"I'm sure you are, Larry. I was just saying maybe he didn't mean it, that's all. That's all I said."

Larry put down his pencil. "No. I don't think that's all you said."

Sherryl looked at the *TV Guide* on the coffee table, considered picking it up. Then she thought she heard Caroline's bedroom door squeak open down the hall.

"What you said was I'm imagining things. Isn't *that* what you said?"

Sherryl crushed out her cigarette. "Larry, I really wish you'd stop snapping at *me* every time you're mad at somebody." She got up and went to the end of the hall. "Caroline? Aren't you supposed to be in bed?"

Caroline's door squeaked shut. Sherryl watched the parallelogram of light on the hall floor diminish to a fine yellow line. "And turn off those lights, young lady. You heard me. Right now," Sherryl said. In high school Billy Mason had a crush on me, she thought, but I wouldn't give him the time of day. That morning she had seen Billy's picture on the cover of *Software World* at the supermarket.

"What I mean is, Larry, is that you're not the *only* person who's had a bad day sometimes—"

Sherryl was turning to face him when the telephone rang.

"Sometimes *my* day hasn't been that hot either," she said, and retreated to the telephone, picked up the receiver. "Hello?"

"Hi. Hello," the voice said. "I was hoping, well, I mean I didn't want to disturb anybody, but I wondered if Mr. Chambers was in. Mr. *Larry* Chambers, I think? Have I got that right?"

"This is his wife. Who's this?"

"Who is it?" Larry asked, picking up his pencil and jotting a number on his notepad.

Sherryl gazed expressionlessly over Larry's head at the dining room window and, beyond, the 7-Eleven marquee. The voice on the phone filled her ears like radio static. "—I mean, I just had the article here a moment ago, let me see . . . Look, tell him Hungry Bear called, and by the time he calls back I'll find the article—wait, in fact here it is right here—no, sorry, *that's* not it. But still, tell him Jim called. Jim Prideux—" Sherryl looked around the kitchen. She had forgotten to clean up after dinner. The sink was filled with dirty dishes, the countertop littered with bread crumbs. Stray Cheerios from that morning's breakfast had attached themselves like barnacles to the Formica table. She pulled up a chair and sat down, feeling suddenly tired. There was a television movie she had been looking forward to all week, and now, by the time she finished her cleaning, the show would practically be half over. She felt like saying to hell with it, to hell with all of it. She just wanted to go to bed. To hell with Larry, Caroline, the dishes, the vacuuming—every damn bit of it. The voice buzzed inconstantly in her ear like a mosquito, something about wolves, Navajo deities, sacred totems, irrepressible dreams of wolves, he wasn't exactly sure . . . Wolves wolves wolves, wolves every-where, she thought, and strengthened her grip on the receiver. "Listen to

me," she said. "Listen to me, Mr. Bear, or Mr. Prideux, or Mr. Whoever
You Are. Listen to me for just one minute, and I'll say this as *nicely* as I can.
Please don't call here anymore. Larry's not interested, *I'm* not interested.
Frankly, Mr. Bear, I don't think *anybody's* interested. I don't think anybody's
really interested at all."

In Sherryl's dream the men and wolves loped together across the white
plain. Larry was there, and Caroline, and Andy and Evelyn and Marty and
Beatrice. Sherryl recognized the mailman, the newspaper boy, supermarket
employees, former boyfriends and lovers. Even her parents were there, keeping pace with wolves under the cold moonlight. Everybody was dressed as
usual: The men wore slacks, ties, cuff links and starched shirts; the women
skirts, blouses, jewelry and high heels. Caroline carried one of her toys, Andy
his briefcase, Marty his racquetball racket and Larry one of his largest gray
Acco-Grip binders. Sherryl raised a greasy spatula in her right hand, a tarnished coffeepot in her left. We forgot to schedule Caroline's dental appointment, she told Larry. When I was a child you treated me as if I was stupid,
she told her father, but I wasn't stupid. The sky is filled with stars, she told
Davey Stewart, her high school sweetheart. The Milky Way: the Wolf's Trail.
But nobody responded, nobody even seemed to notice her. The bright air
was laced with the spoor of caribou. She felt a sudden elbow in her back; she
turned and awoke in a dark room, a stiff bed. I forgot the shopping today, she
thought. There isn't any milk in the house, or any coffee.

Beside her in bed, the man slowly moved.

Sherryl sat up, her pupils gradually dilating. Eventually she discerned the
motel room's clean, uncluttered angles. The thin and fragile dressing table,
the water glasses wrapped in wax paper, the hot plate, the aluminum-foil hot
cocoa packets.

"What's the matter, baby?" Andrew sat up beside her, his arm encircling
her waist. "Nightmare? Tell me, sweetheart. You can tell lover." He kissed
her neck, stroked her warm stomach.

"Please, Andy. Not now. Please." Sherryl climbed out of bed. Her clothes
lay folded on a wooden chair.

"Sorry. Forget it." Andrew rolled over, adjusted his pillow and listened to
the rustle of Sherryl's clothing.

Sherryl stood at the window, gazing out through the blinds. Stars and
moon were occluded by a high haze of lamplight. She heard the distant
hishing of street sweepers, and pulled on her blouse. Then she heard the rain
begin, drumming hollowly against the cheap plywood door.

Andrew took his watch from the end table. The luminous dial said almost
2:00 a.m. "I'll call you," he said.

"No," she said. "I'll call you this time. I need a few days to think." She opened the door and stepped out into the rain. They always do that, she thought. *They* have to be the ones who call, *they* have to be the ones who say when you'll meet or where you'll go. She pulled her coat collar up over her new perm, gripped the iron banister and descended one step at a time on darkling high heels. Puddles were already gathering on the warped cement stairs. "It's as if we don't have any brains of our own," she imagined herself telling Evelyn. "And I'm sure that's just what they think. That we haven't got the brains we were born with. That we have to be told *everything.*" By the time she climbed into the Volvo the rain had ceased, as abruptly as if someone had thrown a switch. Her coat was soaked through, and she laid it out on the backseat to dry.

At this hour, the streets were practically deserted. She drove past a succession of shops and restaurants: Bob's Big Boy, Li'l Pickle Sandwiches, Al's Exotic Birds, Ralph's Market. Inside Long's Drugs empty aisles of hair supplies, pet food, household appliances and vitamin supplements were illuminated by pale, watery fluorescents, like the inside of an aquarium. "It's not as if we couldn't do just as well without them," she would continue, awaiting Evelyn's quick nods of agreement. "I certainly didn't need to get married. I could have done just as well on my own. It's not as if it's some *man's* secret how to get by in this world. It's just a matter of keeping your feet on the ground, being objective about things, not fooling yourself. That's all there is to it. That's the big secret."

As she turned onto Beverly Glen her high beams, sweeping through an alleyway, reflected off a pair of attentive red eyes. Being realistic, she thought, and heard the wolves emerge from alleyways, abandoned buildings, underground parking garages, their black callused paws pattering like rain against the damp streets. They loped alongside her car for short distances, trailed off to gobble stray snails and mice, paused to bite and scratch their fleas. She refused to look, driving on through the deserted city. The alternating traffic lights cast shifting patterns and colors across the glimmering asphalt, like rotating spotlights on aluminum Christmas trees. Wolves, men, lovers, cars, streets, cities, worlds, stars. The real and the unreal, the true and the untrue. Unless you're careful it all starts looking like a dream, it all seems pretty strange and impossible, she thought, while all across the city the wolves began to howl.

THE LAST
AND DREADFUL HOUR

CHARLES L. GRANT

Summer, in Oxrun, died in a storm.

The afternoon had been warm for the last day of September, but the leaves had already started to turn, the ducks on the pond already gone in a twilight flight that called out to the village and brought on the dark. No one wore a coat, but sweaters were taken out to be aired in the yard, gloves were found in drawers and closets, and windows were checked for betrayals of draughts. Fur thickened, pavement hardened, boilers and furnaces practiced their steam.

It was warm for the last day of September, but those leaving work just after five saw the clouds on the horizon, moving toward the valley east of the tracks: white, and puffed, and sharp-edged against the blue. And the same drifting over the hills south and north, like desert clouds building their frozen billowing smoke: white, and puffed, and sharp-edged against the blue. And a single massive cloud that crawled out of the west, its shadow creeping across the fields like a shade drawn against the sun: grey, and boiling, and smothering the blue.

The wind began to blow just after six, in no particular direction as the clouds merged at their rims, forming a funnel above the village that looked up to the blue shrinking to the size of a platter, a coin, an eye that closed tightly when all the clouds turned to black.

Leaves ran in gutters, paper slapped against doors, dust in dark tornadoes bounced across the grass to explode against walls; hats were blown off, faces turned away, and on Fox Road near the cemetery a loose, flapping shutter chipped its paint against clapboard until a hinge snapped, a nail loosened, and it spun to the ground. The flag over the high school entrance began to shred. A line of wash on Barlow Street tore loose and was snagged on the branches of a dying pine. The sidewalk displays in front of Buller's Market were carted inside by clerks, who swore angrily when their aprons whipped their legs and their hair whipped their eyes. Neon flickered on, street lamps cast shadows, the amber light at Mainland Road and the Pike jerked and swayed, danced and spun, until it sputtered, brightened, and winked out without a sound.

The rain began just after seven.

The film in the Regency started just at seven-thirty.

The lights dimmed once, just after eight.

And summer, in Oxrun Station, died in a storm.

The Regency Theater was less than two years new, and had been constructed old-fashioned because the owner was tired of tiny figures on tiny screens pretending to be much larger than they were.

The exterior was deliberately houselike, red brick and white trim, no marquee and no posters, and the ticket booth was flush with the glass doors that flanked it. There were windows as well, white-curtained, with white tasseled shades pulled midway down the sash, and more than one visitor looked in to see what the living room was like.

What they saw was darkly polished black oak wainscoting topped with pearl-and-silver flocked paper, ivy and leaves and just a suggestion of trees; the thick wall-to-wall carpet was Oriental, floral, its background a royal blue and vacuumed three times a night; and along the back wall, between the entrances to the auditorium, were thickly upholstered high-backed couches, Queen Anne chairs, and silver ashtray stands. To the left and right in the corners were red-carpeted staircases leading to the balcony, and in shallow alcoves beside each a small concession stand.

But the Regency's pride was the theater itself.

The screen was a monster that tipped your head back when you sat in the front row, the ceiling slightly domed and painted in constellations that glowed for a moment when the houselights went down; the walls on the sides were draped in dark red velvet, the seats upholstered and wide; and there was a steep-angled balcony that extended ten rows over the main floor. A uniformed usher with a hooded flashlight guided the way to patrons' places; there were Saturday matinees that showed nothing but old horror films, five cartoons, and a trailer, and the manager could usually be found standing stiffly at the back, unafraid to eject the rowdy and keep the popcorn in its boxes.

And as the last show ended, the credits still running and the lights slowly brightening in their bronze brackets on the walls, the electricity failed and the building went dark.

"Oh, wonderful," Ellery muttered and slumped back in his seat, glaring at the dark as if he could bring the lights back simply by threatening them with damnation. It was, without question, the only possible end to an already miserable day, and he wasn't surprised when the manager's voice soon came over the sound system and apologized for the inconvenience, asking the customers still remaining to please stay where they were until the staff came around with lights to guide them out.

Why the hell not, he thought; if I go home, the place will have probably been struck by lightning.

He heard without listening to the voices drifting around him—only a few, if he was right, and someone laughing giddily in the balcony.

A minute passed, too long for his comfort, and a man to his far left began a strident complaint, arguing with someone, evidently his wife. He couldn't see who it was, couldn't see anyone at all, and the more he strained, the closer he came to giving himself a headache. The people in the balcony—there couldn't have been more than two—laughed even louder, and the noise echoed in the huge auditorium, merging, distorting, and soon after, he felt the first tear of perspiration grow cold on his brow.

"Easy, El," he whispered, and pulled his raincoat close to his chest. "Take it easy. It won't last."

But the perspiration was there, and the muffled thunder above, the sounds of things—people!—moving without waiting for someone to help them.

"Easy," he said, but he couldn't help the acid that started to build in his stomach.

He didn't like the dark.

It was stupid, and it was silly, and most certainly childish. But no matter how often he told himself at home that he could easily close the bedroom drapes and keep out the streetlight and moonlight without any problem, he didn't. The shadows were better than no shadows at all, and a lamp burned in the living room until he came down for breakfast.

Another minute, and he shook out his raincoat, touched his throat, and stood, grabbing for the seat in front and sidling to his left until he reached the aisle, proud he hadn't sliced open his shin on the chairs' curved metal legs. The manager once again assured them they would soon be able to see, but he couldn't wait. He wanted to get out. He wanted to see something, even if it were only shadows against a lighter dark.

Then the lobby doors swung open and shimmering white swept down the aisle. There was good-humored applause, suddenly excited chatter, and soon he was able to distinguish black figures easing out of the rows, the complaining man now laughing along with those still upstairs.

He paused for a moment, struggling into his raincoat and scolding himself for almost losing control. But it was, he thought, symptomatic of the way things had been going these past few days—as if he had been latched onto by a gremlin determined to make him look like a fool.

Nice, he thought then; good sane thinking, El. Keep it up, they'll have you safely locked away before you can sneeze.

His arm caught in a sleeve where the lining was frayed. He closed his eyes, took a breath, and rammed it through, smiling when he felt the worn threads tear at the wrist.

And as he watched the others file toward the lobby, he frowned in the realization he had been practically alone for the entire show. Not that it was surprising. The storm had renewed itself vigorously just after he'd decided that sitting home alone wasn't going to do his depression any good. The bars were out because he wasn't much of a drinker, there was no one he could call for a shoulder to use, and going back to the botch he had made of his day's work would only depress him further. So he came to a movie. And even now he'd be hard-pressed to explain what it had been about.

A figure partially blocked the glow at the head of his aisle, large and formless, hands on its wide hips as it kicked doorstops into place. Callum Davidson, the manager, shepherding his people out of the abyss. Ellery sighed and started up, the dim light slowing him so he wouldn't trip on a chair leg or stumble over his own feet. Davidson turned and left; another figure took his place, one with a flashlight that aimed straight into his eyes. He turned his head, raised a hand, and the usher apologized, lowered the beam to the floor, and waited.

At the back row, Ellery smoothed his coat's lapels and turned around, to see the screen framed in black; it looked as if it were glowing.

"Weird, huh?" the usher said, stabbing his flashlight at the stage. "Happens all the time. Absorbs the light or something, Mr. Davidson says, and makes it look like some kind of monster TV screen."

"Seth," Ellery said to the young man sourly, "Mr. Davidson has a lousy imagination."

The usher shrugged.

Easy, Ellery told himself; it isn't the kid's fault.

He turned to apologize, and lifted his head when he heard what he thought was someone falling, and falling hard. Seth heard it, too, and after exchanging alarmed glances, they stepped back down the aisle, trying to see past the flashlight's reach, listening for a moan or a crying or someone swearing as he got back to his feet. But the only sounds were the distant rumble of thunder and the muffled chatter of the people in the lobby.

"I heard it," he said when they reached the first row, the screen looming behind him. "I know I did."

Seth shifted the light from one hand to the other and rubbed his chest nervously. "I know. Me, too. Here," and they moved to the other aisle and

started back up, slowly, then more rapidly as they approached the last seats
and Ellery had about decided they had made a mistake.

They found him in the corner, slumped on the floor.

"Oh, Jesus," the usher said as Ellery squeezed into the row, his shadow
blotting out the fallen man until Seth ran around the back wall and poked the
light through the short drapes that blocked the lobby's glow from the theater.
The brass rings that held the velvet on its rod rattled too much like bones, and
Ellery knelt quickly, reached out a hand and pulled it back.

"You'd better get Callum," he said, and was handed the long silver cylin-
der.

The man was old without an age, his hair sparse and white, his face lightly
tinged as if he had jaundice. His coat was worn, and when Ellery pulled back
a lapel, he saw a suit underneath, a white shirt, a black knitted tie pulled away
from the collar. The eyes were closed, but a touch of his hand to the man's
boney chest and the side of his scrawny neck proved a heartbeat, which made
him sigh and lean back, wipe a hand over his forehead and dry it on his thigh.

Davidson arrived in a hurry and leaned over the wall, staring as Ellery
played the flashlight along the old man's body.

"Is he dead?"

"No."

"What the hell happened?"

"I guess he tripped."

"Wonderful."

"God, you think maybe he had a heart attack or something?" Seth whispered, a suggestion Ellery didn't want to hear and the manager snorted at.

"You know who he is, El?"

He shook his head. "Never saw him before."

"Is there something wrong?" a voice asked, and he looked to the end of
the row, at a young woman peering anxiously through the gloom.

"Toni?" he said.

She took a step in. "Mr. Phillips? Mr. Phillips, are you okay?"

"It's not me, thank god," he answered, stood, and pointed at the old man.
"Let me take a look."

He looked at Davidson and shrugged *why not?*, pressing as best he could
against the seatback behind him while she squeezed past. She was wearing a
white T-shirt and washed-out jeans, and it was all he could do to resist
patting her rump as she passed. When she knelt down, he explained softly to
Callum that she was a student at Hawksted College, her father a doctor and
she studying to be the same. She used to come often to the bookshop, and
there were times, more than several, when he wished he were ten years
younger.

"He's knocked his head pretty good," she said without looking up. "There's a nasty bruise here."

"Heart attack?" Callum asked.

"No, I doubt it. But I think you'd better get a doctor here just in case."

"Toni," Ellery said softly, "we can't leave him there on the floor."

"It's okay to move him, if that's what you're worried about," she answered. "Just be careful of his head, okay?" Then she straightened, rubbed a hand over the back of her neck, and waved him out to the aisle. He grinned and did as he was told, thanked her when she joined him, took her arm and pulled her down a pace while Davidson and Seth moved to carry the old man to the manager's office.

"I haven't seen you for a while," he said quietly, feeling the dark on his back, watching the two men swaying away with their burden.

She looked up at him and, after a long moment's study, smiled sadly. His hand was taken in hers, and he felt the cold there in her long, soft fingers, as he felt a cold he hadn't noticed before filling the auditorium, seeping through the walls from the storm outside. It made him shiver and hunch his shoulders, and she tightened her grip briefly before letting him go.

"I've been around," she whispered.

"Busy with the new semester?" and let her pull him slowly up the aisle toward the light.

She shook her head. "I didn't go back."

"What? No kidding. Well, why not, Toni? I thought you were doing so well."

She stopped and faced him, eyes hidden in shadow, features blurred. "Things are different, Mr. Phillips," she said, in a quiet voice, a low voice.

He wasn't sure what to say, didn't know what she meant and called himself a damned fool for just standing there and smiling.

Then she tilted her head to one side, her lips slightly parted, colorless, and dry. "Have you ever been to the orchard, Mr. Phillips?"

"Huh? What are you . . . what orchard?"

"There's an orchard. On the other side of Mainland Road, on the old Armstrong farm. Some of it's dead, some of it's not."

He shifted to step around her, to move up the aisle back to the others. He hadn't the slightest idea what the hell she was talking about, but he was afraid she had changed too much for him to know her.

"It's really nice there," she said still whispering, taking a sidestep to block him. "I had a picnic there once."

"Picnics are good things," he told her, wincing at how inane he must sound. "I used to go on them myself when I was younger." Thinking: She's on something, that's why she's not in school anymore. What a hell of a thing to happen to such a nice kid. A hell of a thing. "But I have to admit I've never—"

"It's cold there," she said. "Really cold."

He looked over her shoulder for someone to help him, and unconsciously pulled his raincoat closed against the chill that still worked the theater.

"Toni, look, why don't we—"

"Be careful," she whispered then. "I wasn't kidding before. Things are different now, Mr. Phillips. Things aren't ever going to be the same."

And before he could move away, she leaned against him and kissed his cheek, released his hand, and ran away.

Leaving him in the flickering twilight of the auditorium, one finger touching the cold mark of her lips while thunder whispered in the black above his head.

Seconds later, realizing he had been left alone, he rushed into the lobby, paused to let his eyes adjust to the light, then turned left and stepped into Davidson's small, cluttered office beside the concession stand. Seth was waiting glumly by the door. The old man was lying on a leather couch, his overcoat for a blanket.

"Did you call the police, a doctor?" he asked.

Davidson shook his head and pointed to his desk. "Phone's out. Someone will have to go for one."

"He's going to have a hell of a headache when he wakes up," he said, nodding toward a faint bruise on the old man's temple. "He must have hit the wall, or an armrest, on his way down."

"Great. A lawsuit is just what I need."

Ellery hesitated, unsure what to do next. He could offer to wait with Callum until someone came, but he barely knew him, and Davidson's size—well over six feet, with the weight to go with it—made him feel uncomfortable. He smiled weakly, looked again at the unconscious man on the couch, and went into the lobby as the manager began suggesting that Seth, if he were a truly good human being, should volunteer to fetch the doctor.

When the door closed behind him, he headed for the nearest exit, buttoning his coat, preparing to leave. But he stopped when he saw Katherine Avalon, part owner of the record shop, standing in the middle of the floor, head back, staring up at a huge chandelier whose teardrop crystals were reflecting and amplifying the light from the candelabra set at each of the concession counters and on two of the low Sheraton tables between the couches and chairs.

"Wow," she said excitedly. "Hey, look at this. God, they look just like stars!"

No one moved, and he noted with a puzzled frown that if all the people in the lobby were the only ones who had come to the late show that night, the theater had been a lot more empty than it felt.

There were only six, including a couple sitting on the center couch, and another pair much younger on the far staircase, sharing a cigarette.

Something was wrong.

He glanced back at the office.

Something . . . and he saw it. In the glass doors that led to the street. The black outside.

Jesus, he thought, and walked over to take a look.

In the candleglow that stretched weakly to the curb, he saw the rain— sheets and lashes of it exploding on the pavement, driven in hard slants and silvered cyclones by the wind charging down Park Street, sweeping around the corner, spilling over the theater roof, and slamming against the doors. At times it rattled against the glass like pellets of ice, sending white webs to the frames and obscuring the street; then the wind took another direction, and he saw black rivers rushing high in the gutters.

He turned, pointing behind him in amazement, and let his arm drop.

That's what was wrong.

Not the rain—the people. No one had their coats on; no one was leaving.

Flustered for a moment, and blaming his reaction on Toni's odd behavior, he forced himself with a deep breath to relax, understanding that those who stayed behind were probably hoping the rain would ease soon, or the wind calm down, to give them a chance outside without drowning on their feet. Cozy, he thought then; just like in the movies, where everybody gets to know everybody else, secrets are spilled, murders are committed, and when the sun shines again, the hero and heroine walk off to a new life. He chuckled at the images that formed and re-formed, and decided that he might as well do the same. He took off his coat and wandered over to the nearest refreshment stand, grunted when he saw the clerk had already gone, and jumped when a hand lightly tapped his shoulder.

"Nerves, El?" Katherine said.

He laughed and leaned back against the display case. "Just had a sudden attack of the hungries, that's all."

She patted his stomach and shook a finger at him. "Hungries, at your age, will get you a pot."

"At my age, I'm lucky to get the hungries at all," he answered, not at all sure he was making any sense, and knowing he seldom did when she was around. Ever since he had taken the job to manage Yarrow's a year ago, he had not lost a single opportunity to get a glimpse of her whenever he walked to the luncheonette for his noon meal; he had even, for a stretch of three weeks during the winter, tried to time his arrival on Centre Street with hers. It made him feel like a jerk. And he felt even worse when he twice asked her to dinner and was twice refused—politely, even regretfully—but he hadn't found the courage to ask her out again.

A sudden splash of rain against the doors made her turn around. "I think I'm on the Ark, you know?"

Then Seth came out of the office, bundled in a green plastic poncho, a floppy-brimmed hat, and holding an umbrella a dazzling red. He grimaced comically when Ellery lifted an eyebrow, ignored good-natured jeers from the others, and stood at the exit. Waited. Lifted his shoulders and pushed through, and they flinched at the wind that sailed into the room. Several candles went out, and the rest danced unpleasant shadows on the floor and the walls.

The usher hadn't gone two steps before the storm yanked the umbrella from his hands. There was a brilliant burst of blue-white that turned the rain to silver slashes as he hurried to the curb; and in the afterimage, after Seth had vanished, Ellery was sure the boy had thrown up his hands.

"Christ, will you look at that damned rain," a man said from the couch. The woman beside him shifted uneasily. "I think we ought to leave now, Gary. It doesn't look like it's going to get any better." She blinked then when she realized the others were watching, and a faint blush darkened her already darkly rouged cheeks. Her husband leaned toward her and lay a hand on her leg. She sat back, her fingers busily twisting a handkerchief, her eyes on the chandelier.

Ellery looked away, embarrassed for the woman's fear and understanding it perfectly. Storms like this were better suffered at home, not in the company of strangers. He leaned his forearms on the top of the glass case and stared at the empty popcorn machine.

Katherine mimicked his stance and whispered, "Paula Richards."

"What?"

"That's Paula Richards," she said, lowering her voice still further.

"No kidding? Of *the* Richards?"

She nodded.

"I'll be damned."

He had never seen any of that family before, knew them only by reputation as a somewhat reclusive clan, and by their address on Williamston Pike, assuming it was one of the estates that lined the road out to the valley. Once a month, at least since he'd worked there, one of the household staff dropped by the store and ordered over a hundred dollars' worth of books. All sorts of books. All in paperback. And once a month, another staff member came by to pick them up.

A quick guilty glance, and he nodded to himself. She was slender, and rather pretty in spite of the severe tweed suit, the unruffled white blouse, the shoes almost large enough to be brogans. The effect was, in fact, almost pathetic, straight out of a Forties' film, the plain-jane clerk waiting for Cary Grant and getting instead the man he'd guessed rightly was her husband, himself in a dark blue tailored suit, and a pair of sneakers that had seen better days.

Again he turned around, leaned back, stuffed his hands in his pockets. Katherine said something before turning as well, and he stared dumbly at her.

"As a cat," she repeated with a gently mocking smile. "As in 'as nervous as.' That's you."

"It shows?"

A wink for a nod. "Bad day?"

"Bad day. Bad week. Bad month. I think I'll go outside and throw myself into the gutter."

Understatement, he thought. The owners of the bookstore had been watching him closely for the past few weeks, doublechecking his bookkeeping without being obvious about it, suggesting more than once—and kindly, he had to admit—that perhaps he might like to take the vacation time he'd accumulated over the year. But he couldn't leave. From home to store to home again he was safe, prevented by his work and his solitude from making the mistakes that had brought him here in the first place. The bumbling, foolish errors that had cost him his previous job, his previous lover, and all jobs and lovers before them. A therapist had told him—no charge, El, you're a friend—he was tailoring his own excuses for running back home from a world that didn't know he existed. He wasn't sure. It didn't matter. He was home, after twenty years, and nothing had changed.

Katherine lay a hand on his arm, stroked it once, and gave him sympathy with a look. Then she tilted her head toward the office door. "Who's the old guy?"

"I don't know. He fell."

"Is he all right?"

"Toni says so. Just hit his head. Seth's gone for—"

"Toni?" she said, eyes wide now and the smile broad. "Toni who?"

"Toni Keane," he answered peevishly, not liking her tone, thinking she knew of his infatuation and was rubbing it in. "She's Doctor Keane's—" He scanned the lobby for her and frowned. "Guess she's in the ladies' room."

The couple on the balcony steps were whispering and passing another cigarette back and forth, and he watched them for a minute, envious of the boy's hand draped casually over her shoulder, the tips of his fingers just brushing across the top of her breast, envious of the girl's self-assurance that didn't force her to drive them away with a pout for convention. The sexual revolution, he thought glumly; only they didn't come by and draft me. The rats.

Davidson stalked out of the office then, scowling, his raincoat on. "Phone's still out," he announced as he slapped a hat on his head. "Seth's not back. I'll head over to the police, okay, folks? Don't worry about a thing. See you in a minute."

And he was gone before anyone could say a word, the door wind-slammed behind him, rain spattering in on the carpet, the candles dancing and dying again.

Though Ellery waited for it, half expected it, there was no bolt of lightning. The manager strode through the light, into the black, and all they could hear was the hiss of running water.

"I'll be damned," said Gary Richards as he pushed off the couch and walked to the door. "Can you beat that? He just walked out, just like that. God, some people, you know?"

His wife stood as if to join him, saw Ellery and smiled shyly. When he returned the smile, she walked over hesitantly, nodded politely to Katherine, and said, "Excuse me, but you . . . you're the man from Yarrow's, aren't you?"

"And you're the lady who's keeping us in business."

Her laugh was high and quiet, though it didn't quite reach to her eyes. "I like to read," she said apologetically. "There isn't much else to do, really." A movement of her hand. "Gary's always busy with this and that and the business. I—" She paused, ducked her head, lifted it again. "He thinks I'm going to ruin my eyes."

"Never," he said. "Look at me. I read all the time, and I'm only half blind."

Paula Richards stared, then laughed again. "I guess we'd better go. We, uh . . . it doesn't look like it's going to stop anytime soon."

"Think of this as a dream," he said as she turned to leave. "Your head or mine."

Again she blinked. "I read about them, you know. Dreams. It's very interesting."

"Yes, you are," and he smiled, wider when she put a hand to her cheek and looked as if, before she turned away, the one thing in the world she wanted to do most was to wink at him and grin.

As she walked away, Katherine nudged his side with a soft elbow. "That was very nice."

"She seems like a nice woman."

"So am I when you get to know me," she said, and headed for the ladies' room on the lobby's other side.

He gaped, not caring that he probably looked as if he'd just been punched in the stomach. He wasn't so dense that he missed her intent, but the courage to follow her was blocked by a loud round of swearing. Richards was standing by the lefthand exit, his hands on the glass. Paula was behind him, a palm on his shoulder, pulling him back gently.

"No, damnit!" the man said angrily. "I will not calm down!" He turned to the others, face dark and eyes wide in indignation. Even the couple on the staircase looked at him curiously. "It's locked," Richards announced, kicking back with one heel. Then he pushed his wife to one side and tried the other door. "Damn! I don't believe it! Both of them! I mean . . . that stupid manager's locked us all in."

Ellery doubted it. In the first place, it didn't make any sense to do something like that. In the second place, Davidson simply hadn't had the time; he had just walked out into the storm without stopping, without even turning around. But when Richards saw the expression on his face and challenged him with a look, he tried them himself, leaned down and peered at the tiny gap between the door and frame.

"What did I tell you?" Richards said over his shoulder, "The stupid sonofa—"

"It isn't locked," Ellery said, and pointed. "The bolt's not over." When he pushed, however, it didn't give. He pulled, and pulled harder. Pushed a second time and watched as Richards did the same on the other side. "Maybe all the water's warped the frames or something."

"They're aluminum," the man said sarcastically. "How the hell is that gonna warp? Jesus."

"What about the fire exits?"

They turned at the question, saw the boy on the staircase coming down toward them.

"You want to break a leg going in there, Scotty?" Richards said sarcastically as he pointed to the auditorium doors. "It's pitch black, for god's sake. But go ahead, I don't care." He looked at Ellery and rolled his eyes. "The kid's a jerk. He works for his old man, gardening and stuff. The old man couldn't grow sand in a desert."

Ellery said nothing. He didn't know the boy, and right now didn't much care for Gary Richards. He checked the doors again to give himself something to do, knowing it had to be a warp of some kind because doors didn't lock without a bolt turning over, and they sure as hell didn't lock on their own.

Another push for good measure, another pull that nearly wrenched his shoulder, and he went into the office in hopes of finding some sort of clue as to the doors' closing, maybe something to do with new turns in electronics. Scotty was taking the usher's flashlight from a shelf on the wall. They exchanged a look that condemned Richards and, at the same time, forged no abrupt alliances. Then he was gone, and Ellery scratched the side of his nose, rubbed its tip, and knew he was wasting his time. A single candle burned feebly on the desk, and as far as he could tell, there was no exit here. The old man was still on the couch, still unconscious, and snoring. Ellery grinned at him, wished him luck, and returned to the lobby.

The far doors to the auditorium were swinging slowly and soundlessly shut; the young girl was still on the staircase, and she waved to him, grinned, and made a face at Richards. He grinned and waved back, took another step and rubbed his palms briskly. It was getting cold in here, the same flat cold he had felt earlier, and by the expressions on the others, they felt it as well.

The doors stopped swinging.

A fresh fall of rain slapped against the glass, and Paula jumped away as if she'd been drenched. Her husband swore and glared at the pavement, threatening Davidson in absentia and damning the storm in the same breath.

There was thunder. No lightning. The creak of a floorboard, the squeal of a hinge.

Ellery pulled at the bottom of his sport jacket, pulled at his shirt as if he were wearing a tie too tight for his throat. And he watched in amazement as the candles on the refreshment counter across the lobby began to sputter, to smoke, and one by one flare out. It left only six burning, on a table by the wall, and he stared at them, too, waiting for them to die and leave them all in the dark.

As it was, the room pulled in on itself, the light barely reaching the exits, not touching the rain at all. All he could hear then was the hiss, and the slap, the ghosts of the storm scratching to get in.

Ellery pulled back his jacket sleeve and looked at his watch; it was just past eleven. Davidson had left for the police nearly thirty minutes ago, and Scotty had been in the auditorium for just about ten. He considered checking on the boy, but Katherine came out of the rest room and stopped, a hand waving briefly in front of her face until she realized what had happened to the rest of the light. By then he was beside her, explaining quickly about the doors, ignoring the increasingly loud curses Richards was spouting despite his wife's gentle pleading to please stay calm.

Then he heard another voice, plaintive and small. "Scotty?"

It was the girl on the staircase, and without thinking he climbed three steps to sit in front of her, Katherine climbing two more to kneel at her side.

"Hi," he said. "I'm Ellery Phillips."

She was terrified. Her blonde hair had been ribbon-tied into a pony tail, and she had pulled it over her shoulder to stroke it quickly, hold it, while her free hand rubbed her arm for warmth. When he repeated his name and laid a finger on her knee to get her attention, she glanced fearfully at the auditorium doors, back to him, then to Katherine.

"Ginny," she said, sounding no more than six. "Ginny Amerton."

"Oh, yeah," he said with a mock scowl. "Your dad's been trying to sell me a Mercedes for a zillion years. I keep telling him he'll have to pay for half, and he keeps throwing me out."

The smile for his effort was feeble, but it was a smile nonetheless. "We're trapped in here, right?"

He shook his head immediately. "Ginny, how can you get trapped in a movie theater? Scotty's checking the fire exits, right? And if they're locked like these here, we'll . . ." He looked over his shoulder at Richards pacing the lobby, Paula now slumped on the ticket taker's stool. He lowered his voice. "We'll use the creep over there to break the glass."

Katherine laughed quietly, and poked the girl's arm until she broke and laughed too.

Thunder shook the walls.

Another candle went out.

Ellery exaggerated a groan as he stretched his arms over his head and stood. "Guess I'll go see how Scotty's doing." And with a look asked Katherine to stay behind with the girl. She nodded; he smiled and backed down to the floor, telling himself there was nothing to worry about, all will soon be revealed. When Paula saw him moving and half rose from the stool, he pointed to the doors. She shrugged, and Richards gave no indication he either cared or would join him.

Wonderful, he thought as he pushed into the auditorium; this is just great.

And he thought it again when the door closed silently behind him, and the only light came from a pebbled glass square over his shoulder.

He didn't call out; he didn't want to worry Ginny. Instead, he walked to the head of the center aisle and searched for the flashlight's beam, down at the exits flanking the stage, and on either side of him in the wide corridor that ran behind the seats.

Black; nothing but black. And no response when he whispered, "Scotty, hey, Scotty!" as loud as he dared.

Christ, the kid probably fell or something, he decided, and made his way along the wall to the lefthand fire door, grabbed the crossbar, and shoved down. It didn't move. When he tried to pull it up, his hands slipped and he nearly fell on his back. The opposite door was the same—iron, sounding hollow when he kicked it, not budging when he put his shoulder to it and pushed as hard as he could. His soles slipped on the worn carpeting. His palms coated the bar with sweat and his fingers lost their grip.

No sweat, he thought; the other ones.

Down the side aisle, then, keeping one hand on the wall and moving slowly in case he met Scotty along the way, speaking the boy's name and damning him for not answering. He probably thought it was a practical joke. He was probably already back in the lobby, and the others were just waiting to yell "Surprise!" when he came out.

The exits were locked.

He glanced toward the lobby doors to reassure himself of the light, then decided he might as well do a little checking on his own as long as he was here. Just don't take too long, he told himself; don't take too long.

But there was nothing on the stage when he climbed awkwardly up and poked around in the small storage spaces behind the velvet curtains. The screen was fixed to the cinder-block wall behind; there was no room for a door, much less a place for someone to hide.

Damned stupid kid, he thought, dusting off his hands and shirt, hating to think that Richards had been right.

Then he heard a scream, muffled, prolonged, and a sudden babble of voices that sent him leaping to the floor, colliding with a series of armrests until he found the center aisle and charged up. The light from the door window was flickering wildly, and he thought for a moment a fire had broken out—one of the candles had tipped over somehow, igniting the carpet. He was trying to remember if he'd seen a fire extinguisher as he pushed through, and stumbled to a halt.

Gary was standing in front of one of the doors, a chair in his hands. Paula was kneeling on the floor, crying. Katherine and Ginny were waiting at the bottom of the staircase, and it was clear from the girl's face it was she who had screamed.

"What?" he demanded.

Scotty wasn't there.

"What?" Richards said angrily, almost shouting. "Hell, I'll show you what," and he lifted the chair over his head, almost overbalanced before bringing it down on the door.

The glass didn't break.

One of the legs did.

Bewildered, Ellery watched as the man staggered to the door on the right and tried it again, twice, this time sending the seat spinning to the floor. Then he threw the chair as hard as he could against the glass wall of the ticket seller's booth. It trembled, but didn't shatter. As far as Ellery could see, it didn't even crack.

"Scotty," the girl said at last, and they turned one by one. "Where's Scotty? Mr. Phillips, where's Scotty?"

He had no answer to give her, but he began to wonder if this was something more than just a prank. Someone on the outside didn't want them leaving, and he immediately recalled hostage situations he had read about, seen on television, had heard about from customers coming into the store. But it didn't make sense. The only ones here who had any kind of money for things like ransom were the Richards, and by now the street should have been filled with police cars, lights, sirens, with someone from some lunatic paramilitary group making all sorts of demands for the reporters and cameras.

Yet there was nothing out there.

Nothing but the rain, the thunder, the occasional glare of lightning.

And it didn't explain why the glass didn't break.

Oh, god, he thought, and walked over to the door. His breath smoked a circle, and he wiped it away with one finger.

"Somebody? Please, where's Scotty?"

There were no lights at all out there.

The streetlamps were dark, the shops on Centre Street, the houses, even the white globes in front of the police station. No cars passed, no trucks.

He cupped his hands around his eyes and waited for the next bolt, and when it came, he managed not to blink.

Nothing.

No outlines of buildings, no reflections on the road.

The rain, and the curb, and the rushing black water.

He heard footsteps and whirled to see Ginny taking the stairs up two at a time, Katherine with her hand outstretched and looking to him for help. He wanted to shrug, but when Richards continued to do nothing but pace, he trotted over and peered up to the landing where the staircase jogged to the right.

"What happened?"

"She thinks Scotty's hiding up there. She thinks . . . she's got the idea someone drugged the refreshments and now Scotty's gone off the deep end or something."

Her voice was barely under control, and when he put a hand to her shoulder, he could see a throbbing at her temple before she brushed at her hair and covered it.

"Maybe we ought to leave her alone," he said. "She'll be back when she can't find him."

"She could get hurt, El," she said. "That's steep up there. God, suppose she gets to the bottom and falls."

"Scotty didn't come out," he said, hoping it was a question and taking a breath when Katherine shook her head. "Then maybe he climbed up somehow. He could be trying the doors to the fire escape." Then, suddenly, he looked to the stairs and frowned, looked around the lobby and snapped his fingers. "Toni," he said. "Damn, I forgot all about Toni."

When she looked puzzled he reminded her of the girl he had mentioned before this all started.

"Sorry, I don't remember."

He described her.

"Nope. No bells, sorry. She must have left already."

"But how?" he said, struggling with frustration. "The doors, remember?"

"Davidson left. So did that usher. She must have gone out the same way."

He wanted to ask, to demand to know why they couldn't do the same and get the hell home. Instead, he wondered aloud if the young woman wasn't in the ladies' room, until Katherine told him she had been in there alone.

"Oh, Jesus," he said wearily. "Damn, don't tell me she's lying someplace, hurt like Scotty must be. Christ."

Paula was still on the floor, staring into her lap. "The exits are all locked, aren't they."

He wanted to lie, but there was nothing to gain and she would know it anyway. "As far as I can tell, yes. They must be blocked somehow from the outside."

"Great," Richards said bitterly. "Just . . . shit."

"El," Katherine said then. "What the hell's going on?"

"It's my money," Richards said. "That's probably what it is, you know. Any minute now, some asshole is going to pop up through the floor and demand all my money and a fast plane to Cuba." He wrestled off his tie and tossed it aside. "Dumb shit. Who the hell does he think he is?"

Ellery didn't say a word, not surprised the man had come to the same conclusion he had, though he knew it wasn't right, not right at all.

The night was too dark, and . . . he shuddered, exhaled, and exhaled again when he thought he saw the ghost of his breath. A third time proved him wrong, but the cold didn't leave him.

"El?" Katherine said. "El, please, what's going on? Is he right? Is that what it is?"

"I don't know." And he wished they would stop looking to him for answers. He didn't know anything, and he didn't know how to find out, but for the time being, to keep himself from thinking too much, he could get Ginny back here with the rest, and maybe find Toni in the bargain.

Taking one of the candles then, and hissing when a drop of wax landed on his wrist, he cupped his hand around the flame and started up. Katherine moved to go with him, paused halfway to the landing, and changed her mind with a nervous smile. When he reached the turn and looked down, she had already gone back to Paula and was helping her to the couch. He couldn't see Gary at all, only heard him kicking at the pieces of the chair he had broken.

Insane, he thought as he rounded the corner and started up the second flight; it's crazy.

"Ginny!"

At the top of the stairs was a narrow passageway. It ran the width of the building and, like the floor below, had a low wall on the left, broken in the center and both ends for the step-aisles down. The righthand wall was blank save for a pair of large-framed wildlife prints that needed a good dusting.

"Toni?"

There was thunder.

"Toni Keane, where are you? Are you okay?"

He looked down the side aisle, lifting his shoulders against the wintery cold, lifting the candle high and away from his eyes.

"Ginny, c'mon, answer me! He's not up here. C'mon!"

To the center aisle, a draught snaking about his ankles, and he stepped through the gap, took the first step down, and felt his temper begin to flare.

"Toni! Ginny! What the hell's going on?"

Shifting his fingers to escape a run of hot wax. Keeping his face slightly averted so not to be blinded by the white of the flame and the halo around it.

"Damnit, Ginny, will you show yourself for god's sake?"

Another step, and a third.

Candlelight shimmered shadows across the empty seats, shifting them back and forth, raising the far end of the row and rolling the backs toward him like gelid waves in a black sea. It was a dizzying effect, and he closed his eyes for a moment, opened them, and saw the girl pressed against the far wall. Her hands were out to the sides, her eyes so wide he could see nothing but white, and her shirt was pulled out of the waistband of her jeans.

"Jesus, Ginny," he said, not bothering to disguise his relief. He made his way along a row toward her, holding the candle higher. "Jesus, why the hell didn't you answer me, huh? You've got me scared half to death." He tried a laugh and gave it up, shifted the candle into his left hand; and ignored a sudden sharp burning at the base of his thumb. "You haven't seen Toni, have you? No, of course not. You don't even know her. Look, why don't you just—"

Her head began rocking slowly side to side, her outstretched arms were trembling, but she didn't move, didn't speak, and it hit him that she might have found Scotty after all; from the terror she showed him, it wasn't going to be nice.

His attention snapped then to the floors between the rows, but he couldn't see anything down there but a few crushed cigarette butts, burnt matches, an empty box of popcorn, a half-filled paper cup of soda, another one on its side.

And his own shadow darting into the gaps, darting away, disappearing.

He could hear her breathing when he was halfway along—harsh, quick, prelude to a scream.

"Take it easy," he said quietly. "Take it easy, Ginny, it's only me."

He moved again, watching her head rock faster and faster while her legs began to palsy, one heel thumping hollow against the baseboard. Softly, then loudly, and softly again. Her gaze shifting into puzzled focus on his face, her lips quivering for a moment before closing. He smiled at her and checked the rows above and below him, seeing nothing at all until he saw her feet. They were bare, and he realized she had stopped drumming on the wall.

"Okay, Ginny," he said. And stopped.

She had relaxed, and somehow the ribbon from her ponytail had come undone and was draped now over one shoulder, almost lost in the spray of her dark blonde hair. The shirt was open three buttons down, exposing pale breasts against a tanned chest and a small white rose in the center of her bra.

He heard a soft click, looked down, and saw a button bounce on the floor and roll out of sight.

"Ginny, what's—"

The shirt was completely open, and she hadn't moved her hands. The snap of her jeans was undone, the plane of her stomach gold in the candlelight, pushing slowly out, sighing slowly in.

"Ginny," he said harshly, damning his shadow now growing on the wall, covering her, shading her bronze. "Ginny, where is Scotty? Can you tell me where Scotty is? Is he hurt?"

She smiled at him, innocence and seduction. Her jeans were crumpled at her feet, and the shirt slipped over her shoulder while he watched, hissing when it caught at her waist, hissing again when it slid to the floor. He turned away as if looking for someone to witness what was happening here, turned back to see her reach her arms out toward him. Reluctantly, he stepped closer, shaking his head at her, trying by his expression to tell her she didn't know what she was doing.

Wax poured onto his hand, and he cursed, dropped the candle, and the flame died on the wick.

"Goddamn," he muttered, raising an angry fist toward the girl, lowering it slowly when he realized he could still see her. The candle was out. The light hadn't gone. It still lay his hovering shadow over her face, still coated her with colors the flame never had.

Hallelujah, he thought; someone's finally fixed the electricity.

"Okay, kiddo," he said sternly. "Let's stop the nonsense, all right? They'll be coming up to see how you are, and I don't want them to find you like this. So look, do us both a big favor and pick up—"

He had turned to hurry back along the row to the center aisle, and said no more when he saw the exit signs over the fire doors still unlit, the bulbs recessed in the ceiling still dark. A hand grabbed for a seat back. The balcony was black except where he stood.

"Ellery," Ginny whispered, not the voice of a girl.

He ordered himself not to look.

"Ellery."

He didn't understand the light, but he knew full well what the girl wanted, what she was trying to do. Her mind had snapped, no question about it, probably from something she had stumbled on up here, something he hadn't yet seen himself. And if he looked now, he would only encourage her; if he turned, he wouldn't know how to get her dressed again without using force, and he knew what that would look like should anyone come up to see what was taking him so long in his search.

"Ellery."

"Ginny, for Christ's sake, would you knock it off and—"

Her hand gripped his shoulder and twisted viciously, until he either had to turn or sprawl over the chairs. His jacket tore at the seam as if it were paper, his shirt tore as well, and there was a fire along his skin that made him hiss and yank free, stumbling back until he grabbed an armrest and steadied.

"Ellery."

Her eyes were dull orange, her teeth lengthened to fangs, her hair was a nest of spitting black serpents.

He screamed and his left arm lashed out, catching her on the temple and tumbling her into the next row, where she regained her feet before he could turn and run, snakes gone, eyes normal, teeth covered by lips that were shining with the blood streaming from her nose.

She smiled. "Ellery."

And she was naked.

"Ellery."

She climbed agilely over the seat after him, grinning as he backed away while holding his aching shoulder, giggling when he held out a palm to stop her as if he were staving off a vampire with a large silver cross. Then she shuddered, straightened, and ran her hands up her sides until they were cupping her breasts, kneading them, flattening them, slipping one hand down over her stomach, up again, slowly, smearing her blood in pale patterns across her amber skin. Holding out a hand, stretching out a finger, reaching for him, to touch him, before he spun around and tried to run, tripped into the aisle and fell. His head struck a riser, and he grunted in pain; he blinked rapidly to clear his eyes and rolled onto his back.

She was standing over him.

Straddling him.

Bending down in the nonlight until he saw the flesh peeling patches from her cheeks, her forehead, the sides of her nose.

He screamed when she reached for him, her hands nothing but bone that cracked at the joints; screamed again when she took hold of his belt and lifted his hips effortlessly off the floor.

Screamed a third time when she smiled, and the light snapped out.

He assumed he had fainted, blacked out for a second, maybe two, when the thing that was Ginny Amerton hauled his groin toward her teeth. And when consciousness returned, he flailed hysterically at the air, twisting onto a hip, kicking out, grunting, feeling tears in his eyes until, at last, he calmed and lay cheek-down on the steps, gulping for a breath and telling himself over and over and over again that he was all right, he was all right, he was alone up here and he was all right. Something had somehow triggered an hallucination, but he was all right now, and he could stand if he tried.

"All right," he said to hear the sound of his voice. "You're all right, pal. No sweat. Get up and get moving before they think you're dead."

His legs weren't listening. They refused to hold him, the muscles jumping in spasms until he had to grab for an armrest and hauled himself to his knees. Lowered his head. Panted again for air. Ignoring the dark while he listened for footsteps, for the rub of fleshless hand over cloth, over wood, for someone other than himself in the balcony's night.

What he heard was thunder; what he felt was the floor vibrating until the thunder was gone.

He stood at last, not knowing how long it had taken for him to do it without falling down again; he used the seats to pull himself painfully up the aisle, not knowing how he managed to find the strength even to hold on; he used the wall to keep from falling and eventually made it to the top of the staircase, checking behind him twice every step of the way while he talked himself into believing he had imagined the whole thing. And talked again, commanded, when his hands began to shake, so badly his wrists and knuckles began to ache. And a third time when he knew that unless someone talked to him, and talked to him soon, he was going to cry.

If only, he thought, it wasn't so damned dark!

Five minutes while he leaned against the wall and felt the blood on his shoulder and the sweat on his face; and five again while he stared at the faint light on the landing below him. He didn't bother to wonder why he couldn't hear the others, only drinking in the sight like heady gulps of fresh spring air. Calming. Real. No threat or nightmare there.

God, he thought; Jesus God.

He swallowed dryly and coughed, then gripped the banister white-knuckled until he reached the turn. There was silence below, but he forced himself to wait, to claw fingers through his hair, to pull off the jacket and brush a palm over his shirt. Then he stepped around the corner, smiling grimly, eyes narrowed.

The lobby was empty.

Katherine and Paula weren't on the couch, and when he staggered down to the carpet, he couldn't find Gary.

No, he thought; no. They couldn't have gotten out and forgot me. They couldn't!

"Hey, Katherine!" he called as he hurried to the exit. "Mrs. Richards?"

The doors still wouldn't open, the remains of the battered chair still scattered by the ticket booth.

"Katherine?"

The rain washing the glass, the wind bringing in the cold.

"Paula? Gary?"

The office door was open, and he started toward it in a rush, slowed, and moved cautiously though he wasn't sure why. And every step he took, he expected Ginny to leap out at him, shrieking with laughter, the flesh still falling from her skeleton and the blood still running from her nose.

The chandelier trembled; the crystals rang like tiny bells that had never been tuned.

"Look, guys," he said as he stepped over the threshold.

The office was empty, except for the injured man still sleeping on the couch. The candle burning on the desk was much lower, and he could see the bruise on the man's temple darkening, spreading, as if there was hemorrhaging. He hurried over and shook his shoulder, shook it harder when there was nothing but a waggling of the man's head. Holy shit, he thought, and knelt beside him, put a finger to his neck, to his wrist, to find evidence of a heartbeat. It was there, but it was weak, and he licked at his lips as he returned to the lobby.

"I don't get it," he said aloud, hands on his hips. "Hey, Katherine! Mrs. Richards? Paula?" He pushed the auditorium door in and braced it open with one foot. "Gary! Hey, Richards, where the hell are you guys, huh?"

Nothing in there but the dark; even the huge screen had stopped its glowing.

It's all right, he told himself. It's cool, it's all right, they'll be back.

He backed into the lobby and watched the door swing silently shut. A nightmare, he decided; Ginny, the rain—it's a goddamned nightmare, that's all.

Ellery

He whirled to stare at the staircase he'd taken, whirled again to peer at the one on his right. No one was there; no shadows, no nightmare.

But he noticed the men's room door and rushed in, propped it open with a trash can to give him feeble light, and called again for Richards, shutting up instantly when the name echoed flatly off the dull white tiles. The three stall doors were open; water dripped from one of the faucets; a shred of brown paper towel dangled from its dispenser and waved at him in a draught. The stench of stale disinfectant gagged him; the smell of his own sweat was sour and strong.

Without thinking, not daring to think, he crossed to the sink and turned the faucet off with an angry twist, yanked away the strip of toweling and used it to dry his hands, tore off another length and soaked it in warm water. He rinsed his face, dried it, dried his hands twice, all the while avoiding a look at his reflection in the mirror above the basin. He was not a brave man, and was not ashamed to admit it; and he knew that as soon as he saw the look on his face, the look in his eyes, something inside was going to shatter.

He sighed explosively, and moved on his toes to the door so not to have to hear his footsteps.

A look at his watch; it was well past midnight.

A look to the outside; it was still raining hard.

It wasn't until he found himself staring at the candles on the table that he realized he would have to do something soon or they were all going to go out at about the same time; and when they did, he would be alone. In the dark.

Quickly, he pinched out the flames of all but one, sagged into a chair, and stared blindly at the front doors. A single candle wasn't much, but four of them would last a hell of a lot longer one at a time. By then, if he were lucky, it would be daylight and he'd be able to signal someone out on the street to get help, to let him out.

But Davidson had left, and so had Seth and Toni, and in all the time they'd been gone, not one had returned.

Ellery

He ignored it. It was only his nerves playing stupid games.

"I will wake up now," he said loudly, pleased his voice didn't crack or waver. "I will wake up *now*, and I will go home."

It had been a boring film.

"Now! I am waking up right now!"

He couldn't even remember the title, and he had fallen asleep somewhere in the middle, drained because of the problems at the store, weary because he couldn't seem to get his personal life in line, disgusted because he had no one to blame but himself. Every morning without exception, he woke up determined to take charge; and most evenings he returned home, thinking that perhaps his brother during their last meeting two years ago had been right, that he was a loser. Not because he wasn't smart, but because he allowed too many people to have too great a say in what should be his destiny, his own fate.

"I *will* wake up," he said to the empty lobby.

"Then can I wake up too?" Katherine asked him, leaning against the frame of the ladies' room door, her makeup smeared, her eyes red from weeping.

When he spoke her name, his breath was white.

When he took off his jacket to place around her shoulders, a fresh flow of blood stained the sleeve of his white shirt.

When she asked him what happened, he only looked at the stairs.

"Did your brother really call you a loser?"

They were on the couch, his arm around her shoulders, and they were staring at the rain.

He hadn't realized he had been speaking aloud, and he answered her truthfully, making her frown.

"He was wrong, then, wasn't he," she said.

"I guess. I don't know. Sometimes I wonder."

She snuggled closer, laying her head on his shoulder as she drew up her legs, not bothering to adjust the skirt that exposed most of a thigh. He touched her hair. She sighed and told him that not long after he had gone upstairs after Ginny, Richards had decided he and his wife would do what Ellery was obviously incapable of doing—find a way out. The man, she said, had virtually dragged his wife into the auditorium, and when they hadn't returned after fifteen minutes or so, she had gone in to check on them. They were gone. She had called to Ellery from the middle aisle, but he hadn't answered. She could not, however, bring herself to go up the stairs, so she'd gone into the rest room instead. Hidden. And started to cry.

"I want to know what's going on."

"So do I. Believe me, so do I."

"But there has to be a reason!"

"I know, I know."

And he told her about his earlier notion it might be some sort of hostage situation, though not the kind Richards had claimed, or a prank, or maybe someone was out there fiddling around with electronics, which might explain why the doors wouldn't open and the telephone wouldn't work. He knew next to nothing about such things, and could not explain, when asked, why the glass wouldn't break. Nor could he explain what had happened to Ginny.

"Now that has to be a trick," she said in disgust, shivering in spite of the fact he hadn't told her the whole story. "I mean, that kind of weird stuff just doesn't happen."

"Except in dreams," he said quietly.

Without warning she pinched his chest hard and he yelped, almost slapped her when she pinched him again. "Not a dream," she said. "So what the hell is it?"

By his reckoning it wasn't more than fifteen minutes before they roused themselves from the couch in a tacit decision to make a methodical search of the building for the others, and for a way out.

They didn't talk about the storm; they didn't react to the lightning and thunder.

By consent, they began in Davidson's office, not bothering to remain quiet despite the old man's restless sleep. Drawers were opened, emptied, and were empty of keys; they could find no tools, no extra flashlights, nothing on any of the papers they uncovered that would tell them what had gone wrong with the theater tonight. The rug was turned up wherever they could move it, furniture was shifted, a storage closet was found that was completely empty. They tapped the walls for hidden exits, feeling like fools and doing it twice again. He climbed on a chair to tap the ceiling for a trapdoor entrance to a crawlspace or attic; and she stared at the old man for over a full minute, finally leaned down and shouted in his ear, slapped his face hard, and was about to drag him to the floor when Ellery stopped her, grabbing her in his arms and taking her gently out.

"Who *is* he?"

"I don't know."

"Where did he come from?"

"I don't know that either. I just found him, that's all."

"The sonofabitch. I hope he dies."

They searched the rest rooms again, propping open the doors to let some of the candlelight creep in before them.

They each took one of the staircases to the balcony, felt their way along the upstairs wall, and met in the middle. He almost didn't make it. He couldn't look down the aisles, and when Katherine asked him where he had last seen the girl, he couldn't even lift a finger to point. It was too dark up here, darker than it should have been, and it was all he could do to keep from grabbing her and screaming.

In the lobby he hefted the ticket seller's stool and prodded the doors with its thin metal legs, harder each time as frustration shortened his breath and turned his muscles rigid, until he was ramming furiously against the glass, in the corners, in the center, while the rain ran in white-edged sheets and the thunder mocked him and the lightning showed him nothing but his reflection in its glare. His hair darkened with perspiration, his lips were drawn back, teeth bared, tongue flicking; a leg buckled and he was thrown forward, hitting his shoulder against the jamb, and he whirled and threw the stool across the room, shouting wordlessly, fists in the air, then at his temples. Then down at his sides.

Katherine reached into a display case and tossed him a box of candy. He let it bounce off his chest, staring at it dumbly until she picked it up, took his arm, and pulled him down to the floor. She opened the package and gave him a piece.

"It's chewy," she said. "It'll help calm you."

Her hair was in rags across her face, and no matter how often she pushed it away, it returned. Her blouse was stained wet and bunched over her waistband, and somewhere along the line she had tossed the suit's jacket onto the couch.

"I think," she said at last, "this is a judgment of some kind."

His mouth was filled with tasteless candy, but he chewed it anyway, swallowing, sometimes choking.

"I mean, it could be, couldn't it? Like we've been transported somehow to a different plane than the one we live on—you know what I mean? Do you know about planes? Of existence?" He nodded; she nodded back. "So we're here, see, and we're being judged. Like we're already dead. We don't know it, but we are." She grinned. "You must have had some pretty interesting thoughts about women, El, to see Ginny that way."

He spat the candy out behind him, took off his jacket, unbuttoned his shirt, and pulled it down and back roughly to show her his left shoulder. There was a deep, ragged scratch there, and bits of stained white thread sticking to dried blood. "That's not on another plane," he told her sharply, pulling the shirt back on and trying not to wince. "That's here, Katherine. She wasn't an apparition. I saw her. I felt her. She was nothing like a ghost or some kind of an illusion."

"But she had to be, El. Don't be silly. You must have cut yourself when you tripped on the stairs, caught it on the edge of a seat or something."

"I fell later, not then."

She looked down at her shoes. A finger poked at her skirt, flicked at some lint he couldn't see. "You don't think it's a judgment, then?"

"I don't think so, no."

"Then what?"

"If I knew that, we'd be gone, don't you think?"

The strain worked on her face, giving her lines about the mouth and canyons beneath her eyes; smudges of dust hollowed her cheeks and streaked over her brow, and though she had tried to wipe away the results of her weeping, flecks of eye shadow and mascara still clung to her skin.

She's beautiful, he thought, and didn't know the question was coming until his lips moved. "Why didn't you go out with me, Katherine?"

She was startled and leaned away for a second, and he was embarrassed and tried to wave it all aside, telling her with his gestures that it didn't matter, he was being ridiculous, and this was, after all, hardly the time.

"I think," she said, "it was because I felt a little sorry for you."

"You did?"

A nod, a brief smile. "You were trying so hard, El, all those accidental meetings on the street, looking in the store window like you were an urchin begging for food."

"Me?" He didn't know whether to be angry or hurt.

"I didn't want to feel sorry for you, you understand? I wanted to like you without having to feel as if I had to mother you to get your attention." She grinned, like a child who has a wonderful secret. "When you stopped it, I thought you found another girl. Then when I found out—"

"You found out?"

She shrugged. "I asked around."

It was his turn to grin, and feel awfully foolish.

"When I found out you didn't have a girl, I couldn't get the nerve to call you. Stupid, you know? I wanted to—it's the thing we women can do these days—and I just couldn't do it."

"I'll be damned."

Candlelight danced, and the chandelier sang off-key.

There was no doubt about it—he could see his breath now.

And he didn't move when she said, "There's someone in the theater."

He had heard it almost as soon as she had spoken—a low moaning, someone in pain. Instantly, he was on his feet, grabbing her arm and pulling her with him, telling her to hold the doors open while he went inside, following his shadow to the head of the center aisle and seeing, halfway down, a figure sprawled on the floor. He ran to it without thinking, turned it over, and saw Paula staring back at him, terrified. She began crying the moment she recognized him, threw her arms around his neck when he lifted her and carried her back to the couch. Katherine hovered, and sat beside her on the edge of a cushion as soon as he moved away, helplessly waving his hands until he returned to the auditorium and shouted Gary's name. He knew there would be no response, but he kept it up for several minutes, walking up and down the aisles, ignoring the dark that reached out from the stage to drag him back, drag him under, to where the thunder was born.

Ignoring it as long as he could, too angry to yield to the fear lying in ambush, too frightened to dare let his mind out of its cage.

And when at last he returned to the lobby, wiping his face dry with a sleeve, Paula was sitting up and Katherine was leaving the ladies' room, a wad of damp paper towel cupped in her hand. She gave him a *she's all right* smile and returned to the couch, daubing Paula's cheeks, her forehead, until her hand was gently pushed away.

"I'll live," she said. "I got scared in the dark and ran. I think I must have collided with a seat or something." And she looked at Ellery. "Is Gary back yet?"

"No. Look, where were . . . no."

"That's okay." She massaged her forearm absently. "He will be. He doesn't like to leave me alone for very long. He says I could hurt myself because I don't pay attention to what I'm doing. He calls me a hothouse flower." A sigh; a deep breath. "Hothouse flowers are stronger than he thinks."

"Why"—Katherine rose and smoothed her skirt down over her hips— "why don't we check the doors again, huh? God knows there isn't anything else—"

"It's still raining," Paula whispered, wonder softening the hysteria in her voice. "It's still pouring out there, and it isn't even flooded."

When she stopped, her teeth began chattering.

"Good idea," he said to Katherine. "We'll each take a candle and make the rounds. There's got to be something we've missed. Maybe some sort of special emergency exit, one of those flush-to-the-wall doors or something."

He picked up a candle from the table, lighted it, and handed it over. Paula shook her head when he offered her one, pushing back into the couch's corner and holding her arms tight at her sides. Her rouge was gone; there was no blood in her face. Then Katherine headed for the auditorium, stopped, and turned. He was still at the table, looking at the staircases. He couldn't go up there again, not a third time. He didn't care if the place was falling down on their heads, there was nothing anyone could say that would make him climb up there again.

She gave him a smile, pity or sympathy, he didn't know, and he felt no guilt at all when she hurried away, one hand sliding up the brass banister, her shoes at the bottom where she'd kicked them off.

He shook himself to dispell the chill that seemed to deepen for a moment, and winked confidently at Paula before stepping out of the lobby. She whispered something to him—he thought it was *i wish gary were more like you*—but he didn't go back to find out. Whatever it was, it was meant kindly, to be reassuring, and he didn't want to tell her that if Gary were like him, he and his wife would be living someplace far different than their estate on the Pike.

He kept his arm straight out in front of him, the candle at an angle to drop the scalding wax on the floor.

He tried all the doors, pulled aside the wall coverings and examined every inch of brick he could reach, climbed a second time to the stage and hunted for a rear exit he might have overlooked before. All he found was some incomprehensible equipment thrust into the corners, and when he came around the curtain, he glanced up at the balcony to see how Katherine was doing.

There was no light.

He called to her.

There was no answer.

Deciding she had already finished, he moved toward the lobby, thinking about what he'd imagined Paula Richards had said, wondering at the same time why he hadn't panicked. This was, he told himself sardonically, hardly your ordinary predicament, yet he had somehow managed to keep relatively calm, reasonably in control, despite the encounter with. . . . He moistened his lips. He couldn't say it. But there must be something inside him, something he hadn't been able to put to his tongue yet that knew what was happening, or had a fairly good idea; and that influence, felt and not known, must be what was preventing him from dropping off the deep end.

He hurried into the lobby.

He dropped the candle on the floor.

"Oh, god," he said dully. "Oh, my god."

Katherine was sprawled on the carpet under the chandelier, one leg pulled under the other, one hand outstretched and clawed at the air. A candelabrum was lying beside her head, and the left side of her face was covered in red.

"Jesus, Paula, what happened?"

He ran to the fallen woman and put out a hand, drew it back into a fist when he realized she was dead, that the blood on her cheek was already drying.

"Paula, goddamnit, what the hell happened?"

There were tears in his eyes when he looked over his shoulder, and one of them slipped to his cheek when he saw her sitting primly in the middle of the

couch. She was looking at her hands folded neatly in her lap, and she was
smiling.

It came at last, the scream.

It tightened his chest with bands of cold iron, flexed the muscles of his
arms, brought darkred ridges to the sides of his neck.

He looked up to the domed ceiling and saw the nodding shadow of Paula's
head, the crystals on the chandelier refusing the light—and he opened his
mouth to let out the anger, to set free the fear, to demand in the wailing the
explanation rightfully his, for his torment and the dying and the dark that was
spilling down the staircase and across the flowered carpet.

In spite of the candles, the dark was closing in.

The concession stands vanished. The steps were gone in black.

And the scream became raw as he tasted blood in his mouth, the sweat
pouring down his face, the bite of a split knuckle as the scream settled to a
sobbing, to a whimpering, to a harsh and halting breathing that soon dropped
him to his back.

And when that stopped as well, he could hear the old man, and the old
man was snoring.

"Shit!" he yelled, pounded the floor with both fists and rolled over, scrambled to his feet and felt his eyes widen. "Shit!" as he charged into the office
and looked down, his shirt torn off his injured shoulder, his legs snapping
outward, trying to hold him while his hands reached for the wattled throat
and halted less than a finger's length away.

"Get up!" he screamed.

"Fucking bastard, get up!" he shouted, and threw the weathered coat
aside, grabbed the man's lapels and yanked him toward his face. Spittle flew
when he screamed again; the head bobbed and nodded when he shook the
man furiously; a drop of blood landed on a bruised cheek when he bit into
his own lip and threw the old man down.

The eyelids didn't flutter.

The face muscles didn't twitch.

A hand coated with liver spots dangled to the floor.

Rain drummed in cadence; thunder drifted away.

Behind him, so softly, he could hear Paula humming.

"Damn you," he said to the stranger sleeping on the couch, and dropped
to his knees, too weak to tear out the old man's throat, to pummel his chest,
to drag him into the lobby and break a chair or a table or his own hands over
the head that no longer moved.

He sniffed, and the tears stopped, and when the candle on the desk finally
guttered out in a draught, he remembered a rhyme and knew then it was so.

"Wake up," he whispered. "Old man, wake up."

Thunder rattled a picture frame on the wall, and the candle flared again, turned to smoke, and the smoke was a shadow.

"Please. Wake up."

He rocked back onto his heels, pushed himself to his feet, and left. Paula was still on the couch. Katherine's body was gone, and her shoes by the far staircase, the candelabrum, the stains of her blood.

With thumbs pressed to his cheeks, fingers massaging his brow, he walked to the lefthand door and stared out at the rain.

"Paula?"

He could see her in the glass. Pale there as well, her hair fleeing its pins in slow-waving wisps. She was watching him; she heard him.

"Do you . . ."

The cold drifted from the door, touched him, moved on.

". . . do you remember before, when we were talking about dreams?"

After several seconds she nodded. He didn't ask the next question. He waited instead, until she licked her lips several times and made a feeble effort to put her errant hair to rights. A hand to her throat, pulling the skin thoughtfully, inadvertently loosening the high collar's pearl button. The other hand spread in a fan across her chest.

"We all do it," the reflection said though the dark lips didn't move. "We remember sometimes; we forget most of the time."

Yeah, he thought; but you have nightmares just the same.

"They don't always make sense, except to some part of your brain." A brief scowl, a briefer smile. "You're supposed to be working out your daily problems somehow."

Right, he thought; but it doesn't always work.

"Do you dream, Ellery?"

He nodded.

"So do I. It's lovely."

Raining harder, and easing, until the thunder brought it back.

"I read once," she said, "that you do most of your dreaming, the serious stuff, I mean, just before you wake up." A shake of her head; a sighing look at the chandelier. "I don't know about that. I'm no expert."

"I know," he said, and knew she hadn't heard him.

She continued to talk, and he continued to watch the rain, flaring brightly at times like static on a black screen, drops running together in a mockery of tears.

The cold deepened.

The thunder was gone.

Then he heard Gary's name, and he turned as slowly as his legs would allow.

Paula was standing, her eyes closed, lips parted.

He watched without fascination as her hips thickened slightly beneath the confines of the tweed skirt, her waist draw in, her breasts enlarge, the angles of her face sharpen here, and there grow soft;

he watched as the skirt slit up one side and her leg poked through, the stockings gleaming in the light;

he watched her shoulders broaden, her neck slightly lengthen, her hair break free into a cloud about her head;

he watched tendrils of steam lift from her soles and curl up her spine to slip over her shoulders.

She came toward him, and he met her in the center of the room, the solitary candle behind her not giving her a shadow.

"Paula," he said.

And she spat in his face.

it's raining

He took the seat of the chair Gary had broken a hundred years ago and turned it over, tipped the candle he was holding until a thick puddle of wax gathered on the wood bottom. He held the candle in it until the wax hardened, then placed the seat in front of the door.

When he was sure it wouldn't tip, he walked into the office and checked the old man again, his lips in a spare smile when he was satisfied the man was alive, still breathing.

Paula was gone.

She had run into the auditorium, and he hadn't chased her to bring her back; she was still altering her appearance out of the wallflower mold, and he didn't want to know what she would look like at the end.

it's pouring

The dark was still gathering, and the cold turned his breath to a dead white fog.

You're out there, he thought to the village beyond the dark; goddamnit, I know you're out there.

He sat beside the candle and crossed his legs, pulling his jacket over his shoulders in hope of some warmth.

the old man is snoring

Ginny was wrong—this wasn't some test of experimental drugs some idiot had put in the soda or candy.

Gary was wrong—this wasn't a macabre way to get at his fool money.

he hit his head

And Katherine was wrong, and she was too terribly right—it wasn't a dream that belonged to any of them. If it was true, it belonged to the old man sleeping now in Callum's office; and if Paula was right, the hardest part of dreaming didn't come until the end.

All he could do now was wait, and watch the storm, and wonder without answers why the others had been discarded, one by one, why he had been left to live the last hour of dream time, the dreadful hour at the end before the dreamer awoke.

and he went to bed

He sat then, and he waited, and he tried not to think that maybe he was wrong too.

That maybe it wasn't the old man, that it was him after all.

The candle went out.

Rain ticked against the glass.

And he would not close his eyes when the dark swept around him and he could no longer hear the old man in the office.

He would not close his eyes.

"I am here," he said softly to the rain and took a breath. "I am awake. I am."

and he won't get up till morning

Dream Baby

Bruce McAllister

Dream Baby, got me dreamin' sweet dreams
The whole day through.
Dream Baby, got me dreamin' sweet dreams
The night time too.
  —Cindy Walker

I don't know whether I was for or against the war when I went. I joined and became a nurse to help. Isn't that why everyone becomes a nurse? We're told it's a good thing, like being a teacher or a mother. What they don't tell us is that sometimes you can't help.

Our principal gets on the PA one day and tells us how all these boys across the country are going over there for us and getting killed or maimed. Then he tells us that Tony Fischetti and this other kid are dead, killed in action, Purple Hearts and everything. A lot of the girls start crying. I'm crying. I call the Army and tell them my grades are pretty good, I want to go to nursing school and then 'Nam. They say fine, they'll pay for it but I'm obligated if they do. I say it's what I want. I don't know if any other girls from school did it. I really didn't care. I just thought somebody ought to.

I go down and sign up and my dad gets mad. He says I just want to be a whore or a lesbian, because that's what people will think if I go. I say, "Is that what you and Mom think?" He almost hits me. Parents are like that. What other people think is more important than what they think, but you can't tell them that.

I never saw a nurse in 'Nam who was a whore and I only saw one or two who might have been butch. But that's how people thought, back here in the States.

I grew up in Long Beach, California, a sailor town. Sometimes I forget that. Sometimes I forget I wore my hair in a flip and liked miniskirts and black pumps. Sometimes all I can remember is the hospitals.

* * *

I got stationed at Cam Ranh Bay, at the 23rd Medevac, for two months, then the 118th Field General in Saigon, then back to the 23rd. They weren't supposed to move you around like that, but I got moved. That kind of thing happened all the time. Things just weren't done by the book. At the 23rd we were put in a bunch of huts. It was right by the hospital compound, and we had the Navy on one side of us and the Air Force on the other side. We could hear the mortars all night and the next day we'd get to see what they'd done.

It began to get to me after about a week. That's all it took. The big medevac choppers would land and the gurneys would come in. We were the ones who tried to keep them alive, and if they didn't die on us, we'd send them on.

We'd be covered with blood and urine and everything else. We'd have a boy with no arms or no legs, or maybe his legs would be lying beside him on the gurney. We'd have guys with no faces. We'd have stomachs you could hold in your hands. We'd be slapping ringers and plasma into them. We'd have sump pumps going to get the secretions and blood out of them. We'd do this all day, day in and day out.

You'd put them in bags if they didn't make it. You'd change dressings on stumps, and you had this deal with the corpsmen that every fourth day you'd clean the latrines for them if they'd change the dressings. They knew what it was like.

They'd bring in a boy with beautiful brown eyes and you'd just have a chance to look at him, to get a chest cut-down started for a subclavian catheter. He'd say, "Ma'am, am I all right?" and in forty seconds he'd be gone. He'd say "Oh, no" and he'd be gone. His blood would pool on the gurney right through the packs. Some wounds are so bad you can't even plug them. The person just drains away.

You wanted to help but you couldn't. All you could do was watch.

When the dreams started, I thought I was going crazy. It was about the fourth week and I couldn't sleep. I'd close my eyes and think of trip wires. I'd think my bras and everything else had trip wires. I'd be on the john and hear a sound and think that someone was trip-wiring the latch so I'd lose my hands and face when I tried to leave.

I'd dream about wounds, different kinds, and then the next day there would be the wounds I'd dreamed about. I thought it was just coincidence. I'd seen a lot of wounds by then. Everyone was having nightmares. I'd dream about a sucking chest wound and a guy trying to scream, though he couldn't, and the next day I'd have to suck out a chest and listen to a guy try to scream.

I didn't think much about it. I couldn't sleep. That was the important thing. I knew I was going to go crazy if I couldn't sleep.

Sometimes the dreams would have all the details. They'd bring in a guy that looked like someone had taken an icepick to his arms. His arms looked like frankfurters with holes punched in them. That's what shrapnel looks like. You puff up and the bleeding stops. We all knew he was going to die. You can't live through something like that. The system won't take it. He knew he was going to die, but he wasn't making a sound. His face had little holes in it, around his cheeks, and it looked like a catcher's mitt. He had the most beautiful blue eyes, like glass. You know, like that dog, the weimer-something. I'd start shaking because he was in one of my dreams—those holes and his face and eyes. I'd shake for hours, but you couldn't tell anybody about dreams like that.

The guy would die. There wasn't anything I could do.

I didn't understand it. I didn't see a reason for the dreams. They just made it worse.

It got so I didn't want to go to sleep because I didn't want to have them. I didn't want to wake up and have to worry about the dreams all day, wondering if they were going to happen. I didn't want to have to shake all day, wondering.

I'd have this dream about a kid with a bad head wound and a phone call, and the next day they'd wheel in some kid who'd lost a lot of skull and brain and scalp, and the underlying brain would be infected. Then the word would get around that his father, who was a full-bird colonel stationed in Okie, had called and the kid's mother and father would be coming to see him. We all hoped he died before they got there, and he did.

I'd had a dream about him. I'd even dreamed that we wanted him to die before his mom and dad got there, and he did, in the dream he did.

When he died I started screaming and this corpsman who'd been around for a week or two took me by the arm and got me to the john. I'd gotten sick but he held me like my mom would have and all I could do was think what a mess I was, how could he hold me when I was such a mess? I started crying and couldn't stop. I knew everyone thought I was crazy, but I couldn't stop.

After that things got worse. I'd see more than just a face or the wounds. I'd see where the guy lived, where his hometown was and who was going to cry for him if he died. I didn't understand it at first—I didn't even know it was happening. I'd just get pictures, like before, in the dream and they'd bring this guy in the next day or the day after that, and if he could talk, I'd find out that what I'd seen was true. This guy would be dying and not saying a thing and I'd remember him from the dream and I'd say, "You look like a Georgia boy to me." If the morphine was working and he could talk, he'd say, "Who told you that, Lieutenant? All us brothers ain't from Georgia."

I'd make up something, like his voice or a good guess, and if I'd seen other things in the dream—like his girl or wife or mother—I'd tell him about those, too. He wouldn't ask how I knew because it didn't matter. How could it matter? He knew he was dying. They always know. I'd talk to him like I'd known him my whole life and he'd be gone in an hour, or by morning.

I had this dream about a commando type, dressed in tiger cammies, nobody saying a thing about him in the compound—spook stuff, Ibex, MAC SOG, something like that—and I could see his girlfriend in Australia. She had hair just like mine and her eyes were a little like mine and she loved him. She was going out with another guy that night, but she loved him, I could tell. In the dream they brought him into ER with the bottom half of him blown away.

The next morning, first thing, they wheeled this guy in and it was the dream all over again. He was blown apart from the waist down. He was delirious and trying to talk but his jaw wouldn't work. He had tiger cammies on and we cut them off. I was the one who got him and everyone knew he wasn't going to make it. As soon as I saw him I started shaking. I didn't want to see him, I didn't want to look at him. You really don't know what it's like, seeing someone like that and knowing. I didn't want him to die. I never wanted any of them to die.

I said, "Your girl in Australia loves you—she really does." He looked at me and his eyes had that look you get when morphine isn't enough. I could tell he thought I looked like her. He couldn't even see my hair under the cap and he knew I looked like her.

He grabbed my arm and his jaw started slipping and I knew what he wanted me to do. I always knew. I told him about her long black hair and the beaches in Australia and what the people were like there and what there was to do.

He thought I was going to stop talking, so he kept squeezing my arm. I told him what he and his girlfriend had done on a beach outside Melbourne, their favorite beach, and what they'd had to drink that night.

And then—this was the first time I'd done it with anyone—I told him what I'd do for him if I was his girlfriend and we were back in Australia. I said, "I'd wash you real good in the shower. I'd turn the lights down low and I'd put on some nice music. Then, if you were a little slow, I'd help you." It was what his girlfriend always did, I knew that. It wasn't hard to say.

I kept talking, he kept holding my arm, and then he coded on me. They always did. I had a couple of minutes or hours and then they always coded on me, just like in the dreams.

I got good at it. The pictures got better and I could tell them what they wanted to hear and that made it easier. It wasn't just faces and burns and stumps, it was things about them. I'd tell them what their girlfriends and wives would do if they were here. Sometimes it was sexual, sometimes it wasn't. Sometimes I'd just ruffle their hair with my hand and tell them what Colorado looked like in summer, or what the last Doors concert they'd been to was like, or what you could do after dark in Newark.

I start crying in the big room one day and this corpsman takes me by the arm and the next thing I know I'm sitting on the john and he's got a needle in his hand, a 2% solution. He doesn't want to see me hurting so much. I tell him no. Why, I don't know. Every week or so I'd walk into the john and find somebody with a needle in their arm, but it wasn't for me, I thought. People weren't supposed to do that kind of thing. Junkies on the Pike back home did it—we all knew that—but not doctors and medics and nurses. It wasn't right, I told myself.

I didn't start until a couple of weeks later.

There's this guy I want to tell you about. Steve—his name was Steve.

I come in one morning to the big ER room shaking so hard I can't even put my cap on and thinking I should've gotten a needle already, and there's this guy sitting over by a curtain. He's in cammies, his head's wrapped and he's sitting up real straight. I can barely stand up, but there's this guy looking like he's hurting, so I say, "You want to lie down?"

He turns slowly to look at me and I don't believe it. I know this guy from a dream, but I don't see the dream clearly. Here's this guy sitting in a chair in front of me unattended, like he could walk away any second, but I've had a dream about him, so I know he's going to die.

He says he's okay, he's just here to see a buddy. But I'm not listening. I know everything about him. I know about his girlfriend and where he's from and how his mom and dad didn't raise him, but all I can think about is, he's going to die. I'm thinking about the supply room and needles and how it wouldn't take much to get it all over with.

I say, "Cathy misses you, Steve. She wishes you could go to the Branding Iron in Merced tonight, because that band you like is playing. She's done something to her apartment and she wants to show it to you."

He looks at me for a long time and his eyes aren't like the others. I don't want to look back at him. I can see him anyway—in the dream. He's real young. He's got a nice body, good shoulders, and he's got curly blond hair under those clean bandages. He's got eyelashes like a girl, and I see him laughing. He laughs every chance he gets, I know.

Very quietly he says, "What's your name?"

I guess I tell him, because he says, "Can you tell me what she looks like, Mary?"

Everything's wrong. The guy doesn't sound like he's going to die. He's looking at me like he understands.

I say something like "She's tall." I say, "She's got blond hair," but I can barely think.

Very gently he says, "What are her eyes like?"

I don't know. I'm shaking so hard I can barely talk. I can barely remember the dream.

Suddenly I'm talking. "They're green. She wears a lot of mascara, but she's got dark eyebrows, so she isn't really a blond, is she."

He laughs and I jump. "No, she isn't," he says and he's smiling. He takes my hand in his. I'm shaking badly but I let him, like I do the others. I don't say a word.

I'm holding it in. I'm scared to death. I'm cold-turkeying and I'm letting him hold my hand because he's going to die. But it's not true. I dreamed about him, but in the dream he didn't die. I know that now.

He squeezes my hand like we've known each other a long time and he says, "Do you do this for all of them?"

I don't say a thing.

Real quietly he says, "A lot of guys die on you, don't they, Mary."

I can't help it—I start crying. I want to tell him. I want to tell someone, so I do.

When I'm finished he doesn't say something stupid, he doesn't walk away. He doesn't code on me. He starts to tell me a story and I don't understand at first.

There's this G–2 reconnaissance over the border, he says. The insertion's smooth and I'm point, I'm always point. We're humping across paddy dikes like grunts and we hit this treeline. This is a black op, nobody's supposed to know we're here, but somebody does. All of a sudden the goddamn trees are full of Charlie ching-ching snipers. The whole world turns blue—just for me, I mean, it turns blue—and everything starts moving real slow. I can see the first AK rounds coming at me and I step aside nicely just like that, like always.

The world always turns blue like that when he needs it to, he says. That's why they make him point every goddamn time, why they keep using him on special ops to take out infrastructure or long-range recon for intel. Because the world turns blue. And how he's been called in twice to talk about what he's going to do after this war and how they want him to be a killer, he says. The records will say he died in this war and they'll give him a new identity. He doesn't have family, they say. He'll be one of their killers wherever they need him. Because everything turns blue. I don't believe what I'm hearing.

It's like a movie, like that *Manchurian Candidate* thing, and I can't believe it.
They don't care about how he does it, he says. They never do. It can be the
world turning blue or voices in your head or some grabass feeling in your gut,
or, if you want, it can be God or the Devil with horns or Little Green
Martians—it doesn't matter to them what you believe. As long as it works, as
long as you keep coming back from missions, that's all they care about. He
told them no, but they keep on asking. Sometimes he thinks they'll kill his
girlfriend just so he won't have anything to come back to in the States. They
do that kind of thing, he says. I can't believe it.

So everything's turning blue, he says, and I'm floating up out of my body
over this rice paddy, these goddamn ching-ching snipers are darker blue, and
when I come back down I'm moving through this nice blue world and I
know where they are, and I get every goddamn one of them in their trees.

But it doesn't matter, he says. There's this light-weapons sergeant, a guy
they called the Dogman, who's crazy and barks like a dog and makes everyone laugh even if they're bleeding, even if their guts are hanging out. He
scares the VC when he barks. He humps his share and the men love him.

When the world turns blue, the Dogman's in cover, everything's fine, but
then he rubbernecks, the sonuvabitch rubbernecks for the closest ching-
ching—he didn't have to, he just didn't have to—and takes a round high. I
don't see the back of his head explode, so I think he's still alive. I go for him
where he's hanging half out of the treeline, half in a canal full of stinking rice
water. I try to get his body out of the line of fire, but Charlie puts the next
round right in under my arm. I'm holding the Dogman and the round goes
in right under my arm, a fucking heart shot. I can feel it come in. It's for me.
Everything goes slow and blue and I jerk a little—I don't even know I'm
doing it—and the round slides right in under me and into him. They never
get *me*. The fucking world turns blue and everything goes slow and they
never get *me*.

I can always save myself, he says—his name is Steve and he's not smiling
now—but I can't save *them*. What's it worth? What's it worth if you stay alive
and everybody you care about is dead? Even if you get what *they* want.

I know what he means, I know now why he's sitting on a chair nearly
crying, I know where the body is, which curtain it's behind, how close it's
been all this time. I remember the dream now.

Nobody likes to die alone, Steve says. Just like he said it in the dream.

He stays and we talk. We talk about the dreams and his blue world, and we
talk about what we're going to do when we get out of this place and back to
the Big PX, all the fun we're going to have. He starts to tell me about other

guys he knows, guys like him that his people are interested in, but then he stops and I see he's looking past me. I turn around.

There's this guy in civvies at the end of the hallway, just standing there, looking at us. Then he nods at Steve and Steve says, "I got to go."

Real fast I say, "See you at nineteen hundred hours."

He's looking at the guy down the hallway. "Yeah, sure," he says.

When I get off he's there. I haven't thought about a needle all day and it shows. We get a bite to eat and talk some more, and that's that. My room-mate says I can have the room for a couple of hours, but I'm a mess. I'm shaking so bad I can't even think about having a good time with this guy. He looks at me like he knows this, and says his head hurts and we ought to get some sleep.

He gives me a hug. That's it.

The same guy in civvies is waiting for him and they walk away together on Phan Hao Street.

The next day he's gone. I tell myself maybe he was standing down for a couple of days and had to get back, but that doesn't help. I know lots of guys who traveled around in-country AWOL without getting into trouble. What could they do to you? Send you to 'Nam?

I thought maybe he'd call in a couple of days, or write. Later I thought maybe he'd gotten killed, maybe let himself get killed. I really didn't know what to think, but I thought about him a lot.

Ten days later I get transferred. I don't even get orders cut, I don't even get in-country travel paper. No one will tell me a thing—the head nurse, the CO, nobody.

I get scared because I think they're shipping me back to the States because of the smack or the dreams—they've found out about the dreams—and I'm going to be in some VA hospital the rest of my life. That's what I think.

All they'll tell me is that I'm supposed to be at the strip at 0600 hours tomorrow, fatigues and no ID.

I get a needle that night and I barely make it.

This Huey comes in real fast and low and I get dust in my eyes from the prop wash. A guy with a clipboard about twenty yards away signals me and I get on. There's no one there to say good-bye and I never see the 23rd again.

The Huey's empty except for these two pilots who never turn around and this doorgunner who's hanging outside and this other guy who's sitting back with me on the canvas. I think maybe he's the one who's going to explain things, but he just stares for a while and doesn't say a thing. He's a sergeant, a Ranger, I think.

It's supposed to be dangerous to fly at night in Indian Country, I know, but we fly at night. We stop twice and I know we're in Indian Country. This one guy gets off, another guy gets on, and then two more. They seem to know each other and they start laughing. They try to get me to talk. One guy says, "You a Donut Dolly?" and another guy says, "Hell, no, asshole, she's Army, can't you tell? She's got the thousand yards." The third guy says to me, "Don't mind him, ma'am. They don't raise 'em right in Mississippi." They're trying to be nice, but I don't want in.

I don't want to sleep either. But my head's tipped back against the steel and I keep waking up, trying to remember whether I've dreamed about people dying, but I can't. I fall asleep once for a long time and when I wake up I can remember death, but I can't see the faces.

I wake up once and there's automatic weapon fire somewhere below us and maybe the slick gets hit once or twice. Another time I wake up and the three guys are talking quietly, real serious, but I'm hurting from no needle and I don't even listen.

When the rotors change I wake up. It's first light and cool and we're coming in on this big clearing, everything misty and beautiful. It's triple-canopy jungle I've never seen before and I know we're so far from Cam Ranh Bay or Saigon it doesn't matter. I don't see anything that looks like a medevac, just this clearing, like a staging area. There are a lot of guys walking around, a lot of machinery, but it doesn't look like regular Army. It looks like something you hear about but aren't supposed to see, and I'm shaking like a baby.

When we hit the LZ the three guys don't even know I exist and I barely get out of the slick on my own. I can't see because of the wash and suddenly this Green Beanie medic I've never seen before—this captain—has me by the arm and he's taking me somewhere. I tell myself I'm not going back to the Big PX, I'm not going to some VA hospital for the rest of my life, that this is the guy I'm going to be assigned to—they need a nurse out here or something.

I'm not thinking straight. Special Forces medics don't have nurses.

I'm looking around me and I don't believe what I'm seeing. There's bunkers and M-60 emplacements and Montagnard guards on the perimeter and all this beautiful red earth. There's every kind of jungle fatigue and cammie you can think of—stripes and spots and black pajamas like Charlie and everything else. I see Special Forces enlisted everywhere and I know this isn't some little A-camp. I see a dozen guys in real clean fatigues who don't walk like soldiers walk. I see a Special Forces major and he's arguing with one of them.

The captain who's got me by the arm isn't saying a thing. He takes me to this little bunker that's got mosquito netting and a big canvas flap over the front and he puts me inside. It's got a cot. He tells me to lie down and I do. He says, "The CO wants you to get some sleep, Lieutenant. Someone will come by with something in a little while." The way he says it I know he knows about the needles.

I don't know how long I'm in the bunker before someone comes, but I'm in lousy shape. This guy in civvies gives me something to take with a little paper cup and I go ahead and do it. I'm not going to fight it the shape I'm in. I dream, and keep dreaming, and in some of the dreams someone comes by with a glass of water and I take more pills. I can't wake up. All I can do is sleep but I'm not really sleeping and I'm having these dreams that aren't really dreams. Once or twice I hear myself screaming, it hurts so much, and then I dream about a little paper cup and more pills.

When I come out of it, I'm not shaking. I know it's not supposed to be this quick, that what they gave me isn't what people are getting in programs back in the States, and I get scared again. Who are these guys?

I sit in the little bunker all day eating ham-and-motherfuckers from C-rat cans and I tell myself that Steve had something to do with it. I'm scared but it's nice not to be shaking. It's nice not to be thinking about a needle all the time.

The next morning I hear all this noise and I realize we're leaving, the whole camp is leaving. I can hear this noise like a hundred slicks outside and I get up and look through the flap. I've never seen so many choppers. They've got Chinooks and Hueys and Cobras and Loaches and a Skycrane for the SeaBee machines and they're dusting off and dropping in and dusting off again. I've never seen anything like it. I keep looking for Steve. I keep trying to remember the dreams I had while I was out all those days and I can't.

Finally the Green Beanie medic comes back. He doesn't say a word. He just takes me to the LZ and we wait until a slick drops in. All these tiger stripes pile in with us but no one says a thing. No one's joking. I don't understand it. We aren't being hit, we're just moving, but no one's joking.

We set up in a highlands valley northwest of where we'd been, where the jungle is thicker but it's not triple canopy. There's this same beautiful mist and I wonder if we're in some other country, Laos or Cambodia.

They have my bunker dug in about an hour and I'm in it about thirty minutes before this guy appears. I've been looking for Steve, wondering why

I haven't seen him, and feeling pretty good about myself. It's nice not to be shaking, to get the monkey off my back, and I'm ready to thank *somebody*.

This guy opens the flap. He stands there for a moment and there's something familiar about him. He's about thirty and he's in real clean fatigues. He's got MD written all over him—but the kind that never gets any blood on him. I think of VA hospitals, psychiatric wards, and I get scared again.

"How are you feeling, Lieutenant?"

"Fine," I say, but I'm not smiling. I know this guy from the dreams—the little paper cups and pills—and I don't like what I'm feeling.

"Glad to hear it. Remarkable drug, isn't it, Lieutenant?"

I nod. Nothing he says surprises me.

"Someone wants to see you, Lieutenant."

I get up, dreading it. I know he's not talking about Steve.

They've got all the bunkers dug and he takes me to what has to be the CP. There isn't a guy inside who isn't in real clean fatigues. There are three or four guys who have the same look this guy has—MDs that don't ever get their hands dirty—and intel types pointing at maps and pushing things around on a couple of sand-table mock-ups. There's this one guy with his back turned and everyone else keeps checking in with him.

He's tall. He's got a full head of hair but it's going gray. He doesn't even have to turn around and I know.

It's the guy in civvies at the end of the hallway at the 23rd, the guy that walked away with Steve on Phan Hao Street.

He turns around and I don't give him eye contact. He looks at me, smiles, and starts over. There are two guys trailing him and he's got this smile that's supposed to be charming.

"How are you feeling, Lieutenant?" he says.

"Everybody keeps asking me that," I say, and I wonder why I'm being so brave.

"That's because we're interested in you, Lieutenant," he says. He's got this jungle outfit on with gorgeous creases and some canvas jungle boots that breathe nicely. He looks like an ad from a catalog but I know he's no joke, he's no pogue lifer. He's wearing this stuff because he likes it, that's all. He could wear anything he wanted to because he's not military, but he's the CO of this operation, which means he's fighting a war I don't know a thing about.

He tells me he's got some things to straighten out first, but that if I go back to my little bunker he'll be there in an hour. He asks me if I want anything to eat. When I say sure, he tells the MD type to get me something from the mess.

I go back. I wait. When he comes, he's got a file in his hand and there's a young guy with him who's got a cold six-pack of Coke in his hand. I can tell they're cold because the cans are sweating. I can't believe it. We're out here in the middle of nowhere, we're probably not even supposed to be here, and they're bringing me cold Coke.

When the young guy leaves, the CO sits on the edge of the cot and I sit on the other end and he says, "Would you like one, Lieutenant?"

I say, "Yes, sir," and he pops the top with a church key. He doesn't take one himself and suddenly I wish I hadn't said yes. I'm thinking of old movies where Jap officers offer their prisoners a cigarette so they'll owe them one. There's not even any place to put the can down, so I hold it between my hands.

"I'm not sure where to begin, Lieutenant," he says, "but let me assure you you're here because you belong here." He says it gently, real softly, but it gives me a funny feeling. "You're an officer and you've been in-country for some time. I don't need to tell you that we're a very special kind of operation here. What I do need to tell you is that you're one of three hundred we've identified so far in this war. Do you understand?"

I say, "No, sir."

"I think you do, but you're not sure, right? You've accepted your difference—your gift, your curse, your talent, whatever you would like to call it—but you can't as easily accept the fact that so many others might have the same thing, am I right, Mary—may I call you Mary?"

I don't like the way he says it but I say yes.

"We've identified three hundred like you, Mary. That's what I'm saying."

I stare at him. I don't know whether to believe him.

"I'm only sorry, Mary, that you came to our attention so late. Being alone with a gift like yours isn't easy, I'm sure, and finding a community of those who share it—the same gift, the same curse—is essential if the problems that always accompany it are to be worked out successfully, am I correct?"

"Yes."

"We might have lost you, Mary, if Lieutenant Balsam hadn't found you. He almost didn't make the trip, for reasons that will be obvious later. If he hadn't met you, Mary, I'm afraid your hospital would have sent you back to the States for drug abuse if not for what they perceived as an increasingly dysfunctional neurosis. Does this surprise you?"

I say it doesn't.

"I didn't think so. You're a smart girl, Mary."

The voice is gentle, but it's not.

He waits and I don't know what he's waiting for.

I say, "Thank you for whatever it was that—"

"No need to thank us, Mary. Were that particular drug available back home right now, it wouldn't seem like such a gift, would it?"

He's right. He's the kind who's always right and I don't like the feeling.

"Anyway, thanks," I say. I'm wondering where Steve is.

"You're probably wondering where Lieutenant Balsam is, Mary."

I don't bother to nod this time.

"He'll be back in a few days. We have a policy here of not discussing missions—even in the ranks—and as commanding officer I like to set a good example. You can understand, I'm sure." He smiles again and for the first time I see the crow's-feet around his eyes, and how straight his teeth are, and how there are little capillaries broken on his cheeks.

He looks at the Coke in my hands and smiles. Then he opens the file he has. "If we were doing this the right way, Mary, we would get together in a nice air-conditioned building back in the States and go over all of this together, but we're not in any position to do that, are we?

"I don't know how much you've gathered about your gift, Mary, but people who study such things have their own way of talking. They would call yours a 'TPC hybrid with traumatic neurosis, dissociative features.'" He smiled. "That's not as bad as it sounds. It's quite normal. The human psyche always responds to special gifts like yours, and neurosis is simply a mechanism for doing just that. We wouldn't be human if it didn't, would we?"

"No, we wouldn't."

He's smiling at me and I know what he wants me to feel. I feel like a little girl sitting on a chair, being good, listening, and liking it, and that is what he wants.

"Those same people, Mary, would call your dreams 'spontaneous anecdotal material' and your talent a 'REM-state precognition or clairvoyance.' They're not very helpful words. They're the words of people who've never experienced it themselves. Only you, Mary, know what it really feels like inside. Am I right?"

I remember liking how that felt—*only you*. I needed to feel that, and he knew I needed to.

"Not all three hundred are dreamers like you, of course. Some are what those same people would call 'kinetic phenomena generators.' Some are 'tactility-triggered remoters' or 'OBE clears.' Some leave their bodies in a firefight and acquire information that could not be acquired in ordinary ways, which tells us that their talent is indeed authentic. Others see auras when their comrades are about to die, and if they can get those auras to disappear, their friends will live. Others experience only a vague visceral sensation, a gut feeling which tells them where mines and trip wires are. They know, for example, when a crossbow trap will fire and this allows them to knock away the arrows before they can hurt them. Still others receive pictures, like waking dreams, of what will happen in the next minute, hour, or day in combat.

"With very few exceptions, Mary, none of these individuals experienced anything like this as civilians. These episodes are the consequence of combat, of the metabolic and psychological anomalies which life-and-death conditions seem to generate."

He looks at me and his voice changes now, as if on cue. He wants me to feel what he is feeling, and I do, I do. I can't look away from him and I know this is why he is CO.

"It is almost impossible to reproduce them in a laboratory, Mary, and so these remarkable talents remain mere anecdotes, events that happen once or twice within a lifetime—to a brother, a mother, a friend, a fellow soldier in a war. A boy is killed on Kwajalein in 1944. That same night his mother dreams of his death. She has never before dreamed such a dream, and the dream is too accurate to be mere coincidence. He dies. She never has a dream like it again. A reporter for a major newspaper looks out the terminal window at the Boeing 707 he is about to board. He has flown a hundred times before, enjoys air travel, and has no reason to be anxious today. As he looks through the window the plane explodes before his very eyes. He can hear the sound ringing in his ears and the sirens rising in the distance; he can feel the heat of the ignited fuel on his face. Then he blinks. The jet is as it was before —no fire, no sirens, no explosion. He is shaking—he has never experienced anything like this in his life. He does not board the plane, and the next day he hears that its fuel tanks exploded, on the ground, in another city, killing ninety. The man never has such a vision again. He enjoys air travel in the months, and years, ahead, and will die of cardiac arrest on a tennis court twenty years later. You can see the difficulty we have, Mary."

"Yes," I say quietly, moved by what he's said.

"But our difficulty doesn't mean that your dreams are any less real, Mary. It doesn't mean that what you and the three hundred like you in this small theater of war are experiencing isn't real."

"Yes," I say.

He gets up.

"I am going to have one of my colleagues interview you, if that's all right. He will ask you questions about your dreams and he will record what you say. The tapes will remain in my care, so there isn't any need to worry, Mary."

I nod.

"I hope that you will view your stay here as deserved R&R, and as a chance to make contact with others who understand what it is like. For paperwork's sake, I've assigned you to Golf Team. You met three of its members on your flight in, I believe. You may write to your parents as long as you make reference to a medevac unit in Pleiku rather than to our actual operation here. Is that clear?"

He smiles like a friend would, and makes his voice as gentle as he can. "I'm going to leave the rest of the Coke. And a church key. Do I have your permission?" He grins. It's a joke, I realize. I'm supposed to smile. When I do, he smiles back and I know he knows everything, he knows himself, he knows me, what I think of him, what I've been thinking every minute he's been here.

It scares me that he knows.

His name is Bucannon.

The man that came was one of the other MD types from the tent. He asked and I answered. The question that took the longest was "What were your dreams like? Be as specific as possible both about the dream content and its relationship to reality—that is, how accurate the dream was as a predictor of what happened. Describe how the dreams and their relationship to reality (i.e., their accuracy) affected you both psychologically and physically (e.g., sleeplessness, nightmares, inability to concentrate, anxiety, depression, uncontrollable rages, suicidal thoughts, drug abuse)."

It took us six hours and six tapes.

We finished after dark.

I did what I was supposed to do. I hung around Golf Team. There were six guys, this lieutenant named Pagano, who was in charge, and this demo sergeant named Christabel, who was their "talent." He was, I found out, an "OBE clairvoyant with EEG anomalies," which meant that in a firefight he could leave his body just like Steve could. He could leave his body, look back at himself—that's what it felt like—and see how everyone else was doing and maybe save someone's ass. They were a good team. They hadn't lost anybody yet, and they loved to tease this sergeant every chance they got.

We talked about Saigon and what you could get on the black market. We talked about missions, even though we weren't supposed to. The three guys from the slick even got me to talk about the dreams, I was feeling that good, and when I heard they were going out on another mission at 0300 hours the next morning, without the sergeant—some little mission they didn't need him on—I didn't think anything about it.

I woke up in my bunker that night screaming because two of the guys from the slick were dead. I saw them dying out in the jungle, I saw how they died, and suddenly I knew what it was all about, why Bucannon wanted me here.

He came by the bunker at first light. I was still crying. He knelt down beside me and put his hand on my forehead. He made his voice gentle. He said, "What was your dream about, Mary?"

I wouldn't tell him. "You've got to call them back," I said.

"I can't, Mary," he said. "We've lost contact."

He was lying I found out later: he could have called them back—no one was dead yet—but I didn't know that then. So I went ahead and told him about the two I'd dreamed about, the one from Mississippi and the one who'd thought I was a Donut Dolly. He took notes. I was a mess, crying and sweaty, and he pushed the hair away from my forehead and said he would do what he could.

I didn't want him to touch me, but I didn't stop him. I didn't stop him. I didn't leave the bunker for a long time. I couldn't.

No one told me the two guys were dead. No one had to. It was the right kind of dream, just like before. But this time I'd *known* them. I'd met them. I'd laughed with them in the daylight and when they died I wasn't there, it wasn't on some gurney in a room somewhere. It was different.

It was starting up again, I told myself.

I didn't get out of the cot until noon. I was thinking about needles, that was all.

He comes by again at about 1900 hours, just walks in and says, "Why don't you have some dinner, Mary. You must be hungry."

I go to the mess they've thrown together in one of the big bunkers. I think the guys are going to know about the screaming, but all they do is look at me like I'm the only woman in the camp, that's all, and that's okay.

Suddenly I see Steve. He's sitting with three other guys and I get this feeling he doesn't want to see me, that if he did he'd have come looking for me already, and I should turn around and leave. But one of the guys is saying something to him and Steve is turning and I know I'm wrong. He's been waiting for me. He's wearing cammies and they're dirty—he hasn't been back long—and I can tell by the way he gets up and comes toward me he wants to see me.

We go outside and stand where no one can hear us. He says, "Jesus, I'm sorry." I'm not sure what he means.

"Are you okay?" I say, but he doesn't answer.

He's saying, "I wasn't the one who told him about the dreams, Mary, I swear it. All I did was ask for a couple hours' layover to see you, but he doesn't like that—he doesn't like 'variables.' When he gets me back to camp, he has you checked out. The hospital says something about dreams and how crazy you're acting, and he puts it together. He's smart, Mary. He's real smart—"

I tell him to shut up, it isn't his fault, and I'd rather be here than back in the States in some VA program or ward. But he's not listening. "He's got you here for a reason, Mary. He's got all of us here for a reason and if I hadn't asked for those hours he wouldn't know you existed—"

I get mad. I tell him I don't want to hear any more about it, it isn't his fault.

"Okay," he says finally. "Okay." He gives me a smile because he knows I want it. "Want to meet the guys on the team?" he says. "We just got extracted—"

I say sure. We go back in. He gets me some food and then introduces me. They're dirty and tired but they're not complaining. They're still too high off the mission to eat and won't crash for another couple of hours yet. There's an SF medic with the team, and two Navy SEALs because there's a riverine aspect to the mission, and a guy named Moburg, a Marine sniper out of Quantico. Steve's their CO and all I can think about is how young he is. They're all so young.

It turns out Moburg's a talent, too, but it's "anticipatory subliminal"—it only helps him target hits and doesn't help anyone else much. But he's a damn good sniper because of it, they tell me.

The guys give me food from their trays and for the first time that day I'm feeling hungry. I'm eating with guys that are real and alive and I'm really hungry.

Then I notice Steve isn't talking. He's got that same look on his face. I turn around.

Bucannon's in the doorway, looking at us. The other guys haven't seen him, they're still talking and laughing—being raunchy.

Bucannon is looking at us and he's smiling, and I get a chill down my spine like cold water because I know—all of a sudden I know—why I'm sitting here, who wants it this way.

I get up fast. Steve doesn't understand. He says something. I don't answer him, I don't even hear him. I keep going. He's behind me and he wants to know if I'm feeling okay, but I don't want to look back at him, I don't want to look at any of the guys with him, because that's what Bucannon wants.

He's going to send them out again, I tell myself. They just got back, they're tired, and he's going to send them out again, so I can dream about them.

★   ★   ★

I'm not going to go to sleep, I tell myself. I walk the perimeter until they tell me I can't do that anymore, it's too dangerous. Steve follows me and I start screaming at him, but I'm not making any sense. He watches me for a while and then someone comes to get him, and I know he's being told he's got to take his team out again. I ask for some Benzedrine from the Green Beanie medic who brings me aspirin when I want it but he says he can't, that word has come down that he can't. I try writing a letter to my parents but it's 0400 hours and I'm going crazy trying to stay awake because I haven't had more than four hours' sleep for a couple of nights and my body temperature's dropping on the diurnal.

I ask for some beer and they get it for me. I ask for some scotch. They give it to me and I think I've won. I never go to sleep on booze, but Bucannon doesn't know that. I'll stay awake and I won't dream.

But it knocks me out like a light, and I have a dream. One of the guys at the table, one of the two SEALs, is floating down a river. The blood is like a woman's hair streaming out from his head. I don't dream about Steve, just about this SEAL who's floating down a river. It's early in the mission. Somehow I know that.

I don't wake up screaming, because of what they put in the booze. I remember it as soon as I wake up, when I can't do anything about it.

Bucannon comes in at first light. He doesn't say, "If you don't help us, you're going back to Saigon or back to the States with a Section Eight." Instead he comes in and kneels down beside me like some goddamn priest and he says, "I know this is painful, Mary, but I'm sure you can understand."

I say, "Get the hell out of here, motherfucker."

It's like he hasn't heard. He says, "It would help us to know the details of any dream you had last night, Mary."

"You'll let him die anyway," I say.

"I'm sorry, Mary," he says, "but he's already dead. We've received word on one confirmed KIA in Echo Team. All we're interested in is the details of the dream and an approximate time, Mary." He hesitates. "I think he would want you to tell us. I think he would want to feel that it was not in vain, don't you."

He stands up at last.

"I'm going to leave some paper and writing utensils for you. I can understand what you're going through, more than you might imagine, Mary, and I believe that if you give it some thought—if you think about men like Steve and what your dreams could mean to them—you will write down the details of your dream last night."

I scream something at him. When he's gone I cry for a while. Then I go ahead and write down what he wants. I don't know what else to do.

★ ★ ★

I don't go to the mess. Bucannon has food brought to my bunker but I don't eat it.

I ask the Green Beanie medic where Steve is. Is he back yet? He says he can't tell me. I ask him to send a message to Steve for me. He says he can't do that. I tell him he's a straight-leg ass-kisser and ought to have his jump wings shoved, but this doesn't faze him at all. Any other place, I say, you'd be what you were supposed to be—Special Forces and a damn good medic—but Bucannon's got you, doesn't he. He doesn't say a thing.

I stay awake all that night. I ask for coffee and I get it. I bum more coffee off two sentries and drink that, too. I can't believe he's letting me have it. Steve's team is going to be back soon, I tell myself—they're a strike force, not a Lurp—and if I don't sleep, I can't dream.

I do it again the next night and it's easier. I can't believe it's this easy. I keep moving around. I get coffee and I find this sentry who likes to play poker and we play all night. I tell him I'm a talent and will know if someone's trying to come through the wire on us, sapper or whatever, so we can play cards and not worry. He's pure new-guy and he believes me.

Steve'll be back tomorrow, I tell myself. I'm starting to see things and I'm not thinking clearly, but I'm not going to crash. I'm not going to crash until Steve is back. I'm not going to dream about Steve.

At about 0700 hours the next morning we get mortared. The slicks inside the perimeter start revving up, the Skycrane starts hooking its cats and Rome plows, and the whole camp starts to dust off. I hear radios, more slicks and Skycranes being called in. If the NVA had a battalion, they'd be overrunning us, I tell myself, so it's got to be a lot less—company, platoon—and they're just harassing us, but word has come down from somebody that we're supposed to move.

Mortars are whistling in and someone to one side of me says "Incoming— fuck it!" Then I hear this other sound. It's like flies but real loud. It's like this weird whispering. It's a goddamn flechette round, I realize, spraying stuff, and I don't understand. I can hear it, but it's like a memory, a flashback. Everybody's running around me and I'm just standing there and someone's screaming. It's me screaming. I've got flechettes all through me—my chest, my face. I'm torn to pieces. I'm dying. But I'm running toward the slick, the one that's right over there, ready to dust off. Someone's calling to me, screaming at me, and I'm running, but I'm not. I'm on the ground. I'm on the jungle floor with these flechettes in me and I've got a name, a nickname, Kicker, and I'm thinking of a town in Wyoming, near the Montana border, where everybody rides pickup trucks with shotgun racks and waves to everybody else, I grew up there, there's a rodeo every spring with a county fair and I'm thinking about a girl with braids, I'm thinking how I'm going to die here in the middle of this jungle, how we're on some recondo that no one cares about, how Charlie doesn't have flechette rounds, how Bucannon never makes mistakes.

I'm running and screaming and when I get to the slick the Green Beanie medic grabs me, two other guys grab me and haul me in. I look up. It's Bucannon's slick. He's on the radio. I'm lying on a pile of files right beside him and we're up over the jungle now, we're taking the camp somewhere else, where it can start up all over again.

I look at Bucannon. I think he's going to turn any minute and say, "Which ones, Mary? Which ones died from the flechette?" He doesn't.

I look down and see he's put some paper and three pencils beside me on the floor. I can't stand it. I start crying.

I sleep maybe for twenty minutes and have two dreams. Two other guys died out there somewhere with flechettes in them. Two more guys on Steve's team died and I didn't even meet them.

I look up. Bucannon's smiling at me.

"It happened, didn't it, Mary?" he says gently. "It happened in the daylight this time, didn't it?"

At the new camp I stayed awake another night, but it was hard and it didn't make any difference. It probably made it worse. It happened three more times the next day and all sorts of guys saw me. I knew someone would tell Steve. I knew Steve's team was still out there—Echo hadn't come in when the rocketing started—but that he was okay. I'm lying on the ground screaming and crying with shrapnel going through me, my legs are gone, my left eyeball is hanging out on my cheek, and there are pieces of me all over the guy next to me, but I'm not Steve, and that's what matters.

The third time, an AK round goes through my neck so I can't even scream. I fall down and can't get up. Someone kneels down next to me and I think it's Bucannon and I try to hit him. I'm trying to scream even though I can't, but it's not Bucannon, it's one of the guys who was sitting with Steve in the mess. They're back, they're back, I think to myself, but I'm trying to tell this guy that I'm dying, that there's this medic somewhere out there under a beautiful rubber tree who's trying to pull me through, but I'm not going to make it, I'm going to die on him, and he's going to remember it his whole life, wake up in the night crying years later and his wife won't understand.

I want to say, "Tell Steve I've got to get out of here," but I can't. My throat's gone. I'm going out under some rubber tree a hundred klicks away in the middle of Laos, where we're not supposed to be, and I can't say a thing.

This guy who shared his ham-and-motherfuckers with me in the mess, this guy is looking down on me and I think, Oh my God, I'm going to dream about him some night, some day, I'm going to dream about him and because I do he's going to die.

He doesn't say a thing.

He's the one that comes to get me in my hooch two days later when they try to bust me out.

They give me something pretty strong. By the time they come I'm getting the waking dreams, sure, but I'm not screaming anymore. I'm here but I'm not. I'm all these other places, I'm walking into an Arclight, B-52 bombers, my ears are bleeding, I'm the closest man when a big Chinese claymore goes off, my arm's hanging by a string, I'm dying in all these other places and I don't even know I've taken their pills. I'm like a doll when Steve and this guy and three others come, and the guards let them. I'm smiling like an idiot and saying, "Thank you very much," something stupid some USO type would say, and I've got someone holding me up so I don't fall on my face.

There's this Jolly Green Giant out in front of us. It's dawn and everything's beautiful and this chopper is gorgeous. It's Air Force. It's crazy. There are these guys I've never seen before. They've got black berets and they're neat and clean, and they're not Army. I think, Air Commandos! I'm giggling. They're Air Force. They're dandies. They're going to save the day like John Wayne at Iwo Jima. I feel a bullet go through my arm, then another through my leg, and the back of my head blows off, but I don't scream. I just feel the feelings, the ones you feel right before you die—but I don't scream. The Air Force is going to save me. That's funny. I tell myself how Steve had friends in the Air Commandos and how they took him around once in-country for a whole damn week, AWOL, yeah, but maybe it isn't true, maybe I'm dreaming it. I'm still giggling. I'm still saying, "Thank you very much."

We're out maybe fifty klicks and I don't know where we're heading. I don't care. Even if I cared I wouldn't know how far out "safe" was. I hear Steve's voice in the cockpit and a bunch of guys are laughing, so I think safe. They've busted me out because Steve cares and now we're safe. I'm still saying "Thank you" and some guy is saying "You're welcome, baby," and people are laughing and that feels good. If they're all laughing, no one got hurt, I know. If they're all laughing, we're safe. Thank you. Thank you very much.

Then something starts happening in the cockpit. I can't hear with all the wind. Someone says "Shit." Someone says "Cobra." Someone else says "Jesus Christ what the hell." I look out the roaring doorway and I see two black gunships. They're like nothing I've never seen before. No one's laughing. I'm saying "Thank you very much" but no one's laughing.

I find out later there was one behind us, one in front, and one above. They were beautiful. They reared up like snakes when they hit you. They had M-134 Miniguns that could put a round on every square centimeter of a football field within seconds. They had fifty-two white phosphorous rockets apiece and Martin-Marietta laser-guided Copperhead howitzer rounds. They had laser designators and Forward-Looking Infrared Sensors. They were night-black, no insignias of any kind. They were model AH–1G–X and they didn't belong to any regular branch of the military back then. You wouldn't see them until the end of the war.

I remember thinking that there were only two of us with talent on that slick, why couldn't he let us go? Why couldn't he just let us go?

I tried to think of all the things he could do to us, but he didn't do a thing. He didn't have to.

I didn't see Steve for a long time. I went ahead and tried to sleep at night because it was better that way. If I was going to have the dreams, it was better that way. It didn't make me so crazy. I wasn't like a doll someone had to hold up.

I went ahead and wrote the dreams down in a little notebook Bucannon gave me, and I talked to him. I showed him I really wanted to understand, how I wanted to help, because it was easier on everybody this way. He didn't act surprised, and I didn't think he would. He'd always known. Maybe he hadn't known about the guys in the black berets, but he'd known that Steve would try it. He'd known I'd stay awake. He'd known the dreams would move to daylight, from "interrupted REM-state," if I stayed awake. And he'd known he'd get us back.

We talked about how my dreams were changing. I was having them much earlier than "events in real time," he said. The same thing had probably been happening back in ER, he said, but I hadn't known it. The talent was getting stronger, he said, though I couldn't control it yet. I didn't need the "focal stimulus," he said, "the physical correlative." I didn't need to meet people to have the dreams.

"When are we going to do it?" I finally said.

He knew what I meant. He said we didn't want to rush into it, how acting prematurely was worse than not understanding it, how the "fixity of the future" was something no one yet understood, and we didn't want to take a chance on stopping the dreams by trying to tamper with the future.

★   ★   ★

"It won't stop the dreams," I said. "Even if we kept a death from happening, it wouldn't stop the dreams."

He never listened. He wanted them to die. He wanted to take notes on how they died and how my dreams matched their dying, and he wasn't going to call anyone back until he was ready to.

"This isn't war, Mary," he told me one day. "This is a kind of science and it has its own rules. You'll have to trust me, Mary."

He pushed the hair out of my eyes, because I was crying. He wanted to touch me. I know that now.

I tried to get messages out. I tried to figure out who I'd dreamed about. I'd wake up in the middle of the night and try to talk to anybody I could and figure it out. I'd say, "Do you know a guy who's got red hair and is from Alabama?" I'd say, "Do you know an RTO who's short and can't listen to anything except Jefferson Airplane?" Sometimes it would take too long. Sometimes I'd never find out who it was, but if I did, I'd try to get a message out to him. Sometimes he'd already gone out and I'd still try to get someone to send him a message—but that just wasn't done.

I found out later Bucannon got them all. People said yeah, sure, they'd see that the message got to the guy, but Bucannon always got them. He told people to say yes when I asked. He knew. He always knew.

I didn't have a dream about Steve and that was the important thing.

When I finally dreamed that Steve died, that it took more guys in uniforms than you'd think possible—with more weapons than you'd think they'd ever need—in a river valley awfully far away, I didn't tell Bucannon about it. I didn't tell him how Steve was twitching on the red earth up North, his body doing its best to dodge the rounds even though there were just too many of them, twitching and twitching, even after his body wasn't alive anymore.

I cried for a while and then stopped. I wanted to feel something but I couldn't.

I didn't ask for pills or booze and I didn't stay awake the next two nights scared about dreaming it again. There was something I needed to do.

I didn't know how long I had. I didn't know whether Steve's team—the one in the dream—had already gone out or not. I didn't know a thing, but I kept thinking about what Bucannon had said, the "fixity," how maybe the future couldn't be changed, how even if Bucannon hadn't intercepted those messages something else would have kept the future the way it was and those guys would have died anyway.

I found the Green Beanie medic who'd taken me to my hooch that first day. I sat down with him in the mess. One of Bucannon's types was watching us but I sat down anyway. I said, "Has Steve Balsam been sent out yet?" And he said, "I'm not supposed to say, Lieutenant. You know that."

"Yes, Captain, I do know that. I also know that because you took me to my little bunker that day I will probably dream about your death before it happens, if it happens here. I also know that if I tell the people running this project about it, they won't do a thing, even though they know how accurate my dreams are, just like they know how accurate Steve Balsam is, and Blakely, and Corigiollo, and the others, but they won't do a thing about it." I waited. He didn't blink. He was listening.

"I'm in a position, Captain, to let someone know when I have a dream about them. Do you understand?"

He stared at me.

"Yes," he said.

I said, "Has Steve Balsam been sent out yet?"

"No, he hasn't."

"Do you know anything about the mission he is about to go out on?"

He didn't say a thing for a moment. Then he said, "Red Dikes."

"I don't understand, Captain."

He didn't want to have to explain—it made him mad to have to. He looked at the MD type by the door and then he looked back at me.

"You can take out the Red Dikes with a one-K nuclear device, Lieutenant. Everyone knows this. If you do, Hanoi drowns and the North is down. Balsam's team is a twelve-man night insertion beyond the DMZ with special MAC V ordnance from a carrier in the South China Sea. All twelve are talents. Is the picture clear enough, Lieutenant?"

I didn't say a thing. I just looked at him.

Finally I said, "It's a suicide mission, isn't it. The device won't even be real. It's one of Bucannon's ideas—he wants to see how they perform, that's all. They'll never use a nuclear device in Southeast Asia and you know that as well as I do, Captain."

"You never know, Lieutenant."

"Yes, you do." I said it slowly so he would understand.

He looked away.

"When is the team leaving?"

He wouldn't answer anymore. The MD type looked like he was going to walk toward us.

"Captain?" I said.

"Thirty-eight hours. That's what they're saying."

I leaned over.

"Captain," I said. "You know the shape I was in when I got here. I need it again. I need enough of it to get me through a week of this place or I'm not going to make it. You know where to get it. I'll need it tonight."

As I walked by the MD type at the door I wondered how he was going to die, how long it was going to take, and who would do it.

I killed Bucannon the only way I knew how.

I started screaming at first light and when he came to my bunker, I was crying. I told him I'd had a dream about him. I told him I dreamed that his own men, guys in cammies and all of them talents, had killed him, they had killed him because he wasn't using a nurse's dreams to keep their friends alive, because he had my dreams but wasn't doing anything with them, and all their friends were dying.

I looked in his eyes and I told him how scared I was because they killed her too, they killed the nurse who was helping him too.

I told him how big the 9-millimeter holes looked in his fatigues, and how something else was used on his face and stomach, some smaller caliber. I told him how they got him dusted off soon as they could and got him on a sump pump and IV as soon as he hit Saigon, but it just wasn't enough, how he choked to death on his own fluids.

He didn't believe me.

"Was Lieutenant Balsam there?" he asked.

I said no, he wasn't, trying not to cry. I didn't know why, but he wasn't, I said.

His eyes changed. He was staring at me now.

He said, "When will this happen, Mary?"

I said I didn't know—not for a couple of days at least, but I couldn't be sure, how could I be sure? It felt like four, maybe five, days, but I couldn't be sure. I was crying again.

This is what made him believe me in the end.

He knew it would never happen if Steve were there—but if Steve was gone, if the men waited until Steve was gone?

Steve would be gone in a couple of days and there was no way that this nurse, scared and crying, could know this.

He moved me to his bunker and had someone hang canvas to make a hooch for me inside his. He doubled the guards and changed the guards and doubled them again, but I knew he didn't think it was going to happen until Steve left.

I cried that night. He came to my hooch. He said, "Don't be frightened, Mary. No one's going to hurt you. No one's going to hurt anyone."

But he wasn't sure. He hadn't tried to stop a dream from coming true—even though I'd asked him to—and he didn't know whether he could or not.

I told him I wanted him to hold me, someone to hold me. I told him I wanted him to touch my forehead the way he did, to push my hair back the way he did.

At first he didn't understand, but he did it.

I told him I wanted someone to make love to me tonight, because it hadn't happened in so long, not with Steve, not with anyone. He said he understood and that if he'd only known he could have made things easier on me.

He was quiet. He made sure the flaps on my hooch were tight and he undressed in the dark. I held his hand just like I'd held the hands of the others, back in Cam Ranh Bay. I remembered the dream, the real one where I killed him, how I'd held his hand while he got undressed, just like this.

Even in the dark I could see how pale he was and this was like the dream too. He seemed to glow in the dark even though there wasn't any light. I took off my clothes, too. I told him I wanted to do something special for him. He said fine, but we couldn't make much noise. I said there wouldn't be any noise. I told him to lie down on his stomach on the cot. I sounded excited. I even laughed. I told him it was called "around the world" and I liked it best with the man on his stomach. He did what I told him and I kneeled down and lay over him.

I jammed the needle with the morphine into his jugular and when he struggled I held him down with my own weight.

No one came for a long time.

When they did, I was crying and they couldn't get my hand from the needle.

Steve's team wasn't sent. The dreams stopped, just the way Bucannon thought they would. Because I killed a man to keep another alive, the dreams stopped. I tell myself now this was what it was all about. I was supposed to keep someone from dying—that's why the dreams began—and when I did, they could stop, they could finally stop. Bucannon would understand it.

"There is no talent like yours, Mary, that does not operate out of the psychological needs of the individual," he would have said. "You dreamed of death in the hope of stopping it. We both knew that, didn't we. When you killed me to save another, it could end, the dreams could stop, your gift could return to the darkness where it had lain for a million years—so unneeded in civilization, in times of peace, in the humdrum existence of teenagers in Long Beach, California, where fathers believed their daughters to be whores or lesbians if they went to war to keep others alive. Am I right, Mary?"

This is what he would have said.

* * *

They could have killed me. They could have taken me out into the jungle
and killed me. They could have given me a frontal and put me in a military
hospital like the man in '46 who had evidence that Roosevelt knew about the
Japanese attack on Pearl. The agency Bucannon had worked for could have
sent word down to have me pushed from a chopper on the way back to
Saigon, or had me given an overdose, or assigned me to some black op I'd
never come back from. They were a lot things they could have done, and
they didn't.

They didn't because of what Steve and the others did. They told them
you'll have to kill us all if you kill her or hurt her in any way. They told
them you can't send her to jail, you can send her to a hospital but not for
long, and you can't fuck with her head, or there will be stories in the press
and court trials and a bigger mess than My Lai ever was.

It was seventy-six talents who were saying this, so the agency listened.

Steve told me about it the first time he came. I'm here for a year, that's all.
There are ten other women in this wing and we get along—it's like a club.
They leave us alone.

Steve comes to see me once a month. He's married—to the same one in
Merced—and they've got a baby now, but he gets the money to fly down
somehow and he tells me she doesn't mind.

He says the world hasn't turned blue since he got back, except maybe
twice, real fast, on freeways in central California. He says he hasn't floated out
of his body except once, when Cathy was having the baby and it started to
come out wrong. It's fading away, he says, and he says it with a laugh, with
those big eyelashes and those great shoulders.

Some of the others come, too, to see if I'm okay. Most of them got out as
soon as they could. They send me packages and bring me things. We talk
about the mess this country is in, and we talk about getting together, right
after I get out. I don't know if they mean it. I don't know if we should. I tell
Steve it's over, we're back in the Big PX and we don't need it anymore—
Bucannon was right—and maybe we shouldn't get together.

He shakes his head. He gives me a look and I give him a look and we both
know we should have used the room that night in Cam Ranh Bay, when we
had the chance.

"You never know," he says, grinning. "You never know when the baby
might wake up."

That's the way he talks these days, now that he's a father.

"You never know when the baby might wake up."

The Heart's Desire

Chet Williamson

What's yours?"

"It's foolish, Peter. I have none."

"No. *That's* foolish. Everyone has one."

"Not me."

Michael Lindstrom, without a heart's desire, smiled at his friend and sipped from a glass of white wine.

"Come on, Michael," Peter said. "A moment somewhere? Somewhere along the way you lost, but still remember, bright as your youth. If I had one, you had one."

"What *was* yours?"

Peter Riley's face drifted for an instant. "It'll sound . . . stupid. Undoubtedly. But it is *the* time. The *best* time. I was eleven."

"Oh Jesus."

"Hear me out. I was eleven. And I was on a baseball team."

"Little League."

"Nothing so grand. A park league. Summer at the town park. I was not a good player, but I liked it. I wanted to be good. And I practiced every evening, made my dad throw me balls and I'd hit them. Or try to. In those afternoon games I'd stand out in right field, nervous as Hell when I was about to bat. Oh, I got hits. Maybe one out of five or six. Always a single, and usually because somebody bobbled a ball or made a bad throw. But one day —*the* day—I was at bat with a guy on first, one run behind, and two outs. It was the bottom of the seventh—we only played seven—and my whole team was muttering under their breaths, and some out loud. But that first pitch, the very first pitch—well, I belted it. I absolutely ripped that mother. That goddamn ball went back over the left fielder's head, hit, and bounced, and went right into the creek. And by the time the kid fished it out, I was long home, and everyone was yelling and cheering and clapping and pounding my ass off they were so damn happy. It wasn't a championship game or anything like that, but *I* won it. Me. That was the day. And there's never been another to touch it for sweetness."

"Not even when you lost your virginity?"

"I'm not even sure when that was. Technically."

"And you've relived that home run."

"Yeah. Several times."

"Doesn't it lose its novelty?"

"No. Each time there's something new."

"Come on. You can't mean you actually experience it. I can't believe that."

"But I have. It's time travel, Michael, honest to God."

"I also can't believe you're calling it that."

"Me and a hundred other people. And why not? You can't go back physically. That's science fiction. Mentally is the only conceivable way. Your own memory, your subconscious has it all in there. Every tiny detail. And Wagner knows how to make you remember."

"And how much have you paid Wagner all told for that privilege?"

"It's not inexpensive."

"No. That type of thing never is. 'Sell all you have and follow me.' "

"Don't make it sound like a religion."

"I wanted to make it sound like an obsession. Or an addiction."

"It's harmless. Helpful if anything."

"Does Jennifer think it's harmless?"

"Jennifer's been very supportive of it. Of me."

"Financially as well?"

"I can *handle* the cost, Michael."

"Doesn't she get a bit jealous? Of your running away from her back to the town park?"

Peter paused a moment too long. "No. I'm . . . refreshed when I come back from the experience. Renewed. I'm a better husband for it."

"And how long before all that freshness and renewal wear off and things get shabby again?"

Peter laughed. "Michael," he said quickly, "I just can't describe it. It's something you have to experience. I mean, everything is there, the smell of kids, the feel of the sun on your t-shirt, the infield dirt under your Keds— *Keds,* for Christ's sake—the old, taped bat in your hands—*everything.* The sensation is *total.*"

"You sound like you did when you tried to talk me into doing acid in college. Then, if you'll recall the precious sensations, I had to hold you all night while you cried and told me to watch out for the blue willies. What the Hell *were* the blue willies anyway?"

"I don't remember."

"Well, I'm sure Dr. Wagner could remind you."

Michael's wife came up to them. "All right, what are you two up to?" She put an arm around each one, kissing them both soundly.

"Michael is giving me Hell again, Maggie," Peter said.

"Oh, your treatment . . ."

"It's not a treatment," Peter protested.

"Sure it is," said Michael. "Fight reality with a checkup and a check. A big one."

"Michael, it *is* reality."

"No, Peter. *This* is reality. Here and now. That *was* reality."

Peter turned to Maggie.

"Don't get me in this argument," she said.

Peter nodded. "I never *could* talk him into anything, could I? Where's Jennifer?"

"Upstairs," said Maggie. "I think she was going to be sick."

Peter tried to smile. "We all have our ways of escaping from reality, huh? But what's yours, Michael?" Peter turned and disappeared into the crowd.

"You shouldn't be so hard on him," Maggie said, taking her arm from Michael's shoulder.

"I can't approve of what he's doing."

"He seems to be getting something out of it."

"Oh yes. An alcoholic wife."

"Michael . . ."

"They're lies. He's lying to himself, Maggie. He's found one moment of triumph that's become the core of his life, filled with seeds, and he goes back time after time to get one more."

"It's his choice. What can you do?"

"I could expose it."

"Why?"

"It would sell, for one thing. And the other thing is that it makes me angry to see my friend throwing away his money and his life to dreams."

There was that and more, enough to make Michael Lindstrom decide to do an exposé on temporal revisualization, to make him call Dr. Paul Wagner's Park Avenue office for an appointment, to make him lie when he met the doctor, expressing admiration for his work and acknowledging Wagner's compliments toward Michael's own writing with a grace and a gratitude he could not feel. He told Wagner that he wished to do a first-person article on the procedure, and asked for Wagner's cooperation.

Wagner gave a smile of practiced sincerity. "There's no pledge of secrecy, Mr. Lindstrom. I'll be happy to have you as a patient, and you can tell as much or as little as you like. Do you . . . have a certain time in mind that you wish to revisit?"

Michael chuckled. "You make it sound so simple. 'Step into my time machine and let's go.'"

"Hardly that. But it is quite simple, really. When you know how."

"How?"

"Drugs—harmless, government-approved drugs—and hypnosis. It's in your mind, Mr. Lindstrom. It's really all in there."

"This sounds awfully sixtyish—Timothy Leary stuff."

Wagner shrugged. "Styles change. The mind doesn't."

"It's just very hard to believe," said Michael with a penitent's smile, "that it's all still there . . . in as much detail as I've heard about."

"It's there," Wagner said plainly. "Things you didn't even know you'd seen. You'll scarcely believe it. But you'll be there. And so will everything else. Just as it was."

"I assume it's very expensive."

"And I assume your publisher will pay for it, so that needn't worry you."

Michael smiled wryly, thinking it best not to appear too innocent, too trusting. "You doctors."

"Or doctors' *wives*," Wagner said, his smile showing his teeth for the first time. They looked white, and bright, and young, like the rest of him. "Now. Suppose you tell me."

Michael pursed his lips, looked at Wagner, looked down at his hands in his lap, and back up again. "A woman," he lied. "A woman I once knew."

"A lover?"

"Must you know that?"

"I should."

"No. Not a lover. Though I loved her. And I think she loved me. I was young, in college. It was before I met my wife. It was our second, maybe third date, I can't remember. But we were walking on the beach. With no one else around. We must have walked for miles without seeing a soul. And we didn't say a word. Not all the way. Then, when the beach ended . . ."

"Ended?"

"Isn't that strange," said Michael, "but that's how I remember it. It just ended. A cliff, a sea-wall, I don't know."

"You will," Wagner said quietly. "What happened next?"

"I held her. I kissed her. Nothing more. And we walked back. And that day I felt happier, more at peace with myself, than I've been before or since."

"What happened? Between the two of you."

"She died. Three weeks later. Swimming alone on that same beach. Drowned. A young boy saw her go down. They never found her body."

Wagner nodded slowly. "What was her name?"

"Anne." *Beautiful Annabel Lee. In her tomb by the side of the sea.* Michael laughed inside at the lie, the false Anne, the seaside and walk he had never known. "And that," he said aloud, "is the moment I want to reclaim."

"One thing, Mr. Lindstrom," said Wagner with a frown. "What brought you here? Your desire to see and be with this girl again? Or your desire for a story."

"Both. Combined business and pleasure trip."

Wagner looked at him for so long that Michael grew uncomfortable. Finally he spoke. "Ready then?"

"Now?"

"It doesn't take long. A matter of minutes."

"That's not much for the money."

"It will seem far longer, I promise. But first I'll have to ask you to sign this," and he handed Michael a piece of paper and a pen from a desk drawer. "It simply releases me from any legal actions stemming from a psychological complaint. I remain liable, however, for any adverse physical reaction." Michael read it and signed.

Wagner stood and walked to a metal cabinet that contrasted starkly with the tasteful opulence of the room's other furnishings. He returned to Michael's side bearing a tray on which lay an unmarked vial, a syringe, an alcohol swab, and a Band-Aid. "Do you mind needles?" Michael shook his head, shrugged off his jacket, and rolled up his right sleeve. Wagner inserted the syringe in the vial and drew out a cc of thick, milky fluid.

"What is that?" Michael asked.

"Ah. My secret," Wagner replied, wiping the skin over Michael's biceps with the swab. "Safer than aspirin as far as side effects. This'll sting a bit."

The needle slid into Michael's arm, and he looked away. "There," said Wagner. "All there is to it. You'll begin to feel drowsy in a minute or so."

"Do I lie down?" asked Michael, looking in vain for a couch.

"No. Sitting is fine. You won't be aware of your body. Now just relax."

Within seconds, Michael felt a lethargy steal over him, as when he would fall asleep on trains. He closed his eyes. He didn't hear Wagner speaking, could not remember later if Wagner had said anything at all.

The beach appeared slowly, but with such a sense of reality that he felt as if he were awakening from a dream. It was real, it was true, and the wet sand was cool where his bare feet pressed it down. Wind, blowing from a gray sky, ruffled the sleeves of his jacket and played with his hair. The smell of the sea was fresh and strong, and the hand he was holding was warm.

He turned—not his dream-self, he thought, but *he*—and looked at her, and knew that he had never seen her before, but knew that she was here, was real, and that no one would ever be able to take her place. She gazed back at him with deep, thoughtful eyes that had owned him always, then turned her face out to the sea so that the breeze took her hair and made it shimmer like a curtain of obsidian rain.

Had he wanted to speak, he could not have. His knowledge would have choked him. But his voice and thoughts, those of fifty-year-old Michael Lindstrom, were imprisoned within the young body, with whose flesh he saw, and touched, and heard. His consciousness rode above, like a hawk over a storm, observed all, felt, but could not express the feeling. They walked on through the cool day, over the wet sand, and from time to time he would look at her, kiss her cheek or her lips, and when he looked ahead, or down at the sand, he prayed to himself to turn his head, to look at her again, to never look away, never leave her alone, because then she would not vanish, not leave him, not be claimed by the sea.

It was a cliff at the end of the beach. That which he had not remembered, which had never existed, was there now, tall and gray, its lower flanks gleaming with salt spray. He and Anne *(Anne)* watched the waves caress the rock, moved to where beach and sea and cliff all met, then sat in the sand and held each other. Michael shivered as the chill crept over his buttocks and touched the base of his spine. He hugged Anne tighter, thinking, *tighter still never let go never,* and he wanted to crush her to him, make them inseparable for always, but his young arms would not obey old desires.

After too short a time they rose and walked back, back the way they had come. It seemed to Michael that they ran where he would have crawled. He could feel Anne's arm around him, could feel the wind cool his flesh, could feel Anne's hair, black as the sea's depth, brush his cheek, whisper at his ear, and then another reality impinged—a reality of a three-piece suit, a leather chair beneath him, his hands resting on its arms, and Dr. Wagner beside him, gazing into his face with a loving concern.

"Welcome back," Wagner said softly.

Michael could not speak. He felt as though he had been wrenched in time and place, experienced sudden confusion that approached panic before he remembered what he had done, why he was there. He looked at his right hand, and was surprised when he found Anne's hand missing. He spread his fingers apart, examined them, looked down at his shod feet. He could still feel the sand. "It was all a lie," he said huskily. "None of it was true."

"You saw it," said Wagner. "You were there. Weren't you?"

"There was no *there* to be!" Michael said with an anger that startled and unmanned him. He knew that he should have felt smug, triumphant. He felt neither.

"You were lying then," the doctor said. "I suspected you were."

"Did you?"

"Annabel Lee, wasn't that it?" Wagner smiled gently. "A fairly simple allusion."

"If you knew it was a lie, why did you do it? Let me take it?"

"Mr. Lindstrom, half of what my patients want to relive are lies. They never happened. At least not as grandly as most of them remember. But if that's what they want, that's what they can have. At last."

"But that's . . . a fraud . . ."

"Not really. The rooms are inside. I just provide the key."

"For such simple things? My friend, and his home run?"

"Maybe it was, maybe it wasn't. Maybe it was only a single, maybe even only a walk. That doesn't matter. *Now* it's a home run. Not many of us have had those perfect moments. Not even one. Life can be very sad when one has to pretend to remember happiness."

"You sell dreams," Michael said.

"No." Wagner's face was expressionless, his tone flat. "I sell the heart's desire. Sometimes what was, but more often what should have been."

Michael held up an admonishing finger, then saw it tremble, and lowered it guiltily. "I'm going to . . . to tell about this," he said, his lower lip quivering. "This cannot, should not happen."

"If you feel you must, you may," Wagner said calmly. "I'm not sure what exactly you've found that you consider worthy of exposing, but you're welcome to whatever it is. Just one thing—think about it for a day or two. Before you start writing. And ask yourself if your knowledge will make any difference to those who come to me. Ask yourself if they don't already know what you know.

"And ask yourself too, if the truth be known, whether people will stop coming to see me, or whether more will start to come."

Michael tried to stop shaking. "Why do you do this?"

"Because I can. Because it helps to ease the pain."

"What if I don't *want* my pain eased?" Michael flared. "Or what if I *have* no pain?"

"Then you shouldn't have come here. I am, after all, a doctor. My purpose is healing."

Michael made no reply.

"If you have no more questions, there are other patients I must see."

Michael stood up. "This is not . . . the last of this," he said, before he moved to the door.

"No," Dr. Wagner said. "I don't suppose it is."

Maggie was in the kitchen when Michael Lindstrom arrived home. When he embraced her, her bare arms felt rough and leathery, her hair was the

texture of straw against his cheek. Her smile was stiff and unfriendly, a
stranger's smile, and her voice, as she tried to draw out his secrets over dinner,
was cawing, strident. He stayed up late that night, and drank more than was
customary for him.

The following day, when Dr. Wagner was told by his receptionist that
Michael Lindstrom had made a second appointment, he was not surprised.
The doctor prided himself on his ability to recognize deep pain, pain that
would be long in healing, healing that would leave scars as deep as the pain
that had made them necessary.

In the Flesh

Clive Barker

When Cleveland Smith returned to his cell after the interview with the Landing Officer, his new bunkmate was already in residence, staring at the dust-infested sunlight through the reinforced glass window. It was a short display; for less than half an hour each afternoon (clouds permitting) the sun found its way between the wall and the administration building and edged its way along the side of B Wing, not to appear again until the following day.

"You're Tait?" Cleve said.

The prisoner looked away from the sun. Mayflower had said the new boy was twenty-two, but Tait looked five years younger. He had the face of a lost dog. An ugly dog, at that—a dog left by its owners to play in traffic. Eyes too wide, mouth too soft, arms too slender: a born victim. Cleve was irritated to have been encumbered with the boy. Tait was dead weight, and Cleve had no energies to expend on the boy's protection, despite Mayflower's pep talk about extending a welcoming hand.

"Yes," the dog replied. "William."

"People call you William?"

"No," the boy said. "They call me Billy."

"Billy." Cleve nodded, and stepped into the cell. The regime at Pentonville was relatively enlightened; cells were left open for two hours in the mornings, and often two in the afternoon, allowing the cons some freedom of movement. The arrangement had its disadvantages, however, which was where Mayflower's talk came in.

"I've been told to give you some advice."

"Oh?" the boy replied.

"You've not done time before?"

"No."

"Not even Borstal?"

Tait's eyes flickered. "A little."

"So you know what the score is. You know you're easy meat."

"Sure."

"Seems I've been volunteered," Cleve said without appetite, "to keep you from getting mauled."

Tait stared at Cleve with eyes the blue of which was milky, as though the sun were still in them. "Don't put yourself out," the boy said. "You don't owe me anything."

"Damn right I don't. But it seems I got a social responsibility," Cleve said sourly. "And you're it."

Cleve was two months into his sentence for handling marijuana, his third visit to Pentonville. At thirty years of age he was far from obsolete. His body was solid, his face lean and refined; in his court suit he could have passed for a lawyer at ten yards. A little closer, and the viewer might catch the scar on his neck, the result of an attack by a penniless addict, and a certain wariness in his gait, as if with every step forward he was keeping the option of a speedy retreat.

You're still a young man, the last judge had told him; you still have time to change your spots. He hadn't disagreed out loud, but Cleve knew in his heart he was a leopard born and bred. Crime was easy, work was not. Until somebody proved otherwise he would do what he did best, and take the consequences if caught. Doing time wasn't so unpalatable if you had the right attitude toward it. The food was edible, the company select; as long as he had something to keep his mind occupied he was content enough. At present he was reading about sin. Now *there* was a subject. In his time he'd heard so many explanations of how it had come into the world, from probation officers and lawyers and priests. Theories sociological, theological, ideological. Some were worthy of a few minutes' consideration. Most were so absurd (sin from the womb, sin from the state) he laughed in their apologists' faces. None held water for long.

It was a good bone to chew over, though. He needed a problem to occupy the days. And nights; he slept badly in prison. It wasn't *his* guilt that kept him awake but that of others. He was, after all, just a hash pusher, supplying wherever there was a demand: a minor cog in the consumerist machine, he had nothing to feel guilty about. But there were others here, *many* others, it seemed, whose dreams were not so benevolent, nor nights so peaceful. They would cry, they would complain, they would curse judges local and celestial. Their din would have kept the dead awake.

"Is it always like this?" Billy asked Cleve after a week or so. A new inmate was making a ruckus down the landing: one moment tears, the next obscenities.

"Yes. Most of the time," said Cleve. "Some of them need to yell a bit. It keeps their minds from curdling."

"Not you," observed the unmusical voice from the bunk below, "You just read your books and keep out of harm's way. I've watched you. It doesn't bother you, does it?"

"I can live with it," Cleve replied. "I got no wife to come here every week and remind me what I'm missing."

"You been in before?"

"Twice."

The boy hesitated an instant before saying, "I suppose you know your way around the place, do you?"

"Well, I'm not writing a guidebook, but I got the general layout by now." It seemed an odd comment for the boy to make. "Why?"

"I just wondered," said Billy.

"You got a question?"

Tait didn't answer for several seconds, then said: "I heard they used to . . . used to *hang* people here."

Whatever Cleve had been expecting the boy to come out with, that wasn't it. But then he had decided several days back that Billy Tait was a strange one. Sly, sidelong glances from those milky-blue eyes; a way he had of staring at the wall or at the window like a detective at a murder scene, desperate for clues.

Cleve said, "There used to be a hanging shed, I think."

Again silence, and then another inquiry, dropped as lightly as the boy could contrive. "Is it still standing?"

"The shed? I don't know. They don't hang people anymore, Billy, or hadn't you heard?" There was no reply from below. "What's it to you, anyhow?"

"Just curious."

Billy was right; curious he was. So odd, with his vacant stares and his solitary manner, that most of the men kept clear of him. Only Lowell took any interest in him, and his motives for that were unequivocal.

"You want to lend me your lady for the afternoon?" he asked Cleve while they waited in line for breakfast. Tait, who stood within earshot, said nothing; neither did Cleve.

"You hear me? I asked you a question."

"I heard. You leave him alone."

"Share and share alike," Lowell said. "I can do you some favors. We can work something out."

"He's not available."

"Well, why don't I ask *him?*" Lowell said, grinning through his beard. "What do you say, baby?"

Tait looked around at Lowell.

"I say no thank you."

"No *thank you,*" Lowell said, and gave Cleve a second smile, this quite without humor. "You've got him well trained. Does he sit up and beg, too?"

"Take a walk, Lowell," Cleve replied. "He's not available and that's all there is to it."

"You can't keep your eyes on him every minute of the day," Lowell pointed out. "Sooner or later he's going to have to stand on his own two feet. Unless he's better kneeling."

The innuendo won a guffaw from Lowell's cell-mate, Nayler. Neither were men Cleve would have willingly faced in a free-for-all, but his skills as a bluffer were honed razor-sharp, and he used them now.

"You don't want to trouble yourself," he told Lowell. "You can only cover so many scars with a beard."

Lowell looked at Cleve, all humor fled. He clearly couldn't distinguish the truth from bluff, and equally clearly wasn't willing to put his neck on the line.

"Just don't look the other way," he said, and said no more.

The encounter at breakfast wasn't mentioned until that night when the lights had been extinguished. It was Billy who brought it up.

"You shouldn't have done that," he said. "Lowell's a bad bastard. I've heard the talk."

"You want to get raped then, do you?"

"No," he said quickly, "Christ no. I got to be fit."

"You'll be fit for nothing if Lowell gets his hands on you."

Billy slipped out from his bunk and stood in the middle of the cell, barely visible in the gloom. "I suppose you want something in return," he said.

Cleve turned on his pillow and looked at the uncertain silhouette standing a yard from him. "What have you got that I'd want, Billy Boy?" he said.

"What Lowell wanted."

"Is that what you think that bluster was all about? Me staking a claim?"

"Yeah."

"Like you said: no thank you." Cleve rolled over again to face the wall.

"I didn't mean—"

"I don't care what you meant. I just don't want to hear about it, all right? You stay out of Lowell's way, and don't give me shit."

"Hey," Billy murmured, "don't get like that, please. *Please.* You're the only one friend I've got."

"I'm nobody's friend," Cleve said to the wall. "I just don't want any inconvenience. Understand me?"

"No inconvenience," the boy repeated, dull-tongued.

"Right. Now . . . I need my beauty sleep."

Tait said no more but returned to the bottom bunk and lay down, the springs creaking as he did so. Cleve lay in silence, turning the exchange over in his head. He had no wish to lay hands on the boy, but perhaps he had made his point too harshly. Well, it was done.

From below he could hear Billy murmuring to himself, almost inaudibly. He strained to eavesdrop on what the boy was saying. It took several seconds of ear-pricking attention before Cleve realized that Billy Boy was saying his prayers.

Cleve dreamed that night. What of, he couldn't remember in the morning, though as he showered and shaved tantalizing grains of the dream sifted through his head. Scarcely ten minutes went by that morning without something—salt overturned on the breakfast table, the sound of shouts in the exercise yard—promising to break his dream, but the revelation did not come. It left him uncharacteristically edgy and short tempered. When Wesley, a small-time forger whom he knew from his previous vacation here, approached him in the library and started to talk as though they were bosom pals, Cleve told the runt to shut up. But Wesley insisted on speaking.

"You got trouble."

"Oh. How so?"

"That boy of yours. Billy."

"What about him?"

"He's asking questions. He's getting pushy. People don't like it. They're saying you should take him in hand."

"I'm not his keeper."

Wesley pulled a face. "I'm telling you, as a friend."

"Spare me."

"Don't be stupid, Cleveland. You're making enemies."

"Oh?" said Cleve. "Name one."

"Lowell," Wesley said, quick as a flash. "Nayler for another. All kinds of people. They don't like the way Tait is."

"And how is he?" Cleve snapped back.

Wesley made a small grunt of protest. "I'm just trying to tell you," he said. "He's sly. Like a fucking rat. There'll be trouble."

"Spare me the prophecies."

* * *

The law of averages demands the worst prophet be right some of the time: this was Wesley's moment, it seemed. The day after, coming back from the workshop, where he'd exercised his intellect putting wheels on plastic cars, Cleve found Mayflower waiting for him on the landing.

"I asked you to look after William Tait, Smith," the officer said. "Don't you give a damn?"

"What's happened?"

"No, I suppose you don't."

"I asked what happened. Sir."

"Nothing much. Not this time. He's been roughed up, that's all. Seems Lowell has a hankering after him. Am I right?" Mayflower peered at Cleve, and when he got no response went on: "I made an error with you, Smith. I thought there was something worth appealing to under the hard man. My mistake."

Billy was lying on the bunk, his face bruised, his eyes closed. He didn't open them when Cleve came in.

"You O.K.?"

"Sure," the boy said softly.

"No bones broken?"

"I'll survive."

"You've got to understand—"

"*Listen.*" Billy opened his eyes. The pupils had darkened somehow, or that was the trick the light performed with them. "I'm alive, O.K.? I'm not an idiot, you know. I knew what I was letting myself in for, coming here." He spoke as if he'd had a choice in the matter. "I can take Lowell," he went on, "so don't fret." He paused, then said, "You were right."

"About what?"

"About not having friends. I'm on my own, you're on your own. Right? I'm just a slow learner, but I'm getting the hang of it." He smiled to himself.

"You've been asking questions," Cleve said.

"Oh, yeah?" Billy replied off-handedly. "Who says?"

"If you've got questions, ask me. People don't like snoopers. They get suspicious. And then they turn their backs when Lowell and his like get heavy."

Naming the man brought a painful frown to Billy's face. He touched his bruised cheek. "He's dead," the boy murmured, almost to himself.

"Some chance," Cleve commented.

The look that Tait returned could have sliced steel. "I mean it," he said, without a trace of doubt in his voice. "Lowell won't get out alive."

Cleve didn't comment; the boy needed this show of bravado, laughable as it was.

"What do you want to know that you go snooping around?"

"Nothing much," Billy replied. He was no longer looking at Cleve but staring at the bunk above. Quietly, he said, "I just wanted to know where the graves were, that was all."

"The graves?"

"Where they buried the men they'd hanged. Somebody told me there's a rose bush where Crippen's buried. You ever hear that?"

Cleve shook his head. Only now did he remember the boy asking about the hanging shed, and now the graves. Billy looked up at him. The bruise was ripening by the minute.

"You know where they are, Cleve?" he asked. Again, that feigned nonchalance.

"I could find out, if you do me the courtesy of telling me why you want to know."

Billy looked out from the shelter of the bunk. The afternoon sun was describing its short arc on the painted brick of the cell wall. It was weak today. The boy slid his legs off the bunk and sat on the edge of the mattress, staring at the light as he had on that first day.

"My grandfather—that is, my mother's father—was hanged here," he said, his voice raw. "In 1937. Edgar Tait. Edgar Saint Clair Tait."

"I thought you said your *mother's* father?"

"I took his name. I didn't want my father's name. I never belonged to him."

"Nobody belongs to anybody," Cleve replied. "You're your own man."

"But that's not true," Billy said with a tiny shrug, still staring at the light on the wall. His certainty was immovable; the gentility with which he spoke did not undercut the authority of the statement. "I *belong* to my grandfather. I always have."

"You weren't even born when he—"

"That doesn't matter. Coming and going; that's nothing."

Coming and going, Cleve puzzled. Did Tait mean life and death? He had no chance to ask. Billy was talking again, the same subdued but insistent flow.

"He was guilty, of course. Not the way they thought he was, but *guilty*. He knew what he was and what he was capable of; that's guilt, isn't it? He killed four people. Or at least that's what they hanged him for."

"You mean he killed more?"

Billy made another small shrug: numbers didn't matter apparently. "But nobody came to see where they'd laid him to rest. That's not right, is it? They didn't care, I suppose. All the family were glad he was gone, probably. Thought he was wrong in the head from the beginning. But he wasn't. I know he *wasn't*. I've got his hands, and his eyes. So Mama said. She told me all about him, you see, just before she died. Told me things she'd never told anybody, and only told me because of my eyes . . ." He faltered, and put his hand to his lip, as if the fluctuating light on the brick had already mesmerized him into saying too much.

"What did your mother tell you?" Cleve pressed him.

Billy seemed to weigh up alternative responses before offering one. "Just that he and I were *alike* in some ways," he said.

"Crazy, you mean?" Cleve said, only half-joking.

"Something like that," Billy replied, eyes still on the wall. He sighed, then allowed himself a further confession. "That's why I came here. So my grandfather would know he hadn't been forgotten."

"Came here?" said Cleve. "What are you talking about? You were caught and sentenced. You had no choice."

The light on the wall was extinguished as a cloud passed over the sun. Billy looked up at Cleve. The light was there, in his eyes.

"I committed a crime to get here," the boy replied. "It was a deliberate act."

Cleve shook his head. The claim was preposterous.

"I tried before—twice. It's taken time. But I got here, didn't I?"

"Don't take me for a fool, Billy," Cleve warned.

"I don't," the other replied. He stood up now. He seemed somehow lighter for the story he'd told; he even smiled, if tentatively, as he said: "You've been good to me. Don't think I don't know that. I'm grateful. Now"—He faced Cleve before saying—"I want to know where the graves are. Find that out and you won't hear another peep from me, I promise."

Cleve knew next to nothing about the prison or its history, but he knew somebody who did. There was a man by the name of Bishop—so familiar with the inmates that his name had acquired the definite article—who was often at the workshop at the same time as Cleve. The Bishop had been in and out of prison for much of his forty-odd years, mostly for misdemeanors, and, with all the fatalism of a one-legged man who makes a life study of monopedia, had become an expert on prisons and the penal system. Little of his information came from books. He had gleaned the bulk of his knowledge from old lags and screws who wanted to talk the hours away, and by degrees he had turned himself into a walking encyclopedia on crime and punishment. He had made it his trade, and he sold his carefully accrued knowledge by the sentence; sometimes as geographical information to the would-be escapee, sometimes as prison mythology to the godless con in search of a local divinity. Now Cleve sought him out and laid down his payment in tobacco and IOUs.

"What can I do for you?" The Bishop asked. He was heavy but not unhealthily so. The needle-thin cigarettes he was perpetually rolling and smoking were dwarfed by his butcher's fingers, stained sepia by nicotine.

"I want to know about the hangings here."

The Bishop smiled. "Such good stories," he said, and began to tell.

On the plain details, Billy had been substantially correct. There had been hangings in Pentonville up until the middle of the century, but the shed had long since been demolished. On the spot now stood the Probation Office in B Wing. As to the story of Crippen's roses, there was truth in that too. In front of a hut on the grounds, which, The Bishop informed Cleve, was a store for gardening equipment, was a small patch of grass, in the center of which a bush flourished, planted (and at this point The Bishop confessed that he could not tell fact from fiction) in memory of Doctor Crippen, hanged in 1910.

"That's where the graves are?" Cleve asked.

"No, no," The Bishop said, reducing half of one of his skinny cigarettes to ash with a single inhalation. "The graves are alongside the wall, to the left behind the hut. There's a long lawn; you must have seen it."

"No stones?"

"Absolutely not. The plots have always been left unmarked. Only the governor knows who's buried where, and he's probably lost the plans." The Bishop ferreted for his tobacco tin in the breast pocket of his prison-issue shirt and began to roll another cigarette with such familiarity he scarcely glanced down at what he was doing. "Nobody's allowed to come and mourn, you see. Out of sight, out of mind: that's the idea. Of course, that's not the way it works, is it? People forget prime ministers, but they remember murderers. You walk on that lawn, and just six feet under are some of the most notorious men who ever graced this green and pleasant land. And not even a cross to mark the spot. Criminal, isn't it?"

"You know who's buried there?"

"Some very wicked gentlemen," The Bishop replied, as if fondly admonishing them for their mischief mongering.

"You heard of a man called Edgar Tait?"

Bishop raised his eyebrows; the fat of his brow furrowed. "Saint Tait? Oh certainly. He's not easily forgotten."

"What do you know about him?"

"He killed his wife, and then his children. Took a knife to them all, as I live and breathe."

"All?"

The Bishop put the freshly rolled cigarette to his thick lips. "Maybe not all," he said, narrowing his eyes as he tried to recall the specific details.

"Maybe one of them survived. I think perhaps a daughter." He shrugged dismissively. "I'm not very good at remembering the victims. But then, who is?" He fixed his bland gaze on Cleve. "Why are you so interested in Tait? He was hanged before the war."

"Nineteen thirty-seven. He'll be well gone, eh?"

The Bishop raised a cautionary forefinger. "Not so," he said. "You see, the land this prison is built upon has special properties. Bodies buried here don't rot the way they do elsewhere." Cleve shot The Bishop an incredulous glance. "It's true," the fat man protested mildly. "I have it on unimpeachable authority. Take it from me, whenever they've had to exhume a body from the plot it's always been found in almost perfect condition." He paused to light his cigarette and drew upon it, exhaling the smoke through his mouth with his next words. "When the end of the world is upon us, the good men of Marylebone and Camden Town will rise up as rot and bone. But the wicked? They'll dance to Judgment as fresh as the day they dropped. Imagine that." This perverse notion clearly delighted him. His pudgy face puckered and dimpled with pleasure at it. "Ah," he mused, "and who'll be calling who corrupt on *that* fine morning?"

Cleve never worked out precisely how Billy talked his way on to the gardening detail, but he managed it. Perhaps he had appealed directly to Mayflower, who'd persuaded his superiors that the boy could be trusted out in the fresh air. However he worked the maneuver, in the middle of the week following Cleve's discovery of the graves' whereabouts, Billy was out in the cold April morning cutting grass.

What happened that day filtered back down the grapevine around recreation time. Cleve had the story from three independent sources, none of whom had been on the spot. The accounts had a variety of colorations, but were clearly of the same species. The bare bones went as follows:

The gardening detail, made up of four men watched over by a single prison guard, were moving around the blocks, trimming grass and weeding beds in preparation for the spring planting. Custody had been lax, apparently. It was two or three minutes before the guard even noticed that one of his charges had edged to the periphery of the party and slipped away. The alarm was raised. The guards did not have to look far, however. Tait had made no attempt to escape, or if he had he'd been stymied in his bid by a fit of some kind, which had crippled him. He was found (and here the stories parted company considerably) on a large patch of lawn beside the wall, lying on the grass. Some reports claimed he was black in the face, his body knotted up and his tongue all but bitten through; others that he was found facedown, talking to the earth, weeping and cajoling. The consensus was that the boy had lost his mind.

The rumors made Cleve the center of attention, a situation he did not relish. For the next day he was scarcely left alone, men wanting to know what it was like to share a cell with a lunatic. He had nothing to tell, he insisted. Tait had been the perfect cell-mate—quiet, undemanding and unquestionably sane. He told the same story to Mayflower when he was grilled the following day, and later, to the prison doctor. He let not a breath of Tait's interest in the graves be known and made it his business to see The Bishop and request a similar silence of him. The man was willing to oblige only if vouchsafed the full story in due course. This Cleve promised. The Bishop, as befitted his assumed clerisy, was as good as his word.

Billy was gone for two days. In the interim Mayflower disappeared from his duties as Landing Officer. No explanation was given. In his place a man called Devlin was transferred from D Wing. His reputation went before him. He was not, it seemed, a man of rare compassion. The impression was confirmed when, the day of Billy Tait's return, Cleve was summoned into Devlin's office.

"I'm told you and Tait are close," Devlin said. He had a face as giving as granite.

"Not really, sir."

"I'm not going to make Mayflower's mistake, Smith. As far as I'm concerned, Tait is trouble. I'm going to watch him like a hawk, and when I'm not here you're going to do it for me, understand? If he so much as crosses his eyes it's the ghost train. I'll have him out of here and into a special unit before he can fart. Do I make myself clear?"

"Paying your respects, were you?"

Billy had lost weight in the hospital, pounds his scrawny frame could scarcely afford. His shirt hung off his shoulders; his belt was on its tightest notch. The thinning more than ever emphasized his physical vulnerability; a featherweight blow would floor him, Cleve thought. But it lent his face a new, almost desperate, intensity. He seemed all eyes, and those had lost all trace of captured sunlight. Gone, too, was the pretense of vacuity, replaced with an eerie purposefulness.

"I asked a question."

"I heard you," Billy said. There was no sun today, but he looked at the wall anyway. "Yes, if you must know, I was paying my respects."

"I've been told to watch you, by Devlin. He wants you off the Landing. Transferred entirely, maybe."

"Out?" The panicked look Billy gave Cleve was too naked to be met for more than a few seconds. "Away from here, you mean?"

"I would think so."

"They can't!"

"Oh, they can. They call it the ghost train. One minute you're here; the next—"

"No," the boy said, hands suddenly fists. He had begun to shake, and for a moment Cleve feared a second fit. But he seemed, by act of will, to control the tremors, and turned his look back to his cell-mate. The bruises he'd received from Lowell had dulled to yellow-gray, but far from disappeared; his unshaven cheeks were dusted with pale-ginger hair. Looking at him Cleve felt an unwelcome twinge of concern.

"Tell me," Cleve said.

"Tell you what?" Billy asked.

"What happened at the graves."

"I felt dizzy. I fell over. The next thing I knew I was in hospital."

"That's what you told *them,* isn't it?"

"It's the truth."

"Not the way I heard it. Why don't you explain what really happened? I want you to trust me."

"I do," the boy said. "But I have to keep this to myself, see. It's between me and him."

"You and Edgar?" Cleve asked, and Billy nodded. "A man who killed all his family but your mother?"

Billy was clearly startled that Cleve possessed this information. "Yes," he said after consideration. "Yes, he killed them all. He would have killed Mama too if she hadn't escaped. He wanted to wipe the whole family out. So there'd be no heirs to carry the bad blood."

"Your blood's bad, is it?"

Billy allowed himself the slenderest of smiles. "No," he said. "I don't think so. Grandfather was wrong. Times have changed, haven't they?"

He *is* mad, Cleve thought. Lightning-swift, Billy caught the judgment.

"I'm not insane," he said. "You tell them that. Tell Devlin and whoever else asks. Tell them I'm a lamb." The fierceness was back in his eyes. There was nothing lamblike there, though Cleve forbore saying so. "They mustn't move me out, Cleve. Not after getting so close. I've got business here. Important business."

"With a dead man?"

"With a dead man."

★ ★ ★

Whatever new purpose he displayed for Cleve, the shutters went up when Billy got back among the rest of the cons. He responded neither to the questions nor the insults bandied about; his facade of empty-eyed indifference was flawless. Cleve was impressed. The boy had a future as an actor, if he decided to forsake professional lunacy.

But the strain of concealing the newfound urgency in him rapidly began to tell. In a hollowness about the eyes and a jitteriness in his movements; in brooding and unshakable silences. The physical deterioration was apparent to the doctor to whom Billy continued to report; he pronounced the boy suffering from depression and acute insomnia and prescribed sedatives to aid sleep. These pills Billy gave to Cleve, insisting he had no need of them himself. Cleve was grateful. For the first time in many months he began to sleep well, unperturbed by the tears and shouts of his fellow inmates.

By day, the relationship between him and the boy, which had always been vestigial, dwindled down to mere courtesy. Cleve sensed that Billy was closing up entirely, removing himself from merely physical concerns.

It was not the first time he had witnessed such a premeditated withdrawal. His sister-in-law, Rosanna, had died of stomach cancer three years earlier: a protracted and, until the last weeks, steady decline. Cleve had not been close to her, but perhaps that very distance had lent him a perspective on the woman's behavior that the rest of his family had lacked. He had been startled at the systematic way she had prepared herself for death, drawing in her affections until they touched only the most vital figures in her life—her children and her priest—and exiling all others, including her husband of fourteen years.

Now he saw the same dispassion and frugality in Billy. Like a man in training to cross a waterless wasteland and too possessive of his energies to squander them in a single fruitless gesture, the boy was sinking into himself. It was eerie; Cleve became increasingly uncomfortable sharing the twelve feet by eight of the cell with Billy. It was like living with a man on Death Row.

The only consolation was the tranquilizers, which Billy readily charmed the doctor into continuing to supply. They guaranteed Cleve sleep that was restful, and, for several days at least, dreamless.

And then he dreamed the city.

Not the city first; first the desert. An empty expanse of blue-black sand, which stung the soles of his feet as he walked, and was blown up by a cool wind into his nose and eyes and hair. He had been here before, he knew. His dream-self recognized the vista of barren dunes, with neither tree nor habitation to break the monotony. But on previous visits he had come with guides (or such was his half-formed belief); now he was alone, and the clouds above his head were heavy and slate-gray, promising no sun. For what seemed hours he walked the dunes, his feet turned bloody by the sharp sand, his body, dusted by the grains, tinged blue. As exhaustion came close to defeating him, he saw ruins and approached them.

It was no oasis. There was nothing in those empty streets of health or sustenance; no fruitful trees nor sparkling fountains. The city was a conglomeration of houses, or parts of same—sometimes entire floors, sometimes single rooms—thrown down side by side in parodies of urban order. The styles were a hopeless mishmash: fine Georgian establishments standing beside mean tenement buildings with rooms burned out; a house plucked from a terraced row, perfect down to the glazed dog on the windowsill, back to back with a penthouse suite. All were scarred by a rough removal from their context: walls were cracked, offering sly glimpses into private interiors; staircases beetled cloudward without destination; doors flapped open and closed in the wind, letting on to nowhere.

There was life here, Cleve knew. Not just the lizards, rats and butterflies—albinos all—that fluttered and skipped in front of him as he walked the forsaken streets—but *human* life. He sensed that every step he took was watched over, though he saw no sign of human presence—not on his first visit, at least.

On the second, his dream-self forsook the trudge across the wilderness and was delivered directly into the necropolis, his feet, easily tutored, following the same route as he had on his first visit. The constant wind was stronger tonight. It caught the lace curtains in this window, and a tinkling Chinese trinket hanging in that. It carried voices too; horrid and outlandish sounds that came from some distant place far beyond the city. Hearing that whirring and whittering, as of insane children, he was grateful for the streets and the rooms, for their familiarity if not for any comfort they might offer. He had no desire to step into those interiors, voices or no; he did not want to discover what marked out these snatches of architecture that they should have been ripped from their roots and flung down in this whining desolation.

Yet once he had visited the site, his sleeping mind went back there, night upon night; always walking, bloody-footed, seeing only the lizards and the rats and the butterflies, and the black sand on each threshold, blowing into rooms and hallways that never changed from visit to visit; that seemed, from what he could glimpse between the curtains or through a shattered wall, to have been *fixed* somehow at some pivotal moment, with a meal left uneaten on a table set for three (the capon uncarved, the sauces steaming), or a shower left running in a bathroom in which the lamp perpetually swung; and in a room that might have been a lawyer's study a lapdog, or else a wig torn off and flung to the floor, lying discarded on a fine carpet whose intricacies were half devoured by sand.

Only once did he see another human being in the city, and that was Billy. It happened strangely. One night, as he dreamed the streets, he half stirred from sleep. Billy was awake, and standing in the middle of the cell, staring up at the light through the window. It was not moonlight, but the boy bathed in it as if it were. His face was turned up to the window, mouth open and eyes closed. Cleve barely had time to register the trance the boy seemed to be in before the tranquilizers drew him back into his dream. He took a fragment of reality with him however, folding the boy into his sleeping vision. When he reached the city again, there was Billy Tait: standing on the street, his face turned up to the lowering clouds, his mouth open, his eyes closed.

The image lingered only a moment. The next, the boy was away, his heels kicking up black fans of sand. Cleve called after him. Billy ran on however, heedless; and with that inexplicable foreknowledge that dreams bring, Cleve knew where the boy was going. Off to the edge of the city, where the houses petered out and the desert began. Off to meet some friend coming in on that terrible wind, perhaps. Nothing would induce him into pursuit; yet he didn't want to lose contact with the one fellow human he had seen in these destitute streets. He called Billy's name again, more loudly.

This time he felt a hand on his arm, and started up in terror to find himself being jostled awake in his cell.

"It's all right," Billy said. "You're dreaming."

Cleve tried to shake the city out of his head, but for several perilous seconds the dream bled into the waking world, and looking down at the boy he saw Billy's hair lifted by a wind that did not, *could* not, belong in the confines of the cell. "You're dreaming," Billy said again. "Wake up."

Shuddering, Cleve sat fully up on his bunk. The city was receding—was almost gone—but before he lost sight of it entirely he felt the indisputable conviction that Billy *knew* what he was waking Cleve from; that they had been together for a few fragile moments.

"You know, don't you?" he accused the pallid face at his side.

The boy looked bewildered. "What are you talking about?"

Cleve shook his head. The suspicion became more incredible with each step he took from sleep. Even so, when he looked down at Billy's bony hand, which still clung to his arm, he half expected to see flecks of that obsidian grit beneath his fingernails. There was only dirt.

The doubts lingered however, long after reason should have bullied them into surrender. Cleve found himself watching the boy more closely from that night on, waiting for some slip of tongue or eye which would reveal the nature of his game. Such scrutiny was a lost cause. The last traces of accessibility disappeared that night; the boy became—like Rosanna—an indecipherable book, letting no clue as to the nature of his secret world out from beneath his lids. As to the dream—it was not even mentioned again. The only roundabout allusion to that night was Billy's redoubled insistence that Cleve continue to take the sedatives.

"You need your sleep," he said after coming back from the infirmary with a further supply. "Take them."

"You need sleep too," Cleve replied, curious to see how far the boy would push the issue. "I don't need the stuff any more."

"But you do," Billy insisted, proffering the vial of capsules. "You know how bad the noise is."

"Someone said they're addictive," Cleve replied, not taking the pills. "I'll do without."

"No," said Billy, and now Cleve sensed a level of insistence which confirmed his deepest suspicions. The boy *wanted* him drugged, and had all along. "I sleep like a babe," Billy said. "Please take them. They'll only be wasted otherwise."

Cleve shrugged. "If you're sure," he said, content—fears confirmed—to make a show of relenting.

"I'm sure."

"Then thanks." He took the vial.

Billy beamed. With that smile, in a sense, the bad times really began.

That night, Cleve answered the boy's performance with one of his own, appearing to take the tranquilizers as he usually did but failing to swallow them. Once lying on his bunk, face to the wall, he slipped them from his mouth and under his pillow. Then he pretended sleep.

Prison days both began and finished early; by eight forty-five or nine most of the cells in the four wings were in darkness, the inmates locked up until dawn and left to their own devices. Tonight was quieter than most. The weeper in the next cell but one had been transferred to D Wing; there were few other disturbances along the landing. Even without the pill Cleve felt sleep tempting him. From the bunk below he heard practically no sound, except for the occasional sigh. It was impossible to guess if Billy was actually asleep or not. Cleve kept his silence, occasionally stealing a moment-long glance at the luminous face of his watch. The minutes were leaden, and he feared, as the first hours crept by, that all too soon his imitation of sleep would become the real thing. Indeed he was turning this very possibility around in his mind when unconsciousness overcame him.

He woke much later. His sleep position seemed not to have altered. The wall was in front of him, the peeled paint like a dim map of some nameless territory. It took him a minute or two to orient himself. There was no sound from the bunk below. Disguising the gesture as one made in sleep, he drew his arm up within eye range, and looked at the pale green dial of his watch. It was one fifty-one. Several hours yet until dawn. He lay in the position he'd awakened in for a full quarter of an hour, listening for every sound in the cell, trying to locate Billy. He was loath to roll over and look for himself, for fear that the boy was standing in the middle of the cell as he had been the night of the visit to the city.

The world, though benighted, was far from silent. He could hear dull footsteps as somebody paced back and forth in the corresponding cell on the landing above; could hear water rushing in the pipes and the sound of a siren on Caledonian Road. What he couldn't hear was Billy. Not a breath of the boy.

Another quarter of an hour passed, and Cleve could feel the familiar torpor closing in to reclaim him; if he lay still much longer he would fall asleep again, and the next thing he'd know it would be morning. If he was going to learn anything, he had to roll over and *look*. Wisest, he decided, not to attempt to move surreptitiously but to turn over as naturally as possible. This he did, muttering to himself, as if in sleep, to add weight to the illusion. Once he had turned completely, and positioned his hand beside his face to shield his spying, he cautiously opened his eyes.

The cell seemed darker than it had the night he had seen Billy with his face up to the window. As to the boy, he was not visible. Cleve opened his eyes a little wider and scanned the cell as best he could from between his fingers. There was something amiss, but he couldn't quite work out what it was. He lay there for several minutes, waiting for his eyes to become accustomed to the murk. They didn't. The scene in front of him remained unclear, like a painting so encrusted with dirt and varnish its depths refuse the investigating eye. Yet he knew—*knew*—that the shadows in the corners of the cell, and on the opposite wall, were not empty. He wanted to end the anticipation that was making his heart thump, wanted to raise his head from the pebble-filled pillow and call Billy out of hiding. But good sense counseled otherwise. Instead he lay still, and sweated, and watched.

And now he began to realize what was wrong with the scene before him. The concealing shadows fell where no shadows belonged; they spread across the floor where the feeble light from the window should have been falling. Somehow, between window and wall, that light had been choked and devoured. Cleve closed his eyes to give his befuddled mind a chance to rationalize and reject this conclusion. When he opened them again his heart lurched. The shadow, far from losing potency, had grown a little.

He had never been afraid like this before, never felt a coldness in his innards akin to the chill that found him now. It was all he could do to keep his breath even and his hands where they lay. His instinct was to wrap himself up and hide his face like a child. Two thoughts kept him from doing so. One was that the slightest movement might draw unwelcome attention to him. The other, that Billy was somewhere in the cell, and perhaps as threatened by this living darkness as he.

And then, from the bunk below, the boy spoke. His voice was soft, presumably so as not to wake his sleeping cell-mate. It was also eerily intimate. Cleve entertained no thought that Billy was talking in his sleep; the time for willful self-deception was long past. The boy was addressing the darkness; of that unpalatable fact there could be no doubt.

". . . it hurts . . ." he said, with a faint note of accusation. ". . . You didn't tell me how much it hurts. . . ."

Was it Cleve's imagination, or did the wraith of shadows bloom a little in response, like a squid's ink in water? He was horribly afraid.

The boy was speaking again. His voice was so low Cleve could barely catch the words.

". . . it must be soon . . ." he said with quiet urgency. ". . . I'm not afraid. Not afraid."

Again the shadow shifted. This time, when Cleve looked into its heart, he made some sense of the chimerical form it embraced. His throat shook; a cry lodged behind his tongue, hot to be shouted.

". . . all you can teach me . . ." Billy was saying, ". . . quickly . . ." The words came and went, but Cleve barely heard them. His attention was on the curtain of shadow, and the figure—stitched from darkness—that moved in its folds. It was not an illusion. There was a man there: or rather a crude copy of one, its substance tenuous, its outline deteriorating all the time and being hauled back into some semblance of humanity again only with the greatest effort. Of the visitor's features Cleve could see little, but enough to sense deformities paraded like virtues: a face resembling a plate of rotted fruit, pulpy and peeling, swelling here with a nest of flies, and there suddenly fallen away to a pestilent core. How could the boy bring himself to converse so easily with such a *thing*? And yet, putrescence notwithstanding, there was a bitter dignity in the bearing of the creature, in the anguish of its eyes, and the toothless O of its maw.

Suddenly, Billy stood up. The abrupt movement, after so many hushed words, almost unleashed the cry from Cleve's throat. He swallowed it, with difficulty, and closed his eyes down to a slit, staring through the bars of his lashes at what happened next.

Billy was talking again, but now the voice was too low to allow for eavesdropping. He stepped toward the shadow, his body blocking much of the figure on the opposite wall. The cell was no more than two or three strides wide, but by some mellowing of physics, the boy seemed to take five, six, seven steps away from the bunk. Cleve's eyes widened: he knew he was not being watched. The shadow and its acolyte had business between them: it occupied their attention utterly.

Billy's figure was smaller than seemed possible within the confines of the cell, as if he had stepped through the wall and into some other province. And only now, with his eyes wide, did Cleve recognize that place. The darkness from which Billy's visitor was made was cloud-shadow and dust; behind him, barely visible in the bewitched murk, but recognizable to any who had been there, was the city of Cleve's dreams.

Billy had reached his master. The creature towered above him, tattered and spindly, but aching with power. Cleve didn't know how or why the boy had gone to it, and he feared for Billy's safety now that he had, but fear for his own safety shackled him to the bunk. He realized in that moment that he had never loved anyone, man or woman, sufficiently to pursue them into the shadow of that shadow. The thought brought a terrible isolation, knowing that same instant that none, seeing *him* walk to his damnation, would take a single step to claim him from the brink. Lost souls both, he and the boy.

Now Billy's lord was lifting his swollen head, and the incessant wind in those blue streets was rousing his horse mane into furious life. On the wind, the same voices Cleve had heard carried before, the cries of mad children, somewhere between tears and howls. As if encouraged by these voices, the entity reached out toward Billy and embraced him, wrapping the boy round in vapor. Billy did not struggle in his embrace but rather returned it. Cleve, unable to watch this horrid intimacy, closed his eyes against it, and when— seconds? minutes?, later—he opened them again, the encounter seemed to be over. The shadow thing was blowing apart, relinquishing its slender claim to coherence. It fragmented, pieces of its tattered anatomy flying off into the streets like litter before wind. Its departure seemed to signal the dispersal of the entire scene; the streets and houses were already being devoured by dust and distance. Even before the last of the shadow's scraps had been wafted out of sight the city was lost to sight. Cleve was pleased to be rid of it. Reality, grim as it was, was preferable to that desolation. Brick by painted brick the wall was asserting itself again, and Billy, delivered from his master's arms, was back in the solid geometry of the cell, staring up at the light through the window.

Cleve did not sleep again that night. Indeed he wondered, lying on his unyielding mattress and staring up at the stalactites of paint depending from the ceiling, whether he could ever again find safety in sleep.

Sunlight was a showman. It threw its brightness down with such flamboyance, eager as any tinsel-merchant to dazzle and distract. But beneath the gleaming surface it illuminated was another state; one that sunlight—ever the crowd pleaser—conspired to conceal. It was vile and desperate, that condition. Most, blinded by sight, never even glimpsed it. But Cleve knew the state of sunlessness now; had even walked it, in dreams; and though he mourned the loss of his innocence, he knew he could never retrace his steps back into light's hall of mirrors.

He tried his damnedest to keep this change in him from Billy; the last thing he wanted was for the boy to suspect his eavesdropping. But concealment was well nigh impossible. Though the following day Cleve made every show of normality he could contrive, he could not quite cover his unease. It slipped out without his being able to control it, like sweat from his pores. And the boy knew, no doubt of it, he *knew*. Nor was he slow to give voice to his suspicions. When, following the afternoon's workshop, they returned to their cell, Billy was quick to come to the point.

"What's wrong with you today?"

Cleve busied himself with remaking his bed, afraid even to glance at Billy. "Nothing's wrong," he said. "I don't feel particularly well, that's all."

"You have a bad night?" the boy inquired. Cleve could feel Billy's eyes boring into his back.

"No," he said, pacing his denial so that it didn't come too quickly. "I took your pills, like always."

"Good."

The exchange faltered, and Cleve was allowed to finish his bed making in silence. The business could only be extended so long, however. When he turned from the bunk, job done, he found Billy sitting at the small table, with one of Cleve's books open in his lap. He casually flicked through the volume, all sign of his previous suspicion vanished. Cleve knew better than to trust to mere appearances, however.

"Why'd you read these things?" the boy asked.

"Passes the time," Cleve replied, undoing all his labors by clambering up on to the top bunk and stretching out there.

"No. I don't mean why do you read books? I mean, why read *these* books? All this stuff about sin."

Cleve only half heard the question. Lying there on the bunk reminded him all too acutely of how the night had been. Reminded him too that darkness was even now crawling up the side of the world again. At that thought his stomach seemed to aspire to his throat.

"Did you hear me?" the boy asked.

Cleve murmured that he had.

"Well, why then; why the books? About damnation and all?"

"Nobody else takes them out of the library," Cleve replied, having difficulty shaping thoughts to speak when the others, unspoken, were so much more demanding.

"You don't believe it then?"

"No," he replied. "No, I don't believe a word of it."

The boy kept his silence for a while. Though Cleve wasn't looking at him, he could hear Billy turning pages. Then, another question, but spoken more quietly; a confession.

"Do you ever get *afraid?*"

The inquiry startled Cleve from his trance. The conversation had changed back from talk of reading matter to something altogether more pertinent. Why did Billy ask about fear unless he too was afraid?

"What have I got to be scared of?" Cleve asked.

From the corner of his eye he caught the boy shrugging slightly before replying. "Things that happen," he said, his voice soulless. "Things you can't control."

"Yes," Cleve replied, not certain of where this exchange was leading. "Yes, of course. Sometimes I'm scared."

"What do you do then?" Billy asked.

"Nothing *to* do, is there?" Cleve said. His voice was as hushed as Billy's. "I gave up praying the morning my father died."

He heard the soft pat as Billy closed the book and inclined his head sufficiently to catch sight of the boy. Billy could not entirely conceal his agitation. He *is* afraid, Cleve saw; he doesn't want the night to come any more than I do. He found the thought of their shared fear reassuring. Perhaps the boy didn't entirely belong to the shadow; perhaps he could even cajole Billy into pointing their route out of this spiraling nightmare.

He sat upright, his head within inches of the cell ceiling. Billy looked up from his meditations, his face a pallid oval of twitching muscle. Now was the time to speak, Cleve knew; *now,* before the lights were switched out along the landings, and all the cells consigned to shadows. There would be no time then for explanations. The boy would already be half lost to the city and beyond persuasion.

"I have dreams," Cleve said. Billy said nothing but simply stared back, hollow-eyed. "I dream a city."

The boy didn't flinch. He clearly wasn't going to volunteer elucidation; he would have to be bullied into it.

"Do you know what I'm talking about?"

Billy shook his head. "No," he said lightly, "I never dream."

"Everybody dreams."

"Then I just don't remember them."

"I remember mine," Cleve said. He was determined, now that he'd broached the subject, not to let Billy squirm free. "And you're there. You're in that city."

Now the boy flinched; only a treacherous lash but enough to reassure Cleve that he wasn't wasting his breath.

"What is that place, Billy?" he asked.

"How should I know?" the boy returned, about to laugh, then discarding the attempt. "I don't know, do I? They're your dreams."

Before Cleve could reply he heard the voice of one of the guards as he moved along the row of cells, telling the men to bed down for the night. Very soon, the lights would be extinguished and he would be locked up in this narrow cell for ten hours. With Billy; and phantoms.

"Last night," he said, fearful of mentioning what he'd heard and seen without due preparation, but more fearful still of facing another night on the borders of the city, alone in darkness. "Last night I saw . . ." He faltered. Why wouldn't the words come? "Saw . . ."

"Saw what?" the boy demanded, his face inscrutable; whatever sign of apprehension there had been in it had now vanished. Perhaps he too had heard the guard's advance and known that there was nothing to be done; no way of staying the night's advance.

"What did you see?" Billy insisted.

Cleve sighed. "My mother," he replied.

The boy betrayed his relief only in the tenuous smile that crept across his lips.

"Yes . . . I saw my mother. Large as life."

"And it upset you, did it?" Billy asked.

"Sometimes dreams do."

The guard had reached B. 3. 20. "Lights out in two minutes," he said as he passed.

"You should take some more of those pills," Billy advised, putting down the book and crossing to his bunk. "Then you'd be like me. No dreams."

Cleve had lost. He, the arch bluffer, had been outbluffed by the boy, and now had to take the consequences. He lay, facing the ceiling, counting off the seconds until the light went out, while below the boy undressed and slipped between the sheets.

There was still time to jump up and call the guard back; time to beat his head against the door until somebody came. But what would he say to justify his histrionics? That he had bad dreams? Who didn't? That he was afraid of the dark? Who wasn't? They would laugh in his face and tell him to go back to bed, leaving him with all camouflage blown, and the boy and his master waiting at the wall. There was no safety in such tactics.

Nor in prayer either. He had told Billy the truth, about his giving up God when his prayers for his father's life had gone unanswered. Of such divine neglect was atheism made; belief could not be rekindled now, however profound his terror.

Thoughts of his father led inevitably to thoughts of childhood; few other subjects, if any, could have engrossed his mind sufficiently to steal him from his fears but this. When the lights were finally extinguished, his frightened mind took refuge in memories. His heart rate slowed; his fingers ceased to tremble, and eventually, without his being the least aware of it, sleep stole him.

The distractions available to his conscious mind were not available to his unconscious. Once asleep, fond recollection was banished; childhood memories became a thing of the past, and he was back, bloody-footed, in that terrible city.

Or rather, on its borders. For tonight he did not follow the familiar route past the Georgian house and its attendant tenements, but walked instead to the outskirts of the city, where the wind was stronger than ever, and the voices it carried clear. Though he expected with every step he took to see Billy and his dark companion, he saw nobody. Only butterflies accompanied him along the path, luminous as his watch face. They settled on his shoulders and his hair like confetti, then fluttered off again.

He reached the edge of the city without incident and stood, scanning the desert. The clouds, solid as ever, moved overhead with the majesty of juggernauts. The voices seemed closer tonight, he thought, and the passions they expressed less distressing than he had found them previously. Whether the mellowing was in them or in his response to them he couldn't be certain.

And then, as he watched the dunes and the sky, mesmerized by their blankness, he heard a sound and glanced over his shoulder to see a smiling man, dressed in what was surely his Sunday finery, walking out of the city toward him. He was carrying a knife; the blood on it, and on his hand and shirt front, was wet. Even in his dream state, and immune, Cleve was intimidated by the sight and stepped back—a word of self-defense on his lips. The smiling man seemed not to see him however, but advanced past Cleve and out into the desert, dropping the blade as he crossed some invisible boundary. Only now did Cleve see that others had done the same, and that the ground at the city limit was littered with lethal keepsakes—knives, ropes (even a human hand, lopped off at the wrist)—most of which were all but buried.

The wind was bringing the voices again: tatters of senseless songs and half-finished laughter. He looked up from the sand. The exiled man had gone out a hundred yards from the city and was now standing on top of one of the dunes, apparently waiting. The voices were becoming louder all the time.

Cleve was suddenly nervous. Whenever he had been here in the city, and heard this cacophony, the picture he had conjured of its originators had made his blood run cold. Could he now stand and wait for the banshees to appear? Curiosity was discretion's better. He glued his eyes to the ridge over which they would come, his heart thumping, unable to look away. The man in the Sunday suit had begun to take his jacket off. He discarded it and began to loosen his tie.

And now Cleve thought he saw something in the dunes, and the noise rose to an ecstatic howl of welcome. He stared, defying his nerves to betray him, determined to look this horror in its many faces.

Suddenly, above the din of their music, somebody was screaming; a man's voice, but high-pitched, gelded with terror. It did not come from here in the dream-city, but from that other fiction he occupied, the name of which he couldn't quite remember. He pressed his attention back to the dunes, determined not to be denied the sight of the reunion about to take place in front of him. The scream in that nameless elsewhere mounted to a throat-breaking height, and stopped. But now an alarm bell was ringing in its place, more insistent than ever. Cleve could feel his dream slipping.

"No . . ." he murmured, ". . . let me see. . . ."

The dunes were moving. But so was his consciousness—out of the city and back toward his cell. His protests brought him no concession. The desert faded, the city too. He opened his eyes. The lights in the cell were still off: the alarm bell was ringing. There were shouts in cells on the landings above and below, and the sound of guards' voices, raised in a confusion of inquiries and demands.

He lay on his bunk a moment, hoping, even now, to be returned into the enclave of his dream. But no; the alarm was too shrill, the mounting hysteria in the cells around too compelling. He conceded defeat and sat up, wide awake.

"What's going on?" he said to Billy.

The boy was not standing in his place by the wall. Asleep, for once, despite the din.

"Billy?"

Cleve leaned over the edge of his bunk, and peered into the space below. It was empty. The sheets and blankets had been thrown back.

Cleve jumped down from his bunk. The entire contents of the cell could be taken at two glances, there was nowhere to hide. The boy was not to be seen. Had he been spirited away while Cleve slept? It was not unheard of; this was the ghost train of which Devlin had warned: the unexplained removal of difficult prisoners to other establishments. Cleve had never heard of this happening at night, but there was a first time for everything.

He crossed to the door to see if he could make some sense of the shouting outside, but it defied interpretation. The likeliest explanation was a fight, he suspected: two cons who could no longer bear the idea of another hour in the same space. He tried to work out where the initial scream had come from, to his right or left, above or below; but the dream had confounded all direction.

As he stood at the door, hoping a guard might pass by, he felt a change in the air. It was so subtle he scarcely registered it at first. Only when he raised his hand to wipe sleep from his eyes did he realize that his arms were solid gooseflesh.

From behind him he now heard the sound of breathing, or a ragged parody of same.

He mouthed the word "Billy" but didn't speak it. The gooseflesh had found his spine; now he began to shake. The cell *wasn't* empty after all; there was somebody in the tiny space with him.

He screwed his courage tight and forced himself to turn around. The cell was darker than it had been when he awoke; the air was a teasing veil. But Billy was not in the cell; nobody was.

And then the noise came again and drew Cleve's attention to the bottom bunk. The space was pitch black, a shadow—like that on the wall—too profound and too volatile to have natural origins. Out of it, a croaking attempt at breath that might have been the last moments of an asthmatic. He realized that the murk in the cell had its source there—in the narrow space of Billy's bed; the shadow bled onto the floor and curled up like fog on to the top of the bunk.

Cleve's supply of fear was not inexhaustible. In the past several days he had used it up in dreams and waking dreams; he'd sweated, he'd frozen, he'd lived on the edge of sane experience and survived. Now, though his body still insisted on gooseflesh, his mind was not moved to panic. He felt cooler than he ever had, whipped by recent events into a new impartiality. He would *not* cower. He would *not* cover his eyes and pray for morning, because if he did one day he would wake to find himself dead and he'd never know the nature of this mystery.

He took a deep breath and approached the bunk. It had begun to shake. The shrouded occupant in the lower tier was moving about violently.

"Billy," Cleve said.

The shadow moved. It pooled around his feet; it rolled up into his face, smelling of rain on stone, cold and comfortless.

He was standing no more than a yard from the bunk, and still he could make nothing out; the shadow defied him. Not to be denied sight, he reached toward the bed. At his solicitation the veil divided like smoke, and the shape that thrashed on the mattress made itself apparent.

It was Billy, of course; and yet not. A lost Billy, perhaps, or one to come. If so, Cleve wanted no part of a future that could breed such trauma. There, on the lower bunk, lay a dark, wretched shape, still solidifying as Cleve watched, knitting itself together from the shadows. There was something of a rabid fox in its incandescent eyes, in its arsenal of needle-teeth; something of an upturned insect in the way it was half curled upon itself, its back more shell than flesh and more nightmare than either. No part of it was fixed. Whatever figuration it had (perhaps it had many) Cleve was watching the status dissolve. The teeth were growing yet longer and, in so doing, more insubstantial, their matter extruded to the point of frailty, then dispersed like mist; its hooked limbs, pedaling the air, were also growing paltry. Beneath the chaos he saw the ghost of Billy Tait, mouth open and babbling agonies, striving to make itself known. He wanted to reach into the maelstrom and snatch the boy out, but he sensed that the process he was watching had its own momentum and it might be fatal to intervene. Al he could do was stand and watch as Billy's thin white limbs and heaving abdomen writhed to slough off this dire anatomy. The luminous eyes were almost the last to go, spilling out from their sockets on myriad threads and flying off into black vapor.

At last he saw Billy's face, truant clues to its former condition still flickering across it. And then, even these were dispersed, the shadows gone, and only Billy was lying on the bunk, naked and heaving with the exertion of his anguish.

He looked at Cleve, his face innocent of expression.

Cleve remembered how the boy had complained to the creature from the city. *". . . it hurts . . ."* he'd said, hadn't he? *". . . You didn't tell me how much it hurts. . . ."* It was the observable truth. The boy's body was a wasteland of sweat and bone; a more unappetizing sight was scarcely imaginable. But *human;* at least that.

Billy opened his mouth. His lips were ruddy and slick, as if he were wearing lipstick.

"Now . . . ," he said, trying to speak between painful breaths. "Now what shall we do?"

The act of speaking seemed too much for him. He made a gagging sound in the back of his throat, and pressed his hand to his mouth. Cleve moved aside as Billy stood up and stumbled across to the bucket in the corner of the cell, kept there for their night wastes. He failed to reach it before nausea overtook him; fluid splashed between his fingers and hit the floor. Cleve looked away as Billy threw up, preparing himself for the stench he would have to tolerate until slopping-out time the following morning. It was not the smell of vomit that filled the cell, however, but something sweeter and more cloying.

Mystified, Cleve looked back toward the figure crouching in the corner. On the floor between his feet were splashes of dark fluid; rivulets of the same ran down his bare legs. Even in the gloom of the cell, it was unmistakably blood.

In the most well-ordered of prisons violence could—and inevitably did—erupt without warning. The relationship of two cons, incarcerated together for sixteen hours out of every twenty-four, was an unpredictable thing. But as far as had been apparent to either prisoners or guards there had been no bad blood between Lowell and Nayler; nor, until that scream began, had there been a sound from their cell: no argument, no raised voices. What had induced Nayler to spontaneously attack and slaughter his cell-mate, and then inflict devastating wounds upon himself, was a subject for debate in dining hall and exercise yard alike. The why of the problem, however, took second place to the how. The rumors describing the condition of Lowell's body when found defied the imagination; even among men inured against casual brutality the descriptions were met with shock. Lowell had not been much liked; he had been a bully and a cheat. But nothing he'd done deserved such mutilation. The man had been ripped open, his eyes put out, his genitals torn off. Nayler, the only possible antagonist, had then contrived to open up his own belly. He was now in an intensive care unit; the prognosis was not hopeful.

It was easy, with such a buzz of outrage going about the wing, for Cleve to spend the day all but unnoticed. He too had a story to tell: but who would believe it? He barely believed it himself. In fact on and off through the day, when the images came back to him afresh, he asked himself if he was entirely sane. But then sanity was a movable feast, wasn't it? One man's madness might be another's politics. All he knew for certain was that he had seen Billy Tait transform. He clung to that certainty with a tenaciousness born of near despair. If he ceased to believe the evidence of his own eyes, he had no defense left to hold the darkness at bay.

After ablutions and breakfast, the entire wing was confined to cells; workshops, recreation—any activity that required movement around the landings—was canceled while Lowell's cell was photographed and examined, then swabbed out. Following breakfast, Billy slept through the morning; a state more akin to coma than sleep, such was its profundity. When he awoke for lunch he was brighter and more outgoing than Cleve had seen him in weeks. There was no sign beneath the vacuous chatter that he knew what had happened the previous night. In the afternoon Cleve faced him with the truth.

"You killed Lowell," he said. There was no point in trying to pretend ignorance any longer; if the boy didn't remember now what he'd done, he would surely recall in time. And with that memory, how long before he remembered that Cleve had watched him transform? Better to confess it now. "I saw you," Cleve said. "I saw you change. . . ."

Billy didn't seem much disturbed by these revelations.

"Yes," he said. "I killed Lowell. Do you blame me?" The question, begging a hundred others, was put lightly, as a matter of mild interest, no more.

"What happened to you?" Cleve said. "I saw you—*there*"—he pointed, appalled at the memory, at the lower bunk—"you weren't human."

"I didn't mean you to see," the boy replied. "I gave you the pills, didn't I? You shouldn't have spied."

"And the night before . . . ," Cleve said. "I was awake then too."

The boy blinked like a bemused bird, head slightly cocked. "You really have been stupid," he said. "So stupid."

"Whether I like it or not, I'm not out of this," Cleve said. "I have dreams."

"Oh, yes." Now a frown marred the porcelain brow. "Yes. You dream the city, don't you?"

"What is that place, Billy?"

"I read somewhere: *The dead have highways*. You ever hear that? Well . . . they have cities too."

"The dead? You mean it's some kind of ghost town?"

"I never wanted you to become involved. You've been better to me than most here. But I *told* you, I came to Pentonville to do business."

"With Tait."

"That's right."

Cleve wanted to laugh; what he was being told—*a city of the dead?*—only heaped nonsense upon nonsense. And yet his exasperated reason had not sniffed out one explanation more plausible.

"My grandfather killed his children," Billy said, "because he didn't want to pass his condition on to another generation. He learned late, you see. He didn't realize, until he had a wife and children, that he wasn't like most men. He was special. But he didn't *want* the skills he'd been given, and he didn't want his children to survive with that same power in their blood. He would have killed himself, and finished the job, but that my mother escaped. Before he could find her and kill her too, he was arrested."

"And hanged. And buried."

"Hanged and buried, but not *lost*. Nobody's lost, Cleve. Not ever."

"You came here to find him."

"More than find him: make him *help* me. I knew from the age of ten what I was capable of. Not quite consciously, but I had an inkling. And I was afraid. Of course I was afraid: it was a terrible mystery."

"This mutation: you've always done it?"

"No. Only *known* I was capable of it. I came here to make my grandfather tutor me, make him *show me how*. Even now"—he looked down at his wasted arms—"with him teaching me . . . the pain is almost unbearable."

"Why do it then?"

The boy looked at Cleve incredulously. "To be *not* myself; to be smoke and shadow. To be something terrible." He seemed genuinely puzzled by Cleve's unwillingness. "Wouldn't you do the same?"

Cleve shook his head. "What you became last night was repellent."

Billy nodded. "That's what my grandfather thought. At his trial he called himself an abomination. Not that they knew what he was talking about, of course, but that's what he said. He stood up and said: 'I am Satan's excrement' "—Billy smiled at the thought—" 'for God's sake hang me and burn me.' He's changed his mind since then. The century's getting old and stale; it needs new tribes." He looked at Cleve intently. "Don't be afraid," he said. "I won't hurt you, unless you try to tell tales. You won't do that, will you?"

"What could I say that would sound like sanity?" Cleve returned mildly. "No, I won't tell tales."

"Good. And in a little while I'll be gone, and you'll be gone. And you can forget."

"I doubt it."

"Even the dreams will stop when I'm not here. You only share them because you have some mild talents as a sensitive. Trust me. There's nothing to be afraid of."

"The city—"

"What about it?"

"Where are its citizens? I never see anybody. No, that's not quite true. I saw one. A man with a knife . . . going out into the desert . . ."

"I can't help you. I go as a visitor myself. All I know is what my grandfather tells me: that it's a city occupied by dead souls. Whatever you've seen there, forget about it. You don't belong there. You're not dead yet."

Was it wise to believe always what the dead told you? Were they purged of all deceit by the act of dying, and delivered into their new state like saints? Cleve could not believe such naiveté. More likely they took their talents with them, good and bad, and used them as best they could. There would be

shoemakers in paradise, wouldn't there? Foolish to think they'd forgotten
how to sew leather.

So perhaps Edgar Tait *lied* about the city. There was more to that place
than Billy knew. What about the voices on the wind, the man and the knife,
dropping it among a litter of weapons before moving off to God alone knew
where? What ritual was that?

Now—with the fear used up, and no untainted reality left to cling to,
Cleve saw no reason not to go to the city willingly. What could be there, in
those dusty streets, that was worse than what he had seen in the bunk below
him, or what had happened to Lowell and Nayler? Beside such atrocities the
city was a haven. There was a serenity in its empty thoroughfares and plazas; a
sense Cleve had there that all action was over, all rage and distress finished
with; that these interiors (with the bath running and the cup brimming) had
seen the *worst,* and were now content to sit out the millennium. When that
night brought sleep, and the city opened up in front of him, he went into it
not as a frightened man astray in hostile territory but as a visitor content to
relax a while in a place he knew too well to become lost in, but not well
enough to be weary of.

As if in response to this newfound ease, the city opened itself to him.
Wandering the streets, feet bloody as ever, he found the doors open wide, the
curtains at the windows drawn back. He did not disparage the invitation they
offered but went to look more closely at the houses and tenements. On closer
inspection he found them not the paradigms of domestic calm he'd first taken
them for. In each he discovered some sign of violence recently done. In one,
perhaps no more than an overturned chair, or a mark on the floor where a
heel had slid in a spot of blood; in others, the manifestations were more
obvious. A hammer, its claw clotted, had been left on a table laid with
newspapers. There was a room with its floorboards ripped up, and black
plastic parcels, suspiciously slick, laid beside the hole. In one, a mirror had
been shattered; in another, a set of false teeth left beside a hearth in which a
fire flared and spat.

They were murder scenes, all of them. The victims had gone—to other
cities, perhaps, full of slaughtered children and murdered friends—leaving
these tableaux fixed forever in the breathless moments that followed the
crime. Cleve walked down the streets, the perfect voyeur, and peered into
scene after scene, reconstructing in his mind's eye the hours that had preceded the studied stillness of each room. Here a child had died: its cot was
overturned; here someone had been murdered in his bed, the pillow soaked
in blood; the ax on the carpet. Was this damnation then, the killers obliged to
wait out some portion of eternity (all of it, perhaps) in the room they had
murdered in?"

Of the malefactors themselves he saw nothing, though logic implied that they must be close by. Was it that they had the power of invisibility to keep themselves from the prying eyes of touring dreamers like himself; or did a time in this nowhere transform them, so that they were no longer flesh and blood but became part of their cell—a chair, a china doll?

Then he remembered the man at the perimeter who'd come in his fine suit, bloody-handed, and walked out into the desert. *He* had not been invisible.

"Where are you?" he said, standing on the threshold of a mean room, with an open oven and utensils in the sink, water running on them. "Show yourself."

A movement caught his eye, and he glanced across to the door. There was a man standing there. He had been there all along, Cleve realized, but so still, and so perfectly a part of this room, that he had not been visible until he moved his eyes and looked Cleve's way. He felt a twinge of unease, thinking that each room he had peered into had, most likely, contained one or more killers, each similarly camouflaged by stasis. The man, knowing he'd been seen, stepped out of hiding. He was in late middle-age and had cut himself that morning as he shaved.

"Who are you?" he said. "I've seen you before. Walking by."

He spoke softly and sadly—an unlikely killer, Cleve thought.

"Just a visitor," he told the man.

"There are no visitors here," he replied, "only prospective citizens."

Cleve frowned, trying to work out what the man meant. But his dream-mind was sluggish, and before he could solve the riddle of the man's words there were others.

"Do I know you?" the man asked. "I find I forget more and more. That's no use, is it? If I forget I'll never leave, will I?"

"Leave?" Cleve repeated.

"Make an exchange," the man said, realigning his toupee.

"And go where?"

"Back. Do it over."

Now he approached Cleve across the room. He stretched out his hands, palms up; they were blistered.

"You can help me," he said. "I can make a deal with the best of them."

"I don't understand you."

The man clearly thought he was bluffing. His upper lip, which boasted a dyed black mustache, curled. "Yes you do," he said. "You understand perfectly. You just want to sell yourself, the way everybody does. Highest bidder, is it? What are you, an assassin?"

Cleve shook his head. "I'm just dreaming," he replied.

The man's fit of pique subsided. "Be a friend," he said. "I've got no influence; not like some. Some of them, you know, they come here and they're out again in a matter of hours. They're professionals. They make arrangements. But me? With me it was a crime of passion. I didn't come prepared. I'll stay here till I can make a deal. Please be a friend."

"I can't help you," Cleve said, not even certain of what the man was requesting.

The killer nodded. "Of course not," he said, "I didn't expect . . ."

He turned from Cleve and moved to the oven. Heat flared up from it and made a mirage of the hob. Casually, he put one of his blistered palms on the door and closed it; almost as soon as he had done so it creaked open again. "Do you know just how appetizing it is—the smell of cooking flesh?" he said, as he returned to the oven door and attempted to close it a second time. "Can anybody blame me? Really?"

Cleve left him to his ramblings; if there was sense there it was probably not worth his laboring over. The talk of exchanges and of escape from the city: it defied Cleve's comprehension.

He wandered on, tired now of peering into the houses. He'd seen all he wanted to see. Surely morning was close, and the bell would ring on the landing. Perhaps he should even wake himself, he thought, and be done with this tour for the night.

As the thought occurred, he saw the girl. She was no more than six or seven years old, and she was standing at the next intersection. This was no killer, surely. He started toward her. She, either out of shyness or some less benign motive, turned to her right and ran off. Cleve followed. By the time he had reached the intersection she was already a long way down the next street; again he gave chase. As dreams would have such pursuits, the laws of physics did not pertain equally to pursuer and pursued. The girl seemed to move easily, while Cleve struggled against air as thick as treacle. He did not give up, however, but pressed on wherever the girl led. He was soon a good distance from any location he recognized in a warren of yards and alleyways—all, he supposed, scenes of blood-letting. Unlike the main thoroughfares, this ghetto contained few entire spaces, only snatches of geography: a grass verge, more red than green; a piece of scaffolding, with a noose depending from it; a pile of earth. And now, simply, a wall.

The girl had led him into a cul-de-sac; she herself had disappeared how-ever, leaving him facing a plain brick wall, much weathered, with a narrow window in it. He approached: this was clearly what he'd been led here to see. He peered through the reinforced glass, dirtied on his side by an accumula-tion of bird-droppings, and found himself staring into one of the cells at Pentonville. His stomach flipped over. What kind of game was this; led out of a cell and into this dream-city, only to be led back into prison? But a few seconds of study told him that it was not *his* cell. It was Lowell and Nayler's. Theirs were the pictures taped to the gray brick, theirs the blood spread over floor and wall and bunk and door. This was another murder scene.

"My God Almighty," he murmured. "Billy . . ."

He turned away from the wall. In the sand at his feet lizards were mating; the wind that found its way into this backwater brought butterflies. As he watched them dance, the bell rang in B Wing, and it was morning.

It was a trap. Its mechanism was by no means clear to Cleve—but he had no doubt of its purpose. Billy would go to the city, soon. The cell in which he had committed murder already awaited him, and of all the wretched places Cleve had seen in that assemblage of charnel houses surely the tiny, blood-drenched cell was the worst.

The boy could not know what was planned for him; his grandfather had lied about the city by exclusion, failing to tell Billy what special qualifications were required to exist there. And why? Cleve returned to the oblique conversation he'd had with the man in the kitchen. That talk of exchanges, of deal making, of *going back*. Edgar Tait had regretted his sins, hadn't he? He'd decided, as the years passed, that he was *not* the Devil's excrement, that to be returned into the world would not be so bad an idea. Billy was somehow an instrument in that return.

"My grandfather doesn't like you," the boy said when they were locked up again after lunch. For the second consecutive day all recreation and work-shop activities had been canceled, while a cell-by-cell inquiry was undertaken regarding Lowell's and—as of the early hours of that day—Nayler's deaths.

"Doesn't he?" Cleve said. "And why?"

"Says you're too inquisitive. In the city."

Cleve was sitting on the top bunk; Billy on the chair against the opposite wall. The boy's eyes were bloodshot; a small but constant tremor had taken over his body.

"You're going to die," Cleve said. What other way to state that fact was there, but baldly? "I saw . . . in the city . . ."

Billy shook his head. "Sometimes you talk like a crazy man. My grandfather says I shouldn't trust you."

"He's afraid of me, that's why."

Billy laughed derisively. It was an ugly sound, learned, Cleve guessed, from Grandfather Tait. "He's afraid of no one," Billy retorted.

"Afraid of what I'll see. Of what I'll tell you."

"No," said the boy with absolute conviction.

"He told you to kill Lowell, didn't he?"

Billy's head jerked up. "Why'd you say that?"

"You never wanted to murder him. Maybe scare them both a bit, but not *kill* them. It was your loving grandfather's idea."

"Nobody tells me what to do," Billy replied, his gaze icy. "Nobody."

"All right," Cleve conceded, "maybe he *persuaded* you, eh? Told you it was a matter of family pride. Something like that?" The observation clearly touched a nerve; the tremors had increased.

"So? What if he did?"

"I've seen where you're going to go, Billy. A place just waiting for you." The boy stared at Cleve but didn't interrupt. "Only murderers occupy the city, Billy. That's why your grandfather's there. And if he can find a replacement—if he can reach out and make more murder—he can go free."

Billy stood up, face like a fury. All trace of derision had gone. "What do you mean *free?*"

"Back to the world. *Back here.*"

"You're lying."

"Ask him."

"He wouldn't cheat me. His blood's my blood."

"You think he cares? After fifty years in that place, waiting for a chance to be out and away. You think he gives a *damn* how he does it?"

"I'll tell him how you lie," Billy said. The anger was not entirely directed at Cleve; there was an undercurrent of doubt there, which Billy was trying to suppress. "You're dead," he said, "when he finds out how you're trying to poison me against him. You'll see him, then. Oh yes. You'll see him. And you'll wish to Christ you hadn't."

There seemed to be no way out. Even if Cleve could convince the authorities to move him before night fell—(a slim chance indeed; he would have to reverse all that he had claimed about the boy, tell them Billy was dangerously insane, or something similar. Certainly not the truth.)—even if he were to have himself transferred to another cell, there was no promise of safety in such a maneuver. The boy had said he was smoke and shadow. Neither door nor bars could keep such insinuations at bay; the fate of Lowell and Nayler was proof positive of that. Nor was Billy alone. There was Edgar St. Clair Tait to be accounted for, and what powers might he possess? Yet to stay in the same cell with the boy tonight would amount to self-slaughter, wouldn't it? He would be delivering himself into the hands of the beasts.

When they left their cells for the evening meal, Cleve looked around for Devlin, located him, and asked for the opportunity of a short interview, which was granted. After the meal, Cleve reported to the officer.

"You asked me to keep an eye on Billy Tait, sir."

"What about him?"

Cleve had thought hard about what he might tell Devlin that would bring an immediate transfer: nothing had come to mind. He stumbled, hoping for inspiration, but was empty-mouthed.

"I . . . I . . . want to put in a request for a cell transfer."

"Why?"

"The boy's unbalanced," Cleve replied. "I'm afraid he's going to do me harm. Have another of his fits."

"You could lay him flat with one hand tied behind your back. He's worn to the bone." At this point, had he been talking to Mayflower, Cleve might had been able to make a direct appeal to the man. With Devlin such tactics would be doomed from the beginning.

"I don't know why you're complaining. He's been as good as gold," said Devlin, savoring the parody of fond father. "Quiet; always polite. He's no danger to you or anyone."

"You don't know him—"

"What are you trying to pull?"

"Put me in a Rule 43 cell, sir. *Anywhere,* I don't mind. Just get me out of his way. *Please.*"

Devlin didn't reply but stared at Cleve, mystified. At last, he said, "You *are* afraid of him."

"Yes."

"What's wrong with you? You've shared cells with hard men and never turned a hair."

"He's different," Cleve replied; there was little else he could say except: "He's insane. I tell you he's insane."

"All the world's crazy, save thee and me, Smith. Hadn't you heard?" Devlin laughed. "Go back to your cell and stop bellyaching. You don't want a ghost train ride, now do you?"

When Cleve returned to the cell, Billy was writing a letter. Sitting on his bunk, poring over the paper, he looked utterly vulnerable. What Devlin said was true: the boy *was* worn to the bone. It was difficult to believe, looking at the ladder of his vertebrae, visible through his T-shirt, that this frail form could survive the throes of transformation. But then, maybe it would not. Maybe the rigors of change would tear him apart with time. But not soon enough.

"Billy . . ."

The boy didn't take his eyes from his letter.

". . . what I said, about the city . . ."

He stopped writing—

". . . Maybe I *was* imagining it all. Just dreaming."

—and started again.

". . . I only told you because I was afraid for you. That was all. I want us to be friends."

Billy looked up. "It's not in my hands," he said very simply. "Not now. It's up to Grandfather. He may be merciful; he may not."

"Why do you have to tell him?"

"He knows what's in me. He and I . . . we're like one. That's how I know he wouldn't cheat me."

Soon it would be night; the lights would go out along the wing, the shadows would come.

"So I just have to wait, do I?" Cleve said.

Billy nodded. "I'll call him, and then we'll see."

Call him? Cleve thought. Did the old man need summoning from his resting place every night? Was that what he had seen Billy doing, standing in the middle of the cell, eyes closed and face up to the window? If so, perhaps the boy could be *prevented* from putting in his call to the dead.

As the evening deepened Cleve lay on his bunk and thought his options through. Was it better to wait here and see what judgment came from Tait, or attempt to take control of the situation and block the old man's arrival? If he did so, there would be no going back; no room for pleas or apologies: his aggression would undoubtedly breed aggression. If he failed to prevent the boy from calling Tait, it would be the end.

The lights went out. In cells up and down the five landings of B Wing men would be turning their faces to their pillows. Some, perhaps, would lie awake planning their careers when this minor hiccup in their professional lives was over; others would be in the arms of invisible mistresses. Cleve listened to the sounds of the cell: the rattling progress of water in the pipes, the shallow breathing from the bunk below. Sometimes it seemed that he had lived a second lifetime on this stale pillow, marooned in darkness.

The breathing from below soon became practically inaudible; nor was there sound of movement. Perhaps Billy was waiting for Cleve to fall asleep before he made any move. If so, the boy would wait in vain. He would not close his eyes and leave them to slaughter him in his sleep. He wasn't a pig, to be taken uncomplaining to the knife.

Moving as cautiously as possible, so as to arouse no suspicion, Cleve unbuckled his belt and pulled it through the loops of his trousers. He might make a more adequate binding by tearing up his sheet and pillowcase, but he could not do so without arousing Billy's attention. Now he waited, belt in hand, and pretended sleep.

Tonight he was grateful that the noise in the Wing kept stirring him from dozing, because it was fully two hours before Billy moved out of his bunk, two hours in which—despite his fear of what would happen should he sleep —Cleve's eyelids betrayed him on three or four occasions. But others on the landings were tearful tonight; the deaths of Lowell and Nayler had made even the toughest cons jittery. Shouts—and countercalls from those awakened— punctuated the hours. Despite the fatigue in his limbs, sleep did not master him.

When Billy finally got up from the lower bunk it was well past twelve and the landing was all but quiet. Cleve could hear the boy's breath; it was no longer even but had a catch in it. He watched, eyes like slits, as Billy crossed the cell to his familiar place in front of the window. There was no doubt that he was about to call up the old man.

As Billy closed his eyes, Cleve sat up, threw off his blanket and slipped down from the bunk. The boy was slow to respond. Before he quite comprehended what was happening, Cleve had crossed the cell and thrust him back against the wall, hand clamped over Billy's mouth.

"No, you don't," Cleve growled. "I'm not going to go like Lowell." Billy struggled, but Cleve was easily his physical superior.

"He's not going to come tonight," Cleve said, staring into the boy's wide eyes, "because you're not going to call him."

Billy fought more violently to be free, biting hard against his captor's palm. Cleve instinctively removed his hand and in two strides the boy was at the window, reaching up. In his throat, a strange half-song; on his face, sudden and inexplicable tears. Cleve dragged him away.

"Shut your noise up!" he snapped. But the boy continued to make the sound. Cleve hit him, open-handed but hard, across the face. *"Shut up!"* he said. Still the boy refused to cease his singing; now the music had taken on another rhythm. Again Cleve hit him, and again. But the assault failed to silence him. There was a whisper of change in the air of the cell, a shifting in its chiaroscuro. The shadows were moving.

Panic took Cleve. Without warning he made a fist and punched the boy hard in the stomach. As Billy doubled up an upper-cut caught his jaw. It drove his head back against the wall, his skull connecting with the brick. Billy's legs gave and he collapsed. A featherweight, Cleve had once thought, and it was true. Two good punches and the boy was laid out cold.

Cleve glanced around the cell. The movement in the shadows had been arrested; they trembled though, like greyhounds awaiting release. Heart hammering, he carried Billy back to his bunk and laid him down. There was no sign of consciousness returning; the boy lay limply on the mattress while Cleve tore up his sheet and gagged him, thrusting a ball of fabric into the boy's mouth to prevent him from making a sound behind his gag. He then proceeded to tie Billy to the bunk, using both his own belt and the boy's, supplemented with further makeshift bindings of torn sheets. It took several minutes to finish the job. As Cleve was lashing the boy's legs together, Billy began to stir. His eyes flickered open, full of puzzlement. Then, realizing his situation, he began to thrash his head from side to side; there was little else he could do to signal his protest.

"No, Billy," Cleve murmured to him, throwing a blanket across his bound body to keep the fact from any guard who might look in through the peep-hole before morning, "tonight, you don't bring him. Everything I said was true, boy. He wants out, and he's using you to escape." Cleve took hold of Billy's head, fingers pressed against his cheeks. "He's not your friend. *I am*. Always have been." Billy tried to shake his head from Cleve's grip but couldn't. "Don't waste your energy," Cleve advised. "It's going to be a long night."

He left the boy on the bunk, crossed the cell to the wall, and slid down it to sit on his haunches and watch. He would stay awake until dawn, and then, when there was some light to think by, he'd work out his next move. For now, he was content that his crude tactics had worked.

The boy had stopped trying to fight; he had clearly realized the bonds were too expertly tied to be loosened. A kind of calm descended on the cell: Cleve sitting in the patch of light that fell through the window, the boy lying in the gloom of the lower bunk, breathing steadily through his nostrils. Cleve glanced at his watch. It was twelve fifty-four. When was morning? He didn't know. Five hours, at least. He put his head back, and stared at the light.

It mesmerized him. The minutes ticked by slowly but steadily, and the light did not change. Sometimes a guard would advance along the landing, and Billy, hearing the footsteps, would begin his struggling afresh. But no-body looked into the cell. The two prisoners were left to their thoughts; Cleve to wonder if there would ever come a time when he could be free of the shadow behind him, Billy to think whatever thoughts came to bound monsters. And still the dead-of-night minutes went, minutes that crept across the mind like dutiful school-children, one upon the heels of the next, and after sixty had passed that sum was called an hour. And dawn was closer by that span, wasn't it? But then so was death, and so, presumably, the end of the world: that glorious Last Trump of which The Bishop had spoken so fondly, when the dead men under the lawn outside would rise as fresh as yesterday's bread and go out to meet their Maker. And sitting there against the wall, listening to Billy's inhalations and exhalations, and watching the light in the glass and through the glass, Cleve knew without doubt that even if he escaped this trap, it was only a temporary respite; that this long night, its minutes, its hours, were a foretaste of a longer vigil. He almost despaired then; felt his soul sink into a hole from which there seemed to be no hope of retrieval. *Here* was the real world; he wept. Not joy, not light, not looking forward; only this waiting in ignorance, without hope, even of fear, for fear came only to those with dreams to lose. The hole was deep and dim. He peered up out of it at the light through the window, and his thoughts became one wretched round. He forgot the bunk and the boy lying there. He forgot the numbness that had overtaken his legs. He might, given time, have forgotten even the simple act of taking breath but for the smell of urine that pricked him from his fugue.

He looked toward the bunk. The boy was voiding his bladder, but that act was simply a symptom of something else altogether. Beneath the blanket, Billy's body was moving in a dozen ways that his bonds should have prevented. It took Cleve a few moments to shake off lethargy, and seconds more to realize what was happening. Billy was changing.

Cleve tried to stand upright, but his lower limbs were dead from sitting still for so long. He almost fell forward across the cell, and only prevented himself by throwing out an arm to grasp the chair. His eyes were glued to the gloom of the lower bunk. The movements were increasing in scale and complexity. The blanket was pitched off. Beneath it Billy's body was already beyond recognition; the same terrible procedure as he had seen before, but in reverse. Matter gathering in buzzing clouds about the body, and congealing into atrocious forms. Limbs and organs summoned from the ineffable, teeth shaping themselves like needles and plunging into place in a head grown large and swelling still. He begged for Billy to stop, but with every drawn breath there was less of humanity to appeal to. The strength the boy had lacked was granted to the beast; it had already broken almost all its constraints, and now, as Cleve watched, it struggled free of the last, and rolled off the bunk onto the floor of the cell.

Cleve backed off toward the door, his eyes scanning Billy's mutated form. He remembered his mother's horror at earwigs and saw something of that insect in this anatomy: the way it bent its shiny back upon itself, exposing the paddling intracacies that lined its abdomen. Elsewhere, no analogy offered a hold on the sight. Its head was rife with tongues, that licked its eyes clean in place of lids, and ran back and forth across its teeth, wetting and rewetting them constantly; from seeping holes along its flanks came a sewer stench. Yet even now there was a residue of something human trapped in this foulness, its rumor only serving to heighten the filth of the whole. Seeing its hooks and its spines, Cleve remembered Lowell's rising scream and felt his own throat pulse, ready to loose a sound its equal should the beast turn on him.

But Billy had other intentions. He moved—limbs in horrible array—to the window and clambered up, pressing his head against the glass like a leech.

The music he made was not like his previous song—but Cleve had no doubt it was the same summoning. He turned to the door and began to beat upon it, hoping that Billy would be too distracted with his call to turn on him before assistance came.

"Quick! For Christ's sake! Quick!" He yelled as loudly as exhaustion would allow, and glanced over his shoulder once to see if Billy was coming for him. He was not; he was still clamped to the window, though his call had all but faltered. Its purpose was achieved. Darkness was tyrant in the cell.

Panicking, Cleve turned back to the door and renewed his tattoo. There was somebody running along the landing now; he could hear shouts and imprecations from other cells. "Jesus Christ, help me!" he shouted. He could feel a chill at his back. He didn't need to turn to know what was happening behind him. The shadow growing, the wall dissolving so that the city and its occupant could come through. Tait was here. He could feel the man's presence, vast and dark. Tait the child killer, Tait the shadow-thing, Tait the transformer. Cleve beat on the door till his hands bled. The feet seemed a continent away. Were they coming? Were they coming?

The chill behind him became a blast. He saw his shadow thrown up on to the door by flickering blue light; smelled sand and blood.

And then, the voice. Not the boy, but that of his grandfather, of Edgar St. Clair Tait. This was the man who had pronounced himself the Devil's excrement, and hearing that abhorrent voice, Cleve believed both in hell and its master, believed himself already in the bowels of Satan, a witness to its wonders.

"You are too inquisitive," Edgar said. "It's time you went to bed."

Cleve didn't want to turn. The last thought in his head was that he *should* turn and look at the speaker. But he was no longer subject to his own will; Tait had fingers in his head and was dabbling there. He turned, and looked.

The hanged man was in the cell. He was not that beast Cleve had half seen, that face of pulp and eggs. He was here in the flesh; dressed for another age, and not without charm. His face was well made; his brow wide, his eyes unflinching. He still wore his wedding ring on the hand that stroked Billy's bowed head like that of a pet dog.

"Time to die, Mr. Smith," he said.

On the landing outside, Cleve heard Devlin shouting. He had no breath left to answer with. But he heard keys in the lock or was that some illusion his mind had made to placate his panic?

The tiny cell was full of wind. It threw over the chair and table, and lifted the sheets into the air like childhood ghosts. And now it took Tait, and the boy with him; sucked them back into the receding perspectives of the city.

"Come on now," Tait demanded, his face corrupting, "we need you, body and soul. Come with us, Mr. Smith. We won't be denied."

"No!" Cleve yelled back at his tormentor. The suction was plucking at his fingers, at his eyeballs. "I won't—"

Behind him, the door was rattling.

"I won't, you hear!"

Suddenly, the door was thrust open, and threw him forward into the vortex of fog and dust that was sucking Tait and his grandchild away. He almost went with them but for a hand that grabbed at his shirt and dragged him back from the brink, even as consciousness gave itself up.

Somewhere, far away, Devlin began to laugh like a hyena. He's lost his mind, Cleve decided; and the image his darkening thoughts evoked was one of the contents of Devlin's brain escaping through his mouth like a flock of flying dogs.

He awoke in dreams; and in the city. He awoke remembering his last conscious moments: Devlin's hysteria, the hand arresting his fall as the two figures were sucked away in front of him. He had followed them, it seemed, unable to prevent his comatose mind from retreading the familiar route to the murderers' metropolis. But Tait had not won yet. He was still only *dreaming* his presence here. His corporeal self was still in Pentonville; his dislocation from it informed his every step.

He listened to the wind. It was eloquent as ever: the voices coming and going with each gritty gust, but never, even when the wind died to a whisper, disappearing entirely. As he listened he heard a shout. In this mute city the sound was a shock; it startled rats from their nests and birds up from some secluded plaza.

Curious, he pursued the sound, whose echoes were almost traced on the air. As he hurried down the empty streets he heard further raised voices, and now men and women were appearing at the doors and windows of their cells. So many faces, and nothing in common between one and the next to confirm the hopes of a physiognomist. Murder had as many faces as it had occurrences. The only common quality was one of wretchedness, of minds despairing after an age at the site of their crime. He glanced at them as he went, sufficiently distracted by their looks not to notice where the shout was leading him until he found himself once more in the ghetto to which he had been led by the child.

Now he rounded a corner, and at the end of the cul-de-sac he'd seen from his previous visit here (the wall, the window, the bloody chamber beyond) he saw Billy, writhing in the sand at Tait's feet. The boy was half himself and half that beast he had become in front of Cleve's eyes. The better part was convulsing in its attempt to climb free of the other, but without success. In one moment the boy's body would surface, white and frail, only to be subsumed the next into the flux of transformation. Was that an arm forming, and being snatched away again before it could gain fingers?; was that a face pressed from the house of tongues that was the beast's head? The sight defied analysis. As soon as Cleve fixed upon some recognizable feature it was drowned again.

Edgar Tait looked up from the struggle in front of him, and bared his teeth at Cleve. It was a display a shark might have envied.

"He doubted me, Mr. Smith," the monster said, "and came looking for his cell."

A mouth appeared from the patchwork on the sand and gave out a sharp cry, full of pain and terror.

"Now he wants to be away from me," Tait said. "You sowed the doubt. He must suffer the consequences." He pointed a trembling finger at Cleve, and in the act of pointing the limb transformed, flesh becoming bruised leather. "You came where you were not wanted, and look at the agonies you've brought."

Tait kicked the thing at his feet. It rolled over on to its back, vomiting.

"He needs me," Tait said. "Don't you have the sense to see that? Without me, he's lost."

Cleve didn't reply to the hanged man but instead addressed the beast on the sand.

"Billy?" he said, calling the boy out of the flux.

"Lost," Tait said.

"Billy," Cleve repeated. "Listen to me. . . ."

"He won't go back now," Tait said. "You're just dreaming this. But he's *here,* in the flesh.

"Billy," Cleve persevered. "Do you hear me? It's me; it's Cleve."

The boy seemed to pause in its gyrations for an instant, as if hearing the appeal. Cleve said Billy's name again, and again.

It was one of the first skills the human child learned: to call itself something. If anything could reach the boy it was surely his own name.

"Billy . . . Billy . . ." At the repeated word, the body rolled itself over.

Tait seemed to have become uneasy. The confidence he'd displayed was now silenced. His body was darkening, the head becoming bulbous. Cleve tried to keep his eyes off the subtle distortions in Edgar's anatomy and concentrate on winning Billy back. The repetition of the name was paying dividends; the beast was being subdued. Moment by moment there was more of the boy emerging. He looked pitiful; skin-and-bones on the black sand. But his face was almost reconstructed now, and his eyes were on Cleve.

"Billy . . . ?"

He nodded. His hair was plastered to his forehead with sweat; his limbs were in a spasm.

"You know where you are? *Who* you are?"

At first it seemed as though comprehension escaped the boy. And then— by degrees—recognition formed in his eyes, and with it came a terror of the man standing over him.

Cleve glanced up at Tait. In the few seconds since he had last looked all but a few human characteristics had been erased from his head and upper torso, revealing corruptions more profound than those of his grandchild. Billy gazed up over his shoulder like a whipped dog.

"*You belong to me,*" Tait pronounced, through features barely capable of speech. Billy saw the limbs descending to snatch at him, and rose from his prone position to escape them, but he was too late. Cleve saw the spiked hook of Tait's limb wrap itself around Billy's neck, and draw him close. Blood leapt from the slit windpipe, and with it the whine of escaping air.

Cleve yelled.

"With me," Tait said, the words deteriorating into gibberish.

Suddenly the narrow cul-de-sac was filling up with brightness, and the boy and Tait and the city were being bleached out. Cleve tried to hold on to them, but they were slipping from him; and in their place another concrete reality: a light, a face (faces) and a voice calling him out of one absurdity and into another.

The doctor's hand was on his face. It felt clammy.

"What on earth were you dreaming about?" he asked, the perfect idiot.

Billy had gone.

Of all the mysteries that the governor—and Devlin and the other guards who had stepped into cell B. 3. 20 that night—had to face, the total disappearance of William Tait from an unbreached cell was the most perplexing. Of the vision that had set Devlin giggling like a loon nothing was said; easier to believe in some collective delusion than that they'd seen some objective reality. When Cleve attempted to articulate the events of that night, and of the many nights previous to that, his monologue, interrupted often by his tears and silences, was met with feigned understanding and sideways glances. He told the story over several times, however, despite their condescension, and they, looking no doubt for a clue among his lunatic fables as to the reality of Billy Tait's Houdini act, attended every word. When they found nothing among his tales to advance their investigations, they began to lose their tempers with him. Consolation was replaced with threats. They demanded, voices louder each time they asked the question, where Billy had gone. Cleve answered the only way he knew how. "To the city," he told them. "He's a murderer, you see."

"And his body?" the governor said. "Where do you suppose his *body* is?"

Cleve didn't know, and said so. It wasn't until much later, four full days later in fact, that he was standing by the window watching the gardening detail bearing this spring's plantings cross between wings, that he remembered the lawn.

He found Mayflower, who had been returned to B Wing in lieu of Devlin, and told the officer the thought that had come to him. "He's in the grave," he said. "He's with his grandfather. Smoke and shadow."

They dug up the coffin by cover of night, an elaborate shield of poles and tarpaulins erected to keep proceedings from prying eyes, and lamps, bright as day but not so warm, trained on the labors of the men volunteered as an exhumation party. Cleve's answer to the riddle of Tait's disappearance had met with almost universal bafflement, but no explanation—however absurd— was being overlooked in a mystery so intractable. Thus they gathered at the unmarked grave to turn earth that looked not to have been disturbed in five decades: the governor, a selection of Home Office officials, a pathologist and Devlin. One of the doctors, believing that Cleve's morbid delusion would be best countered if he viewed the contents of the coffin and saw his error with his own eyes, convinced the governor that Cleve should also be numbered among the spectators.

There was little in the confines of Edgar St. Clair Tait's coffin that Cleve had not seen before. The corpse of the murderer—returned here (as smoke perhaps?) neither quite beast nor quite human, and preserved, as The Bishop had promised, as undecayed as the day of his execution—shared the coffin with Billy Tait, who lay, naked as a babe, in his grandfather's embrace. Edgar's corrupted limb was still wound around Billy's neck, and the walls of the coffin were dark with congealed blood. But Billy's face was not besmirched. *He looks like a doll,* one of the doctors observed. Cleve wanted to reply that no doll had such tear stains on its cheeks, nor such despair in its eyes, but the thought refused to become words.

Cleve was released from Pentonville three weeks later after special application to the Parole Board, with only two-thirds of his sentence completed. He returned, within half a year, to the only profession that he had ever known. Any hope he might have had of release from his dreams was short-lived. The place was with him still: neither so focused nor so easily traversed now that Billy—whose mind had opened that door—was gone, but still a potent terror, the lingering presence of which wearied Cleve.

Sometimes the dreams would almost recede completely, only to return again with terrible potency. It took Cleve several months before he began to grasp the pattern of this vacillation. *People* brought the dream to him. If he spent time with somebody who had murderous intentions, the city came back. Nor were such people so rare. As he grew more sensitive to the lethal streak in those around him he found himself scarcely able to walk the street. They were *everywhere,* these embryonic killers, people wearing smart clothes and sunny expressions were striding the pavement and imagining, as they strode, the deaths of their employers and their spouses, of soap-opera stars and incompetent tailors. The world had murder on its mind, and he could no longer bear its thoughts.

Only heroin offered some release from the burden of experience. He had never done much intravenous H, but it rapidly became heaven and earth to him. It was an expensive addiction however, and one which his increasingly truncated circle of professional contacts could scarcely hope to finance. It was a man called Grimm, a fellow addict so desperate to avoid reality he could get high on fermented milk, who suggested that Cleve might want to do some work to earn him a fee the equal of his appetite. It seemed like a wise idea. A meeting was arranged, and a proposal put. The fee for the job was so high it could not be refused by a man so in need of money. The job, of course, was murder.

"There are no visitors here, only prospective citizens." He had been told that once, though he no longer quite remembered by whom, and he believed in prophecies. If he didn't commit murder now, it would only be a matter of time until he did.

But though the details of the assassination that he undertook had a terrible familiarity to him, he had not anticipated the collision of circumstances by which he ended fleeing from the scene of his crime barefoot, and running so hard on pavement and tarmac that by the time the police cornered him and shot him down his feet were bloody, and ready at last to tread the streets of the city—just as he had in dreams.

The room he'd killed in was waiting for him, and he lived there, hiding his head from any who appeared in the street outside, for several months. (He assumed time passed here, by the beard he'd grown; though sleep came seldom, and day never.) After a while, however, he braved the cool wind and the butterflies and took himself off to the city perimeters, where the houses petered out and the desert took over. He went, not to see the dunes, but to listen to the voices that came always, rising and falling, like the howls of jackals or children.

He stayed there a long while, and the wind conspired with the desert to bury him. But he was not disappointed with the fruit of his vigil. For one day (or year), he saw a man come to the place and drop a gun in the sand, then wander out into the desert, where, after a while, the makers of the voices came to meet him, loping and wild, dancing on their crutches. They surrounded him, laughing. He went with them, laughing. And though distance and the wind smudged the sight, Cleve was certain he saw the man picked up by one of the celebrants, and taken on to its shoulders as a boy, thence snatched into another's arms as a baby, until, at the limit of his senses, he heard the man bawl as he was delivered back into life. He went away content, knowing at last how sin (and he) had come into the world.